PENGUIN BOOKS

AN ALBANY TRIO

William Kennedy is a novelist who began his writing career as a journalist. His novel, *Ironweed*, received both the Pulitzer Prize and the National Book Critics Circle Award for fiction. His nonfiction collection, *Riding The Yellow Trolley Car*, was published in 1993. That year he was elected to membership in The American Academy of Arts and Letters. Mr. Kennedy's newest novel, *The Flaming Corsage* is available in the Viking edition.

AN ALBANY TRIO

THREE NOVELS FROM THE ALBANY CYCLE

Legs · Billy Phelan's Greatest Game · Ironweed

WILLIAM KENNEDY

PENGUIN BOOKS

PENGUIN BOOKS
Published by the Penguin Group
Penguin Books USA Inc., 375 Hudson Street, New York, New York 10014, U.S.A.
Penguin Books Ltd, 27 Wrights Lane, London W8 5TZ, England
Penguin Books Australia Ltd, Ringwood, Victoria, Australia
Penguin Books Canada Ltd, 10 Alcorn Avenue, Toronto, Ontario, Canada M4V 3B2
Penguin Books (N.Z.) Ltd, 182–190 Wairau Road, Auckland 10, New Zealand

Penguin Books Ltd, Registered Offices: Harmondsworth, Middlesex, England

This volume first published in Penguin Books 1996

3 5 7 9 10 8 6 4

Legs first published in the United States of America
by Coward, McCann & Geoghegan, Inc. 1975
Published in Penguin Books 1983
Copyright © William Kennedy, 1975
All rights reserved

Billy Phelan's Greatest Game first published in the United States of America
by The Viking Press 1978
Published in Penguin Books 1983
Copyright © William Kennedy, 1978
All rights reserved

Ironweed first published in the United States of America by The Viking Press 1983
Published in Penguin Books 1984
Copyright © William Kennedy, 1979, 1981, 1983
All rights reserved

Portions of *Ironweed* were originally published in *Epoch*.

Grateful acknowledgment is made for permission to reprint an excerpt from "Bye, Bye, Blackbird," lyrics by Mort Dixon and music by Ray Henderson. Copyright 1926 by Warner Bros. Inc.;
copyright © renewed. All rights reserved. Used by permission.

Introduction copyright © Trolley Car Unlimited Incorporated, 1996
All rights reserved

LIBRARY OF CONGRESS CATALOGING IN PUBLICATION DATA
Kennedy, William, 1928–
An Albany trio/William Kennedy
p. cm.
Contents: Legs—Billy Phelan's greatest game—Ironweed.
ISBN 0 14 02.5786 1
1. Albany (N.Y.)—Fiction.   2. Diamond, Legs, 1895 or 6–1931—
Fiction.   3. Kidnapping—New York (State)—Albany—Fiction.
4. Criminals—New York (State)—Albany—Fiction.   5. Gamblers—New
York (State)—Albany—Fiction.   6. Family—New York (State)—Albany—
Fiction.   I. Title.
PS3561.E428A77   1996
813'.54—dc20   95–50540

Contents

PRELUDE IN A SALOON
vii

LEGS
1

BILLY PHELAN'S GREATEST GAME
233

IRONWEED
443

Prelude in a Saloon

IF DANIEL QUINN had interviewed the old gangster, the interview would have been arranged by Quinn's uncle, Billy Phelan. Quinn would have been writing his second novel and having a difficult time with it; for it kept growing larger with his discoveries of such people as the old gangster, whose name was Morty Besch. Morty had worked for Jack Diamond at the end, had slept in the same room with him, could describe the scars on his body, the holes left in his arms by bullet wounds.

Morty owned the Elite Club, a saloon where he would sit for his interview. It was on Hudson Avenue in Albany and was once a speakeasy. Jack Diamond had roomed upstairs on nights when he was changing his address to stay alive. The saloon had one large front room with a bar, a pendulum clock, a television set, a calendar with a naked woman sitting on the hood of a car, and a wall menu noting the oxtail soup and the ham and cheese sandwich you might, on one of his good days, persuade George the bartender to serve you. The soup, three cans of it, had been sitting on a shelf under the menu for six years.

The back room of the Elite Club had three booths, and Quinn and his Uncle Billy sat in one to wait for Morty to come downstairs and talk about Jack Diamond.

"You think he knows who killed Diamond?" Quinn asked.

"He coulda done it himself," Billy said. "He was one of the last ones to see him."

It was summer but the bar was cool, for no sunlight ever penetrated its sanctum, so when Morty came downstairs from where he had lived with his sister until she died, he was wearing a green cardigan. There is a photo of him from the *New York Mirror* in 1932 when he was running with Fats McCarthy and the Vincent Coll gang, and he is dapper in his fedora and double-breasted overcoat and necktie, lighting a cigarette. This was what he looked like when he knew Jack, who checked out in 1931. Seventy now, solid gray, with a paunch and an ailing prostate, Morty had quit whiskey, but would smoke and sip short beers during the interview. So would Billy and Quinn; and Quinn would buy all the beer as a way of thanking Morty for his conversation.

"Jack never cared about being rich," Morty said to Quinn, who took notes in a composition book. "He wanted what money could buy—the action. Shooting crap, beautiful women, picking up checks. He was the smartest man on Broadway. Things he said, he gotta've read them someplace. He'd write four, five letters in a beautiful hand while he was talking to you. He got letters from women, priests. He was always the life of the party, always being admired, a pleasant, humorous guy. We'd all enjoy him if he was sitting here with us."

"They shot him so many times, he must have lived in fear," Quinn said.

"Self-preservation," Morty said. "He was ready to meet fear."

"He wants to know who killed Diamond," Billy said to Morty. "I told him not to ask any questions." This was the main question Quinn couldn't ask but Billy could, for he had been friends with Morty for thirty years; also Billy knew Morty would not give a direct answer to such a question.

"I was with Jack one night on Ten Broeck Street," Morty said, "him and me and Cap Benedict, a cop who was on Jack's payroll. We saw somebody across the street and we ducked behind a couple of trees. We all three had pistols but they wouldn't'a helped. Guys across the street had machine guns. They didn't shoot us because they recognized Cap Benedict and didn't want to kill a cop. Towns close down to you when you kill a cop."

"I heard about that," Quinn said. "That was Honey Curry and his pals. An Albany cop told me that story."

"Is that so," said Morty.

"Curry. The cop swore it was true," Quinn said.

"Cops do that," Morty said. "Cops like to swear."

"I knew Curry," Billy said. "He hung around with Hubert Maloy, who worked for Diamond."

Quinn remembered Billy's link to Maloy and Curry when Charlie Boy McCall was kidnapped, and now he thought he should write about that too, the kidnapping a logical extension of the life and times of Jack Diamond.

This book was getting too fat.

Quinn had decided years earlier, after becoming obsessed with Albany's history, to write one large book that would tell everything about the town. He would go all the way back to the old Dutchmen, and move up to the Revolution, and then to the Irish coming in to build the canal, and the local stops on the Underground Railway, and Albany's 44th regiment leaving to take on the Rebs. He would bring Melville into the book, and Henry James, and Grover Cleveland, and T.R. racing newspaper reporters up the Capitol steps, and Billy Barnes running the town like a fiefdom for two decades at the turn of the century. He would chart the rise of the Patsy McCall political machine that would become invincible, unspeakable, hilarious, and would write of Jack (Legs) Diamond's presence on the Albany nightscape during Prohibition, and of Al Smith and F.D.R. not getting along, and of Dewey trying to break the McCall machine. He would write about the town during the second war, when Billy went into the army, and he'd use the gambling lives of his father and Billy, and the heroic home lives of his mother and grandmother, Peg and Annie. He would find a way to bring in his grandfather Francis Phelan, the baseball hero, and his grandfather-namesake Daniel Quinn, whom he never knew, but whose recorded adventures shaped his imagination, and, hey, he would put himself someplace in the middle of it all.

The book got so big that Quinn decided to focus only on the early politics of the McCall machine, and maybe the kidnapping of Charlie Boy McCall. He started writing that, but when he tried to fold Jack Diamond's story into it, because Jack had been murdered in Albany in that era, Jack delivered an ultimatum: Write me my own book, or else.

So Quinn put the politicians aside and wrote Jack's book, and now—would you believe it?—*Billy* was imposing himself on Jack's book in the same way: Time for *my* story, nephew.

"Curry, Maloy, and Morrie Berman," Billy said. "They staked me one night in the first pool match I had with Doc Fay and I won, but just. I hadda work like hell for it. And Maloy comes over after I win and says, 'You didn't have to worry, Billy. If you'da lost to that guy we'da taken the money away from him and give it back to you.' I liked Maloy. He was nuts."

"Everybody's nuts," Morty said. "That's what makes it dangerous."

Quinn talked to Morty for several hours, several times, and turned pieces of him into criminal voices when he wrote the Jack Diamond book. One voice belonged to Hubert Maloy, who made the leap from Jack's book to the next book, about Billy, a natural progression: home-grown talent on the hometown stage, a long-running show.

Quinn played pool with Billy at the Howard Street tables and Billy taught him about safe shots, the secret of Billy's success as a hustler: don't leave the other guy anything to shoot at.

"When I played Doc Fay," Billy said, "the bet was even money and the joint was packed. Betting was heavy against me because the Doc was good, but I knew I could beat him. He was a better shot but I played safe better than him. I bet forty bucks, all I had, and when I won, the Doc paid me in two twenty-dollar gold pieces. I gave them to your father to take home and pay the rent."

When he began thinking about Billy's life, Quinn saw it was dense with gameplaying and that he had inherited that in part from *his* father, Francis, a baseball player. Quinn would remember (he was ten at the time) when Francis came back to Albany after being away for so many years; and Quinn would look back at an early story he'd written about Francis, who wasn't really his grandfather in that old story, wasn't even married. Here is a fragment of how Quinn saw him then:

He came through the door with an off-balance bounce, slamming it with a clatter that threatened to shatter the glass. He was middle-aged and off the street. A vagrant in any town. The men at the bar and the dart-shooters stared at him.

"Francis," the bartender said. "Been a long time."

"Hello, Charlie, old pal, old pal. Double rye."

The bartender set it up and Francis drank it.

"Gimme another, Charlie."

"How long you been gone, Francis?" and Charlie poured a second double.

"Whataya think, Charlie, don't you remember?"

"All I see is you changed. You look like a different person. You ain't been taking care of yourself."

"Whatayou saying, I'm a bum in my hometown? Maybe I'm a bum in Kansas City, but in this town I got a home. Where do you get off telling me I don't look good? I'll knock your goddamn teeth out. Gimme another double."

"You ain't paid for the last one. The first was on the house."

"Why you cheap bastard. All these years you don't even buy a drink?"

"This ain't a charity bazaar."

"You're goddamn right it ain't. You get treated like a god-damn wino in your hometown."

"You better go home and sleep it off. Come in tomorrow when you're straightened out."

"Don't do me no goddamn favors. I don't need any of you bastards."

Francis pulled his fedora forward and straightened the brim. It was a stylish movement. He tried to button his coat but it had no buttons. He tried to open the door but couldn't. A dart-shooter opened it for him and he staggered out.

"Pikers," he said.

"Nice guy," the dart-shooter said.

"He was a good fellow sober," Charlie said.

"The look of him, he hasn't been sober in years."

"He'll be sober tomorrow. They bury his mother."

"Oh," said the dart-shooter.

"He's probably celebrating," Charlie said.

Francis rose up from that story and walked into Billy's book, where Quinn reimagined him as Billy's runaway father. Quinn tried to give him the complexity that was his due, tried to illuminate his life before and after his return to the home he'd abandoned twenty-two years earlier. As he invented this new Francis on the pages of Billy's story, Quinn would hear the man speak so vividly that he would feel another ultimatum rising, from Francis: Where the hell is *my* book?

So, as he had with Jack Diamond and Billy, Quinn would write Francis his own book and also would stop thinking that he was writing individual stories about individual people, although they were that. He would see that he was creating an open-ended cycle of lives: the story of one man or woman begetting another, all of them counting time in the shared continuum of common ground, common history. Quinn also saw that this was becoming what he set out to write: one book, a prolonged conversation with time that would be as large as his understanding, and perhaps larger if he got lucky.

Quinn saw that he was creating himself as judge and jury of time gone, which curiously became his vital principle of time present. This flirtation with time he loved, and was bored writing anything that was not this. The links between these individual columns of time had riveted his mind on recognizable change, not only in the people of his stories: their maturing, their triumphs, their failures, as they struggled in ignorance with the forces that shaped their acts; but also on the change in time itself, how it lived and died as people did. Men and women moved through their days believing their folly was high wisdom, unaware their wisdom was high nonsense. Yet in tracking the history of those dead faiths and dead eras, Quinn came to see that the way people clung to their ignorant beliefs was what shaped the conscience of their age. However dead those beliefs were now, they had once elevated men to heroism and bliss, reduced them to cowardice and sorrow.

Quinn would view his works as tragicomedies of such lives, and he would access their history not in order to replay it, or revise it, but to inhabit it. He would try to create books that were as different from one another as Jack Diamond was from Billy, as Billy was from Francis, and yet the books would be as kindred as blood: a mosaic of space, a collage of time that would continue as long as he did, and no longer.

In the back room of the Elite Club, Quinn did not yet know these things about himself and his work, and was busy taking notes on Morty Besch's truth about Jack Diamond.

"He wanted to live from day to day," Morty said. "He wanted to hijack, rob, plunder. He wanted the excitement. Nonsensical when you look back. Risking your life all the way up for a chunk of fast money. But when you're a kid it's thrilling. There was seven of us in this speakeasy on Broadway, and a week later only two of us left. The other five died with their shoes on, shooting it out on the street."

Billy was no hoodlum but Quinn saw he was like Diamond and Morty in that the action of the game was what mattered. Even losing, if that's how it turned out, freed you from the responsibility and the folly of money.

Billy: free like his runaway father, free from every oppressive illusion of the humdrum life, so that even his lies to himself became a form of glory dreaming, a vitalizing source of authority and wisdom.

"Jack had a million but he went broke," Morty said.

"I went broke without a million," Billy said.

"You were always broke," Morty said.

"I could get a buck."

"You were like one of them damn communists, never interested in money," Morty said.

"The only thing worse than a communist is a sticky drinker," Billy said. "Buy a drink, nephew."

"Right. But how come you didn't die like those other guys?" Quinn asked Morty.

"Lucky," Morty said. "And like Billy, I knew how to play safe."

The Billy safe shot: you work it out alone, keep the other fellow in trouble, no foolish bravado, wait for the right time, the right chance, you know it when you see it, refuse to be negated, for the ultimate strength is surviving long enough to win.

Quinn made a note on what he had to learn. Then he bought another round.

Legs

This is for Pete McDonald, a first-rate relative,
and for all the archetypes lurking in
Ruth Tarson's lake house

People like killers. And if one feels sympathy for the victims it's by way of thanking them for letting themselves be killed.

—EUGENE IONESCO

Jack's Alive

"I REALLY DON'T THINK HE'S DEAD," I said to my three very old friends.
"You what?" said Packy Delaney, dropsical now, and with only four teeth left. Elephantiasis had taken over his legs and now one thigh was the size of two. Ah time.

"He don't mean it," Flossie said, dragging on and then stubbing out another in her chain of smokes, washing the fumes down with muscatel, and never mind trying to list *her* ailments. ("Roaches in your liver," Flossie's doc had told her. "Go on home and die at your own speed.")

Tipper Kelley eyed me and knew I was serious.

"He means it, all right," said Tipper, still the dap newsman, but in a 1948 double-breasted. "But of course he's full of what they call the old bully-bull-bullshit because I was there. You *know* I was there, Delaney."

"Don't I know it," said the Pack.

"Me and Bones McDowell," said the Tip. "Bones sat on his chest."

"We know the rest," said Packy.

"It's not respectful to Bones' memory to say he sat on the man's chest of his own accord," Tipper said. "Bones was the finest reporter I ever worked with. No. Bones wouldn't of done that to any man, drunk or sober, him or Jack the corpse, God rest his soul. Both their souls, if Jack had a soul."

"He had a soul all right," said Flossie. "I saw that and everything else he had too."

"We'll hear about that another time," said Tipper, "I'm now talking about Bones, who with myself was the first up the stairs before the cops, and Jack's wife there in the hallway, crying the buckets. The door was open, so Bones pushed it the rest of the way open and in he snuck and no light in the room but what was coming in the window. The cops pulled up then and we heard their car door slam and Bones says to me, 'Come inside and we'll get a look before they kick us the hell out,' and he took a step and tripped, the simple bastard, and sprawled backward over the bed, right on top of poor Jack in his underwear, who of course didn't feel a thing. Bones got blood all over the seat of his pants."

"Tipper," said Packy, "that's a goddamn pack of lies and you know it. You haven't got the truth in you, and neither did Bones McDowell."

"So in comes big Barney Duffy with his flashlight and shines it on Bones sitting on poor Jack's chest. 'Sweet mother of mine,' says Barney and he grabbed Bones by the collar and elbow and lifted him off poor Jack like a dirty sock. 'Haven'tcha no manners atall?' Barney says to him. 'I meant no harm,' says Bones. 'It's a nasty thing you've done,' says Barney, 'sittin' on a dead man's chest.' 'On the grave of me mother I tripped and fell,' says Bones. 'Don't be swearing on your mother at a filthy time like this,' says Barney, 'you ought to be ashamed.' 'Oh I am,' says Bones, 'on the grave of me mother I am.' And then Barney threw us both out, and I said to Bones on the way down the stairs, 'I didn't know your mother was in the grave,' and he says to me, 'Well, she's not, the old fart-in-the-bottle, but she oughta be.'"

"You never got a good look at the corpse," Packy said to Tip, "and don't tell me you did. But you know damn well that I did. I saw what they did to him when he was over at Keenan the undertaker's for the autopsy. Thirty-nine bullets. They walked in there while he was sleeping and shot him thirty-nine times. I counted the bullet holes. You know what that means? They had seven pistols between the pair of them."

"Say what you will," I told them, savoring Packy's senile memory, remembering that autopsy myself, remembering Jack's face intact but the back of his head blown away by not thirty-nine but only three soft-nosed .38-caliber bullets: one through his right jaw, tearing the neck muscle, cutting the spinal cord, and coming out through the neck and falling on the bed; another entering his skull near the right ear and moving upward through his brain, fracturing his skull, and remaining in the fracture; and the third, entering the left temple, taking a straight course across the brain and stopping just above the right ear.

"I still don't think he's dead."

x   x   x

I had come to see Jack as not merely the dude of all gangsters, the most active brain in the New York underworld, but as one of the truly new American Irishmen of his day; Horatio Alger out of Finn McCool and Jesse James, shaping the dream that you could grow up in America and shoot your way to glory and riches. I've said it again and again to my friends who question the ethics of this somewhat unorthodox memoir: "If you liked Carnegie and Custer, you'll love Diamond." He was almost as famous as Lindbergh while his light burned. "The Most Picturesque Racketeer in the Underworld," the New York *American* called him; "Most Publicized of Public Enemies," said the *Post*; "Most Shot-At Man in America," said the *Mirror*.

Does anyone think these superlatives were casually earned? Why he was a pioneer, the founder of the first truly modern gang, the dauphin of the town for years. He filled the tabloids—never easy. He advanced the cause of joyful corruption and vice. He put the drop of the creature on the parched tongues of millions. He filled the pipes that pacify the troubled, loaded the needles that puncture anxiety bubbles. He helped the world kick the gong around, Jack did. And was he thanked for this benevolence? Hardly. The final historical image that endures is that corpse clad in underwear, flat-assed out in bed, broke and alone.

That's what finally caught me, I think: the vision of Jack Diamond alone, rare sight, anomalous event, pungent irony. Consider the slightly deaf sage of Pompeii, his fly open, feet apart, hand at crotch, wetting surreptitiously against the garden wall when the lava hits the house. Why he never even heard the rumbles. Who among the archaeologists could know what glories that man created on earth, what truths he represented, what love and wisdom he propagated before the deluge of lava eternalized him as The Pisser? And so it is with Jack Diamond's last image. It wouldn't matter if he'd sold toilet paper or milk bottles for a living, but he was an original man and he needs an original epitaph, even if it does come four and a half decades late. I say to you, my reader, that here was a singular being in a singular land, a fusion of the individual life flux with the clear and violent light of American reality, with the fundamental Columbian brilliance that illuminates this bloody republic. Jack was a confusion to me. I relished his company, he made me laugh. Yet wasn't I fearful in the presence of this man for whom violence and death were well-oiled tools of the trade? Yes, ah yes. The answer is yes. But fear is a cheap emotion, however full of wisdom. And, emotionally speaking, I've always thought of myself as a man of expensive taste.

I chose the Kenmore to talk to Packy, Tipper, and Flossie because if Jack's ghost walked anywhere, it was in that bar, that old shut-down Rain-Bo room with its peeling paint and its glory unimaginable now beneath all that emptiness. In the 1920's and 1930's the Kenmore was the Number One nightclub between New York and the Canadian border. Even during the Depression you needed a reservation on weekends to dance in evening clothes to the most popular bands in the country:

Rudy Vallee and Ben Bernie and Red Nichols and Russ Morgan and Hal Kemp and the Dorsey Brothers and all the rest who came before and after them. Naturally, limelighter that he was, Jack lived there. And so why wouldn't I choose the place to talk to three old friends, savor their memories and ring them in on my story?

I called Flossie first, for we'd had a thing of sorts between us, and I'll get to that. She was pretty back in those days, like a canary, all yellow-haired and soft and with the innocence of a birdsong, even though she was one of the loveliest whores north of Yonkers: The Queen of Stars, she called herself then. Packy's Parody Club had burned years before and he was now tending bar at the Kenmore, and so I said can we meet there and can you get hold of Tipper? And she said Tipper had quit the newspaper business finally but would be on tap, and he was. And so there we were at the Kenmore bar, me looking up at the smoky old pair of David Lithgow murals, showing the hunt, you know. Eight pink-coated huntsmen on horseback were riding out from the mansion in the first mural, at least forty-five hounds at their heels, heading into the woods. They were back indoors in the second painting, toasting and laughing by the fire while one of their number held the dead fox up by the tail. Dead fox.

"I was sitting where you're sitting," Packy said to me, "and saw a barman work up an order for Jack's table, four rum Cokes. All he poured was one shot of rum, split it over the top of the four and didn't stir them, so the suckers could taste the fruit of his heavy hand. 'I saw that,' I told him after the waiter picked the order up, 'and I want you to know Jack Diamond is a friend of mine.' The thieving bastard turned green and I didn't pay for another drink in this joint till Jack died."

"His name had power," Tipper said.

"It still does," I said. "Didn't he bring us together here?"

And I told them I was writing about him then, and they told me some of their truths, and secret lies, just as Jack had, and his wife Alice and his lovely light o' love, Kiki, had years ago. I liked all their lies best, for I think they are the brightest part of anybody's history.

I began by recalling that my life changed on a summer day in 1930 when I was sitting in the second-floor library of the Knights of Columbus, overlooking Clinton Square and two blocks up from the Kenmore bar. I was killing time until the pinochle crowd turned up, or a pool partner, and I was reading Rabelais, my gift to the library. It was the only book on The Index in the library and the only one I ever looked at.

That empty afternoon, and that book, gave me the insight that my life was a stupendous bore, and that it could use a little Gargantuan dimension. And so I said yes, I would take Jack Diamond up on his telephone invitation of that morning to come down to his place for Sunday dinner, three days hence. It was the Sunday I was to speak at the police communion breakfast, for I was one of Albany's noted communion breakfast intellectuals in those days. I would speak, all right, and then I would walk down to Union Station and take the west shore train to Catskill to listen to whatever that strange and vicious charmer had to say to an Albany barrister.

Jack Sauce

I MET JACK IN 1925 when he and his brother Eddie were personally running booze down from Canada. Jack stopped at the Kenmore even then, and he and Eddie and some more of their crew were at the table next to me, talking about Al Jolson. From what he said, Jack was clearly a Jolson fan, and so was I, and I listened to him express amazement that anybody could be as good at anything as Jolson was, but that he was also the most conceited son of a bitch in shoe leather. I broke into the conversation and said something windy, like: "He sings, whistles, dances, gives out the jokes and patter and it's all emotion, all a revelation of who he is. I don't care how much he's rehearsed, it's still rare because it's pure. He's so at home in himself he can't make a false gesture. Everything he does is more of that self that's made a million, ten, twenty million, whatever it is. People find this very special and they'll pay to see it. Even his trouble is important because it gives him diversity, pathos, and those qualities turn up in his voice. Everything he does funnels in and out of him through his talent. Sure he's conceited, but that's only a cover-up for his fear that he'll be exposed as the desolated, impoverished, scrawny, fearful hyena that he probably thinks is his true image, but that he can't admit to anybody without destroying his soul."

It all stunned Jack, who was a sucker for slick talk, and he bought me drinks for an hour. The next day he called to say he was sending me six quarts of Scotch and could I get him a pistol permit from Albany County? I liked the Scotch so I got him the permit.

I didn't have anything to do with him after that until 1929 when I represented Joe Vignola in the Hotsy Totsy case. And a story, which I pieced together very painfully from Joe, Jack, and half a dozen others, goes with that. It begins the night Benny Shapiro knocked out Kid Murphy in eight rounds at the Garden in '29. Jack, a serious fan of Benny's, won two grand that night taking the short end of seven to five.

"Stop by the club later," Benny remembered Jack telling him in the dressing room after the fight. "We'll have a little celebration."

"I got to meet a guy, Jack," Benny said.

"Bring her along."

"I'll try to make it, but I might be late."

"We'll wait," said Jack.

*   *   *

Herman Zuckman came hustling toward the bar as Jack walked into the Hotsy Totsy Club with Elaine Walsh, a singer and his special friend of the moment, on his arm. Fat Herman had been sole owner of the Hotsy until Jack Diamond decided to join him as a fifty-fifty partner. The club was on Broadway, near Fifty-fourth, top of the second-floor stairs, music by a six-piece jazz band, and tonight Joe Vignola, the singing waiter, doubling on violin.

All thirty tables in the bar area were full, despite Mayor Walker's nightlife curfew to keep decent people away from racketeers, bad beer, and worse liquor. Wood alcohol. Rubbing alcohol. The finest. Imported by Jack from the cellars of Newark and Brooklyn. Drink me. The bartenders were working hard, but there was too much work for the pair, Walter Rudolph, old rum-runner with a bad liver, and Lukas, a new man. Jack took off his coat, a Palm Beach, and his hat, a white sailor straw, and rolled up his sleeves to help the barmen. Elaine Walsh sat at the end of the bar and listened to the music. "I'm just a vagabond lover," Joe Vignola was singing. Joe Vignola, a merger of John Gilbert and Oliver Hardy, fiddled a chorus, then went back to delivering drinks.

Saul Baker, silent doorman, sat by the door with two pistols in his pockets, one on his hip, another inside his coat, and smiled at arriving customers. Just out of Sing Sing, a holdup man in need, pudgy Saul had found a survival point in the spiritual soup kitchen of Jack Diamond. Let no hungry thief pass my door. Don't try to tell Saul Baker Jack Diamond is a heartless man.

Charlie Filetti sat at the end of the bar. Filetti, it would soon be disclosed, had recently banked twenty-five thousand dollars in one day, a fragment of profit from his partnership with Jack Diamond in the shakedown of bucket-shop proprietors, shady dealers in the stock market.

"Who won the fight, Jack?" Filetti asked.

"Benny. KO in eight. He ruined the bum."

"I lose three hundred."

"You bet against Benny?" Jack stopped working.

"You got more confidence in him than I got. A lot of people don't like him ducking Corrigan."

"Ducking? Did you say ducking?"

"I'm saying what's being said. I like Benny good enough."

"Benny ducks nobody."

"Okay, Jack, but I'm telling you what talk's around town. They say you can make Benny lose, but you can't make him win."

"It was on the level tonight. You think I'd back a mug who runs? You should've seen him take Murphy apart. Murphy's a lunk. Hits like half a pound of sausage. Benny ate him up."

"I like Benny," Filetti said. "Don't get me wrong. I just like what Murphy did in his last fight. Murphy looked good that night I saw him."

"You don't know, Charlie. You shouldn't bet on fights. You just don't know. Ain't that right, Walter? He don't know?"

"I don't follow the fights, Jack," Walter Rudolph said. "I got out of the habit in stir. Last fight I saw was in '23. Benny Leonard whippin' a guy I don't even remember."

"How about you, pal?" Jack asked Lukas, the new bar-man. "You follow the fights? You know Benny Shapiro?"

"I see his name in the papers, that's all. To tell you the truth, Mr. Diamond, I watch baseball."

"Nobody knows," Jack said. He looked at Elaine. "But Elaine knows, don't you, baby? Tell them what you said tonight at the fight."

"I don't want to say, Jack." She smiled.

"Go ahead."

"It makes me blush."

"Never mind that, just tell them what you said."

"All right. I said Benny fights as good as Jack Diamond makes love."

Everybody at the bar laughed, after Jack laughed.

"That means he's a cinch to be champ," Jack said.

x   x   x

The mood of the club was on the rise and midnight seemed only a beginning. But forty minutes behind the bar was enough for Jack. Jack, though he had tended bar in his time, was not required to do manual labor. He was a club owner. But it's a kick to do what you don't have to do, right? Jack put on his coat and sat alongside Elaine. He put his hand under her loose blond hair, held her neck, kissed her once as everyone looked in other directions. Nobody looked when Jack kissed his ladies in public.

"Jack is back," he said.

"I'm glad to see him," Elaine said.

Benny Shapiro walked through the door and Jack leaped off his chair and hugged him with one arm, walked him to a bar stool.

"I'm a little late," Benny said.

"Where's the girl?"

"No girl, Jack. I told you it was a man. I owed some insurance."

"Insurance? You win a fight, break a man's nose, and then go out and pay your insurance?"

"For my father. I already stalled the guy two weeks. He was waiting. Woulda canceled the old man out in the morning. I figure, pay the bill before I blow the dough."

"Why don't you tell somebody these things? Who is this prick insurance man?"

"It's okay, Jack, it's all over."

"Imagine a guy like this?" Jack said to everybody.

"I told you I always liked Benny," Filetti said.

"Get us a table, Herman," Jack said. "Benny's here."

Herman Zuckman, counting money behind the bar, turned to Jack with an amazed look.

"I'm busy here, Jack."

"Just get us a table, Herman."

"The tables are all full, Jack. You can see that. We already turned away three dozen people. Maybe more."

"Herman, here beside me is the next welterweight champion of the world who's come to see us, and all you're doing is standing there making the wrong kind of noise."

Herman put the money in a strongbox under the bar, then moved two couples away from a table. He gave them seats at the bar and bought them a bottle of champagne.

"You feeling all right?" Jack asked Benny when they all sat down. "No damage?"

"No damage, just a little headache."

"Too much worrying about insurance. Don't worry anymore about shit like that."

"Maybe he's got a headache because he got hit in the head," Charlie Filetti said.

"He didn't get hit in the head," Jack said. "Murphy couldn't find Benny's head. Murphy couldn't find his own ass with a compass. But Benny found Murphy's head. And his nose."

"How does it feel to break a man's nose?" Elaine asked.

"That's a funny question," Benny said. "But to tell the truth you don't even know you're doing it. It's just another punch. Maybe it feels solid, maybe it don't."

"You don't feel the crunch, what the hell good is it?" Jack said.

Filetti laughed. "Jack likes to feel it happen when the noses break, right Jack?"

Jack mock-backhanded Filetti, who told him: "Don't get *your* nose out of joint, partner"—and he laughed some more. "I remember the night that big Texas oil bozo gave Jack lip. He's about six eight and Jack breaks a bottle across his face at the table, and then *you* couldn't stop laughing, Jack. The son of a bitch didn't know what hit him. Just sat there moppin' up his blood. Next day I go around to tell him what it costs to give lip to Jack and he says he wants to apologize. Gives me a grand to make Jack feel good. Remember that, Jack?"

Jack grinned.

*   *   *

The Reagans, Billy and Tim, came into the club and everybody knew it. They were brawny boys from the Lower West Side, dockworkers as soon as they knew they were men, that God had put muscles in their backs to alert them to that fact. Behind his back people called Billy The Omadhaun, a name he'd earned at seventeen when in a drunken rage he threw repeated football blocks at the crumbling brick tenement he lived in. Apart from the bleeding scrapes and gouges all over his body, an examination disclosed he had also broken both shoulders. His brother Tim, a man of somewhat larger wit, discovered upon his return from the Army in 1919 that beer-loading was no more strenuous than ship-loading, and far more lucrative. Proprietorship of a small speakeasy followed, as Tim pursued a prevailing dictum that to establish a speakeasy what you needed was one room, one bottle of whiskey, and one customer.

"That's a noisy bunch," Elaine said when they came in.

"It's the Reagans," said Filetti. "Bad news."

"They're tough monkeys," Jack said, "but they're pretty good boys."

"The big one's got a fist like a watermelon," Benny said.

"That's Billy," Jack said. "He's tough as he is thick."

Jack waved to the Reagans, and Tim Reagan waved and said, "Hello, Jack, howsa boy?"

"How's the gin in this joint?" Billy asked Joe Vignola in a voice that carried around the room. Herman Zuckman looked up. Customers eyed the Reagans.

"The best English gin is all we serve," Vignola told him. "Right off the boat for fancy drinkers like yourselves."

"Right out of Jack's dirty bathtub," Billy said.

"No homemade merchandise here," Vignola said. "Our customers get only the real stuff."

"If he didn't make it then he stole it," Billy said. He looked over at Jack Diamond. "Ain't that so, Jack?"

"If you say so, Billy," Jack said.

"Hey, he can get in trouble with that kind of talk," Filetti said.

"Forget it," Jack said. "Who listens to a drunk donkey Irishman?"

"Three of the good gins," Billy told Vignola. "Right away."

"Comin' up," said Vignola, and he rolled his eyes, dropped the serving tray he carried under his arm, but caught it just before it hit the floor, then lofted it and caught it again, well over his head, and spun it on the index finger of his left hand: a juggler's routine. Others laughed. The Reagans did not.

"Get the goddamn gin and never mind the clown act," Billy Reagan said. "You hear me, you waiter baloney? Get the gin."

Jack immediately went to the Reagan table and stood over big-fisted Billy. He poked Billy's shoulder with one finger. "You got no patience. Make noise in your own joint, but have a little patience when you're in somebody else's."

"I keep telling him he's ignorant," Tim Reagan said. "Sit down, Jack, don't mind him. Have a drink. Meet Teddy Carson from Philly. We been tellin' him about you, how you come a long way from Philadelphia."

"How you makin' out, Jack?" Teddy Carson said, another big fist. He shook Jack's hand, cracking knuckles. "Some boys I know in Philly talk about you a lot. Duke Gleason, Wiggles Mason. Wiggles said he knew you as a kid."

"He knocked a tooth out on me. I never got even."

"That's what he told me."

"You tell him I said hello."

"He'll be glad to hear that."

"Pull up a chair, Jack," Tim said.

"I got a party over there."

"Bring 'em over. Make the party bigger."

Saul Baker left his post by the door when Jack went back to his own table. "That's a bunch of shitheads, Jack. You want 'em thrown out?"

"It's all right, Saul." Pudgy little Saul Baker, chastising three elephants.

"I hate a big mouth."

"Don't get excited."

Jack said he wanted to have a drink with the Reagans. "We'll all go over," he said to Filetti, Elaine, and Benny.

"What the hell for?" said Filetti.

"It'll keep 'em quiet. They're noisy, but I like them. And there's a guy from Philly knows friends of mine."

Jack signaled Herman to move the table as Joe Vignola finally brought drinks to the Reagans.

"You call this gin?" Billy said to Vignola, holding up a glass of whiskey. "Are you tryna be a funny guy? Are you lookin' for a fight?"

"Gin's gone," Vignola said.

"I think you're lookin' for a fight," Billy said.

"No, I was looking for the gin," Vignola said, laughing, moving away.

"This is some dump you got here, Jack," Billy called out.

Herman and a waiter moved Jack's table next to the Reagans, but Jack did not sit down.

"Let me tell you something, Billy," Jack said, looking down at him. "I think your mouth is too big. I said it before. Do I make myself clear?"

"I told you to shut your goddamn trap," Tim told Billy, and when Billy nodded and drank his whiskey, Jack let everybody sit down and be introduced. Charlie Filetti sat in a quiet pout. Elaine had swallowed enough whiskey so that it made no difference where she sat, as long as it was next to Jack. Jack talked about Philadelphia to Teddy Carson, but then he saw nobody was talking to Benny.

"Listen," Jack said, "I want to raise a toast to Benny here, a man who just won a battle, man headed for the welterweight crown."

"Benny?" said Billy Reagan. "Benny who?"

"Benny Shapiro, you lug," Tim Reagan said. "Right here. The fighter. Jack just introduced you."

"Benny Shapiro," Billy said. He pondered it. "That's a yid name." He pondered it further. "What I think is yids make lousy fighters."

Everybody looked at Billy, then at Benny.

"The yid runs, is how I see it," Billy said. "Now take Benny there and the way he runs out on Corrigan. Wouldn't meet an Irishman."

"Are you gonna shut up, Billy?" Tim Reagan said.

"What do you call Murphy?" Benny said to Billy. "Last time I saw him tonight he's got rosin all over his back."

"I seen you box, yid. You stink."

"You dumb fucking donkey," Jack said. "Shut your stupid mouth."

"You wanna shut my mouth, Jack? Where I come from, the middle name is fight. That's how you shut the mouth."

Billy pushed his chair away from the table, straddling it, ready to move. As he did, Jack tossed his drink at Billy and lunged at his face with the empty glass. But Billy only blinked and grabbed Jack's hand in flight, held it like a toy.

Saul Baker snatched a gun from his coat at Jack's curse and looked for a clear shot at Billy. Then Tim Reagan grabbed Saul's arm and wrestled for the gun. Women shrieked and ran at the sight of pistols, and men turned over tables to hide. Herman Zuckman yelled for the band to play louder, and customers scrambled for cover to the insanely loud strains of the "Jazz Me Blues." Elaine Walsh backed into a checkroom, Benny Shapiro, Joe Vignola, and four others there ahead of her. The bartenders ducked below bar level as Billy knocked Jack backward over chairs.

"Yes, sir," Billy said, "the middle name is fight."

Tim Reagan twisted the pistol out of Saul Baker's grip as Teddy Carson fired the first shot. It hit Saul just above the right eye as he was reaching for his second pistol, on his hip.

The second shot was Charlie Filetti's. It grazed Billy's skull, knocking him down. Filetti fired again, hitting Carson, who fell and slithered behind a table.

Jack Diamond, rising slowly with his pistol in his hand, looked at the only standing enemy, Tim Reagan, who was holding Saul's pistol. Jack shot Tim in the stomach. As Tim fell, he shot a hole in the ceiling. Standing then, Jack fired into Tim's forehead. The head gave a sudden twist and Jack fired two more bullets into it. He fired his last two shots into Tim's groin, pulling the trigger three times on empty chambers. Then he stood looking down at Tim Reagan.

Billy opened his eyes to see his bleeding brother beside him on the floor. Billy shook Tim's arm and grunted "Timbo," but his brother stayed limp. Jack cracked Billy on the head with the butt of his empty pistol and Billy went flat.

"Let's go, Jack, let's move," Charlie Filetti said.

Jack looked up and saw Elaine's terrified face peering at him from the checkroom. The bartenders' faces were as white as their aprons. All faces looked at Jack as Filetti grabbed his arm and pulled. Jack tossed his pistol onto Billy's chest and it bounced off onto the floor.

Jack, Out of Doors

JACK LIVED THE FUGITIVE LIFE after the Hotsy, the most hunted man in America, and eventually he wound up in the Catskills. I don't think I'd have ever seen him again if the 1925 meeting in the Kenmore had been our only encounter. But I know my involvement in the Hotsy case brought me back to his mind, even though we never met face to face during it. And when the heat was off in midsummer of 1930, when the Hotsy was merely history, Jack picked me out of whatever odd pigeonhole he'd put me in, called me up and asked me to Sunday dinner.

"I'm sorry," he said when he called, "but I haven't seen you since that night we talked in the Kenmore. That's been quite a while and I can't remember what you look like. I'll send a driver to pick you up, but how will he recognize you?"

"I look like St. Thomas Aquinas," I said, "and I wear a white Panama hat with a black band. Rather beat up, that hat. You couldn't miss it in a million."

"Come early," he said. "I got something I'd like to show you."

*   *   *

Joe (Speed) Fogarty picked me up at the Catskill railroad station, and when I saw him I said, "Eddie Diamond, right?"

"No," he said. "Eddie died in January. Fogarty's the name."

"You look like his twin."

"So I'm told."

"You're Mr. Diamond's driver—or is he called Legs?"

"Nobody who knows him calls him anything but Jack. And I do what he asks me to do."

"Very loyal of you."

18

"That's the right word. Jack likes loyalty. He talks about it."

"What does he say?"

"He says, 'Pal, I'd like you to be loyal. Or else I'll break your fucking neck.' "

"The direct approach."

We got into Jack's custom, two-tone (green and gray) Cadillac sedan with whitewalls and bulletproof glass, armor panels, and the hidden pistol and rifle racks. The latter were features I didn't know existed until the following year when Jack had the occasion to open the pistol rack one fateful night. Now what I noticed were the black leather seats and the wooden dashboard with more gauges than any car seemed to need.

"How far is it to Jack's house?" I asked.

"We're not going to Jack's house. He's waiting for you over at the Biondo farm."

"That wouldn't be Jimmy Biondo, would it?"

"You know Jimmy?"

"I met him once."

"Just once? Lucky you. The bum is a throwback. Belongs in a tree."

"I'd tend to sympathize with that view. I met him during the Hotsy Totsy business. We swapped views one day about a client of mine, Joe Vignola."

"Joe. Poor Joe"—and Fogarty gave a sad little chuckle. "Some guys'd be unlucky even if they were born with rabbits' feet instead of thumbs."

"Then you knew Joe."

"I used to go to the Hotsy when I was in New York even before I knew Jack. It was quite a place before the big blowup. Plenty of action, plenty of gash. I met my wife there, Miss Miserable of 1929."

"So you're married."

"Was. It broke up in four months. That dame would break up a high mass."

It was Sunday morning, not quite noon, when Fogarty left the station in Catskill and headed west toward East Durham, where Jimmy Biondo lived. My head was full of Catskill images, old Rip Van Winkle who probably would have been hustling applejack instead of sleeping it off if he'd been alive now, and those old Dutchmen with their magical ninepins that lulled you into oblivion and the headless horseman riding like a spook through Sleepy Hollow and throwing his head at the trembling Ichabod. The Catskills were magical for me because of their stories, as well as their beauty, and I was full of both, despite the little crater of acid in the pit of my stomach. After all, I was actually going to Sunday dinner with one of the most notorious men in America. Me. From Albany.

"You know, two and a half hours ago I was talking to a whole roomful of cops."

"Cops? I didn't know cops worked in Albany on Sunday."

"Communion breakfast. I was the speaker and I told them a few stories and then looked out over their scrubbed faces and their shiny buttons and explained that they were our most important weapon in saving the nation from the worst scourge in its history."

"What scourge?"

"Gangsterism."

Fogarty didn't laugh. It was one of his rare humor failures.

*   *   *

Fogarty was the only man I ever met through Jack who wasn't afraid to tell me what was really on his mind. There was an innocence about him that survived all the horror, all the fear, all the crooked action, and it survived because Jack allowed it to survive. Until he didn't allow it anymore.

Fogarty told me he was eleven when he understood his own weak spot. It was his nose. When tapped on the nose in a fight, he bled, and the sight and feel of the blood made him vomit. While he vomited, the other guy punched him senseless. Fogarty avoided fistfights, but when they were unavoidable he packed his nose with the cotton he always carried. He usually lost his fights, but after he understood his nose, he never again bled to the vomit point.

He was thirty-five when I got to know him, pretty well recovered from a case of TB he'd picked up during his last year of college. He had a Fordham stringency that had gone sour on religion, but he still read books, liked O'Neill, and could talk a little Hamlet, because he'd played Laertes once in school. Jack used him as a driver but also trusted him with money and let him keep the books on beer distribution. But his main role was as Jack's sidekick. He looked like Eddie. And Eddie had died of TB.

Fogarty was working as a bartender for Charlie Northrup when he first met Jack. He talked flatteringly about Jack's history when they sat across from each other at Northrup's roadhouse bar. Jack was new in the mountains and he quizzed Fogarty on the scene. What about the sheriff and the judges? Were they womanizers? Gamblers? Queers? Drunks? Merely greedy? Who ran beer in the mountains besides Northrup and the Clemente brothers?

Fogarty gave Jack the answers, and Jack hired him away from Northrup and gave him the pearl-handled .32 Eddie Diamond once owned. Fogarty carried it without loading it, giving it the equivalent menace of a one-pound rock. "You boys don't know it, but I've got you all covered with a one-pound rock."

"I don't want to get into any heavy stuff" is what he explained to Jack when he took the pistol.

And Jack told him: "I know you better than that, Speed. I don't ask my tailor to fix my teeth."

This arrangement suited Fogarty down to his socks. He could move among the big fellows, the tough fellows, without danger to himself. If he did not fight, he would not bleed.

x   x   x

Fogarty turned onto a winding narrow dirt road that climbed a few minor hills and then flattened out on a plateau surrounded by trees. Jimmy Biondo's place was an old white farmhouse with green shutters and green shingled roof. It sat at the end of the drive, and behind it stood a large unpainted barn as dilapidated as the house was elegant. Three moving shapes sat on the long front porch, rocking in green wicker rockers, their faces hidden from me by the newspapers they were all reading. The faces opened themselves to us when Fogarty stopped on the grass beside the house, and Jack, the first to stand, threw down the paper and bounded down the stairs to greet me. The woman, Alice, held the paper in her lap and looked at me with a smile. The second man was Jimmy Biondo, who owned the place but no longer used it, and rented it to Jack. He detached himself from Andy Gump to give me a look.

"Welcome to God's country, Marcus," Jack said. He was in white ducks, brown and white wing tips, and a yellow silk sport shirt. A tan blazer hung on the back of his rocker.

"God's country?" I said. "Fogarty told me Jimmy Biondo owned this place."

Jack laughed and Jimmy actually smiled. A smile from Jimmy lit up the world like a three-watt bulb.

"Look at this guy," Jack said to his wife and Jimmy, "a lawyer with a sense of humor. Didn't I tell you he was beautiful?"

"I only let my mother call me beautiful," I said.

What can I say? Jack laughed again. He liked my lines. Maybe it was my delivery or my funny old hat. Fogarty recognized me from the hat as soon as he saw me. It was all discolored at the front from where I touched it, crown and brim; the brim was split on the side and the black band raveling a little. It happened to be my favorite hat. People don't understand that some men need tradition as much as others need innovation. I doffed the hat when Alice came down the steps and characteristically asked me after our handshake, "Are you hungry? Have you had breakfast?"

"Catholic eggs and Irish bacon. That's extra greasy. About three hours ago at a communion breakfast."

"We just came from church, too," Alice said.

Oh? But I didn't say oh. I just repeated the story about my speech on the scourge of gangsterism. Jack listened with straight face, and I thought, Oh Christ, another humor failure.

"I know what you mean," he said. "Some of my best friends have been taken by that scourge." Then he smiled, a very small smile, a smile you might call wry, or knowing, or ironic, or possibly ominous, which is how I looked at it and was why I laughed my courtroom laugh. That laugh, as they used to say in the Albany papers, is booming and infectious, and it had the effect of making Jack's line seem like the joke of the year.

Jack responded by standing up and jiggling, a moving glob of electricity, a live wire snaking its way around the porch. I knew then that this man was alive in a way I was not. I saw the vital principle of his elbow, the cut of his smile, the twist of his pronged fingers. Whatever you looked at was in odd motion. He hit you, slapped you with his palm, punched you with a light fist, clapped you on the shoulder, ridding himself of electricity to avoid exploding. He was conveying it to you, generating himself into yourself whether you wanted to receive him or not. You felt something had descended upon him, tongues of fire maybe or his phlogiston itself, burning its way into your own spirit.

I liked it.

It was an improvement on pinochle.

I mounted the steps and shook hands with Biondo and told him how overjoyed I was to see him again. He gave me a nod and an individualized twitch of each nostril, which I considered high graciousness. I would describe Jimmy as a giant maggot, an abominable toad with twelve-ounce eyelids and an emancipated nose that had nothing to do with the rest of his face. He was a globular figure of uncertain substance. Maybe all hotdog meat, goat's ears and pig's noses inside that salmony, shantung sportshirt. You said killer as soon as you looked at him, but he was not a killer. He was more complex than that.

"How's your buddy Joe Vignola?" he asked me. And he grunted a laugh, which went like this: "Hug, hug, hug."

"Joe is recovering nicely," I said, an exaggeration. Joe was in awful shape. But I should give Jimmy Biondo satisfaction?

"Dumb," said Jimmy. "Dumb, dumb, dumb."

"He never hurt anybody," I said.

"Dumb," said Jimmy, shaking his head, drawing out the sound like a short siren. "Dumb waiter," he said, and he laughed like a sneeze.

"I felt so sorry for his family," Alice said.

"Feel sorry for your own family," Jack said. "The son of a bitch was a stool pigeon."

"I'll feel sorry for anybody I feel like feeling sorry for," Alice said in modified spitfire manner, a trait I somehow didn't expect from the wife of Jack Diamond. Did I think he'd marry a placid cow? No. I thought he'd dominate any woman he chose to live with. We know from the movies, don't we, that one well-placed grapefruit in the kisser and the women learn who's boss? *Public Enemy*, the Cagney movie with that famed grapefruit scene, was touted as the real story of Jack Diamond when it played Albany. The advertising linked it unmistakably to his current escapades: "You read about him on yesterday's front pages in this newspaper. Now see the story behind the headlines," etc. But like everything else that ever had anything to do with Jack in the movies, it never had anything to do with Jack.

Well, we got past Joe Vignola as a topic, and then after a few anxious grunts from Jimmy ("Guh, guh, guh,"), he got up and announced his departure. Fogarty would take him to Hudson, across the river, and he'd take a train to Manhattan. His and Jack's presence on this front porch was not explained to me, but I didn't pry. I didn't know until much later that they were partners of a kind. His departure improved the conversation, and Alice said she and Jack had been to mass over at Sacred Heart in Cairo where she, and once in a while he, went on Sunday, and that Jack had given money for the new church organ and that she brought up Texas Guinan one summer to raise money at a church lawn party and Jack was going to bring Al Jolson up and so on. Revelatory.

An old colored man came to the foot of the front steps and said to Jack, "The tahger's ready, Mist' Jack." Tahger? Tiger? Could he be keeping a tiger? Was that what he wanted to show me?

"Okay, Jess," Jack said. "And will you bring out two quarts of rye and two quarts of champagne and leave 'em here on the porch?"

Jesse nodded and moved off slowly, a man who looked far older than his years, actually a stoop-backed fifty, a Georgia cotton chopper most of his days and then a stable hand. Jack met him in '29 through a Georgia horse breeder who had brought him to Churchill Downs as a stable boy. Jack heard Jesse had made moonshine back home and hired him on the spot at a hundred a week, a pay raise of about eight hundred percent, to come north with his two teen-aged sons and no wife and be plumber for an applejack still Jack and Biondo owned jointly, and which, since that time, had functioned night and day in a desolated patch of woods a quarter of a mile from the patch of porch on which I was rocking.

So the old man went for the rye and champagne, and I mentally alerted my whistle to coming attractions. Then Alice looked at Jack and Jack looked at me and I looked at both of them, wondering what all the silent looking was for. And then Jack asked me a question: "Ever fire a machine gun, Marcus?"

✻   ✻   ✻

We walked to the garage-cooler, which is what it turned out to be, as luxuriously appointed a tumbledown barn as you'd be likely to find anywhere in America, with a beer refrigeration unit; a storage room for wine and champagne, paneled in knotty pine; a large area where three trucks could comfortably park; and a total absence of hay, hornets, barnsmell, cowflop, or chickenshit.

"No," I had told Jack, in answer to his question, "I am a machine-gun virgin."

"Time you shot the wad," Jack said, and he went dancing down the stairs and around the corner toward the barn, obviously leading both me and Alice, before we were out of our chairs.

"He's a nut on machine guns," Alice said. "He's been waiting till you got here to try it out. You don't have to do it, you know, just because he suggests it."

I nodded my head yes, shook it no, shrugged, and, I suppose, looked generally baffled and stupid. Alice and I walked across the side lawn to the barn where Jack had already pried up a floorboard and was lifting out a Thompson submachine gun, plus half a dozen boxes of bullets.

"Brand-new yesterday from Philadelphia," he said. "I been anxious to test it." He dislodged the magazine, loaded it, replaced it with what, despite my amateurism in the matter, I would call know-how. "I heard about a guy could change one of these drums in four seconds," he said. "That's handy in a tight spot."

He stood up and pointed it at the far end of the barn where a target was tacked on a windowless wall. The target was a crudely drawn face with the name Dutch Schultz lettered beneath.

"I had a couple of hundred of these printed up a few years ago," he said, "when Schultz and me weren't getting along. He looks just like that, the greedy prick. I drew it myself."

"You get along all right now with him?"

"Sure. We're pals again," Jack said and he let go with a long blast that nicked the Schultz forehead in two or three places.

"A little off," Jack observed, "but he'd have noticed."

"Let me try," Alice said. She took the gun from Jack, who parted with it reluctantly, then fired a long burst which roamed the wall without touching the target. With a second burst she hit the paper's edge, but not Schultz.

"I'm better with a rifle."

"You're better with a frying pan," Jack said. "Let Marcus try it."

"It's really out of my line," I said.

"Go on," Jack said. "You may never get another chance, unless you come to work for me."

"I've got nothing against Mr. Schultz."

"He wouldn't mind. Lotsa people shoot at him."

Jack put the gun in my hands, and I held it like a watermelon. Ridiculous. I put my right hand on the pistol grip, grabbed the other handgrip with the left, and raised the stock into my armpit. Absurd. Uncomfortable.

"Up a little," Jack said. "Against the shoulder."

I touched the trigger, raised the gun. Why? It was wobbly, cold. I pointed it at Schultz. Sunday morning. Body of Christ still undigested in some internal region, memory of prayer and holy bacon grease on my tongue. I touched the trigger seriously, pulled the gun tighter to my shoulder. Old feeling. Comfortable with a weapon against the pectoral. Like Army days, days in the woods as a kid. Put it down, fool.

"For chrissake, Marcus, give it a blast," Jack said.

Really childish not to. Raising the flag of morality. Powerful Irish Catholic magic at work that prohibits shooting effigies on the side of a barn. Bless me Father for I have sinned. I shot at Mr. Schultz's picture. And did you hit it, son? No, Father, I missed. For your penance say two rosaries and try again for the son of a bitch.

"Honest, Marcus," Alice said, "it won't bite."

Ladies' Auxiliary heard from. Altar Rosary Society Member attends machine-gun outing after mass, prods lawyer to take part. What a long distance between Marcus and Jack Diamond. Millenniums of psychology, civilization, experience, turpitude. Man also develops milquetoasts by natural selection. Would I defend him if some shooters walked through the barn door? What difference from defending him in court? And what of Jack's right to justice, freedom, life? Is the form of defense the only differentiating factor? What a morally confounded fellow Marcus is, perplexed by Mr. Thompson's invention.

I pressed the trigger. Bullets exploded in my ears, my hands, my shoulders, my blood, my brain. The spew of death was a personal tremor that even jogged my scrotum.

"Close, off the right ear," Jack said. "Try again."

I let go with another burst, feeling confident. No pain. It's easy. I leveled the weapon, squeezed off another.

"Got him. Eyeball high. No more Maggie's Drawers for Marcus. You want a job riding shotgun?"

Jack reached for the gun, but I held onto it, facing the ease with which I had become new. Do something new and you are new. How boring it is not to fire machine guns. I fired again and eliminated the Schultz mouth.

"Jesus, look at that," Jack said.

I gave him the gun and he looked at me. Me. Sandlot kid hits grand slam off thirty-game winner, first time at bat.

"How the hell did you do that?" Jack asked me.

"It's all a matter of the eyeball," I said. "I also shoot a pretty fair game of pool."

"I'm impressed," Jack said. He gave me another amazed look and put the weapon to his shoulder. But then he decided the shooting was over. What if he missed the target now? Bum of bums.

"Let's have lunch and toast your sharpshooting," he said.

"Oh nonsense," Alice said, "let's toast something important, like the beautiful day and the beautiful summer and having friends to dinner. Are you our friend, Marcus?"

I smiled at Alice to imply I was her friend, and Jack's, too. And I was then, yes I was. I was intuitively in sympathy with this man and woman who had just introduced me to the rattling, stammering splatter of violent death. Gee, ain't it swell?

We walked back to the porch where Fogarty was reading Krazy Kat.

"I heard the shooting," Fogarty said, "who won?"

"Marcus won," Alice said.

"I wiped out Mr. Schultz's mouth, if that's a win."

"Just what he deserves. The prick killed a kid cousin of mine last week in Jersey."

And so I had moral support for my little moral collapse—which sent a thrill through me, made me comfortable again on this glorious Sunday in the mountains.

*   *   *

We got into the car and left the Biondo place, Alice and I in the back seat, Jack up front with Fogarty. Alice previewed our Sunday dinner for me: roast beef and baked potatoes, and did I like my beef rare the way Jack liked it, and asparagus from their own garden, which Tamu, their

Japanese gardener, had raised, and apple pie by their colored maid, Cordelia.

Alice bulged out of her pink summer cotton in various places, and my feeling was that she was ready instantly to let it all flop out whenever Jack gave the signal. All love, all ampleness, all ripeness, would fall upon the bed, or the ground, or on him, and be his for the romping. Appleness, leaves, blue sky, white sheets, erect, red nipples, full buttocks, superb moistness at the intersection, warm wet lips, hair flying, craziness of joy, pleasure, wonder, mountains climbable with a stride after such sex.

I liked her.

Oxie was asleep on the enclosed porch when we arrived, more formally known as Mendel (The Ox) Feinstein, one of the permanent cadre. Oxie was a bull-necked weightlifter with no back teeth, who'd done a four-year stretch for armed robbery of a shoe store. The judge specified he do the full four because, when he held up the lady shoe clerk, he also took the shoes she was wearing. Justice puts its foot down on Oxie.

He got up immediately when the key turned in the front door. We all watched as Alice stopped to coo at two canaries in a silver cage on the porch. When she went on to the kitchen, Fogarty sat down on the sofa with Oxie, who made a surreptitious gesture to Jack.

"Marion called about a half hour ago," he whispered.

"Here?"

Oxie nodded and Jack made facial note of a transgression by Marion.

"She wants you to see her this afternoon. Important, she said."

"Goddamn it," Jack said, and he went into the living room and up the stairs two at a time, leaving me on the porch with the boys. Fogarty solved my curiosity, whispering: "Marion's his friend. Those two canaries there—he calls one Alice, one Marion." Oxie thought that was the funniest thing he'd heard all week, and while he and Fogarty enjoyed the secret, I went into the living room, which was furnished to Alice's taste: overstuffed mohair chairs and sofa; walnut coffee table; matching end tables and table lamps, their shades wrapped in cellophane; double-thick Persian rug, probably worth a fortune if Jack hadn't lifted it. My guess was he'd bought it hot; for while he loved the splendid things of life, he had no inclination to pay for them. He did let Alice pick out the furniture, for the hot items he kept bringing home clashed with her plans, such as they were. She'd lined the walls with framed calendar art and holy pictures—a sepia print of the Madonna returning from Calvary and an incendiary, bleeding sacred heart with a cross blooming atop the bloody fire. One wall was hung with a magnificent blue silk tapestry, a souvenir from Jack's days as a silk thief. Three items caught my eye on a small bookshelf otherwise full of Zane Grey and James Oliver Curwood items: a copy of Rabelais, an encyclopedia of Freemasonry, and the Douay Bible sandwiched between them.

When he came down, I asked about the books. The Freemasonry? Yeah, he was a Mason. "Good for business," he said. "Every place you go in this country, the Protestant sons of bitches got the money locked up." And Rabelais? Jack picked up the book, fondled it.

"A lawyer gave it to me when I had my accident in 1927." (He meant when he was shot three times by the Lepke mob when they ambushed and killed Little Augie Orgen.) "Terrific book. You ever read it? Some screwball that Rab-a-lee."

I said I knew the book but avoided mentioning the coincidence of Rabelais being here and also in the K. of C. library, where I made my decision to come here, and in the additional fact that a lawyer had given the book to Jack. I would let it all settle, let the headiness go out of it. Otherwise, it would sound like some kind of weird, fawning lie.

Alice heard us talking and came into the living room in her apron. "Those damn Masons," she said. "I can't get him away from that nonsense." To rile her, Jack kept a picture of an all-seeing eye inside a triangle, a weird God-figure in the Masonic symbology, on the wall in the upstairs bathroom. Alice raised this issue, obviously a recurring one.

"It sees you, Alice," Jack told her, "even when you pee."

"My God doesn't watch me when I pee," Alice said. "My God is a gentleman."

"As I get it," Jack said, "your God is two gentlemen and a bird."

He opened the Rabelais to a page and began reading, walking to the kitchen doorway to serenade Alice with the flow. He read of Gargantua's arrival in Paris, his swiping of the Notre Dame Cathedral bells for his giant horse, and then his perching on the cathedral roof to rest while mobs of tiny Parisians stared up at him. And so he decided to give them wine.

" 'He undid his magnificent codpiece' "—Jack read with mock robustness; his voice was not robust but of a moderately high pitch, excitable, capable of tremolos—" 'and bringing out his john-thomas, pissed on them so fiercely that he drowned two hundred and sixty thousand, four hundred and eighteen persons, not counting the women and small children.' "

"My God, John," Alice said, "do you have to read *that*?"

"Piss on 'em," Jack said. "I always felt that way." And holding the book and talking again to me, he said, "You know what my full name is? John Thomas Diamond." And he laughed even harder.

✻   ✻   ✻

Jack threw the book on the sofa and went quickly out to the porch, then to the car, and came back with a bottle of champagne in each hand. He put both bottles on the coffee table, got four glasses from the china closet.

"Alice, Speed, you want champagne?" They both said no and he didn't ask Oxie. Why waste champagne on a fellow who'd rather drink feet juice? He poured our champagne, the real goods.

"Here's to a fruitful legal relationship," Jack said, rather elegantly, I patronizingly thought. I sipped and he gulped and poured himself another. That disappeared and another followed that, two and a half glasses in one minute.

"Thirsty," he explained, "and that's prime stuff." But he was getting outside his skin. He finished what was in his glass and then stared at me while I drank and told him my experiences with bad champagne. He interrupted me, perfectly, at a pause, with obvious intentions of letting me continue, and said: "I don't want to interrupt your story, but how about a walk? It's a great day and I want to show you a piece of land."

He led the way out the back door and along a stream that ran parallel to the highway, and at a narrow point we leaped across the stream and into the woods, all soft with pine needles, quiet and cool, a young forest with the old granddaddy trees felled long ago by loggers, and the new trees—pines, white birches, maples, ash—tall but small of girth, reaching up for sunlight. A cat named Pistol followed at Jack's heel like an obedience-trained dog. He was an outdoor cat and had picked us up as we left the back steps, where he'd been sitting, gnawing gently on a squirrel that wasn't quite dead and that still had the good sense to run away whenever Pistol relaxed his teeth. But that old squirrel never got far from the next pounce.

Jack walked rapidly, stepping over the carcasses of old trees, almost running, moving uphill, slipping but never falling, surefooted as the cat. He turned around to check me out and at each turn motioned to me with his right hand, backs of fingers upright toward me, bending them toward himself in a come-on gesture. He said nothing, but even today I can remember that gesture and the anxious look on his face. He was not mindful of anything else except me and his destination and whatever obstacle he and the cat might have to dodge or leap over: an old log, jutting rocks, half-exposed boulders, fallen limbs, entire dead trees, the residual corpses of the forest. Then I saw a clearing and Jack stopped at its edge to wait for me. He pointed across a meadow, a golden oval that rolled upward, a lone, dead apple tree in the center like the stem and root of a vast yellow mushroom turned upside down. Beyond the tree an old house stood on the meadow's crest and Jack said that was where we were going.

He walked with me now, calmed, it seemed, by the meadow or perhaps the sight of the house, all that speed from the forest faded now into a relaxed smile, which I noticed just about the time he asked me: "Why'd you come down here today, Marcus?"

"I was invited. And I was curious. I'm still curious."

"I thought maybe I could talk you into going to work for me."

"As a lawyer or riding shotgun?"

"I was thinking maybe you'd set up a branch of your office in Catskill."

That was funny and I laughed. Without even telling me what he wanted of me, he was moving me into his backyard.

"That doesn't make much sense," I said. "My practice is in Albany and so is my future."

"What's in the future?"

"Politics. Maybe Congress, if the slot opens up. Not very complicated really. It's all done with machinery."

"Rothstein had two district attorneys on his payroll."

"Rothstein?"

"Arnold Rothstein. I used to work with him. And he had a platoon of judges. Why did you get me a pistol permit?"

"I don't really have a reason."

"You knew I was no altar boy."

"It cost me nothing. I remember we had a good conversation at the Kenmore. Then you sent me the Scotch."

He clapped me on the shoulder. Electric gesture.

"I think you're a thief in your heart, Marcus."

"No, stealing's not my line. But I admit to a corrupt nature. Profligacy, sloth, licentiousness, gluttony, pride. Proud of it all. That's closer to my center."

"I'll give you five hundred a month."

"To do what?"

"Be available. Be around when I need a lawyer. Fix my traffic tickets. Get my boys out of jail when they get drunk or go wild."

"How many boys?"

"Five, six. Maybe two dozen sometimes."

"Is that all? Doesn't seem like a full-time job."

"You do more, I pay you more."

"What more might I do?"

"Maybe you could move some money for me. I want to start some accounts in other banks up this way, and I don't want to be connected to them."

"So you want a lawyer on the payroll."

"Rothstein had Bill Fallon. Paid him a weekly salary. You know who Fallon was?"

"Every lawyer in the U.S. knows who Fallon was."

"He defended me and Eddie when we got mixed up in a couple of scrapes. He wound up a drunk. You a drunk?"

"Not yet."

"Drunks are worthless."

We were almost at the old house, a paintless structure with all its windows and doors boarded up and behind it a small barn, or maybe it was a stable, with its eyes gouged out and holes in its roof. The panorama from this point was incredible, a one-hundred-and-eighty-degree vision of natural grandeur. I could see why Jack liked the spot.

"I know the old man who owns this," he said. "He owns the whole field, but the son of a bitch won't sell. He owns half the mountainside. A stubborn old Dutchman, and he won't sell. I want you to work on him. I don't care what the price is."

"You want the house? The field? What?"

"I want all you can get, the whole hill and the forest. I want this yellow field. Everything between here and my place. Things are going good now and they can only get better. I want to build up here. A big place. A place to live good. I saw one in Westchester, a great place I liked. Roomy. A millionaire owned it. Used to work for Woodrow Wilson. Had a big fireplace. Look at this rock."

He picked up a purple stone lying at our feet.

"Plenty of this around," he said. "Have the fireplace made out of it. Maybe face part of the house with it. You ever see a house faced with purple rock?"

"Never."

"Me either. That's why I want it."

"You're settling in here in the Catskills then, permanently?"

"Right. I'm settling in. Plenty of work around here." He gave me a conspiratorial smile. "Lots of apple trees. Lots of thirsty people." He looked over at the house. "Van Wie is his name. He's about seventy now. He used to farm a little up here a few years ago." Jack walked over to the shed and looked inside. Grass was growing inside it, and hornets, birds, and spiders were living in the eaves. Birdshit and cobwebs were everywhere.

"Eddie and me did the old man a favor in here one day," Jack said, reminding me and himself, and, in his way, reminding me to remind the

old man too that when Jack Diamond did you a favor, you didn't turn
your back on him. He turned suddenly to me, not at all relaxed now,
but with that anxious face I saw as he was moving through the forest.

"Are you with me?"

"I could use the money," I said. "I usually lose at pinochle."

*   *   *

I can recall now the quality of the light at that moment when I went to
work for Jack. The sun was dappling his shoulders as he peered into
the shadows of the empty stable with its random birdshit, with his faithful cat Pistol (Marion later had a poodle named Machine Gun), rubbing
its sides against Jack's pants legs, his head against Jack's shoe, the sun
also dappling the black and white of Pistol's tiger tom fur as it sent its
electricity into Jack the way Jack sent his own vital current into others.
I mentioned to Jack that he looked like a man remembering something
a man doesn't want to remember and he said yes, that was a thousand
percent, and he told me the two interlocking memories he was resisting.

One was of another summer day in 1927 when old man Van Wie
came down the meadow past the apple tree, which was not dead then,
and into the forest where Jack and Eddie Diamond were firing pistols
at a target nailed to a dead, fallen tree, recreation therapy for Eddie,
for whom the house, which would later be described as Jack's fortress,
had been purchased: mountain retreat for tubercular brother.

The gunfire brought the old man, who might have guessed the oc-
cupation of his neighbors but not their identities; for Jack and Eddie
were the Schaefer brothers back then, a pseudonym lifted from Jack's
in-laws; and Jack was not yet as famous a face as he would be later in
that same year when Lepke bullets would not quite kill him. The farmer
did not speak until both Jack and Eddie had given him their full attention. He then said simply, "There is a mad cat. Will you shoot it before
it bites on my cow? It already bit on my wife." Then the old man waited
for a reply, staring past his flat nose and drooping mustache, which,
like his hair, he had dyed black, giving him the comic look of a Keystone
Kop; which was perhaps why Jack said to him, "Why don't you call
the troopers? Or the sheriff. Have them do it."

"They'd be all week," said the old man. "Might be it's got the
rabies."

"How'll we find him?" Jack asked.

"I chased him with the pitchfork and he ran in the barn. I locked
him in."

"Is the cow in there?"

"No. Cow's out in the field."

"Then he can't get at the cow. You got him trapped."

"He might get out. That's a right old barn."

Jack turned to Eddie, and they smiled at the prospect of making a mad cat hunt together, the way they had once hunted rats and woodchucks in the Philadelphia dumps. But Eddie could not walk all the way to the farmer's house, and so they went back and got Jack's car, and with old man Van Wie they drove to the barn which had not yet had its eyes gouged out or holes made in its roof. And with guns drawn and the farmer behind them with his pitchfork, they entered the barn.

"What's going to stop him from biting hell out of us?" Jack said.

"I expect you'll shoot him 'fore he gets a chance at that," the old man said.

Jack saw the cat first, yellowish orange and brown and curled up on some hay, and quiet. It looked at them and didn't move, but then it opened its mouth and hissed without sound.

"That don't look like a mad cat to me," Jack said.

"You didn't see it bite on my wife or leap on the lampshade and then try to run up the curtain. Maybe it's quiet 'cause I whacked it with the fork. Maybe I knocked it lame."

"It looks like Sugarpuss," Eddie said.

"I know," Jack said. "I'm not going to kill it."

The mad cat looked at the men, orange and silent and no longer disturbed by their intrusion or fearful of their menace.

"You shoot it if you want," Jack said.

"I don't want to shoot it," Eddie said.

"Look out," old man Van Wie said, pushing past the brothers and sticking his pitchfork through the cat, which squealed and wriggled and tried to leap off the fork. But it was impaled and the farmer held it out to the brothers, an offering.

"Now shoot it," the old man said.

Jack kept his arm at his side, pistol down, watching the cat squeal and squirm upside down on the fork. Eddie put three bullets in its head, and the old man, saying only "Obliged" and grabbing a shovel off a nail, carried the carcass out to the yard to bury what remained of madness. And Jack then was triggered into his second cat memory of eighteen years before, when he was twelve, when he said to Eddie that he wanted to furnish the warehouse and Eddie did not understand. The warehouse was enormous, longer than some city blocks, empty for as long as they had been alive. It was made of corrugated metal and wooden beams and had scores of windows that could be broken but not shattered. Jack discovered it, and with Eddie, they imagined its vast empty floor space full of automobiles and machinery and great crated mysteries. At one end an office looked down on the emptiness from second-story level. There was no staircase to it, but Jack found a way. He rigged a climbing rope, stolen from a livery stable, over a wooden crossbeam, the stairway's one remnant. He worked two hours to maneuver a loop upward that would secure the rope, then shinnied up. It was 1909 and his mother had been dead two months. His brother was eight and spent two days learning how to shinny up to the office.

The brothers looked out the office windows at a fragment of Philadelphia's freight yards, at lines of empty boxcars, stacks of crossties, piles of telegraph poles covered with creosote. They watched trains arrive and then leave for places they knew only from the names painted on the cars—Baltimore and Ohio, New York Central, Susquehanna, Lackawanna, Erie, Delaware and Hudson, Boston and Albany—and they imagined themselves in these places, on these rivers. From the windows they saw a hobo open a freight-car door from inside, and they assumed he'd just awakened from a night's sleep. They saw him jump down and saw that a bull saw, too, and was chasing him. The hobo had only one shoe, the other foot wrapped in newspaper and tied with string. The bull outran him and beat him with a club, and when the hobo went down, he stayed down. The bull left him where he fell.

"The bastard," Jack said. "He'd do the same to us."

But the Diamond brothers always outran the bulls, outscrambled them beneath the cars.

Jack brought a chair to the office and a jug of water with a cork in it, candles, matches, a slingshot with a supply of stones, half a dozen pulp novels of the wild West, a cushion, and, when he could steal it from his father's jug, some dago red. He kept the hobo's hat, which was worn through at the crown from being fingered and had spots of blood on the brim. Jack took it off the hobo after he and Eddie went down to help him and found he was dead. The hobo was a young man, which shocked the brothers. Jack hung the hat on a nail in the office and let no one wear it.

The brothers were asleep in the office the day the orange cat came in. It had climbed one of the wooden pillars and found its way along a crossbeam. A dog was after it, barking at the foot of the pillar. Jack gave it water in the candle dish, petted it, and called it Sugarpuss. The dog kept barking and Jack fired stones at it with his slingshot. When it wouldn't leave, Jack shinnied down, clubbed it with a two-by-four, cut its throat, and threw it out by the crossties.

Sugarpuss remained the mascot of the brothers and the select group of friends they allowed up the rope. It lived in the warehouse, and all the gang brought it food. During the winter Jack found Sugarpuss outside, frozen in the ice, its head almost eaten off where another animal had gotten it. He insisted it be given a decent burial and immediately got another cat to replace it. But the second cat ran away, an early lesson in subtraction for Jack.

*   *   *

We came out of the woods onto the highway and walked back toward Jack's house. A car passed us, and a middle-aged man and woman waved and tooted at Jack, who explained they were neighbors and that he'd had an ambulance take their kid to Albany Hospital, some thirty miles away, about six months back when the local sawbones didn't know what ailed the boy. Jack footed the bill for examinations and a week's stay in the hospital, and the kid came out in good shape. An old woman down the road had a problem with her cow after her shed collapsed, and so Jack paid for a new shed. People in Acra and Catskill told these stories when the papers said Jack was a heartless killer.

Jack's Uncle Tim was working on the rosebushes when we reached the house. The lawn had been freshly cut, some grass raked into piles on the front walk. Tamu was watering the flower beds of large and small marigolds, dahlias, snapdragons, on the sunny side of the brown shingled house. The flowers reached up toward a second-story window where, it was authoritatively reported in the press at a later date, Jack had his machine guns mounted. The fortress notion was comic but not entirely without foundation, for Jack did have floodlights on the house to illuminate all approaches, and the maple trees on the lawn were painted white to a point higher than a man, so anyone crossing in front of one was an instant target. Jack installed the lights back in 1928 when he was feuding with Schultz and Rothstein, right after a trio of hirelings tried to kill Eddie in Denver. Eddie went to Denver because the Catskills hadn't solved his lung problems, and Denver must have helped, for when they shot at him he leaped out of his car and outran the killers. One killer, when he saw Eddie'd gotten away, grabbed a bull terrier pup in front of somebody's house and shot off one of its paws, an odd substitute for murder. But then I guess in any realm of life you solve your needs any way you can.

Jack and I stood on the lawn and watched the grooming of the landscape. Domestic felicity. Back to the soil. Country squirearch. It didn't conform to my preconceptions of Jack, but standing alongside him, I had to admit it didn't sit so badly on him either.

"Pretty good life you've got here," I told him. He wanted to hear that.

"Beats hell out of being at the bottom of the river," he said.

"A striking truth."

"But this is nothing, Marcus, nothing. Give me a year, maybe even six months, you'll see something really special."

"The house, you mean, the purple house?"

"The house, the grounds, this whole goddamn county."

He squinted at me then and I waited for clarification.

"It's a big place, Marcus, and they pack in the tourists all summer long. You know how many speakeasies in this one county? Two hundred and thirty. I don't even know how many hotels yet, but I'm finding out. And every goddamn one of them can handle beer. Will handle beer."

"Who's servicing them now?"

"What's the difference?"

"I don't know what the difference is, except competition."

"We'll solve that," Jack said. "Come on, let's have some champagne."

Pistol, who had followed us out of the woods and along the road, pounced on a mole that made the mistake of coming out of his tunnel. The cat took him to the back steps and played with him alongside the carcass of the squirrel, who had died of wounds. Or perhaps Pistol had finished him off when he decided to take a walk with us. He let the mole run away a little, just as he'd let the squirrel, then he pounced.

We were hardly inside the house when Alice called out to Jack, "Will you come here please?" She was on the front porch, with Oxie and Fogarty still on the sofa. They were not moving, not speaking, not looking at Alice or at Jack or at me either when we got there. They both stared out toward the road.

Alice opened the canary cage and said to Jack, "Which one do you call Marion?"

Jack quickly turned to Fogarty and Oxie.

"Don't look at them, they didn't tell me," Alice said. "I just heard them talking. Is it the one with the black spot on its head?"

Jack didn't answer, didn't move. Alice grabbed the bird with the black spot and held it in her fist.

"You don't have to tell me—the black spot's for her black hair. Isn't it? Isn't it?"

When Jack said nothing, Alice wrung the bird's neck and threw it back in the cage. "That's how much I love you," she said and started past Jack, toward the living room, but he grabbed her and pulled her back. He reached for the second bird and squeezed it to death with one hand, then shoved the twitching, eyebleeding corpse down the crevice of Alice's breasts. "I love you too," he said.

That solved everything for the canaries.

*   *   *

We left the house immediately, with a "Come on, Marcus" the only words Jack said. Fogarty followed him wordlessly, like Pistol. "Haines Falls," Jack said in a flat, hostile voice.

Fogarty leaned over the seat to tell Jack, "We didn't know she was listening or we . . ."

"Shut your fucking mouth."

We drove a few miles in silence, and then Jack said in a tone that eliminated the canary episode from history, "I'm going to Europe. Ever been to Europe?"

"I was there with the AEF," I said. "But it was a Cook's Tour. I was in a headquarters company in Paris. Army law clerk."

"I was in Paris. I went AWOL to see it."

"Smart move."

"When they caught up with me, they sent me back to the States. But that was a long time ago. I mean lately. You been to Europe lately?"

"No, that was the one and only."

"Fantastic place, Europe. Fantastic. I'd go all the time if I could. I like Heidelberg. If you go to Heidelberg, you got to eat at the castle. I like London, too. A polite town. Got class. You want to go to Europe with me, Marcus?"

"Me go to Europe? When? For how long?"

"What the hell's the difference? Those are old lady questions. We go and we come back when we feel like it. I do a little business and we have ourselves some fun. Paris is big fun, I mean big fun."

"What about your business here? All those hotels. All those speak-easies."

"Yeah, well, somebody'll look after it. And it won't be all that long of a trip. Goddamn it, a man needs change. We get old fast. I'm an old son of a bitch, I feel old, I could die any time. I almost died twice already, really close. So goddamn stupid to die when there's so many other things to do. Jesus, I learned that a long time ago; I learned it in Paris from an old crone—old Algerian chambermaid with her fingers all turned into claws and her back crooked and every goddamn step she took full of needles. Pain. Pain she wanted to scream about but didn't. Tough old baby. I think she was a whore when she was young, and me and Buster Deegan from Cleveland, we went AWOL together to see Paris before they shot us in some muddy fucking trench, and we wind up talking every morning to this old dame who spoke a little English. She wore a terrycloth robe—maybe she didn't even own a dress—and a rag on her head and house slippers because her feet couldn't stand shoes. We double-tipped her every day and she smiled at us, and one day she says to me, 'M'sieur, do you have fun in Paris?' I said I was having a pretty good time. 'You must, M'sieur,' she said to me. 'It is necessary.' Then she give me a very serious look, like a teacher giving you the word, and she smiled. And I knew she was saying to me, yeah, man, I got pain now, but I had my day long, long ago, and I still remember that, I remember it all the time."

I'd been watching Jack have fun all day, first with his machine gun and then his champagne and his Rabelais and his dream of a purple mansion; but his fun was nervous, a frenetic motion game that seemed less like fun than like a release of energy that would explode his inner organs if he held it in.

We were climbing a mountain by this time, along a two-lane road that wound upward and seemed really about as wide as a footpath when it snaked along the edges of some very deep and sudden drops. I saw a creek at one point, visible at the bottom of a gorge. When you looked up, you saw mountains to the left, and you climbed and climbed and climbed and then made a hairpin turn and saw a waterfall cascading down the side of a great cliff.

"Get a look at that," Jack said, pointing. "Is that some sight?"

And at another sharp turn he told Fogarty to stop, and we both got out and looked back down the mountain to see how far and how steeply we had climbed; and then he pointed upward where you could see more mountains beyond mountains. The stop was clearly a ritual for Jack, as was pointing out the waterfall. It was his mountain range somehow, and he had a proprietor's interest in it. We made a cigarette stop as we entered Haines Falls, a store where Jack knew they carried Rameses, his exotic, Pharaonic brand, and he dragged me to the souvenir counter and urged me to buy something.

"Buy your wife a balsam pillow or an Indian head scarf."

"My wife and I split up two years ago."

"Then you got no reason not to go to Europe. How about a cigarette box for yourself or a pinetree ashtray?"

I thought he was kidding, but he was insisting; a souvenir to seal our bargain, a trinket to affirm the working relationship. He fingered the dishes and glassware with their gaudy Catskill vistas, the thermometers framed in pine, toothbrush holders, inkstands, lampstands, photo albums, all with souvenir inscriptions burned into them, commemorating vacation time spent in this never-never land in the clouds. I finally agreed on a glass paperweight with an Indian chief in full war bonnet inside it, and Jack bought it. Forty-nine cents. The action was outrageously sentimental, the equivalent of his attitude toward that Algerian crone or the deceased brother, from whom, I would later come to know, Jack felt all his good luck had come. "All my troubles happened after Eddie died," Jack told me in the final summer of his life when he was learning how to die. Thus his replacement of the brother with Fogarty had a talismanic element to it. Talismanic paperweight, talismanic brother-substitute, talismanic memory of the Arthritic Witch of Fun. And here we were in old talismanic Haines Falls, the highest town in the Catskills, Jack said, and of course, of course, the proper place for him to stash the queenly consort of his fantasy life, the most beautiful girl I've ever known.

*   *   *

Jack said he once saw Charlie Northrup belly-bump a man with such force that the man did a back-flip over a table. Charlie was physical power, about six four and two forty. He had a wide, teeth-ridden smile and blond hair the color and straightness of straw, combed sideways like a well-groomed hick in a tintype. He was the first thing we saw when we entered Mike Brady's Top o' the Mountain House at Haines Falls. He was at the middle of the bar, standing in brogans with his ankles crossed, his sportshirt stained with sweat from armpit to armpit, drinking beer, talking with the bartender, and smiling. Charlie's smile went away when he met Jack eyeball to eyeball.

"Missed you the other night, Charlie," Jack said.

"Yeah. I think you're gonna keep missing me, Jack."

"That's a wrong attitude."

"May be. But I'm stuck with it."

"Don't be stupid, Charlie. You're not stupid."

"That's right, Jack. I'm not stupid."

Jack's face had all the expression of an ice cube, Charlie's full of overheated juices. He was telling Jack now about something I had no clue to; but from their tone there were confidences between them. It turned out Charlie was responsible for Jack being in the Masons. They had been young thieves together on Manhattan's West Side in 1914, running with The Gophers, a gang Owney Madden led until he went to jail for murder. They both wound up in the Bronx about 1925, with Charlie gone semi-straight as a numbers writer and Jack a feared figure in the New York underworld because of his insane gang tactics and his association with the powerful Arnold Rothstein. Jack had also opened a place he called The Bronx Theatrical Club, whose main theatrical element was Jack's presence as a performing psychopath. I say performing because I don't think Jack was psychopathic in its extreme sense.

He was aberrated, yes, eccentric, but his deeds were willful and logical, part of a career pattern, even those that seemed most spontaneous and most horrendous. He was rising in the world, a celebrated hijacker, and Charlie was a working stiff with money problems. Charlie married Jimmy Biondo's sister and they vacationed in the Catskills. When times got very rough in New York, Charlie and some two-bit Jersey thieves bought a defunct brewery in Kingston and went into shoestring bootlegging. In the years after, Charlie opened his roadhouse and also became the biggest beer distributor in Greene and Ulster counties. He was tough, with a reputation for muscle if you didn't pay promptly for your goods. But he was different from Jack. Just a bootlegger. Just a businessman.

"I'm having a little meeting tomorrow night," Jack told him, "for those who couldn't make it to the last one."

"I'm booked up."

"Unbook, Charlie. It's at the Aratoga. Eight o'clock. And I'm all business, Charlie. All business."

"I never knew you to be anything else, Jack."

"Charlie, old brother, don't have me send for you."

Jack left it there, turned his back on Charlie and walked down the bar and into the table area where only one table was occupied: by that beauty in a white linen suit and white pumps; and at the table with her a five-foot-five, one-eyed, waterheaded gnome. This was Murray (The Goose) Pucinski who'd worked for Jack for the past five years.

"Oh, God, Jack, oh, God where've you been?" was Kiki's greeting. She stood to hug him.

Jack squeezed her and gave her a quick kiss, then sat alongside her.

"She behaving herself, Goose?" Jack asked the waterhead.

Goose nodded.

"How could anybody misbehave up here?" Kiki said, looking me over. I was struck by the idea of misbehaving with her. That was the first logical thing to consider when you looked at Kiki. The second was the flawless quality of her face, even underneath all that professionally applied makeup; a dense rather than a delicate beauty, large, dark eyes, a mouth of soft, round promise, and an abundance of hair, not black as Alice had said, but auburn, a glorious Titian mop. Her expression, as we visually introduced ourselves, was one of anxious innocence. I use the phrase to describe a moral condition in fragments, anxious to be gone, but with a large segment still intact. The condition was visible in the eyes, which for all their sexual innuendo and expertise, for all their knowledge of how beauty rises in the world, were in awe, I suspect, of her rarefied situation: its prisonerlike quality, its dangers, its potential cruelties, and its exhilarating glimpses of evil. By eye contact alone, and this done in a few seconds, she conveyed to me precisely how uneasy she was with The Goose as her chaperon. A quick glance at him, then at me, then a lift of the eyebrows and twist of the pursed lips, was my clue that The Goose was a guardian of negative entertainment value.

"I wanna dance," she said to Jack. "Jackie, I'm dying to dance. Speed, play us something so we can dance."

"It's too early to dance," Jack said.

"No, it isn't"—and her entire body did a shimmy in anticipation. "Come on, Joey, come on, puh-leeeze."

"My fingers don't wake up till nine o'clock at night," Fogarty said. "Or after six beers."

"Aw, Joey."

Fogarty hadn't sat down yet. He looked at Jack who smiled and shrugged, and so Fogarty went to the piano on the elevated bandstand and, with what I'd call a semipro's know-how, snapped out a peppy version of "Twelfth Street Rag." Kiki was up with the first four bars, pulling Jack to his feet. Jack reluctantly took an armful of Kiki, then whisked her around in a very respectable foxtrot, dancing on the balls of his feet with sureness and lightness. Fogarty segued into the "Charleston" and then the "Black Bottom," and Kiki split from Jack and broke into bouncily professional arm maneuvers and kicks, showing a bit of garter.

Interested as I was in Kiki's star and garter performance, it was Jack who took my attention. Was Legs Diamond really about to perform in public? He stood still when Kiki broke away, watched her for a step or two, then assessed his audience, especially the bar where Charlie Northrup and the barkeep were giving Jack full eyeball.

"C'mon, Jackie," said Kiki, her breasts in fascinating upheaval. Jack looked at her and his feet began to move, left out, right kick, right back, left back, basic, guarded, small-dimensioned movements, and then "C'mon, dance," Kiki urged, and he gave up his consciousness of the crowd and then left out, right kick, right back, left back expanded, vitalized, and he was dancing, arms swinging, dancing, Jack Diamond, who seemed to do everything well, was dancing the Charleston and Black Bottom, dancing them perfectly, the way all America had always wanted to be able to dance them—energetically, controlled, as professionally graceful as his partner who had danced these dances for money in Broadway shows, who had danced them for Ziegfeld; and now she was dancing on the mountaintop with the king of the mountain, and they were king and queen of motion together, fluid with Fogarty's melody and beat.

And then above the music, above the pounding of Fogarty's foot, above the heavy breathing and shuffling of Jack and Kiki and above the concentration that we of the small audience were fixing on the performance, there came the laughter. You resisted acknowledging that it was laughter, for there was nothing funny going on in the room and so it must be something else, you said to yourself. But it grew in strength and strangeness, for once you did acknowledge that yes, that's laughter all right, and you said, somebody's laughing at them, and you remembered where you were and who you were with, you turned (and we all turned) and saw Charlie Northrup at the end of the bar, pounding the bar with the open palm of his right hand, laughing too hard. The bartender told him a joke, was my thought, but then Charlie lifted the palm and pointed to Jack and Kiki and spluttered to the barman and we all heard, because Fogarty had heard the laughing and stopped playing and so there was no music when Charlie said, "Dancin' . . . the big man's dancin' . . . dancin' the Charleston on Sunday afternoon . . ." and then Jack stopped. And Kiki stopped six beats after the music had and said, "What happened?"

Jack led her to the table and said, "We're going to have a drink," and moved her arm and made sure she sat down before he walked to the bar and spoke to Charlie Northrup in such a low voice that we couldn't hear. Charlie had stopped laughing by then and had taken a mouthful of beer while he listened to whatever it was Jack said. Then he swallowed the beer, and with a mirthless smile he retorted to Jack, who did not wait for the retort but was already walking back toward us.

"I'm trembling, brother," Charlie called to him. "Trembling." He took another mouthful of beer, swished it around in his mouth, and spat it in a long arc after Jack. Not hitting him, or meaning to, but spitting as a child spits when he can think of no words as venomous as his saliva. Then he turned away from the direction of his spit, swallowed the last of his beer, and walked his great hulk out of the bar.

Holy Flying Christ, I said to myself when I understood Charlie's laughter and saw the arc of beer, for I understood much more than what we were all seeing. I was remembering what Jack's stylized terror could do to a man, remembering Joe Vignola, my client in the Hotsy Totsy case, a man visited not by Jack's vengeance but merely by the specter of it. I was remembering Joe on his cot in the Tombs, tracing with his eye a maze a prisoner before him had drawn on the wall, losing the way, tracing with his finger, but the finger too big, then finding a broom straw and tracing with that. And scratching his message above the maze with a spoon: *Joe Vignola never hurt nobody, but they put him in jail anyway.* Joe was dreaming of smuggling a gun in via his wife's brassiere, but he couldn't conceive of how to ask her to do such an embarrassing thing. And the district attorney was explaining almost daily to him, it's just routine, Joe, we hold 'em all the time in cases like this, an outrage, as you know, what happened, and we must have witnesses, must have them. Also a precautionary measure, as I'm sure you're aware, Joe, you're safer here. But I want to go home, Joe said, and the DA said, well, if you insist, but that's twenty thousand. Twenty thou? Twenty thou. I'm not guilty, you've got the wrong man. Oh no, said the DA, you're the right man. You're the one who saw Legs Diamond and his friends being naughty at the Hotsy Totsy. I'm not the only one, Joe said. Right, Joe, you are not the only one. We have other witnesses. We have the bartender. We have Billy Reagan, too, who is coming along nicely. An open-and-shut case, as they say.

✼   ✼   ✼

Joe Vignola was in jail eight days when his wife got a phone call. Somebody, no name, told her: Look on such and such a page of the *Daily News* about what happened to Walter Rudolph. Walter Rudolph was the DA's corroborating witness, and two kids had found him lying off the Bordentown Turnpike near South Amboy, wearing his blue serge suit, his straw hat alongside him, eleven machine-gun slugs in him.

I was called into the case at this point. Vignola's lawyer was suddenly inaccessible to Vignola's wife, and an old show business friend of mine, Lew Miller, who produced Broadway shows and had patronized the Hotsy and gotten to know Joe Vignola well enough to go to bat for him, called me up and asked me to see what I could do for the poor bird.

Memory of my first interrogation of Joe:

Why did you tell the cops what you saw? Why did you identify photos of Jack Diamond and Charlie Filetti for the grand jury?

Because I wanted people to know I had nothing to do with it. Because I didn't want them to put me in jail for withholding evidence. And a cop slapped me twice.

But why, really, Joe? Did you want your name in the papers, too?

No, because Billy Reagan had talked and would be the main witness and because the cops had at least twenty-five other witnesses who were in the club, and they told the same story I did, the DA said.

But, Joe, knowing what we know about Jack Diamond and people like him, how could you do it? Was it time to die?

Not at all. Basically, I don't approve of murder, or Jack Diamond or Charlie Filetti either. I was brought up a Catholic and I know the value of honesty. I know what a citizen has to do in cases like this. Don't I hear it in church and on the radio and in the papers about being a good citizen? We can't let these bums take over America. If I don't stand up and fight, how can I expect the next guy to stand up? How could I look myself in the mirror?

But why, Joe? Lay off the bullshit and tell me for chrissake, why?

Why? Because it takes big balls. Because Jack Diamond was always cracking wise about the guineas and nobody is going to say that Joe Vignola is a yellow-bellied guinea. Joe Vignola is an Italian-descent American with big balls.

> Big balls, Joe? Was that really it?
> Right.
> You dumb bastard.

I got in touch with the lawyer for Charlie Filetti, who they caught in Chicago and hit with murder one. They hadn't picked up Jack. I told the lawyer poor Joe was of no use to the prosecution because he would not be able to remember anything at the time, and that I wanted to be in touch with somebody in the Diamond gang who I could relay this message to at first hand so that Jack would also know what Joe was up to, which was not much. The lawyer put me on to Jimmy Biondo, who met me at the Silver Slipper on Forty-eighth Street one night. We talked briefly, as follows:

"You guarantee he's no pigeon?"

"I guarantee," I said.

"How?"

"Every way but in writing."

"The bum. The fuckin' bum."

"He's all right. He won't talk. Lay off the telephone threats. He's got three kids and a nice wife. He's a nice Italian boy like yourself. He doesn't want to hurt anybody. He's an altar boy."

"Funeral for altar boys," said eloquent Jimmy.

"I guarantee you. What do you want from me? I'm his lawyer. He can't fire me. He hasn't even paid me yet."

"Fuckin' . . ." said Jimmy.

"Easy does it. He won't talk."

"Fuck . . ."

"I guarantee."

"You guarantee?"

"I guarantee."

"You better fuckin' guarantee."

"I said I guarantee, and when I say I guarantee, I guarantee."

"Fuckin' well better . . ."

"Right, Jimmy. You got my word. Joe won't talk."
"Fuck."

*   *   *

Joe told me Jack Diamond, disguised as a Boy Scout, came through the bars of his cell one night and stood alongside Joe's bunk as he slept. "It's time to have your ears pierced," Jack said to Joe, and he shoved the blade of his Scout knife into Joe's left ear. Joe's brain leaked out through the hole.

"Help me," Joe yelled. "My ear is leaking." From the next cell somebody yelled, "Shut up, you looney son of a bitch."

But Joe didn't feel he was looney. He told the Bellevue alienist how it was when they wanted to know why he hid food under the bedclothes.

"That was for Legs Diamond. If he wants a bite to eat and I got nothing, that's trouble."

"Did it occur to you that the food would rot and give off a stench?"

"Rotten, it doesn't really matter. It's the offer that counts."

"Why did you cover your head with the blanket?"

"I wanted to be alone."

"But you were alone."

"I didn't want visitors."

"The blanket kept them away?"

"No, I could see them through the blanket. But it was better than nothing."

"Why did you hide the spoon?"

"So my visitors would have something to eat with."

"Then why did you scratch at the concrete floor with it?"

"I wanted to dig a place to hide so the visitors couldn't find me."

"How did you tear up your fingers?"

"When they took my spoon away."

"You dug at the concrete with your fingers?"

"I knew it'd take a long time; the nails'd have to grow back before I could dig again."

"Who visited you?"

"Diamond came every night. Herman Zuckman came, cut up the middle and half a dozen iron bars inside him, and wire wrapped around his stomach to keep the bars from falling out. He dripped muck and seaweed all over. 'What did you do wrong, Herman?' I said to him.

" 'Jew people have a tough life,' " he said.

"And I told him, 'You think it's easy being Italian?' "

"Any other visitors?"

"Walter Rudolph came in to cheer me up and I saw daylight through his bullet holes."

The night the dead fish leaped out of Herman's tuxedo Joe finally won his straitjacket.

                        *   *   *

The judge ordered the acquittal of Filetti after four days of trial, saying that the state had utterly failed to prove its case. Jack, still a fugitive, was never mentioned during the trial. Of the fifteen witnesses who testified, not one claimed to have seen Filetti actually shoot anybody. Joe Vignola, who was described as the state's most important witness, said he was dozing in another room when the shooting broke out and he saw nothing. His speech was incoherent most of the time.

Billy Reagan testified he was too drunk after drinking twenty shots of gin to remember what happened. Also, Tim Reagan's last words, originally said to have incriminated Diamond and Filetti, were not about them at all, a detective testified, but rather a violent string of curses.

                        *   *   *

Jack was a fugitive for eight months, and most of his gang, which was an amalgam of old-timers and remnants of Little Augie Orgen's Lower East Side Jews, drifted into other allegiances. The bond had not been strong to begin with. Jack took the gang over after he and Augie were both shot in a labor racketeering feud. Augie died, but you can't kill Legs Diamond.

Eddie Diamond died in January, 1930. Jack was still a fugitive when he met Kiki Roberts in April at the Club Abbey, and he immediately dropped Elaine Walsh. Half a dozen gangland murders were credited to his feud with Dutch Schultz during these months.

He saw the Jack Sharkey-Tommy Loughran fight at Yankee Stadium, as did Al Smith, David Belasco, John McGraw, and half the celebrities of New York. Jack couldn't miss such a show, even if he did have to raise a mustache and sit in an upper deck to avoid recognition. He bet on Loughran, like himself a Philadelphia mick; but Sharkey, the Boston sailor, won.

The crest of his life collapsed with the Hotsy shooting. All he'd been building to for most of a decade—his beer and booze operations, the labor racketeering he built with and inherited in part from Little Augie, his protection of the crooked bucketshops which bilked stock market suckers, an inheritance from Rothstein, his connections with the dope market, and, most ignominiously, his abstract aspiration to the leadership mantle that would somehow simulate Rothstein's—all this was Jack's life-sized sculpture, blown apart by gunpowder.

Dummy, you shoot people in your own club?

Jack got the word from Owney Madden, his old mentor from Go-

pher days, a quiet, behind-the-scenes fellow who, after doing his murder
bit, came out of Sing Sing in 1923 and with a minimum of fanfare
became the Duke of New York, the potentate of beer and political
power in the city's underworld. Madden brought Jack the consensus
sentiment from half a dozen underworld powerhouses: Go someplace
else, Jack. Go someplace else and be crazy. For your own good, go. Or
we'll have to kill you.

Jack's pistol had punctuated a decade and scribbled a finale to a
segment of his own life. He had waged war on Schultz, Rothstein, and
half a dozen lesser gang leaders in the Bronx, Jersey, and Manhattan,
but he could not war against a consortium of gangs and he moved to
the Catskills. I knew some of this, and I was certain Charlie Northrup
knew much more, which is why Charlie's spitting beer at Jack and
mocking him to his face did not seem, to say the least, to be in Charlie's
own best interest.

*   *   *

After Charlie walked out of the Top o' the Mountain House Kiki said
she was sick of the place and wanted to go someplace and have fun,
and Jack-the-fun-seeker said okay, and we stopped at a hot dog stand,
Kiki's choice, and sought out an aerial bowling alley which intrigued
her and was a first for me. A genuine bowling ball was suspended on a
long cable, and you stood aloof from the pins below and let the ball fly
like a cannon shot. It then truly or falsely spun through the air and
knocked over all the pins your luck and skill permitted. Kiki scored
sixty-eight and almost brained the pinboy with a premature salvo, Jack
got one fourteen and I won the day with one sixty-four. Jack was coming to respect my eye at least as much as he respected my legal acuity.

From bowling we went to miniature golf, where we played eighteen
holes. Some holes you climbed stairs to and putted downhill. Kiki went
first at one of those, and when you stood to the rear of her, as Jack and
I did—Fogarty and The Goose were consuming soda pop elsewhere—
you had total visibility of the girl's apparatus. She wore rolled silk stockings with frilly black garters about five inches above the knee, the sheerest pair of lace panties I'd theretofore seen, and areas of the most
interesting flesh likely to be found on any mountain anywhere, and I
also include the valleys.

I see her there yet. I see her also crossing and uncrossing her silki-
ness, hinting at secret reaches, dark arenas of mystery difficult to reach,
full of jewels of improbable value, full of the *promise* of tawdriness, of
illicitness, of furtiveness, of wickedness, with possibly blue rouge on the
nipples, and arcane exotica revealed when she slips down the elastic
waistband of those sheerest of sheers. They infected my imagination,

those dark, those sheer, those elasticized arenas of that gorgeous girl's life.

I did not know that the infection would be prophetic of Kiki, prophetic of revelations of flesh, prophetic of panties. Nor did I know that this afternoon, with its sprinkles of rain interrupting our sport, would be the inspiration for Jack to initiate his organized shakedown of hot dog stands and miniature golf courses all over Greene and Ulster counties.

*   *   *

Kiki showed me a clipping once with a coincidence that made her believe in destiny. It was an item out of Winchell, which said, "Dot and Dash is a mustache. Yaffle is an arrest. Long cut short is a sawed-off shotgun. White is pure alcohol. Simple Simon is a diamond. . . ." It appeared the day before Kiki met Jack at a nightclub party, and she was just about to go into rehearsal for a new musical, *Simple Simon.*

I look back to those early days and see Kiki developing in the role of woman as sprite, woman as goddess, woman as imp. Her beauty and her radiance beyond beauty were charms she used on Jack, but used with such indifference that they became subtle, perhaps even secret, weapons. I cite the dance floor episode at the Top o' the Mountain House as an example, for she had small interest in whether it was Jack who danced with her or not. Her need was to exult in her profession, which had not been chosen casually, which reflected a self dancing alone beneath all the glitter of her Broadway life. "I must practice my steps," she said numerous times in my presence, and then with a small radio Jack had given her she would find suitable music and, oblivious of others, go into her dance, a tippy-tap-toe routine of cosmic simplicity. She was not a good dancer, just a dancer, just a chorus girl. This is not a pejorative reduction, for it is all but impossible for anyone to be as good a chorus girl as Kiki proved to be, proved it not only on stage—Ziegfeld said she was the purest example of sexual nonchalance he'd ever seen —but also in her photogenicity, her inability to utter a complex sentence, her candor with newspapermen, her willingness to trivialize, monumentalize, exalt, and exploit her love for Jack by selling her memoirs to the tabloids—twice—and herself to a burlesque circuit for the fulfillable professional years of her beauty and the tenacious years of Jack's public name. More abstractly she personified her calling in her walk, in her breathing, in the toss of her head, in her simultaneous eagerness and reluctance to please a lover, in her willingness to court wickedness without approving of it, and in her willingness to conform to the hallowed twentieth-century chorus-girl stereotype that Ziegfeld, George White, Nils T. Granlund, the Minskys, and so many more men, whose business was flesh, had incarnated, and which Walter Winchell, Ed Sullivan, Odd McIntyre, Damon Runyon, Louis Sobol, and so many others, whose business was to muse and gossip on the ways of this incarnated flesh, had mythicized. And as surely as Jack loved pistols, rifles, machine guns—loved their noise, their weight, their force, the power they passed to him, their sleekness, their mechanical perfections, their oily surfaces as balm for his ulcerated gangster soul—so did he cherish the weaponistic charms of Kiki. And as the guns also became his trouble as well as his beloved, so became Kiki. She did not know such ambivalence was possible when she met Jack, but her time alone with The Goose on the mountaintop was the beginning of her wisdom, painful wisdom which love alone could relieve.

*   *   *

A quick summer storm blew up and it started to rain as Fogarty drove Kiki, Jack, and me back to Haines Falls after the golf. There was talk of dinner, which I declined, explaining I had to get back to Albany. But no, no, Jack wouldn't hear of my leaving. Wasn't I done out of a champagne lunch by the canary scene? We went to the Top o' the Mountain House to freshen up before we ate, and Jack gave me the room The Goose had been using, next to Kiki's. Jack joined Kiki in her room for what I presumed was a little mattress action, and I pursued a catnap. But the walls were thin and I was treated instead to a memorably candid conversation:

"I'm going back to New York," Kiki said.

"You don't mean it," Jack said.

"I don't care what you do. I'm not staying in this prison with that goon. He never says a word."

"He's not good at talking. He's good at other things. Like you."

"I hate having a bodyguard."

"But your body deserves guarding."

"It deserves more than that."

"You're very irritable tonight."

"You're damn right I am."

"You've got a right to be, but don't swear. It's not ladylike."

"You're not so particular in bed about ladylike."

"We're not in bed now."

"Well, I don't know why we're not. I don't see you for two days and you show up with a stranger and don't even try to be alone with me."

"You want a bed, do you? What do you want to put in it?"

"How's this? How does it look?"

"Looks like it's worth putting money into."

"I don't want money in it."

"Then I'll have to think of something else."

"I love to kiss your scars," Kiki said after a while.

"Maybe you'll kiss them all away," Jack said.

"I wouldn't want to do that. I love you the way you are."

"And you're the most perfect thing I've ever seen. I deserve you. And you don't have any scars."

"I'm getting one."

"Where?"

"Inside. You cut me and let me bleed, and then I heal and you leave me to go back to your wife."

"Someday I'll marry you."

"Marry me now, Jackie."

"It's complicated. I can't leave her. She's in a bad way lately, depressed, sick."

"She goes to the movies. She's old and fat."

"I've got a lot of money in her name."

"She could run off with it, wipe you out."

"Where could she run I couldn't find her?"

"You trust her, but you don't trust me alone."

"She's never alone."

"What is she to you? What can she give you I can't?"

"I don't know. She likes animals."

"I like animals."

"No, you don't. You never had a pet in your life."

"But I like them. I'll get a pet. I'll get a cat. Then will you marry me?"

"Later I'll marry you."

"Am I your real lay?"

"More than that."

"Not much more."

"Don't be stupid. I could lay half the town if I wanted to—Catskill, Albany, New York, any town. Unlimited what I could lay. Unlimited."

"I want a set of those Chinese balls. The metal ones."

"Where'd you hear about those?"

"I get around. I get left alone a lot now, but I didn't always."

"What would you do with them?"

"What everybody does. Wear them. Then when nobody's around to take care of me and I get all hot and bothered, I'd just squeeze them and they'd make me feel good. I want them."

"Will you settle for an Irish set?"

"Can I keep them with me?"

"I'll see they don't get out of range."
"Well, see to it then."

*   *   *

"Everything was still incredible with me and Jack back then," Kiki said to me much later, remembering the sweet time. "It was thrilling just to see him from a new angle, his back, or his stomach, any part of his bare skin. He had gouges and scars from knife fights when he was a kid, and where he'd been shot and kicked and beaten with clubs and boards and pipes. I got sad up on the mountain one night looking at them all. But he said they didn't hurt him anymore, and the more I looked at them and touched them, the more they made his body special, the way his head was special. It wasn't an all white and smooth and fatty body like some I've seen but the body of a man who'd gone through a whole lot of hell. There was a long red scar on his stomach just above his belly button, where he'd almost died from a cut in a knife fight over a girl when he was fifteen. I ran my tongue over it and it felt hot. I could almost taste how much it hurt when he'd got it and what it meant now. To me it meant he was alive, that he didn't die easy. Some people could cut their little toe and give up and bleed to death. Jack never gave up, not his body, not anything."

*   *   *

Well, we all did have dinner on the mountain, and then I insisted on leaving. "It's been a special day," I told Jack, "but an odd one."
"What's so odd about it?"
"Well, how about buying a paperweight for starters?"
"Seems like an ordinary day to me," he said. I assumed he was kidding. But then he said, "Come to dinner next week. I'll have Alice cook up another roast. I'll call you during the week to set it up. And think about Europe."
So I said I would and turned to Kiki, whom I'd spoken about forty words to all day. But I'd smiled her into my goodwill and stared her into my memory indelibly, and I said, "Maybe I'll see you again, too," and before she could speak Jack said, "Oh you'll see her all right. She'll be around."
"I'll be around he says," Kiki said to me in a smart-ass tone, like Alice's whippy retort had been earlier in the day. Then she took my hand, a sensuous moment.
Everything seemed quite real as I stood there, but I knew when I got back to Albany the day would seem to have been invented by a mind with a faulty gyroscope. It had the quality of a daydream after

eight whiskeys. Even the car I was to ride down in—Jack's second buggy, a snazzy, wire-wheeled, cream-colored Packard roadster The Goose was using to chauffeur Kiki around the mountains—had an unreal resonance.

I know the why of this, but I know it only now as I write these words. It took me forty-three years to make the connection between Jack and Gatsby. It should have been quicker, for he told me he met Fitzgerald on a transatlantic voyage in 1926, on the dope-buying trip that got him into federal trouble. We never talked specifically about Gatsby, only about Fitzgerald, who, Jack said, was like two people, a condescending young drunk the first time they met, an apologetic, decent man the second time. The roadster was long and bright and with double windshields, and exterior toolbox, and a tan leather interior, the tan a substitute, for Gatsby's interior was "a sort of green leather conservatory." But otherwise it was a facsimile of the Gatsby machine, and of that I'm as certain as you can be in a case like this. Jack probably read *Gatsby* for the same reason he read every newspaper story and book and saw every movie about gangland. I know he saw Von Sternberg's *Underworld* twice; we did talk about that. It was one way of keeping tabs on his profession, not pretension to culture. He mocked Waxey Gordon to me once for lining his walls with morocco-bound sets of Emerson and Dickens. "They're just another kind of wallpaper to the bum," Jack said.

I accept Jack's Gatsby connection because he knew Edward Fuller, Fitzgerald's neighbor on Long Island who was the inspiration for Gatsby. Fuller and Rothstein were thick in stocks, bonds, and bucketshops when Jack was bodyguarding Rothstein. And, of course, Fitzgerald painted a grotesque, comic picture of Rothstein himself in *Gatsby*, wearing human molar cuff buttons and spouting a thick Jewish accent, another reason Jack would have read the book.

I rode with The Goose in Jack's roadster and tried to make a little conversation.

"You known Jack long?"

"Yeah," said Murray, and then nothing for about three miles.

"Where'd you meet him?"

"Th'army," said Murray, not spending two words where one would do.

"You've been working with him since then?"

"No, I did time. Jack, too."

"Ah."

"I got nine kids."

Murray looked at me when he said this, and I guess I paused long enough before I said, "Have you?" to provoke him.

"You don't believe me?"

"Sure I believe you. Why shouldn't I?"

"People don't believe I got nine kids."

"If you say it, I believe it. That's a lot of kids. Nobody lies about things like that."

"I don't see them. Once a year. Maybe, maybe not. But I send 'em plenty."

"Uh-huh."

"They don't know what I do for a living."

"Oh?"

Then we had another mile or so of silence, except for the thunder and lightning and the heavy rain, which kept Murray creeping slowly along the snaky road down the mountain. I judged him to be about forty-five, but he was hard to read. He might've seemed older because of the menace he transmitted, even when he talked about his kids. His mouth curled down into a snarleyow smile, his lone eye like a flat spring, tightly coiled, ready to dilate instantly into violent glare. He was obviously the pro killer in the gang, which I deduced as soon as I saw him. Oxie may have had some deadly innings in his career, but he looked more like a strongarm who would beat you to death by mistake. Murray's clothes were a shade too small for him, giving him a puffy, spaghetti-filled look. I thought I detected tomato sauce stains on his coat and pants and even his eyepatch. I choose to believe he was merely a slob rather than inefficient enough to walk around with bloodstains from his last victim. I doubt Jack would have approved of that sort of coarseness.

"You workin' for Jack now?" Murray asked me.

"Tentatively," I said, wondering whether he understood the word, so I added, "for the time being I guess I am."

"Jack is a pisser."

"Is he?"

"He's crazy."

"Is that so?"

"That's why I work for him. You never know what'll happen next."

"That's a good reason."

"He was crazy in the Army. I think he was always crazy."

"Some of us are."

"I said to myself after he done what he done to me, this is a crazy guy you got to watch out for because he does crazy stuff."

"What did he do to you?"

"What did he do to me? What did he do to me?"

"Right."

"I was in the stockade at Fort Jay for raping a colonel's wife, a bum rap. I only did her a favor after she caught me in the house and I rapped her one and she fell down. Her dress goes up and she says, 'I suppose you're gonna strip and rape me,' and I hadn't figured on it, but you take what comes. So I'm in for that, plus burglary and kickin' an MP when Jack comes in to wait for his court-martial.

" 'Whatcha in for?' I asked him.

" 'Desertion and carrying a pistol.'

" 'That's heavy duty.'

" 'I figure I'll do a little time,' he said. 'They want my ass.'

" 'Likewise,' I said and told him my story.

" 'What'd you do before you got in?' he asks me and I tell him, 'I was a burglar.' He got a kick out of that because he done a bit for the same thing when he was a kid. So we talk and Jack gets a pint of whiskey from the corporal who made bedcheck. I don't drink that shit, so Jack asks me if I wanna drink some rain instead. It's raining out just like now, and Jack puts a cup out the window. Took about five minutes to fill it up part way, and by that time Jack's whiskey is most gone and he gets the cup of rain and gives it to me.

" 'I don't want no rain,' I says to him. 'It's dirty.'

" 'Who says it's dirty?'

" 'Everybody says.'

" 'They're wrong,' he says. 'Best water there is.'

" 'You drink it,' I says, 'I don't want no part of any dirty, shitty rain.'

" 'Goddamn it, I told you rain wasn't dirty. You think I'd drink rain if it was dirty?' And he takes a drink of it.

" 'Anybody who'd drink rain'd shit in church,' I says to him.

" 'Did you say shit in church?'

" 'Shit in church and then kick it out in the aisle.'

" 'That's a goddamn lie. I'd never shit in church.'

" 'If you'd drink rain, you'd shit in church all right.'

" 'Not me. I'd never shit in church. You hear that, goddamn it? Never!'

" 'All them rain drinkers. They all shit in church.'

" 'Not me, no sir. Why do you say that?'

" 'I never knew an Irishman wouldn't shit in church if he thought he could get away with it.'

" 'Irishmen don't shit in church. I don't believe that.'

" 'I seen four Irishmen at the same time, all taking a shit in church.'

" 'Polacks shit in church.'

" 'I once seen an Irishman shit right in the holy water fountain.'

" 'That's a goddamn lie.'

" 'Then I seen two Irishmen takin' shits in the confessional boxes and about a dozen more takin' shits up on the altar all at once. I seen one Irishman shit during a funeral. Irishmen don't know no better.'

"I was layin' on my cot while this was going on. Then Jack got up and punched me in the right eye so hard I lost the sight of it. Jesus, that was a crazy thing to do. I didn't even see it comin'. I had to kick him all over the room, broke ribs and stuff. The guards pulled me off him. I woulda killed him if I knew the eye was gone, but I didn't know it then. When I saw him a week later he got down on his knees and asked me to forgive him what he done. I said, 'Fuck you, Jack,' and left him on his knees. But we shook hands before I left and I told him 'Okay, don't worry about it.' But I was still sore about it. I done six years because the MP I kicked died, and when I come out I looked Jack up because I figure he owes me a job. He thought he did a tough thing about the eye, but shit, once you get used to one eye it's just as good as two. And workin' for Jack, you get to do everything you got to do, so I got no complaints."

＊　　　＊　　　＊

We were about halfway down the mountain when Murray hit the brakes, but not soon enough, and we skidded into a rock slide and smashed into a boulder that must've just landed because other little rocks kept bouncing off the car. Both of us hit the windshield, and I got a hell of a bump and a four-day headache out of it. Murray's forehead was cut, a horizontal gash like a split seam.

"We better haul ass before another one falls on top of us," Murray said, a thought I hadn't had yet since I was preoccupied with my pain. He tried backing up, but the car made a weird noise and was hard to move. He got out in the rain and so I got out after him. There was about one foot between me and about a four-hundred-foot drop, so I got carefully back inside and out Murray's door. He was pulling on the front left fender, which was smashed and rubbing against the wheel. Murray was a small man but a strong one, for the fender came almost straight at this tug. He cut his right hand on the edge of it, and when I offered him my pocket handkerchief, he shook his head and scooped up a handful of earth and grass and patted it on his forehead and then globbed a wad into his sliced right palm.

"Get in," he said, his face and hand smeared and dripping with bloody mud.

"I'll drive," I told him.

"No, I'll handle it."

"You're in no shape to drive."

"This is not your car, mister," he said in a tone that was unarguably the last word.

"All right, then, back up and turn around. I'll direct you. You're damn near over the edge right there, and it's one hell of a long way down."

It was dark now and I was wet to the underwear, standing in the middle of desolation, maybe about to be buried in a landslide, giving traffic directions to a bleeding, one-eyed psychopath who was, with one hand, trying to drive a mythic vehicle backwards up an enchanted mountain.

I'd come a long way from the K. of C. library.

Johnny Raw, Jack Gentleman

Jack came to Albany to see me four days after my time on the mountain. He was full of Europe and its glories, the spas at Bad Homburg and Wiesbaden, the roulette and baccarat in the casinos where croupiers spoke six languages, the eloquent slenderness of the Parisian whore. He came to my office with Fogarty; he was in town on other business we didn't discuss but which I presume was beer supply for his expanding clientele. He handed me five hundred cash as my initial retainer.

"What do I do for this?"

"Buy a ticket to Europe."

"Jack, I've got no good reason to go to Europe."

"You owe it to your body," he said. "All that great wine and great food."

"All right, maybe," I said. But what, really, did I need with this kind of action? Where was the profit? Jack merely said he'd be in touch within the week and that was that.

Then I got a weird call at three the next morning from him, saying he'd decided to go to New York immediately instead of next week and leave for Europe in the afternoon if he got the booking, and was I ready, did I live in control of the quick decision or was I going to take a week to think it over? It meant being in Manhattan in about nine or ten hours and committing myself to the booking and turning off my practice. He kept saying, "Well? Well? What do you think?" And so I said, "All right, yes," against all sane judgment, and he said, "You're a winner, Marcus," and I rolled over and went back for two more hours. Then I closed off my Albany life with four phone calls and caught the ten thirty train to New York.

*   *   *

A fox terrier leaped overboard, an apparent suicide, the day the news broke aboard ship that Charlie Northrup's bloodstained Buick was found in a Sixty-first Street garage near the Brooklyn Army Base. The garage was owned by Vannie Higgins, a pal of Jack's and the crown prince of Long Island rum-runners. Oxie and a Brooklyn couple, the wife a pal of Alice's, were arrested in their apartment with an arsenal: tear-gas grenades, ammo, flares, fountain-pen pistols, bulletproof vests, and enough explosives to blow up a city block. Brooklyn war with Capone, said the papers. Oxie said only that he was sleeping on Jack's porch at Acra when two men he wouldn't identify woke him and offered him fifty bucks to take the Buick to New York and dump it. Cops saw him and the other man near a Fifty-eighth Street pier acting suspiciously, and Oxie admitted that the blocks in the Buick were to be used to run it over the stringpiece.

We were two days out of New York on the *Belgenland*, bound for Plymouth and Brussels, and suddenly our foursome—Jack, Count Duschene, Classy Willie Green, and myself—was the center of all attention. Jack was traveling under the name of John Nolan, a name of notable nautical import, and he got away with it until the radio brought news bulletins from the New York City police commissioner, a feisty old Irishman named Devane, that Jack was fleeing from a foul murder and was now on the high seas, bound for England to buy dope.

He wasn't wanted by the police, but Devane felt it his duty to alert the nations of Europe that a fiend was approaching. The Northrup car was the subject of daily bulletins in the ship's newspaper, and as the mystery of what happened to Charlie intensified, so did Jack's celebrity. Passengers snapped his picture, asked for his autograph, assured him they didn't believe such a nice person as he was would have anything to do with such terrible goings on.

The fox terrier: He appeared as I stood on the sports deck near the rail, while Jack was shooting skeet. I saw nothing chasing the dog, which came at me in a blur of brown and white, but there must have been something, for he was panicky or perhaps suddenly maddened. He took a corner at high speed, dead-ended into a bulkhead, turned around, and leaped through the rail, flailing like a crazy-legged circus clown falling off a tightrope into a net. I saw him surface once, go into a wave, bob up again, and then vanish. I doubt anyone else saw it.

A man finally came toward me at a brisk pace and asked if I'd seen his dog, and I said, yes, I'd just seen it leap overboard.

"Leap overboard?" the man said, stunned by the concept.

"Yes. He leaped."

"He wasn't thrown?"

"Nobody threw him, I can tell you that. He jumped."

"A dog wouldn't leap overboard like that."

He looked at me, beginning to believe I'd killed his dog. I assured him I'd never seen such a thing either, but that it was true, and just then he looked past me and said, "That's Legs Diamond," the dog instantly forgotten, the man already turning to someone to pass along his discovery. In a matter of minutes a dozen people were watching Jack shoot. He had been reloading during my encounter and saw the crowd before he put the shotgun again to his shoulder. He fired, missed, fired, missed. The crowd tittered, but he looked at them and silenced the titters. He fired again, missed again, fired again, missed again, and thrust the gun angrily at the man in charge of lofting the clay pigeons. Then he and I went quickly down to the parlor where Classy Willie and The Count, a dapper pair, were jointly relieving four other passengers of their vacation money in a poker game. I knew neither The Count nor Willie before I boarded the ship with Jack, but it turned out that The Count was Jack's international associate, an expert bottom dealer who spoke French, German, and Spanish and did not lose his head in the presence of too many forks, and that Classy Willie was a card thief, specializing in ocean liners, who had been hired by Jimmy Biondo to represent him in the dope deal. Willie had a certain suavity behind his pencil-line mustache, but he was also known for his erratic violence on behalf of his employer.

I understood these relationships only much later. At this point in the trip I assumed both men worked for Jack.

I asked Jack about Oxie and the car and he said, "I take no responsibility for mugs like him once they're out of my sight."

"Goddamn it, Jack, you've got me involved in the biggest murder case in upstate New York in Christ knows how long and you give me this evasive routine?"

"Who said you're involved? I'm not even involved."

"You're involved. On the radio is involved."

"Tomorrow there'll be an earthquake in Peru and they'll try to stick me with it."

"Bullshit."

"Shove your bullshit up your ass," he said and walked away.

But he came back an hour later and sat down beside me in a deck-chair, where I was brooding on my stupidity and reading Ernest Dimnet on how to think better, and he said, "How's things now?"

"I'm still involved."

"You worry a lot, Marcus. That's a bad sign. Gets you into trouble."

"I'm in trouble now because I didn't worry enough."

"Listen, you got nothing to be afraid of. Nobody's after your ass, nobody wants to put you on the spot. I never knew a fucking lawyer yet couldn't talk his way out of a sandstorm. You'll do all right if you don't lose your head."

"There was blood in that car, and Oxie was with it. And Oxie is your man."

"Somebody could've had a nosebleed. For chrissake, don't fuck me AROUND!" And he walked away from me again.

We didn't speak a direct word to each other, apart from pass the salt, for two days. My plan was to get off at Plymouth and get the next boat home. I observed him from a distance, seeing people go out of their way for a look at him playing cards in his shirtsleeves. I saw a blond librarian ask him to dance and begin a thing with him. He was a bootlegger and, as such, had celebrity status, plus permission from the social order to kill, maim, and befoul the legal system, for wasn't he performing a social mission for the masses? The system would stay healthy by having life both ways: first, relishing Jack's achievement while it served a function, then slavering sensually when his head, no longer necessary, rolled. This insight softened my hard line of Northrup. Maybe it was all a bootlegger's feud, which somehow made the consequent death okay. Let others assess the moral obliquity in this.

Jack went through a tango with the librarian, who was from Minneapolis, a fetchingly rinsed-out blonde who wore schoolmarmish tweed suits with low-cut blouses beneath. You saw the blouses only when she peeled off the top covering as the dancing went on and on. Jack invited her to eat with us when he started up with her, and he saw to it that none of us lingered over coffee.

Then one day at dinner she wasn't there. Her empty chair went unremarked upon until Jack himself gestured toward it and said, "She wanted my autograph on her briefs," which I thought was a quaint euphemism for Jack.

Everyone laughed at the absurdity, even me.

"I gave her a bullet," Jack said, and I fell into uncertainty until he added, "She says to me, 'It's the right shape but the wrong size.' And I told her, 'Use it sideways.' "

We were swilling duck à l'orange when the librarian came up to the table with her jacket off and put her face inches away from Jack's.

"You turn women into swine," she said.

Jack nodded and bit the duck.

*   *   *

The morning news was that the search for Charlie Northrup had turned into one of the biggest manhunts in New York State history. He was presumed dead, but where? On top of this came a cable from Jimmy Biondo to Classy Willie, precipitating an impromptu meeting of our small quartet in Jack's cabin. Willie arrived, visibly equipped with a pistol for the first time since we boarded ship. Sensing tension, I got up to leave. But Jack said stick around, and so I did.

"Jimmy wants to call off the deal," Willie said to Jack, the first time a deal had been mentioned on the trip.

"Is that so?"

Willie handed the cable to Jack, who read it to us. "Tell our friend we can't stay with him," it said.

"I wonder what he's worried about?" Jack said.

Classy Willie didn't say anything.

"Do you know what he means, Willie?"

"He's talking about the money. Wants me to take it back to him."

"Our money?"

"Jimmy figures it's his money until we make the buy."

"Until I make the buy," Jack said.

"You know what I mean, Jack."

"No, Willie, I can't say that I do. You're a card thief. I never knew a card thief who could talk straight."

"Jimmy must figure you're too hot. The radio says they won't let you into England."

"I wasn't going to England."

"You know what I'm talking about, Jack."

"I suppose I do, Willie. I suppose I do." Jack put on his weary tone of voice. "But I'll tell you the truth, Willie, I'm not even thinking about money. What I'm thinking about is jewels."

"What jewels?"

"I got eighty grand worth and I don't know how to get them off the boat. They'll go through my luggage with a microscope."

"Let your friend Marcus carry them," Willie said. "He's legitimate."

"Not interested, thank you," I said.

"That's not a bad idea, Marcus," Jack said.

"It's a terrible idea, Jack. I want no part of hot merchandise. No part whatever. Not my line of work."

"If Marcus says no, it's no," Jack said. "We'll have to find another way."

I believe Jack already knew what he was going to do with the jewels and was merely testing me for a reaction. My reaction was so instantaneous he didn't even press it a second time. I was more attuned to Classy Willie's problem. If Biondo ever had any sense at all, he wouldn't have sent a dapper thief, a man long known as the Beau Brummell of Forty-eighth Street, to play watchdog to a man as devious as Jack.

"Jimmy wants me to get off at England and come back home with the cash," Willie said. "That was the plan if there was a hitch. He said he talked to you about it."

"I do remember something like that," Jack said. "But how do I know you won't take the cash and hop a boat for the Fiji Islands? I already told you I don't trust card thieves, Willie. I couldn't jeopardize Jimmy's money that way. No. We'll get to Germany and make the deal, and we'll all be a little fatter when we get home. Am I right, Count?"

"The beer is good in Germany," said The Count, a diplomat. "You don't have to needle it."

The façade of the deal was that Jack was to buy booze and wines, and ship them from Bremen to somewhere off Long Island. That's what I was told, by Jack. But Devane was right that Jack was after dope—heroin, which Jack had been buying in Germany since '26 when Rothstein was financing the imports. A federal charge Jack had been dodging successfully since then had come with the bustup of an elaborate smuggling scheme in which Jack was a key figure. The present destination was Frankfurt and, after the deal was wrapped up, a week's vacation in Paris. I remember when we got back to the States that a federal narcotics nabob told the press that Jack's dope smuggling made his booze and beer business look like penny-candy stuff. But people didn't pay attention to such official guff. Their image of Jack was fixed. He was a bootlegger. Locking him into dope was only a source of confusion.

*   *   *

I have vivid recollections of Jack and the press meeting in the hallways of courthouses, at piers and railroad stations in New York, Philadelphia, Albany, Catskill. I remember the aggression the newsmen always showed, persistent in their need to embarrass him with gross questions, but persistent also in their need to show him affection, to laugh harder than necessary at his *bons mots*, to draw ambivalent pleasure from his presence—a man they loved to punish, a man they punished with an odd kind of love. When the British newsmen invaded the *Belgenland* on our arrival in Plymouth, some thirty reporters and cameramen pushed their way into Jack's stateroom to be greeted by the presence himself, clad in black slippers, sky-blue silk pajamas with a white chalk stripe, a navy-blue silk robe, and a Rameses between index and middle fingers. The British behaved no differently from their American brethren, except that Jack's being a foreigner diminished their need to insult him for the sake of the homeland. But their self-righteousness shone through in their questions: Why does America tolerate gangsters? How long have you been a gangster? Was Mr. Charles Northrup murdered at your order? Do you think gangsterism will end when Prohibition ends? How many men have you killed in your life? What about Capone and your Brooklyn arsenal?

Jack treated them like children, laughing at their requests for a laundry list of his victims. "First off, boys, I'm not a gangster, only a bootlegger. There are no gangsters in America. Too easy to get rich other ways. I'm just a civilized citizen. Not a dese, dem, and dose guy. Just a man of the people, trying to make a dollar. Over here getting the cure. Got some stomach trouble and I was advised to go to Vichy and Wiesbaden and take the waters. Brooklyn arsenal? I own nothing in Brooklyn. Capone used to work for me years ago, driving a truck, but I haven't seen him in years. That feud is a lot of nonsense. I get along with people. I'm a legitimate citizen. You newspaper guys scream at the cops to pick me up, and they hold me a few days and find out I'm clean and let me go. I'm not claiming you treat me wrong, but I never see anybody write big headlines when they tell me the charge don't stick. I'm sick of headlines, boys. I came to Europe to get away from it all for a while. Leave that hubbub behind. Make a kind of grand tour on my own, take the waters and cure what ails me. You can understand that, can't you, fellows?"

Sure they could.

Jack's fame at this point was staggering. About four hundred Englishmen had come to the pier by six thirty just to get a glimpse of him. The press of the whole Western world was following our transatlantic voyage, front-paging it with an intensity not quite up to what they did for Byrd, Peary, and other world travelers, but I'll bet with more reader interest. One English paper was so anxious for a story that it invented a phone interview with Jack two days before our boat reached an English pier. "I'm here in London on a secret mission," they quoted him as saying.

So the newsmen, installing Jack in the same hierarchy where they placed royalty, heroes, and movie stars, created him anew as they enshrined him. They invented a version of him with each story they wrote, added to his evil luster by imagining crimes for him to commit, embellishing his history, humanizing him, defining him through their own fantasies and projections. This voyage had the effect of taking Jack Diamond away from himself, of making him a product of the collective imagination. Jack had imagined his fame all his life and now it was imagining him. A year hence he would be saying that "publicity helps the punk" to another set of newsmen, aware how pernicious a commodity it could be. But now he was an addict, a grotesquely needy man, parched for glory, famished for public love, dying for the chance at last to be everybody's wicked pet.

He called the stateroom press conference to a halt after fifteen minutes and said he had to get dressed. The newsmen waited and he joined them on deck, clad now in his blue pinstriped suit, his wide-brimmed white felt hat, his seven-and-a-half-B black wingtips, his purple tie, and his Knight Templar pin in his lapel.

"Hello, boys," he said, "what else do you want from me?"

They talked for another quarter hour and asked, among other things, about that lapel pin; and a story goes with that.

When we talked after the press left, Jack told me that Charlie Northrup was why he was in the Masons. Back in the Bronx in the mid-twenties Jack was playing cards in the back room of his garish Theatrical Club, orange and black decor, and Charlie was sitting in. For no reason he could remember, Jack wondered out loud what a jack was, the picture card. Charlie told him the symbolic meaning of a knave among kings and queens, and Jack liked the whole idea.

Charlie talked about the Masons and their symbols, and it was like the dawn of a new era for Jack. He pumped Charlie for more, then talked him into proposing him as a candidate in the order. He went through in a whoosh and obviously with attention to all the arcane mumbo jumbo he had to memorize. The Masonic books I inherited from him were well marked and annotated in the margins, in his handwriting.

Alongside one section on an old Templar rite of initiation, a Christly pilgrimage through red, blue, black, and then the final white veils of the temple, Jack had noted: "Good stuff. Sounds like one of my dreams."

❋   ❋   ❋

Just after meeting the British press Jack complained to me of itching hands, small red dots which gave up a clear fluid when squeezed. The broken pustules then burned like dots of acid. A passenger shot off three of his toes at skeet and blamed Jack for hexing the weapon. Then the Minneapolis librarian cut her wrists, but chose against death and summoned help. Her condition became common knowledge on the ship.

I saw Jack on deck alone after that, toying with a rosary, the first time I knew he carried one. He was not praying—only staring at it, strung like webbing through his fingers, as if it were a strange, incomprehensible object.

* * *

The night we were steaming toward Plymouth, a steward came to Jack's room with a message from the captain that the British authorities had definitely proclaimed Jack *persona non grata*. Stay out, you bum. The message jolted him, for it suddenly put our destination in jeopardy. What would Belgium do? And Germany?

Jack came to my stateroom and said he wanted to go up on deck and talk, that he didn't trust the walls. So we walked in the sea-sweetened night along the main deck where a few night walkers took the air, most memorably a rheumatic old aristocratic woman with a belief in the curative power of voyaging that was so religious she left her deckchair only during storms and meals, and to sleep and, I presume, to pee. She chewed tobacco and had a small pewter spittoon alongside her chair which she would pick up and spit her little bloody gobs into in a most feminine manner, that is, through taut, narrow lips.

She was the only witness to my conversation with Jack, and her presence and periodic spitting were the only intrusions on our conversation, apart from the splash of the sea, as we talked and walked, up and then back, in our desolated section of deck. We talked only of Jack's rejection by England until he decided to get to the point.

"Marcus, I want you to do me a favor."

"A legal one?"

"No."

"I thought as much. The jewels. I told you I want no part of it, Jack."

"Listen to me. This is a lot of money. Do you believe in money?"

"I do."

"So do I."

"But I don't want to go to jail to get it."

"How many lawyers you know ever went to jail?"

"A few, and you'd have a point if we were back in Albany."

"I told you a long time ago you were a thief in your heart."

"No, we're still not talking about thievery."

"Right. This is just a proposition. You don't have to take it."

Jack then took from his inside coat pocket a long slender box, and we paused under one of the wall lights so I could view its contents: an array of gems, rings, and necklaces. Some jewel thief had stolen them, fenced them, and they'd found their way to Jack, the internationalist, who would refence them in Europe. I knew he hadn't stolen them. He wasn't above such activity, just afield of it. No longer a burglar. He'd failed at that as a teen-ager and graduated to the activity that conformed to his talent, which was not stealth but menace.

"They don't take up much space," Jack said, and I nodded and made no answer.

"I planned to get rid of them in Brussels, but they're too hot to carry. I mean look at that"—and he held up a ruby for me to admire. "It's kind of famous, I'm told, and where it came from is even more famous."

"I don't think I'm interested."

"My suitcase has special bindings for this stuff. You could get it off the boat and through customs. But not me, not now."

I toyed with it. NOTED UPSTATE LAWYER CAUGHT WITH MRS. ASTOR'S FAVORITE RUBY, Or was it Mrs. Carnegie's? Or that tobacco-chewing lady aristocrat behind us, whoever she might be?

"If you don't handle them, I dump them. Now."

"Dump them?"

"Overboard."

"Christ, why do that? Why not hide them in a chandelier and come back later for them? Isn't that how it's done?"

"Fuck 'em," Jack said. "I don't want anything to do with this goddamn boat again once I get off it. It's a jinx."

"A jinx? You don't really believe in jinxes."

"I'd be fucking well dead if I didn't. Are you game? Yes or no."

"No."

He walked to the railing and I trailed him, expecting the next ploy in the act. A final appeal to my greed.

"You wanna watch?" he said, and so I moved alongside him in time to see him tip the box and see, yes, jewels falling, a few, and disappearing in shadow long before they hit the water. He tipped the box further and a few more plummeted toward the deep, then he shook it empty, looked at me, and, while looking, let the box flutter toward the water. It flipped a few times, made a silent plop we could see because it was white, and was then glommed by the blackness.

*   *   *

Jack was in shirtsleeves, sitting alone at the card table where Classy Willie fleeced the suckers, when I came up for brunch one day. I ate and then watched Jack playing solitaire and losing. I sat across from him and said, "I was planning to get off this tub and go home, but I think I'll stay on for the full treatment."

"Good. What changed your mind?"

"I don't know. Maybe the jewels. But I think I decided to trust you. Is that a mistake?"

"Trust me with anything but women and money."

"I also want a straight answer on Charlie Northrup. Is that asking too much?"

Jack mused, then with high seriousness said, "I think he's dead. But I'm not sure. If he's dead, it wasn't murder. That I am sure of."

"That's straight?"

"That's as straight as I can say it."

"Then I guess I have to believe it. Deal the cards."

He picked them up and shuffled. "Blackjack," he said and, after burying a card, dealt us both a hand. I had eighteen. He had twenty, which he showed me before I could bet. I looked blank and he said only, "Watch," and then dealt six hands, face up. I got between thirteen and seventeen in all six. He got twenty four times and two blackjacks.

"Impressive. Are you always that lucky?"

"They're marked," he said. "Never play cards with a thief." He tossed the deck on the table, leaned back, and looked at me.

"You think I killed Northrup."

"You say you didn't. I told you I accept that."

"You don't convince me."

"Maybe it's the other way around."

He put his coat on and stood up. "Let's go out on deck. I'll tell you a couple of stories." I followed and we found our way back to the desolate spot where he'd dumped the jewels. The old lady was there, and it was still as private as any place on deck.

"How are you today?" Jack said to the old dame, who took the remark first as an intrusion, then looked at Jack as if he were invisible. He shrugged and we walked to the rail and looked down at the waves and at our foamy wake.

"I dumped a guy in the water once over marked cards."

I nodded, waited. He stared out at the ocean and went on: "A card game in a hotel. It was the first time I ever met Rothstein. I was working as a strikebreaker with Little Augie, breakin' heads, just out of jail. A bum. I was a bum. Augie says to me, 'You wanna work strongarm at a card game?' And I said all right and he sent me to this hotel room and there's Rothstein, the cocksucker, and he says to me, 'What happened to your head?' 'Nothin' happened to it,' I said. 'That haircut,' he said. 'You look like a skinned rabbit, skinned by somebody who don't know how to skin. Get a haircut for pity's sake.' Can you imagine that son of a bitch? He's got seventy-six grand in his pocket, he told me so, and he tells me get a haircut. Arrogant bastard. He was right about the haircut. A barber-school job. Awful. I tell you I was a bum on the street and I looked like one. But he made me feel like a zero.

"So the game went on and there's this high roller—let me call him Wilson—who's challenging Rothstein. There's other players, but he wants to beat A. R., who's the king. And he's doing it. Wins eleven thousand one hand, eight the next, in five thousand-dollar freezeout. Rothstein has two men in the bathroom looking over the decks Wilson brought, and they find the marks, little tits on the design in the corner. First-rate work by the designer. Rothstein hears the news and calls a break but doesn't let on, and then tells me to brain Wilson if he gets out of hand, and I say all right because he's paying me. He bottom-deals Wilson a six and Wilson calls him on it. Then A. R. says never mind about bottom dealing, what about a man who brings paper into a legitimate game? And when Wilson stood up, I brained him. Didn't kill him. Just coldcocked him and he went down. When he came to, they told me to take him someplace he wouldn't be a bother. They didn't say kill him. I took him to the river with a driver and walked him to the edge of a dock. He offered me four grand, all he had left from the game, and I took it. Then I shot him three times and dumped him in. It turned out he had three kids. He was a cheater, but he was complicated. He looked at me and said, 'Why? I give you the four grand.' His life had to be complicated with three kids and I killed him. I wanted the four grand bad and I knew he had it. But I never killed anybody before and I tell you I blame Rothstein. Maybe I wouldn't have killed him if he didn't say that about the haircut, make me feel I was such a bum. I knew I was a bum, but I didn't think it showed so much. With the four grand I wasn't a bum anymore. I bought a new suit and got a haircut at the Waldorf-Astoria."

*   *   *

The money inspired Jack. He and his brother Eddie met one Ace O'Hagan, who drove for Big Bill Dwyer, the king of Rum Row. Dwyer had the Coast Guard, Jersey City, and part of Long Island on his payroll, and Jack gave Ace fifty to connect him to Dwyer for a job. Ace called Dwyer from the bar where he and the Diamond boys were drinking and found Dwyer was partying and wouldn't be back. Then, in the back of Jack's car, with Eddie driving, Jack had another idea and stuck a pistol in O'Hagan's ear and asked for the location of Dwyer's most vulnerable drop.

"He wouldn't tell me," Jack said, "so I smashed his nose with the pistol and he flooded himself. Bled all the way to the Bronx where I knew we could get a truck. I told him I'd burn his toes to cinders if he didn't tell me, and he told and we packed his nose with toilet paper and headed for Dwyer's smallest drop in White Plains. I cooked up a story that we were sent to load up the truck for a millionaire named Riley, a fellow Dwyer was doing business with, and Ace was the convincer. He talked the two guys guarding the drop into loading the truck with Scotch and champagne, and on the way back to the city, he says to me, 'Dwyer'll kill you.' And I said, 'Bill's a nice guy from what I hear. He wouldn't hurt a fellow with a little ambition.'

"Then we took Ace to the hospital and I paid to get his nose fixed up. We kept him at our rooms till I figured out what to do next, and during the night he says to Eddie, 'He's going to kill me, isn't he?' And Ed told him, 'No, I don't think so. If he was going to kill you, why would he pay for your nose?'"

⁂   ⁂   ⁂

Jack then went to Rothstein with a proposition.

"Listen, I have quite a lot of booze. I mean quite a lot."

"What are you asking?" Rothstein said, surprised Jack had anything of value besides his pistol.

"The going rate."

"The rate varies. Quality talks."

"Taste it yourself."

"I drink very little. Only at bar mitzvahs and weddings. But I have a friend who drinks nicely and understands what he drinks."

Jack led Rothstein and friend to the West Side garage where the booze truck was parked. The genuine article, said the taster.

"I take it you imported these goods yourself," A. R. said.

"Since when does Arnold Rothstein worry about such details?"

"In some ways, I'm particular about whose pockets my friends pick."

"I'll tell you straight. It's Dwyer's stock."

Rothstein laughed and laughed and laughed.

"That's quite a daring thing, to do this to Big Bill. And I'm laughing also because Bill owes me for several loads of whiskey for which he borrowed a certain sum, and so it's just possible you're trying to sell me goods with a personal interest to me."

"Dwyer doesn't have to know you bought the stuff."

Rothstein laughed again at this devious fellow.

"If I had two more trucks, I could get you this much twice over," Jack said. "That's also part of my proposition. Fit me out with two fast trucks and I'll keep you hip-deep in booze."

"You're moving very fast," said A. R.

"Just a young fellow trying to get ahead," said Jack.

Rothstein came to an end of business dealing with Dwyer as a result of Jack Diamond, the underworld *arriviste*, who, the day after Rothstein bought him two trucks, went back to the White Plains drop and, with his new assistants, and their new shotguns, newly sawed off, cleaned the place out down to the last bottle.

✻   ✻   ✻

Jack was notorious as a hijacker by 1925, Rothstein's crazy—his own man, however—nabob at his Theatrical Club by then, and making enemies like rabbits make rabbits.

"I felt the pellets hit me before I heard the noise, and I saw the cut barrel sticking out of the window as the car passed before I felt the pain. I scrunched sideways below the bottom level of the window so they couldn't fire another one except through the metal door, and while I was down I heard their wheels scream, and I knew I had to come up to steer when I felt the bullet hit my right heel. I didn't run into anything because there was nothing to hit, just traffic way off and no intersection or parked cars. I was around a Hundred and Sixth Street when I looked up and saw them going away. I knew I had to stop. Make them think I was out of it. I veered off to the curb and put my head back on the seat, like a collapse. Wet with blood, and then the pain came. Bloody heel. A woman looked in at me, scared, and ran off. I saw the car away up the block, turning off Fifth, probably coming back to inspect their work. My car was stalled by this time. I started it and saw my hat on the floor, a new straw sailor, the brim half shot off. I lifted my foot, trying not to let the heel touch the floor, put the car in gear, clutch, gas. Goddamn but that pain was heavy. People were out there hiding behind parked cars. I had to get away, so I turned off Fifth then, touched my head. The blood was everywhere and the fucking pain was incredible. I headed for Mount Sinai, the only hospital I knew, a few blocks back on Fifth. 'Don't let the toes go dead or I'm through driving. Don't think about the blood. Move the toes.' You know what else I thought? I wondered could you buy an artificial heel. They weren't following me. Probably pissed now that they knew they didn't kill me. My vision was going on me, the pain getting to where it counted. 'Don't black out now, tough monkey. Here we go.' Then, Jesus, a red light. I was afraid if I ran it I'd get hit, and then I'd be dead for sure. Bleed to death. So I waited for the light, if you can believe that, a goddamn lake of blood on the floor and another lake I'm sitting in. My ass floating in blood, ruining the suit, the hat already ruined. I didn't see the face behind the muzzle of the shotgun, but I saw the driver. Ace O'Hagan. He'd be smiling, remembering the night his own blood flowed all over the seat. Ace would pay. And Ace would tell me who the shooter was because Ace couldn't take the pain. I promised I'd make him pick me out a new suit and hat before I did the son of a bitch. Then I was almost to the hospital, and I remembered my pistol and threw it out the window. Didn't want to get caught with that goddamn thing. I opened the car door and I remember thinking to myself, is my underwear clean? Imagine that? I moved the bum leg then, limped toward the door, and I started to spin. I spun through the doorway and began to topple and just inside, mother, here comes the floor.

✳   ✳   ✳

"It was a guinea mob from the Bronx did it. I'd lifted some of their dope. But I got the bum who led them. He floated up the East River wearing a stolen watch. The boys dressed like cops the day they went to his house to get him. O'Hagan, that prick, I got him good, too. The fish ate his fingers. And he named the shooter like I knew he would. A greaseball from St. Louis. I got *him* in a whorehouse."

✳   ✳   ✳

It wasn't until after Jack died that I heard the whorehouse story. Flossie told it to me one night at Packy Delaney's Parody Club in Albany, one of Jack's latter-day hangouts. The Floss worked at Packy's as a singer and free-lance source of joy. She and I had no secrets, physical or professional, from each other.

"He was a handsome boy," she began, "with hair like Valentino, shiny and straight and with a blue tint to it because it was so black. Maybe that's why they called him Billy Blue. And they always said from St. Loo whenever they said his name. Billy Blue from St. Loo. I don't think his real name was Blue because he was Italian, like Valentino. He talked and laughed at the bar just like a regular fella, but you know they just ain't no regular fellas anymore, not since I was a kid in school. They all got their specialties. I never would've figured him for what he was. I never even figured him for carryin' a gun. He looked too pretty.

"I was working in Loretta's place on East Thirty-third Street, her own house which she'd lived in alone since her husband was clubbed to death by two fellas he tried to cheat with loaded dice. Loretta had been in the life when she was young and went back to it after that happened. It was a nice place, an old town house with all her old kerosene lamps turned into electric, and nice paintings of New York in the old days, and a whole lineup of teapots she'd collected when she went straight. We were as good as there was in the city and we got a lot of the swells, but we also got a lot of business from hoodlums with big money. Billy was one of those.

" 'What's your name?' he says to me when he come in.

" 'The Queen of Stars, that's my name.'

" 'Beautiful Queen of Stars,' he says to me. 'I'm going to screw love into you.'

"Nobody knew my real name and they never would. And it's not Flossie neither. My old man would've died of shame if he knew what I was doin', and I didn't want to hurt him more than I already done. So I picked Queen of Stars when Loretta asked me what my name was. I was thinking of Queen of Diamonds, but I never figured I'd ever get any diamonds, and I was dead right about that. All I ever got was rhinestones. So I said Stars because I had as much right to them as anybody livin'. Then Loretta said okay and we went from there to business, that lousy business. You couldn't get out once you were in because they hooked you. They even charged you for the towels. And the meals? You'd think it was some swanky place the way they priced everything. Then they took half what you made, and by the time you were done payin', what you had left wasn't worth sockin' away. And try and quit. Marlene got it with a blackjack in the alley, and she didn't quit anymore. They even beat up Loretta once after she complained about how much she had to pay the guys up above. The only thing to do was forget it. Just work and don't try to beat 'em out of anything because you couldn't. They were bastards, all of 'em, and a girl had no chance. I saved what I could and figured when I got enough money, I'd make a move. But I never did because I never knew where to move to.

"So Billy Blue, he called me by my full name anyway. Some of them called me Queenie and most everybody that knew me good called me Stars, but he was one of the few called me the whole thing. I liked him. Most of them I didn't like, but most I didn't even look at. Billy was pretty to look at. He got me to sit on the edge of my oak dresser, and then he walked into me. He had his pistol in his hand and stuck it in my mouth and told me to suck it. Jeez, that got me. I was scared as hell. It tasted like sour, oily stuff and I kept thinking, if he gets too excited when he comes, he'll blow a hole in my head. But what could I do?

" 'You like my pistol?' he asks me.

"Now what do you say to a goofy question like that? I couldn't say anything anyway with the thing in my mouth, but I tried to smile and I give him a nod and he seemed to like that. You can't understand how a nice-lookin' fella like that could be so bugs. The first bug I ever had stuck a feather duster up his hiney, his own duster he brought with him, and jumped around the room makin' noises like a turkey. All I did was sit on the bed so he could look at me while he did his gobbles.

"So I'm on the table and Billy's doing his stuff and I got the pistol in my mouth when the door opens and in comes Jack Diamond and two other guys, one of them was The Goose with his one eye and the other was fat Jimmy Biondo, and they got guns out, but not Jack, who was just lookin' around with them eyes of his that looked right through doors and walls, and The Goose shoots twice. One bullet hit the mirror of my oak dresser. The other one got Billy in the right shoulder, and he let go the pistol, which fell out of my mouth onto the floor and cut my lip. Billy didn't fall. He just spun around and stared at the men, with nothing on him at all but the safety.

"Jack looked at me and said, 'It's all right, Stars, don't worry about anything.'

"I was scared as hell, but I felt sorry for Billy because he looked so pretty, even if he was bugs. I started to get off the table, but The Goose says to me 'Just stay there,' and so I did, because he was the meanest-looking guy I ever saw. Jack was just lookin' at Billy and gettin' red in the face. You could see how mad he was, but he didn't talk. He just stared, and all of a sudden he takes a gun out of his coat pocket and shoots Billy in the stomach three times, and Billy falls sideways on my bed, bleedin' all over the new yellow blanket I had to pay eleven bucks for after a customer peed all over my other one and the pee smell wouldn't wash out.

"Loretta came runnin' then, and was she mad.

" 'Why the hell'd you do that here?' she asked Jack. 'What'm I supposed to do with him? Goddamn it all, Jack, I can't handle this.'

"Billy was moanin' a little bit, so I sat down alongside him, just to be near him. He looked at me like he wanted me to do somethin' for him, get a doctor or somebody, but I couldn't do anything except look at him and nod my head, I was so scared. I thought if they decided to leave maybe I could help him then.

" 'We'll take him with us,' Jack said. 'Wrap him up.'

"The Goose and Biondo walked over to the bed and stood over Billy. Billy's eyes were still open and he looked at me.

" 'It's sloppy,' The Goose said, and he took an ice pick out of his coat and punched it half a dozen times through Billy's temples, first one side then the other. It happened so fast I couldn't not look. Then he and Jimmy Biondo wrapped Billy in my yellow blanket and carried him down the back way to the alley. Billy was still straight up and still had the safety on. I'd told him I was clean, that I got regular checkups, but he wore it anyway. I didn't see The Goose or Biondo again for years, but I saw Jack quite a lot. He was our protector. That's what they called him anyway. Some protector. It was him and his guys beat up Loretta and Marlene—the bastards, the things they could do and then be so nice. But they also took care nobody shook us down and nobody arrested us. I don't know how he did it, but Jack kept the cops away, and my whole life I never been in jail except for being drunk. Jack didn't own us, though. I always heard Arnold Rothstein did, but I never knew for sure. Loretta never told us anything. Jack did own some places later and got me a job in a House of All Nations he was partners in, up in Montreal. I was supposed to be either a Swede or a Dutchie because of my blond hair. Jack brought me back down to Albany a couple of years later and I've been here ever since.

"I really hardly knew him, saw him in Loretta's a few times, that's all, until he gave Billy Blue his. Then one night about a month later he come in and buys me a real drink. None of thàt circus water Loretta dished us out when the chumps were buying. Jack brought the real stuff for us.

" 'I'm sorry about that whole scene, Stars,' he said, 'but we had to settle a score. Your guinea friend tried to kill me six months ago.'

"Jack took my fingers and ran them over the back of his head where he said there were still some shotgun pellets. It was very bumpy behind his left ear.

" 'Were you scared, Stars?'

" 'Was I! I been sick over it. I can't sleep.'

" 'Poor kid. I was really sorry to do that to you.'

"He was still holding my hand and then he rubbed my hair. The first thing you know we were back up in my room and we really got to know one another, I'll tell the world."

                              *   *   *

The Wilson, Rothstein, O'Hagan, and Blue confessions came out of Jack so totally without reservation that I told him, "I believe you about Northrup now."

"Sometimes I tell the truth."

"I don't know as I'm so sure why you've told me all these stories, though."

"I want you to know who you're working for."

"You seem to trust me."

"If you ever said anything, you'd be dead. But you know some people well enough they'd never talk. I know you."

"I take that as a compliment, but I'm not looking for information. Now or ever."

"I know that. You wouldn't get a comma out of me if I didn't want to give it. I told you, I want you to know who I am. And who I used to be. I changed. Did you get that? I come a long way. A long fucking way. A man don't have to stay a bum forever."

"I see what you mean."

"Yeah, maybe you do. You listen pretty good. People got to have somebody listen to them."

"I get paid for that."

"I'm not talking about pay."

"I am. I'm for sale. It's why I went to law school. I listen for money. I also listen for other reasons that have nothing to do with money. You're talking about the other reasons. I know that."

"I knew you knew, you son of a bitch. I knew it that night you cut Jolson up that you talked my language. That's why I sent you the Scotch."

"You're a prescient man."

"You bet your ass. What does that mean?"

"You don't have to know."

"Blow it out your whistle, you overeducated prick."

But he laughed when he said it.

*   *   *

My memories of Jack in Europe during our first stops are like picture postcards. In the first he walks off the *Belgenland* at Antwerp in company of two courteous, nervous Belgian gendarmes in their kicky bucket hats and shoulder straps. He had hoped to sneak off the ship alone and meet us later, but helpful passengers pointed him out to the cops and they nailed him near the gangway.

Down he went but not without verbal battle, assertion of his rights as an American citizen, profession of innocence. In the postcard Jack wears his cocoa-brown suit and white hat and is held by his left arm, slightly aloft. The holder of the arm walks slightly to the rear of him down the gangplank. The second officer walks to their rear entirely, an observer. The pair of ceremonial hats and Jack's oversized white fedora dominate the picture. They led the angry Jack to an auto, guided him into the back seat, and sat on either side of him. A small crowd followed the action. The car turned a corner off the pier into the thick of an army that had been lying in wait for the new invasion of Flanders. Poppies perhaps at the ready, fields of crosses under contract in anticipation of battle with the booze boche from the west. Four armored cars waited, along with six others like the one carrying Jack, each with four men within and at least fifty foot-patrolmen armed with clubs or rifles.

You can see Jack's strong suit was menace.

*   *   *

We left Belgium the next day, the twerps, as Jack called them, finally deciding Jack must be expelled by train. Jack chose Germany as his destination and we bought tickets. The American embassy involved itself by not involving itself, and so Jack was shunted eastward to Aachen, where the Belgian cops left off and the German *Polizei* took over. A pair of beefy Germans in mufti held his arms as he looked over his shoulder and said to me through a frantic, twisted mouth: "Goddamn it, Marcus, get me a goddamn lawyer."

*   *   *

Instead of turning the money over to Classy Willie, Jack gave a hundred and eighty thousand of it to me, some in a money belt, which gave me immediate abdominal tensions, and the rest inside my Ernest Dimnet best seller, *The Art of Thinking*, out of which we cut most of the pages. I carried thirty thousand in thousand-dollar bills in the book and kept the book in the pocket of my hound's-tooth sport jacket until I reached Albany. The money that didn't fit into the book and the money belt we rolled up and slid into the slots in Jack's bag reserved for the jewels. And the bag became mine.

*   *   *

Police were still dragging lakes all over the Catskills. They preferred to do that rather than follow the tip that led to a six-mile stretch of highway near Saugerties that was paved the day after Charlie disappeared.

Jack's home was searched; Alice was nowhere to be found. A shotgun and rifle in a closet were confiscated. Fogarty was seminude with a buxom Catskill waitress of comparable nudity when the raid came.

Life went on.

*   *   *

I noticed that Jack had a luminous quality at certain moments, when he stood in shadow. I suspect a derangement of my vision even now, for I remember that the luminosity intensified when Jack said that I should carry a pistol to protect myself (he meant to protect his money) and then offered me one, which I refused.

"I'll carry the stuff, but I won't defend it," I said. "If you want that kind of protection give it to The Count to take home."

Since that perception of Jack's luminosity, I've read of scientists working to demystify psychic phenomena who claim to have photographed energy emitted by flowers and leaves. They photograph them while they are living, then cut them and photograph them in progressive stages of dying. The scientists say that the intense light in the living flower or leaf is energy, and that the luminous quality fades slowly until desiccation, at which point it vanishes.

I already spoke of Jack's energy as I saw it that memorable Sunday in the Catskills. The luminosity was further evidence of it, and this finally persuaded me of a world run not by a hierarchy of talents but by a hierarchy of shining energetics. In isolation or defeat some men lapse into melancholia, even catatonia, the death of motion a commonplace symptom. But Jack was volatile in his intensifying solitude, reacting with anger to his buffetings, also trying to convince, bribe, sweet-talk, harass his way out. At Aachen he argued with the German cops, saying, yes, he had the same name as the famous gangster, but he wasn't the same man. In protest of their disbelief he did a kind of Indian war dance in the aisle of the first-class coach, a dance at which one could only marvel. Ah, the creative power of the indignant liar.

I remember my own excitement, the surge of energy I felt rising in myself from some arcane storage area of the psyche when I strapped on the money belt. No longer the voyeur at the conspiracy, I was now an accessory, and the consequence was intoxicating. I felt a need to drink, to further loosen my control center, and I did.

At the bar I found a woman I'd flirted with a day or so earlier and coaxed her back to my cabin. I did not wait to strip her, or myself, but raised her dress swiftly, pulled her underclothing off one leg, and entered her as she sat on the bed, ripping her and myself in the process so that we both bled. I never knew her name. I have no recollection of the color of her hair, the shape of her face, or any word she might have said, but I still have an indelible memory of her pubic region, its color and its shape, at the moment I assaulted it.

*　　　*　　　*

No one suspected me of carrying The Great Wad, not even Classy Willie. I passed along the sap question to Willie over drinks on the train out of Belgium. "Did Jack ever give you back Biondo's bankroll?" He gave me a hangdog look that deflated his dapper façade and reduced him forever in my mind to the status of junior villain.

The Berlin lawyer I contacted when Jack was grabbed at Aachen and held for four days was named Schwarzkopf, his name the gift of a German detective who took a liking to Jack and spoke English to him, calling him "der Schack," a mythic nickname the German press had invented. (The French called Jack Monsieur Diamant; the Italians, Giovanni Diamante; and he was "Cunning Jackie" to the British.)

Schwarzkopf turned out to be one of Berlin's leading criminal lawyers, but he failed to delay Jack's deportation for even a day. He even failed, when it became clear that Germany was not an open door, to get Jack aboard the liner I'd booked us on out of Bremen. The liner said no.

Nevertheless, Jack commissioned Schwarzkopf with a one grand retainer to sue the German government for mistreatment and expenses, and to grease enough levers to get him back into Germany when the fuss went away. It was typical of Jack not to yield to what other men would consider the inevitable.

When we met Schwarzkopf in the palm garden of the Bremen hotel where Jack was staying, he brought along his nephew, a young, half-drunk playwright named Weissberg, who in turn brought along a gum-chewing, small-breasted, brassiereless, and dirty little whore, dirtier than street whores need to be. She spoke only three words near the end of our conversation, stroking Weissberg's silky black mustache and calling him *"Mein schön scheizekopf."*

Weissberg had written a well-received play about burglars, pimps, and pickpockets in Berlin, but he'd never met anybody in the under-world with the exalted status of Jack and so he'd persuaded Schwarz-kopf to arrange a meeting. The violinist and accordion player were sending out Straussian strains suitable to palm gardens as we all drank our dunkelbock and schnapps under an open sky. The tables were small, and so Classy Willie and The Count, who both carried weapons now, sat apart from our quartet, just as Fogarty and The Goose had on the mountain. Jack, like the aristocratic Germans around us, had an acute sense of class distinction.

Jack's German mood, after he was refused first-class passage, seemed, finally, glum. That's how I read it, and I was wrong. He was more disturbed than that, but I was unable to perceive it. I excuse myself for this failure of perception, for I think he was concealing it even from himself. It was Weissberg who brought him to explosion. Weissberg began with questions, not unlike the press, only more penetrating.

"Do you know anyone in the underworld who has a conscience, Herr Diamond?"

"I don't know anybody in the underworld. I'm only a bootlegger."

"What are your feelings about willful murder?"

"I try to avoid it."

"I have known people who would steal and yet would not maim another person. I know people who would maim and yet stop short of murder. And I know of men who claim that they could murder in anger but never in cold blood. Is this the way the underworld is morally structured?"

Jack seemed to like that question. Possibly he'd thought of its im-port over the years without ever raising the question quite so precisely. He squinted at the playwright, who talked with a cigarette constantly at the corner of his mouth, never removing it, letting the ashes fall as they would, on his chest or into the schnapps, or snorting them away with nasal winds. He was accomplished at this gesture, which I guessed he'd adopted when he first entered the underworld milieu.

"There's always a guy," Jack said to him, "who's ready to do what you won't do."

"What is your limit? What is it you will not do?"

"I've done everything at least twice," Jack said with a satiric snicker, "and I sleep like a baby."

"*Wunderbar!*" said Weissberg, and he threw his arms in the air and arched his body backward in the chair in a physical demonstration of Eureka! We listened to more waltz music and we drank our legal alcohol and we watched the playwright commune silently, smilingly, with this sudden inflation of meaning. He threw off the half inch of cigarette from his lip and leaned toward Jack.

"I want to write a play about your life," he said. "I want to come to America and live with you. I don't care what might happen in your life, and I fully expect you'll kill me if you think I'm informing on you. I want to see you eat and breathe and sleep and work and do your bootleg things and steal and rob and kill. I want to witness everything and write a great play, and I will give it all to you, all my glory, all my money. I want only the opportunity to write what I believe, which is that there are similarities among the great artist, the great whore, and the great criminal. The great artist is the work he does which outlives him. The great whore lives in the memory of ineffable sensual gratification that outlasts the liaison; she is also the beauty of the parts, as is art. And she is the perversion of love, as art is the exquisite perversion of reality. Of course, with both artist and whore, the rewards are ever-greater recompense, ever-greater renown. And I see the great criminal shining through the bold perversion of his deeds, in his willingness to scale the highest moral barriers (and what is morality to the whore, the artist?). In all three professions is the willingness to withhold nothing from one's work. All three, when they achieve greatness, have also an undeniable high style which separates them from the pedestrian mobs. For how could we tell a great criminal from a thug in the alley, or a great whore from a street slut, if it were not for style? Yesssss, Herr Diamond, yesssss! It is abandon, first, which goes without saying, but it is finally style that makes *you* great and will make *me* great, and it is why we are drinking here together in this elegant hotel and listening to this elegant music and drinking this elegant schnapps.

"My little piglet here," he said, turning to his own whore, who understood no English, and whose breasts look like two fried eggs in my memory, "knows nothing of style and can never be more than a gutter animal. She is a filthy woman and I do enjoy this. I enjoy paying her and stealing back the money. I enjoy infecting her with my diseases and then paying her doctor bills. I enjoy squeezing her nipples until she screams. She is a superb companion, for she is stupid and knows nothing of me. She is not capable of even conceiving of how the great whores of Germany function today. I will have them, too, in time. But now my piglet exalts my young life.

"And you, sir, are a great man and have achieved great things. I can see in your eyes that you have leaped all moral and social barriers, that you are no prisoner of creeds and dogmas. You are intelligent, Herr Diamond. You live in the mind as well as on the street of bullets and blood. I too live in the mind and in the heart. My art is my soul. It is my body. Everything I do contributes to my art. We live, you and I, Herr Diamond, in the higher realms of the superman. We have each overcome our troublesome self. We exist in the world of will. We have created the world before which we can kneel. I speak Nietzsche's words. Do you know him? He says clearly that he who must be a creator in good and evil has first to be a destroyer and break values. We have both destroyed, Herr Diamond. We have both broken old values. We have both gone into the higher planes where the supermen dwell, and we will always triumph over the spirits of defeat that try to pull us down. Will you let me live with you and write your story—our story? Will you do this, Herr Diamond?"

Jack gave it a few seconds, letting it all settle, watching those electric eyes under Weissberg's bushy black brows. Then he went over to The Count's table and came back with The Count's small .25-caliber pistol half-concealed from the two dozen customers who sat in the garden's magical twilight, letting Strauss, the gentle swaying of the potted palms, and the intoxicating mellowness of the afternoon's first drinks lull them into sweet escape. Jack pulled his chair close to Weissberg's until they were knee to knee, and he then showed the playwright the pistol, holding it loosely in his palm. He said nothing at all for perhaps a minute, only held the weapon as a display item. Then suddenly and with eyes turned snakish, with a grimace of hate and viciousness whose like I had never seen before on his face, he nosed the barrel downward and fired one shot into the grass between Weissberg's feet, which were about six inches from each other. The downward course of the firing, the small caliber of the weapon, the shot muffled by pants legs and overwhelmed by music, created a noise that did not disrupt. A few people turned our way, but since we seemed at ease, no disturbance in process, the noise was assumed to be something as trivial as a broken glass. Jack took no notice of any external reaction. He said to Weissberg, "You're a kid, a fool."

The pistol was already in his pocket as he stood up and tossed a handful of deutsche marks on the table to pay for the drinks.

"My beautiful shithead," said the dirty little whore, stroking Weissberg's mustache, which by then was wet with tears, as wet as the front of his pants. Weissberg, the young playwright, had very suddenly liquefied.

*   *   *

Jack was two days out of Hamburg on the freighter *Hannover*, the only passenger, before he heard the strange melodic chaos coming up from below. He went through corridors and down a stairway where he found the forty-five hundred canaries the *Hannover* was bringing to the American bird-cage crowd. The Hartz Mountain birds, yellow and green, stopped singing when Jack entered their prison, and he thought: *They've smelled me.* But canaries are idiots of smell and wizards of hearing and love. The prison was moist and hot and Jack began to sweat. A sailor feeding the birds looked up and said, "I'm feedin' the birds."

"So I see."

"If you don't feed 'em, they drop dead."

"Is that so?"

"They eat a lot of food."

"You wouldn't think it to look at them."

"They do, though."

"Everybody needs a square meal," Jack said.

"Canaries especially."

"Can I help you feed them?"

"Nah. They wouldn't like you."

"What makes you think they wouldn't like me?"

"They know who you are."

"The canaries know me?"

"You saw the way they quit singin' when you come in?"

"I figured they were afraid of people."

"They love people. They're afraid of you."

"You're full of shit," Jack said.

"No, I'm not," said the sailor.

Jack opened a cage to gentle one of the birds. It pecked once at his knuckle. He lifted the bird out and saw it was dead. He put it in his pocket and opened another cage. That bird flew out, silently, and perched on top of the highest stack of cages, beyond Jack's reach unless he used the sailor's ladder. The bird twisted its tail and shat on the floor in front of Jack.

"I told you," the sailor said. "They don't want nothin' to do with you."

"What've they got against me?"

"Ask them. If you know what music is all about, you can figure out what they're sayin'. You know how they learn to sing so good? Listenin' to flutes and fiddles."

Jack listened, but all he heard was silence. The bird shat at him again. Jack yelled, "Fuck you, birdies," to the canaries and went back topside.

*   *   *

Jack heard from the radio operator that he was still steady news across the world, that now everyone knew he was on a ship with forty-five hundred canaries and that the corpse of Charlie Northrup had still not turned up. The sailor who fed the birds came up from below one morning, and Jack detected traces of the Northrup mouth on the man, a semitaut rubber band with the round edges downward turning. No smile, no smile. When the sailor opened the hatch, Jack heard the music of the birds. He inched toward it as it grew more and more glorious. The song heightened his sense of his own insignificance. What song did *he* sing? Yet it unaccountably pleased him to be nothing on the high seas, a just reward somehow; and now the birds were singing of justice. Jack remembered how satisfying it was to be shot and to linger at the edge of genuine nothingness. He remembered touching the Kiki silk and strong Alice's forehead. How rich! How something! And the vibrancy of command. Ah yes, that was *some*thing. Get down, he said to a nigger truck driver one night on the Lake George road; and the nigger showed him a knife, stupid nigger, and Jack fired one shot through his forehead. When Murray opened the door, the nigger fell out. Power! And when they got Augie—the lovely pain under Jack's own heart. Bang! And in the gut. Bang! Bang! Fantastic! Let us, then, be up and doing, with a heart for any fate.

"How's all the birdies?" Jack asked the sailor.

"Very sad," said the sailor. "They sing to overcome their sadness."

"That's not why birds sing," Jack said.

"Sure it is."

"Are you positive?"

"I live with birds. I'm part bird myself. You should see my skin up close. Just like feathers."

"That's very unusual," Jack said.

The sailor rolled up his sleeve to show Jack his biceps, which were covered with brown feathers.

"Now do you believe me?" the sailor asked.

"I certainly do. It's absolutely amazing."

"I used to be a barn swallow before I became a sailor."

"You like it better as a bird or this way?"

"I had more fun as a bird."

"I would've given nine to five you'd say that," Jack said.

*   *   *

A sailor told me a story when I boarded the *Hannover* back in the States.

"A strange man, der Schack, und I like him," the sailor said. "Good company, many stories, full of the blood that makes a man come to life as thousands around him become dead. A natural man. A man who knows where to find Canis Major. I watch him by the railing, looking out at the waves, not moving. He looks, he trembles. He holds himself as you hold a woman. He is a man of trouble. The captain sends me to his cabin when he does not come to breakfast, und on the table by the bed are three birds, all dead. Der Schack is sick. He says he vill take only soup. For three days he stays in the room und just before Philadelphia he comes to me und says he wants to buy three birds to take home. 'They are my friends,' he says. When I get the birds for him, he wants to pay me, but I say, 'No, Schack, they are a gift.' In his cabin I look for the three dead ones, but they are gone."

*   *   *

I beat Jack home, caught a liner a day and a half after he left Hamburg, and probably passed his floating birdhouse before it was out of the English Channel. The money passed back to America with me without incident, and so, I thought, had I, for I had been a passive adjunct to Jack's notoriety, a shadowy figure in the case, as they say. But my shadow ran ahead of me, and when I returned to Albany and rented a safe-deposit box for the cash, I found I was locally notorious. My picture had been taken in Germany with Jack, and it had smiled all over the local papers. My legal maneuvering on the Continent, however marginal and unpublic, had been ferreted out by German newsmen and duly heralded at home.

I'd told Jack in Hamburg, when we shook hands at the gangplank, that I'd meet him when he docked in the U.S. and I'd bring Fogarty with me. But Fogarty, I discovered, couldn't leave the state, and Jack was coming in to Philadelphia. The federals had Fogarty on three trivial charges while·they tried to link him to a rum-boat raid they'd made at Briarcliff Manor, a hundred-and-twenty-five-thousand-dollar haul of booze, the week before we left for Europe. This was the first I'd heard of the raid or of Fogarty's arrest. He'd been waiting in a truck as the boat docked, and when he spotted a cop, he tried to make a run. They charged him with vagrancy, speeding, and failing to give a good account of himself, my favorite misdemeanor.

"They can't tie me to it," Fogarty said on the phone from Acra. "I never went near the boat. I was in the truck taking a nap."

"Excellent alibi. Was it Jack's booze?"

"I wouldn't know."

"As one Irishman to another, I don't trust you either."

So I drove to Philadelphia by myself.

The reception for Jack was hardly equal to the hero welcomes America gives its Lindys, but it surpassed anything I'd been involved in personally since the armistice. I talked my way onto the cutter that was to bring a customs inspector out to meet the *Hannover* at quarantine on Marcus Hook. A dozen newsmen were also aboard, the avant-garde eyeballs of the waiting masses.

We saw Jack on the bridge with the captain when we pulled alongside. The captain called out, "No press, no press," when the customs inspector began to board, and Jack added his greeting: "Any reporter comes near me I'll knock his fucking brains out." The press grumbled and took pictures, and then Jack saw me and I climbed aboard.

"I was just passing by," I said, "and thought I might borrow a cup of birdseed."

Jack grinned and shook hands, looking like an ad for what an ocean voyage can do for the complexion. He was in his favorite suit—the blue double-breasted—with a light gray fedora, a baby blue tie, and a white silk shirt.

"I'm big pals with these birds," he said. "Some of them whistle better than Jolson."

"You're looking fit."

"Greatest trip of my life," he said. The captain was a hell of a fellow, the food was great, the sea air did wonders for his stomach and blah blah blah. Marvelous how he could lie. I told him about the reception he was going to get, some evidence of it already in view: tugs, police launches, chartered press boats, that customs cutter, all of them steaming along with us as we glided up the Delaware toward Pier Thirty-four. Jack's navy.

"I'd estimate three thousand people and a hundred cops," I said.

"Three thousand? They gonna throw confetti or rocks?"

"Palm fronds is my guess."

I told him about Fogarty's travel restrictions, and asked:

"Was that your booze they got on that boat?"

"Mostly mine," he said. "I had a partner."

"A sizable loss—a hundred and twenty-five thousand dollars."

"More. Add another twenty-five."

"Were you on the scene?"

"Not at the dock. I was someplace else, waiting. And nobody showed. My old pal Charlie Northrup worked that one up."

"He was your partner?"

"He tipped the feds."

"Ah. So that's what this is all about."

"No, that's not even half of it. What about Jimmy Biondo?"

"I had a call from him. He wants his money."

"I don't blame him, but he's not going to get it."

"He threatened me. He thinks maybe I've got it. I didn't think he was that bright."

"How did he threaten you?"

"He said he'd make me dead."

"Don't pay any attention to that bullshit."

"It's not something I hear every day."

"I'll fix the son of a bitch."

"Why don't you just give him back his money?"

"Because I'm going back to Germany."

"Oh, Christ, Jack. Don't you learn?"

When he talked to Schwarzkopf about greasing the way for a return trip, I took it as the necessary response of an angry reject. I couldn't imagine him really risking a second international fiasco. But I was making a logical assumption and Jack was working out of other file cabinets: his faith in his ability to triumph over hostility, his refusal to recognize failure even after it had kicked him in the crotch, and, of course, his enduring greed. As a disinterested observer I might have accepted all but the greed as admirable behavior, but now with Biondo on my back as well as Jack's, such perseverance struck me as an open invitation to assassination.

"Let's get it straight, Jack. I'm not comfortable."

"Who the hell is?"

"I used to be. I want to get rid of that money and I want to get rid of Jimmy Biondo. I went along for the ride, but it's turned into something else. You don't know how big this Northrup thing is. In the papers every day. Biggest corpse hunt in years, which raises our old question again. Is he or isn't he? I've got to know this time."

We were on the forward deck, watching the boats watch us. The captain and his sailors were nowhere near us, but Jack looked behind and then spoke so no breeze would carry the words aft.

"Yeah," he said.

"Great. Jesus Christ, that's great news."

"It wasn't my fault."

"No?"

"It was a mistake."

"Then that makes everything all right."

"Don't fuck around with this, Marcus. I said it was a mistake."

"It's a mistake I'm here."

"Then get the fuck off."

"When it's over. I don't quit on my clients."

I think I knew even as I said it that there would be no quitting. Certainly I sensed the possibility, for just as Jack's life had taken a turning in Europe, so had mine. Our public association had done me in with the Albany crowd. They could do beer business all year long with Jack, but after mass on Sunday they could also tut-tut over the awful gangsterism fouling the city. It followed they could not run a man for the Congress who was seeking justice for an animal like Jack. Forget about Congress, was the word passed to me at the Elks Club bar after I came home from Germany. When I think back now to whether the Congress or the time with Jack would have given me more insight into American life, I always lean to Jack. In the Congress I would have learned how rudimentary hypocrisy is turned into patriotism, into national policy, and into the law, and how hypocrites become heroes of the people. What I learned from Jack was that politicians imitated his style without comprehending it, without understanding that their venality was *only* hypocritical. Jack failed thoroughly as a hypocrite. He was a liar, of course, a perjurer, all of that, but he was also a venal man of integrity, for he never ceased to renew his vulnerability to punishment, death, and damnation. It is one thing to be corrupt. It is another to behave in a psychologically responsible way toward your own evil.

*   *   *

The police came aboard, just like Belgium, with a warrant for Jack as a suspicious character. Jack was afraid of the mob, afraid he was too much of a target, but the cops formed a wedge around him and moved him through. The crowd pushed and broke the wedge, calling out hellos and welcome backs to Jack; and some even held up autograph books and pencils. When all that failed, the fan club began to reach out to feel him, shake his hand. A woman who couldn't reach him hit his arm with a newspaper and apologized—"I only wanted to touch you, lover"— and a young man made a flying leap at Jack's coat, got a cop's instead, also got clubbed.

"Murderer," someone called out.

"Go home. We don't want you here."

"Don't mind them, Jack."

"You look great, Legs."

"He's only a bird in a gilded cage."

"Give us a smile, Legs," a photographer said and Jack swung at him, missed.

"Hello, cuz!" came a yell and Jack turned to see his cousin William, an ironworker. Jack asked the cops to let him through, and William, six four with major muscles and the facial blotch of a serious beer drinker, moved in beside the car where Jack was now ringed by police.

"Lookin' snappy, Jack," William said.

"Wish I could say the same for you, Will."

"What's that you got there in the lapel?"

"Knight Templar pin, Will."

"Son of a bitch, Jack, ain't that a Protestant bunch?"

"It's good for business, Will."

"You even turned on your own religion."

"Ah shit, Will, have you got anything to tell me? How's Aunt Elly?"

"She's fit."

"Does she need anything?"

"Nobody needs anything from you."

"Well, it was nice seeing you, Will. Give my regards to the worms."

"We know who the worm in this family is, cousin."

And Jack got into the car.

"What do you think of the killing of the dry agent yesterday at the Rising Sun Brewery in Newark?" a reporter asked through the window.

"First I heard of it, but it's the most foolish thing in the world. It'll cramp business for a month."

"Can you whistle for us?" another reporter asked.

"Up your whistle, punk," Jack said, and the reporter faded.

"How did you find Europe?"

"I got off the boat and there it was."

"Who was the blonde you were with in Hamburg?"

"A Red Cross nurse I hired to take my pulse."

"How well did you know Charlie Northrup?"

"A personal friend."

"The police think you killed him."

"Never trust what a cop or a woman thinks."

No longer amused, the cops shoved the reporters back and made a path for the car. Jack waved to me as it pulled away, smiling, happy to be vulnerable again. My subconscious works in musical ways at times and as I wrote that last sentence I heard an old melody float up and I couldn't say why. But I trust my music and when I sang it all the way through I could hear a jazz band playing it in raucous ragtime, Jack giving me that going-away smile on the pier forty-two years ago, soothed by the music, which I hear clearly, with a twist all my own:

It goes Na-Da, Na-Da,
Na-Da-Na-Da nil-nil-nil.

Jack was twenty hours in jail. His aunt sent him a box of molasses cookies, and I sent him two corned beefs on rye. Commissioner Devane in New York had asked Philadelphia to hold Jack, but they found nothing to prosecute and by midmorning I'd worked out a release arrangement. We'd announce we were leaving town, assuring the citizenry that no carpetbaggers would invade the territory of the local hoodlums. Jack wanted only two hours to visit relatives and the judge said all right, so we went through a four-minute court ritual. But the judge found it necessary to give Jack a dig: "This court considers the attention you have received from the press and from the vast numbers of people who gathered at the pier to witness your arrival, to be twin aberrations of the public mind, aberrations which find value in things that are worth nothing at all. I speak for the decent people of this city in saying that Philadelphia doesn't want you any more than Europe did. Get out of this city and stay out."

In the car, Jack looked like a man trying to see through a rain of cotton balls. The reporters tailed us, so he said, "Skip the relatives, head for New York." We lost the last of the press about thirty miles out of the city. It was a decent fall day, a little cloudy, but with a lot of new color in the world. But then it started to drizzle and the road got foggy. The fog seemed to buoy Jack's spirits and he talked about his women. He'd left his canaries on the ship and now wanted to buy something for Alice and Kiki, so we stopped at Newark, which he seemed to know as well as he knew Manhattan.

"Dogs," he said. "Alice loves dogs."

We went to three pet shops before we found a pair of gray Brussels griffons. They appealed to Jack because he could claim he'd bought them in Belgium. There were four in the litter and I suggested another pair for Kiki.

"She'd lose them or let them die," he said, and so we found a jewelry store and he bought her an eight-hundred-dollar diamond, elaborately set ("A diamond from my Diamond," she quickly dubbed it).

I'd expected him to emphasize one or the other woman when he arrived, depending on his mood: horny or homey. But he balanced them neatly, emphasizing neither, impatient to see them both, moving neither away from one nor toward the other but rather toting one on each shoulder into some imagined triad of love, a sweet roundelay which would obviate any choice of either/or and would offer instead the more bountiful alternative of both. More power to you, old boy.

But his mood was not bountiful at the moment. We came out of the jewelry store and got in the car, and he looked at me and said, "Did you ever feel dead?"

"Not entirely. I woke up once and felt my leg was dead. Not pins and needles but genuinely dead. But that's as far as I ever got."

"I feel like I died last week."

"You've had a pretty negative experience. It's understandable."

"I didn't even feel like this when I *was* dying."

"Go someplace and sleep it off. Always works for me when I hit bottom."

"Some cocaine would fix my head."

"I'll stop at the next drugstore."

"Let's get a drink. Turn right, we'll go to Nannery's"—and we hunted down a small speakeasy where Jack knew the doorman and got the biggest hello of the week from half the people in the place.

"I just heard about you on the radio ten minutes ago," Tommy Nannery told him, a spiffy little bald-headed Irishman with oversize ears. He kept clapping Jack on the back and he put a bottle of rye in front of us. "They sure gave you a lot of shit over there, Jack," Nannery said.

"It wasn't so bad," Jack said. "Don't believe all that horseshit you read in the papers. I had a good time. I got healthy on the ocean."

"I didn't believe any of it," Nannery said. "Talkin' here the other night about it I says to a fellow, they don't shove Jack Diamond around like that, I don't care who they are. Jack has got friends a way up. Am I right?"

"You're right, Tommy. Here's to my friends."

Jack drank about three straight ones while I was getting halfway through my first. He put a twenty on the bar and said he'd take the bottle.

"My treat, Jack, my treat," Nannery said. "Glad to see you back in Newark."

"It's nice to have good friends," Jack said. "Tommy, it's nice."

He had another two fast ones before we left, and in the car he sat with the bottle between his legs, swilling it as we went. When I got into Manhattan, he was out of his depression with a vengeance, also out of control with good old Marcus at the wheel. I'd every intention of dropping him in the city and going straight on to Albany with a demarcating flourish. The end. For the peculiar vanity that had first sent me to Catskill on that odd summer Sunday, the need for feeding the neglected negative elements of my too-white Irish soul, the willful tar-and-feather job on my conscience, all that seemed silly now. Childish man. Eternal boy. Bit of a rascal. Unpredictable Marcus. The wiping away of my political future, however casually I'd considered it in the past, the prospect of assassination, and my excursion into quasi-rape convinced me my life had changed in startling ways I wouldn't yet say I regretted. But what would I do with such developments? Underneath, I knew I was still straight, still balancing the either/or while Jack plunged ahead with diamonds and doggies toward the twin-peaked glory of bothness. I felt suddenly like a child.

I looked at Jack and saw him whiten. Was that a bad bit of barley he was swilling? But the bottle was two-thirds down. He was suddenly quite drunk, and without a sound or a move toward the door, he puked in his lap, onto the seat, onto the gearshift, the floormat, the open ashtray, my shoes, my socks, my trousers, and the Philadelphia *Inquirer* I'd bought before going to court, Jack's face in closeup staring up from it at Jack, receiving mouth-to-mouth vomit.

"Fucking ocean," Jack said, and he collapsed backward with his eyes closed, lapsing into a ragged flow of mumbles as I looked frantically for a gas station. He rattled on about being offered fifteen hundred a month to perform in a German cabaret, and twenty-five thousand by an English news syndicate for his life story and a blank check by the *Daily News* for the same thing. I'd heard all this in Germany and was now far more interested in any sign of the flying red horse on Eleventh Avenue, steed that would deliver me from puke.

" 'Magine 'em asking Rothstein?" Jack said, eyes closed, words all tongued. " 'Magine him packin' 'em in?"

"No, I can't imagine it," I said, distracted still. Jack opened his eyes when I spoke.

"Wha'?"

"I said I couldn't imagine it."

" 'Magine wha'?"

"Rothstein onstage."

"Where?"

"Forget it."

"They wouldn't put that bum onstage," he said and he closed his eyes. He snapped to when I hosed down his lap and shoes at the gas station, and by the time we got to the Monticello Hotel where Kiki was waiting, he was purged, stinking and still drunk but purged of salt air and European poisons, cured by America's best home remedy. And good old Uncle Marcus was still there, guiding him with as little guidance as possible toward the elevator. Upstairs, Jack could lie down and think about puke and poison. He could discover in quiet what his body already understood: that his fame hadn't answered the basic question he had asked himself all his life, was still asking.

Playing the Jack

Jimmy Biondo visited Kiki three hours before we knocked on her door. The result was still on her face. She'd met him with Jack frequently, and so, when he knocked, she let him in. He then dumped his froggy body into the only easy chair in the room, keeping his hat on and dripping sweat off his chin onto his bow tie.

"Where's your friend Diamond?"

"He hasn't called me yet."

"Don't lie to me, girlie."

"I don't lie to people and don't call me girlie, you big lug."

"Your friend's got trouble."

"What kind of trouble?"

"He's gunna grow great big holes in his belly."

"He better not hear you say that."

"He'll hear it all right. He'll hear it."

"Listen, I don't want to talk to you and I'll thank you to leave."

"I'll tank you to leave."

"So get lost."

"Shut up, you dumb cunt."

"Oh! I'm tellin' Jack."

"Just right. And tell him I want my money and tell him he shouldn'a done what he done to Charlie Northrup."

"He didn't do anything to Charlie Northrup."

"You dumb cunt, what do you know? You think he's a nice guy, wouldn't hurt anybody? I wanna tell you what a nice guy your boyfriend is and what nice guys he's got workin' for him. You ever hear of Joe Rock? Your boyfriend's pals took him up inna woods, and when he said he wooden pay off the ransom, Murray the Goose pulls himself off inna cloth and rubs it in Joe's eyes and ties the rag on the eyes and Joe goes blind because The Goose has got the clap and the syph, both kinds of diseases, and that's your boyfriend Jack Diamond. I tell you this because Joe Rock was a business associate of mine. And after your boyfriend burns up Red Moran inna car over inna Newark dump and finds out Moran's girl knows who done it, he ties her up with sewer grates and dumps her inna river while she's still kickin'. That's your boyfriend Jack Diamond. How you like your boyfriend now, you dumb cunt?"

"Oh, oh, oh!" said Kiki as Joe left the room.

✻   ✻   ✻

After we heard her story Jack shoved a fifty into my hand with the suggestion: "How you like to take a pretty girl out to dinner?" He called somebody and went out with word to us that he'd be back in a few hours and was gone before I found the way to tell him we were quits. I can't say the idea of Kiki's company repelled me, but I was intimidated. I've talked about her beauty, and it was never greater than at that moment. She'd been primping for Jack, calling up all her considerable wisdom of sex and vanity, and had created a face I've since thought of as The Broadway Gardenia. It was structured with eyebrow pencil, mascara, an awareness of the shape of the hairline and the fall of the loose curl. It was beauty that was natural and artificial at once, and the blend created this flower child of the Follies. No carefree Atlanta belle, no windblown, wheat-haired Kansas virgin, no Oriental blossom, or long-stemmed Parisian rose could quite match her. Beauty, after all, is regional. I remember the high value the Germans put on their rose-cheeked Fräuleins. And to me the cheeks were just blotchy.

"Are you leaving me alone?" Kiki said as Jack kissed her.

"I'll be back." He had sobered considerably in less than ten minutes.

"I don't want to be alone anymore. He might come in again."

"Marcus is here."

That's when he gave me the fifty and left. Kiki sat on the bed looking at the door, and when she decided he was definitely gone, she said, "All right, goddamn it," and went to the mirror and looked at her face and took out some black wax I've since learned is called beading and heated it in a spoon and dabbed it on her eyelids with a toothpick. Her eyes didn't need such excess, but when she looked at me, I saw something new: not excess but heightening. Magic beyond magic. I've never known another woman in the world who used that stuff and only one who even knew what it was. It was an object out of Kiki's mystical beauty kit like all her other creams and powders and soft pencils and lip brushes, and as I looked at the bottles and jars on the dressers, they all illuminated something central to her life: the studied passivity of being beautiful, of being an object to be studied, of being Jack's object. Her radio was on the dresser and exaggerated the passivity for me— lying there waiting for Jack, always waiting for Jack, and letting the music possess her as a substitute; the pink rubber douche equipment on top of the toilet tank—more proof of Kiki as Jack's vulnerable receptacle.

She stood, after she finished her eyebrows, and lifted her dress over her head, a navy-blue satin sheath with silver spangles on the bodice— Jack loved spangles. Her slip went part way up, and there flashed another view of some of the underneath dimension, to which I reacted by saying, memorably, "Whoops." She laughed and I stood up and said, "I'll meet you in the lobby."

"Why?"

"Give you a little privacy."

"Listen, I'm all fed up with privacy. Stick around. You won't see half what you'd see if I was in one of my costumes. I'm just changing my dress."

She moved around in her slip, sat down at the dressing table and combed the hair she had mussed, then turned quickly, faced me, giving me a full central view of upper, gartered thigh, and I thought, oh, oh, if I do what I am being tempted to do, I will end up with very substantial trouble; thinking also: vengeful concubine. But I was wrong there.

"You know," she said, "I don't know why I'm here."

"In this room or on this earth?"

"In this room waiting for that son of a bitch to come and see me whenever he goddamn feels like it, even after I tell him a story like I told him about Jimmy Biondo."

I sensed she was talking to me this way because she had taken her dress off and felt powerful. She was a sexual figure without the dress and merely a vulnerable beauty with it. Sitting there giving me an ample vision of her hinterlands was a gesture of power. Tenors shatter glassware. Strongmen bend iron bars. Sexual powerhouses show you their powersources. It reassures them in the place where they are strongest, and weakest, that they are significant, that the stares that automatically snap toward that sweet region of shadow are stares of substance and identification. With this stare, I thee covet. Desirable. Yes, yes, folks, see that? I'm desirable and everything is going to be all right. Feeling powerful, she could talk tough.

"Do you work for him all the time now, Mr. Gorman?" That "Mr." destroyed my fantasy of being seduced. A disappointment and a relief.

"I've done some things for him."

"Do you remember Charlie Northrup from that day up on the mountain?"

"I do indeed."

"Do you think Jack really did something to him? Hurt him?"

"I have no firsthand information on that."

"I don't think Jack would kill him like that Biondo man said. And what he said about that man's eyes and that girl in the river. Jack wouldn't do that stuff."

"I'm sure he wouldn't."

"I couldn't stay with him if he did that stuff."

"I understand."

"I'd leave right now if I thought he did that stuff. You think I could love a man who could do something to somebody's eyes like that?"

"Didn't you say it was Murray who did that?"

"That's what Biondo said, but he said Jack knew about it."

"Well, you can't believe Biondo."

"That's just what I think.

"I know Jack liked Charlie Northrup. When he spit that beer at Jack up on the mountain, Jack told me that night, 'If I didn't like that guy, he'd be in a lot of trouble.' Everybody thinks Jack is such a tough guy, but he's really sweet and gentle and never hurts nobody. I never even saw him pop the guts on a fly. Jack is a gentleman always and one of the tenderest, sweetest human persons I've ever come across, and I've come across my share of persons and they're not all human, I'll tell you that. I saw him with Charlie Northrup up in the mountains, and they were talking together and walking around the front yard. So I know Jack wouldn't hurt him. It's a bunch of lies what's in the papers because I know what I saw."

"That happened *after* that day we were all on the mountain?"

"Five days after. I counted the days. I always count the days. At Biondo's farm up there. Jack said staying up on the mountain was too far away for me, and he moved me down to the farm for a few days."

"What about dinner?"

"Jesse cooked for me. The old nigger man who runs the still."

"I mean now."

"Oh, now. All I have to do is put my dress on."

She closed her gates of power and stood up.

"You know," she said, "I like you. I could talk to you. Don't take this the wrong way now."

"I take it as a statement of friendship."

"That's just what I mean. Some people you talk to them and ka-zoom, it's a pass, just because you said something nice."

"You like me because I didn't make a pass?"

"Because you wanted to and didn't and you had such a good chance."

"You're a perceptive girl."

"What's that mean?"

"You see inside people."

"I see how they look at me, that's all."

"Not many people see that much."

"You see, I knew I could talk to you. You don't make me feel like a dumb bunny."

✻   ✻   ✻

The night I went to dinner with Kiki, Tony (The Boy) Amapola was shot through the head and neck four times and dumped outside Hackensack. The papers said he was a close pal of Jimmy Biondo's and that Biondo was Capone's man in town, which wasn't true. Another victim of another beer war, was the consensus, but I suggest he was a victim of Jimmy's bad manners toward ladies.

I sat talking with Kiki that night until Jack came back around midnight, and then I drove to Albany without telling him I was all through. A call from Jesse Franklin was waiting for me when I got to the office the next day, asking me to come and see him. I don't think I'd have remembered him if Kiki hadn't mentioned him as her cook at the farm the night before. I called him back and got a hotel which turned out to be a flophouse for Negroes in Albany's South End. I told him to come and see me, but he said he couldn't, and would I come to see him? I never met a client in a flophouse before, so I said I would.

It turned out to be the ground floor of an old converted livery stable with a dozen cots, two of which were occupied: one by a man wheezing and ranting in a drunken, mumbly wine coma, and the other by Jesse, who sat on his cot like a bronze sculpture of despair, a weary old man with nubby white hair, wearing ratty overalls and staring downward, watching the roaches play around his muddy shoes. He hadn't been out of the flop in three weeks except to go to a corner store and buy food, then come back and sleep and wait.

"You remember me, Mr. Gorman?"

"I was talking about you with Kiki Roberts only last night."

"Pretty lady."

"That's her truth all right."

"She didn't see nothin' what I seen, what I wants to tell you 'bout. Nobody seen what I seen."

"Why do you want to tell me about it?"

"I got some money. I can pay."

"I would expect it."

"I sent my boys away but I don't wanna go myself, don't know where to go. Only one place to go I know of is back to the farm and work for Mr. Jack, but I don't wanna go back there. Can't go back to that old place after what I seen. I fear 'bout those men. I know the police lookin' for me too 'cause they askin' Mr. Fogarty 'bout me before he go to jail and I don't want no police, so I highfoots it up to Albany 'cause I know they got coloreds up here plenty and nobody know me, and then I know I gonna run out of money and have to be on the road and I gonna get picked up sure as Jesus. So I been sittin' here thinkin' 'bout what I gonna do and I remember Mr. Jack got a lawyer friend in Albany. I been sittin' here three weeks tryin' to 'member your name. Then yesterday this old bum he fall right in front of me, right there by them little roaches, and he got a newspaper in his pocket and I seen your picture and Mr. Jack's picture and I say, that's my man all right, that's my man. Man who runs this place got me your phone number all right. I gets picked up you goin' help me?"

"I'll help you if I can, but I've got to know what this is all about."

"Yep. I gonna tell you but nobody else. No how. What I see I don't want no more part of. I see it when I just about finished at the still for about five hours, sun goin' down and I throwed down my head to sleep off the miseries when I heerd this automobile pull up in front of the barn. I sleeps in the back of the house, so I look out and see Mr. Fogarty openin' the barn doors and other fellas Mr. Jack have around him all the time in the car and they drives right inside. Now I never did see this before. Mr. Jack use that barn for storage and he don't want no automobiles drivin' in and out of where he keep his beer and his whiskey 'cept for loadin' and that ain't no loadin' car I see. But Jesse ain't about to tell them fellas they can't use Mr. Jack's barn. Bye'em bye, Mr. Fogarty he come in the house and then he and Miss Kiki go out with Mr. Jack. I spies out the window at the gay-rage and I sees the light on there. I don't see nobody comin' or goin' out of that old place so I figure it ain't none of Jesse's business and I tries to go back and sleep. Bye'em bye, I hear that car again and it's dark now and in a little bit Mr. Fogarty comes in and gets some old newspapers and calls up to Jesse, is you up there and I say I is and he say Mr. Jack say for me not to go near the still tonight and I say okay by me and I don't ask why because Jesse ain't a man who asks why to Mr. Jack and his friends. Mr. Fogarty carries them papers back out and about twenty minutes go by and I heerd that car again and I sits right up in the bed and says, well they's done whatever they's done and I look out the window and they's no light in the gay-rage and I call down the stairs to Mr. Fogarty, but he don't say nothin' back and nobody else does neither, and I know my boys won't, 'cause they sleep like fishbones on the bottom of a mud pond, and so I think of what they been doin' in the gay-rage and I can't figure it out. But I say to myself, Jesse, you ought to know what's goin' on hereabouts since this is where you livin' and maybe they up to somethin' you don't want yourself fixed up in. So I takes my flashlight and I spokes quiet like down them stairs and out into the backyard and they's no light in the gay-rage so I sprites 'round by the back in case somebody pull up. And inside it's the same old gay-rage, a couple three newspapers on the floor 'longside the wheelbarra. Coolin' room's the same as usual and Mr. Jack's tahger's on the back wall's the same as usual and all the tools on the bench. I can't see no difference nowhere. Then I see in the corner of the coolin' room a big piece of somethin' all wrapped up and I knows this wasn't there before and I knows what I think it is soon as I sees it. And I shines the light on it. It look like a rug all rolled up 'cept it ain't no rug. It's canvas we throwed over the beer barrels first time the roof leaked. And I goes over and touches that canvas with my toe and it is solid. It feel just like I 'spect it to feel. And Jesse beginnin' to worry what gonna happen if he caught here with this thing alone. But I got to make sure it's what I think, so I puts my whole foot on it and feel how it feels, and it ain't exactly like what I 'spect, so I touches it with my hand. And that ain't exactly like I 'spect either and so I opens one end of the canvas to peek inside and see what is this thing that ain't like what it ought to be like, and out come this here head. All by itself. It roll out just a little bit, and I tell you if I ain't 'lectrified dead now, I don't know why I ain't. And I highfoots it out of that barn and back into the house and up them stairs and back to my own room and under the covers so's I can think by myself what I ought to do. And I thinks. And I thinks. And I don't hear nobody comin' back. Then I say to myself, Jesse, if somebody do come back, you is in mighty trouble. Because that head ain't where it ought to be and they is goin' to know somebody been out peekin' into that canvas. And first thing, they comin' back in here and say to you, Jesse, why you foolin' around with that head out in that barn? What you say then, old man? So bye'em bye, I sits up, and gets up, and goes downstairs and out to the gay-rage and what scare me now ain't that head, but them lights of the car if they come shootin' back in the road. But I say to myself, Jesse, you got to go put that head back where you got it. So I goes back in the coolin' room and shines the light down and sees the old head lookin' up at me three feet out from the end of the canvas where it rolled. And

I gets a good look at that face which I can't reckonize and maybe nobody on this earth gonna reckonize over again, because it been beat so bad it ain't no face at all. It just a head full of beat-up old flesh. I feels sorry for that poor fella 'cause he got his. No doubt 'bout that. But I say, Jesse, feel sorry for this man when you gets back to your bed. Right now, get yourself busy puttin' that head back in with the rest of him. Now I don't like it nohow, but I pick up that old head and opens up the canvas so's I can put it back in and, oh God A'mighty, there's two hands and a foot side by side like the Lord never intended nobody's hands and foot to be put together. And I opens up the canvas wider and oh God A'mighty, they ain't one whole piece of that poor fella no more. He is in ten, fifteen pieces, oh my Jesus, I gonna die. I put that head back where it used to be and fold that canvas up the way it used to be. Then I look around on the floor for any little blood drippin's I might of spilt, but I can't see none. I can't see none they might of left either, so I guess they got it all mopped up with them newspapers Mr. Fogarty picked out. Oh, sweet Jesus. And I go back out of the coolin' room then, and back into the house. I ain't worried now whether they gonna find me out there, because they ain't. It just like it was before I seen it the first time. Now I'se worryin' about somethin' else, which is how I gonna get myself and the boys out of this here butcher shop. I sure can't do it right away or they gonna know I knows more'n I s'pose to know. So I lays there thinkin' 'bout how long it'd be before it be right for me to go my own way and take my boys with me. And wonderin' where we gonna go, 'cause we ain't had no job good as this in mighty a year. But I ain't worryin' now 'bout no job. I worryin' 'bout the jailhouse gettin' me, and what my boys gonna do then? I'se still thinkin' 'bout this when I hears the car pull into the yard and I looks out and there comes Mr. Murray and somebody I can't see and they pulls in the gay-rage again but with one of Mr. Jack's trucks and stays 'bout five minutes and they back out and close the door. Then goodbye. They gone. I know the canvas and the head and the rest of the pieces of that poor ol' boy done gone too, but I don't move, 'cause it's daylight just beginnin', and ain't nobody gonna see Jesse Franklin in that barn today. Not any of those fellas, not Mr. Jack, not any stranger, not Jesse hisself. Jesse is gonna stay clear of that ol' gay-rage till somebody come who got business to do in it. And when it all simmer down, Jesse gonna take his boys and he goin' waaaay 'way from here. These is bad people, cut a man up like that. How he gonna make it all back together again come judgment time? Bad people, doin' that to a man."

*   *   *

It was Fogarty who told me how Charlie Northrup got it, told me later when he was figuring out where his life went, still drunk, still ready to muzzle any pussy that showed itself. He never changed and I always liked him and I knew all along why Jack kept him on—because he was the opposite of Murray. He was Fogarty, the group's nice guy. I liked him in that context, probably because of the contrast. I no longer think it strange that Jack had both kinds—Fogarty kind, Murray kind—working for him. Jack lived a long time, for Jack, and I credit it to his sense of balance, even in violent matters, even in the choice of killers and drivers, his sense that all ranges of the self must be appeased, and yet only appeased, not indulged. I make no case for Jack as a moderate, only as a man in touch with primal needs. He read them, he answered them, until he stopped functioning in balance. That's when the final trouble began.

Charlie Northrup drove his car to the Biondo farm at dusk to keep his appointment with Jack. Fogarty said Murray and Oxie were on the porch, rocking in the squeaky, green rockers while Jack waited inside.

"I don't go inside," Charlie said at the foot of the steps.

"Then you wait there," Murray said, and he went for Jack, who came out through the screen door and walked down the stairs and put his hand out to shake Charlie's hand. But it wasn't there.

"Never mind jerking me off," Charlie said. "Get to the point."

"Don't talk nasty, Charlie," Jack said, "or I'll forget we're brothers."

"Brothers. You got some rotten fucking way of being a brother. What you done to me, you're a bum in my book, a bum in spades."

"Listen, Charlie. I got something to say to you. I ought to blow your face off. Anybody talks to the federals has a right to get their face blown off, isn't that so?"

Fogarty said Charlie shut up at that point, that he obviously didn't think Jack knew.

"I got some good friends who happen to be federals," Jack said.

Charlie kept quiet.

"But the way I look at it, Charlie, I blow your face off and I lose all that money I'd have had if the federals didn't pick up my cargo. And what I figure is, set up a working relationship with Charlie and he'll pay me back what I lost. All we do is cooperate and the problem is solved."

"Cooperate," said Charlie, "means I give you my shirt and kiss your ass for taking it."

"Partners, Charlie. That's what I got in mind. Partners in an expanding business. I produce the business, you provide the product. We split seventy-thirty till you pay off the debt, then we reduce it, fifty-fifty, because we're brothers. Business doubles, triples at higher prices and a locked-up market. It's brilliant, Charlie, brilliant."

"You know I got partners already. They're nobody's patsies."

"I take the risk about your partners."

"I don't want no part of you," Charlie said. "I wouldn't hold onto you in an earthquake."

Charlie stopped walking. They were under the maples, a few feet from the porch, Jack in a tan suit and Charlie in his sweat shirt.

"I said it before, Jack. Stuff it up your ass. You're not talking to a man without power. Play with me you're not playing with some apple-knocker up here, some dummy saloonkeeper. You know my friends. I'm done talking about it."

He walked away from Jack, toward his car.

"You stupid fucking donkey," Jack said, and he looked up at Oxie and Murray, who stood up and pointed their pistols at Charlie. Fogarty remembered only his own rocker squeaking at that point. He kept rocking until Murray gave him the gesture and then he got out of the chair and in behind the wheel of Northrup's car and drove it back into the garage with Oxie and Murray inside it holding their pistols against Charlie's belly. Fogarty remembered Jack climbing the porch steps and watching them all get in the car.

"Now, Charlie," he said, "you got to get a lesson in manners."

*   *   *

Murray always wore steel-toed shoes and I never knew that either until Fogarty told me this whole story. He used a gun or the long, pointed, three-cornered file he carried (his improvement on the ice pick Flossie remembered) when necessary, but he used his feet when he could. The story is he took lessons from a French killer he met in jail and who used to box savate style. Murray had the rep of being able to kill you with one kick.

He kicked Charlie in the belly as soon as they got out of the car. Charlie doubled up but charged Murray head down, two hundred and forty pounds of wild bull. Murray sidestepped and kicked Charlie in the leg. Charlie crashed into a wall and bounced off it like a rubber rhino. Murray the shrimp gave a high kick and caught Charlie under the chin, and as Charlie wobbled, Murray kicked him in the kneecap and he went down. Murray kicked him in the groin, creased his face, crunched his nose with the side of his shoe. He danced around Charlie, kicking elbows, ribs, shins, calves, and thighs, kicking ass and back and then kicking Charlie's face lightly, left foot, right foot, lightly but still

a kick, drawing blood, rolling the head from side to side like a leaky
soccer ball.

*   *   *

Fogarty left the garage and went inside the house. He poured himself a
double whiskey and stood looking at a fly on the front screen door.
Jack and Kiki came down the stairs, Jack carrying Kiki's suitcase.

"Can I see you, Jack?" he said and they went out on the porch,
and Fogarty said, "I don't need that stuff going on back there. That
cocksucker's not going to leave any face on the man."

"All right. The Goose and Oxie can handle it alone."

"The Goose is a fucking maniac. He oughta be in a cage."

"The Goose knows what he's doing. He won't hurt him too bad."

"He's gonna kill him. You said you didn't want to kill him."

"The Goose won't kill him. He's done this before."

"He's a sick son of a bitch."

"Listen, don't get your balls out of joint. Drive us to town. Have
a drink in the village while we have dinner. Change your mood."

So Fogarty drove them in, and Jack checked Kiki in at the Saulpaugh to get her away from the farm. He moved her around like a
checker. Fogarty drove Jack back to his own house at midnight and
went to sleep himself on the porch sofa where he was awakened at two
in the morning by the private buzzer, the one under the second porch
step. Jack was at the door almost as soon as Fogarty got himself off the
sofa. Jack was wide awake, in his red silk pajamas and red silk robe. It
was Oxie at the door.

"Northrup's shot," Oxie said.

"Who shot him?"

"Murray."

"What the hell for?"

"He had to. He acted up."

"Where are they?"

"In Northrup's car, in the driveway."

"You half-witted cocksucker, you brought him here?"

"We didn't want to leave him no place."

"Get him over to the farm. I'll meet you there in ten minutes."

Fogarty pulled up behind the Northrup car which Oxie had parked
in shadows on the farm's entrance road.

"He looks dead," Jack said when he looked at Charlie's crumpled
frame in the back seat. The seat was full of blood near his head.

"He ain't peeped," Murray said. "I think he's a cold fishy."

Jack picked up Charlie's hand, felt it, dropped it.

"What happened?"

"I was past Newburgh when he got the rope off," Murray said.

"Who tied him up?"

"Me," said Murray.

"He got free and swung a tire iron and hit me in the neck," Murray said. "Almost broke my neck."

"I was followin' in our car and I saw him swerve, almost go in a ditch," Oxie said.

"Where'd he get a tire iron?"

"It musta been down behind the seat," Murray said. "It wasn't on the floor when we put him in."

Jack kept nodding, then threw up his hands in a small gesture.

"You had to shoot him?"

"It was only one shot, a fluke. What am I supposed to do about a guy with a tire iron?"

"You're a fucking maniac. You know what this could cost me? Front pages. Not to mention a fucking war." He hit the roof of the car with his fist.

"What do we do with him?" Oxie asked.

"Get some weights, we'll put him in the river," said Murray.

"Goddamn this," Jack said. He kicked Northrup's fender. Then he said, "No, the river he could float up. Take him in the woods and bury him. No, wait, they could still find the son of a bitch. I want no evidence on this. Burn him."

"Burn him?" Fogarty said.

"Use the fire out at the still. You can make it as big as you want, nobody pays attention." And then he said to Fogarty, "If he's dead, he's dead, right? A lump of mud."

"What about Jesse and his kids?"

"Go see them. Tell them to stay away from the still tonight."

"You can't burn a man's body in that pit out there," Fogarty said. "It's big but not that big."

"I'll take care of that," Murray said. "I'll trim off the edges."

"Christ Almighty."

"Try not to burn down the woods," Jack said. "When you're done, let me know. And you won't be done till there's nothing left, even if it takes two days. And then you clean out the pit and sift the ashes and smash the teeth and the bones that don't burn, especially the teeth. And scatter the pieces and the dust someplace else."

"Gotcha," said Murray. It was his kind of night.

"Speed, you better give 'em a hand," Jack said. "Drive and stand guard. He don't have to touch anything," Jack told Murray.

"What does he ever touch?" Murray said.

Fogarty's stomach was burbling as he drove Northrup's car inside the barn. Murray said he needed a lot of newspapers, and so Fogarty went into the house and got some and told Jesse to stay clear of the still until he was told he could go back. Fogarty walked slowly back to the barn, feeling like he might puke. When he saw what Murray had already done to Charlie with the hatchet, it shot out of him like a geyser.

"Tough guy," Murray said.

*   *   *

"Marcus," Kiki said from the other end of the phone, and it was the first time she called me that, "I'm so damn lonely."

"Where's your friend?"

"I thought you might know."

"I haven't seen him since the night I took you to dinner."

"I've seen him twice since then. Twice in seventeen days. He's up in the country with her all the time. Christ, what does he see in that fat old cow? What's the matter with me? I wash my armpits."

"He's all business these days. He'll turn up."

"I'm getting bedsores waiting. What he don't know is I'm not waiting anymore. I'm going into a new show. I just couldn't cut it anymore, sitting, waiting. Maybe he sees me dancing again he'll think twice about playing titball with his fat-assed wife. I bet when she takes off her brassiere they bounce off her toes."

Kiki was tight, another road to power.

"What's the show and when does it open? I wouldn't miss that."

"*Smiles* is the name of it, and I do one routine by myself, a tap number. It's swell, Marcus, but I'd rather make love."

"Sure. Had any more visits from Jimmy Biondo?"

"Nobody visits me. Why don't you come down to the city and see me? Just to talk, now. Don't let the little lady give you the wrong impression."

"Maybe I will," I said, "next time I'm down there on business."

I had no pressing business in New York, but I made it a point to go, and I presume it was for the same reason I'd helped old Jesse frame a new identity for himself and then got him a job in Boston—because I was now addicted to entering the world of Jack Diamond as fully as possible. I was unable not to stick around and see how it all turned out. And yes, I know, even as a spectator, I was condoning the worst sort of behavior. Absolute worst. I know, I know.

I called Jack when I decided to go down, for I had no wish to put myself in the middle of the big romance.

"Great," he said. "Take her to a movie. I'll be down Friday and we'll all go out."

"You know I still have some of your belongings."

"Hang onto them."

"I'd rather not."

"Only for a little while more."

"A very little while."

"What's the problem? They taking up too much room?"

"Only in my head."

"Clean out your head. Go see Marion."

So I did and we went to dinner and talked and talked, and then I took her to see Garbo in *Flesh and the Devil* in a place that hadn't yet converted to talkies. Kiki was a Garbo fanatic and looked on herself as a *femme fatale* even though she was nothing of the sort. The main thing she had in common with Garbo was beauty. There is a photo of Garbo at fifteen that has something of Kiki about it, but after that the ladies were not playing the same game. "The spiritually erotic rules over the sensually erotic in her life," an astrologist once said of Garbo, which was a pretty fair critical summary of her movie self at least.

Kiki was something else: a bread-and-butter sensualist, a let's-put-it-all-on-the-table-folks kind of girl. She actually enjoyed the feeling of being wicked. In the movie Garbo rushes to save her two loves from a duel, repentant that she started it all as a way of simplifying her choice between them. She falls through the ice on the way and it's good-bye Greta. Kiki leaned over to me and whispered, "That's what you get for being a good girl."

Kiki started out with the glitter dream, a bathing beauty at fifteen, a Follies' girl at eighteen, a gangster's doll at twenty. She yearned for spangles and got them quickly, then found she didn't really want them except for what they did for her head. They preserved her spangly mood. She was in spangles when she met Jack at the Club Abbey during his fugitive time, and he loved them almost as much as he loved her face.

"I always knew exactly how pretty I was," she told me, "and I knew I could write my own ticket in show business, even though I don't dance or sing so great. I don't kid myself. But whatever you can get out of this business with good looks, I'm going to get. Then when I met Jack it changed. My life started going someplace, someplace weird and good. I wanted to feel that good thing in me, and when I did it with Jack, I knew I didn't care about show business except as a way to stay alive and keep myself out front. I'm Jack's girl, but that's not all I am, and supposing he drops me? But I know he won't do that because what we have is so great. We go out, me and Jack, out to the best places with the best people, rich people, I mean, society people, famous people like politicians and actors and they fall all over us. I know they envy us because of what we've got and what we are. They all want to make sex with us and kiss us and love us. All of them. They look up my dress and down my front and touch me any place they can, stroke my wrist or hair or pat my fanny and say excuse me, or take my hand and say something nice and stupid, but it's all an excuse to touch. And when practically everybody you come across does this to you, women too, then you know you're special, maybe not forever, but for now. Then you go home and he puts it up in you and you wrap around him and you come and he comes, and it mixes up together and it's even greater than what was already great, but it's still the same fantastic thing. You're in love and you're wanted by everybody, and is anything ever better than that? One night, when Jack was in me, I thought, Marion, he's not fucking you, he's fucking himself. Even then I loved him more than I'd ever loved anything on earth. He was stabbing me and I was smothering him. We were killing everything that deserved to die because it wasn't as rich as it could be. We were killing the empty times, and then we'd die with them and wake up and kill them again until there wasn't anything left to kill and we'd be alive in a way that you can never die when you feel like that because you own your life and nothing can ruin you.

"And then he leaves me here for seventeen days and keeps track of everygoddamnbody I buy a paper off or smile at in the lobby, and so I stay in and practice my dance steps and listen to Rudy Vallee and Kate Smith, and I don't even have a view of the park because Jack doesn't want to be a target from the trees. This is a nice little suite and all, and do I mean little. Because you can lose your mind staying in two rooms, and so I fix my hair and pluck my eyebrows. I know when every hair in my eyebrows first pokes its way out. I watch it grow. I take a hot bath and I rub myself off to forget what I want. One day I did that four times and that's not healthy for a young person like me and I'll tell you straight, I'm to the point where I'm not going to be so damn particular who's inside me when I want to feel that good thing. But I never cheated on him yet, and I don't want to. I don't want to leave him, and that's the God's truth. I almost said I can't leave him, but I know I can. I can leave if I want. But I don't want to leave. That's why I took the job in *Smiles*. To show him I can leave him, even when I don't want to."

* * *

At 9:30 P.M. on Saturday, October 11, 1930, three men, later identified as members of the Vincent Coll gang, walked into the Pup Club on West Fifty-first Street in Manhattan. One walked up to the short one-eyed man at the bar and said softly to him, "Murray?" The one-eyed man turned on his stool and faced two guns.

"You're out, Murray," the man who had spoken to him said, and the other two fired six bullets into him. Then they left.

An hour and a half later, in an eighth-floor room at the Monticello Hotel, across the hall from the room occupied by Marion Roberts, two men stepped off the elevator at the same time that two others were touching the top step of the stairs leading to the eighth floor. The four fanned out into the cul-de-sacs of the hallways and returned to the elevator with an all clear, and Jimmy Biondo stepped out past a blanched elevator man. The five men, Jimmy at the center, walked down the hall to Room 824 and knocked three times, then twice, then once, and the door opened on Jack Diamond in shirtsleeves, a pistol on the arm of the chair he was sitting in. Count Duschene said he stood to Jack's left, and at other points around the room were the men who had confronted Murray earlier in the evening: Vincent Coll, Edward (Fats McCarthy) Popke, and Hubert Maloy.

"Hey, Jimmy," Jack said. "Glad you could come. How you getting along?"

Pear-shaped Jimmy, still mistrusting the room, stared at all faces before settling on Jack's and saying, "Whatayou got to offer aside from my money?"

"Sit down, Jimmy, chair there for you. Let's talk a little."

"Nothing to talk about. Where's the money?"

"The money is in good hands. Don't worry about that."

"Whose good hands?"

"What's the difference if it's safe?"

"Never mind the horseshit, where's the money?"

"What would you say if I told you it's on its way back to Germany?"

"I'd tell you you ain't got very fucking long to live."

"I'm going back there, Jimmy, and this time I'll get in. Don't you like instant seven-to-one on your money?"

"I like my money."

"We made a deal. I want to keep my part of the bargain is all."

"No deal. Tony Amapola knows how you deal. Charlie Northrup knows how you deal."

"I knew you'd think of me when Tony got it. But I had nothing to do with that. I like Tony. Always did. As for Charlie I do know what happened. It was a free-lance job. Charlie made enemies up in the country. But Charlie and I were as close as you and Tony. We were like brothers."

"Charlie had a different story. He said you were a fuckhead."

"You don't believe me, ask any of these boys who it was gave it to Charlie."

Jimmy looked around, settled on Fats McCarthy. Fats nodded at him.

"Murray The Goose," Fats said. "He give it to Charlie."

"You heard yet what happened to Murray The Goose?" Jack asked Jimmy.

"No."

"Somebody just dealt him out, up in the Pup Club. Walked in and boom-boom-boom. Cooked The Goose. Somebody got even for Charlie is how I read it. Now how do you like your friends?"

"It's a fact," The Count said. "I happened to be in the club at the time."

"There's a coincidence for you," Jack said.

"Puttin' it on The Goose don't mean he was even in the same state."

"Ask around. Don't tell me you didn't hear the rumors."

"I hear nothin'."

"You oughta listen a little instead of talking so much about money. There's more to life than money, Jimmy."

"Fuck life. I been listenin' too long. I been listenin' to your bullshit here five minutes, and I don't see no money onna fuckin' table. I tell you what—you got a telephone I make a call to an old frienda yours. Charlie Lucky."

"Always glad to say hello to Charlie."

"He be glad to say hello to you too because half the two hundred come outa his pocket. Whataya think of that, you Irish fuck?"

"I'll tell you what, you guinea fuck, call Charlie. He tells me it's half his I'll have it for him in the morning."

Jimmy moved his elbow at one of his young gunmen: early twentyish, pencil-line mustache. The gunman dialed, said something in Italian, waited, handed the phone to Jimmy.

"That you, Charlie?" Jimmy said. "I'm with our friend. He wants to know were you my silent partner. Okay. Sure." He handed Jack the phone.

"Charlie, how you doin'? You staying thin? Right, Charlie, that's the only way. You were. You did. So. Yeah. Now I get it. You're not saying this just for Jimmy. You wouldn't con me after all these years. Right. I understand. Let's have a drink one of these days, Charlie. Any time. Beautiful."

Jack hung up and turned to Jimmy. "He said he loaned you twenty grand at fourteen percent."

"He don't say that."

"I just talked to the man. Did you hear me talk to him? What am I, a guy who makes up stories you see with your own eyes?"

"He's in for half, no interest."

"I tell you what, Jimmy. I'll have twenty available in the morning. I'll call you and tell you where to pick it up and you can pay Charlie back. Meantime we still got a deal with what's left."

"Charlie, give me a hundred, you fuckheaded fuck!" Jimmy screamed and stood up, and everybody's pistol came out at the same time. Jack didn't touch his. All the pistols were pointed at all the other pistols. Anybody moved it was ten-way suicide.

"We don't seem to be getting anyplace," Jack said. He lit a Rameses and sat down and crossed his legs. "Why don't you go have a drink and think about life, Jimmy? Think about how rich you'll be when I come back with all that beautiful white stuff. A million four. Is that hard to take or is that hard to take?"

"I'm talkin' to a dead man," Jimmy said.

"Dead men pay no debts, Jimmy."

"Keep lookin' for me," Jimmy said.

"Watch yourself crossing the street," Jack said.

These were atrocious melodramatics, and I would not give them the time of day, despite my trust in Fogarty, except that when Jimmy and his friends left the Monticello and walked down West Sixty-fourth Street, a car came in their direction at low speed and two shotgun blasts from a back window blew apart two of Jimmy's shooters. Jimmy and the other two escaped with only a certain loss of dignity.

Count Duschene later remembered Jack's reaction when he heard the news: "Mustache cocksuckers. Fast as you knock 'em off they bring in another boatload." The rest of the news came out in the morning paper: Murray, with six bullets in him, was not yet dead.

*   *   *

Kiki said that the positively worst time of her life was when she was hiding at Madge's apartment and the knock came on the door and Madge turned to her and said, "Get in the bedroom and hide." So she went first behind Madge's big Morris chair, but then she said to herself, Gee, they'd look here right away, and so she started to roll under Madge's canopy bed with the beaded curtain, but then she said to herself, Won't they look under here, too? And so she stood in the closet behind Madge's summer and winter dresses and coats until she realized that anybody opening the door would look right through the hangers into her great big beautiful brown eyes, and so she took Madge's dyed muskrat everybody thought was mink off the wooden hanger and covered herself with it and rolled into the smallest ball she could make out of herself and faced the wall with her rounded back to the door so they would think the coat had fallen off the hanger on top of a pile of shoes

and little boxes and galoshes. And then they'd go away. Yes. Go away.
Let me alone.

Right then, Kiki would have said if anyone had asked her, she or-
dinarily didn't like to be alone. But now it was quite necessary, for she
had to figure out what she was going to do with her life. She never had
to hide in a closet before, ever. Jack's fault. Her fault too for staying
with him, waiting for him. She had decided to leave him for good, truly
leave this time and not just go back into show business or take a train
home to Boston with her mad money. No. This was the end. Nothing
on earth could make her stay with Jack Diamond for another day because he truly did kill people.

She had read all the news stories when he was in Europe, but she
didn't read past the parts where they began to say things about him.
She'd just throw the papers in the bottom of her closet for Jack because
she knew how he loved to save clippings about himself. And what a big
stack it got to be! She didn't even read any of the long series of articles
they wrote about him because the first one began by calling him Eggs
Diamond. Because eggs are yellow. And though she knew Jack wasn't
yellow, she didn't really know what color he was. She didn't know
anything really deep about him except what he said and what she
wanted him to say and what he said was "You're gorgeous in my life"
and "You're the most beautiful thing in the world. I deserve you." And
she said to that, "And I deserve you, too." And they went into their silk
cocoon then. Her warm bed with the pink silk sheets and her white silk
nightgown and Jack in his yellow silk pajamas with the green dragon
on them, and slowly they took the silk off one another and just smothered themselves in the cocoon and fucked and fucked and fucked. And
when they were all through they went to sleep and woke up, and then
they fucked and fucked some more and took a shower and went to see
Jolson again in *Mammy*, and had dinner and came back to the cocoon,
and didn't they fuck even more? They certainly did. Oh, wasn't that the
cat's knickers? Vo-de-oh-do! There was never anything like that in her
life before Jack, though she knew about fucking all right, all right. But
fucking is one thing and fucking with Jack was another thing altogether.
It was not the glitter. Sometimes when you fucked it was just to get
something or because you thought you ought to or because you liked
his looks and he was nice to you and it was expected of you and you
wanted to do what was expected. It was your role to fuck men who
were nice because you're only young once, isn't that so? Isn't that why
you wanted to be in the glitter dream? To glitter by yourself? And what
better way to glitter than to fuck whenever you felt like it? Fuck the
best people, the most beautiful people. Do you like to fuck? Oh, I love
it, don't you?

But then she met Jack and she didn't want anybody but him. Now it wasn't just liking to fuck. It was liking to fuck Jack. And it was feeling wanted and taken and also taking and also wanting, which was the key to the thing that changed in her. She wanted in a new way. Jack taught her that. She wanted not just for the moment or the hour or the day, but she wanted permanently.

"We'll always live in the cocoon, won't we?"

"Sure, kid."

"We'll make love even when you're seventy-five, won't we?"

"No, kid. I'm not going to live to be seventy-five. I didn't expect to make it to thirty-three."

And that changed her again. She wanted him and wanted what he gave her forever and ever, but now she had to think about outliving him, of this maybe being that last time she would ever put her arms around him and bite his ear and play with his candy cane because then he might get up and get dressed and go out and die. Well, then she wanted him more than ever. She didn't know why. She just called it love because that's what everybody else called it. But it wasn't only that, because now she wanted not just Jack himself but Jack who was going to die. She wanted to kiss and fuck somebody who was going to die. Because when he died, then you had something nobody else could ever get again.

And then Jimmy Biondo came and talked to her and she said she didn't believe what he said about Jack being so awful. But she went and read all the papers she was saving in the closet and oh, the things they said that Jack did all his life, and she couldn't believe her eyes because they were so awful, so many killings and torturing people and burning prostitutes with cigarettes. Oh, oh, oh! And so she knew then she would leave him. She knew it and she knew it and she knew it all Saturday night even after he came to her room and they went into the cocoon killing the bad things. She forgot while that was happening that she was going to leave him, for how can you leave a person when they're making you forget the bad things? But when it was over she remembered and when she went to sleep alongside him she thought of it and she was still thinking about it when she woke up and saw him drinking the orange juice he'd ordered for them both, with toast and eggs and coffee and a steak for him, and she thought of it while he ate the steak in his blue pajamas with the red racehorses on them. I am seeing you eat your last piece of steak. I am seeing you wear your last pajamas. She would kill him in her mind and that would be the end of Jack Diamond for Marion Roberts. So long, Jackie boy. I loved your candy. Gee it was swell. But you're dead now for me. You're mine forever. Marion Roberts is not going to go on living her life as a gangster's doll, a gangster's

moll. Marion Roberts is her own woman and she is not going to live
for fucking. She is not going to live for any one man. She is not going
to live for killing because she knows better. She knows how good life
is and how hard it is to make life good. She's going to move on to
something else. She can go on dancing. She will find a way to live out
her life without gangster Jackie.

But then she wondered: What is it about a gangster like him? Why
did I take up with him? Why didn't I believe what everybody said about
him, that I might wind up in the river, that I might get shot in bed with
him, that he might ruin my face if he ever caught me cheating? Because
gangsters are evil and don't care about anybody but themselves. Why
didn't she believe those things? Because she wanted it all out of life, all
all all there was to get. The top, the tip, the end, the reach, the most,
the greatest, the flashiest, the best, the biggest, the wildest, the craziest,
the worst.

Why did Kiki want the worst? Because she was a criminal too? A
criminal of love? Birds of a feather, Marion. You knew even as you
were saying that you were leaving him that you wouldn't leave. You
knew as you read about the torture he did and the killing he did that
you wouldn't give him up because you knew about the other side of
that glorious man, with his candy up in your sweet place and his mouth
on yours. You wouldn't give that up.

Even when those men came to the hotel this morning and Jack went
to meet them and said to them while you were lying there in the half-
empty cocoon, even when he said: "Hello, boys, how are you? Be right
with you," and said to you that he'd only be a few minutes, and that
he had some business to finish up, and went out in the hallway still in
his blue pajamas with the red racehorses and the darker blue robe with
the white sash and the white diamond embroidered on the breast pocket,
even then you knew.

You got up and went into the shower and you let it smother you
like you smothered him and you were standing in that sweet heat after
love in the morning when you heard the shots: two, four, six, then none,
then three more and another and another and another. And you froze
in all that heat because you said to yourself (Oh, God forgive you for
saying it), you said: That murdering bastard, he's killed somebody else.

*   *   *

Later, when she started to dance, she remembered looking at her feet
and said to herself: These are going to be the most famous legs on
Broadway. And she danced on that for five minutes to the piano man's
rippling repetition of a tune of four-four tempo whose name she
couldn't remember any more than she could remember the piano man's

name or the director's name or the name of the musical itself. Black mesh stockings enveloped her most famous legs. White trunks covered her most famous hips. A white blouse tied at the midriff covered her most famous breasts. And black patent leather tap shoes covered her most famous toes, which nobody realized yet were famous. She thought of how people would behave when they found out how famous they were and tried to let that thought crowd out the rest. But she couldn't. Because her mind went back to what it was that was going to make her toes so famous and she stopped dancing, seeing it all again, seeing herself see it this time and knowing she was webbed in something that wasn't even going to be possible to get out of. So she looked at the piano man and then at the director, and while the other girls went on dancing, she decided to fall down.

The next thing she knew she was sitting at her mirror with all her theatrical makeup on the table in front of her, and the calico kitten Jack had won for her at the Coney Island shooting gallery, all cuddly and sleepy in the middle of the table. In the mirror she saw Madge Conroy sitting on a chair beside her, and Bubble, the chorus boy who had helped Madge pick her off the floor. They both stared at her.

"She finally blinked," Bubble said.

"You all right?" Madge asked.

"Close your eyes, for heaven's sake," Bubble said, "before they explode all over us."

The mirror was outlined by a dozen bare bulbs, all illuminating her face, so famous to be, so unknown to even its own exploding eyes. Why aren't you running away, pretty lady in the brilliant mirror? What brought you to the theater? Is it that you don't know what to be afraid of yet? Do you think the theater will protect you? Do you think the mirror will?

Bubble said, "Mirror, mirror on the wall, who's got the Kikiest eyes of all?"

"Shut up," Madge said, "and get her a drink someplace." Madge rubbed Kiki's wrists as Bubble went away.

"Oh, Madge, I just got to talk to somebody."

"I had a hunch you did. I kept watching you dancing out there. You looked like somebody kidnapped your brain. Like a zombie."

"Honest to God, Madge, it's something awful. It's so awful."

Bubble came back with an unlabeled half-pint. Madge grabbed it and looked at it, smelled it and poured Kiki a drink. She capped the bottle, set it on Kiki's table, and told Bubble, "Will you please, please, please get lost?"

"What's the *matter* with her?"

"I'll find out if you let us be."

"Yes, nursie."

"You oughta be rehearsing out there," Kiki said to Madge.

"They can do without me. I know the routine."

"It was so awful. Honest to God, this is the worst thing that ever happened to me."

"What? What the hell happened?"

"I can't tell you here. Can we go someplace? I don't know what to do, Madge. Honest to God I don't."

"We can go over to my apartment. Change your clothes."

But it took so much effort for Kiki to take off her trunks that she left on the rest, her mesh stockings and the rehearsal blouse and only put on her skirt and street shoes. She threw her other street clothes and the trunks and tap shoes into her red patent-leather hatbox and saw, as she did, her street makeup and her purse, the only things she took when she ran out of the hotel.

"I'm ready," she said to Madge.

*   *   *

"You better buy a paper," Kiki told Madge when they came to a newsstand at Broadway and Forty-seventh. And as Madge did and after Kiki saw her utter a small "Oh" and throw her face into the paper, Kiki turned to see an old man in a gray bowler, with a yellowing white walrus mustache and pince-nez specs, wearing a frock coat with lapel gardenia and a brocaded yellow vest across which dangled an old watch chain and fob in the design of a mermaid. Blank cards, an ink bottle, and a quill pen lay in front of him on a table that folded into a suitcase. Samples of his script-for-sale, tacked to the table's drop-leaf front, were splendid with antique swirls, curlicues, and elegant hills, valleys, and ovals.

"I hope you're in show business, young lady," the old gent said to her over his pince-nez.

"As a matter of fact, I am."

"It's the only safe place for talentless beauty, miss."

"You've got some crust saying I don't have any talent."

"Anywhere else you'll be destroyed."

"As a matter of fact, I'm quitting show business."

"A disastrous move."

"But none of *your* business."

"Forgive me for speaking so freely, but you look to me like a bird wounded in the heart, the brain, and between the legs, and we in the Audubon Society do what we can for the wounded. My card."

"I'm Jack Diamond's girl. What about that?"

"Ah, then, ah. I had no way of knowing"—and the old man retrieved his card and handed her another. "Jack Diamond is an entirely safe place. You have nothing to fear, my dear, as long as you have a role in Jack Diamond's hilarious tragedy."

She looked at the card and saw in the obsolete glory of his pen strokes the biography of her vampy, bondaged, satin-slippered addiction. The card read: "There is no good and bad in the elfin realm." When she looked up, the man had packed his table and was halfway down the block.

❊   ❊   ❊

Kiki looked over Madge's shoulder at the headline which read: JACK DIAMOND SHOT FIVE TIMES BY GUNMEN IN 64TH STREET HOTEL.

"I was there," Kiki told Madge.

"You didn't shoot him, did you?"

"Oh, Madge, I love him."

"What's that got to do with it? Come on, we've got to get you off the street."

And so they took a cab to Madge's place and Kiki had a stiff drink, a very stiff one, and then she started to weep. So Madge held her hand and Kiki knew that even though Madge was her friend that she was touching her because she was a special person. Because Madge never touched her like that before, stroking the back of her hand, patting it with her fingertips; and Kiki felt good because somebody was being nice to her and she finally told Madge then how she heard the shots as she stood in the shower. And she thought somebody would come in and shoot her. And she would die in the bathtub, her blood going down the drain. Maybe Jack would be the one to shoot her. Why did Kiki think that about Jack?

Then she heard the running in the corridor, and she said to herself, why, Jack wouldn't run away and leave me, and so she quickly got into her pink robe and went next door to Jack's own room and saw the door open and Jack on the floor with his eyes open but not moving, looking up at her. And she said, "Oh, Jackie, you're dead," but he said, "No I'm not, help me up," and they were just the best old words she'd ever heard and she put her arms under him and lifted him and he put one of his hands over his stomach and the other over his chest to hold in the blood where they'd shot him. Blood was coming down his face and all down his blue pajamas so you couldn't even see the red racehorses anymore.

"Get the whiskey," Jack told her when she had him sitting on the bed, and she looked around the room and couldn't see it, and Jack said, "In the bathroom," and when she got it, he said, "In my mouth," and she wiped the blood off his lips and poured in the whiskey. Too much.

He choked and coughed and new blood spurted out of one of the holes in his chest, and like a little fountain turned on and off by the pumping of his heart, it flowed down over his fingers.

"Get The Count," he said, "across the hall," and she knocked on The Count's door until her knuckles hurt and he came to Jack's room and Jack said to her then: "Get the hell out of here and don't come back and don't admit you were here or you're all washed up." And Kiki nodded but didn't understand and said to Madge, "How would I be washed up, Madge? Did he mean in show business?" And Madge said, "Go on," so she said The Count called a doctor as she was leaving and then took Jack to another room in the hotel, down the hall, because Jack said the killers might come back to see if they did the job right. And Kiki, still in her pink robe, backed down the hallway toward her own room, and watched The Count walking and holding Jack, who was bent like a wishbone, and in they went to another room, which was when Kiki decided she would go to the theater and behave like nothing at all had happened. And things went along perfectly well, didn't they? They went along fine, just fine until she saw it all again while she was dancing. What she saw was that little spurt of blood coming out of Jack's chest like a fountain after she gave him too much whiskey. That was when she decided to fall down.

Madge read in the paper that two gunmen came running out of the hotel about the time Jack was shot and got into a car with its motor running and its door open and drove off with their New Jersey license plates. Those men, awful men, had shot Jack two places in the chest and once in the stomach and once in the thigh and once in the forehead, and the doctor said he was certainly not going to be able to go on living with all those holes in himself. The paper made no mention of the pretty little lady who was the first to see it all, but Kiki knew that her time of attention was going to come.

She caught the faintest smell of mothballs in Madge's closet, and she thought of marriage because only married people need mothballs. Kiki would never keep anything long enough to worry about moths unless she happened to be married. Last year's things? She stuck them away and bought new ones and let the moths have their fun. Kiki never thought of herself as married, even though she and Jack talked about it all the time. She talked about it and Jack tried to change the subject, is more like it.

"I'll marry you someday, kid," he told her once, but she didn't believe that and wasn't even sure she wanted to believe it. Kiki doing the wash. Kiki beating the rugs. Kiki making fudge. It was certainly a laughing matter.

When the second knock on the door came, just seconds after Madge told her to hide in the bedroom (and she was in the closet by then, under the muskrat and smelling the mothballs by then), she heard Madge say to somebody, "What the hell are you bothering me for? You have no right to come in here." But they didn't go away. Kiki heard them walking in the rooms and heard them just outside the door, so she breathed so silently that not even a moth would have known she was there.

Who are those men is what Kiki wanted to know. Are they after me? And at that the light flashed into the closet and the muskrat unwrapped itself from her back and a hand grabbed her and two great big faces stared down at her.

"Go away," she said. "I don't know you men." And she pulled one of Madge's dresses over her face. She could hear Madge saying, "I had no idea she was involved in any shooting. I certainly wouldn't have brought her into my own home if I thought she was mixed up in any sort of nasty shooting business. I don't want this kind of publicity."

But they put Madge's picture in the papers too. With her legs crossed.

*   *   *

Jack didn't die. He became more famous than ever. Both the *News* and the *Mirror* ran series on him for weeks. The *News* also ran Kiki's memoirs: How I went from bathing beauty to the Ziegfeld chorus to Jack Diamond's lap. She and Jack were Pyramus and Thisbe for the world and no breakfast table was without them for at least a month. Kiki overnight became as famous as most actresses, her greatest photo (that gorgeous pout at the police station) on every page one.

Jack recovered at Polyclinic Hospital, and when he came to and saw where he was, he asked to be moved into the room where Rothstein had died. The similarities to this and A. R.'s shooting, both shot in a hotel, both mysterious about their assailants, money owed being at the center of both cases, and Jack being A. R.'s man of yore, were carefully noted by the press. You'd think it was the governor who'd got it, with all the bulletins on conditions and the endless calls from the public. The hospital disliked the limelight and worried too about the bill until a delivery boy brought in an anonymous thirty-five hundred dollars in crumpled fifties and twenties and a few big ones with a note: "See Jack Diamond gets the best." This the work of Owney Madden.

Of course Jack never said who shot him. Strangers he could never possibly identify, he told Devane. Didn't get a good look at them. But the would-be assassins were neutral underworld figures, not Jack's enemies and not in Biondo's or Luciano's circle (nor Dutch Schultz's either, who was generally credited with the work at the time). Their neutrality was why Jack let them in.

Their function was to retrieve Charlie Lucky's money, but Jack refused to give it back, claiming finally that Luciano was lying about his role in the transaction. This was not only Jack's error, but also his willful need to affront peril. The visitors' instructions were simple: Get *all* the money or kill him.

He was sitting on the bed when they took out their guns. He ran at them, swinging the pillow off the bed, swinging in rage and terror, and though both men emptied their pistols, the pillow deflected both their attention and their aim so that only five of twelve bullets hit him.

But five is a lot. And the men ran, leaving him for dead.

                    *   *   *

The Count called me to say that Jack mentioned me just before he went unconscious from his wounds. "Have Marcus take care of Alice and see she doesn't get the short end from those shitkickers up in the country," he told The Count. Then when Alice called me from the hospital and said Jack wanted to see me, I went down, and it turned out he wanted to make his will: a surreptitious ten thousand to Kiki, a token bequest, no more; everything else to Alice. The arrangement seemed to speak for itself: Alice, the true love. But Jack wasn't that easy to read even when he spelled it out himself. Money was only the measure of his guilt and his sense of duty, a pair of admitted formidables, but not his answer to his enduring question.

He was in good spirits when I saw him, his bed near the window so he could hear the city, the roar of the fans spiraling upward from Madison Square Garden during the fights, all the cars on Broadway squealing and tooting, the sirens and bells and yells and shouts of the city wafting Jackward to comfort him, the small comfort being all he would have for two and a half months, for Jack Diamond the organism, was playing tag with adhesions, abscesses and lungs which had the congenital strength of tissue paper.

Jack's mail came in sacks and stacks, hundreds upon hundreds of letters during the first weeks, then dwindling to maybe a steady twenty-five a day for a month. A good many were sob stories, asking for his money when he shuffled off. Get well wishes ran second, and dead last were the handful who wanted him dead: filthy dog, dirty scum. Women were motherly, forgiving, and, on occasion, uninhibited: "Please come to my home as soon as you are up and around and I will romp you back to good health. First you can take me on the dining room table, and then in the bathroom on our new green seat, and the third time (I know you will be able to dominate me thrice) on my husband's side of the bed."

"Please when you are feeling better I would like you to please come and drown our six kittens," another woman wrote. "My husband lost everything in the crash. We cannot afford to feed six more mouths, and children come before cats. But I am much too chickenhearted to kill them myself and know you are strong enough to oblige."

"I have a foolproof plan for pass-posting the bookie I bet with," wrote a horseplayer, "but, of course, I will need protection from his violence, which is where you come in as my partner."

"Dear Mr. Legs," a woman wrote, "all my life I work for my boy. Now he gonna go way and leave his momma. He is no dam good. I hope he die. I hope you shoot him for me. I will pay what you think up to fifty-five dollars, which is all the extra I got. But he deserve it for doing such a thing to his momma who gave him her life. His name is Tommy."

"Dear Sir," wrote a man, "I read in the papers where you have been a professional killer. I would like to hire you to remove me from this life. I suppose a man in your position gets many requests like this from people who find existence unbearable. I have a special way I would prefer to die. This would be in lightly cooked lamb fat in my marble bathtub with my posterior region raised so you may shoot several small-caliber bullets into my anus at no quicker than thirty-second intervals until I am dead."

A package came which the police traced, thinking someone was trying to make good on the numerous threats that Jack would never leave the hospital alive. An eight-year-old girl from Reading, Pennsylvania, had sent it—an ounce of holy oil from the shrine of Ste. Anne de Beaupré.

"I read about Mr. Diamond being shot and how his arm is paralyzed, and I have been taught in school to help those who are down and out," the child told police.

"Punk kid," Jack said. "What does she mean down and out?"

*   *   *

On the street in front of Polyclinic little clusters of Jack's fans would gather. A sightseeing bus would pass and the announcer would say, "On your right, folks, is where the notorious Jewish gangster Legs Diamond is dying," and all would crane but none would ever see the lip quivering as he slept or the few gray hairs among all the chestnut, or the pouches of experience under his eyes, or the way his ears stuck out, and how his eyes were separated by a vertical furrow of care just above the nose, or that nose: hooked, Grecian, not Jewish, not Barrymore's either, merely a creditable piece of work he'd kept from damage, now snorting air. He was twelve pounds under his normal one fifty-two and still five ten and a half while I sat beside his bed with his last will and testament in my pocket for his signature. And he wheezed just like other Americans in their sleep.

I'd been fumbling through a prayer book on Jack's bedside table while he slept and I had turned up a credo I no more accepted as mere coincidence than I did the congruence of his and my pleasure in Rabelais; which is to say I suspected a pattern hovering over our relationship. The credo read:

> You work much harm in these parts, destroying and slaying God's creatures without his leave; and not only have you slain and devoured beasts of the field but you have dared to destroy and slay men made to the image of God: wherefore you are worthy of the gallows as a most wicked thief and murderer; all folk cry out and murmur against you. But I would make peace, Brother Wolf, between them and you, and they shall obtain for you so long as you live, a continual sustenance from the men of this city so that you shall no more suffer hunger, for well I know that you have done all this harm to satisfy your hunger. . . .

This paraphrased perfectly my private plot to forget Charlie Northrup the way everybody else was forgetting him. He was gone off page one, only a subordinate clause in Jack's delightful story. Charlie, thanks for giving us so much of your time. Such fun having a cadaver in the scenario, especially one we can't locate. But, Charl, please excuse us while we say a little prayer for Jack.

I remember also the passing thought that maybe it would be better if Jack never woke up, and then I remember seeing him wide awake, swathed in hospital-white hygienic purity.

"Hey, Marcus," he said, "great to wake up to a friendly face instead of some snooping cop. How's your ballocks?"

"Friendly toward ladies," I said, and when he laughed he winced with pain.

"I been dreaming," he said. "Talking to God. No joke."

"Uh-oh."

"Why the hell is it I'm not dead? You figured it out?"

"They were bum shooters? You're not ready to die?"

"No, it's because I'm in God's grace."

"Is that a fact? God told you that?"

"I'm convinced. I thought I was just lucky back in '25 when they hit me. Then when Augie got it, I thought maybe I was as strong as a man can be, you know, in health. But now I think it's because God wants me to live."

He was not quite sitting up in bed, his prayer book there all soft and black on the white table and his rosary twined around the corner post of his bed, shiny black beads capturing the white tubing. Did he appreciate the contrast? I'm convinced he created it.

"You've got the disease of sanctity," I told him.

"No, that's not it."

"You've got it the way dogs get fleas. It's common after assassination attempts. It accounts for the closeness between the church and aging dictators. It's a kind of infestation. Look at this room." Alice had hung a crucifix over the bed and set a statue of the virgin on the windowsill. The room had been priest-ridden since Jack moved into it, the first a stranger who came to hear his confession and inquired who shot him. Even through quasi-delirium Jack recognized a Devane stooge. The next, a Baltimore chum of Alice's who dropped in without the press learning his name, comforted Jack, blessed him through opiated haze, then told newsmen: "Don't ask me to tell you anything about that poor suffering boy in there." And then came good Father Skelly from Cairo, indebted to Jack for the heavenly music in his church.

"God won't forget that you gave us a new organ," said the priest to the resurrecting Jack.

"Will God do the same for us when ours gets old?" Jack asked.

The priest heard his confession amid the two bouquets of roses Alice renewed every three days until Jack said the joint smelled like a wake, and so she replaced them with a potted geranium and a single red wax rose in a vase on the bedside table.

"I thought you'd given up the holy smoke," I said. "I thought you had something else going for you."

"What the hell am I supposed to do after people keep shooting me and I don't die? I'm beginning to think I'm being saved."

"For dessert? Looks classic to me, Jack. Shoot a man full of bullets and he's a candidate for blessedness."

"What about you and your communion breakfasts? Big-shot Catholic."

"Don't be misled. That's just part of being an Albany Democrat."

"So you're a Democrat and I got fleas. But it turns out I don't mind them."

"I can see that, and it all ties in. Confession, sanctity, priests. Yes, it goes with having yourself shot."

"Come again?"

"The shooting. I've assumed all along that you rigged it."

"You're not making sense."

"Could it have happened without your approval? You saw them alone, you know what they were. I know what such go-betweens can be, and I'm not even in your business. And you never had any intention of turning over that money. You asked for exactly what you got. Am I exaggerating?"

"You got some wild imagination, pal. I see why you score in court."

But when he looked at me, that furrow of care between his eyes turned into a question mark. He ran his fingertips along the adhesive tape of his chest bandage, pleasurably some might say, as he looked at the author of the bold judgment. Jack Diamond having himself shot? Ridiculous. He fingered the rosary entwined over his right shoulder on the bed, played the beads with his fingertips as if they were keys on an instrument that would deliver the music he wanted to hear. Organ music. A sound like Skelly's new machine. No words to it, just the music they play at benediction after the high mass. Yes, there are words. From a long time ago. The *"Tantum Ergo."* All Latin words you never forget, but who the hell knows what they mean? *"Tantum ergo sacramentum, veneremur cernui; et antiquum documentum, Novo cedat ritui."*

A bridge.

A certain light.

Something was happening to him, Jack now knew.

*   *   *

"I want you to talk for me," he said. He had recovered from my impertinence, was restoring the client-attorney relation, putting me in my place. "I want you to talk to some people upstate. A few judges and cops, couple of businessmen, and find out what they think of my setup now. Fogarty's handling it, but he can't talk to those birds. He's too much of a kid. I got through to all those bastards personally, sent them whiskey, supported their election campaigns, gave 'em direct grease. All them bums owe me favors, but the noise in the papers about me, I don't know now whether it scares 'em or not."

" 'Pardon me, your honor, but are you still in the market for a little greasy green as a way of encouraging Jack Diamond with his bootlegging, his shakedowns, and his quirky habit of making competitors vanish?' Is that my question?"

"Any fucking way you like to put it, Marcus. You're the talker. They all know my line of work. It'll be simpler if I still got the okay, but I don't really give a goddamn whether they like it or not. Jack Diamond's got a future in the Catskills."

"Don't you think you ought to get straight first?"

"You don't understand, Marcus. You can carve out a whole goddamn empire up there if you do it right. Capone did it in Cicero. Sure there's a lot of roads to cover, but that's all right. I don't mind the work. But if I slow now, somebody else covers those roads. And it's not like I got all the time in the world. The guineas'll be after me now."

"You think they won't ride up to the Catskills?"

"Sure, but up there I'll be ready. That's my ball park."

I've often vacillated about whether Jack's life was tragic, comic, a bit of both, or merely a pathetic muddle. I admit the muddle theory moved me most at this point. Here he was, refocusing his entire history, as if it had just begun, on the dream of boundless empire. It was a formidable readjustment and I considered it desperate, but maybe others would find it only confused and ridiculous. In any case, given the lengths he was willing to go to carry it off, it laid open his genuine obsession.

I might have credited the whole conversation about the Catskills to Jack's extraordinary greed if it hadn't been for one thing he said to me. It took me back to 1928 when Jack was arrested with his mob in a pair of elegant offices on the fourteenth and fifteenth floor of the Paramount Building, right on Times Square. Some address. Some height. Loftiness is my business, said the second-story man.

Now Jack gave me a wink and ran his hand sensuously along the edge of the chest bandage that was giving him such pleasure. "Marcus," he said, "who else do you know collects mountains?"

I've been in Catskill maybe a dozen and a half times, most of those visits brief, on behalf of Jack. I don't really know the place, never needed to. It's a nice enough village, built on the west bank of the Hudson River about a hundred or so miles north of the Hotsy Totsy Club. Henry Hudson docked near this spot to trade with the Indians and then went on up to Albany, just like Jack. The village had some five thousand people in this year of 1931 I'm writing about. It had a main street called Main Street, a Catskill National Bank, a Catskill Savings Bank, a Catskill Hardware and so on. Formal social action happened at the IOOF, the Masonic Temple, the Rebekah Lodge, the American Legion, the PTA, the Women's Progressive Club, the White Shrine, the country club, the Elks. Minstrel shows drew a good audience and visiting theater companies played at the Brooks Opera House. The local weekly serialized a new Curwood novel at the end of 1931, which Jack would have read avidly if he'd not been elsewhere. The local daily serialized what Jack was doing in lieu of reading Curwood.

Catskill was, and still is, the seat of Greene County, and just off Main Street to the north is the four-story county jail, where Oxie Feinstein was the most celebrated resident on this particular day. Before I was done with Jack, there would be a few more stellar inmates.

The Chamber of Commerce billed the village as the gateway to the

Catskills. The Day Line boats docked at Catskill Landing, and tourists were made conscious of the old Dutch traditions whenever they were commercially applicable. A Dutch friend of mine from law school, Warren Van Deusen, walked me through the city one day and showed me, among other points of interest, the home of Thomas Cole on Spring Street. Cole was the big dad of the nineteenth-century's Hudson River school of painting, and one of his works "Prometheus Bound," a classic landscape, I remember particularly well, for it reminded me of Jack. There was this giant, dwarfed by the landscape, chained to his purple cliff in loincloth and flowing beard (emanating waves of phlogiston, I'll wager) and wondering when the eagle was going to come back and gnaw away a few more of his vitals.

I called Van Deusen, who was involved in Republican county politics, as a way of beginning my assignment for Jack. In the early days of our law practice, his in Catskill, mine in Albany, I recommended him to a client who turned into very decent money for Van, and he'd been trying for years to repay the favor. I decided to give him the chance and told him to take me to lunch, which he did. We dined among men with heavy watch chains and heavier bellies. Warren, still a young man, had acquired a roll of well-to-do burgher girth himself since I'd last seen him, and when we strolled together up Main Street, I felt I was at the very center of America's well-fed, Depression complacency. It was an Indian summer day, which lightened the weight of my heavy question to Warren, that being: "What does this town think of Jack Diamond?"

"A hero, if you can believe it," Van said. "But a hero they fear, a hero they wished lived someplace else."

"Do you think he's a hero?"

"You asked about the town's feelings. My private theory is he's a punishment inflicted on us for the sins of the old patroons. But maybe that's just my Dutch guilt coming out."

"You know Jack personally?"

"I've seen him in some of our best speakeasies and roadhouses. And like most of the town, I at least once made it a point to be passing by that little barbershop right across the street there when he and his chums pulled up at eleven o'clock one morning. They always came at eleven for their ritual daily shave, hair trim, shampoo, hot towels, shoe shine, and maybe a treatment by the manicurist from up the street."

"Every day?"

"Whatever else I say about him, I'll never accuse him of being ill-groomed."

"I can't imagine this being the extent of your knowledge, a political fellow like yourself."

Van gave me a long quiet look that told me the subject was taboo, if I wanted to talk about a subsidy from Jack—that he was not in the market and knew no one who was.

"I know all the gossip," he said, finessing it. "Everybody does. He's the biggest name we've had locally since Rip Van Winkle woke up. I know his wife, too; I mean, I've seen her. Alice. Not a bad-looking woman. Saw her awhile back at the Community Theater, as a matter of fact. They change the movie four times a week and she sees them all. People seem to like her, but they don't know why she stays with Diamond. Yet they kind of like him, too—I suppose in the same way you find him acceptable."

"I accept him as a client."

"Sure, Marcus, And what about that European jaunt? Your picture even made the Catskill paper, you know."

"Someday when I understand it all better, I'll tell you about that trip. Right now all I want to know is what this town thinks."

"What for?"

"Grounding purposes, I suppose. Better my understanding of the little corner of the world where my candle burns from time to time."

Van looked at me with his flat Dutch face that seemed as blond as his hair. He was smiling, a pleasant way of calling me a liar. Van and I knew each other's facial meanings from days when our faces were less guarded. We both knew the giveaway smirks, the twitches, puckers, and sneers.

"Now I get it," he said. "It's him. He wants to know if the town's changed, how we take to his new notoriety. Is he worried?"

"What are you talking about?"

"All right, Marcus, so you won't play straight. Come on, I want to show you something."

We walked awhile, Van singling out certain landmarks for my education: There stood the garage the Clemente brothers used before Jack terrorized them out of the beer business. Over that way is a soft drink distributor's warehouse, which Diamond also took over. This was news to me. But I suppose when you set out to corner the thirst market, you corner it all.

Then Van turned in at the Elks' Club and led me to the bar. I ordered a glass of spring water and Van a beer, and then he motioned to the bartender, a man who might have been twenty-eight or forty-five, with a muscular neck; large, furlable ears; and a cowlick at the crown of his head. His name was Frank DuBois and Van said he was a straight arrow, a countryman of old Huguenot stock, and a first-class bartender.

"I was just about to tell Marcus here about your visit from the Diamond boys," Van said to him, "but I know you tell it better."

DuBois snuffed a little air, readying his tale for the four-hundredth telling, and said, "They come in all right, right through that door. Come right behind the bar here, unhitched the beer tap and rolled the barrel right out the door. 'Say,' I says to 'em, 'what'd ya do that for?' And one of them pokes me with a gun and says it's because we wasn't buying the good Canadian beer and they'd deliver us some in the mornin'. 'Yeah,' I says, 'that's just fine, but what about tonight? What do the fellas drink tonight?' 'Not this,' said one of 'em, and he shoots a couple of holes in the barrels we got. Not a fella I'd seen around before, and don't want to see him again either. Then they went out back, two of 'em, and shot up the barrels out there. Took me and Pete Gressel half a day to get the place mopped up and dried out. Dangdest mess you ever saw."

"You know the fellow who poked the gun at you?" I asked.

"I knew him all right. Joe Fogarty. Call him Speed, they do. Nervous fella. Been around this town a long time. I seen him plenty with the Diamond bunch."

"When was all this?"

"Friday week, 'bout eleven at night. Had to close up and go home. No beer to serve. No people neither, once they saw who it was come in."

"Is that the right kind of beer Van's drinking now?"

"You betcha, brother. Nobody wants no guns pokin' at them they can help it. Membership here likes peace and quiet. Nobody lookin' for trouble with Legs Diamond. He's a member this here club, you know. In good standin' too. Paid up dues and well liked till all this happen. Don't know what the others think now."

It was tidy. If Jack let his men point a gun at his own club, what other club could be safe? DuBois moved up the bar and Van said quietly, "A lot of people aren't just accepting this kind of thing, Marcus."

"I don't know what that means, not accepting."

"I'll let you use your imagination."

"Vigilantes?"

"That's not impossible but not likely either, given the people I'm talking about. At least not at the moment."

"What people *are* you talking about?"

"I have to exercise a little discretion too, Marcus. But I don't mean helpless people like Frank here."

"Then all you've got for me is a vague, implied resistance, but without any form to it. People thinking how to answer Jack?"

"More than vague. More than thinking about it."

"Van, you're not telling me much. I thought I could count on your candor. What the hell good are riddles?"

"What the hell good is Jack Diamond?"

Which was the same old question I'd been diddling with since the start. Van's expression conveyed that he knew the answer and I never would. He was wrong.

John Thomson's Man

WHEN THE POLICE WENT THROUGH JACK'S HOUSE in one of their fine-combings near the end, somebody turned up a piece of plaster, one side covered with the old-time mattress ticking wallpaper. The paper was marked with twenty-five odd squiggles, which the police presumed were some more code notations of booze deliveries; and they saved the plaster along with Jack's coded notebooks and file cards on customers and connections all over the United States and in half a dozen foreign countries.

I asked Alice about the plaster before she was killed, for it turned up in the belongings they returned to her, through my intervention, after Jack died. When she saw it she laughed a soft little laugh and told me the squiggle marks were hers; that she'd made them the first weekend she and Jack were married; that they stayed in an Atlantic City hotel and hardly went out except to eat and that they'd made it together twenty-five times. After number five, she said, she knew they'd only just started and she kept the score on the wall next to the bed. And when they checked out, Jack got the tire iron from the car and hacked out the plaster with all the squiggles on it. They kept it in their dresser drawer until the police took it away. Alice made Jack give the hotel clerk twenty-five dollars for the broken wall. A dollar a squiggle. Half the price of professional action.

I thought of Warren Van Deusen telling me people didn't understand why Alice stayed with Jack. She had her reasons. Her memories were like those squiggles. She was profoundly in love with the man, gave him her life at the outset and never wanted anyone else. She was in love with loving him too, and knew it, liked the way it looked. She won a bundle of psychic points sitting at his bedside after the Monticello, cooing into his ear while the reporters listened at the door and the nurses and orderlies carried messages to tabloid snoops. Alice heroine. Sweet Alice. Alice Blue. When the crash comes they always go back to their wives. Faithful spouse. Betrayed, yet staunch. Adversity no match for Alice. The greatest of the underworld women. Paragon of wifely virtue. Never did a wrong thing in her life. The better half of that bum, all right, all right.

Texas Guinan let her have a limousine, with chauffeur, all the time she was in New York, so she wouldn't have to worry about hawking taxis to and from Jack's bedside. The press gave Kiki the play at first, but then they caught up with Alice at the police station (that's where Kiki and Alice first met; they glowered at each other, didn't speak). The press boys tried to make her the second act of the drama, but Alice wouldn't play.

"Did you know the Roberts girl?"

"No."

"Did you know any of his friends?"

"He had many friends, but I'm not sure I knew them."

"Did you know his enemies?"

"He didn't have any enemies."

Alice was no sap, had no need for publicity. Not then. It was all happening in her ball park anyway, whether she talked or not.

"You know," she said to me after the shooting, "I hardly even brought up the subject of Marion with him. Only enough to let him know I wasn't going to die over it, that I was bigger than that. I was just as sweet as I could be. Gave him the biggest old smile I could and told him I remembered the squiggles and let him lay there and fry."

*   *   *

She said she was thinking about her Mormon dream and how it didn't make any sense when she had it, even after she told John about it and they talked about him having another wife. It was in the time of the roses, after he was shot the first time, on Fifth Avenue, when he was afraid he would die before he had done what he set out to do. He saw girls at his Theatrical Club. She knew that. But that was a trivial thing in the life of Alice Diamond because she had John as a husband, and that superseded any girl. Alice Diamond was bona fide. The real thing. A wife. And don't you forget it, John Diamond. A wife. For life.

She sat on the arm of his chair one night in the living room and told him she dreamed he'd brought home a second wife. He stood alongside the woman in the dream and said to Alice, "Well, we'll all be together from now on." And Alice said, "Not on your Philadelphia tintype." But even as she said no to him she knew it was not no. Never a total no to anything John wanted. Then the other wife came in and started taking over little things Alice used to do for John. But after Alice told him the dream, he said, "Alice, I love you, nobody else." And Alice said to him, "No, you've got another wife." And they both laughed when he said to her, "Alice, we'll be together as long as we live."

Alice did not think her dream would ever come true. Maybe he'd see a woman now and then. But to move into a hotel, to keep a woman permanently, to see her just hours after he'd seen Alice, and maybe even after he'd *been with* Alice, was terrible. It was not incomprehensible. How, after all, could *anything* be incomprehensible to a person like Alice, who knew what everybody along Broadway thinks, wants, does, and won't do? Alice was as smart about life as anybody she ever came up against. She knew the worst often happened, worse than the worst you can imagine, and so you made provisions. Her prayer book helped her make provision for the worst: for the sick, the dying, for a happy death, for the departed, for the faithful departed, for the souls in Purgatory, for the end of man, for release from Purgatorial fire. Even a special one for John. She knew she was deceived by John's capacity for passion, and so she sat by his bed and read the *Prayer to Overcome Passions and to Acquire Perfection*: "Through the infinite merits of Thy painful sufferings, give John strength and courage to destroy every evil passion which sways his heart, supremely to hate all sin, and thus to become a saint."

Saint John of the Bullets.

"Alice, there you are, Alice," Jack said when he woke up and saw her. The beginning and the end of his first coherent sentence.

She smiled at him, picked up the wax rose she'd brought him, the one rose, the secret nobody else knew, and said, "It's wax, John. Do you remember?" The corners of his mouth eased upward and he said, "Sure," so softly she could barely hear it. Then she ran her fingers ever so softly through his hair. Bittykittymins. Sweet baby. Son of a bitch. Bittykittymins. And when he was really awake for the first time, when he'd even had a little bouillon and she'd combed his hair and they put a new hospital gown on him, she said to him in her silent heart: I wish you had died.

"How are you, kid?" she said out loud, the first time in a long, long while she called him kid, the code word.

"I might make it."

"I think you might."

"They got me good this time."

"They always get you good."

"This time it hurt more."

"Everybody got hurt this time."

Alice was hurt, and she knew why. Because she loved an evil person and always would. She now wondered about her remarkable desire to see Jack dead. She had at times wished death to bad persons. Because Alice was good. Alice would not stay long in Purgatory. Because she was good. But now she wanted to die herself when she wished John dead and saw how deeply evil she herself was. She prayed to Jesus to let her want John to live. Let me not think that he's evil. Or me either. I know he's a good man in certain ways. Don't tell me I should've married somebody pure and holy. They would've bored the ass off me years ago. After all, I didn't marry a priest, Jesus. I married a thief. And landed on the front pages alongside him. My hubbydubbylubbybubby. People asking me questions. Coming for interviews. Forced to hide. Hide my light under the bushel. It will shine brighter for all that hiding. Light polishes itself under the bushel. What an awful thing for Alice to think: polishing up her own private brilliance through the troubles of Johnny-victim-on-the-boat. Oh, Alice. How awful you really are. It is so enormously wrong and wicked and evil and terrible, loving John for the wrong reasons; wanting him dead; profiteering from your marriage. Alice was evil and she truly hated herself.

But listen, kiddo, Alice knew she was married to one of the rottenest sons of bitches to come along in this century. Just the fact that she was able to sit there stroking his fingers and the back of his hand and running her hand through his bittykittymins gave her the evidence of her moral bankruptcy. Yet she was still trying to reform John. She didn't want him to be a Mason on the square. She wanted a genuine four-cornered Catholic. Four corners on my bed. Four angels overhead. Matthew, Mark, Luke, John. Bless the bed we all lie on. She put a rosary around his neck while he lay under the influence of drugs to invoke grace and secret blessings God couldn't possibly deliver publicly to such a person. Hypocrisy for her to do that. Yes, another sin, Alice. But she knew that without being a hypocrite she could never love John.

Knowing this, knowing how evil she was for being married to evil, she therefore knew she must stay married to it, knew she must suffer all the evil that evil brings. For how else could a girl, an Irish Catholic girl brought up to respect grace and transubstantiation, ever get to heaven? How else could a girl hold her head up in her family? How else could a girl ever show her face among her peers, let alone her sneering inferiors, unless she expiated her awfulness, that black terribleness of marrying and loving evil, except by staying married to it?

Suffer the evil to come unto me, said doughty Alice. Perhaps she enjoyed that evil too much. More than she could ever expiate. Perhaps she will merit longer and more excruciating punishment than she can yet imagine. Yes, the very worst may be in store for this little lady.

But she sat there with the villain, stroking, cooing, telling the Good Lord Above: Go ahead and do me, Lord. I can take it.

*   *   *

Sitting beside his hospital bed watching him breathe perhaps the final breaths of his life, she knew he was unquestionably hers now forever. Nothing and nobody could part them. She had withstood the most scandalous time and had not stopped loving him. She was the victim of love: sucker and patsy for her own sloppy heart. But from suckerdom comes wisdom the careful lover never understands.

"I'm sorry what this is doing to you," John said to Alice.

"Are you, John? Or is that just another apology?"

"It's a bad time for you, Al, I know. But this ain't exactly a great big bed of roses I got myself into."

"You'll get out of it."

"We both will. We'll have a special time when I get my ass up out of here."

"Give your ass a rest."

"Anything you say."

"Give everybody's ass a rest."

"Whose ass you talking about now?"

"Maybe you could figure it out if you live long enough."

"I'm in no condition to tire anybody out."

"That's a nice change. I also mean no visitors. I already put up with more than I can stand, but I won't put up with her here."

"She hasn't shown up yet. And if she does, it won't be my doing. But she won't."

"The police won't let her out of custody, that's why she won't."

"She knows better. She knows her place."

"Oh? And just what the hell *is* her place?"

"No place. Nothing. She knows she's got no hold on me."

"That's why you kept her in the hotel."

"I was doing her a favor."

"How often? Twice a night?"

"I saw her now and then, no more. A friend. A date when I was in town looking for company."

"The whole world's got it figured out, John. Don't start with the fairy tales."

She was talking to him as if he had the strength of a healthy man, but he was only an itty-bitty piece of himself, a lump of torn-up flesh. Why did Alice talk so tough to a sick lump? Because she knew the lump was tough. She was tough too. A pair of tough monkeys, is how John always said he saw this husband-wife team. Yes, it's why we get along, was Alice's way of looking at this toughness. She always treated him this way, even when he was most vulnerable, told him exactly what she thought. There now. See? See his hand move off the sheet and onto her knee? See his fingers raise the hem of her skirt? Feel him touch her with his fingertips on the flesh above her stocking? Home territory. Jack is coming home. Jack is not discouraged by her tough line. Tough monkey, my husband.

When Alice felt these fingers on herself she looked at the single wax rose on the bedside table and remembered the early growth of the rose. There will always be a wax rose in our life, Alice now insisted, and in his own way Jack remembered it too. With a tea rose in his lapel when he wore his tux. Never a gardenia. Never a white carnation. Always the red, red rose.

It was after the Fifth Avenue shooting in 1925 and he sat in the living room of their house on 136th Street in the Bronx with the top and back of his head shaved and bandaged, wearing the old blue wool bathrobe with the holes in the elbows, sitting alone on the sofa, looking at the floor and drinking coffee royals because he liked their name and potency; eating saltine crackers with peanut butter but no meals, awake all night for a week but saying almost nothing, just making soft whimpering sounds like a dog dreaming of his enemies. Keeping Alice awake until her ear got used to the rhythms of the whimpers. When the rhythm was right, she could always sleep.

She had tried the rosary, but he wasn't ready for that, and so it only sat on the coffee table alongside the wax roses in the orange and black Japanese vase. She had tried to calm him, too, by reading from the prayer book, but he wouldn't listen. He was as far from religion as he'd ever been. Alice told him he should take the shooting as a warning from God to get out of the rackets or die in the bullet rain.

"I don't want to be like that woman in Brooklyn who lost a husband and two sons in the gang wars," Alice said to him. But that had no effect. Alice didn't know what would have any effect.

"Come on out, boy," she had said one day, a little whisper in his ear. "We all know you're hiding in there."

But all he ever asked was did you call in my numbers: 356, 880, and 855. Jackie, Jack and John out of the dream book. Jack always played numbers, from the time he ran them as a teen-ager. Now he played five dollars on each number and she never knew whether he hit them or not. Her game was not played with numbers.

She would also turn the radio on for him, but when she'd leave the room, he'd turn it off.

"Jesus, they really almost got me, almost wiped me out," he said one night and shook his head as if this were an incredible possibility, some wild fancy that had nothing to do with the real life and potential of John Thomas Diamond. That was when Alice knew he was not going to quit the rackets, that he was committed to them with a fervor which matched her own religious faith.

"They can't keep me down forever" had been his phrase from when she first knew him. She hoped he would find another way up, but this thought still was the central meaning of his whimpers.

The bridge lamp was on the night Alice got out of bed, unable to accept the animal noises John was making. They had become more growls than whimpers or the whisperings of troubled sleep. She saw him on the floor where he'd slid off the couch. He was pointing his pistol at the Japanese vase.

"Are you going to shoot the roses, John?"

He let his hand fall, and after a while she took the pistol. She helped him back onto the sofa and then knelt in front of him in her nightgown, not even a robe over it, and herself visible right through the sheer silk. Her amply visible self.

"I can't sleep no more," he said to her. "I close my eyes and I see my mother screaming every time she breathes."

"It's all right, boy. It's going to be all right."

And then Alice rose half up out of her kneeling position, but without sitting either, stretched herself lengthwise and leaning, a terribly uncomfortable position as she recalls it. But John could see all of her very private self that way, feel her all along his arm and his hip and his good leg that wasn't shot. And without the pistol his hand was free. First she said the Our Father to him just to put the closeness of God into his head again and then she maneuvered herself until her perfect center was against the back of his hand. Then she moved ever so slightly so he could feel where he was, even if he couldn't see it or didn't sense it.

Did this maneuvering work? Alice put an arm around his neck and kissed him lightly on the ear. He turned his hand so the knuckles faced away from her. Then, with a little bit of help, that sheer silk nightgown rose to the demands of the moment. John said she smelled like grass in the morning with dew on it, and she said he smelled like a puppyduppy, and with both their hands where they had every right in the world to be, Mr. and Mrs. John Diamond fell asleep on the sofa in their very own parlor. And they slept through the night.

*   *   *

When they killed Alice, she was sitting at the kitchen table of her Brooklyn apartment looking at old clippings of herself and Jack. One clip, of which she had seven copies, showed her beside his bed of Polyclinic pain. She sat beneath her cloche hat in that old clip, a few tufts of blond hair (not yet dyed Titian to match that of Kiki, The Titian-Haired Beauty of the tabloids; not yet dyed saffron to glamorize her for her Diamond Widow stage career) sticking out from underneath. She was all trim and tailored in the gray tweed suit Jack had helped her choose. "My hero!" was what Alice had written on the clipping.

I imagine her in her final kitchen remembering that bedside scene and all that came later up in Acra when Jack left the Polyclinic bed: Alice nursing her John back to health, massaging his back with rubbing alcohol, taking him for walks in the woods with some of the boys fanning out ahead and behind them, making him toddies and cooking him beef stew and dumplings and tapioca pudding. Now he was more handsome than he'd ever been in his life. Oh, brilliant boy of mine! Hero of the strife! From New Year's Day, 1931, when he left the hospital, on through early April, she possessed him exclusively. Oh, rapturous time! Nothing like it ever before, ever again. What a bitter cup it was for Alice to leave him after that.

She told me she left him the day after Lew Edwards and I paid a curious visit to idyllic Acra. Lew was a Broadway producer, dead now, who grew up next door to me in North Albany, became the impresario of most of Public School 20's undergraduate productions, and went on to produce plays for Jeanne Eagels, Helen Morgan, and Clifton Webb. Lew knew Jack casually, knew also my connection with Jack, and called me with an idea. I told him it was sensational and would probably die at first exposure to Jack. Lew said it was worth the chance and we met at the Hudson train station. I drove down from Albany to pick him up, we had lunch in Catskill, took a short walk to buy the papers, a fateful purchase, and then drove out to Jack's.

The chief change from my summer visit was the set of outside guards at the house, a pair of heavies I'd never seen before who sat in a parked Packard and periodically left the driveway to explore the road down toward Cairo and up toward South Durham for visitors who looked like they might want to blow Jack's head off. When that pair drove off, another pair on duty on the porch took up driveway positions in a second car, and a set from the cottage took up posts on the porch as inside guards.

"Just like Buckingham Palace," Lew said.

Alice gave me a big hello with a smooch I remember. That tempting appleness. Fullness. Pungent wetness I remember thee well. But she meant nothing by such a lovely kiss except hello, my friend. Then she said to me: "Marcus, he's wonderful. He looks better than he has in years. I swear he's even handsomer now than when I married him. And it's better other ways too."

She shook Lew's hand and took my arm and walked me into the living room and whispered: "He's all through with her, Marcus, he really is. He hasn't seen her since the shooting, only once. She came to the hospital one day when I wasn't there, but I heard about it. Now she's all a part of the past. Oh, Marcus, you can't imagine how glorious it's been these past few months. We've been so damned happy you wouldn't believe we were the same people you saw the last time you were here."

She said he was upstairs napping now, and while she went up to rouse him, Cordelia, the maid, mixed us a drink. Jack came down groggy—and in shirtsleeves, baggy pants and slippers—and gave us a few vague minutes. Then we were a group—Jack and Alice on the sofa with Alice's pair of long-legged dolls in crinoline between them, his hand in hers across the dolls, Lew and I in the overstuffed chairs as witnesses to this domestic tranquillity.

"So you've got a deal," Jack said, and Lew immediately went for his cigar case to get a grip on something. Jack had met Lew five years back when Lew butted aggressively into a bar conversation Jack was having, without knowing who Jack was. That's another story, but it turned out Lew gave Jack a pair of theater tickets that introduced him to Helen Morgan, who became one of Jack's abstract passions. He never could understand why Morgan was so good, why she moved him so. It was perverse of him to want to understand the secrets of individual talent, to want secret keys to success. He was still talking about La Morgan the night he died.

"I got a million-dollar idea for you, Jack," Lew said, stuffing a cigar in his mush but not lighting it.

"My favorite kind."

"And you don't have to do a thing for a year."

"It gets better."

"I like it too," said Alice.

"You've got to be one of the most famous, pardon the expression, criminals in the East, am I right?"

"I wouldn't admit to any wrongdoing," Jack said. "I just make my way the best I can."

"Sure, Jack, sure," said Lew. "But plenty of people take you for a criminal. Am I right?"

"I got a bad press, no doubt about that."

"Bad press is a good press for this idea," said Lew. "The more people think you're a bad-ass bastard, the easier we make you a star."

"He's already a star," Alice said. "Too much of a one."

"You mean a Broadway star?" Jack asked. "I carry a tune, but I'm no Morgan."

"Not Broadway. I mean all of America. I can make you the biggest thing since Billy Sunday and Aimee Semple McPherson. An evangelist. A preacher."

"A preacher?" Jack said, and he gave it the big ho-de-ho-ho.

"A preacher how?" Alice said, leaning forward.

Lew said, "If you'll excuse me for saying it, there's about a hundred million people in this country know your name, and they figure you're one mean son of a bitch. Is this more or less true or am I mistaken?"

"Go on," Jack said. "What else?"

"So this mean son of a bitch, this Legs Diamond, this bootlegger, this gang leader, he gives it all up. Quits cold. Goes straight. And a year later he hears the voice of the Holy Spirit. He is touched by a whole damn flock of flaming doves or tongues or whatever the hell they send down to touch guys with, and he becomes an apostle for the Big Fellow. He goes barnstorming, first on a shoestring. A spiritual peanut vendor is all he is. A man with a simple commitment to God and against Satan and his works. He talks to anybody who'll sit still for half an hour. The press picks him up immediately and treats him like a crazy. But also it's a hell of a story for them. Whatsisname, on the road to Damascus. You know the routine. Doesn't care about gin, gangs, guns, gals or gelt anymore. All he wants is to send out the word of God to the people. The people! They'll sell their kids for a ticket. Tickets so scarce you've got to hire a manager, and pretty soon you, he, winds up on the vaude circuits, touches every state, SRO all over. A genuine American freak. Then he gets word from God he shouldn't play theaters with those evil actors. Oughta talk in churches. Of course the churches won't have him. Fiend turned inside out is still a fiend. And a fake. A show biz figure. So he has to play stadiums now, and instead of six hundred he draws maybe twenty thousand and winds up in Yankee Stadium with a turnaway crowd, a full orchestra, four hundred converts around him, the best press agent in town, and the first million-dollar gate that isn't a heavy-weight fight. More? Sure. He builds his own temple and they come from all over the world to hear him speak. Then, at his peak, he moves off to Paris, London, Berlin. And hey. Rome."

Lew fell against his chairback and lit the cigar he'd been using as a pointer, a round little man with a low forehead, thick black hair, and a constant faceful of that stogie. He worked at being a Broadway character, structured comic lines to deliver ad lib at the right moment: "Jack Johnson got the worst deal of any nigger since Othello" is one of his I never forgot.

Lew had bought the New York *Daily Mirror* and read bits of it in the car on the way to Jack's, and now he pulled it out of his right coat pocket in a gesture he said later was caused by discomfort from the bulk, and tossed it onto the coffee table. Jack opened it, almost as a reflex, and skimmed the headlines while all the silence was drumming at us. Jack turned the pages, barely looking at them, then stopped and said to Lew: "How the hell could I preach anything anybody'd believe? I haven't made a speech since high school when I did something from Lincoln. I'm no speaker, Lew."

"I'd make you one," Lew said. "I'd get you drama coaches, speech coaches, singing teachers. Why, for Christ's sake, you'd be a voice to reckon with in six months. I seen this happen on Broadway."

"I think it's a fantastic idea," Alice said. She stood up and paced in front of the couch nervously.

"You know the power you'd have, Jack?" Lew asked. "Hell, we might even get a new American church going. Sell stock in it. I'd buy some myself. A man like you carrying the word to America what the rackets are all about, giving people the lowdown on the secret life of their country. Jesus, I get the shivers thinking how you'd say it. Snarling, by God. Snarling at those suckers for God Almighty. Your stories don't have to be true but they'll sound true anyway. Jesus, it's so rich I can hear the swoons already. I could put together a team of writers'd give you the goddamnedest supply of hoopla America ever heard. Force-feed 'em their own home-grown bullshit. Tell 'em you've gotten inside their souls and know what they need. They need more truth from you, that's what they need. Can't you see those hicks who read everything they can lay hands on about crooks and killers? Organ music with it. 'The Star-Spangled Banner.' 'Holy, Holy, Holy.' You know what Oscar Wilde said, don't you? Americans love heroes, especially crooked ones. Twenty to one you'd get a movie. Maybe they'd even run you for Congress. A star, Jack, I mean a goddamn one hundred percent true-blue American star. How does it grab you?"

Alice exploded before Jack could say anything at all.

"John, it's absolutely perfect. Did you ever believe anybody'd ask you to do anything as marvelous as this? And you can do it. Everything he said was true. You'd be wonderful. I've heard you talk when you're excited about something and I know you can do it. You know you can act, you did it in high school, oh, I know it's right for you."

Jack closed the newspaper and folded it. He crossed his legs, left foot on right knee and tapped the paper on his shoe.

"You'd like to do a little barnstorming, would you?" he said to her.

"I'd love to go with you."

Alice's faith. Love alone. She really believed Jack could do anything. Such an idea also had pragmatic appeal: saving herself from damnation. Show business? So what? As to the stardom, well, the truth is, Alice could no longer get along without it. Yet this promised stardom without taint. Oh, it was sweet! The promise of life renewed for Alice. And her John the agent of renewal.

"What's your reaction, Marcus?" Jack said. And when I chuckled, he frowned.

"I can see it all. I really can see you up there on the altar, giving us all a lesson in brimstone. I think Lew is right. I think it'd work. People would pay just to see you sit there, but if you started saving their souls, well, that's an idea that's worth a million without even counting next month's house." And I laughed again. "What sort of robes would you wear? Holy Roman or Masonic?"

Maybe that did it, because Jack laughed then too. He tapped Alice lightly on the knee with the newspaper and tossed it on the coffee table in front of her. It's curious that I remember every move that newspaper made, not that Alice would've missed its message without us, although I suppose that's possible. The point is that Lew and I, on our mission for American evangelism, were innocent bearers of the hot news.

Jack stood up. "It's a joke," he said.

"No," said Lew, "I'm being straight."

"Make a funny story back in Lindy's if I said yes."

"Jack," said Lew, who was suddenly drained of facial blood by the remark, "this is an honest-to-God idea I had and told nobody but Marcus and now you and your wife. Nobody else."

Jack gave him a short look and figured out from his new complexion that he wasn't practical-joking.

"Okay, Lew. Okay. Let's say it's a nice try then. But not for me. Maybe it'd make a bundle, but it rubs me wrong. I feel like a stool pigeon just thinking about it."

"No names, Jack, nobody's asking for names. Tell stories, that's all. It's what you know about how it all works."

"That's what I mean. You don't tell the suckers how the game is played."

Alice picked up the *Mirror* and slowly and methodically rolled it into a bat. She tapped it against her palm the way a cop plays with a sap. I thought she was going to let Jack have a fast one across the nose. Good-bye barnstorm. Good-bye private Diamond altar. Good-bye salvation, for now.

Her crestfallen scene reveals to me at this remove that she really didn't understand Jack as well as I thought she did. She knew him better than anyone on earth, but she didn't understand how he could possibly be true to his nature. She really thought he was a crook, all the way through to the dirty underwear of his psyche.

"It'd be fun, Lew," Jack said, starting to pace now himself, relaxed that it was over and he could talk about it and add it to his bag of offers. "It'd be a hell of a lot of fun. New kind of take. And I know I got a little ham in me. Yeah, it'd be a good time, but I couldn't take it for long. I couldn't live up to the part."

Alice left the room and carried the newspaper with her. It looked like a nightstick now. I can see her unrolling it and reading it in the kitchen, although I was not in the kitchen. She turns the pages angrily, not seeing the headlines, the photos, the words. She stops at Winchell because everybody stops there and reads him. She is not really reading. Her eyes have stopped at his block of black and white, and she stares down at it, thinking of getting off the train in Omaha and Denver and Boston and Tallahassee and spreading the word of John and God and standing in the wings holding her John's robe, making him tea, no more whiskey, washing his socks, answering his mail, refusing interviews. Damn, damn, damn, thinks Alice, and she sees his name in Winchell.

In the living room, standing on his purple Turkish rug, framing himself against the blue silk he'd stolen from a Jersey boxcar eight years before, Jack was saying he couldn't be a hypocrite.

"That sound funny coming from me, Lew?"

"Not a bit, Jack. I understand." But I could see Lew too, watching a million-dollar idea curl up in the smoke of another Broadway pipe dream.

"Hypocrite? What the hell was he talking about?" Lew asked me later when we were on the way back to the Hudson station. "Does he think I don't know who he is?"

"He had something else in mind, I'm sure," I said. "He knows you know who he is. He knows everybody knows. But he obviously doesn't think what he's doing is hypocritical."

Lew shook his head. "All the nuts ain't on the sundaes."

Lew too. Victim of tunnel vision: A man's a thief, he's dishonest. What we didn't know as we listened to Jack was that he was in the midst of a delicate, supremely honest balancing act that would bring his life together if it worked, let it function as a unified whole and not as warring factions. Maybe Jack thought he was being honest in his retreat from page one, in his acquiescence to Alice's implorings that he become a private man, a country man, a home man, a husband. This behavior generated in Lew's head the idea that if Jack could only stay down long enough, he was fodder for American sainthood.

But Lew's conversion plan was false because Jack's behavior in retreat was false. Jack wasn't a private but a public man, not a country squire but a city slicker, not a home but a hotel room man, not a husband but a cocksmith, not an American saint but an insatiable extortionist. ("Fuck 'em," he said when I told him about Warren Van

Deusen's vigilantes.) And he was not the sum of all these life-styles either, but a fusion beyond them all.

In a small way this was about to be demonstrated. Shirtsleeved, Jack shook our hands, walked us to the front door, apologized for not standing there with us, but said he didn't want to make it too easy for any passing shooters, and thanked us for livening up his afternoon.

The liveliness was just beginning.

*   *   *

The Winchell item in the *Mirror* read: "Stagehands in the Chicago theater where Kiki Roberts is dancing in 'Flying High' under the name of Doris Kane can set their watch by the phone call she gets every night at 7:30. You guessed the caller: Legs Diamond. . . ."

*   *   *

"You son of a bitch, you said you weren't talking to her."

"Don't believe everything you read."

"You're always out of the house at that hour."

"Doesn't mean a thing."

"You promised me, you bastard. You promised me."

"I talked to her once in four months, that's all."

"I don't believe that either."

"Believe Winchell then."

"I thought you were being straight with me."

"You were right. I was. I didn't see her, I didn't see nobody."

"After all the goddamn nursing and handholding."

"I'm fond of the girl. I heard she was having some trouble and I called her. She's all right."

"I don't believe that. You're a liar."

"What's that on your housedress?"

"Where?"

"By the pocket."

"A spot."

"A spot of what?"

"What's the difference what the spot is. It's a spot."

"I paid to have that housedress cleaned and pressed and starched. The least you could do is keep it clean."

"I do keep it clean. Shut up about the housedress."

"I pay for the laundry and you put these things on and dirty them up. Goddamn money going down the goddamn laundry sink."

"I'm leaving."

"What's that in your hair?"

"Where?"

"Behind your right ear. There's something white. Is that gray hair?"

"It might be. God knows I've got a right to some."

"Gray hair. So that's what you've come to. I spend money so you can get your hair bleached half the colors of the goddamn rainbow and you stand there and talk to me with gray hair."

"I'm going upstairs to pack."

"What's that on your leg?"

"Where?"

"Right there on the thigh."

"Don't touch me. I don't want you to touch me."

"What is it?"

"It's a run in my stocking."

"Goddamn money for silk stockings and look what happens to them."

"Get your hand away. I don't want to feel you. Go on, get it away. I don't want your hand there. No. Not there either. No. You won't get it that way anymore. Not after this. No. Don't you dare do that to me with Cordelia in the kitchen and after what I just read. You've lied once too often. I'm packing and nobody on God's earth can do anything to stop me."

"What if I moved her in with us?"

"Oh."

"We could work it out."

"Oh!"

"She's a great girl and she thinks the world of you. Sit down. Let's talk about it."

∗   ∗   ∗

Kiki lay naked on the bed that was all hers and which stood where Alice's had stood before Jack had it taken out and bought the new one. She was thinking of the evening being unfinished, of the fudge that hadn't hardened the last time she touched it, and of Jack lying asleep in his own room, his heavy breathing audible to Kiki, who could not sleep and who resented the uselessness of her nakedness.

They had been together in her bed at early evening, hadn't eaten any supper because they were going to have dinner out later. The fudge was already in the fridge then. Jack was naked too, lying on his back, smoking and staring at the wall with the prints of the Michelangelo sketches, the punishment of Tityus and the head of a giant, prints Jack told her he bought because Arnold Rothstein liked them and said Michelangelo was the best artist who ever brushed a stroke. Jack said Kiki should look at the pictures and learn about art and not be so stupid about it. But the giant had an ugly head and she didn't like the one with the bird in it either, so she looked at Jack instead of dopey pictures. She wanted to touch him, not look at him, but she knew it wouldn't be right because there was no spark in him. He was collapsed and he had tried but wasn't in the mood. He started out in the mood, but the mood left him. He needed a rest, maybe.

He wouldn't look at her. She kept looking at him but he wouldn't look back, so she got up and said, "I'm going downstairs and see if that fudge is hard yet."

"Put something on."

"I'll put my apron on."

"Take a housecoat. There may be somebody on the porch."

"They're all out in the cottage playing pool or in the car watching the road. I know they are."

"I don't want you showing off your ass to the hired help."

She put on one of Alice's aprons, inside out so it wouldn't look too familiar to Jack, and went downstairs. She looked in the mirror and knew anybody could see a little bit of her tail if there was anybody to see it, but there wasn't. She didn't want clothes on. She didn't want to start something and then have to take the clothes off in a hurry and maybe lose the spark, which she would try to reignite when she went back upstairs. She wanted Jack to see as much of her as he could as often as he could, wanted to reach him with all she could reach him with. She had the house now. She had beaten Alice. She had Jack. She did not plan to let go of him.

The fudge was still soft to her touch. She left another fingerprint in it. She had made it for Jack, but it wasn't hardening. It had been in the fridge twenty-eight hours, and it wasn't any harder now than it was after the first hour.

"What do you like—chocolate or penuche?" she had asked him the day before.

"Penuche's the white one with nuts, right?"

"Right."

"That's the one."

"That's the one I like too."

"How come you know so much about fudge?"

"It's the only thing I ever learned how to cook from my mother. I haven't made it in five or six years, but I want to do it for you."

The kitchen had all the new appliances, Frigidaire, Mixmaster, chrome orange juice squeezer, a machine for toasting two slices of bread. But, for all its qualities, Kiki couldn't find the ingredients she remembered from her mother's recipe. So she used two recipes, her own and one out of Alice's *Fanny Farmer Cook Book*, mixed them up together and cooked them and poured it all into a tin pie plate and set it on the top shelf of the fridge. But it didn't harden. She tasted it and it was sweet and delicious, but it was goo after an hour. Now it was still goo.

"It's all goo," she told Jack when she went back upstairs. She stood alongside him and took off her apron. He didn't reach for her.

"Let's go out," he said, and he rolled across the bed, away from her, and stood up. He put on his robe and went into his own room to dress. Even when Alice was there he had had his own room. Even at the hotel he had kept his own room to go to when he and Kiki had finished making love.

"Are you angry because the fudge didn't harden?"

"For crissakes, no. You got other talents."

"Do you wish I could cook?"

"No. I cook good enough for both of us."

And he did, too. Why Jack made the best chicken cacciatore Kiki ever ate, and he cooked a roast of lamb with garlic and spices that was fantastic. Jack could do anything in life. Kiki could only do about three things. She could dance a little and she could love a man and she could be pretty. But she could do those things a thousand times better than most women. She knew about men, knew what men told her. They told her she was very good at love and that she was pretty. They also liked to talk about her parts. They all (and Jack too) told her she was lovely everyplace. So Kiki didn't need to learn about cooking. She wasn't going to tie in with anybody as a kitchen slave and a fat mommy. She wore an apron, but she wore it her way, with nothing underneath it. If Jack wanted a cook, he wouldn't have got rid of Alice. Kiki would just go on being Kiki, somebody strange. She didn't know how she was strange. She knew she wasn't smart enough to understand the reasons behind that sort of thing. I mean I know it already, she said to herself. I don't have to figure it out. I know it and I'm living it.

Kiki thought about these things as she was lying naked in her bed wishing the fudge would harden. Earlier in the night, after Jack had rolled out of her bed, they'd gone out, had eaten steaks at the New York Restaurant in Catskill, one of the best, then had drinks at Sweeney's club, a good-time speakeasy. It was on the way home that everything was so beautiful and quiet. She felt strange then. She and Jack were in the back seat and Fogarty was driving. She was holding Jack's hand, and they were just sitting there, a little glassy-eyed from the booze, yes, but that wasn't the reason it was so beautiful. It was beautiful because they were together as they deserved to be and because they didn't have to say anything to each other.

She remembered looking ahead on the road and looking out the window she'd rolled down and feeling the car was moving without a motor. She couldn't hear noise, couldn't see anything but the lights on the road and the darkened farmhouses and the open fields that were all so brightly lighted by the new moon. The stars were out too, on this silent, this special night. It was positively breathtaking, is how Kiki later described the scene and the mood that preceded the vision of the truck.

That damn truck.

Why did it have to be there ahead of them?

Why couldn't Joe have taken another road and not seen it?

Oh, jeez, wouldn't everything in her whole life have been sweet if they just hadn't seen that truck?

x   x   x

When he saw the old man in the truck, got a good look and saw the side of his face with its bumpkin stupid smile, Jack felt his heart leap up. When Fogarty said, "Streeter from Cairo—he hauls cider, but we never caught him with any," Jack felt the flush in his neck. He had no pistol with him, but he opened the gun rack in the back of the front seat and unclipped one of the .38's. He rolled down the window on his side, renewed.

"Jack, what's going to happen?" Kiki asked.

"Just a little business. Nothing to get excited about."

"Jack, don't get, don't get me, don't get . . ."

"Just shut up and stay in the car."

They were on Jefferson Avenue, heading out of Catskill when the trucker saw Jack's pistol pointing at him. Fogarty cruised at equal speed with the truck until Streeter pulled to the side of the road across from a cemetery. Jack was the first out, his pistol pointed upward. He saw the barrels on the truck and quick-counted more than fifteen. Son of a bitch. He saw the shitkicker's cap, country costume, and he hated the man for wearing it. Country son of a bitch, where Jack had to live.

"Get down out of that truck."

Streeter slid off the seat and stepped down, and Jack saw the second head, another cap on it, sliding across the seat and stepping down, a baby-faced teen-ager with a wide forehead, a widow's peak, and a pointy chin that gave his face the look of a heart.

"How many more you got in there?" Jack said.

"No more. Just me and the boy."

"Who is he?"

"Bartlett, Dickie Bartlett."

"What's he to you?"

"A helper."

Streeter's moon face was full of rotten teeth and a grin.

"So you're Streeter, the wise guy from Cairo," Jack said.

Streeter nodded, very slightly, the grin stayed in place and Jack punched it, cutting the flesh of the cheekbone.

"Put your hands up higher or I'll split your fucking head."

Jack poked Streeter's chest with the pistol barrel. The Bartlett boy's hands shot up higher than Streeter's. Jack saw Fogarty with a pistol in his hand.

"What's in the barrels?"

"Hard cider," said Streeter through his grin.

"Not beer or white?"

"I don't haul beer, or white either. I ain't in the booze business."

"You better be telling the truth, old man. You know who I am?"

"Yes, I know."

"I know you too. You been hauling too many barrels."

"Haulin's what I do."

"Hauling barrels is dangerous business when they might have beer or white in them."

"Nothing but cider in them barrels."

"We'll see. Now move."

"Move where?"

"Into the car, goddamn it," Jack said, and he slapped Streeter on the back of the head with his gun hand. He knocked off the goddamn stinking cap. Streeter bent to pick it up and turned to Jack with his grin. He couldn't really be grinning.

"Where you taking that cider?"

"Up home, and some over to Bartlett's."

"The kid?"

"His old man."

"You got a still yourself?"

"No."

"Bartlett got a still?"

"Not that I know of."

"What's all the cider for then?"

"Drink some, make vinegar, bottle some, sell some of that to stores up in the hollow, sell what's left to neighbors. Or anybody."

"Where's the still?"

"Ain't no still I know of."

"Who do you know's got a still?"

"Never hear of nobody with a still."

"You heard I run the only stills that run in this county? You heard that?"

"Yes siree, I heard that."

"So who runs a still takes that much cider?"

"Ain't that much when you cut it up."

"We'll see how much it is," Jack said. He told Kiki to sit in front and he put Streeter and Bartlett in the back seat. He pulled their caps down over their eyes and sat in front with Kiki while Fogarty drove the truck inside the cemetery entrance. Fogarty was gone ten minutes, which passed in silence, and when he came back, he said, "Looks like it's all hard cider. Twenty-four barrels." And he slipped behind the wheel. Jack rode with his arm over the back seat and his pistol pointed at the roof. No one spoke all the way to Acra, and Streeter and Bartlett barely moved. They sat with their hands in their laps and their caps over their eyes. When they got out of the car inside the garage, Jack made them face the wall and tied their hands behind them. Fogarty backed the car out, closed the door, and took Kiki inside the house. Jack sat Streeter and Bartlett on the floor against a ladder.

Shovels hung over the old man's head like a set of assorted guillotines. Jack remembered shovels on the wall of the cellar in The Village where the Neary mob took him so long ago when they thought he'd hijacked a load of their beer—and he had. They tied him to a chair with wire around his arms and legs, then worked him over. They got weary and left him, bloody and half conscious, to go to sleep. He was fully awake and moved his arms back and forth against the wire's twist until he ripped his shirt. He sawed steadily with the wire until it ripped the top off his right bicep and let him slip his arm out of the bond. He climbed up a coal chute and out a window, leaving pieces of the bicep on the twist of wire, and on the floor: skin, flesh, plenty of blood. Bled all the way home. Bicep flat now. Long, rough scar there now. Some Nearys paid for that scar.

He looked at the old man and saw the ropes hanging on the wall behind him, can of kerosene in the corner, paintbrushes soaking in turpentine. Rakes, pickax. Old man another object. Another tool. Jack hated all tools that refused to yield their secrets. Jack was humiliated before the inanimate world. He hated it, kicked it when it affronted him. He shot a car once that betrayed him by refusing to start. Blew holes in its radiator.

The point where the hanging rope bellied out on the garage wall looked to Jack like the fixed smile on Streeter's face. Streeter was crazy to keep smiling. He wasn't worth a goddamn to anybody if he was crazy. You can kill crazies. No loss. Jack made ready to kill yet another man. Wilson, the first one he killed. Wilson, the card cheat. Fuck you, cheater, you're dead. I'm sorry for your kids.

In the years after he dumped Wilson in the river Jack used Rothstein's insurance connections to insure family men he was going to remove from life. He made an arrangement with a thieving insurance salesman, sent him around to the family well in advance of the removal date. When the deal was sealed, give Jack a few weeks, then bingo!

"You got any insurance, old man?"

"No."

"You got any family?"

"Wife."

"Too bad. She's going to have to bury you best she can. Unless you tell me where that still is you got hid."

"Ain't got no still hid nowheres, mister. I told you that."

"Better think again, old man. You know where the still is, kid?" Dickie Bartlett shook his head and turned to the wall. Only a kid. But if Jack killed one, he would have to kill two. Tough break, kid.

"Take off your shoes."

Streeter slowly untied the rawhide laces of his high shoe-boots without altering his grin. He pulled off one shoe and Jack smelled his foot, his sweaty white wool sock, his long underwear tucked inside the sock. Country leg, country foot, country stink. Jack looked back at the grin, which seemed as fixed as the shape of the nose that hovered above it. But you don't fix a grin permanently. Jack knew. That old son of a bitch is defying me, is what he thought. He hasn't got a chance and yet he's defying Jack Diamond's law, Jack Diamond's threat, Jack Diamond himself. That grinning façade is a fake and Jack will remove it. Jack knows all there is to know about fake façades. He remembered his own grin in one of the newspapers as he went into court in Philadelphia. Tough monkey, smilin' through. They won't get to me. And then in the courtroom he knew how empty that smile was, how profoundly he had failed to create the image he wanted to present to the people of Philadelphia, not only on his return but all his life, all through boyhood, to live down the desertion charge in the Army, and, worse, the charge that he stole from his buddies. Not true. So many of the things they said about Jack were untrue and yet they stuck.

He was a nobody in the Philadelphia court. Humiliated. Arrested coming in, then kicked out. And stay out, you bum. I speak for the decent people of this city in saying that Philadelphia doesn't want you any more than Europe did. Vomit. Puke, puke. Vomit. Country feet smelled like vomit. Jack's family witnessing it all in the courtroom. Jack always loved them in his way. Jack dumped about eight cigarettes out of his Rameses pack and pocketed them. He twisted the pack and lit it with a loose match, showed the burning cellophane and paper to Streeter, who never lost his grin. Jack said, "Where's the still?"

"Jee-zus, mister, I ain't seen no still. I ain't and that's a positive fact, I tell you."

Jack touched the fire to the sock and then to the edge of the underwear. Streeter shook it and the fire went out. Jack burned his own hand, dropped the flaming paper and let it burn out. Fogarty came back in then, pistol in hand.

"Kneel on him," Jack said, and with pistol pointed at Streeter's head, Fogarty knelt on the old man's calf. The pistol wasn't loaded, Fogarty said later. He was taking no chances shooting anybody accidentally. It had been loaded when they stopped Streeter's truck because he felt when he traveled the roads with Jack he was bodyguard as well as chauffeur, and he would stand no chance of coping with a set of killers on wheels if his gun was empty. But now he wasn't a bodyguard anymore.

"He's a tough old buzzard," Jack said.

"Why don't you tell him what he wants to know?" Fogarty said conspiratorially to Streeter.

"Can't tell what I don't know," Streeter said. The grin was there. The flame had not changed it. Jack knew now he would remove that grin with flame. Finding the still was receding in importance, but such a grin of defiance is worth punishing. Asks for punishing. Will always get what it asks for. The Alabama sergeant who tormented Jack and other New York types in the platoon because of their defiance. "New Yoahk mothahfucks." Restriction. Punishment. KP over and over. Passes denied. And then Jack swung and got the son bitch in the leg with an iron bar. Had to go AWOL after that, couldn't even go back. That was when they got him, in New Yoahk. Did defiance win the day for Jack? It was satisfying, but Jack admits it did not win the day. Should have shot the son bitch in some ditch off-post. Let the rats eat him.

"Where's that still, you old son bitch?"

"Hey, mister, I'd tell you if I knew. You think I'd keep anythin' back if I knew? I dunno, mister, I just plain dunno."

Jack lit the sock, got it flaming this time, and the old man yelled, shook his whole leg again and rocked Fogarty off it. The flame went out again. Jack looked, saw the grin. The old man is totally insane. Should be bugged. Crazy as they make 'em. Crazy part of a man that takes any kind of punishment, suffers all humiliations. No pride.

"You old son bitch, ain't you got no pride? Tell me the goddamn answer to my question. Ain't you got no sense? I'm gonna hang your ass off a tree you don't tell me what I want to know."

But you can't really punish a crazy like that, Jack. He loves it. That's why he's sitting there grinning. Some black streak across his brain makes him crazier than a dog with his head where his ass oughta be.

He's making *you* crazy now, Jack. Got you talking about hanging. You can't be serious, can you?

"All right, old man, get up. Speed, get that rope."

"What you got in mind, Jack?"

"I'm gonna hang his Cairo country ass from that maple tree outside."

"Hey," said Streeter, "you ain't really gonna hang me?"

"I'm gonna hang you like a side of beef," Jack said. "I'm gonna pop your eyes like busted eggs. I'm gonna make your tongue stretch so far out you'll be lickin' your toes."

"I ain't done nothin' to nobody, mister. Why you gonna hang me?"

"Because you're lyin' to me, old man."

"No, sir, I ain't lyin'. I ain't lyin'."

"How old are you right now?"

"Fifty."

"You ain't as old as I thought, but you ain't gonna be fifty-one. You're a stubborn buzzard, but you ain't gonna be fifty-one. Bring him out."

Fogarty led the old man outside with only one shoe, and Jack threw the rope over the limb of the maple. He tied a knot, looped the rope through the opening in the knot—a loop that would work like an animal's choker chain—and slipped it over Streeter's neck. Jack pulled open a button, one down from the collar, to give the rope plenty of room.

"Jack," Fogarty said, shaking his head. Jack tugged the rope until he took up all the slack and the rope rose straight up from Streeter's neck.

"One more chance," Jack said. "Where is that goddamn still you were headed for?"

"Jee-zus Keh-ryst, mister, there just ain't no still, you think I'm kiddin' you? You got a rope around my neck. You think I wouldn't tell you anything I knew if I knew it? Jee-zus, mister, I don't want to die."

"Listen, Jack. I don't think we ought to do this." Fogarty was trembling. The poor goddamn trucker. Like watching a movie and knowing how it ends, Fogarty said later.

"Shitkicker!" Jack yelled. "Where is it? SHITKICKER! SHITKICKER!"

Before the old man could answer, Jack tugged at the rope and up went Streeter. But he had worked one hand loose and he made a leap as Jack tugged. He grabbed the rope over his head and held it.

"Retie the son of a bitch," Jack said, and Fogarty knew then he was party to a murder. Full accomplice now and the tied-up Bartlett

kid a witness. There would be a second murder on this night. Fogarty,
how far you've come under Jack's leadership. He tied the old man's
hands, and Jack then wound the rope around both his own arms and
his waist so it wouldn't slip, and he jerked it again and moved backward. The old man's eyes bugged as he rose off the ground. His tongue
came out and he went limp. The Bartlett kid yelled and then started to
cry, and Jack let go of the rope. The old man crumpled.

"He's all right," Jack said. "The old son of a bitch is too miserable
to die. Hit him with some water."

Fogarty half-filled a pail from an outside faucet and threw it on
Streeter. The old man opened his eyes.

"You know, just maybe he's telling the truth," Fogarty said.

"He's lying."

"He's doing one hell of a good job."

Jack took Fogarty's pistol and waved it under Streeter's nose. *At
least he can't kill him with that,* Fogarty thought.

"It's too much work to hang you," Jack said to Streeter, "so I'm
gonna blow your head all over the lawn. I'll give you one more chance."

The old man shook his head and closed his eyes. His grin was gone.
I finally got rid of that, is what Jack thought. But then he was suddenly
enraged again at the old man. You made me do this to you, was the
nature of Jack's accusation. You turned me into a goddamn sadist because of your goddamn stinking country stubbornness. He laid the
barrel of the pistol against the old man's head and then he thought:
Fogarty. And he checked the cylinder. No bullets. He gave Fogarty a
look of contempt and handed him back the empty pistol. He took his
own .38 from his coat pocket, and Streeter, watching everything, started
to tremble, his lip turned down now. Smile not only gone, but that face
unable even to remember that it had smiled even once in all its fifty
years. Jack fired one shot. It exploded alongside Streeter's right ear. The
old man's head jerked and Jack fired again, alongside the other ear.

"You got something to tell me now, shitkicker?" Jack said.

The old man opened his eyes, saucers of terror. He shook his head.
Jack put the pistol between his eyes, held it there for seconds of silence.
Then he let it fall away with a weariness. He stayed on his haunches in
front of Streeter, just staring. Just staring and saying nothing.

"You win, old man," he finally said. "You're a tough monkey."

Jack stood up slowly and pocketed his pistol. Fogarty and one of
the porch guards drove Streeter and Bartlett back to their truck. Fogarty
ripped out their ignition wires and told them not to call the police. He
drove back to Acra and slept the sleep of a confused man.

*   *   *

When Speed had brought her from the car into the house, Kiki had said to him, "What's going to happen with those men?"

"I don't know. Probably just some talk."

"Oh, God, Joe, don't let him hurt them. I don't want to be mixed up in that kind of shit again, please, Joe."

"I'll do what I can do, but you know Jack's got a mind of his own."

"I'll go and see him. Or maybe you could tell him to come in. Maybe if I asked him not to do anything, for me, don't do it for me, he wouldn't do it."

"I'll tell him you said it."

"You're a nice guy, Joe."

"You go to bed and stay upstairs. Do what I tell you."

"Yes, Joe."

Kiki was thinking that Joe really and truly was a nice guy and that maybe she could make it with him if only she wasn't tied up with Jack. Of course, she wouldn't do anything while she was thick with Jack. But it was nice to think about Joe and his red hair and think about how nice he would be to play with. He was nicer than Jack, but then she didn't love Jack because he was nice.

She worried whether Jack had killed the two men when she later heard the two shots and the screaming. But she had thought the worst at the Monticello, thought Jack had killed *those* men when they had really tried to kill him. She didn't want to think bad things about Jack again. But she lived half an hour with uncertainty. Then Jack came into her room and said the men were gone and nobody got hurt.

"Did you get the information you wanted?" she asked.

"Yeah, I don't want to talk about it."

"Oh, good. Are you done now?"

"All done."

"Then we can finish the evening the way we intended."

"It's finished."

"I mean really finished."

"And I mean really finished."

He kissed her on the cheek and went to his bedroom. He didn't come back to see her or ask her to come to him. She tried to sleep, but she kept wanting to finish the evening, continue from where she and Jack had left off in the car in the silence and the chilliness and the brightness of the new moon on the open fields. She wanted to lie alongside Jack and comfort him because she knew from the way he was behaving that he had the blues. If she went in and loved him, he would feel better. Yet she felt he didn't really want that, and she rolled over and tossed and turned, curled and uncurled for another hour before she decided: Maybe he really does want it. So then, yes, she ought to do it.

She got up and very quietly tiptoed into Jack's room and stood naked alongside his bed. Jack was deeply asleep. She touched his ear and ran her fingers down his cheek, and all of a sudden she was looking down the barrel of his .38 and he was bending her fingers back so far she was screaming. Nobody came to help her. She thought of that later. Jack could have killed her and nobody would have tried to stop him. Not even Joe.

"You crazy bitch! What were you trying to do?"

"I just wanted to love you."

"Never, never wake me up that way. Don't ever touch me. Call me and I'll hear it, but don't touch me."

Kiki was weeping because her hand hurt so much. She couldn't bend her fingers. When she tried to bend them, she fainted. When she came to, she was in a chair and Jack was all white in the face, looking at her. He was slapping her cheek lightly just as she came out of it.

"It hurts an awful lot."

"We'll go get a doctor. I'm sorry, Marion, I'm really sorry I hurt you."

"I know you are, Jack."

"I don't want to hurt you."

"I know you don't."

"I love you so much I'm half nuts sometimes."

"Oh, Jackie, you're not nuts, you're wonderful and I don't care if you hurt me. It was an accident. It was all my fault."

"We'll go get the doc out of bed."

"He'll fix me up fine, and then we can come back and finish the evening."

"Yeah, that's a swell idea."

The coroner was Jack's doctor, and they got him out of bed. He bandaged her hand and said she'd have to have a cast made at the hospital next day, and he gave her pills for her pain. She told him she'd been rehearsing her dance steps and had fallen down. He didn't seem to believe that, but Jack didn't care what he believed, so she didn't either. After the doctor's they went back home. Jack said he was too tired to make love and that they'd do it in the morning. Kiki tossed and turned for a while and then went down to the kitchen and checked the fudge again, felt it with the fingers of her good hand. It was still goo, so she put it out on the back porch for the cat.

x   x   x

Clem Streeter told his story around Catskill for years. He was a celebrity because of it, stopped often by people and asked for another rendition. I was being shaved in a Catskill barber chair the year beer came back,

and Jack was, of course, long gone. But Clem was telling the story yet
again for half a dozen locals.

"The jedge in Catskill axed me what I wanted the pistol *per*mit
for," he said, "and I told him 'bout how that Legs Diamond feller
burned my feet and hung me from a sugar maple th'other night up at
his garage. 'That so?' axed the jedge. 'I jes told you it were,' I said.
People standin' 'round the courthouse heard what we was sayin' and
they come over to listen better. 'You made a complaint yet against this
Diamond person?' the jedge axes me. But I tell him, only complaint I
made so far was to the wife. That jedge he don't know what to do with
hisself he's so took out by what I'm sayin'. I didn't mean to upset the
jedge. But he says, 'I guess we better get the sheriff on this one and
maybe the DA,' and they both of 'em come in after a little bit and I tell
'em my story, how they poked guns outen the winders of their car and
we stopped the truck, me and Dickie Bartlett. They made us git down,
but I didn't git fast enough for Diamond, so he hit me with his fist and
said, 'Put up your hands or I'll split your effin' head.' Then they hauled
us up to Diamond's place with our caps pulled down so we wouldn't
know where we was goin', but I see the road anyway out under the side
of the cap and I know that place of his with the lights real well. Am I
sure it was Diamond, the jedge axes. 'Acourse I'm sure. I seen him plenty
over at the garage in Cairo. He had a woman in the car with him, and
I recognized the other feller who did the drivin' 'cause he stopped my
truck another night I was haulin' empty barrels 'bout a month back.'
'So this here's Streeter, the wise guy from Cairo,' Diamond says to me
and he cuffs me on the jaw with his fist, just like that, afore I said a
word. Then up in the garage they tried to burn me up. 'What'd they do
that for?' the jedge axes me, and I says, "Cause he wants to know where
there's a still I'm s'posed to know about. But I told Diamond I don't
know nothin' 'bout no still.' And the jedge says, 'Why'd he think you
did?' And I says, "Cause I'm haulin' twenty-four barrels of hard cider
I'd picked up down at Post's Cider Mill.' 'Who for?' says the jedge. 'For
me,' I says. 'I like cider. Drink a bunch of it.' 'Cause I ain't about to
tell no jedge or nobody else 'bout the still me and old Cy Bartlett got
between us. We do right nice business with that old still. Make up to a
hundred, hundred and thirty dollars apiece some weeks off the fellers
who ain't got no stills and need a little 'jack to keep the blood pumpin'.
That Diamond feller, he surely did want to get our still away from us.
I knew that right off. Did me a lot of damage, I'll say. But sheeeeee.
Them fellers with guns is all talk. Hell, they don't never kill nobody.
They just like to throw a scare into folks so's they can get their own
way. Son of a bee if I was gonna give up a hundred and thirty dollars
a week for some New York feller.'"

Jack Among the Maids

THE STREETER INCIDENT TOOK PLACE IN MID-APRIL, 1931. Eight days later, the following document was released in the Capitol at Albany:

Pursuant to section 62 of the Executive Law, I hereby require that you, the Attorney General of this state, attend in person or by your assistants or deputies, a regular special and trial term of the Supreme Court appointed to be held in and for the County of Greene for the month of April, 1931, and as such term as may hereafter be continued, and that you in person or by said assistants or deputies appear before the grand jury or grand juries which shall be drawn and sit for any later term or terms of said court for the purpose of managing and conducting in said court and before said grand jury and said other grand juries, any and all proceedings, examinations and inquiries, and any and all criminal actions and proceedings which may be taken by or before said grand jury concerning any and all kinds and—or—criminal offences, alleged to have been committed by John Diamond, also known as Jack (Legs) Diamond and—or—any person or persons acting in concert with him, and further to manage, prosecute and conduct the trial of any indictments found by said grand jury or grand juries at said term or terms of said court or of any other court at which any and all such indictments may hereafter be tried, and that in person or by your assistants or deputies you supersede the district attorney of the County of Greene in all matters herein specified and you exercise all the powers and perform all the

duties conferred upon you by Section 62 of the Executive Law
and this requirement thereunder; and that in such proceedings
and actions the District Attorney of Greene County shall only
exercise such powers and perform such duties as are required
of him by you or by the assistants or deputies attorney general
so attending.

> Franklin Delano Roosevelt
> Governor of the State of New York

Jack thus became the first gangster of the Prohibition Era to have
the official weight of an entire state, plus the gobble of its officialese,
directed at him. I find this notable.

I did what little I could to throw a counterweight when the time
came. I cited the whole affair as a cynical political response to the harsh
spotlight that Judge Seabury, his reformers, and the Republican jackals
were, at the moment, shining on the gangsterism and corruption so
prevalent in New York City's Tammany Hall, with Democratic Gentleman Jimmy Walker the chief illuminated goat. FDR, I argued when I
pleaded Jack's case in the press, was making my client the goat in a
Republican stronghold. I voiced particular outrage at superseding the
Greene County District Attorney.

But my counterweight didn't weigh much. Jack went to jail and I
understood the spadework done in Albany by Van Deusen's vigilantes.
FDR even sent his personal bodyguard to Catskill as an observer when
the swarm of state police and state attorneys moved toward Jack's
jugular.

*   *   *

Knute Rockne told his men: "Don't be a bad loser, but don't lose."

*   *   *

Fogarty got me out of bed to tell me Jack had been arrested and that
he himself was going into hiding. Jack and Kiki were in the parlor at
Acra, and Fogarty was playing pool in the cottage when the trooper
rang the bell under the second step. Three times. Jack's straight neighbors thought three was the insider's ring, but it was the ring only for
straights.

Jack tried to talk the trooper into letting him surrender in the morning by himself, avoid the ignominy of it, but the trooper said nix, and
so Jack wound up on a hard cot in a white-washed third-floor cell of
the county jail. Tidy and warm, not quite durance vile, as one journalist

wrote, but vile enough for the King Cobra of the Catskills, as he was now known in the press.

I worked on the bail, which was a formidable twenty-five thousand dollars: ten each for assaulting Streeter and Bartlett, five for the kidnapping. Uh-oh, I said, when I heard the news, heard especially how young Bartlett was. What we now are dealing with, I told Fogarty, and Jack too, is not a bootleggers' feud, which is what it was in a left-handed way, but the abduction of children in the dead of night. Not a necessary social misdemeanor, as most bootlegging was contemporaneously regarded, but a high crime in any age.

I called Warren Van Deusen to see if I could pry Jack loose by greasing local pols, but found him haughtily supporting the state's heavy anti-Jack thrust. "Kidnapping kids now, is he? I hear he's holding up bread truck drivers too. What's next? Disemboweling old ladies?" I wrote off Warren as unreliable, a man given to facile outrage, who didn't understand the process he was enmeshed in.

It has long been my contention that Jack was not only a political pawn through Streeter, but a pawn of the entire decade. Politicans used him, and others like him, to carry off any vileness that served their ends, beginning with the manipulation of strikebreakers as the decade began and ending with the manipulation of stockbrokers at the end of the crash, a lovely, full, capitalistic circle. Thereafter the pols rejected Jack as unworthy, and tried to destroy him.

But it was Jack and a handful of others—Madden, Schultz, Capone, Luciano—who reversed the process, who became manipulators of the pols, who left a legacy of money and guns that would dominate the American city on through the 1970's. Jack was too interested in private goals to see the potential that 1931 offered to the bright student of urban life. Yet he was unquestionably an ancestral paradigm for modern urban political gangsters, upon whom his pioneering and his example were obviously not lost.

I hesitate to develop all the analogies I see in this, for I don't want to trivialize Jack's achievement by linking him to lesser latter-day figures such as Richard Nixon, who left significant history in his wake, but no legend; whose corruption, overwhelmingly venal and invariably hypocritical, lacked the admirably white core fantasy that can give evil a mythical dimension. Only boobs and shitheads rooted for Nixon in his troubled time, but heroes and poets followed Jack's tribulations with curiosity, ambivalent benevolence, and a sense of mystery at the meaning of their own response.

*   *   *

Fogarty, sitting at a bar and waiting for a female form to brighten his life, and meanwhile telling a story about a gang-bang, felt alive for the first time in a week, for the first time since they hauled Jack in and he took off up the mountain. A week in a cabin alone, only one day out for groceries and the paper, is enough to grow hair on a wart, shrivel a gonad.

Fogarty found solitude unbearably full of evaporated milk and tuna fish, beans and cheese, stale bread and bad coffee, memories of forced bed-rest, stultifying boredom with one's own thought. And then to run out of candles.

The old shack on stilts was down the mountain from Haines Falls, half a mile in an old dirt road, then a quarter of a mile walk with the groceries. He walked down from the cabin to his old car every morning and every night to make sure it was still there and to start it. Then he walked alone in the woods looking at the same trees, same squirrels, same chipmunks and rabbits, same goddamn birds with all that useless song, and came back and slept and ate and thought about women, and read the only book in the cabin, *The World Almanac*. He related to the ads—no end to life's jokes:

Last Year's Pay Looks Like Small Change to These Men Today; Raised Their Pay 500% When They Discovered Salesmanship . . . Have YOU Progressed During the Past Three Years? . . . Ask Your Dealer for Crescent Guns, 12-16-20-410 Gauge . . . A Challenge Made Me Popular! . . . This Man Wouldn't Stay Down . . . It Pays to Read Law . . . Success—Will You Pay the Price? . . . Finest of All Cast Bronze Sarcophagi.

Fogarty closed the book, took a walk in the dark. A wild bird call scared him, and he retreated to the cabin to find only half a candle left, not enough to get him through the night. It's time, he said. It was ten o'clock. The Top o' the Mountain House would have some action and he needed a drink, needed people, needed a look at a woman, needed news. His old relic of a Studebaker started all right. Would he ever again see his new Olds, sitting back in the shed behind his house in Catskill? No chance to take it when he left Jack's in such a hurry.

There were four men at the bar, two couples at one table in the back room. He checked them all, knew nobody, but they looked safe. The bartender, a kid named Reilly he'd talked to, but never pressured, was okay. Fogarty ordered applejack on ice. He made it, sold it, liked it. Jack hated it. He had three and was already half an hour into a

conversation with Reilly, feeling good again, telling about the night he
and eight guys were lined up in a yard on 101st Street for a girl named
Maisie who was spread out under a bush, taking on the line.

"I was about fourth and didn't even know who she was. We just
heard it was on and got in line. Then when I saw her, I said to myself,
'Holy beazastards,' because I knew Maisie, and her brother Rick is my
pal and he's in line right behind me. So I said to him, 'I just got a look,
she's a dog, let's beat it,' and I grabbed his arm and pulled, but he was
ready, you know, and I couldn't talk him out of it. He had to see her
for himself. And when he saw her, he pulled off the guy on her and
whipped him, and then beat hell out of Maisie. Next day everybody
had trouble looking Rick in the eye. Guys he knew were there all said
they were behind him in the line and didn't know who she was either.
Maisie was back a couple of nights later, and we all got her without
Rick breaking it up."

Fogarty paused nostalgically. "I got in line twice."

The barman liked the story, bought Fogarty a drink, and said, "You
know, was a guy in here last night askin' about your friend Diamond.
Guy with a bandage on his eye."

"A bandage? You don't mean an eyepatch?"

"No, a bandage. Adhesive and gauze stuff."

"What'd he want?"

"Dunno. Asks has Jack Diamond been in much and when was the
last time."

"You know him?"

"Never seen him before."

"You remember a guy named Murray? Called him The Goose."

"No."

"Nuts."

"You know this guy with the eye?"

"I don't know. Could be he's a friend of ours. Your phone
working?"

"End of the bar."

Fogarty felt the blood rise in his chest, felt needed. Reilly had told
him Jack was out on bail, so it was important for him to know Murray
was around, if he was. All week in the woods Fogarty had cursed Jack,
vowed to quit him, leave the country; that if this thing straightened out,
he'd find a new connection; that he couldn't go on working with a man
who wasn't playing with a full deck. Northrup first, then Streeter.
Crazy. But now that feeling was gone, and he wanted to talk to Jack,
warn him, protect his life.

"Don't touch that phone."

Fogarty turned to see old man Brady, the owner, standing alongside him with his hand on a pistol in his belt.

"Get out of here," Brady said.

"I just want to make a call."

"Make it someplace else. You or none of your bunch are welcome here. We're all through kissing your ass."

Brady's beer belly and soiled shirt pushed against the pistol. The spiderweb veins in Brady's cheeks Fogarty would remember when he was dying, for they would look like the crystalline glaze that covered his own eyes in his last days. Brady with the whiskey webs. Old lush. Throwing me out.

"If it wasn't for your father," Brady said, "I'd shoot you now. He was a decent man. I don't know how in the hell he ever got you."

Fogarty would remember that drops of sweat had run off Brady's spiderwebs one day long ago, the day Fogarty stood in front of him at the bar and told him how much of Jack's beer he would handle a week. Told him. Two of Jack's transient gunmen stood behind him to reinforce the message.

"You're lucky I don't call the troopers and turn you in," old Brady said to him now, "but I wouldn't do that to a son of your father's. Remember the favor that decent man did for you from his grave, you dirty whelp. You dirty, dirty whelp. Go on, get out of here."

He moved his fingers around the butt of his pistol, and Fogarty went out into the night to find Jack.

*   *   *

Fogarty stopped the car and loaded his pistol, Eddie Diamond's .32. If he saw Murray, he would shoot first, other things being equal. He wouldn't shoot him in public. Fogarty marveled at his own aggression, but then he knew The Goose, knew Jack's story of how The Goose stalked a man once who went to the same movie house every week. The Goose sat in the lobby until the man arrived, then shoved a gun in his face, and blew half the head off the wrong man. A week later he was in the same lobby when the right man arrived, and he blew off half the correct head. Jack liked to tell Goose stories, how Goose once said of himself: "I'm mean as a mad hairy." What would The Goose have done to Streeter? Old man'd be stretched now, and the kid too. Was Fogarty the difference between life and death on that night?

He wanted to buy a paper, find out what was happening. He hadn't asked many questions at the bar, didn't want to seem ignorant. But he knew from a conversation with Marcus after Jack's arrest, plus something Reilly said, that the state was sitting heavily on Jack. Old man

Brady's behavior meant everybody'd be tough now. Jack is down and so is Fogarty, so put on your kicking shoes, folks.

Was it all over? No more money ("The boss needs a loan") coming in from the hotels and boardinghouses? No more still? Yes, there would be beer runs. There would always be beer runs. And there were the stashes of booze, if nobody found them. Reilly said four of Jack's men, all picked up at the cottage, were booked on vagrancy, no visible income. But they couldn't say that about Fogarty with his three bank accounts, fifteen thousand dollars deposited in one during the past six months. But he couldn't go near them until he knew his status.

Yet he knew what that had to be. Fugitive. They'd try to hang him by the balls. Jack's closest associate. Jack's pal. Jack's bodyguard. A laugh. But he did carry a loaded gun, finally, just for Jack. Why did Joe Fogarty feel the need to protect Jack Diamond? Because there was a bond. Friendship. Brothers, in a way. Jack talked about Eddie, gave him Eddie's pistol, and they swapped TB stories. Eddie was a bleeder. Always had the streak in his sputum the last year of his life, almost never out of bed or a wheelchair except when he came to New York to help Jack during the Hotsy. No wonder Jack loved him. Jack cried when he talked about Eddie: "He used to bleed so bad they put ice on his chest, made him suck ice too, and the poor guy couldn't move."

Fogarty knew. He'd seen all that, spent five and a half years in sanitariums, twenty-eight months in bed for twenty-four hours a day. Got up only when they made the bed, a bed bath twice a week. Galloping TB is what Fogarty had, and if they hadn't used the pneumo he'd have been dead long ago. Blew air into his lungs, collapsed it, pushed up the poison. Hole in the bronchus, and when the air went in, the pus came up and out his mouth. A basinful of greenish-yellow pus. But after five months that didn't work anymore and the pus stayed in, and he had to lie still for those years.

Death?

Joe Fogarty wasn't afraid of death anymore, only bleeding. He died every day for years. What he was afraid of was lying still and not dying.

"Remember your fibrosis," the nurses would say. "Don't raise your arms above your head. Don't even move when you do pee-pee."

The woodpeckers would come around and tap his chest with stethoscopes and fingers, listen to his percussion. "Cough and say ninety-nine." It must heal, you know. Give yourself a chance to heal. Terrific advice. Bring your tissue together. Heal. Oh, nice. Fight off the poison. Of course. Then show a streak in the sputum and they don't let you brush your teeth by yourself anymore. A long time ago, all that;

and Fogarty finally got well. And met Jack. And did he then make up for those months in bed doing nothing? Ahhhhhh.

*   *   *

"So you think The Goose is back?" Jack said.

"Who else?"

"Maybe you're right. But maybe it was just a one-eyed tourist. Tourists always asking about me."

"You want to take that chance?"

"Not with The Goose. He'll find a way if he's up here. I should stay away from the window."

"You been going out?"

"No, just sticking close here. But we'll go out now."

"Take me with you," Kiki said. She was alone on the couch, knees visible, no stockings, slippers on. But sweeeet lover, did she look good to the Speeder.

"No," said Jack. "You stay home."

"I don't want to be here alone."

"I'll call the neighbor."

"That old cow, I don't want her here."

"She'll be company. We won't be long."

"Where you going?"

"Down the road, make some calls, then we'll be back."

"You'll be out all night."

"Marion, you're a pain in the ass."

"I'm going back to Chicago."

"That show closed."

"You think that show is the only offer I got out there?"

"You can't come with us. I'll bring home spaghetti."

"I want to do something."

"We'll do something when I get back. We'll eat spaghetti."

"I want to hear some music."

"Turn on the radio. Put on a record."

"Oh, shit, Jack. Shit, shit, shit."

"That's better. Have a sherry."

Fogarty finished his double rye and Jack swigged the last of his coffee royal, and they went out the back door. Jack stopped, said, "We'll take your car. Nobody'd look for me in that jalop."

"Nobody looking for me at all?"

"Not yet, but that don't mean they won't be out with a posse to-morrow. They'll get to you, all right, but tonight you're a free citizen. Take it from me, and Marcus. He's down at the Saulpaugh while this stuff is going on. We talked before you got here. Joe, I'm glad you came down."

Jack clapped him on the shoulder. The old jalop was wheezing along. Fogarty smiled, remembered his plan to break with Jack. What a crazy idea.

Jack had taken a rifle from the hall closet, loaded it with dumdums, and thrown it on the back seat. He wouldn't carry a pistol with all the heat on. He'd also put on his gray topcoat, fedora, and maroon tie with a black pearl tie tack. Fogarty, you bum, you wore a linty black sweater and those baggy slacks you slept in all week.

"It's like a dog race," Jack said.

"What is?" Fogarty asked, thinking immediately of himself as a dog.

"This thing. I'm the rabbit. And who'll get it first?"

"Nobody gets those rabbits. The dogs always come up empty."

"The feds are coming into it. The state, all the goddamn cops in the East, Biondo and his guinea friends, Charlie Lucky's pals, and now maybe Murray out there, driving around, trying to make a plan. The good thing about Murray is he can never figure out how to get near anybody. Once he gets near you, so long. But unless you figured it out for him, he could think all month without getting the idea to maybe ring the doorbell."

"Maybe you ought to get away from here."

"They're all keeping track of me. Let's see what news we come up with. Hey, you're heating up."

The temperature gauge was near two twenty when they pulled into the parking lot at Jimmy Wynne's Aratoga Inn on the Acra-Catskill Road. Fogarty unscrewed the radiator cap and let it breathe and blow, and then they went inside, Fogarty with his two pistols Jack didn't even know he had. Fogarty was ready for Murray, who was absent from the gathering of twelve at the bar. It was quiet, the musicians on a break. Fogarty asked Dick Fegan, the bartender, bald at twenty-five, if he'd seen Murray. Fegan said he hadn't seen Murray in months, and Jack went for the telephone. Fogarty dumped four quarts of water into the car radiator and went back in to find Jack off the phone with a Vichy water in front of him, talking about heavyweights to the clarinet player. Heavyweights. "I lost seven grand on Loughran," Jack was saying. "I thought he was the best, gave seven to five, and he didn't last three rounds. Sharkey murdered him. He says, 'Let me sit down, I don't know where I am,' and then he tried to walk through the ropes. Last time I ever bet on anybody from Philadelphia." Jack will talk to anybody about anything, anytime. Why shouldn't people like him?

"Seven grand," said the clarinet player.

"Yeah, I was crazy."

It seemed like a slip, Jack mentioning money. He never got specific about that, so why now? Must be nervous. Jack went back to the phone and made another call.

"He said he lost seven grand on one fight," the clarinetist said to Fogarty.

"Probably did. He always spent."

"But no more, eh?"

It sounded to Fogarty like a line at a wake. That man in the coffin is dead. Fogarty didn't like the feeling he got from shifting from that thought to a thought about Murray walking in the door. But Murray would have to come through the inn's glassed-in porch. Plenty of time to see him. What made Fogarty think he'd pick the one spot in the mountains where Jack happened to be at this odd moment? Did he think maybe he followed the car? Or that he'd been waiting near here for Jack to show up?

"He's probably still got a few dollars in his pocket," Fogarty said to the clarinetist.

"I wouldn't doubt that."

"You sounded like you did."

"No, not at all."

"You sounded like you were saying he's a has-been."

"You got me wrong. I didn't mean that at all. Listen, that's not what I meant. Dick, give us a drink here. I was just asking a question. Hell, Jesus, it was just a goddamn silly question."

"I get you now," Fogarty said.

Wasn't it funny how fast Fogarty could turn somebody's head around? Power in the word. In any word from Fogarty. In the way people looked at him. But it was changing. Maybe you wouldn't think so, sitting here at the Aratoga, and Jack being respected and Fogarty being respected, with maybe that hint of new tension in the air. But it definitely was changing. Little signs: Jack's living room being different, messy, papers on the floor, the chairs not where they used to be. Authority slipping away from Fogarty, authority that he knew Jack well, could talk all about him, talk for him. Dirty dishes on the dining room table. Picture of Eddie on the coffee table never there before, which meant something Fogarty didn't understand. The parties at Jack's; they were over too, at least for now. Even priests used to come. Neighbors, sometimes a cop or a judge from the city, actors and musicians and so many beautiful women. Women liked Jack and the feeling rubbed off to the benefit of Jack's friends. Jack the pivot man at every party. Funny son of a bitch when he gets a few drinks in. Fogarty couldn't remember one funny joke Jack ever told, but all his stories were funny. Just the way he used his voice. Yes. The story about Murray shooting the wrong man. Split your gut listening to Jack tell it. A good singing voice, too. Second tenor. Loves barbershop. "My Mother's Rosary." A great swipe in the middle of that. One of Jack's favorites.

"Well, that's some kind of news," Jack said, sitting back down beside Fogarty. "Somebody saw him at the Five O'Clock Club last night."

"Last night? He must've gone back down."

"If he was ever up here."

"Don't you think he must've been?"

"After this, maybe not. He's not the only one-eyed bum in the state. The point is, where is he now? Last night is a long time ago. He could be here in a few hours. They're still checking him out. Give me a small whiskey, Dick."

And he went back to the phone. Everybody was watching him now. Silence at the bar. Whispers. The clarinetist moved away and stayed away. Dick Fegan set up Jack's drink and moved away. They're watching you, too, Joe. Jack's closest associate. Fogarty drank alone while Jack talked on the phone. The whiskey eased his tension, but didn't erase it. Jack came back and sipped his whiskey, all eyes on him again. When he looked up, they looked away. They always watched him, but never with such grim faces. More finality. Man dying alone in an alley. There's Jack Diamond over there, that vanishing species. That pilot fish with him is another endangered item.

"I can't sit still," Jack said, and he stood up behind the barstool. "I been like this for two days."

"Let's go someplace else."

"They're going to call me. Then we'll move."

The musicians started up, a decent sound. "Muskrat Ramble." Sounds of life. Memories of dancing. Like old times. Memories of holding women. Got to get back to that.

Three-quarters of an hour passed, with Jack moving back and forth between the bar and the phone, then pacing up and down, plenty nervous. If Jack is that nervous, it's worse than Fogarty thought. Pacing. Jack's all alone and he knows it. And you know what that means, Joe? You know who else is alone if Jack is?

On his deathbed, when fibrosis was again relevant to him, Fogarty would recall how aware he was at this moment, not only of being alone, but of being sick again, of being physically weak with that peculiar early weakness in the chest that he recognized so quickly, so intimately. He would recall that he saw Dick Fegan pick up a lemon to squeeze it for a whiskey sour a customer had ordered. The customer was wearing a sport coat with checks so large Fogarty thought of a horse blanket. He would remember he saw these things, also saw Jack move out of his sight, out onto the porch just as the first blast smashed the window.

*   *   *

Fogarty ordered a hot dog and a chocolate milk and watched a fly that had either survived the winter or was getting an early start on the summer. The fly was inspecting the open hot dog roll.

"Get that goddamn fly off my bun," Fogarty told the Greek.

The Greek was sweaty and hairy. He worked hard. He worked alone in the all-night EAT. Fogarty has a loaded pistol in his pocket, which is something you don't know about Fogarty, Greek. The fly could be a cluster fly. Crazy. Flies into things. Fast, but drunk. Few people realize where the cluster fly comes from. He comes from a goddamn worm. He is an earthworm. A worm that turns into a fly. This is the sort of information you do not come by easily. Not unless you lie on your back for a long, long time and read the only goddamn book or magazine or newspaper in the room. And when you've read it all and there's nobody to talk to you, you read it again and find plenty of things you missed the first time around. All about worms and flies. There is no end to the details of life you can discover when you are flat on your back for a long, long time.

"That goddamn fly is on my bun."

There is a certain amount of sadness in an earthworm turning into a fly. But then it is one hell of a lot better than staying an earthworm or a maggot.

"You gonna let that goddamn fly eat my bun, or do I have to kill the goddamn thing myself?"

The Greek looked at Fogarty for the first time. What he saw made him turn away and find the flyswatter. Naturally the goddamn fly was nowhere to be found.

Fogarty had parked his 1927 Studebaker in front of the EAT, which was situated on Route 9-W maybe eight or nine miles south of Kingston at a crossroads. The name of the EAT was EAT, and the Greek was apparently the one-man Greek EAT owner who was now looking for the fly while Fogarty's hot dog was being calcified.

"That's enough on the dog," Fogarty said to the Greek, who was at the other end of the counter and did not see the fly return to the bun. Fogarty saw and he heard his pistol go off at about the same moment the bullet flecked away slivers from the EAT's wooden cutting board. There was a second and then a third and a fourth report from the pistol. The fourth shot pierced the hot dog roll. None of the shots touched the fly. The Greek fled to a back room after the first shot.

Fogarty rejected the entire idea of a hot dog and left the EAT. He climbed into his Studebaker and nosed onto 9-W, destination Yonkers, his sister Peg's, which he knew was a bad idea, but he'd call first and get Peg's advice on where else he might stay. He could stay nowhere in the Catskills. That world exploded with the ten shotgun blasts from a pair of Browning automatic repeaters, fired at Jack as he paced in and out of the porch of the Aratoga. A pair of shooters fired from the parking lot, then stopped and drove away. Somebody snapped out the lights inside at the sound of those shots and everybody hit the floor. Fogarty heard: "Speed, help me," and he crawled out to the porch to see Jack on his stomach, blood bubbling out of holes in his back.

"Bum shooting," Jack said. "Better luck next time."

But he was flat amid the millions of bits of glass, and hurting, and Fogarty got on the phone and called Padalino, the undertaker, and told him to send over his hearse because he was not calling the cops in yet.

When it was obvious the shooting was over, the musicians and customers came out to look at Jack on the floor of the porch and Dick Fegan went for the phone. But Fogarty said, "No cops until we get out," and everyone waited for Padalino.

"Find Alice, keep an eye on her," Jack said to Fogarty.

"Sure, Jack. Sure I will."

"They're putting me in the meat wagon," Jack said when Fogarty and Fegan lifted him gently, carefully into the hearse. By then Fogarty had cut Jack's shirt away and tied up the wounds with clean bar towels. He kept bleeding, but not so much.

"I'll follow you," Fogarty told Padalino, and when they were near Coxsackie, he parked his Studebaker at a closed gas station and got into the hearse alongside Jack. He fed Jack sips of the whiskey he had the presence of mind to take from the bar, tippled two himself, but only two, for he needed to be alert. He kept watching out the window of the rear door. He thought the hearse was being followed, but then it wasn't. Then it was again and then, outside Selkirk, it wasn't anymore. He sat by the rear door of the hearse with a gun in each hand while Jack bled and bled. I know nothing about shooting left-handed, Fogarty thought. But he held both guns, Jack's and Eddie's, a pair. Come on now, you bastards.

"Hurts, Speed. Really hurts. I can't tell where I'm hit."

They'd hit him with four half-ounce pellets. They'd fired ten double-ought shells with nine pellets to a shell. Somebody counted eighty some holes in the windows, the siding, and the inside porch walls. Ninety pellets out of two shotguns, and they only hit him with four, part of one shell. It really *was* bum shooting, Jack. You ought to be dead, and then some.

But maybe he is by this time, Fogarty thought, for he'd left Jack at the Albany Hospital, checked him into emergency under a fake name, called Marcus and got Padalino to take him back to his car at Coxsackie. Then, with the leftover whiskey in his lap, he headed south, only to have a fly land on his hot dog bun. Bun with a hole in it now.

The temperature gauge on the Studebaker was back in the red, almost to 220 again. He drove toward the first possible water, but saw no houses, no gas station. When the needle reached the top of the gauge and the motor began to steam and clank, he finished the whiskey dregs, shut off the ignition, threw the keys over his shoulder into the weeds and started walking.

Four cars passed him in fifteen minutes. The fifth picked him up when he waved his arms in the middle of the road, and drove him three miles to the roadblock where eight state troopers with shotguns, rifles, and pistols were waiting for him.

Poem from the Albany *Times-Union*

Long sleeping Rip Van Winkle seems
At last arousing from his dreams,
And reaching for the gun at hand
To drive invaders from his land.
The Catskills peace and quiet deep
Have been too much disturbed for sleep.
The uproars that such shootings make
Have got the sleeper wide awake.

Fogarty called me and asked me to appear for him at the arraignment, which I did. The charges had piled up: Kidnapping, assault, weapons possession, and, in less than two weeks, the federal investigators also charged both him and Jack with multiple Prohibition Law violations. His bail was seventeen thousand five hundred dollars and climbing. He said he knew a wealthy woman, an old flame who still liked him and would help, and I called her. She said she'd guarantee five thousand dollars, all she could get without her husband knowing. Fogarty had more in the bank, enough to cover the bail, but unfortunately his accounts, like Jack's and Alice's, were all sequestered.

Two of Jack's transient henchmen—a strange, flabby young man who wore a black wig that looked like linguine covered with shoe polish, and a furtive little blond rat named Albert—also inquired after my services, but I said I was overloaded.

"What are you going to do about bail?" I asked Fogarty, and he suggested Jack. But Jack was having trouble raising his own, for much of his cash was also impounded.

Beyond Jack, the woman, and his own inaccessible account, Fogarty had no idea where to get cash. His new Oldsmobile was repossessed for nonpayment a week after his arrest.

"How do you plan to pay me?" I asked him.

"I can't right now, but that money in the bank is still mine."

"Not if they prove it was booze profits."

"You mean they can take it?"

"I'd say they already have."

I liked Joe well enough—a pleasant, forthright fellow. But my legal career was built on defending not pleasant people, but people who paid my fee. I follow a basic rule of legal practice: Establish the price, get the money, then go to work. Some lawyers dabble in charity cases, which, I suspect, is whitewash for their chicanery more often than not. But I've never needed such washing. It was not one of Jack's problems either. What he did that had a charitable element to it was natural, not compensatory behavior. He liked the woman whose cow needed a shed, and so he had one built. He disliked old Streeter and showed it, which cost him his empire. I've absorbed considerable outrage over Jack's behavior with Streeter, but few people consider that he didn't *really* hurt the old man. A few burns to the feet and ankles are picayune compared to what might have happened. I understand behavior under stress, and I know Streeter lived to an old age and Jack did not, principally because Jack, when tested, was really not the Moloch he was made out to be.

Seeing events from this perspective, I felt and still feel justified in defending Jack. Fogarty took a fall—twelve and a half to fifteen, but served only six because of illness. I feel bad that anyone has to go to prison, but Fogarty was Jack's spiritual brother, not mine, and I am neither Jesus Christ nor any lesser facsimile. I save my clients when I can, but I reserve the right of selective salvation.

※   ※   ※

Jack took pellets in the right lung, liver, and back, and his left arm was again badly fractured. The pellet in his lung stayed there and seemed to do him little harm. The papers had him near death for three days, but Doc Madison, my own physician, operated on him and said he probably wasn't even close to dying. He beat off an infection, was out of danger in ten days, and out of the hospital in four and a half weeks. One hundred troopers lined the road for forty-seven miles between Albany and Catskill the day he left the hospital for jail, to discourage loyalists from snatching away FDR's prize. New floodlights were installed on the Greene County jail (lit up the world wherever he went, Jack did), and the guard trebled to keep the star boarders inside: Jack, Fogarty, and Oxie, who had gained fifty pounds in the eight months he'd been there.

The feds indicted Jack on fourteen charges: coercion, Sullivan Law and Prohibition Law violations, conspiracy etc., and it was two weeks before we could raise the new bail to put him back on the street. It really wasn't the street, but the luxurious Kenmore Hotel in Albany, a suite of rooms protected by inside and downstairs guards.

The troopers and the revenue men continued their probing of the mountains. They found Jack's books with records of his plane rentals, his commissioning the building of an oceangoing speedboat. They found the empty dovecotes where he kept his carrier pigeons, his way of beating the phone taps. They found his still on the Biondo farm, and, from the records and notations, they also began turning up stashes of whiskey, wine, and cordials of staggering dimension.

The neatly kept files and records showed Jack's tie-in with five other mobs: Madden's, Vannie Higgins', Coll's, and two in Jersey; distribution tie-ins throughout eighteen counties in the state; brewery connections in Troy, Fort Edward, Coney Island, Manhattan, Yonkers, and Jack's (formerly Charlie Northrup's) plant at Kingston; plus dozens of storage dumps and way stations all through the Adirondacks and Catskills, from the Canadian border to just west of Times Square.

The first main haul was evaluated at a mere $10,000 retail, but they kept hauling and hauling. Remember these booze-on-hand statistics the next time anyone tells you Jack ran a two-bit operation. (Source, federal): 350,000 pints and 300,000 quarts of rye whiskey, worth $4 a pint retail, or about $3.8 million; 200,000 quarts of champagne at $10 a bottle, or $2 million; 100,000 half-kegs of wine worth $2.5 million, plus 80,000 fifths of cordials and miscellany for a grand estimated total of $10 million. Not a bad accumulation for a little street kid from Philly.

Catskill was looking forward to Jack's trial, which was going to be great for tourism. The first nationwide radio hookup of any trial in American history was planned, and I think somehow they would've sold tickets to it. A hundred businessmen, many of them hotel and boardinghouse operators, paying up to three hundred dollars in seasonal tribute to the emperor, held a meeting at the Chamber of Commerce, a meeting remarkable for its anonymity. Fifty newsmen were in town covering every development, but none of the hundred attendees at that meeting were identified.

What they did was unanimously ratify a proclamation calling on one another not to be afraid to testify against Jack and the boys. Getting tough with the wolf in the cage. There was even talk around town of burning down Jack's house. And finally, what Warren Van Deusen had been trying and not trying to tell me about Jack was that half a hundred people had written FDR letters over the past two months, detailing Jack's depredations. It was that supply of complaints, capped by the

Streeter episode, which fired old Franklin to do what he did. That and politics.

The abandoned getaway car of Jack's would-be killers turned up with a flat tire on Prospect Avenue in Catskill, behind the courthouse. The Browning repeaters were still in it, along with a Luger, a .38 Smith and Wesson, and two heavy Colt automatics with two-inch barrels, all fully loaded. The car had a phony Manhattan registration in the name of Wolfe, a nice touch, and when perspective was gained, nobody blamed Murray for the big do. Too neat. Too well planned. A Biondo job was Jack's guess.

My chief contribution to the history of these events was to snatch the circus away from the Catskill greed mob. They squawked that Jack was robbing them again, taking away their chance to make a big tourist dollar. What I did was win us a change of venue on grounds that a fair trial was impossible in Greene County. The judge agreed and FDR didn't fight us. He hopscotched us up to Rensselaer County. With Troy, the county seat, being my old stamping grounds, I felt like Br'er Rabbit being tossed into the briar patch.

Attorney General Bennett paid homage to Jack at the annual communion breakfast of the Holy Name Society of the Church of St. Rose of Lima in Brooklyn. In celebration of Mother's Day he said that if men of Diamond's type had listened to the guidance of their mothers, they would not be what they were today.

"One of the greatest examples of mother's care," the attorney general said, "is the result which the lack of it has shown in the life of Legs Diamond. Diamond never had a mother's loving care nor the proper training. Environment has played a large part in making him the notorious character he is today. A mother is the greatest gift a man ever had."

*   *   *

Alice came out of the elevator, walked softly on the rich, blue carpet toward the suite, and saw a form which stopped all her random thought about past trouble and future anguish. The light let her see the hairdo, and the hair was chestnut, not Titian; and the face was hidden under half a veil on the little clawclutch of a maroon hat. But Alice knew Kiki when she saw her, didn't she? Kiki was locking the door to the room next to Alice's. Then she came toward the elevator, seeming not to recognize Alice. Was it her? Alice had seen her in the flesh only once. She was smaller now than her photos made her out to be. And younger. Her face looked big in the papers. And at the police station. She had sat there at the station and let them take her picture. Crossed her legs for them.

She passed within inches of Alice, explaining herself with the violent fumes of her perfume. It *was* her. But if it truly was, why didn't she give some form of recognition, some gesture, some look? Alice decided that, finally, Kiki didn't have the courage to say hello. Coward type. Brazen street slut. Values of an alleycat. Rut whore. Was it really her? Why was she here? Would Jack know?

*   *   *

Kiki saw Alice coming as soon as she stepped out of the room, and she immediately turned away to lock the door. She recognized the fat calves under the long skirt with the ragged hem. On the long chance Alice wouldn't recognize her, Kiki chose to ignore her, for she feared Alice would turn her in. Kiki the fugitive. But would Alice run that risk? Jack would kill her for that, wouldn't he? Kitchen cow.

Why did life always seem to be saltwater life for Kiki, never life with a sweetness? Violence always taking Jack away. Violence always bringing back the old sow. Meat and potatoes pig. Why was fate so awful to Kiki? And then for people to say she had put the finger on Jack. What an awful thing to think. The cow passed her by and said nothing. Didn't recognize her. Kiki kept on walking to the elevator, then turned to see Alice entering the room next to Kiki's own. But how could that be? Would Alice break into Kiki's room? But for what? Why would she rent a room next to Kiki's? How would she know which one Kiki was in? Kiki would tell Jack about this, all right. But, Fat Mama, why are you here?

*   *   *

The Kenmore had status appeal to Jack: historic haven of gentility from the mauve decade until Prohibition exploded the purple into scarlet splashes. Its reputation was akin to Saratoga's Grand Union in Diamond Jim's and Richard Canfield's day. It was where Matthew Arnold stayed when he came to Albany, and Mark Twain too, on the night he lobbied for osteopathy in the Capitol. It was where Ulysses S. Grant occasionally dined. Al Smith's son lived there when Al was governor, and it was the dining room where any governor was most likely to turn up in the new century. It boasted eventually of Albany's longest bar, always busy with the chatter of legislators, the room where a proper gentleman from Albany's Quality Row could get elegantly swozzled among his peers.

Sure Jack knew this, even if he didn't know the details, for the tradition was visible and tangible, in the old marble, in the polished brass and mahogany, in the curly maple in the lobby, in the stained glass, and the enduring absence of the hoi polloi. Jack was always tuned in to any evidence of other people's refinement.

He dominates more memories of the place even now than Vincent Lopez or Rudy Vallee or Phil Romano or Doc Peyton or the Dorsey Brothers or any other of the greater or lesser musicians who held sway in the Rain-Bo room for so long, but whose light is already dim, whose music has faded away, whose mythology has not been handed on.

Jack didn't create the ambience that made the Kenmore so appealing, but he enhanced it in its raffish new age. He danced, he laughed, he wore the best, and moved with the fastest. But I well knew he had conceived that style long ago in desperation and was bearing it along cautiously now, like a fragile golden egg. He was frail, down eighteen pounds again, eyes abulge again, cheekbones prominent again, left arm all but limp, and periodically wincing when he felt that double-ought pellet bobbling about in his liver. But more troubling than this was the diminishing amount of time left for him to carry out the task at hand: the balancing of the forces of his life in a way that would give him ease, let him think well of himself, show him the completion of a pattern that at least would look *something* like the one he had devised as a young man: Young Jack—that desperate fellow he could barely remember and could not drive out.

Empire gone, exchequer sequestered, future wholly imperfect, it occurred to Jack that the remaining values of his life inhered chiefly in his women. Naturally, he decided to collect them, protect them, and install them in the current safe-deposit box of his life, which at the moment was a six-room second-floor suite in the Kenmore.

x   x   x

"Marcus, you won't believe what I'm saying, but it's a true. I'm in the kitchen one day and the boss come in and says, Sal, you busy? I say no, not too much. He says, I gotta friend of mine in such and such a room and his name is Jack Legs Dime. Have you heard him? Well, I say, in the newspape, yes. He says you wanna be his waiter from now on while he stays uppa here? You go upstays every morning eight thirty breakfast, noon if he's a call, maybe sandwich now and then, don't worry dinner. Take care of him and his friends and he pay you. I say, sure, it's all right with me. So every morning I used to knock on the door with the same breakfast—little steak and egg overlight for Jack, coffee, toast, buns, some scramble eggs for everybody, some cornflakes, milk, plenty potsa coffee, all on the wagon, and Hubert, this rough-lookin' bast with a puggy nose, he's got a goddama gun in both hands. I say Hubert, you son um a bitch I won't come up here no more if you don't put them guns away. I talk to him like that more for joke than anything else. So I see Jack Dime and I give him the breakfast and sometime breakfast for two, three extra people they call to tell me about and Jack call to somebody and says, hey, give Sal twenty-five dollar. He says to me, will that be enough? I say Yeah, Legs, plenty. More than what I expect. Just take care a me and my friends and you down for twenty-five a day, how's that? Beautiful. Jesa Christ, them days twenty-five dollar, who the hell ever seen twenty-five dollar like that? Every day was a different five, six new people, I guess they talking about Jack's trial coming up. And one day Jack call the next room and say, hey, Coll, you wanna eat some breakfas? I gotta breakfas here. Hey, Legs, I say, that Vince Coll? He supposed to be you enemy it says in the pape. Jack says no, he's a good friend a mine. And I pour Coll a coffee and some toast. Then three, four weeks later I met another fellow, Schultz. I say, Hey, Legs, you and Schultz, you supposed to be the worst enemies. And he says no, only sometimes. Now we get along pretty nice. So I pour Schultz a coffee and some toast. I say, Hey, Jack, they's a big fight tonight, who you like, we bet a dollar. Nah, he says, them fighters all crooks. Punks, no good. Then how about baseball, I says. Yeah, he says, I bet you a dollar. I take the Yanks. Legs like Babe Ruth and Bill Dickey. Then one day he says to me, Sal, I want you to meet my wife, Mrs. Jack Legs Dime. I say it's a pleasure, and then another day I go up and he says, Sal, I want you to meet my friend, Miss Kiki Roberts. And Kiki she says hello and I say it's a pleasure. Jesa Christ, I wonder how the hell Jack Dime got these women together. I see them sit down together, have breakfast, and then go out together and shop down the stores on Pearl Street while Jack stay home. I say to Freddie Robin, the detective sergeant who sits in the lobby looking for punks who don't look right and who ask funny questions about Legs and I say, Freddie, son um a bitch, it's magic. He got the both women up there. Freddie says you think that's something you ought to see them Sunday morn. All in church together. No, I say. Yeah, Freddie say. All in the same pew, seven o'clock mass Saint Mary's. No, I say. Don't tell me no, Freddie says, when I get paid to go watch them. So I says this I got to see for myself and next Sunday seven o'clock mass son um a bitch they don't all come in, first Kiki, then Alice, then Jack, and little ways back in another pew, Freddie. Alice goes a communion and Jack and Kiki sit still. Then later every Friday I see the monsignor come into the hotel and go upstairs. To hear the confessions, Freddie says, and he thinks sometimes they go to communion right in the room. Hey, I says to Freddie, I don't know nobody gets a communion in this hotel. How they get away with that when they all living together in the same rooms? I took a peek one day, the women got a room each, and Legs, he got a room all his own and the bodyguards got a room and they got other rooms for people in and out, transaction business. Course when I was up there, everything was mum. Nobody say anything, and when I go back for the dishes and the wagon Legs is maybe getting a shave and a haircut, every day, saying the rosary beads. They got a candle in every room, burn all day long, and a statue of Saint Anthony and the Blessed Virgin, which, I figure out, maybe is through Alice, who is on the quiet side, maybe because she got too damn much on her mind. She don't smile much at me. Hello, Sal, good morning, Sal, always nice, but not like Kiki, who says, Sal, how are you this morning, pretty good? Howsa weather outside? She liked to talk, some girl, Kiki. Wow! Freddie says to me, Sal, you think they all wind up in bed together? I laugh like hell. Freddie, I say, how the hell anybody going to do anything with a woman when another woman alongside you? No, that's not it. Bad as the guy might be, if I had a swear, put my hands to God and say would the guy do anything like that, I would say no. Maybe he got a desire to stay with his wife, then he call his wife into his room. He gotta desire to stay with his girlfriend, he call his girlfriend. It's the only thing I can see. Nine time out of ten I would say his girlfriend. On the other hand, he had to take care of his wife too. She wasn't so bad-looking, and after all it was a legitimate wife. You ask me was he an animal, a beast—I say no. He was a fanat. If he wasn't a fanat, why the hell he got Saint Anthony up there? He must've had some kind of good in him, I gotta say it. Not for the moneywise he gave me. I wouldn't judge him for that. But I couldn't say nothing bad toward the guy. I never even hear him curse. Very refine. Pardon me, pardon me. If he sneeze sometime, it's pardon me, tank you, see ya tomorra. But, actually speaking, who's a know what the hell really goes on upstays?"

                    ✕   ✕   ✕

The night I went to dinner with Jack, Alice, and Kiki at the Kenmore, the ménage seemed to be functioning the way Jack wanted it to function. He'd called me to come down and see him, talk about the trial, and, more important, he wanted to pay me. I'd already told him I was fond of him as a friend, even though I disagreed with some of his behavior, and I enjoyed his company. However, I said, all that has nothing to do with business. If I work for you, I expect to get paid, and now that you've got your bank accounts under government lock and key, what are you going to do about my fee, which, I explained, would be ten thousand dollars payable in advance? I knew two aspiring criminal lawyers who waited until after trial for their pay and are waiting yet.

"Jack, let's face it," I said, "you're a crook."

He laughed and said, "Marcus, you're twice the crook I'll ever be," which pleased me because it implied prowess in a world alien to me, even if it wasn't true. What he was really doing was admiring my willingness to structure an alibi for his trial, give it a reasonableness that smacked lovingly of truth. I had fifteen witnesses lined up three weeks before we went to trial, and all were ready to testify, in authenticatingly eccentric and voluminous detail, that Jack had been in Albany the night Streeter and the kid were abducted. Waiters saw him, a manicurist, a desk clerk, a physiotherapist, a car salesman, a bootblack, a barber, a garment executive from the Bronx, and more.

I arrived at Jack's Kenmore suite half an hour ahead of schedule and was let in by Hubert Maloy, the plump Irish kid from Troy whom Jack had hired away from Vincent Coll as his inside guard. Hubert knew me and let me sit in the parlor. I immediately caught the odor of exotic incense and saw a wisp of smoke curling upward from an open door to one of the bedrooms. I glimpsed Alice on her hands and knees with a brushbroom, pushing a lemon back and forth on the rug in front of the incense, which burned in a tin dish. The scene was so weird it embarrassed me. It was like intruding on someone's humiliating dream. Alice was in her slip and stocking feet, a long run in the stocking most visible to me. Her hair was uncombed and she was without the protection of makeup. I quietly got up from the chair and moved to another one, where I wouldn't be able to see her room.

Jack arrived with Kiki about ten minutes later, and Alice emerged from the incense room like a new woman, hair combed, lipstick in place, lovely wildflower housecoat covering slip and run. She kissed Jack on the check, kissed me too, and said to Kiki: "Your black dress came from the cleaners, Marion. It's in the closet."

"Oh terrific, thanks," said a smiling, amiable, grateful Kiki.

Such was the nature of the interchanges I observed, and I won't bore you further with the banality of their civility. Jack took me aside, and when we'd finished updating the state of the trial, and of our witnesses (our foreboding reserved not for this but for the federal trial), Jack handed me a white envelope with twenty five-hundred-dollar bills.

"That suit you?"

"Seems to be in order. I'll accept it only if you tell me where it came from."

"It's not hot, if that's your worry."

"That's my worry."

"It's fresh from Madden. All legitimate. My fee for transferring some cash."

The cash, I would perceive before the week was out, was the ransom paid for Big Frenchy DeMange, Owney Madden's partner in the country's biggest brewery. Vincent Coll, Fats McCarthy, and another fellow whose name I never caught, whisked Big Frenchy off a corner in midtown Manhattan and returned him intact several hours later after the delivery of thirty-five thousand dollars to Jack, who, despite being on bail, left the state and drove to Jersey to pick it up. Madden knew Coll and McCarthy were basically cretins and that Jack was more than the innocent intermediary in such a neat snatch, and so Madden-Diamond relations were sorely, but not permanently, ruptured. I had little interest in any of that. I merely assured Jack he would now have the best defense money could buy.

Kiki had flopped into the chair from which I'd witnessed Alice's lemon brushing, and she said to Jack when he and I broke from conference: "I wanna go eat, Jackie." I saw Alice wince at the "Jackie." Jack looked at me and said, "Join us for dinner?" and I said why not and he said, "All right, ladies, get yourself spiffy," and twenty minutes and two old-fashioneds later we were all in the elevator, descending to the Rain-Bo room, my own pot of gold tucked away in a breast pocket, Jack's twin receptacles on either side of him, exuding love, need, perfume, promise, and lightly controlled confusion; also present: Hubert, the troll protecting all treasures.

For purposes of polite camouflage, Kiki clutched my arm as we moved toward Jack's corner table in the large room. "You know," she said to me softly, "Jack gave me a gift just before we came down."

"No, I didn't know."

"Five hundred dollars."

"That's a lovely gift."

"In a single bill."

"A single bill. Well, you don't see many of them."

"I never saw one before."

"I hope you put it in a safe place."

"Oh, I did, I'm wearing it."

"Wearing it?"

"In my panties."

Two days later Kiki would take the bill—well stained by then not only with her most private secretions, but also with Jack's—to Madame Amalia, a Spanish gypsy crone who ran a tearoom on Hudson Avenue, and paid the going fee of twenty-five dollars for the hex of a lover's erstwhile possession, hex that would drive the wedge between man and wife. Knowing whose wife was being hexed and wedged, Madame Amalia was careful not to make the five-hundred-dollar bill disappear.

"Did you see the new picture of me and Jack?" Alice asked me across the table.

"No, not yet."

"We had it taken this week. We never had a good picture of us together, just the ones the newspapermen snap."

"You have it there, do you?"

"Sure do." And she handed it over.

"It's a good picture all right."

"We never even had one taken on our honeymoon."

"You're both smiling here."

"I told Jack I wanted us to be happy together for always, even if it was only in a picture."

Despite such healthy overtness, the good Alice had pushed the lemon back and forth in front of the incense for three months, a ritual learned from her maid Cordelia, a child of Puerto Rico, where the occult is still as common as the sand and the sea. The lemon embodied Alice's bitter wish that Jack see Kiki as the witch Alice knew her to be, witch of caprice and beauty beyond Alice's understanding; for beauty to Alice was makeshift—nice clothing, properly colored hair, not being fat. And Kiki's beauty, ineffable as the Holy Ghost, was a hateful riddle.

✻   ✻   ✻

When Jack's lucky blue suit came back from the hotel cleaners, a silver rosary came with it in the key pocket. I always suspected Alice's fine Irish Catholic hand at work in that pocket. The night of our Rain-Bo dinner Jack pulled out a handful of change when he sent Hubert for the *Daily News*, and when I saw the rosary I said, "New prayer implement there?" which embarrassed him. He nodded and dropped it back into his pocket.

He had examined it carefully when it turned up in that pocket, looked at its cross, which had what seemed to be hieroglyphics on it, and at the tiny sliver of wood inside the cross (which opened like a locket), wood that might well, the monsignor suggested, have been a piece of the true cross. The hieroglyphics and the sliver had no more meaning for Jack than the Hail Marys, the Our Fathers, and the Glory Bes he recited as his fingers breezed along the beads. His scrutiny of the cross was a search for a coded message from his mother, whose rosary, he was beginning to believe, had been providentially returned to him. For he remembered clearly the silver rosary on her dresser and, again, twined in her hands when she lay in her coffin. He studied it until its hieroglyphics yielded their true meaning: scratches. The sliver of wood, he decided, was too new to have been at Calvary. Piece of a toothpick from Lindy's more like it. Yet he fondled those silver beads, recited those holy rote phrases as if he, too, were rolling a lemon or hexing money, and he offered up the cheapjack stuff of his ragged optimism to the only mystical being he truly understood.

Himself.

No one else had the power to change the life at hand.

*   *   *

How does a mythical figure ask a lady to dance? As if Jack didn't have enough problems, now he was faced with this. Moreover, when he has a choice of two ladies, which one does he single out to be the first around whom he will publicly wrap what is left of his arms as he spins through waves of power, private unity, and the love of all eyes? These questions shaped themselves as wordless desires in Jack's head as he read his own spoken words about his own mythic nature.

When Hubert came back with four copies of the *Daily News*, everyone at the table opened to the first of a three-part interview with Jack by John O'Donnell. It was said to be Jack's first since all his trouble, and he corroborated that right there in the *News'* very bold type:

> **"I haven't been talking out of vanity—the fact that I've never given out my side before would show pretty clearly that I'm not publicity mad."**

Reasonable remark, Jack. Not publicity mad anymore. Too busy using interviews like these to generate sympathy for your cause, for the saving of your one and only ass, to worry about publicity for vanity's sake. Jack could be more pragmatic, now that he's a myth. But was he really a myth? Well, who's to say? But he does note a mythic development in his life in that bold, bold *Daily News* type:

> **"Here's what I think. This stuff written about me has created a mythical figure in the public mind. Now I'm Jack Diamond and I've got to defend myself against the mythical crimes of the mythical Legs."**

Legs. Who the hell was this Legs anyway? Who here in the Rain-Bo room really knows Legs?

"Hello, Legs."

"How ya doin', Legs?"

"Good luck on the trial, Legs."

"Glad to see you up and around, Legs."

"Have a drink, Legs?"

"We'd like you to join our party if you get a minute, Mr. Legs."

Only a handful in the joint really knew him, and those few called him Jack. The rest clustered 'round the mythic light, retelling stories of origins:

"They call him Legs because he always runs out on his friends."

"They call him Legs because his legs start up at his chest bone."

"They call him Legs because he could outrun any cop at all when he was a kid package thief."

"They call him Legs because he danced so much and so well."

Shall we dance! Who first?

"This is a good interview, Jack," said Marcus. "Good for the trial. Bound to generate some goodwill somewhere."

"I don't like the picture they put with it," Alice said. "You look too thin."

"I am too thin," Jack said.

"I like it," Kiki said.

"I knew you would," Alice said.

"I like it when your hat is turned up like that," Kiki said.

"So do I," Alice said.

"Find your own things to like," Kiki said.

Who first?

Dance with Alice and have the band play "Happy Days and Lonely Nights," your favorite, Jack. Dance with Marion and have them play "My Extraordinary Gal," your favorite, Jack.

"Is it true what he says there about Legs and Augie?" Kiki asked.

"All true," Jack said.

"As a matter of fact I was never called Legs until after that Little Augie affair. Look it up and see for yourself. It don't make much difference, but that's a fact. My friends or my family have never called me Legs. When the name Legs appeared under a picture, people who didn't know me picked it up and I've been called Legs in the newspapers ever since."

O'Donnell explained that Eddie Diamond was once called Eddie Leggie ("Leggie," a criminal nickname out of the nineteenth-century slums) and that somehow it got put on Jack. Cop told a newsman about it. Newsman got it wrong. Caption in the paper referred to Jack as Legs. And there was magic forever after.

"I didn't know that," Kiki said. "Is it really true, Jackie?"

"All the garbage they ever wrote about me is true to people who don't know me."

The music started again after a break, and Jack looked anxiously from woman to woman, faced once again with priority. Did his two women think of him as Legs? Absurd. They knew who he was. If anybody *ever* knew he was Jack Diamond and not Legs Diamond, it was those two ladies. They loved him for his own reasons, not other people's. For his body. For the way he talked to them. For the way he loved them. For the way his face was shaped. For the ten thousand spoken and unspoken reasons he was what he was. It wasn't necessary for Jack to dwell on such matters, for he had verified this truth often. What was necessary now was to keep the women together, keep them from repelling each other like a matched pair of magnets. This matched pair would work as a team, draw the carriage of Jack's future. Fugitive Kiki, wanted as a Streeter witness, needed the protection of Jack's friends until the charge against her went away. She would stick, all right. And Alice? Why, she would stick through anything. Who could doubt that at this late date?

A voluptuous woman in a silver sheath with shoulder straps of silver cord paused at the table with her escort.

"This one here is Legs," she said to the escort. "I'd know him anywhere, even if he is only a ridiculous bag of bones."

"Who the hell are you?" Jack asked her.

"I saw your picture in the paper, Legs," she said.

"That explains it."

She looked at Alice and Kiki, then rolled down the right strap of her gown and revealed a firm, substantial, well-rounded, unsupported breast.

"How do you like it?" she said to Jack.

"It seems adequate, but I'm not interested."

"You've had a look anyway, and that counts for something, doesn't it, sweetheart?" she said to her escort.

"It better, by God," said the escort.

"I can also get milk out of it if you ever feel the need," she said, squeezing her nipple forward between two fingers and squirting a fine stream into Jack's empty coffee cup.

"I'll save that till later," Jack said.

"Oh, he's so intelligent," the woman said, tucking herself back into her dress and moving off.

"I think we should order," Kiki said. "I'm ravished."

"You mean famished," Jack said.

"Yes, whatever I mean."

"And no more interruptions," said Alice.

Jack signaled the waiter and told him, "A large tomato surprise."

"One for everybody?"

"One for me," Jack said. "I have no power over what other people want."

The waiter leaned over and spoke into Jack's face so all could hear. "They tell *me* you've got the power of ten thousand Indians."

Jack picked up his butter knife and stared at the waiter, prepared to drive the blade through the back of that servile hand. He would take him outside, kick him down the stairs, break his goddamn snotty face.

"The way I get it," the waiter said, backing away, speaking directly to Jack, "you know it all. You know who the unknown soldier is and who shot him."

"Where do they get these people?" Jack asked. But before anyone could respond, the waiter's voice carried across the room from the kitchen, "A tomato surprise for the lady killer," and the room's eyes swarmed over Jack in a new way.

Jack straightened his tie, aware his collar was too big for his neck, aware his suit had the ill fit of adolescence because of his lost weight. He felt young, brushed his hair back from his ears with the heels of both hands, thought of the work that lay ahead of him, the physical work adolescents must do. They must grow. They must do the chores of life, must gain in strength and wisdom to cope with the hostile time of manhood. The work of Jack's life lay stretched out ahead of him. On the dance floor, for instance.

He started to get up, but Alice grabbed his arm and whispered in his ear: "Do you remember, Jack, the time you stole the fox collar coat I wanted so much, but then I took it back and you insisted and went back and stole it all over again? Oh, how I loved you for that."

"I remember," he said softly to her. "I could never forget that coat."

Kiki watched their intimacy, then leaned toward Jack and whispered, "I've got my legs open, Jackie."

"Have you, kid?"

"Yes. And now I'm opening my nether lips."

"You are?"

"Yes. And now I'm closing them. And now I'm opening them again."

"You know, kid, you're all right. Yes, sir, you're all right."

He stood up then and said, "I'm going to dance."

Alice looked at Kiki, Kiki at Alice, the ultimate decision blooming at long last. They both looked to Jack for his choice, but he made none. He got up from his chair at last and, with his left arm swinging limply, his right shoulder curled in a way to give his movement the quality of a young man in full swagger, he headed for the dance floor where a half dozen couples were twirling about to a waltz. When Jack put a foot on the dance floor, some, then all couples stopped and the band trailed off. But Jack turned to the bandstand, motioned for the music to continue. Then he looked at Kiki and Alice, who stood just off the edge of the floor.

"My arm, Marion," he said. "Take my arm."

And while Alice's eyes instantly filled with tears at the choice, Kiki gripped Jack's all but useless left hand with her own and raised it. As she moved toward him for the dancer's embrace, he said, "My right arm, Alice," and Alice's face broke into a roseate smile of tears as she raised Jack's right hand outward.

The women needed no further instruction. They joined their own hands and stepped onto the dance floor with their man. Then, as the orchestra broke into the waltz of now and forever, the waltz that all America, all Europe, was dancing to—"Two Hearts in Three-Quarter Time," its arithmetic obviously calculated in heaven—Alice, Marion, and Jack stepped forward into the music, into the dance of their lives.

"One-two-three, one-two-three, one-two-three, one-two-three," Jack counted. And they twirled on their own axis and spun around the room to the waltz like a perfect circle as the slowly growing applause of the entire room carried them up, up, and up into the ethereal sphere where people truly know how to be happy.

Jack-in-the-Box

I'LL SPARE YOU THE DETAILS of the summer's two trials, which produced few surprises beyond my own splendid rhetoric and, in the Troy trial, a perjury indictment for one of our witnesses whose vigorous support of Jack's alibi was, alas, provably untrue. I presume the July verdict must be counted a surprise, being for acquittal of Jack on a charge of assaulting Streeter. The courtroom burst into applause and shouts when the verdict was read. Alice ran down the aisle in her lovely pink frock with the poppy print and her floppy picture hat, leaned over the rail and gave Jack a wet one with gush. "Oh, my darling boy!" And three hundred people standing outside the Rensselaer County courthouse in Troy, because there were no seats left in the courtroom, sent up a cheer heard 'round the world. Moralists cited that cheer as proof of America's utter decadence and depravity, rooting for a dog-rat like Diamond. How little they understood Jack's appeal to those everyday folk on the sidewalk.

I must admit that the attorney general lined up an impressive supply of witnesses to prove conclusively to any logician that Jack was in Sweeney's speakeasy in Catskill the night Streeter was lifted. But once I identified Streeter as a bootlegger, the issue became a gangster argument about a load of booze, not the torture of innocence. And Jack was home free.

It wasn't so easy to confuse the issue at the federal trial in Manhattan. All that the federal lawyers (young Tom Dewey among them) had to do was connect Jack with the still, which wasn't much of a problem, and *they* were home free. The Catskill burghers, including my friend Warren Van Deusen, spouted for the prosecution, and so did some of Jack's former drivers; but most damning was Fogarty, who called Jack a double-crossing rat who wouldn't put up money for a lawyer, who let this poor, defenseless, tubercular henchman, who had trusted him, take the rap alone and penniless. Alice was in court again, with Eddie's seven-year-old son, a marvelously sympathetic prop, and Jack broke into genuine tears when a newsman asked him in the hallway if the boy really was his nephew. But those feds nailed our boy. My rhetoric had no resonance in that alien courtroom: too many indignant businessmen, too much faceless justice, too far from home, too much Fogarty. In an earlier trial at Catskill, the state had managed to convict Fogarty on the same Streeter charge Jack was acquitted of, which was poetic justice for the turncoat as I see it. Jack drew four years, the maximum, and not really a whole lot, but enough of a prospect to spoil the summer.

Jack had been making plans to merge with Vincent Coll and Fats McCarthy, substitute their mob for his own, refurbish the Catskill scene, and maybe put a toe in the door of the Adirondacks. But Johnny Broderick and a squad of New York dicks followed Coll's crowd up from Manhattan and raided them in Coxsackie, hauling in about a dozen. They missed Coll and McCarthy, who along with a few stragglers holed up in an artist's home in Averill Park, a crossroads summer town east of Troy, where Jack and Coll occasionally met and tried to cook up a future for themselves.

It was a depressing time for Jack. Kiki had to take an apartment away from the Kenmore when the state police began to breathe heavily around the lobby, and Alice was delighted to get rid of the competition. But Jack took Kiki out regularly and brought her back to the hotel for visits after the first trial, and Alice finally said good-bye forever, folks, and went to live in her Manhattan apartment on Seventy-second Street.

The acquittal in Troy came in early July, the federal conviction in early August, and the state announced it would try Jack on a second Streeter charge, kidnapping, in December. It was a very long, very hot summer for all of us, but especially Jack, like the predator wolf pushed ever farther from civilization by angry men, who was learning the hard way how to die.

                                    *   *   *

Jack's federal conviction drove a spike of gloom into everybody. Jack insisted on trying to buy a retrial, his hangover from the days when Rothstein had money in everybody's mouth, all the way up to the Presidential cabinet. That money had bought Jack a delay on a federal charge of smuggling heroin for Rothstein, the noted bowling pin case, and Jack died without ever having to face up to the evidence against him.

"The fuckers are all the same, all the way to the top," he said to me one night. "They'll do you any favor you can pay for."

But times had changed to a certain unpredictable degree in Manhattan, especially for people like Jack. The new federal crowd was young, imbued with Seaburyism, and still unbuyable. Even if we had found somebody to buy, there was the case of the diminishing bankroll. The first thing Jack did after he got out of the Catskill jail on bail was to take the one hundred and eighty thousand dollars I'd held for him in safe deposit. That still seemed like a lot of money to me, but it wasn't for Jack. He owed everybody: me, the hospital, the doc, his barber, his waiter, the hotel, his driver, Hubert the bodyguard, infinite numbers of bartenders who would now and in the future provide him with service. He was keeping apartments in Troy, Watervliet, Albany, East Greenbush, a house in Petersburg, and probably six or eight other cities I don't know about. He was keeping Kiki. He was subsidizing Alice in Manhattan. And, and most costly of all, he was paying off politicians everywhere to keep his freedom, keeping them from infecting him with further trouble. The one hundred and eighty thousand dollars went in a few months, or so Jack said, though I think he must have kept a secret nest egg somewhere, and if he did, of course, he kept it utterly to himself. He didn't leave the egg with me. I also know Vincent Coll offered him a loan of ten thousand dollars after a nifty Coll snatch of a Saratoga gambler, and a handsome ransom of sixty-five thousand dollars; and Jack took it.

He coped with the money problem like the pragmatist he had come to be. He went back to work. I met him at the Albany Elks Club bar on a steamy August evening after a day at Saratoga had given me nothing but the aesthetic boredom of picking losers under the elms of the track's stylish old clubhouse and paddock. I came back to town alone, feeling curiously empty for no reason I could explain. The emptiness was a new development. I decided, after six beers, that I hadn't felt this way since that day I was sitting alone in the K. of C. library. And when this thought registered, I knew the problem was Jack-related. My life was far from empty professionally. Since Jack's acquittal in Troy the calls were flooding in and I could name my price for trial work. Was it, then, the loss of a political career? Like an amputated leg, that particular part of me did pain, even though it wasn't there, and yet I was simultaneously relieved at never having to be a politician. It was such a vapid way to spend your life, and a slavish game, too, slavish to the political clubroom crowd, even to the Elks Club where I was standing, a superb fragment of all I found stagnant, repulsive, and so smugly corrupt in Albany. The Democratic bagman, though it was two months till election, was already in his corner of the card room (two city detectives watching the door), accepting tithes from everybody who fed at the county courthouse or city hall troughs—janitors, lawyers growing fat from the surrogate court, vendors, bankers, cops, firemen, secretaries, clerks, contractors. The pattern was consistent with Jack's notion of how an empire should be run. Everybody pays.

Just as I liked Jack, I also liked the old bagman. He was a dandy and a curmudgeon and a wily and wise old Irishman who had read his Yeats and Wilde as well as his Croker and Tweed. I also liked the men who were next to me at the bar. They were men I'd been raised with, men who knew my father and my uncles: tradesmen and sportswriters and other lawyers and politicians and factory hands who liked pinochle and euchre and salesmen who liked to bowl and drink beer, and, of course, of course, Jack.

Most of the Elks who talked frankly with me were confused by his presence. They knew what his minions had done at the Elks Club in Catskill, which bothered them far more than the kidnapping of Streeter or making Charlie Northrup disappear. They didn't really want Jack around. But they were also awed when he walked in, flattered when he bought them a drink, and marked forever when he put his arm on their shoulder and talked baseball with them. Hello, Bill! Hello, Jack! Brotherrrrrrrrrrrrr!

"Counselor," Jack said to me when he moved in alongside me at the bar, "I'm going to buy you a new hat."

"So you're at that again," I said.

"The heat must've got to it, Marcus. It's dead for sure. Take a look."

I looked at my trusty old Panama, which had aged considerably since I last examined it, I must admit.

"Well, it's getting old, Jack, but then so are we all. And I do feel compassion for things that are deteriorating visibly."

"Whataya say, you want to take a ride?"

"Sounds sinister, Jack. My father warned me about taking rides with strange gangsters."

"Little business trip, and what the hell, it's too goddamn hot to stand here smelling armpits. The air'll do you good. Blow the stink off you."

"You're right, I could stand a change. Who's driving?"

"Hubert."

"Ah, Hubert. I still find it hard to believe you've got somebody named Hubert in your employ."

"Good kid, Hubert. Does what he's told."

We left the bar and walked out to the top of the club's stone stoop, which faced on State Street. It was middle evening, the streetlights on, but the sun still making long shadows. We looked up toward Capitol Park, where Hubert went for the car, where General Philip Sheridan, another Albany Irishman, sat astride his horse, riding into eternity. There were only the two of us on the stoop, which struck me as unnecessarily foolish, given the recurring rumor of gunmen out to get Jack.

"We make nice targets for your friends here," I said.

"Fuck it. You can't live like a rat in a hole forever."

I could only agree with that, which straightened my back. How little encouragement it takes to place oneself in jeopardy.

"What's this business trip you've got planned?"

"A small delivery to a customer."

"You don't mean you want me to join you on a booze run."

"Relax, would I do that to you? We won't be in the same vehicle with the stuff. And it's only beer. We'll follow the truck, well back. Plenty safe. Up to Troy, back down to Packy Delaney's. It's a favor for Packy and I'm glad to do it. I like The Pack."

"I do myself."

"I'm glad for the ride, too," Jack said. "Jesus, I get bored easy lately."

"We've got the same affliction."

Hubert pulled up and we headed for Stell's, a busy Troy brewery run by a gang of beer-savvy Dutchmen Jack had been doing business with for years. But the pickup and delivery of the moment would be a departure for Jack: made in a borrowed truck by the man himself, notable status reduction. His excuse was he was doing Packy a favor. "He's in a bind with his Albany supplier, hates the beer he has, but he's gotta take it." It proved to be the other way around, Packy responding to Jack's request for a loan with a pragmatic substitute—a deal. Packy would buy the beer at Jack's price, even though he didn't need it; Jack would show a profit, Packy would avoid making a cash loan that would probably never be repaid, and Packy would have the beer, at least, to show for his investment.

We drove up Broadway and through North Albany, past the streets of my own neighborhood: Emmett, Albany, Mohawk, Genesee, Erie, then the park in front of Sacred Heart Church on Walter and North Second Streets, a view which provided me with a pang of recognition and a sliver of insight which made this trip worth recording. I remembered how my father looked, sitting on a park bench in the years just before his death, teeth too prominent, like a skull's mindless grin, his brain almost as white as his hair, watching the trolleys go to Troy and back. I tried to imagine what that man, who never stole a nickel in his life, would make of his son being on Jack's payroll, a speculation which, I know, reveals more of me than of the old man.

My father was not a religious man in his youth and middle years. He routinely did his Easter duty, kept the Commandments, but often slept through the Sunday slate of masses. Yet he ended his days at daily mass, even serving for the priest when the altar boy of the day overslept. I've long tried to persuade myself that his final conversion to piety was more than simplistic fear of the next, for my father was complex, a teacher, a Latin scholar who named me for his favorite Stoic. Remembering him, then, at that moment by the park when I was also conscious of how Jack was regularly telling his beads, and when I was questioning my own irrational reading of Aquinas long after I'd lost my faith, I knew all three of us were hounded by religious confusion: Jack out of Saint Anne's, both my father and I out of Sacred Heart, products all of the ecclesiastical Irish sweat glands, obeisant before the void, trying to discover something.

And as we passed Sacred Heart, I looked at Jack and said to him, "My old man used to sit in that park and watch the world go by when he got old."

Jack craned his neck for a look, smiling at the thought. His own yellowing skin, and his teeth with too much prominence, gave me back the face of my father. And I thought then that I knew what they were both looking for. I thought: They have misplaced tomorrow and are looking for it. And the search is ruining today.

※   ※   ※

We stopped at a garage on Fourth Street in Troy to pick up the truck Jack was borrowing from a fellow named Curley, who once drove for him. Curley had gone off on his own and now had a fleet of Macks and Reos which did heavy duty on the highways on behalf of public thirst. Hubert got the keys for our truck and drove it from a back lot to the gas pump in front of the garage, where a kid attendant in overalls gassed us up with Socony.

"You want any cupcakes tonight, Legs?" the kid asked.

"Why not?" Jack said and gave him a ten-dollar bill. When the tank was full, the kid ran across the street to an old lady's grocery and came back with three cupcakes in cellophane and an opened bottle of sarsaparilla. Jack ate a cake and sucked at the soda for the kid, who wanted to be near Jack, do things for him.

"You think you can beat that federal rap on an appeal, Legs?"

"A sure thing, kid. Don't bet against me."

The kid—with his freckles, his large Irish teeth, and a cowlick his barber didn't understand—laughed and said, "Bet against you? Never do that."

"Listen, kid," Jack said, and I can hear Cagney telling Billy Halop almost the same thing years later, "don't get the wrong idea about me. I'm not going to live much longer. I got more metal in me than I got bones. Stay in school. The rackets are a bum life. There ain't no heroes in the rackets."

"I heard you were on the spot," the kid said. "That true?"

Jack gave him a happy grin. "I been on the spot all my life."

"I heard a rumor there's guys around want to get you."

"The word's even out to the kids," Jack said to me.

"I wouldn't tell 'em nothing if they come here," the kid said.

"Attaboy," Jack said.

"You know I didn't say nothin' about the panel truck."

"I know that."

"I heard one of the guys looking for you is called Goose."

"Yeah? What else do you hear?"

"That they were asking questions up in Foley's last week."

"Nothing since then?"

"Nothing."

"I heard about that," Jack said. "It's all over with. The Goose flew south."

"It's okay then," the kid said. "Good news."

"Give your old lady some good news, kid. Don't mess in the rackets."

"Okay, Legs."

Jack tipped him five and got behind the wheel of his Lincoln, which he was buying on time. Within a month he'd be too broke to keep it. I got in and we followed Hubert to the brewery, where Jack paid for the beer and saw it loaded. Then we headed for Packy's in downtown Albany. We took a back road from Troy through North Greenbush and into Rensselaer, a town like Albany, where Jack was safe passing through with wet goods, across the Dunn Bridge and up to Packy's on Green Street.

"What was that panel truck the kid mentioned?" I asked when we were rolling again.

"Heavy load of booze. We parked it there one night we were being chased. Oxie sat in it all night with a machine gun."

"That was nice advice you gave the kid. But I can't believe you don't want disciples in your own image, like the rest of us."

"Kid's too soft," Jack said. "If he was tougher, I'd tell him, 'Go ahead kid, see how tough you really are,' line him up behind all the other tough guys waiting to die young, let him take his chances. Sure I'd tell him about the easy money, easy pussy, living high. But I like that kid."

"You liked Fogarty too. Why'd you take him in?"

"He reminded me of Eddie."

"But you let him sink."

"Did I? You had more say over that than me."

"I told you I get paid for what I do. And it was you who said the hell with him, that he was never any good."

"He wasn't. You saw he turned stool pigeon. He was a weak sister. What'd he expect me to do, mother him? Rothstein not only dumped me, he tried to kill me. But I never blew the whistle on him. Never trust a pussy freak. Fogarty's cock ran ahead of him like a headlight. Made a sucker of a good guy. Why not let him sink? I'd let anybody sink except Eddie. And Alice and Marion. I'd even let you sink, Marcus."

"I know. And I'd do the same for you, Jack. But the difference is that I'm just a businessman and you're a prick in your heart."

"Pricks are the only ones got it made in this world."

"That's a chump's line."

"Maybe. I look like a chump these days."

"Chumps never know who their real friends are."

"Friends," said Jack. "I got no friends. You and me, we're just knockin' around, passing the time. You're all right, Marcus, and I always said so, but I only had one friend my whole goddamn life. My brother Eddie. Came down from Saranac when he was dying to help me during the Hotsy thing. Christ, we set up a meeting in the subway, Twenty-eighth Street, and he was all dressed up, coconut straw, brown palm beach, and a new white silk shirt with a lemon tie, looked like a million except you could've got two other guys inside the suit with him. He wanted to make collections for me, wanted to run the operation while I was hiding out. Said he'd do anything and the poor bastard could hardly breathe. We talked an hour, and when we got up to go, I was holding him and he started giving me the Holy Roller malarkey. He got religion up in Saranac and they were calling him The Saint. Used to go around visiting in his wheelchair, seeing guys who couldn't move a muscle, who were afraid to fucking breathe. Really selling me hard, and so I said to him, forget that guff, Ed, it's not my style. You'll come around, he said, and I say in a pig's whistle, and he keeps at it, so I finally say will you for crissake shut up about it? And we're up in the street by then, so I hailed a taxi to get him back to the Commodore where he had a room. And when I let go of his arm, he fell down and Christ Jesus, he let out a cough I thought his whole insides was liquid. Death rattle is what it was. Fantastic horrible goddamn gurgle. He only lasted a couple of months more. Shortened his life coming down to help me out. Couldn't do a goddamn thing for anybody, but he tried, the son of a bitch tried with all he fucking had. That's what's friends, Marcus. That's what I call friends."

Jack, the gush, was crying.

                              *   *   *

Old Joe Delaney opened The Parody Club in 1894 to appease a capricious thirst that took hold of him at odd hours, often after the city's saloons had closed. He ran it until 1919 and dated his retirement to the day a hod carrier swooned at the bar and crumpled like a corpse. Delaney's son Packy (né Patrick), apprenticing as a bartender after a stint with the AEF, looked the hoddy over, kicked his ass, and yelled in his ear, "Get up and go home, you stewbum."

"A born saloonkeeper," the elder Delaney rejoiced, yielding swiftly then to the pull of retirement in his favorite chair, where he died five years later with a bent elbow and foam on his handlebars.

Music greeted us when we walked through the old swinging doors, original doors that led to the Delaney time capsule. We walked under a four-globed chandelier and a four-bladed ceiling fan, past photos on the walls of old railroad men, old politicians, old bare-knuckle fighters, dead Maud Gonne's likeness sketched on a handbill announcing her appearance at Hibernian Hall to raise funds for a free Ireland, defunct Hibernian Society marching down State Street on a sunny Saint Patrick's Day in '95, disbanded private fire companies standing at attention in front of their pumpers, K. of C. beer drinkers, long in their graves, tapping a keg at a McKown's Grove clambake. I went back to Packy's now and again until the place burned down in 1942, when fire dumped all that old history of faces into the powdery ashpit. Nothing ever changed there, till then.

Flossie was making the music when we walked in, the piano being her second talented instrument of pleasure. Flossie was a saucy blond cupcake then, not working directly out of Packy's, where sins of the flesh were traditionally prohibited on premises. But she was advertising from the piano bench and specializing in private sessions to augment her income after her musical workday. Ah, Floss. How well I remember your fingers, so educated to the music of joy.

She was jangling away at the keyboard while Packy and another man delivered up some two-part harmony, not half-bad, of "Arrah-Go-On, I'm Gonna Go Back to Oregon," a song from the war years.

"Now this is something like it," Jack said, and he walked ahead of me past the crowded bar toward an empty back table that gave a view of the door. Hubert, having deposited the truck for unloading inside

Packy's garage, followed us; but Jack told him, "Watch the door and the street." And without a word Hubert went to the end of the bar and stood there alone while Packy pined for Oregon, where they'd call him Uncle Pat, not Uncle John. He gave Jack a smile on that line and an extended left arm that welcomed and introduced the hero to the customers who hadn't yet recognized him; Jack waved to half a dozen men at the bar looking our way.

"You know those fellows?" he asked me.

"I guess I've seen one or two around town."

"All thieves or hustlers. This is a good place to buy yourself a new suit or a new radio cheap."

Jack bought the drinks himself at the bar, then settled into a chair and gave full attention to Flossie's piano and Packy's baritone. Packy came to the table when his harmony ran out.

"Fellow singing with me says he knows you, Jack."

"I don't place him."

"Retired railroad cop and not a bad fellow for a cop. Nice tenor too, and he carries a tune. Hey, Milligan."

The tenor came over and looked at us through cataract lenses. His hair was pure white and standing tall, and his magnified eyes and cryptic smile gave him the look of a man in disguise.

"You don't remember me," he said to Jack.

"Give me a clue."

"Silk. New Jersey. 1924."

"Ah, right. I make you now. You pinched me."

"You've got it. You were stealing the railroad blind, you and your brother."

"I remember. You were in the house when I came home. Sure, I remember you now, you son of a bitch. You sapped me."

"Only after you tried to kick me in the balls."

"I forgot that."

"You were out of jail quicker than I put you in."

"I had some classy political connections in those days."

"I know all about it. You remember anything else about that night? Remember singing a song coming up the stairs?"

"A song."

"It was a favorite of mine and I said to myself, now this can't be such a bad fellow if he knows a song like that. Just about then you saw me and tried to kick me in the crotch."

"I can't remember any song, Milligan, that your name?"

"Milligan's right. You were drunk and howling it out like a banshee. Listen, see if you remember."

He backstepped and put his hand on his stomach, then gave us:

> There's an old time melody,
> I heard long ago . . .

"I damn well remember that," Jack said. "One of my favorites."

> Mother called it the rosary,
> She sang it soft and low . . .

Jack nodded, grinned, sat back, and listened as most of the customers were also listening now, not merely to Milligan, but to Milligan singing for Legs Diamond.

> Without any rhyme,
> I mean without any prose,
> I even forgot
> How the melody goes . . .

Flossie found Milligan's key and trilled some soft background chords, a flicker of faint melody.

> But ten baby fingers . . .

And then Jack could hold it back no longer and added a spoken line: "And ten baby toes . . ." And then together he and Milligan finished the song:

> She'd watch them by the setting sun,
> And when her daily work was done,
> She'd count them each and every one,
> That was my Mother's ro-sa-reeeeeeee.

Flossie gave them a re-intro, and with Jack on melody, Milligan on first tenor, and Packy on baritone, the harmonizers sang mournfully, joyously, and profoundly out of the musical realm of their Irish Catholic souls. They sang for all the children who ever had mothers, for all the mothers who ever had children, and when it was over, Jack called out, "Flossie, love, let's do it again."

"Anything for you, Jack. Anything you want."

And the harmonizers moved closer together, their arms on each other's shoulders, and began once more:

> There's an old time melody,
> I heard long ago . . .

We sang songs that way for three hours and drove everybody out of the bar, including the bartender. Packy made our drinks and Flossie stayed and played for us, long after her advertising day had ended without a client. But I think the Floss anticipated things to come, and rejected all Johns who had no hint of transcendence about their requests. I was drinking beer and Jack was not quite reckless, but was at the boilermakers. And so both of us were a little slow on the uptake when Hubert, back in from a reconnaissance walk up the block, quickstepped over to our table and spoke his first words of the musical evening: "There's a guy in a car across the street, Jack. Two guys, in fact. One at the wheel looks like he's got that eyepatch you been looking for."

*   *   *

"Would that be The Goose?" Packy asked. "I heard he was around asking questions about you."

"Probably him," Jack said.

"Then we've got to get you out of here," said The Pack.

Of our little group of six, only Milligan did not know The Goose. But he asked no questions. The song was over, and Flossie's face showed it. Jack, on the other hand, seemed without tension, which, of course, he was not. Yet his control under the circumstances was almost equal to having none.

"It's tricky with The Goose," he said. "He might break in here any minute and start blasting. That's nonprofessional, but he's crazy all the way now. People have to remember that."

"Sure he's crazy," said Packy. "In and out of town all summer asking questions."

"He's made a game of it," Jack said. "He wants me to sweat."

"But now he's outside," Hubert said, understandably perplexed by a discussion at such a moment. My own first thoughts were to evacuate the uninvolved from the premises, myself included. Yet it seemed cowardly to think of running away from only the possibility of somebody else's trouble. Yet there *was* the Hotsy to recall, where innocents were nicked by crossfire. So if you didn't run away, you might eventually be obliged to duck. It was the price of being Jack's companion.

"Oh, sweet mother," Flossie said when the reality of The Goose hit her. Her face collapsed then, perhaps into a vision of Billy Blue. She was having a good time just before Billy got it, too.

"I'll call the dicks, have 'em come down and pick him up," said Packy, nerve ends flaring, spinning on a proprietor's understandable confusion.

"Pick him up for what?" Jack said. "Sitting in a car?"

"I can think of half a dozen charges if necessary," I said. "Getting them here seems to be the priority."

Packy was already at the phone. Hubert locked the front door and said the two men were still in the maroon sedan, fifty feet from The Parody, across the street.

"Maybe you should just stay here all night," I said.

Jack nodded, aware of that possibility. Milligan pushed his chair away from the table, but didn't get up, an ambiguous gesture which suited an ex-cop in such a situation.

"You don't know if they'll come or not," Packy said after his call. "I got Conlon on the desk, the prick. You never know what they're gonna do for you. Or to you. He said the lieutenant was at a big fire up in the West Albany railroad shops. He'll try to tear a car loose. The prick, the prick."

"They want me dead, too," Jack said.

"I never liked that Conlon," Milligan said, "but I never took a backstep from him or any of them up there. I'll call him."

"It's not your problem, Milligan," Jack said, amused by the old man's concern.

"I always try to keep down violence in the city," said Milligan. "Valuable citizens involved here"—and he gave me a quick eye and a wink and went to the phone. I was left to look at Jack, who'd barely been able to move a shotglass with his left arm all night. He was living mainly by the use of one hand, a liability, should he be forced to confront The Goose in any physical way. Hubert was a good shot, which was one reason Jack hired him; but so was The Goose, and who knew about his faceless helper? Jack would be on the short end of any fight, a fact I was just coming to understand.

Milligan came back. "I called Cap Ronan, but no answer. Maybe he's out at the fire, too. Then I called Conlon again and told him the trouble here personally. He got the message." Milligan sat down and waited, though he was free to leave. But he would then miss how it all came out, miss the test of cop-to-cop influence.

No police came. Sorry, Milligan.

I've since concluded Jack was right. They would have welcomed his assassination, were perhaps even aware one was impending. The police were called often about Jack during this period: Did Diamond get it yet? . . . He's going to get it tonight. I sensed then, my innocence on such matters at last thinning out, that Jack was not really an enemy of the police as much as he was an object of their envy. I can imagine a roomful of them talking about ways to annihilate his privilege.

Hubert announced from the door: "They put their headlights on. They're moving."

"Thank God," said the Floss.

"They're probably not going anyplace," Jack said. And he was right again. Within a few minutes they had parked facing the opposite direction, on The Parody side of the street now, still about fifty feet away.

"They just wanted to look in," Jack said.

The car movement prodded all of us except Jack into standing up and moving around. We turned our attention to each other, and finally, one by one, to Jack for the decision was his alone. Go or stay? Barricade or open season? Packy would probably resent, but maybe not resist a barricade fight. Damage would be minimal, apart from any death, but the legend would be immortal, a shrine of gold established in perpetuity.

Only Hubert lacked doubt about what he was to do. His pistol was already part of our little group because of the way he kept fingering it inside his coat pocket. Jack knew what he was doing when he hired Hubert.

"You have an extra pistol?" Jack asked Packy.

"How many? I got a collection."

"Two then, and shells."

Packy unlocked a closet beneath the back bar and brought out a pair of unmatched handguns, one an old Smith and Wesson .32 which I came to know well, its patent dating to 1877, an ugly little bone-handled, hammerless bellygun that was giving in to rust and had its serial number at the base of the butt filed away. No serious gunfighter would have given it room in the cellar. Packy had probably bartered it for beer. Useless, foolhardy, aggravating weapon. It had a broken mechanism behind the firing pin then and still has, but under ideal circumstances it would fire, and it still will. Ugly, deformed little death messenger, like a cobra on a crutch.

"This is insane," I finally said. "We sit here watching a man prepare for a gun battle, and we know damn well there are other ways to solve the problem. The whole world hasn't gone nuts. Why not call the *state* police?"

"Call the governor," Jack said. "He'll want to keep me healthy."

"Not a bad idea," I said.

"Call my relatives in Philadelphia," Jack said. "Call your own relatives. Call all your friends and tell them we've got an open house here, free booze. Build up a mob in fifteen minutes."

"Another brilliant idea," I said.

"But what do I do tomorrow night?" Jack said.

He loaded one of Packy's pistols while we thought about that one. Flossie decided she was not ready for fatalism.

"If you go upstairs, he'll never find you," she said.

"Where upstairs?"

"My upstairs. Where I go in a pinch."

"You got a place upstairs?"

"A place, yeah. But not really a place."

"He comes in here, don't you figure he'll look upstairs?"

"He'd never find my place, that's the whole point. If you're up there and we go, and the place is dark, he'd never find you in a thousand years. It ain't even in this same building."

"The Goose is thick, but thorough," Jack said. "I wouldn't trust him not to find it."

"Then let's go meet the Polack son of a bitch on the street," Hubert said. "Goddamn fucking sitting ducks here, the hell with it."

"None of this makes sense," I said. "Going, staying, not getting any help, not even trying to get any."

"One night at a time," Jack said. "You work it out slow. I know a lot of dead guys tried to solve a whole thing all at once when they weren't ready. And listen. It's also time you all cleared out."

"I think I'll have another beer," I said, and I sat down at the end barstool farthest from the door. Milligan sat alongside me and said, "I'll have one for the road."

"I'll be closing up after one drink," Packy said, going behind the bar. "I'll put the lights out and leave. I'll get a cop down here if I have to drag him down with a towrope."

Jack shrugged.

"Upstairs then," he said to Flossie. "I guess that's the place."

"Follow me," she said.

"Is there a way back down except through here?"

"Two stairways," Packy said. "It's an old loft. They used to have a peanut butter factory up there."

"Jesus, a peanut butter factory?"

"It faces the other side, on Dongan Avenue, and there's no windows. Flossie is right. Nobody'd ever think we were connected to it. Just a quirk of these antique buildings. They made connections you wouldn't believe in these old relics."

"Nothing'll happen if The Goose *doesn't* come in here," I said. "Isn't that right?"

"I don't think he'll come inside anyplace," Jack said, "and he don't want to hurt anybody but me. But he's a maniac, so how do you know anything he'll do? You all should wait for Flossie to come back down and then clear the hell out of here. Hubert and I can wait it out."

That seemed workable. But I said, "I'll keep you company," and Jack laughed and laughed. I didn't think it was that funny, but he said,

"All right, let's move," and I took my bottle of beer and followed him and Hubert to the place where there was no longer any peanut butter.

✻   ✻   ✻

Flossie led us up an unsafe staircase, through musty corridors, through a rough doorway in the brick wall of another building, and through still more corridors, all in darkness, each of us holding the hand of the other. When she finally lit a kerosene lamp, we were in the loft, a large empty space with a warped floor, a skylight with some of its panes broken and now an access route to a pigeon perch. The pigeons had created a pair of three-inch stalagmites with their droppings, rather brilliant aim, as I remember it. The room held only an old Army cot with an olive-drab blanket and a pillow without a pillowcase. A raw wooden box stood alongside the bed for use as a table, and a straight-back wooden chair stood alongside that. There was nothing else in the room except for the cobwebs, the dust, the rat leavings, and a plentiful scatter of peanut shells.

"You know, Jack," Flossie said, "I never use this place except in special emergencies that can't wait. I keep a sheet downstairs. I could go get it."

"Maybe another time, kid," Jack said, and squeezed her rump with his good hand.

"You haven't grabbed me in years, Jack."

"I'd love to think about getting back to that."

"Well, don't you neglect it. Oh, sweet Jesus, look at that."

She pointed to a wall behind Jack where an enormous rat, bigger than a jackrabbit I'd say, looked out at us, his eyes shining red in the light, white markings under his jaw. He was halfway out of a hole in the wall, about four feet from the floor. He looked like a picture on the wall. As the light reached him, we could see he was gray, brown, and white, the weirdest, handsomest rat I ever saw, and in the weirdest position. A bizarre exhibit, if stuffed, I thought.

"I never saw *him* up here before," Flossie said.

The rat watched us with brazen calm.

"He was here first tonight," Jack said, and he sat on the bed and took off his suit coat. Flossie put the lamp on the box table and told us, "I'll come back and let you know what's going on. I don't know if Delaney's going out, but I'm damn well staying."

"Lovely, Flossie, lovely," said Jack.

"He'd never find his way up here, Jack," she said. "Just stay put."

"I want Hubert to check all the stairs. Can he be seen from outside if he walks with the lamp?"

"Not a chance."

Flossie took the lamp, leaving Jack and me in darkness, the stars and a bright moony sky the only source of our light.

"Some great place to wind up," Jack said.

"I'm sitting down while I consider it," I said and groped toward the chair. "I mean while I consider what the hell I'm doing here."

"You're crazy. I always knew it. You wear crazy hats."

Flossie came back with the kerosene lamp and put it back on the box.

"I lit one of my candles and gave it to Hubert," she said. "I'll be back."

Some moths joined us in the new light and Jack sat down on the cot. The rat was still watching us. Jack put the two pistols Packy gave him on the box. He also took a small automatic out of his back pocket. It fit in his palm, the same kind of item he fired between Weissberg's feet in Germany.

"You've been carrying that around?"

"A fella needs a friend," he said.

"That'd be lovely, picked up with a gun at this point. How many trials do you think you can take?"

"Hey, Marcus, I'm tryin' to stay alive. You understand that?"

"Let Hubert carry the weapons. That's what he's for."

"Right. Soon as I hear The Goose is gone. Long as he's in town there's liable to be shooting, and I might stay alive if I can shoot back. You on tap for that?"

He picked up the Smith and Wesson and handed it to me.

"The Goose only wants me, but he'd shoot anything that moved or breathed. I don't want to make it tough for you, old pal, but that's where you're livin' right this minute. You're breathing."

He had a point. I loaded the weapon. In a pinch I could say I pocketed the pistol when we all fled from the maniac.

Jack fell backward on Flossie's dusty cot and said to me, "Marcus, I decided something. Right now there's nothing in the whole fucking world I want to steal."

I thought that was a great line and it was my turn to laugh. Jack laughed, too, then said, "Why is that so funny?"

"Why? Well, here I am, full of beer and holding a gun, joined up with a wild man to hide from a psychopath, watching the stars, staring at a red-eyed rat, and listening to Jack Diamond, a master thief of our day, telling me he's all through stealing. Jesus Christ, this is an insane life, and I don't know the why of any of it."

"Well, I don't either. I don't say I'm swearing off, because I am what I am. But I say I don't want to steal anything now. I don't want to make another run. I don't want to fight The Goose. I suppose I will, sooner or later, him or some other bum they send."

"Who is they?"

"Take your pick. They get in line to shoot at me."

"But you won't shoot back anymore?"

"I don't know. Maybe, maybe not."

"The papers would eat this up. Jack Diamond's vengeance ends in peanut butter factory."

"Anybody can get revenge. All it costs is a few dollars. I don't want to touch it anymore, not personally."

"Are you just tired? Weary?"

"Maybe something like that."

"You don't believe in God, so it's not your conscience."

"No."

"It's caution, but not just caution."

"No."

"It's self-preservation, but not just that either."

"You could say that."

"Now I've got it. You don't know what's going on either."

"Right, pal."

"The mystery of Jack Diamond's new life, or how he found peace among the peanut shells."

I was too tired, too hot, too drunk to sit up any longer. I slid off the chair onto the floor, clutching the remnants of my beer in my left hand, the snotty little Smith and Wesson in my right, believing with an odd, probably impeachable faith, that if I survived this night I would surely become rich somehow and that I would tell the story of the red-eyed rat to my friends, my clients and my grandchildren. The phrase "If I survived" gave me a vicious whack across the back of the head. That was a temporary terror, and it eventually left me. But after this night I knew I would never again feel safe under any circumstances. Degeneration of even a marginal sense of security. Kings would die in the bed-chambers of their castles. Assassination squads would reach the inner sanctum of the Presidential palace. The lock on the bedroom window would not withstand the crowbar.

Such silly things. Of course, this goes on, Marcus, of course. Mild paranoia is your problem.

Yes. That's it. It goes on and finally I know it. I truly know it and feel it.

No. There is more to it than that. Jack knows more.

*   *   *

Flossie came running. Cops down in the street. Taking Goose away. You can come down. Packy's buying. Milligan got through.

Six detectives, oh, yes. How lovely.

Jack leaped off the bed and was gone before I could sit up.

"Are you comin' too, love? Or can't you move?" the Floss asked me. In my alcoholic kerosene light she was the Cleopatra of peanut-butterland. Her blond hair was the gold of an Egyptian sarcophagus, her eyes the Kohinoor diamond times two.

"Don't go, Flossie," I said and stunned her. I'd known the Floss now and again, sumptuous knowledge, but not in a couple of years. It was past, my interest in professionals. I had a secretary, Frances. But now Flossie's breasts rose and fell beneath her little cotton transparency in a way that had been inviting all of us all night long, and when she had half turned to leave, when my words of invitation stopped her, I caught a vision of her callipygian subtleties, like the ongoing night, never really revealed to these eyes before.

She came toward me as I lay flat on my back, ever so little bounce in the splendid upheaval of her chest, vision too of calf without blemish, without trace of muscular impurity. None like Floss on this earth to-night, not for Marcus.

"Do you want something from me?" she said, bending forward, improving the vision fiftyfold, breathing her sweet, alcoholic whore's breath at me. I loosened my hand from the beer and reached for her, touched her below the elbow, first flesh upon first flesh of the evening. Client at last.

"Come up on the cot, love," she said, but I shook my head and pulled the blanket to the floor. She doubled it as the moon shone on her. The rat was watching us. I raised the pistol and potshot it, thinking of it dying with a bullet through its head and hanging there on the wall; then thinking of framing it or stuffing it in that position, photographing the totality of the creature in its limp deathperch and titling it "Night Comes to the Peanut Butter Factory."

My shot missed and the rat disappeared back into the wall.

"Jesus, Mary, and Holy Saint Joseph," Flossie said at the shot, which sounded like a cannon. "What are you doing?"

"Potting the rat."

"Oh, honeyboy, you're so drunk. Give us that pistol."

"Of course, Flossie"—and she put it on the table out of my reach. The stars shone on her then as she unbuttoned her blouse, unhooked her skirt, folded the clothes carefully and lay them at the foot of the cot. She wore nothing beneath them, the final glory. She helped prepare me as the men moved in with the peanut butter machine and the women arrived to uncrate the nuts.

"It's been a while, hasn't it?" the Floss said to me.

"Only yesterday, Floss, only yesterday."

"Sometimes I feel that way, Marcus, but not tonight."

"It's always yesterday, Floss. That's what's so great."

"Tonight is something else."

"What is it?"

"It's better. It's got some passion in it."

"Lovely passion."

"I don't get at it very often."

"None of us do."

The rat came back to his perch and watched us. The sodden air rose up through the skylight and mated with the nighttime breezes. The machine began to whirr and a gorgeous ribbon of golden peanut butter flowed smoothly out of its jaws. Soon there were jars of it, crates of jars, stacks of crates.

"Isn't it lovely?" said Flossie, flat on her back.

"It's the most ineffable of products," I said. "The secret substance of life. If only the alchemists knew of this."

"Who were the alchemists?" she asked.

"Shhhh," I said.

And instead of talking, Flossie made me a peanut butter sandwich, and we fortified ourselves against the terror.

Jack O' The Clock

JACK WALKED UP SECOND STREET IN TROY, dressed in his double-breasted chinchilla coat and brown velour fedora, walked between his attorney and his wife, a family man today, Kiki discreetly tucked away in the love nest. Jack walked with his hands in his pocket, the press swarming toward him as he was recognized. How do you feel, Legs? Any statement, Mr. Gorman? Do you have faith in your husband's innocence, Mrs. Diamond?

"You guys are responsible for all this," Jack said to the newsmen. "I wouldn't be in trouble if it wasn't for you sonsabitches."

"Keep out the cuss words, boys," I said to the press. I smiled my Irish inheritance, easing the boys.

"What'll you make your case on, counselor?" Tipper Kelly said. "Same as the first trial? An alibi?"

"Our case is based wholly on self-defense," I said.

Self-defense against a kidnapping charge. Jack laughed. His loyal wife laughed. The newsmen laughed and made notes. A *bon mot* to start the day.

"How do you feel about all this, Mrs. Diamond?"

"I'll always be at his side," said Alice.

"Don't bother her," said Jack.

"She's just a loyal wife to a man in trouble," I said. "That's why she's here."

"That's right," said Alice. "I'm a loyal wife. I'll always be loyal, even after they kill him."

"We mustn't anticipate events," I said.

The gray neo-classical Rensselaer County courthouse, with its granite pillars, stood tall over Legs Diamond: legs of Colossus, as this peanut man walked beneath them. Birds roosted on the upper ledges. A stars and stripes snapped in the breeze. As Legs brushed the wall with his shoulder, dust fell from the pillars.

The Pathé News cameraman noted the action and the consequence and asked Legs to come back and do it again. But, of course, Legs could not commit precisely the same act a second time, since every act enhanced or diminished him as well as the world around him. Yet it was that precise moment, that push, that almost imperceptible fall of dust, the cameraman wanted on film.

As the crowd moved into the courtroom the cameraman exercising a bit of creative enterprise, lifted Legs Diamond's coat and hat from the cloakroom. He dressed his slightly built assistant cameraman in the garments and sent him up the stairs to brush the wall for a repeat performance.

The Pathé News cameraman then filmed it all. Inspecting the floor for a closeup, he discovered that the dust that fell was not dust at all, but pigeon shit.

*   *   *

In the crowded hallway of the courthouse, during a brief moment when no one was holding his arm, a youth Jack did not know separated himself from the mob and whispered, "You're gonna get it, Diamond, no matter what happens here. Wanna take it now?" Jack looked at the kid—maybe nineteen, maybe twenty-two, with a little fuzz on his lip and a bad haircut—and he laughed. The kid eased himself back into the crowd, and Jack, pulled by me toward the courtroom, lost sight of him.

"Kid was braggin'," Jack said, telling me about the threat. "He looked like a hundred-dollar pay killer. Too green to be in the big money." Jack shook his head in a way I took to be an amused recognition of his own lowly condition. *They send punk kids after me.*

But I also saw a spot of white on his lower lip, a spot of bloodlessness. He bit at the spot, again and again. The bite hardened his face, as if he were sucking the blood out of the point of his own fear, so that when the threat became tangible it would not bleed him into weakness. It struck me as a strange form of courage, but not as I knew it for myself: no intellectual girding, but rather a physiological act: a Jack Diamond of another day, recollected not by the brain but by the body, his back to a cave full of unexplored dangers of its own, staring out beyond a puny fire, waiting for the unspecified enemy who tonight, or tomorrow night, or the next, would throw a shadow across that indefensible hearth.

*   *   *

By eight o'clock on the evening of the first day of Jack's second Troy trial, both the prosecution and the defense attorneys had exhausted their peremptory challenges and the final juror was at last chosen. He was an auto mechanic who joined two farmers, a printer, an engineer, a mason, a lumber dealer, an electrical worker, two laborers, a merchant, and a plant foreman as the peers, the twelve-headed judge, of Legs Diamond. I had sought to relieve the maleness by accepting two female jurors, but Jack's appeal to women had been too widely documented for the prosecution to take such a risk, and both were challenged.

The prosecution's chief trial counsel was a man named Clarence Knought, who wore a gray, hard-finish, three-button herringbone with vest, gray tie, watch chain, and rimless glasses. His thin lips, receding hairline, gaunt figure, and voice, which lacked modulation but gained relentless moral rectitude through its monotony, provided the jury with the living image of New York State integrity, American Puritanism, and the Columbian quest for perfect justice. He spoke for twenty minutes, outlining the case against Legs Diamond, whom he called Diamond. He recapitulated the kidnapping of Streeter and Bartlett in his opening summary, savoring the punching of Streeter, the death threats, the burning and the hanging, details which landed on the jurors' faces like flying cockroaches. The recapitulation set off an uncontrollable twitching in one juror's cheek, dilated just about every eye, wrinkled eyebrows, and dried up lips. Having filled the jurors with terror, Knought congratulated them.

"You are privileged," he told them. "You have the chance to rid this nation of one of its worst scourges. You have the chance to put behind bars this man Diamond, this figure of unmitigated evil, this conscienceless devil who has been arrested twenty-five times for every crime from simple assault to foul, vicious murder, whose association with the worst men of our time has been widely reported in the press and whose record of having cheated justice again and again is an appalling blot on our national image. Shall this nation be ruled by the rod? Shall this ogre of bestial behavior paralyze every decent man's heart? You twelve can end this travesty, put him in the penitentiary where he belongs."

Knought breathed fury, thumped the railing of the jury box with his fist, then walked to his chair and sat down in a cloud of legitimized wrath.

I rose slowly from my chair alongside Jack, this thought in my head as I did: O *priggish stringbean, thank you for befouling my client with your excremental denunciation, with the ordurous funk of your morality, for you now give me the opportunity to wipe this beshitted coun-*

tenance clean and show the human face beneath the fetid desecration.

My image before the jury was calculatedly bumpkinish, my clothes workingman's best, aspiring to shabby genteel. I tweaked my bow tie and ran my fingers through my unruly head of hair, which I was told, seemed as gifted with wild statement as the brain it covered. The head was leonine, the mane controlled just this side of bushy frazzle. I wore an apple-red vest, high contrast to my baggy-kneed brown tweed suit. I tucked thumbs in vest and unleashed the major weapon of the defense—my voice—that timbre of significance, that resonant spume of the believer, that majestic chord of a man consecrated to the revelation of boilingly passionate truths. I said:

"I expect low blows from the prosecution's lawyers—all seven of them. Are you aware, my friends, that the state has seven lawyers climbing over one another in a frantic effort to railroad one frail man into jail? Yes, I expected their low blows, but never such base name calling as we have just heard—'figure of unmitigated evil,' 'conscienceless devil,' 'ogre of bestial behavior.' I would never have dreamed of telling you what I am about to tell if this champion of self-righteousness had not been so vitriolic a few moments ago, so full of acid and poison toward my client. But I will tell you now. I will tell you of the little old lady—no, I won't disguise her vocation, not now. A little old Catholic nun, she was, and she came to this courtroom less than an hour ago to talk with Jack Diamond, only a few steps from where you are seated. She didn't see him, for he was otherwise occupied. She saw me, however, and I will see to it that she gets her wish, for she came here for one reason only—to see the man who was once a boy at her knee. Jackie Diamond was the name she knew him by, a boy she described as one of the most devout Catholic children she has ever known. She sees that boy still in the face of the man you know as Legs Diamond, that mythical figure of unmitigated evil the prosecutor has invented. This woman had heard such cruel insults hurled before at the boy she knew. She had heard them for years. She had read them in the newspapers. But that little old woman, that creature of God Almighty's very own army, sat down in that room with me for five minutes and talked to me about Jackie Diamond's prayers, his prayers for his mother, a woman who died too early, about the Diamond home and family in Philadelphia. And when she was through with her reminiscing she told me precisely what she thought about all those accusations against the boy whose gaunt, troubled face she hardly recognized when she saw it across the room. 'They're all lies. Mr. Gorman,' she said to me, 'fiendish lies! Now that I have seen his face for myself I know those were lies, Mr. Gorman. I teach children, Mr. Gorman, and I have boys and girls in my charge who delight in drowning puppies and stabbing cats and watching them slowly perish, and I know evil when I see it in the eyes of a human being. I came here today to see for myself whether my memory had deceived me, whether I knew good when I saw it, whether I knew evil. I have now seen the eyes of Jack Diamond in this room and I am as certain as I am of God's love that whatever on earth that man may have done, he is not an evil man. I have verified this for myself, Mr. Gorman. I have verified it.' "

When I finished the rest of my oratory and sat down at the table, Jack leaned over and whispered: "That nun business was terrific. Where did you dig her up?"

"She wandered in during the recess," I said, eyes downcast, scribbling a businesslike doodle on a yellow pad. "She's a regular in the courthouse. Collects nickels for the poor."

"Does she really know anything about me?"

I looked at my client, astounded.

"How the hell should I know?" I retorted.

*   *   *

The trial proceeded as the first one had in July, with two parades of witnesses for and against Jack. We used fewer for the defense, treading lightly after the perjury indictment from the first trial.

I made two points I remember fondly. The first was a countercharacterization of Streeter, who had been dubbed "a son of the soil," by the prosecution. I had not thought to say it in July, but we rise to our challenges, and I said he might better be called a son of the apple tree, which once again reduced the kidnapping to a bootleggers' feud.

I also asked a juror, a wretched little popinjay, whether he thought God loved Legs Diamond. "God made little green apples," he said to me crisply, "but he also put worms in 'em." He got a laugh at Jack's expense, but I liked his theology and kept him. He wore an orange shirt and I knew my man. He'd have been in line for Jack's autograph if he hadn't been on the jury. He turned out to be a vigorous partisan for acquittal. Jack was, of course acquitted, December 17, 1931, at 8:03 P.M. The crowd in the street sent up its usual cheer.

I was standing at Keeler's Men's Bar in Albany a week after the trial, talking to the barman about Jack, and I resurrected a story he told me about a day in 1927 when he was walking in Central Park with his brother Eddie and Eddie's baby boy. Jack had the boy in his arms, and they'd paused on a hill which I can picture even now. Jack was tossing the boy and catching him when he saw a car coming with a gun barrel sticking out its window, a vision to which he had been long sensitized. He tossed the baby feet-first into a bushy blue spruce, yelling the news to brother Ed, and both dove in the opposite direction from the baby as the machine gun chopped up the sod where they'd been standing.

Nobody was hit: the baby bounced off the tree and rolled to safety under a lilac bush. And after I'd told this tale, a fellow tippler at the bar asked, "How many people did he kill?" I said I didn't know, and then, without apparent malice, without actually responding to my baby story, the fellow said, "Yeah, I remember a lot of otherwise intelligent people used to think he was a nice guy."

I told the man he was a horse's ass and walked to the other end of the bar to finish my drink. Intelligent people? The man was an insurance salesman. What could he possibly know about intelligent people?

I am bored by people who keep returning life to a moral plane, as if we were reducible, now, to some Biblical concept or its opposite, as if all our history and prehistory had not conditioned us for what we've become. It's enough to make a moral nigger out of a man. The niggers are down there, no doubt about it. But Jack didn't put them there and neither did I. When we get off the moral gold standard, when the man of enormous wealth is of no more importance to anybody than the man in rags, then maybe we'll look back at our own day as a day of justifiable social wrath.

Meantime, the game is rising, not leveling.

Jack taught me that.

Cured me.

(Brother Wolf, are you listening?)

Dove Street runs north and south in Albany through what for years was the rooming house district on the fringe of downtown. Number 67 sits on the west side of the street between Hudson Avenue and Jay Street, a two-story brick building with a six-step wooden stoop, a building not unlike the house on East Albert Street in Philadelphia where Jack lived as a child. The basement shoemaker, the druggist up the block, the grocery and garage at the corner of Hudson Avenue, the nurses and the masseuse next door and across the street and all other life-support systems in the neighborhood were dark at 4:15 A.M. on Friday, December 18, 1931, when Jack pulled up in front of 67 Dove in his hired cab, Frankie Teller at the wheel.

Teller parked and ran around to open the passenger door, took Jack's arm, helped him out. Teller held the arm while Jack stood up, and together they walked raggedly up the stoop. Jack found his key, but it remained for Teller to open the door with it. The two men then walked up the stairs together and into the room at the front of the house, overlooking the street. Jack took off his hat, and then, with Teller's help, his coat, and sat on the side of the bed, which was angled diagonally, foot facing the windows that looked down on the street.

"Frankie," Jack said. And he smiled at his driver.

"Yeah, Jack."

"Frankie, I'll duke you tomorrow."

"Sure, Jack, don't worry about it."

"Duke you in the morning."

"Sure, Jack, sure. Anything else I can do for you? You all right here alone?"

"Just get outa here and let me sleep."

"Right away. Just want you settled in all right."

"I'm in."

"Tomorrow, then."

"Tomorrow," Jack said.

Frankie Teller went downstairs and got into his car and drove south on Dove Street, back to Packy's to carry the news that Jack was tucked in. A block to the north on the west side of the street a dark red sedan idled with its lights out.

During the eight hours and fifteen minutes that elapsed between his acquittal and the moment when he sat on the bed and looked into the mirror of the scratched and flaking oak dresser in his Dove Street room, Jack had been seeking an antidote to false elation. The jury foreman's saying not guilty created an instant giddiness in him that he recognized. He'd felt it when he saw Streeter's truck in front of him on the road, and he felt it on the ship when he decided not to give Biondo back his money. He could drown in reasons for not yielding the cash and for giving Streeter the heat. But none explained why a man would keep anything that brought on that much trouble, or why a man would jeopardize his entire setup in life for a truckload of cider. And so he feared the giddiness, knew it was to be resisted.

When he'd tossed his forty-dollar brown velour hat onto the bed, it had hit the threadbare spread and rolled off. He folded his brown chinchilla coat (two grand, legitimately acquired) over the footboard, and it too slipped to the floor. When he left the courthouse and saw the newsmen backing away from him in the corridor, saw them on the steps and in the streets with their cameras, he had the impulse to reach into his coat pocket and find the rotten eggs to throw at the bastards. And this was the Jack Diamond who once hired a press agent to get his name around.

He sat on the bed, unable to see the condition of his eyes, which were heavy-lidded with whiskey—too little light in the room and in his brain. He squinted at the mirror, but saw only his squint returned. He felt an irritation of the penis from his lovemaking and adjusted his shorts where they rubbed. He remembered Alice's kiss before he left the party, a wet one. She opened her mouth slightly, as she always did when she had a few whiskeys in. He reached into his pocket, felt a card, and looked at it. Packy's speakeasy card. The Parody Association, members only. Jack had seen it on the bar during the party, never owned one, never needed one, but picked it up and pocketed it out of habit. There was a time when he could enter any speakeasy on his name alone, but now people imitated him, even made collections in his name. I'm Legs Diamond. Oh sure, and I'm Herbert Hoover. He used the cards now because he no longer even looked like his own pictures.

Fifty people were in The Parody when Marcus gave his victory toast, the words floating now somewhere behind Jack's squint.

"To Jack Diamond's ability to escape from the clutches of righteous official indignation, which would so dearly love to murder him in his bed. . . ."

Fifty people with glasses in the air. Would've been more, but Jack said keep it small, it ain't the circus. But it was, in its own way, what with Packy and Marcus and Sal from the Kenmore, and Hubert and Hooker Ryan the old fighter, and Tipper Kelly the newsie, and Flossie, who came with the place.

Jack told me to bring Frances, my secretary, who still thought Jack was the devil, even though he'd been acquitted twice. "Show her the devil face to face," Jack said, but when he saw her he mistrusted her face. Lovely Irish face. Reminded Jack of his first wife, Katherine, he married in '17. Army bride. Prettiest Irish kid you ever saw, and she left him because he used coke. Crazy young Jack.

Crazy Jack owes Marcus. Five grand. Coming in the morning from Madden. Where would Jack Diamond be without Uncle Owney? Pay you in the morning, Marcus. Meet you at your office at eleven. Cash on the barrelhead. Jack would be a semifree man, walking Albany's streets, a little less intimidated by the weight of his own future. Maybe his head would clear now that he'd won a second acquittal. They could go on trying him on gun charges, but Marcus said the state boys were whipped, would never try him again with Streeter the adversary witness. The federals were the problem, with four years facing him and no end of other charges pending. No end, even if he reversed the conviction with an appeal. But Jack would worry about the federals when he got well. The immediate future lay in South Carolina. A beachfront spot where he'd holed up when Rothstein and Schultz were both gunning for him in '27. Beautiful old house on a sand dune back from the ocean. Sea air good for the lungs.

Lung talk: Do you know why Jack Diamond can drink so much whiskey? Because he has TB and the fever burns up the alcohol. Facts. Left lung is congested. But, Jack, really now, you never had TB in your life. What will jail do to your lungs? What will it do to your brain, for that matter? Bore you? You'll have to play a lot of dominoes in jail. Boring dominoes. But you knew that. You were always ready to play dominoes, right? That's part of the game, right?

Wrong. Not part of Jack's game.

Jack took off the coat of his lucky blue suit and hung it on the back of the chair. Suit needs a pressing, Marcus told him, even before the trial began. But Jack told Marcus, told the press boys too: "This is my lucky suit and I'm not parting with it. If we win, I'll get it pressed to celebrate." The suit coat fell to the floor in a pile.

Jack took the change out of his pants pockets, his nail file and comb, his white monogrammed handkerchief, and put them on top of the dresser that one of his obituary writers, Meyer Berger, would describe as tawdry. Jack's ethereal mother, starched and bright in a new green frying pan apron, held up Jack's bulletproof vest. "You didn't wear this," she said. "I told you not go out without it, Jackie. Remember what happened to Caesar?" They rendered old Caesar, Jack was about to say when he felt a new surge of giddiness. It was bringing him a breakthrough perception. I am on the verge of getting it all wrapped up, he said to the steam heat that hissed at him from the radiator. I hear it coming. I have been true to everything in life.

> "I toast also to his uncanny ability to bloom in hostile seasons and to survive the blasts of doom. Jack, we need only your presence to light us up like Times Square in fervid and electric animation. You are the undercurrent of our lives. You turn on our light. . . ."

Freddie Robin, the cop, who stopped in for a quick one, had the glass in his hand when good old Marcus started the toast. And Milligan, the railroad dick alongside him, had a glass in the air, too. Pair of cops toasting Jack's glorious beswogglement of law and order. Hah! And alongside them the priest and the screwball.

"Who the hell is that screwball, anyway?" Jack said to Hubert, who began sniffing. The screwball was talking to everybody, wanted to meet everybody at the party. Looks like a killer to you, does he, Jack? No. But maybe like a cop. Like a federal stooge. They like to crash my parties.

Hubert got his name. He was Mr. Biswanger from Buffalo. A lightning rod salesman. What's he doing at your party, Jack? Trying to hustle you a sample to wear behind your ear? He came with the priest, Hubert reported. And the priest came to Albany to see Marcus. Is that true, Marcus? Marcus says yes, but adds, "He just tagged along, Jack, after a legal chat. I didn't bring the clergy. But they have an affinity for you, like cops. The underside of everybody's life, is what you turn out to be, Jack."

Jack undid his tie, blue with diagonal white stripes, and hung it on the upright pole of the dresser mirror. It slid off. Priests and cops toasting Jack. It's like those Chinese bandits, Jack. Nobody can tell the good from the bad. China will always have bandits, right? So, fellow Chinks, let's sit back and enjoy them.

"To his talent for making virtue seem unwholesome and for instilling vicarious amorality in the hearts of multitudes. . . ."

Alice gave Flossie the fish eye when she kidded Jack about pigeons in the loft and fondled his earlobe. Then Frances gave Flossie the fish eye when the Floss kidded Marcus about pigeons in the loft and fondled his earlobe. The Floss moved alongside the piano, and while the pianoman played "It's a Sin to Tell a Lie," she shook her ass to that sweet and gracious waltz, turning, pivoting, shaking. Disgusting. Gorgeous. Oh, Floss, ya look like Mae West. Harpy. Sweetmeat. Goddess of perfume.

"Who is she?" Alice asked.

"Flossie, she works here," Jack said

"She knows you pretty well to play with your ear."

"Nah, she does that with all the boys. Great girl, the Floss."

"I never knew anybody who liked ears like that."

"You don't get around, Alice. I keep telling you that."

"I know you think I'm jealous of all the harpies in the world, but I'm really not, John. Just remember that the truest love is bright green. Avoid substitutes."

From Buffalo the hunger marchers began their walk toward Washington. John D. Rockefeller, in Ormond, Florida, told newsreel microphones that "better times are coming," and he wished the world a Merry Christmas. In Vienna a grand jury unanimously acquitted Dr. Walter Pfrimer and seven other Fascist Party leaders of charges of high treason stemming from an attempted putsch. A speedy recovery was predicted for Pola Negri.

Jack took off the signet ring that no longer fit, that had been bothering him all day. He wore it because it was lucky, like his suit, gift from the old man in high school: D is also for Dear Daddy. Dead Dad. Defunct Diamond. Sorry, old fellow. Jack listened to the candles burning on the altar of Saint Anne's church. They made the sound of leaves

falling into a pond where a calico cat was slowly drowning. In the
shadow of the first pillar the old man cried as the candles danced. When
the mass was ended, when Jack the small priest had blown out the
authenticating candle of his mother's life, the old man stood up and
turned to pity, politics, and drink. And, oh, how they laughed back in
Cavan. Publicans did not complain when the laughter died and you
threw your arms around yourself in a fit of need. "Nobody knows what
it's like until they lose their wife," old Jack said. "Then you eat Thanksgiving dinner alone." Young Jack looked on. "Just a weak old man. He
cried more than I did. I cried only once."

Jack dropped the signet ring with a clunk into the tawdry dresser
alongside two holy pictures (Stephen and Mary) Alice had brought him
from New York, alongside the letters, the holy fan mail. Jack kept one
letter: "God bless you, son, from a mother with a large family." And
God bless you too, mother, going away.

The giddiness was turning to smiles. Jack looked at himself in the
mirror and smiled at the peeling mercury. His smile was backward.
What else was backward? He was. All. All backward in the mirror
image. Nobody would ever know which image was the real Jack. Only
Jack knows that, and he giggled with the knowledge that he alone was
privy to the secret. What a wonderful feeling! A vision of the Jack nobody knows. Fuck that stupid Legs, right Jack? What'd he ever do
for you?

One of Marcus' law partners came to the party to meet Legs
Diamond—a kid with wide eyes when he shook the hand that shook
the Catskills. Hubert brought two poker players from Troy, and they
talked to Jack about a little game some night. Love to, boys. Packy had
rounded up the musicians, piano, banjoman, drummer. Marcus asked
Alice to dance and then Jack took an armful of Frances and foxtrotted
around to "Ain't Misbehavin'."

"I must say you're a wonderful dancer," said Frances.

And why, miss, must you say it? Jack dancing with yesterday in his
arms. Thank you, young woman out of yesterday.

"You know I never think of you as dancing or doing anything like
this."

"What *do* you think of me doing?"

"Terrible things," she said. She spoke sternly. Scolded, Jack relaxed,
touched her hair with his fingertips, remembering his Army bride.

"Your hair reminds me of Helen Morgan," he said.

Frances blushed.

Doc Madison pulled his wife to her feet, stepped into a snappy
foxtrot with the same certainty he revealed when he removed the filling

from Jack, all those double-ought pellets, restoring life to the dying
frame. We're all so full of life now, Doc. And ain't it great? So many
thanks, Doc.

> ". . . perhaps you all noticed the lofty stained-glass windows
> of the court house annex this afternoon as the sun streamed
> through, as the light fell about our Jack's frail but sturdy
> shoulder, illuminating in those windows both New York's and
> Jack's splendid virtues . . . industry, law, peace, learning, pros-
> perity . . ."

The courtroom felt like a church still, old Presbyterian palace de-
sanctified years ago; choir loft over Jack's head, judges sitting where the
pulpit used to be, truncated suns over the door, ecclesiastical fenestra-
tion and only the faces on the walls different now: clergy and the Jesus
crowd replaced with jurists. But retributionists all.

Frankie Teller, of course, came to the party, and so did one of the
Falzo boys who ran four houses on The Line in Troy, squiring one of
his beauties. Jack asked Johnny Dyke, the Albany bookie, to come by,
and Mushy Tarsky too, who ran the grocery on Hudson Avenue where
Jack bought ham and cheese sandwiches for three weeks when he and
two boys never went off the block because of The Goose. Jack's Uncle
Tim, who had hung on at Acra since the roof fell in, waiting for Jack
to return to the homestead, came up for the celebration.

Tuohey and Spivak, the bagmen detectives from the gambling
squad, dropped in for a look and brought greetings from the Democratic
organization.

Marion did not come.

Couldn't do that. Alice would've blown up if she showed. Jack sent
Hubert and Frankie Teller up with a pint of whiskey to keep her happy,
but she was gone. Note on the door: "Going to Boston to see Mama."
Frankie brought the note back, and Jack said, "Go look for her, she's
on the street. Try the station, and find her. She wouldn't go without
seeing me." It took Frankie and Hubert an hour, and they found her
walking back up Ten Broeck Street toward her apartment house, Number Twenty-one, upstairs. Hubert says he told her, "Jack is worried
about you, Marion," and then she said, "You tell him I'm goddamn
good and mad. I'll stay till the morning, but then I'm leaving; I'm not
putting up with this. One of the biggest nights of his life, and he leaves
me alone four hours while he sits around partying with his cow, and I
have to go to the talkies to keep myself busy. The talkies on a night
like this."

So Hubert called Jack with the news, and Jack went back to the table and told Alice a fib. Bones McDowell, a newsman, calling with death-threat information. Gotta go see him, Al. But she'd been waiting for this, Jack. She knows you, Jack, you and your fake excuses. Then Jack said, "Listen, Al, I know you're having a good time, but why don't you come with me? It's business, but Bones is only a newspaperman with some maybe important dope, and it ain't big business or trouble, and I won't be long. Come with me."

She believed that and gave Jack the wet one with the lips apart, he can see them now, and her tongue just dancing and saying, Come on in, boy, and she smiled too and winked at him, and he let his hand slide down and pat her on the benevolent behind, secretly, so the priest wouldn't be scandalized, so that all the eyes that were never off either of them all night would see something, yes, but not enough to talk dirty about such a sweet, clean woman. And then he let go of her. And she leaned back and gave him a smile, a real smile, crinkling her blue-green eyes and saying, "No, I'll stay here with Kitty and Johnny," Ed's wife and the boy alongside her, family lady to the end, the end. He gave her one final peck and looked at her green cloche hat with the little wispy curls of Titian, color of winners, sticking out from underneath.

"Don't be long," she said. "It's such a swell party."

"I'll be back in half an hour," Jack said, running his fingertips lightly down her cheek. "You can count on that."

He stood up then. It was one o'clock and thirty people still at the party when he turned his back on the crowd and walked the length of the bar, past all the enduring dead on the walls, and then out through Packy's swinging doors.

Now Playing in Albany, December 18, 1931

STRAND: (The clearest picture, the best sound in New York State), George Bancroft in *Rich Man's Folly*.

HARMANUS BLEECKER HALL: (Albany's Palace of Entertainment), Ronald Colman in *The Unholy Garden*.

LELAND: (Where the talkies are better), Billie Dove in *The Age for Love*.

PALACE: (Showplace of The Capital), Leo Carillo in *The Guilty Generation*.

MADISON: Mae Clarke in *Waterloo Bridge*.

COLONIAL: Ann Harding in *Devotion*.

PARAMOUNT: Wheeler and Woolsey in *Hook, Line and Sinker*.

PARAMOUNT: Marian Nixon and Neil Hamilton in *Ex Flame* (a modernized version of *East Lynne*).

ALBANY: Wheeler and Woolsey in *Caught Plastered*.

Jack, sitting on his bed in the rooming house, took off the blue pants, pulled them over the scuffy black shoes, the dark-blue socks with the white clocks. He hung the pants on the open drawer of the tawdry dresser, and they stayed there a few seconds before they fell to the floor. Jack had drunk too much with too many. And yet he was lucid when he left the party, pushed by the whiskey into clarity and anticipation of the sweets of love; that face of perfect worship, the excitement of the body of perfect satisfaction, so wholly Jack's, so fully responsive to his touches, his needs. Climbing the stairs to her apartment, he already relished the look of her, the way she would smile when he greeted her with a kiss, the sweetness of presence alone when they sat and faced each other. This did not change. The power of sweetness had not faded in the almost two years he'd known her.

"They tell me you're going to Boston."

"I really am."

"Without even saying good-bye?"

"What's another good-bye? We're always saying that."

"You're not going anyplace. Tomorrow we'll go down to the mountains, have a drink with old Brady up at Haines Falls. Weather's still pretty good."

"You say that, but we won't go."

"Sure. I'll have Frankie pick you up at noon and meet me at Marcus' office, and we'll go from there."

"What about your darling Alice?"

"I'll send her out shopping."

"Something'll happen and we won't go."

"Yes, we'll go. You can count on it. You got my word."

Jack, euphoric now, opened Marion's robe, gazed on her garden of ecstasy. Always a vision. Now better than ever. Jack had been down. He had hit bottom. But like an astral rubber ball, he was bouncing back toward the stars. When he held Marion in his arms, he felt the giddiness. "Top of the goddamn world," he said into her ear. "I'm on top of the goddamn world."

"That's nice, Jackie."

"I'm a winner again."

"That's really nice."

Jack knew that winners celebrated with biological food. You found the most beautiful woman on the Eastern Seaboard. You took your body to where she waited. You turned off her radio, then gave her body to your body. Your body would thank you for such a gift. Your body would be a happy body.

Jack laughed out loud, once, in his bed, a resonant "Haw!"

Moonshine was down to thirty-five cents a pint, and kids were sipping it with two straws. Iced beer was down to five dollars a gallon, and you could get it delivered home. College girls were pledging not to call for drinks costing more than a nickel when their boyfriends took them out for a good time. Dorothy Dix found this a step in the right direction, for matrimony was waning in popularity, a direct result of the high cost of living.

Jack remembered the night he penetrated to the center of Kiki's treasure at Haines Falls and struck something solid.

"What the hell is that?"

"A cork," she said.

"A cork? How'd it get up there?"

"I took it off a gallon of dago red and put it up there. It's my Italian chastity cork."

"What the hell's the matter with you?"

"I'm not taking it out till you promise to marry me."

But she got over that, and when he entered her on this euphoric night in Albany there was no cork, no ultimatum; no climax either. Jack erected, Marion lubricious, they could've danced all night. But Jack wearied of the effort, and Marion ran out of her capacity to groan with pleasure. They rolled away from each other and let the sweat slowly cool, the breathing return to normal, the artifacts dry.

He pulled off one shoe without opening the laces, let it drop. He took off the second shoe, noted its scuffiness and remembered the night he surrendered on the Hotsy charges. He walked into the Forty-seventh Street station house in his navy-blue chesterfield with the velvet lapels, white on white silk scarf, the midnight-blue serge double-breasted, the gray and black dragon tie, and the shoes so highly polished they could pass for patent leather, the derby heightening the tone of his special condition. Jack was on top that night, too, remembering Vinnie Raymond from East Albert Street, who walked by the Diamond house every night in *his* derby and *his* high-polish shoes and spats, on his way to life. The image of that man's perfection was still in the mind that controlled the scuffed shoe, down at the heel. Then he let it too, drop.

Jack heard the horn blowing in the street outside Marion's Ten Broeck Street apartment. He raised the window.

"It's gettin' late, Jack," Frankie Teller called up to him. "You said half an hour. It's going on two hours. You know what Alice told me. You get him back here to this party, back here to me."

But no partying remained in Jack. He would not return to any festive scene, festive drunks, festive Alice. He closed the window and looked at Marion, who had wrapped herself in a beige floor-length silk robe, gift from Jack six months ago when he had money for anything. The gown had one large brown flower below the knee, same color as the stripe around the small lapel. So gorgeous. Will ever a woman look more gorgeous to Jack than this one?

"You treat women like animals," Marion said.

"Ah, don't fight me tonight, baby. I'm feelin' good."

"Like cats. You treat us like damn old cats. Pet us and pussy us up and scratch our neck."

Jack laughed, fell back on the pillow of his own rooming house bed and laughed and laughed and laughed. She was right. You look a cat in the eye and demand a love song. It sits there, and if it likes you at all, it doesn't run away. It wants its goddamn neck scratched. Wants you to play with its whiskers. Give it what it wants, it turns on its motor. He laughed and raised his feet off the floor and saw his socks, still on.

He sat up and took off one sock, dropped it onto one shoe, missed.

". . . I toast his defiance, his plan not to seduce the world
but to terrify it, to spit in the eye of the public which says no
Moloch shall pass . . ."

Jack would not begin life again in the same way. Adirondacks? Vermont? Maybe. But Coll was in jail, his mob busted up after a shoot-out in Averill Park and a roundup in Manhattan. Jack would have to recruit from scratch, and the prospect was wearying. So many dead and gone. Mike Sullivan, Fatty Walsh, Eddie. He reached for the second sock, remembering all the old boys, friends and enemies. Brocco. Babe. Frenchy. Shorty. Pretty. Mattie. Hymie. Fogarty. Dead, gone off, or in jail. And he seemed to himself, for the first time, a curiously perishable item among many such items, a thing of just so many seasons. When does the season end? He has survived again and again to another day, to try yet again to change what he had never been able to change. Would Jack Diamond ever really change? Or would he wake tomorrow out of this euphoria and begin to do what he had done every other day of his senior life? Was there any reason to doubt that recurring pattern? In the morning he would pay Marcus what he owed and take Kiki for a ride and hustle Alice and keep her happy somehow and try to figure out what next. Where was the money coming from? Something would come up.

He would solve it—he, Jack Diamond, who is what was designed, what was made this morning, yesterday, and the day before out of his own private clay.

Ah. What was designed.

This perception arrived as Jack dropped his second sock to the floor and leaned toward the dresser and saw the rosary in the top drawer.

He thought then of saying it again. But no. No rosary. No prayer. No remorse. Jack is so happy with his perception of being what was designed, so released from the struggle to change, that he begins with a low rumble that rises from the sewers of madness; and yet he is not mad, only enlightened, or could they be the same condition? The rumble grows and rises to his throat where it becomes a cackle, and then into his nose where he begins to snort its joy, and into his eyes which cry with this pervasive mirth. Now his whole being—body, mind, and the spirit of nothing that he has at last recognized in the mirror—is convulsed with an ecstasy of recognition.

> ". . . Jack, when you finally decide to go, when you are only a fading memory along Broadway, a name in the old police files and yellowing tabloids, then we will not grieve. Yet we will be empty because our friend Jack, the nonpareil, the nonesuch, the grand confusion of our lives, has left us. The outer limit of boldness is what your behavior has been, Jack, and even if Christ came to town, I'm not sure He'd be seen on the same hill with you. Nevertheless, I think I speak for all when I say we're rooting for you. And so here's to your good health, and to ours, and let me add a safe home, Jacko, a safe home."

Jack heard the cheer go up out in the street in front of the courthouse. But he knew they were cheering for the wrong man.

"I know that son of a bitch," Jack said as he entered his final dream. "He was never any good."

*   *   *

Mrs. Laura Woods, the landlady at 67 Dove, said she heard two men climb the carpeted stairs past the potted fern and enter the front room where the noted guest, who had originally rented the room as Mr. Kelly, was sleeping. She heard the shots, three into Jack's head, three into the wall, and then heard one man say, "Let's make sure. I been waiting a long time for this." And the second man said, "Oh, hell, that's enough for him."

Mrs. Woods telephoned The Parody Club where she knew Mrs. Diamond was partying. It was 6:55 A.M. before the family notified the police and by then Doc Madison had said yes, death seemed to have at last set in for Jack. When the detectives arrived, Alice was holding a bloody handkerchief, with which she had wiped the face of the corpse with the goggle eyes.

"Oh, my beloved boy," she was saying over and over, "I didn't do it, I didn't do it."

". . . Months ago," Winchell wrote, "we called him 'On His Last Legs' Diamond. . . ."

Jack wore his tuxedo and signet ring and held his rosary at the wake, which was given at the home of Alice's relatives in Maspeth, Long Island. The family sent four floral tributes, and I paid for one-third of the fifth, a pillow of red roses, the other two-thirds kicked in by Packy and Flossie, and signed, "Your pals." An eight-foot bleeding heart was dedicated to "Uncle John," and Alice sent a five-and-a-half-foot-high floral chair of yellow tea roses and lilies of the valley. On a gauze streamer in two-inch gold letters across the chairback she had inscribed: VACANT CHAIR, TO MY OWN, AFTER ALL, YOUR LOVING WIFE.

Owney Madden paid for the coffin, a dark mahogany box worth eight hundred dollars. Jack had seven hundred dollars' worth of industrial insurance once, but the company canceled it. The plan was to bury Jack in Calvary Cemetery alongside Eddie, but the church wouldn't let him be put in consecrated ground. Wouldn't allow a mass either. And the permission for the final prayer by a priest at the wake house, which I negotiated with Cardinal Hayes, was withdrawn at the last minute, putting the women in tears. A thirteen-year-old cousin of Jack's said the rosary in place of the priest, as a thousand people stood outside the house in the rain.

It rained yellow mud into the grave. A couple of hundred of Jack's fans went to the cemetery with the family and the press. Somebody from the undertakers picked up a shovel and tried to drive the photographers away from the graveside, but none of them gave an inch, and when the man screamed at them, the photographers chased him up a tree. Jack belonged to them.

It was all over quickly. Alice, heavily veiled, said, "Good-bye, boy, good-bye," when they began to fill the grave, and then she walked away with a single red rose in her hand. Ten minutes later most of the flowers on the grave were gone. Souvenirs.

*   *   *

When Kiki began her five-a-day stint at the Academy of Music on Fourteenth Street ("See Kiki, the Gangster's Gal"), fifteen hundred people were in line before the theater opened at eleven in the morning, and the manager sold two hundred and fifty SRO tickets. "She is better box office than Peaches Browning," the manager said, "and Peaches was the best I ever had here." Sidney Skolsky reported Alice was in the balcony at the opening to see the wicked child (she was just twenty-two) tippy-tap-toe to the tune of twin banjos, then take four bows and never mention Jack. But Sidney was wrong. Alice didn't see the show. I called her to offer a bit of consolation after I'd read about Kiki's success.

"Only eighteen days, Marcus," Alice said. "He's dead only eighteen days and she's out there with banjos, dancing on his grave. She could at least have waited a month."

My advice was to stop competing with Kiki for a dead man, but it was an absurd suggestion to a gladiator, and the first time I made the mistake of thinking Jack was totally dead. Alice had already hired a writer and was putting together a skit that would be staged, thirty-five days after Jack's murder, on the boards of the Central Theater in the Bronx. The theme was crime doesn't pay. In one moment of the drama Alice interrupted a holdup, disarmed the gunman, and guarded him with his own gun until the police arrived. Then she said to the audience, "You can't make a dime with any of them. The straight and narrow is the only way," which brought to mind the era when she banked eighteen thousand dollars in about six months at Acra. Ambivalence, you're beautiful.

Kiki and Alice both took their acts on the road, in vaudeville and on the Minsky burlesque circuit, outraging any number of actors, the Marx Brothers among them. "A damn shame and a disgrace," said Groucho of Kiki's sixteen-week contract, "especially when so many actors are out of work. For what she is getting they could have hired five good acts, people who know their business. She's nothing but a gangster's moll."

The girls both played the same big towns, and both scandalized the smaller ones, Alice barred from Paterson, Kiki hustled out of Allentown, Alice presuming to teach a moral lesson with her act, Kiki the successful sinner against holy matrimony. Who drew the crowds? Ah.

By spring Kiki was still traveling, but Alice was no longer a serious road attraction. Alice and I talked a few times because she was having money problems, worried about the mortgage on the Acra house. She said then she was going to open at Coney Island and she chided me for never seeing her perform. So I said I'd come and catch her opener.

There is a photograph of her as she looked on the day her show opened on the boardwalk. I was standing behind the news cameraman as he caught her by surprise, and I remember her face before, during, and after the click: the change from uncertainty to hostility to a smile at me. Her hair is parted and wavy, falling over her forehead and covering her ears. A poster behind her advertises Siamese twins joined at the shoulder blades, and there is a girl outlined by a dozen long-bladed knives. A midget is in the photo, being held aloft by a man with dark, oily hair and a pencil-thin mustache. The sign says SIDE SHOW in large letters and to the right: BEAUTIFUL MRS. JACK LEGS DIAMOND IN PERSON.

The weather was unseasonably warm that afternoon, mobs on the boardwalk in shirtsleeves and unnecessary furs, camp chairs on the sand, and young girls blooming in summer dresses as Beautiful Mrs. Jack walked onto the simple unpainted board stage.

From the other direction came the tuxedo man with the little mustache. He introduced Alice, then asked if she wanted to say anything at the start.

"Mr. Diamond was a loving and devoted husband," she said. "Much that was stated and printed about him was untrue."

"People find it difficult to understand why a woman would stay married to a gangster," said the tuxedo man.

"Mr. Diamond was no gangster. He wouldn't have known how to be a gangster."

"It's been said he was a sadistic killer."

"He was a man in love with all of nature, and he celebrated life. I never saw him kill even a fly."

"How, then, would you say he got the reputation for being a gangster and a killer?"

"He did some very foolish things when he was young, but he regretted them later in life."

So it went. The sixteen customers paid ten cents each to enter, and after the show Alice also sold four photos of herself and Jack, the one with "my hero" written on the clipping found in her apartment a year later when they put a bullet in her temple. The photos also sold for a dime, which brought the gross for the first performance to two dollars.

"Not much of a crowd," she said to me when she came off the stage. Her eyes were heavy and she couldn't manage a smile.

"You'll do better when the hot days come along."

"The hot days are all over with, Marcus."

"Hey, that's kind of maudlin."

"No, just honest. Nothing's like it used to be. Nothing."

"You look as good as ever. You're not going under, I can see that."

"No, I don't go under. But I'm all hollow inside. If I went in for a swim I'd float away like an old bottle."

"Come on, I'll buy you a drink."

She knew a speakeasy a few blocks off the boardwalk, upstairs over a hot dog stand, and we settled into a corner and talked over her travels, and her fulfilling of her own fragment of Lew Edwards' dream: John the Priest on the boards of America. He was there. The presence within Alice.

"Are you staying alive on this spiel?" I asked her.

"You mean money? No, not anymore. But I've got a little coming in from a dock union John did some favors for. One of his little legacies to me was how and why he did the favors, and who paid off. And when I told them what I had, they kept up the payments."

"Amazing."

"What?"

"That he's still taking care of you."

"But she's living off him, too. That's what galls me."

"I know. I read the papers. Did you ever catch her act?"

"Are you serious? I wouldn't go within three miles of her footprints."

"She stopped by to see me when she played a club in Troy. She spoke well of you, I must say. 'The old war-horse,' she said to me, 'they can't beat her.' "

Alice laughed, tossed her hair, which was back to its natural color—a deep chestnut—but still a false color, for after Jack died, her roots went white in two days. But it looked right, now. Authentic Alice. She tossed that authentic hair in triumph, then tossed off a shot of straight gin.

"She meant *she* couldn't beat me."

"Maybe that's what she meant. I only agreed with her."

"She never knew John, not till near the end. When she moved into Acra she thought she had him. Then, when I walked out of the Kenmore she thought she had him again. But she didn't know him."

"I thought *she* left the Kenmore."

"She did. The police came looking and John put her in a rooming house in Watervliet, then one in Troy. He moved her around, but he kept bringing her back to the Rain-Bo room and I refused to take it. I told John that the day I left. I wasn't gone three days when he called me to come back up and set up a house or an apartment. But I didn't want Albany anymore, so he came to New York when he wanted to see me. It must've killed her."

I remember Jack telling a story twice in my presence about how he met Alice. "I pulled up to a red light at Fifty-ninth Street and she jumped in and I couldn't get her out."

In its way it was a true story. Jack couldn't kick her out of his life; Alice couldn't leave. Her wish was to be buried on top of him, but she didn't get that wish either. She had to settle for a spot alongside; and buried, like Jack, without benefit of the religion she loved so well. Her murderers took her future away from her, and that, too, was related to Jack. She was about to open a tearoom on Jones' Walk at Coney, which would have been a speakeasy within hours, and was also lending her

name to a sheet to be called *Diamond Widow's Racing Form*. She'd
gotten the reputation of being a crack shot from practicing at the Coney
shooting galleries and practicing in her backyard with a pistol too, so
went the story. And in certain Coney and Brooklyn bars, when she was
escorted by gangsters who found her company improved their social
status, she would announce with alcoholic belligerence that she could
whip any man in the house in a fight. They also said she was threatening
to reveal who killed Jack, but I never believed that. I don't think she
knew any more than the rest of us. We all had our theories.

I remember her sitting at that Coney table, head back, laughing
that triumphant laugh of power. I never saw her again. I talked to her
by phone some months later when she was trying to save Acra from
foreclosure and she was even talking of getting a few boys together
again to hustle some drink among the summer tourists. But she just
couldn't put that much money together (sixty-five hundred dollars was
due) and she lost the house. I did what I could, which was to delay the
finale. She wrote me a thanks-for-everything note, which was our last
communication. Here's the last paragraph of that letter:

> Jack once told me when he was tipsy that "If you can't make
> 'em laugh, don't make 'em cry." I don't know what in hell he
> meant by that, do you? It sounds like a sappy line he heard
> from some sentimental old vaudevillian. But he said it to me
> and he did mean something by it, and I've been trying to figure
> it out ever since. The only thing I can come up with is that
> maybe he thought of himself as some kind of entertainer and,
> in a way, that's pretty true. He sure gave me a good time. And
> other people I won't name. God I miss him.

She signed it "love and a smooch, just one." she was dead a month
later, sixty-four dollars behind in her thirty-two-dollar-a-month rent for
the Brooklyn apartment. Her legacy was that trunkful of photographs
and clippings, the two Brussels griffons she always thought Jack bought
in Europe, and a dinner ring, a wedding ring, and a brooch, all set with
diamonds.

She was a diamond, of course.

They never found her killers either.

*   *   *

I saw Marion for the last time in 1936 at the old Howard Theater in
Boston, another backstage encounter. But then again why not? Maybe
Jack hit the real truth with that line of his. The lives of Kiki and Alice
were both theatrical productions; both were superb in their roles as

temptress and loyal wife, and as leading ladies of underworld drama. Marion was headlining a burlesque extravaganza called *The Pepper Pot Revue* when I read the item in the *Globe* about her being robbed, and I went downtown and saw her, just before her seven o'clock show.

She was sitting in one of the Howard's large dressing rooms, listening to Bing Crosby on the radio crooning a slow-tempo version of "Nice Work If You Can Get It." She wore a fading orchid robe of silk over her costume, wore it loosely, permitting me a glimpse of the flesh-colored patches which made scant effort to cover her attractions. She worked on her toes with two ostrich-feather fans, one of which would fall away by number's end, revealing unclothed expanses of the whitest of white American beauty flesh. She billed herself out front as "Jack (Legs) Diamond's Lovely Light o'Love," a phrase first applied to her after the Monticello shooting by a romantic caption writer. Her semipro toe dance, four a day, five on Saturday, was an improvement over her tippy-tap-toe routine, for the flesh was where her talent lay.

"You're still making the headlines," I told her when the stage doorman showed me where she was.

Her robe flowed open, and she gave me a superb hug, my first full-length, unencumbered encounter with all that sensual resilience, and after the preliminaries were done with, she reached in a drawer, put a finger through an aperture in a pair of yellow silk panties with a border of small white flowers and dangled them in front of me.

"That's the item?"

"That's them. Isn't it ridiculous?"

"The publicity wasn't bad, good for the show."

"But it's so . . . so cheap and awful." She broke down, mopped her eyes with the panties that an MIT student had stolen from her as a fraternity initiation prank. He left an ignominious fifty-cent piece in their place, saying, when they nabbed him at the stage door with the hot garment in his pants pocket, "I would've left more, only I didn't have change."

I was baffled by her tears, which were flowing not from the cheapness of the deed, for she was beyond that, inured. I then considered that maybe the fifty cents was not enough. But would five or fifty dollars have been enough for the girl who once wore a five-hundred-dollar negotiable hymen inside another such garment? No, she was crying because I was witness to both past and present in this actual moment, and she hadn't been prepared to go over it all again on such short notice. She knew I remembered Ziegfeld and all her promise of greater Broadway glory, plus a Hollywood future. But Ziegfeld turned her down after Jack died, and Will Hays wouldn't let her get a foothold in Hollywood: No molls need apply. And finally, as we talked, she brought it out, tears gone, panties there to haunt both of us (I remembered the vision at the miniature golf course, in her Monticello room, and I thought, Pursue it now; nothing bars the way now; no fear, no betrayal intervening between you and that bound-to-be-lovely by-way), and she said: "It's so shitty, Marcus. It seems once fate puts the finger on you, you're through."

"You're still in the paper, kiddo; you're in big letters out front, and you look like seven or eight million dollars. Eight. I know a few young ladies with less to point to."

"You were always nice, Marcus. But you know I still miss Jack. Miss him. After all these years."

Would the maudlin time never end?

"You're keeping him alive," I said. "Look at it that way. He's on the signs out front, too."

"He wouldn't like his name there."

"Sure he would, as long as you were tied to it."

"No, not Jack. He liked it respectable, the two-faced son of a bitch. He left me that night to go home to bed so Alice wouldn't come find him, so he could be there in bed ahead of her. Imagine a man like him thinking like that?"

"Who said he did that?"

"Frankie Teller told me. Jack mumbled it in the cab when they left my place."

She let the old memories run by in silence, then she said, "But I was the last one to see him," and she meant, to make love to him. "He always left Old Lady Prune to come to me. I don't think she had a crotch." And then Kiki laughed and laughed, as triumphantly as Alice had in the Coney speakeasy.

I bought her a sandwich between shows, then took her back to the theater. I kissed her good-bye on the cheek, but she turned and gave me her mouth as I was leaving, a gift. But she didn't linger over it.

"Thanks for coming," she said, and I didn't know whether to leave or not. Then she said, "I could've made it with you, Marcus. I think I could've. But he spoiled me, you know."

"Sometimes friends should just stay friends."

"He spoiled me for so many men. I never thought any man could do that to me."

"You'll never be spoiled for me."

"Come and see me again, Marcus. Next time you see me on a marquee someplace."

"You can bank on that," I said.

But I never did. Her name turned up in the papers when she married a couple of times, never with success. About 1941 a patient treated in

Bellevue's alcoholic ward gave the name of Kiki Roberts, but the story
that it was the real Kiki was denied in the press the next day. She was
hurt in a theater fire in Newark somewhere around that time, and a
friend of mine from Albany saw her back in Boston in a small club
during the middle years of the war, still known professionally as Jack's
sweetheart, not stripping any longer, just singing torch songs, like "Broken Hearted," a tune from '27, the year they killed Little Augie and
shot Jack full of holes, the year he became famous for the first time for
not dying. You can't kill Legs Diamond. I've heard Kiki died in Detroit,
Jersey, and Boston, that she went crazy, broke her back and had a metal
backbone put in, got fat, grew old beautifully, turned lesbian, and that
she still turns up in Troy and Catskill and Albany bars whose owners
remember Jack. I don't believe any of it. I don't know what happened
to her.

*   *   *

That isn't the end of the story, of course. Didn't I, like everybody else
who knew him, end up on a barstool telling Jack's tale again, forty-
three years later, telling it my own way? And weren't Tipper and The
Pack and Flossie there with me, ready, as always with the ear, ready
too to dredge up yet another story of their own? The magazines never
stopped retelling Jack's story either, and somebody put it out in book
form once, a silly work, and somebody else made a bum movie of it.
But nobody ever came anywhere near getting it right, and I mean right,
not straight, for accuracy about Jack wasn't possible. His history was
as crooked as the line between his brain and his heart. I stand on this:
that Packy's dog story was closer to the truth about Jack and his world
than any other word ever written or spoken about him.

We were all there in the dingy old Kenmore when Packy told it,
old folks together, wearying of talk of any kind by now, all of us deep
into the drink, anxious to move along to something else, and yet not
quite able to let go. I remember I was winding up, telling what happened
to The Goose, who at age sixty-eight homosexually assaulted a young
boy in a prison shower and was stabbed in his good eye for his efforts.
And Oxie, who did seven long ones and then dropped dead of a heart
attack on a Bronx street corner after a month of freedom. And Fogarty,
who was let out of jail because of his sickness and wasted away with
TB in the isolation ward of the Ann Lee Home in Albany, and who
called me at the end to handle his legacy, which consisted of Big Frenchy
DeMange's diamond wristwatch. Jack gave it to him as a souvenir after
the Big Frenchy snatch, and Fogarty kept it in a safe-deposit box and
never sold it, even when he didn't have a dime.

My three old friends didn't know either that Jack never paid me for the second trial, nor had he ever paid Doc Madison a nickel for all the doc's attention to his wounds.

"He stole from us all, to the very end," I said.

"Yes, Marcus," said Flossie, the loyal crone, misty-eyed over her wine, profoundly in love with all that was and would never be again, "but he had a right to. He was magic. He had power. Power over people. Power over animals. He had a tan collie could count to fifty-two and do subtraction."

"I wrote a story about his dog," said the Tipper. "It was a black and white bull terrier named Clancy. I went and fed him when they all left Acra and forgot he was there. Smartest dog I ever saw. Jack taught him how to toe dance."

"It was a white poodle," said Packy. "He brought it with him right here where we're sitting one night in the middle of '31. There was a bunch of us and Jack decides he'll take a walk, and we all say, okay, we'll all take a walk. But Jack says he needs his sweater because the night air gets chilly, and we all say, you're right, Jack, it sure gets chilly."

"Jack could turn on the electric light sometimes, just by snapping his fingers," Flossie said.

"So Jack says to the white poodle, 'Listen here, dog, go up and get my black sweater,' and that damn dog got up and went out to the lobby and pushed the elevator button and went up to Jack's suite and barked, and Hubert Maloy let him in."

"Jack could run right up the wall and halfway across the ceiling when he got a good running start," Flossie said.

"We all waited, but the poodle didn't come back, and Jack finally says, 'Where the hell is that dog of mine?' And somebody says maybe he went to the show to see the new Rin-Tin-Tin, and Jack says, 'No, he already saw it.' Jack got so fidgety he finally goes upstairs himself and we all follow, and Jack is sayin' when he walks into his room, 'Come on, you son of a bitch, where's my goddamn sweater?' "

"Jack could outrun a rabbit," Flossie said.

"Well, let me tell you, it took the wind right out of Jack when he saw that damn dog sitting on the sofa with the sweater, sewin' on a button that was missin' off the pocket."

"Jack could tie both his shoes at once," Flossie said.

Jacked Up

Jack (Legs) Diamond, aged thirty-four years, five months, seven days, and several hours, sat up in bed in his underwear and stared into the mirror at his new condition: incipiently dead.

"Those simple bastards," he said, "they finally did it right."

He moved without being able to move, thought out of his dead brain, smiled with an immobile mouth, his face intact but the back of his head blown away. Already aware he was moving outside time, he saw the yellow fluid coming to his eyes, trickling out his nose, his ears, down the corners of his mouth. He felt tricklings from his rectum, his penis, old friend, and knew those too were the yellow. He turned his head and saw the yellow coming out his wounds, on top of his congealing blood. He had known the yellow would come, for he had been at the edge before. But he always failed to understand the why of it. The wisdom of equality, the Book of the Dead said, but that made no sense. Death did make sense. It was a gift. The dead thanked you with stupid eyes.

"Do you think I worry because I'm dead?" Jack asked aloud.

The yellow oozed its curious answer.

The press of death was deranging. He was fully aware of the pressure, like earth sinking into water. Yet there was time left for certain visitors who were crowding into the room. Rothstein stepped out of the crowd and inspected the crown of Jack's head. He fingered that bloody skull like a father fondling the fontanel of his infant son—and who with a better right? He pulled out two hairs from the center of the scalp.

"What odds that I find the answer, big dad?" Jack said.

Rothstein mulled the question, turned for an estimate to Runyon, who spoke out of a cancerously doomed larynx.

"I've said it before," said Damon. "All life is nine to five against."

"You hear that?" A. R. asked.

"I hear it."

"I must call against."

"Then up yours," said Jack. "I'll make it my way."

"Always headstrong," said A. R.

I took Jack by the arm, guided him back from the mirror to lie on his right side, the lying posture of a lion. I pressed my fingers against the arteries on both sides of his throat.

"It's time, Jack," I said. "It's coming."

"I'm not sure I'll know it when it comes."

"I'll tell you this. It looks like a thought, like a cloudless sky. It looks like nothing at all."

"Like nothing?"

"Like nothing."

"I'll recognize it," Jack said. "I know what that looks like."

"Say a prayer," I suggested.

"I did."

"Say another."

"I knew a guy once had trouble cheating because his wife was always praying for him."

"Try to be serious. It's your last chance."

Jack concentrated, whispered, "Dear God, turn me onto the Great White Way." He felt the onset of clammy coldness then, as if this body were fully immersed in water. He remembered Rothstein's prayer and said that too, "O Lord, God of Abraham, keep me alive and smart. The rest I'll figure out for myself."

"Perfect," said A. R.

"Dummy," I said, "you're dead. What kind of a thing is it, asking to stay alive?"

I eased the pressure on Jack's arteries and pressed his nerve of eternal sleep. Then I knelt beside him, seeing the water of his life sinking into fire, waiting for his final exit from that useless body. But if Jack left his body through the ear instead of the top of the head where Rothstein had pulled out the hairs, he might come back in the next life as a fairy musician.

"Jesus," Jack said when I told him, "imagine that?"

"Easy, now," I said, "easy. Out through the top."

Then he was out, just fine, standing in front of the mirror, seeing no more blood, no more yellow.

"Am I completely dead?" he asked, and knew then his last human feeling: his body being blown to atoms, the feeling of fire sinking into air. He looked around the room, but could see no one any longer, though we were all there, watching. He felt his absent pupils dilate to receive the light, which was his own light as well as everyone else's. When the light came, it was not the brilliant whiteness Jack expected, but a yellowish, grayish light that made no one blink. The motion of the light was perceptible. It swirled around Jack's neck like a muffler, rose up past his eyes and hairline like a tornado in crescendo, spun round his entire head with what was obviously a potentially dazzling ferocity, reduced in effect now by the horrendous life-tone of Jack Diamond. It was obvious to everyone that given propitious conditions it could centripetally slurp the entire spirit of Jack into the vortex and make off with it forever; but now it moved only like a bit of fog on a sunny morning, coiled by a frolicsome breeze, then gone, with not enough force to slurp up a toupee.

As Jack's awareness of the light peaked, he was already falling backward. Though he had no arms, he waved them frantically to right himself, and as he fell, twisting and flailing against this ignominious new development, he delivered up one, final, well-modulated sentence before he disappeared into the void, into the darkness where the white was still elusive.

"Honest to God, Marcus," he said going away, "I really don't think I'm dead."

Billy Phelan's Greatest Game

For Brendan Christopher Kennedy,
a nifty kid

Because the city of Albany exists in the real world, readers may be led to believe that the characters who populate the Albany in this book are therefore real people. But there are no authentically real people in these pages. Some local and national celebrities are so indelibly connected to the era of the story that it would have been silly not to present them under their real names. But wherever a character has a role of even minor significance in this story, both name and actions are fictional. Any reality attaching to any character is the result of the author's creation, or of his own interpretation of history. This applies not only to Martin Daugherty and Billy Phelan, to Albany politicians, newsmen, and gamblers, but also to Franklin D. Roosevelt, Thomas E. Dewey, Henry James, Damon Runyon, William Randolph Hearst, and any number of other creatures of the American imagination.

WILLIAM KENNEDY

I

MARTIN DAUGHERTY, age fifty and now the scorekeeper, observed it all as Billy Phelan, working on a perfect game, walked with the arrogance of a young, untried eagle toward the ball return, scooped up his black, two-finger ball, tossed it like a juggler from right to left hand, then held it in his left palm, weightlessly. Billy rubbed his right palm and fingers on the hollow cone of chalk in the brass dish atop the ball rack, wiped off the excess with a pull-stroke of the towel. He faced the pins, eyed his spot down where the wood of the alley changed color, at a point seven boards in from the right edge. And then, looking to Martin like pure energy in shoes, he shuffled: left foot, right foot, left-right-left and slide, right hand pushing out, then back, like a pendulum, as he moved, wrist turning slightly at the back of the arc. His arm, pure control in shirtsleeves to Martin, swung forward, and the ball glided almost silently down the polished alley, rolled through the seventh board's darkness, curving minimally as it moved, curving more sharply as it neared the pins, and struck solidly between the headpin and the three pin, scattering all in a jamboree of spins and jigs.

"Attaway, Billy," said his backer, Morrie Berman, clapping twice. "Lotta mix, lotta mix."

"Ball is working all right," Billy said.

Billy stood long-legged and thin, waiting for Bugs, the cross-eyed pinboy, to send back the ball. When it snapped up from underneath the curved wooden ball return, Billy lifted it off, faced the fresh setup on alley nine, shuffled, thrust, and threw yet another strike: eight in a row now.

Martin Daugherty noted the strike on the scoresheet, which showed no numbers, only the eight strike marks: bad luck to fill in the score while a man is still striking. Martin was already thinking of writing his next column about this game, provided Billy carried it off. He would point out how some men moved through the daily sludge of their lives and then, with a stroke, cut away the sludge and transformed themselves. Yet what they became was not the result of a sudden act, but the culmination of all they had ever done: a triumph for self-development, the end of something general, the beginning of something specific.

To Martin, Billy Phelan, on an early Thursday morning in late October, 1938, already seemed more specific than most men. Billy seemed fully defined at thirty-one (the age when Martin had been advised by his father that he was a failure).

Billy was not a half-bad bowler: 185 average in the K. of C. league, where Martin bowled with him Thursday nights. But he was not a serious match for Scotty Streck, who led the City League, the fastest league in town, with a 206 average. Scotty lived with his bowling ball as if it were a third testicle, and when he found Billy and Martin playing eight ball at a pool table in the Downtown Health and Amusement Club, the city's only twenty-four-hour gamester's palace, no women, no mixed leagues, please, beer on tap till 4:00 A.M., maybe 5:00, but no whiskey on premises, why then Scotty's question was: Wanna bowl some jackpots, Billy? Sure, with a twenty-pin spot, Billy said. Give you fifty-five for three games, offered the Scotcheroo. Not enough, but all right, said Billy, five bucks? Five bucks fine, said Scotty.

And so it was on, with the loser to pay for the bowling, twenty cents a game. Scotty's first game was 212. Billy turned in a sad 143, with five splits, too heavy on the headpin, putting him sixty-nine pins down, his spot eliminated.

Billy found the pocket in the second game and rolled 226. But Scotty had also discovered where the pocket lurked, and threw 236 to increase his lead to seventy-nine pins. Now in the eighth frame of the final game, the match was evening out, Scotty steady with spares and doubles, but his lead fading fast in front of Billy's homestretch run toward perfection.

Word of a possible 300 game with a bet on it drew the bar stragglers, the fag-end bowlers, the night manager, the all-night pinboys, even the sweeper, to alleys nine and ten in the cavernous old room, spectators at the wonder. No one spoke to Billy about the unbroken string of strikes, also bad luck. But it was legitimate to talk of the bet: two hundred dollars, between Morrie Berman and Charlie Boy McCall, the significance being in the sanctified presence of Charlie Boy, a soft, likeable kid gone to early bloat, but nevertheless the most powerful young man in town, son of the man who controlled all the gambling, all of it, in the city of Albany, and nephew of the two politicians who ran the city

itself, all of it, and Albany County, all of that too: Irish-American po-
tentates of the night and the day.

Martin knew all the McCall brothers, had gone to school with
them, saw them grow up in the world and take power over it. They all,
including young Charlie Boy, the only heir, still lived on Colonie Street
in Arbor Hill, where Martin and his father used to live, where Billy
Phelan used to live. There was nothing that Charlie Boy could not get,
any time, any place in this town; and when he came into the old Downtown alleys with Scotty, and when Scotty quickly found Billy to play
with, Charlie just as quickly found Morrie Berman, a swarthy ex-pimp
and gambler who would bet on the behavior of bumblebees. A week
ago Martin had seen Morrie open a welsher's forehead with a shotglass
at Brockley's bar on Broadway over a three-hundred-dollar dart game:
heavy bettor, Morrie, but he paid when he lost and he demanded the
same from others. Martin knew Morrie's reputation better than he knew
the man: a fellow who used to drink around town with Legs Diamond
and had hoodlums for pals. But Morrie wasn't quite a hoodlum himself,
as far as Martin could tell. He was the son of a politically radical Jew,
grandson of a superb old Sheridan Avenue tailor. In Morrie the worthy
Berman family strain had gone slightly askew.

The bet between Charlie Boy and Morrie had begun at one hundred
dollars and stayed there for two games, with Martin holding the money.
But when Morrie saw that Billy had unquestionably found the pocket
at the windup of the second game, he offered to raise the ante another
hundred; folly, perhaps, for his boy Billy was seventy-nine pins down.
Well yes, but that was really only twenty-four down with the fifty-five-
pin spot, and you go with the hot instrument. Charlie Boy quickly
agreed to the raise, what's another hundred, and Billy then stood up
and rolled his eight strikes, striking somberness into Charlie Boy's
mood, and vengeance into Scotty's educated right hand.

Martin knew Scotty Streck and admired his talent without liking
him. Scotty worked in the West Albany railroad shops, a short, muscular, brush-cut, bandy-legged native of the West End German neighborhood of Cabbagetown. He was twenty-six and had been bowling
since he was old enough to lift a duckpin ball. At age sixteen he was a
precociously unreal star with a 195 average. He bowled now almost
every night of his life, bowled in matches all over the country and clearly
coveted a national reputation. But to Martin he lacked champion style:
a hothead, generous neither with himself nor with others. He'd been
nicknamed Scotty for his closeness with money, never known to bet
more than five dollars on himself. Yet he thrived on competition and
traveled with a backer, who, as often as not, was his childhood pal,
Charlie McCall. No matter what he did or didn't do, Scotty was still

the best bowler in town, and bowling freaks, who abounded in Albany, gathered round to watch when he came out to play.

The freaks now sat on folding chairs and benches behind the only game in process in the old alleys, alleys which had been housed in two other buildings and moved twice before being installed here on State Street, just up from Broadway in an old dancing academy. They were venerable, quirky boards, whose history now spoke to Martin. He looked the crowd over: men sitting among unswept papers, dust, and cigar butts, bathing in the raw incandescence of naked bulbs, surrounded by spittoons; a nocturnal bunch in shirtsleeves and baggy clothes, their hands full of meaningful drink, fixated on an ancient game with origins in Christian ritual, a game brought to this city centuries ago by nameless old Dutchmen and now a captive of the indoor sports of the city. The game abided in such windowless, smoky lofts as this one, which smelled of beer, cigar smoke and alley wax, an unhealthy ambience which nevertheless nourished exquisite nighttime skills.

These men, part of Broadway's action-easy, gravy-vested sporting mob, carefully studied such artists of the game as Scotty, with his high-level consistency, and Billy, who might achieve perfection tonight through a burst of accuracy, and converted them into objects of community affection. The mob would make these artists sports-page heroes, enter them into the hall of small fame that existed only in the mob mind, which venerated all winners.

After Billy rolled his eighth strike, Scotty stood, danced his bob and weave toward the foul line, and threw the ball with a corkscrewed arm, sent it spinning and hooking toward the one-three pocket. It was a perfect hit, but a dead one somehow, and he left the eight and ten pins perversely standing: the strike split, all but impossible to make.

"Dirty son of a biiiiiitch!" Scotty screamed at the pair of uncooperative pins, silencing all hubbub behind him, sending waves of uh-oh through the spectators, who knew very well how it went when a man began to fall apart at the elbow.

"You think maybe I'm getting to him?" Billy whispered to Martin.

"He can't even stand to lose a fiver, can he?"

Scotty tried for the split, ticking the eight, leaving the ten.

"Let's *get* it now, Scotty," Charlie Boy McCall said. "In there, buddy."

Scotty nodded at Charlie Boy, retrieved his ball and faced the new setup, bobbed, weaved, corkscrewed, and crossed over to the one-two pocket, Jersey hit, leaving the five pin. He made the spare easily, but sparing is not how you pick up pinnage against the hottest of the hot.

Billy might have been hot every night if he'd been as single-minded as Scotty about the game. But Martin knew Billy to be a generalist, a man in need of the sweetness of miscellany. Billy's best game was pool, but he'd never be anything like a national champion at that either, didn't think that way, didn't have the need that comes with obsessive special- ization. Billy roamed through the grandness of all games, yeoman here, journeyman there, low-level maestro unlikely to transcend, either as gambler, card dealer, dice or pool shooter. He'd been a decent shortstop in the city-wide Twilight League as a young man. He was a champion drinker who could go for three days on the sauce and not yield to sleep, a double-twenty specialist at the dart board, a chancy, small-time bookie, and so on and so on and so on, and why, Martin Daugherty, are you so obsessed with Billy Phelan? Why make a heroic *picaro* out of a simple chump?

Well, says Martin, haven't I known him since he was a sausage? Haven't I seen him grow stridently into young manhood while I slip and slide softly into moribund middle age? Why, I knew him when he had a father, knew his father too, knew him when that father abdicated, and I ached for the boy then and have ever since, for I know how it is to live in the inescapable presence of the absence of the father.

Martin had watched Billy move into street-corner life after his fa- ther left, saw him hanging around Ronan's clubroom, saw him organize the Sunday morning crap game in Bohen's barn after nine o'clock mass, saw him become a pinboy at the K. of C. to earn some change. That was where the boy learned how to bowl, sneaking free games after Duffy, the custodian, went off to the movies.

Martin was there the afternoon the pinboys went wild and rolled balls up and down the middle of the alleys at one another, reveling in a boyish exuberance that went bad when Billy tried to scoop up one of those missiles like a hot grounder and smashed his third finger between that onrushing ball and another one lying loose on the runway. Smash and blood, and Martin moved in and took him (he was fourteen, the same age as Martin's own son is this early morning) over to the Ho- meopathic Hospital on North Pearl Street and saw to it that the intern called a surgeon, who came and sewed up the smash, but never splinted it, just wrapped it with its stitches and taped it to Billy's pinky and said: That's the best anybody can do with this mess; nothing left there to splint. And Billy healed, crediting it to the influence of the healthy pinky. The nail and some bone grew back crookedly, and Martin can now see the twist and puff of Billy's memorable deformity. But what does a sassy fellow like Billy need with a perfectly formed third finger? The twist lends character to the hand that holds the deck, that palms the two- finger ball, that holds the stick at the crap table, that builds the cockeyed bridge for the educated cue.

If Martin had his way, he would infuse a little of Billy's scarred sassiness into his own son's manner, a boy too tame, too subservient to the priests. Martin might even profit by injecting some sass into his own acquiescent life.

Consider that: a sassy Martin Daugherty.

Well, that may not be all that likely, really. Difficult to acquire such things.

Billy's native arrogance might well have been a gift of miffed genes, then come to splendid definition through the tests to which a street like Broadway puts a young man on the make: tests designed to refine a breed, enforce a code, exclude all simps and gumps, and deliver into the city's life a man worthy of functioning in this age of nocturnal supremacy. Men like Billy Phelan, forged in the brass of Broadway, send, in the time of their splendor, telegraphic statements of mission: I, you bums, am a winner. And that message, however devoid of Christ-like other-cheekery, dooms the faint-hearted Scottys of the night, who must sludge along, never knowing how it feels to spill over with the small change of sassiness, how it feels to leave the spillover there on the floor, more where that came from, pal. Leave it for the sweeper.

Billy went for his ball, kissed it once, massaged it, chalked and toweled his right hand, spat in the spittoon to lighten his burden, bent slightly at the waist, shuffled and slid, and bazoo-bazoo, boys, threw another strike: not *just* another strike, but a titanic blast this time which sent all pins flying pitward, the cleanest of clean hits, perfection unto tidiness, bespeaking power battening on power, control escalating.

Billy looked at no one.

Nine in a row, but still nobody said anything except hey, and yeah-yeah, with a bit more applause offered up. Billy waited for the ball to come back, rubbing his feet on the floor dirt just beyond the runway, dusting his soles with slide insurance, then picked up the ball and sidled back to the runway of alley nine for his last frame. And then he rolled it, folks, and boom-boom went the pins, zot-zot, you sons of bitches, ten in a row now, and a cheer went up, but still no comment, ten straight and his score (even though Martin hadn't filled in any numbers yet) is 280, with two more balls yet to come, twenty more pins to go. Is Billy Phelan ready for perfection? Can you handle it, kid? What will you do with it if you get it?

Billy had already won the match; no way for Scotty to catch him, given that spot. But now it looked as if Billy would beat Scotty without the spot, and, tied to a perfect game, the win would surely make the sports pages later in the week.

Scotty stood up and walked to the end of the ball return to wait. He chalked his hands, rubbed them together, played with the towel, as Billy bent over to pick up his ball.

"You ever throw three hundred anyplace before?" Scotty asked.

"I ain't thrown it *here* yet," Billy said.

So he did it, Martin thought. Scotty's chin trembled as he watched Billy. Scotty, the nervous sportsman. Did saying what he had just said mean that the man lacked all character? Did only relentless winning define his being? Was the fear of losing sufficient cause for him to try to foul another man's luck? Why of course it was, Martin. Of course it was.

Billy threw, but it was a Jersey hit, his first crossover in the game. The ball's mixing power overcame imprecision, however, and the pins spun and rolled, toppling the stubborn ten pin, and giving Billy his eleventh strike. Scotty pulled at the towel and sat down.

"You prick," Morrie Berman said to him. "What'd you say that to him for?"

"Say what?"

"No class," said Morrie. "Class'll tell in the shit house, and you got no class."

Billy picked up his ball and faced the pins for the last act. He called out to Bugs, the pinboy: "Four pin is off the spot," and he pointed to it. Martin saw he was right, and Bugs moved the pin back into proper position. Billy kissed the ball, shuffled and threw, and the ball went elegantly forward, perfect line, perfect break, perfect one-three pocket hit. Nine pins flew away. The four pin never moved.

"Two-ninety-nine," Martin said out loud, and the mob gave its full yell and applause and then stood up to rubber-neck at the scoresheet, which Martin was filling in at last, thirty pins a frame, twenty-nine in the last one. He put down the crayon to shake hands with Billy, who stood over the table, ogling his own nifty numbers.

"Some performance, Billy," said Charlie Boy McCall, standing to stretch his babyfat. "I should learn not to bet against you. You remember the last time?"

"Pool match at the K. of C."

"I bet twenty bucks on some other guy."

"Live and learn, Charlie, live and learn."

"You were always good at everything," Charlie said. "How do you explain that?"

"I say my prayers and vote the right ticket."

"That ain't enough in this town," Charlie said.

"I come from Colonie Street."

"That says it," said Charlie, who still lived on Colonie Street.

"Scotty still has to finish two frames," Martin announced to all; for Scotty was already at alley ten, facing down the burden of second best. The crowd politely sat and watched him throw a strike. He moved to alley nine and with a Jersey hit left the baby split. He cursed inaudibly, then made the split. With his one remaining ball he threw a perfect strike for a game of 219, a total of 667. Billy's total was 668.

"Billy Phelan wins the match by one pin, without using any of the spot," Martin was delighted to announce, and he read aloud the game scores and totals of both men. Then he handed the bet money to Morrie Berman.

"I don't even feel bad," Charlie Boy said. "That was a hell of a thing to watch. When you got to lose, it's nice to lose to somebody who knows what he's doing."

"Yeah, you were hot all right," Scotty said, handing Billy a five-dollar bill. "Really hot."

"Hot, my ass," Morrie Berman said to Scotty. "You hexed him, you bastard. He might've gone all the way if you didn't say anything, but you hexed him, talking about it."

The crowd was already moving away, back to the bar, the sweeper confronting those cigar butts at last. New people were arriving, waiters and bartenders who would roll in the Nighthawk League, which started at 3:00 A.M. It was now two-thirty in the morning.

"Listen, you mocky bastard," Scotty said, "I don't have to take any noise from you." Scotty's fists were doubled, his face flushed, his chin in vigorous tremolo. Martin's later vision of Scotty's coloration and form at this moment was that of a large, crimson firecracker.

"Hold on here, hold on," Charlie McCall said. "Cool down, Scotty. No damage done. Cool down, no trouble now." Charlie was about eight feet away from the two men when he spoke, too far to do anything when Morrie started his lunge. But Martin saw it coming and jumped between the two, throwing his full weight into Morrie, his junior by thirty pounds, and knocking him backward into a folding chair, on which he sat without deliberation. Others sealed off Scotty from further attack and Billy held Morrie fast in the chair with two hands.

"Easy does it, man," Billy said, "I don't give a damn what he did."

"The cheap fink," Morrie said. "He wouldn't give a sick whore a hairpin."

Martin laughed at the line. Others laughed. Morrie smiled. Here was a line for the Broadway annals. Epitaph for the Scotcheroo: It was reliably reported during his lifetime that he would not give a sick whore a hairpin. Perhaps this enhanced ignominy was also entering Scotty's head after the laughter, or perhaps it was the result of *his* genetic gift, or simply the losing, and the unbearable self-laceration that went with it. Whatever it was, Scotty doubled up, gasping, burping. He threw his arms around his own chest, wobbled, took a short step, and fell forward, gashing his left cheek on a spittoon. He rolled onto his side, arms still aclutch, eyes squeezing out the agony in his chest.

The mob gawked and Morrie stood up to look. Martin bent over the fallen man, then lifted him up from the floor and stretched him out on the bench from which he had risen to hex Billy. Martin blotted the gash with Scotty's own shirttail, and then opened his left eyelid. Martin looked up at the awestruck mob and asked: "Anybody here a doctor?" And he answered himself: "No, of course not," and looked then at the night manager and said, "Call an ambulance, Al," even though he knew Scotty was already beyond help. Scotty: Game over.

How odd to Martin, seeing a champion die in the embrace of shame, egotism, and fear of failure. Martin trembled at a potential vision of himself also prostrate before such forces, done in by a shame too great to endure, and so now is the time to double up and die. Martin saw his own father curdled by shame, his mother crippled by it twice: her own and her husband's. And Martin himself had been bewildered and thrust into silence and timidity by it (but was that the true cause?). Jesus, man, pay attention here. Somebody lies dead in front of you and you're busy exploring the origins of your own timidity. Martin, as was said of your famous father, your sense of priority is bowlegged.

Martin straightened Scotty's arm along his side, stared at the closed right eye, the half-open left eye, and sat down in the scorekeeper's chair to search pointlessly for vital signs in this dead hero of very recent yore. Finally, he closed the left eye with his thumb.

"He's really gone," he told everybody, and they all seemed to wheeze inwardly. Then they really did disperse until only Charlie Boy McCall, face gone white, sat down at Scotty's feet and stared fully at the end of something. And he said, in his native way, "Holy Mother of God, that was a quick decision."

"Somebody we should call, Charlie?" Martin asked the shocked young man.

"His wife," said Charlie. "He's got two kids."

"Very tough. Very. Anybody else? What about his father?"

"Dead," said Charlie. "His mother's in Florida. His wife's the one."

"I'll be glad to call her," Martin said. "But then again maybe you ought to do that, Charlie. You're so much closer."

"I'll take care of it, Martin."

And Martin nodded and moved away from dead Scotty, who was true to the end to the insulting intent of his public name: tightwad of heart, parsimonious dwarf of soul.

"I never bowled a guy to death before," Billy said.

"No jokes now," Martin said.

"I told you he was a busher," Billy said.

"All right but not now."

"Screw the son of a bitch," Morrie said to them both, said it softly, and then went over to Charlie and said, "I know he was your friend, Charlie, and I'm sorry. But I haven't liked him for years. We never got along."

"Please don't say any more," Charlie said with bowed head.

"I just want you personally to know I'm sorry. Because I know how close you two guys were. I'da liked him if I could, but Jesus Christ, I don't want *you* sore at me, Charlie. You get what I mean?"

"I get it. I'm not sore at you."

"I'm glad you say that because sometimes when you fight a guy his friends turn into your enemies, even though they got nothin' against you themselves. You see what I mean?"

"I see, and I've got nothing against you, Morris. You're just a punk, you've always been a punk, and the fact is I never liked you and like you a hell of a lot less than that right now. Good night, Morris."

And Charlie Boy turned away from Morrie Berman to study the corpse of his friend.

Martin Daugherty, infused with new wisdom by the entire set of events, communicated across the miles of the city to his senile father in the nursing home bed. You see, Papa, Martin said into the microphone of the filial network, it's very clear to me now. The secret of Scotty's death lies in the simple truth uncovered by Morrie Berman: that Scotty would not give a sick whore a hairpin. And Papa, I tell you that we must all give hairpins to sick whores. It is essential. Do you hear me? Can you understand? We must give hairpins to sick whores whenever they require them. What better thing can a man do?

II

MARTIN DAUGHERTY, wearing bathrobe and slippers, sat at his kitchen table, bleeding from sardonic wounds. In the name of the Father, in the name of the Son, who will savor the Father when the Son is gone? He salted his oatmeal and spiced it with raisins, those wrinkled and puny symbols of his own dark and shriveling years. He chewed a single raisin, thinking of Scotty dead, his own son gone to the seminary. But the boy was alive and free to change his mind in time, and the bitter-sweetness of this thought flowed on his tongue: treasure lurking among the wrinkles.

"You're mad entirely," Mary Daugherty said when she saw him smiling and chewing, grim and crazy. She broke into laughter, the lilt of Connacht, a callous response to madness in her morning kitchen.

"You can bet your sweet Irish ass I'm mad," Martin said. "I dreamed of Peter, carried through the streets by pederast priests."

That stopped her laughter, all right.

"You're at the priests again, are you? Why don't you let it alone? He may not even take to it."

"They'll see he does. Fill him full of that windy God shit, called to the front, cherub off Main Street. Give the helping hand to others, learn to talk to the birds and make a bridge to the next world. Why did God make you if it wasn't to save all those wretched bastards who aren't airy and elite enough to be penniless saviors?"

"You're worried he'll be penniless, is that it?"

"I'm worried he'll be saved entirely by priests."

*　　*　　*

The boy, Peter, had been sitting in a web of ropes, suspended beyond the edge of the flat roof of home. Billy Phelan, in another suspended web, sat beside Peter, both of them looking at Martin as they lounged in the ropes, which were all that lay between them and the earth. Martin marveled at the construction of the webs, which defied gravity. And then Peter leaped off the web, face forward, and plummeted two stories. His body hit, then his head, two separate impacts, and he lay still. Two priests in sackcloth scooped him into a wheelbarrow with their shovels and one of them pushed him off into the crowded street. Billy Phelan never moved from his web. Martin, suddenly on the street, followed the wheelbarrow through the rubble but lost it. In a vacant lot he confronted a band of children Peter's age. They jogged in an ominous circle which Martin could not escape. A small girl threw a stone which struck Martin on the head. A small boy loped toward Martin with an upraised knife, and the circle closed in. Martin rushed to meet the knife-wielding attacker and flew at the boy's chest with both feet.

He awoke and squinted toward the foot of the bed, where the figure of an adolescent, wearing a sweater of elaborate patterns, leaned back in a chair, feet propped on the bedcovers. But the figure was perhaps beyond adolescence. Its head was an animal's, with pointed snout. A fox? A fawn? A lamb? Martin sat up, resting on his elbow for a closer look. The figure remained in focus, but the head was still blurred. Martin rubbed his eyes. The figure leaned back on the legs of the chair, feet crossed at the ankles, leisurely observing Martin. And then it vanished, not as a dream fading into wakefulness, but with a filmmaker's magic: suddenly, wholly gone.

Martin, half-erect, leaning on his elbow, heard Mary say the oatmeal was on the table. He thought of the illustrated Bible he had leafed through when he'd come home after Scotty's death, compulsively searching through the Old Testament for an equivalent of the man's sudden departure. He had found nothing that satisfied him, but he'd put out the light thinking of the engraving of Abraham and the bound Isaac, with the ram breaking through the bushes, and he had equated Isaac with his son, Peter, sacrificed to someone else's faith: first communion, confirmation, thrust into the hands of nuns and priests, then smothered by the fears of a mother who still believed making love standing up damned you forever.

Had Martin's fuzzy, half-animal bedside visitor been the ram that saved Isaac from the knife? In a ski sweater? What did it have to do with Peter? Martin opened the Bible to the engraving. The sweatered animal at bedside bore no resemblance to the ram of salvation. Martin re-read what he had written years ago above the engraving after his first reading of the Abraham story: We are all in conspiracy against the next man. He could not now explain what precisely he had meant by that phrase.

* * *

It had been years since the inexplicable touched Martin's life. Now, eating his oatmeal, he examined this new vision, trying to connect it to the dream of Peter falling out of the web, to Peter's face as he left home two days before, a fourteen-year-old boy about to become a high school sophomore, seduced by God's holy messengers to enter a twig-bending preseminary school. Peter: the centerpiece of his life, the only child he would have. He raged silently at the priests who had stolen him away, priests who would teach the boy to pile up a fortune from the coal collection, to scold the poor for their indolence. The assistant pastor of Sacred Heart Church had only recently sermonized on the folly of striving for golden brown toast and the fatuity of the lyrics of "Tea for Two." There was a suburban priest who kept a pet duck on a leash. One in Troy chased a nubile child around the parish house. Priests in their cups. Priests in their beggars' robes. Priests in their eunuch suits. There were saints among them, men of pure love, and one such had inspired Peter, given him the life of Saint Francis to read, encouraging selflessness, fanaticism, poverty, bird calls.

Months ago, when he was shaping his decision, the boy sat at this same kitchen table poking at his own raisins, extolling the goodness of priests. Do you know any good men who aren't priests? Martin asked him.

You, said the boy.

How did I make it without the priesthood?

I don't know, but maybe sometimes you aren't good. Are you always good?

By no means.

Then did you ever know any men good enough to talk to the birds?

Plenty. Neil O'Connor talked to his ducks all day long. After four pints Marty Sheehan'd have long talks with Lackey Quinlan's goose.

But did the birds talk back?

You couldn't shut them up once they got going, said Martin.

Balance: that was what he wanted to induce in Peter. Be reverent also in the presence of the absence of God.

"I just don't want them to drown him in their holy water," Martin said to Mary Daugherty. "And I don't want him to be afraid to tell them to shove their incense up their chalices if he feels like coming home. There'll be none of that failed priest business in this house the

way it was with Chickie Phelan." (And Martin then sensed, unreason-
ably, that Chick would call him on the telephone, soon; perhaps this
morning.) "His mother and sisters wanted Chick to bring a little bit of
heaven into the back parlor, and when he couldn't do it, they never
forgave him. And another thing. I always wanted Peter to grow up here,
grow up and beget. I don't want to see the end of the Daughertys after
the trouble of centuries took us this far."

"You want another Daugherty? Another son? Is that what you're
saying to me?"

"It's that I hate to see the end of a line. Any line. Think of all the
Daughertys back beyond Patrick. Pirates stole *him* you know, made him
a slave. That's how *he* got into the saint business."

"Ah," said Mary, "you're a talky man."

"I am."

"Are you through now?"

"I am."

"Why don't you be talky like that with the boy?"

"I was."

"You told him all that?"

"I did."

"Well, then?" said the wife and mother of the family. "Well?"

"Just about right," said Martin.

*   *   *

The talk had calmed him, and real and present things took his attention:
his wife and her behind, jiggling while she stirred the eggs. Those splendid puffs of Irish history, those sweet curves of the Western world,
sloping imagistically toward him: roundaceous beneath the black and
yellow kimono he'd given her for the New York vacation. The memory
of coupling in their stateroom on the night boat, the memory of their
most recent coupling—was it three, four days ago?—suggested to Martin that screwing your wife is like striking out the pitcher. Martin's
attitude, however, was that there was little point in screwing anyone
else. Was this a moralistic judgment because of his trauma with Melissa
Spencer, or merely an apology for apathetic constancy? Melissa in his
mind again. She would be in town now with the pseudoscandalous
show. She would not call him. He would not call her. Yet he felt they
would very probably meet.

The phone rang and Miss Irish Ass of 1919 callipygiated across the
room and answered it. "Oh yes, yes, Chick, he's here, yes. Imagine that,
and he was just talking about you."

"Well, Chickie," said Martin, "are you ready for the big move today? Is your pencil sharpened?"

"Something big, Martin, really big."

"Big enough," said Martin; for Chick had been the first to reveal to him the plan concocted by Patsy McCall, leader of the Albany Democratic Party, to take control of the American Labor Party's local wing on this, the final day of voter registration. Loyal Democrats, of which Chick was one, would register A.L.P., infiltrate the ranks, and push out the vile Bolsheviks and godless socialists who stank up the city with their radical ways. Patsy McCall and his Democrats would save the city from the red stink.

"No, Martin, it's not that," Chick said. "It's Charlie Boy. The police are next door, and Maloney too. Him and half the damn McCall family's been coming and going over here all night long. He's gone, Martin. Charlie's gone. I think they grabbed him."

"Grabbed him?"

"Kidnapped. They've been using the phone here since four-thirty this morning. A regular parade. They'll be back, I know it, but you're the one should know about this. I owe you that."

"Are you sure of this, Chickie?"

"They're on the way back now. I see Maloney coming down their stoop. Martin, they took Charlie out of his car about four o'clock this morning. His mother got up in the night and saw the car door wide open and nobody inside. A bunch of cigarettes on the running board. And he's gone. I heard them say that. Now, you don't know nothing from here, don't you know, and say a prayer for the boy, Martin, say a prayer. Oh Jesus, the things that go on."

And Chick hung up.

Martin looked at the kitchen wall, dirty tan, needing paint. Shabby wall. Shabby story. Charlie Boy taken. The loss, the theft of children. Charlie was hardly a child, yet his father, Bindy McCall, would still think of him as one.

"What was that?" Mary asked.

"Just some talk about a story."

"Who or what was grabbed? I heard you say grabbed."

"You're fond of that word, are you?"

"It's got a bit of a ring to it."

"You don't have to wait for a ring to get grabbed."

"I knew that good and early, thanks be to God."

And then, Martin grabbed the queenly rump he had lived with for sixteen years, massaged it through the kimono, and walked quickly out of the kitchen to his study. He sat in the reading rocker alongside a stack of Albany newspapers taller than a small boy, and reached for the phone. Already he could see the front pages, the splash, boom, bang, the sad, sad whoopee of the headlines. The extras. The photos. These are the McCall brothers. Here a recap of their extraordinary control of Albany for seventeen years. Here their simple homes. And now this. Here Charlie Boy's car. Here the spot where. Here the running board where the cigarettes fell. Here some famous kidnappings. Wheeeeee.

Martin dialed.

"Yeah," said Patsy McCall's unmistakable sandpaper voice box after the phone rang once.

"Martin Daugherty, Patsy."

"Yeah."

"I hear there's been some trouble."

Silence.

"Is that right or wrong?"

"No trouble here."

"I hear there's a lot of activity over at your place and that maybe something bad happened."

Silence.

"Is that right or wrong, Patsy?"

"No trouble here."

"Are you going to be there a while? All right if I come down?"

"Come down if you like, Martin. Bulldogs wouldn't keep the likes of you off the stoop."

"That's right, Patsy. I'll be there in fifteen minutes. Ten."

"There's nothing going on here."

"Right, Patsy, see you in a little while."

"Don't bring nobody."

❊   ❊   ❊

In his bedroom, moving at full speed, Martin took off his blue flannel bathrobe, spotted with egg drippings and coffee dribbles, pulled on his pants over the underwear he'd slept in and decided not to tell his wife the news. She was a remote cousin to Charlie's mother and would want to lend whatever strength she had to the troubled family, a surge of good will that would now be intrusive.

The McCalls' loss intensified Martin's own. But where his was merely doleful, theirs was potentially tragic. Trouble. People he knew, sometimes his kin, deeply in trouble, was what had often generated his inexplicable visions. Ten years without this kind of divination, now suddenly back: the certainty Chick would call; the bizarre bedside visitor heralding the unknown; the death of Scotty followed by the kidnapping of Charlie. Coincidental trouble.

The inexplicable had first appeared a quarter century ago in late October, 1913, when, fresh from a six-month journalistic foray in England and Ireland, Martin found himself in Albany, walking purposefully but against logic north on North Pearl Street, when he should have been walking west on State Street toward the Capitol, where he had an appointment to interview the new governor, a namesake, Martin H. Glynn, an Albany editor, politician, and orator interested in Ireland's troubles. But a counterimpulse was on him and he continued on Pearl Street to the Pruyn Library, where he saw his cousin, a fireman with steamer eight, sitting on the family wagon, the reins of the old horse sitting loosely on his knees. He was wearing his knitted blue watch cap, a familiar garment to Martin. As their eyes met, the cousin smiled, lifted a pistol from his lap, pointed it at the horse, then turned it to his right temple and pulled the trigger. He died without further ado, leaving the family no explanation for his act, and was smiling still when Martin caught the reins of the startled horse and reached his cousin's side.

Nothing like that happened to Martin again until 1925, the year he published his collection of short stories. But he recognized the same irrational impulse when he was drawn, without reason, to visit the lawyer handling his father's libel suit against an Albany newspaper, which had resurrected the old man's scandal with Melissa. Martin found the lawyer at home, in robust health, and they talked of Martin's father, who at that point was living in New York City. Two hours after their talk the lawyer died of a heart attack walking up Maiden Lane, and the task of finding a new lawyer for his father fell to Martin.

That same year Martin tuned in the radio at mid-morning, an uncharacteristic move, and heard of the sinking of the excursion steamer *Sweethearts* in the Hudson River below Kingston. He later learned that a girl he once loved had gone down with the boat. He began after this to perceive also things not related to trouble. He foresaw by a week that a *Times-Union* photographer would win six thousand dollars in the Albany baseball pool. He was off by only one day in his prediction of when his father would win the libel suit. He knew a love affair would develop between his wife's niece from Galway and an Albany bartender, two months before the niece arrived in Albany. He predicted that on the day of that love's first bloom it would be raining, a thunderstorm, and so it was.

Martin's insights took the shape of crude imagery, like photographs intuited from the radio. He came to consider himself a mystical naturalist, insisting to himself and to others that he did not seriously believe in ghosts, miracles, resurrection, heaven, or hell. He seasoned any account of his beliefs and his bizarre intuition with a remark he credited to his mother: There's no Santa Claus and there's no devil. Your father's both. He dwelled on his visions and found them comforting, even when they were false and led him nowhere and revealed nothing. He felt they put him in touch with life in a way he had never experienced it before, possessor of a power which not even his famous and notorious father, in whose humiliating shadow he had lived all his years, understood. His father was possessed rather by concrete visions of the Irish in the New World, struggling to throw off the filth of poverty, oppression, and degradation, and rising to a higher plane of life, where they would be the equals of all those arrived Americans who manipulated the nation's power, wealth, and culture. Martin was bored with the yearnings of the immigrant hordes and sought something more abstract: to love oneself and one's opposite. He preferred personal insight to social justice, though he wrote of both frequently in his column, which was a confusion of radicalism, spiritual exploration, and foolery. He was a comedian who sympathized with Heywood Broun, Tom Mooney, and all Wobblies, who drank champagne with John McCormack, beer with Mencken, went to the track with Damon Runyon, wrote public love letters to Marlene Dietrich whenever her films played Albany, and who viewed America's detachment from the Spanish Civil War as an exercise in evil by omission.

He also wrote endlessly on a novel, a work he hoped would convey his version of the meaning of his father's scandalous life. He had written twelve hundred pages, aspiring to perhaps two hundred or less, and could not finish it. At age fifty he viewed himself, after publication of two books of non-fiction, one on the war, the other a personal account of the Irish troubles, plus the short story collection and innumerable articles for national magazines, as a conundrum, a man unable to define his commitment or understand the secret of his own navel, a literary gnome. He seriously valued almost nothing he wrote, except for the unfinished novel.

He was viewed by the readers of the *Times-Union*, which carried his column five days a week, as a mundane poet, a penny-whistle philosopher, a provocative half-radical man nobody had to take seriously, for he wasn't quite serious about himself. He championed dowsing and ouija boards and sought to rehabilitate Henry James, Sr., the noted Albanian and Swedenborgian. He claimed that men of truest vision were, like James, always considered freaks, and he formed the International Brotherhood of Crackpots by way of giving them a bargaining agent, and attracted two thousand members.

His column was frequently reprinted nationally, but he chose not to syndicate it, fearing he would lose his strength, which was his Albany constituency, if his subject matter went national. He never wrote of his own gift of foresight.

The true scope of that gift was known to no one, and only his family and a few friends knew it existed at all. The source of it was wondered at suspiciously by his Irish-born wife, who had been taught in the rocky wastes of Connemara that druids roamed the land, even to this day.

The gift left Martin in 1928 after his fortieth birthday debauch with Melissa, the actress, his father's erstwhile mistress, the woman who was the cause of the paternal scandal. Martin returned home from the debauch, stinking of simony, and severely ill with what the family doctor simplistically diagnosed as alcoholic soak. Within a week Martin accurately sensed that his mystical talent was gone. He recuperated from the ensuing depression after a week, but rid himself of the simoniacal stink only when he acceded to his wife's suggestion, and, after a decade of considering himself not only not a Catholic but not even a Christian, he sought out the priest in the Lithuanian church who spoke and understood English only primitively, uttered a confession of absurd sins (I burned my wife's toenail parings three times) and then made his Easter Duty at Sacred Heart Church, driving out the odor of simony with ritual sacrilege.

He shoved his arms into the fresh shirt Mary Daugherty had ironed. A fresh shirt every day, Mary insisted, or you'll blow us all out the window with the B.O. Martin pushed into his black shoes, gone gray with months of scuffs and the denial of polish, threw a tie once around his neck in a loose knot, and thrust himself into his much abused suit coat. A *sughan*, Mary said. You've made a *sughan* of it. Ah well, all things come alike to all, the clean and the unclean, the pressed and the unimpressed.

In the bathroom he brushed away the taste of oatmeal, splashed his face with cold water, flattened his cowlick with the hairbrush, and then salt-stepped down the stairs, saying as he sped through the kitchen: "I've got a hell of a story, I think, Mary. I'll call you."

"What about your coffee? What about your eggs?"

But he was already gone, this aging firefly who never seemed to his wife to have grown up quite like other men, gone on another story.

*   *   *

Martin Daugherty had once lived in Arbor Hill, where the McCalls and the Phelans lived, but fire destroyed the house of his childhood and adolescence, and the smoke poisoned Katrina Daugherty, his mother, who escaped the flames only to die on the sidewalk of Colonie Street in her husband's arms, quoting Verlaine to him: ". . . you loved me so!" "Quite likely—I forget."

The fire began in the Christian Brothers School next door, old Brother William turned to a kneeling cinder by the hellish flames. The fire leaped across the alley and consumed the Daugherty house, claiming not only its second victim in Martin's mother, but also his father's accumulation of a lifetime of books, papers, and clippings that attested to his fame and infamy, and two unfinished plays. Edward Daugherty left Arbor Hill forever after the fire and moved into the North End of the city, politely evicting the tenants in his own father's former home on Main Street.

This was the house Edward Daugherty's parents had built on the edge of the Erie Canal the year before Martin was born, and had lived in until they died. After Edward's first stroke, Martin moved into the house also, with his wife and son, to nurse his father back to independence. But the man was never to be well again, and Martin remained in the house even until now, curator of what he had come to call the Daugherty Museum.

Martin parked his car on Colonie Street in front of the vacant lot where his former home had stood before it burned. He stepped out onto the sidewalk where he'd once pitched pennies and election cards, and the charred roots of his early life moved beneath his feet. Chick Phelan peered out of the upstairs bay window of the house next to the empty lot. Martin did not wave. He looked fleetingly at the outline of the foundation of the old place, slowly being buried by the sod of time.

Patsy McCall's house was kitty-corner to the empty lot and Martin crossed the street and climbed the stoop. He, the Phelans, the McCalls (Bindy lived two doors above Patsy), and all the other youths of the street had spent uncountable nights on this stoop, talking, it now seemed, of three subjects: baseball, the inaccessibility of the myriad burgeoning breasts that were poking themselves into the eyeballs and fluid dreams of every boy on the street, and politics: Would you work for Billy Barnes? Never. Packy McCabe? Sure. Who's the man this election? Did you hear how the Wally-Os stole a ballot box in the Fifth Ward and Corky Ronan chased 'em and got it back and bit off one of their ears?

Martin looked at his watch: eight thirty-five. He rang the doorbell and Dick Maloney, district attorney of Albany County, a short, squat man with an argumentive mouth, answered.

"You're up early, Dick, me boy."

"Am I?"

"Are you in possession of any news?"

"There's no news I know of."

And Maloney pointed toward the dining room, where Martin found Patsy and Matt McCall, the political leaders of the city and county for seventeen years. Cronies of both brothers sat with them at the huge round table, its white tablecloth soiled with coffee stains and littered with cups, ashes, and butts. On the wall the painted fruit was ripening in the bowl and the folks were still up at Golgotha. Alongside hung

framed, autographed photos of Jim Jeffries, Charlie Murphy of Tammany, Al Smith as presidential candidate, and James Oliver Plunkett,
who had inscribed the photo with one of his more memorable lines:
"Government of the people, by the people who were elected to govern
them."

   "Morning, gentlemen," Martin said with somber restraint.

   "We're not offering coffee," said Patsy, looking his usual, overstuffed self. With his tight haircut, rounded jowls, and steel-rimmed
specs, this Irish-American chieftain looked very like a Prussian puffball
out of uniform.

   "Then thanks for nothing," said Martin.

   The cronies, Poop Powell, an ex-hurley player and ex-cop who
drove for the McCalls, and Freddie Gallagher, a childhood pal of Matt's
who found that this friendship alone was the secret of survival in the
world, rose from the table and went into the parlor without a word or
a nod. Martin sat in a vacated chair and said to Patsy, "There's something tough going on, I understand."

   "No, nothing," said Patsy.

   The McCalls' faces were abulge with uncompromising gravity. For
all their power they seemed suddenly powerless confronting personal
loss. But many men had passed into oblivion for misjudging the Mc-
Calls' way with power. Patsy demonstrated it first in 1919 when he
campaigned in his sailor suit for the post of city assessor and won, oh
wondrous victory. It was the wedge which broke the hold the dirty black
Republican sons of bitches had had on the city since '99. Into the chink
Patsy made in the old machine, the Democrats, two years later, drove
a new machine, the Nonesuch, with the McCalls at the wheel: Patsy,
the savior, the *sine qua non*, becoming the party leader and patron;
Matt, the lawyer, becoming the political strategist and spokesman; and
Benjamin, called Bindy, the sport, taking over as Mayor of Nighttime
City.

   The three brothers, in an alliance with a handful of Protestant Yankee aristocrats who ran the formal business of the city, developed a
stupendous omnipotence over both county and city, which vibrated
power strings even to the White House. Democratic aspirants made
indispensable quadrennial pilgrimages to genuflect in the McCall cathedral and plead for support. The machine brushed the lives of every
Albany citizen from diapers to dotage. George Quinn often talked of
the day he leaped off the train at Van Woert Street, coming back in
uniform from France, and was asked for five dollars by John Kelleher
on behalf of Patsy's campaign for the assessorship. George gave not five
but fifteen and had that to brag about for the rest of his life.

   "I have to say it," Martin said, looking at Patsy, his closest friend among the brothers. "There's a rumor around that Charlie was kidnapped last night."

The gravity of the faces did not change, nor did the noncommittal expressions.

"Nothing to that," said Matt, a tall, solid man, still looking like the fullback he once was, never a puffball; handsome and with a movie actor's crop of black hair. When he gained power, Matt put his college football coach on the Supreme Court bench.

"Is Charlie here?" Martin asked him.

"He went to New York," Matt said.

"When was that?"

"None of your goddamn business," said Patsy.

"Patsy, listen. I'm telling you the rumor is out. If it's fake and you don't squelch it, you'll have reporters crawling in the windows."

"Not these windows I won't. And why should I deny something that hasn't happened? What the hell do you think I am, a goddamn fool?"

The rising anger. Familiar. The man was a paragon of wrath when cornered. Unreason itself. He put Jigger Begley in tears for coming drunk to a rally, and a week later Jigger, Patsy's lifelong friend, quit his job in the soap factory, moved to Cleveland, and for all anybody knew was there yet. Power in the voice.

Martin's personal view was this: that I do not fear the McCalls; that this is my town as much as theirs and I won't leave it for any of them. Martin had committed himself to Albany in part because of the McCalls, because of the promise of a city run by his childhood friends. But he'd also come back to his native city in 1921, after two years with the A.E.F. and a year and a half in Ireland and England after that, because he sensed he would be nothing without his roots, and when, in 1922, he was certain of this truth he went back to Ireland and brought Maire Kiley out of her Gaelic wilderness in Carraroe, married her in Galway, and came to Albany forever, or at least sixteen years now seemed like forever. So to hell with Patsy and his mouth and the whole bunch of them and their power. Martin Daugherty's complacency is superior to whatever abstract whip they hold over him. But then again, old fellow, there's no need to make enemies needlessly, or to let the tone of a man's voice turn your head.

"One question then," Martin said with his mildest voice, "and then I'm done with questions."

The brothers waited solemnly.

"Is Bindy in town?"

"He's in Baltimore," said Matt. "At the races with his wife."

Martin nodded, waited, then said, "Patsy, Matt. You say there's nothing going on and I have to accept that, even though Maloney looks like he's about to have twins on the stair carpet. But very obviously something *is* happening, and you don't want it out. All right, so be it. I give you my word, and I pledge Em Jones's word, that the *Times-Union* will not print a line about this thing, whatever it is. Not the rumor, not the denial of the rumor, not any speculation. We will not mention Charlie, or Bindy, or either of you in any context other than conventional history, until you give the go-ahead. I don't break confidences without good reason and you both know that about me all my life. And I'll tell you one more thing. Emory will do anything in his power to put the newspaper behind you in any situation such as the hypothetical one we've not been discussing here. I repeat. Not discussing. Under no circumstances have we been discussing anything here this morning. But if the paper can do anything at all, then it will. I pledge that as true as I stand here talking about nothing whatsoever."

The faces remained grave. Then Patsy's mouth wrinkled sideways into the makings of a small grin.

"You're all right, Martin," he said. "For a North Ender."

Martin stood and shook Matt's hand, then Patsy's.

"If anything should come up we'll let you know," Matt said. "And thanks."

"It's what's right," Martin said, standing up, thinking: I've still got the gift of tongues. For it was as true as love that by talking a bit of gibberish he had verified, beyond doubt, that Charlie Boy McCall had, indeed, been grabbed.

"You know I saw Charlie last night down at the Downtown alleys. We were there when Scotty Streck dropped dead. I suppose you know about that one."

"We knew he was there," Patsy said. "We didn't know who else."

"We're working on that," Matt said.

"I can tell you who was there to the man," Martin said, and he ticked off names of all present except the sweeper and one bar customer, whom he identified by looks. Matt made notes on it all.

"What was Berman doing there?" Patsy asked.

"I don't know. He just turned up at the bar."

"Was he there before Charlie got there?"

"I can't be sure of that."

"Do you think he knew Charlie would be at the alleys?"

"I couldn't say."

"Do you know Berman?"

"I've been in his company, but we're not close."

"Who is close to him?"

Martin shook his head, thinking of faces but connecting no one intimately to the man. Then he said, "Billy Phelan seems to know him. Berman backed him in last night's match and did the same once before, when Billy played pool. He seems to like Billy."

"Do you trust Phelan?" Matt asked.

"No man in his right mind would trust him with his woman, but otherwise he's as good as gold, solid as they come."

"We want to keep tabs on that Berman fellow," Patsy said.

"You think he's connected to this situation?" and both Patsy and Matt shrugged without incriminating Berman, but clearly admitting there certainly was a situation.

"We're keeping tabs on a lot of people," Patsy said. "Can you ask young Phelan to hang around a while with Berman, the next few days, say, and let us know where he goes and what he says?"

"Ahhhhh," said Martin, "that's tricky but I guess I can ask."

"Don't you think he'll do it?"

"I wouldn't know, but it is touchy. Being an informer's not Billy's style."

"Informer?" said Patsy, bristling.

"It's how he might look at it."

"That's not how I look at it."

"I'll ask him," Martin said. "I can certainly ask him."

"We'll take good care of him if he helps us," Matt said. "He can count on that."

"I don't think he's after that either."

"Everybody's after that," Patsy said.

"Billy's headstrong," Martin said, standing up.

"So am I," said Patsy. "Keep in touch."

"Bulldogs," said Martin.

III

M ARTIN DROVE DOWNTOWN and parked on Broadway near the Plaza, as usual, and headed, he thought, for the *Times-Union*. But instead of turning up Beaver Street, he walked south on Broadway, all the way to Madison Avenue. He turned up Madison, realizing then that he was bound for Spanish George's bar. He had no urge to drink and certainly no reason to confront either George or any of his customers, especially at this hour. George, notorious in the city's South End, ran a bar and flophouse in Shanks's old three-story livery stable. He had come to America from Spain to build the Barge Canal and stayed on to establish an empire in the dregs, where winos paid to collapse on his cots after they had all but croaked on his wine.

The sour air assaulted Martin as he stepped inside the bar, but he understood the impulse that was on him and did not retreat. His will seemed unfettered, yet somehow suspended. He knew he was obeying something other than will and that it might, or might not, reveal its purpose. In the years when this came as a regular impulse, he often found himself sitting in churches, standing in front of grocery stores, or riding trolleys, waiting for revelation. But the trolley often reached the end of the line and took him back to his starting point without producing an encounter, and he would resume the previous path of his day, feeling duped by useless caprice. Yet the encounters which did prove meaningful, or even prophetic of disaster or good fortune, were of such weight that he could not help but follow the impulse once he recognized it for what it was. He came to believe that the useless journeys did not arise from the same source as those with genuine meaning, but were rather his misreadings of his own mood, his own imagination, a duping of self with counterfeit expectations. Five such fruitless trips in four days after his debauch made him aware his gift had fled. Now, as he gagged on the wine-pukish rancidity of George's, on the dead-rat stink and the vile-body decay that entered your system with every breath, he was certain that the impulse was the same as it had always been, whether true or false; and what he was doing was giving his mystical renewal a chance to prove itself. He ordered a bottle of beer and when George was looking elsewhere he wiped its neck clean with his handkerchief and drank from the bottle.

"I don't see you too much," George said to him.

George was, as usual, wearing his filthy sombrero and his six-gun in the embroidered leather holster, and looked very like a Mexican *bandido*. The gun, presumably, was not loaded, or so the police had ordered. But any wino aggressive on muscatel could not be so sure of that, and so George, by force of costume alone, maintained order on his premises.

"That's true, George," Martin said. "I keep pretty busy uptown. Not much on this edge of things lately."

"I see you writing in the paper."

"Still at it. Right you are."

"You never write me a story any more."

"I've done you, George, again and again. You've ceased to be newsy. If you decide to renovate the premises and put in a bridal suite, then maybe I'll work up a story."

"No money in that stuff."

"You're probably right. Honeymooners are bum spenders. But business is good, I suppose?"

"Always lousy. You like a sandwich? Fry an egg for you?"

"I just had breakfast, thanks. The beer is fine."

"Okay," George said, and he pushed Martin's dollar back to him.

Martin sensed a presence then and looked toward the door to see a tall, shambling man in a suit coat of brown twill, collar up, lighting a cigarette as he moved toward the bar. Despite what the years had done to the man, Martin instantly recognized Francis Phelan, Billy's father, and he knew his own presence here had a purpose. Forced confluence of Martin and the Phelans: Billy and Chick, now Francis, and yet more than that. The McCalls were part of it. And Martin's father, too, in his bed of senility; and Melissa, in town in the old man's play. A labyrinth.

"Francis," said Martin, and Francis turned and squinted through half-waking eyes, pitiable visage. Martin vividly remembered the original: Franny Phelan: Albany's best-known ballplayer in his time. And he remembered too the dreadful day in 1901 when the scabs and the militia were trying to drive a single trolley through a mob on Broadway in front of Union Station, and Franny, in front of the Railroad YMCA, hurling a smooth round stone like a fast ball, and laying open the skull of the scab conductor. The militia fired wildly into the crowd as other stones flew, and in retaliation for the dead scab, two men who had nothing to do with the violence, a businessman and a shopper, were shot dead. And Franny became a fugitive, his exile proving to be the compost for his talent. He fled west, using an alias, and got a job in Dayton playing pro ball. When he came home again to live, he returned to life on the road every summer for years, the last three as a big leaguer with Washington. Franny Phelan, a razzmatazz third baseman, maestro of the hidden ball trick.

Such a long time ago. And now Franny is back, the bloom of drink in every pore, the flesh ready to bleed through the sheerest of skin. He puffed his cigarette, dropped the lit match to the floor, inhaled, and then looked searchingly at Martin, who followed the progress of the match, watched its flame slowly burn out on the grease of George's floor.

"Ah, how are you, Martin?" Francis said.

"I'm well enough, Fran, and how are you keeping yourself?"

"Keeping?" He smiled. "Orange soda, with ice," he told George.

"What color orange has your money got?" George said.

"Take it here," said Martin, pushing the dollar back to George. And George then poured Francis a glass of soda over ice, a jelly glass with a ridged rim.

"It's been years," Martin said. "Years and years."

"I guess so," said Francis. He sipped the soda, once, twice. "Goddamn throat's burning up." He raised the glass. "Cheers."

"To you," Martin said, raising the bottle, "back in Albany."

"I only came to vote," said Francis, smiling.

"To vote?"

"To register. They still pay for that here, don't they?"

"Ah, yes, of course. I understand. Yes, I believe they do."

"I did it before. Registered fourteen times one year. Twenty-eight bucks."

"The price is up to five now. It must've been a long while ago you did that."

"I don't remember. I don't remember much of anything any more."

"How long has it been? Twenty years, it must be."

"Twenty-two. I do remember that. Nineteen-sixteen."

"Twenty-two years. You see the family?"

"No, I don't go through that business."

"I talked to Chick this morning."

"Fuck him."

"Well, I always get along pretty well with him. And he always thought well of you."

"Fuck 'em all."

"You don't see your kids either?"

"No, I don't see nobody." He sipped the soda. "You see the boy?"

"Quite often. He's a first-rate citizen, and good looking, with some of your features. I was with him last night. He bowled two-ninety-nine in a match game."

"Yeah."

"You want to see him? I could set that up."

"No, hell no. None of that old shit. That's old shit. I'm out of it, Martin. Don't do nothin' like that to me."

"If you say so."

"Yeah, I do. No percentage in that."

"You here for a while?"

"No, passing through, that's all. Get the money and get gone."

"Very strange development, running into you here. Anything I can do for you, Franny?" Franny, the public name. What a hell of a ball player, gone to hell.

"I could use a pack of smokes."

"What's your brand?"

Francis snorted. "Old Golds. Why not?"

Martin pushed a quarter at George and George fished for the cigarettes and bounced them on the bar in front of Francis.

"That's two I owe you, Martin. What're you doin' for yourself?"

"I write for the morning paper, a daily column."

"A writer like your father."

"No, not like that. Not anything like that. Just a column."

"You were always a smart kid. You always wrote something. Your father still alive?"

"Oh yes," and ancient times rolled back, the years before and after the turn of the century when the Phelans and Daughertys were next-door neighbors and Martin's mother was alive in her eccentric isolation. Francis was the handyman who fixed whatever went wrong in the Daugherty home, Edward Daugherty cosmically beyond manual labor, Martin a boyish student of Francis's carpentry skills as he put on the new roof or enlarged the barn to house two carriages instead of one. He was installing a new railing on the back stoop the summer morning Martin's mother came down that same stoop naked, bound for the carriage barn with her shopping bag. Francis wrapped her in a piece of awning and walked her back into the house, the first indication to anyone except Edward Daugherty that something was distracting her.

Edward Daugherty used Francis as the prototype for the fugitive hero in his play about the trolley strike, *The Car Barns*, in which heroic Francis, the scab-killer, was immortalized. Legends and destinies worked out over the back fence. Or over a beer and an orange soda.

"He's in a nursing home now," Martin said of his father. "Pretty senile, but he has his moments when a good deal of it comes back. Those are the worst times."

"That's how it goes," Francis said.

"For some people."

"Yeah. Some don't get that far."

"I have the feeling I ought to do something for you, Fran," Martin said. "Something besides a pack of cigarettes and a glass of soda. Why do I feel that?"

"Damned if I know, Martin. Nothing I want out of you."

"Well, I'm around. I'm in the book, up on Main Street in the North End now. And you can always leave a message at the *Times-Union*."

"Okay, Martin, and thanks for that," and Francis extended his right hand, which was missing two joints on the index finger. He will throw no more baseballs. Martin shook the hand and its stumpy digit.

"Don't blow any whistles on me, Martin. I don't need that kind of scene."

"It's your life," Martin said, but even as he said it he was adding silently: but not entirely yours. Life hardly goes by ones.

*   *   *

Martin bought an *Armstrong* at Jerry's newsroom, just up from the paper, and then an egg sandwich and coffee to go at Farrell's lunchroom, three doors down, and with breakfast and horses in hand he crossed Beaver Street, climbed the paintless, gray, footworn, and crooked staircase to the *Times-Union* city room, and settled in at his desk, a bruised oak antique at which the Albany contemporaries of Mark Twain might have worked. Across the room Joe Leahy, the only other citizen on duty and a squeaker of a kid, was opening mail at the city desk and tending the early phone. The only other life sign was the clacking of the Associated Press and International News Service teletypes, plus the Hearst wire, which carried the words of The Chief: editorials, advisories, exclusive stories on Marion Davies.

Martin never looked at the machine without remembering the night Willie Powers, the night slot man, went to lunch and came back pickled, then failed to notice an advisory that The Chief was changing his front-page editorial on Roosevelt, changing it drastically from soft- to hard-line antipathy, for the following day. Willie failed to notice not only the advisory but also the editorial which followed it, and so the *Times-Union* the next morning carried The Chief's qualified praise of F.D.R., while the rest of the Hearst press across the nation carried The Chief's virulent attack on the president, his ancestors, his wife, his children, his dog.

There is no record of Hearst's ever having visited the *Times-Union* city room, but a week later, during a stopover at the Albany station on the Twentieth Century, The Chief received Emory Jones, who presented him with the day's final edition, an especially handsome, newsy product by local standards. The Chief looked at the paper, then without a word let it fall to the floor of his private compartment, and jumped up and down on it with both feet until Emory fled in terror.

Martin fished up salt, pepper, saccharin, and spoon to garnish his sandwich and coffee and, as he ate, studied the entries in the *Armstrong*. There in the third at Laurel loomed a hunch, if ever a hunch there was: Charley Horse, seven-to-one on the morning line. He circled it, uncradled the phone receiver and dialed the operator: Madge, lively crone.

"Any messages for me, kiddo?"

"Who'd call you, you old bastard? Wait while I look. Yes, Chick Phelan called. Not that long ago. He didn't leave a number."

"You heard from Emory? He coming in?"

"Not a word from him."

"Then give me a line."

Martin dialed home and told Mary the news and swore her to secrecy. Then he called Chick's home. The phone rang but nobody answered. He dialed the home of Emory Jones, the Welsh rarebit, the boss of bosses, editor of editors, a heroic Hearstian for almost as many years as Hearst had owned newspapers, a man who lived and died for the big story, who coveted the Pulitzer Prize he would never win and hooted the bootlickers and eggsuckers who waltzed off with it year after year. Martin would now bring him the word on the Charlie Boy story, fracture his morning serenity.

Martin remembered the last big Albany story, the night word arrived that a local man wanted for a triple murder in Canada would probably try to return to the U.S. Which border crossing he had in mind was uncertain, so Em Jones studied the map and decided the fellow would cross at Montreal. But on the off chance he would go elsewhere Emory also alerted border police at Niagara Falls, Baudette, Minnesota, and Blaine, Washington, to our man perhaps en route. When the four calls were made Emory sat down at the city desk, lit up a stogie, and propped up his feet to wait for the capture. We got him surrounded, he said.

"Em, that you?"

"Ynnnnnh."

"I've got a bit of news."

"Ynnnh."

"Charlie McCall was kidnapped during the night."

Emory yawned. "You drunken son of a bitch."

"I'm not drunk, nor have I been, nor will I be."

"Then you mean it? You mean it?" Emory stood up. Even through the telephone, Martin observed that.

"I just left Patsy and Matt, and Maloney too, all at Patsy's house, and I pledged in your name we wouldn't run a story on it."

"Now I know you're lying." Emory sat down.

"Emory, you better get down here. This town is getting ready to turn itself inside out."

The editor of editors fell silent.

"You really do mean it?"

"Whoever grabbed Charlie meant it, too."

"But you didn't tell Patsy that about no story. You wouldn't say that."

"I did."

"You needle-brained meathead. What in the sweet Christ's name possessed you?"

"My Celtic wisdom."

"Your Celtic ass is right between your eyes, that's your wisdom. I'm coming down. And you better figure a way to undo that pledge, for your own sake. And this better be real. Is it real?"

"Em, are your teeth real?"

"Half and half."

"Then Em, this story is even more real than your teeth."

*   *   *

Martin found two more Chuck and Charlie horses in the *Armstrong*, checked his wallet, and lumped all but his last ten on the bunch, across the board, plus a parlay. Never a hunch like this one. He called the bets in to Billy Phelan, the opening move in his effort to bring Billy into the McCall camp, not that Billy would require much persuasion. Billy was a Colonie Streeter, was he not? Grew up three doors up from Patsy and next door to Bindy, knew Charlie Boy all his life. But Billy was an odd duck, a loner, you bet, erratic in a way Martin was not. Billy was self-possessed, even as a boy, but then again he had to be, did he not? Fatherless from age nine, when Francis Phelan left home, left wife, son, and daughter forever, or at least until this morning.

Martin's problem was similar, but turned inside out: too much father, too much influence, too much fame, too much scandal, but also too much absence as the great man pursued his greatness. And these, my friends, are forces that deprived a young man of self-possession and defined his life as a question mark, unlike Billy Phelan's forces, which defined *his* life as an exclamation point.

When his bets were made Martin swallowed the last of his coffee and went to the morgue and pulled all files on the McCalls. They should have had a file cabinet to themselves, given the coverage of their lives through the years, but thieves walked abroad. No clips remained of Patsy's victory in 1919, or even of the Democratic sweep of the city in 1921. Stories on the 1931 legislative probe into the city's assessment racket were gone. So were all reports on Patsy's doing six months for contempt in the baseball-pool scandal.

This was historical revisionism through burglary. Had freelancers looking for yet another magazine piece on the notorious McCalls done the filching? Or was it McCall loyalist reporters, who doubled on the city payroll as sidewalk inspectors? The lightfingering effectively kept past history out of the ready reach of reform-minded newsmen, or others snooping on behalf of uplift: Tom Dewey, the redoubtable D.A., for instance, who was making noises like a governor: Elect me, folks, and I'll send the McCall bunch swirling down the sinkhole of their own oily unguents.

Joe Leahy saw Martin shuffling through the McCall files and wondered aloud, "What's up with them?"

"Ahh," said Martin with theatrical weariness, "a backgrounder on them and the A.L.P. Big power move that comes to a head tonight when the enrollment figures come in."

"The McCalls taking on the reds? Can they really do it?"

"The power of prayer is with them. The bishop's behind Patsy all the way."

"You writing something for the first edition?"

"Nothing for the first. When it happens, it happens."

Martin turned back to the folders and Leahy walked off, a good Catholic boy who loved Franco and hated the reds. Untrustworthy with anything meaningful. Martin leafed through the Charlie Boy file, all innocuous stuff. Promoted to major in the National Guard. Engaged to sweet-faced Patricia Brennan. Initiated into the B.P.O.E. lodge number forty-nine. Named vice-president of the family brewery. Shown visiting Jimmy Braddock in his dressing room in Chicago before the fight with Joe Louis. Shown with his favorite riding horse, a thoroughbred named Macushla, birthday gift from Uncle Patsy of political fame, who keeps horses on a small Virginia farm.

Charlie was pudgy, the face of a smiling marshmallow on the torso of a left tackle. There he stood in his major's suit, all Sam Browne and no wrinkles. Where are you this minute, Charlie Boy? Tied to a bed?

Gun at your brain? How much do they say your life is worth? Have they already killed you?

Martin remembered Charlie's confirmation, the boy kissing the bishop's ring; then at the party Bindy gave afterward at the Hampton Hotel, the bishop kissing Bindy's foot. That was the year the McCalls all but donated the old city almshouse to the Catholic diocese as a site for the new Christian Brothers Academy, the military high school where Charlie would become a cadet captain. Martin's wife, Maire, now called Mary, a third or maybe fourth cousin to Bindy's wife, sang "Come Back to Erin" at the confirmation party, accompanied on the piano by Mrs. Dillon, the organist at St. Joseph's Church, whose son was simple-minded. And Mary, when the bishop congratulated her on her voice and patted her on the hand, felt fully at home in America for the first time since Martin had snatched her away from Ireland.

Martin's recollection of Charlie Boy on that afternoon was obscured by memories of Bindy and Patsy and Matt, whom he saw yet at a table in a far corner, objects of veneration, Albany's own Trinity.

The perils of being born, like himself, to a man of such fame and notoriety sent Martin into commiseration with Charlie. Bindy was an eminence, the power on the street. "Celebrated sporting figure" and "a member of the downtown fraternity" was as far as the papers ever went by way of identifying him. Cautious journalism. No one mentioned his direct power over the city's illegal gambling. No editor would let a writer write it. It was the received wisdom that no one minds the elephant in the parlor if nobody mentions it's there. Martin's own decision to tell Patsy there would be no story on the kidnapping: Was that conspiratorial genuflection? No end to the veneration of power, for the news is out: The McCalls hurl thunderbolts when affronted.

The memory of their confrontation with *The Albany Sentinel* was still fresh. *The Sentinel* had prospered as an opposition voice to the McCalls in the early days of the machine, but its success was due less to its political point of view than to the gossip it carried. In 1925 the paper dredged up "The Love Nest Tragedy of 1908" involving Edward Daugherty and Melissa Spencer, purporting to have discovered two dozen torchy love letters from the famous playwright to the now beloved star of the silent screen. The letters were crude forgeries and Melissa ignored them. But Edward Daugherty halted their publication with an injunction and a libel suit. Patsy McCall saw to it that the judge in the case was attuned to the local realities, saw to it also that a hand-picked jury gave proper consideration to Patsy's former Colonie Street neighbor. *The Sentinel* publicly admitted the forgery and paid nominal libel damages. But it then found its advertisers withdrawing *en masse* and its tax assessment quintupled. Within a month the ragbag sons of bitches closed up shop and left town, and moral serenity returned to Albany as McCall Democracy won the day.

"Aren't you a little early this morning?"

Marlene Whiteson, a reporter whose stories were so sugary that you risked diabetic coma if you read them regularly, stood in front of Martin's desk, inside her unnecessary girdle, oozing even at this hour the desire but not quite the will, never quite the will, to shed those restrictive stays, leap onto the desk, and do a goat dance with him, or with anyone. But Marlene was an illusionist, her sexuality the disappearing rabbit: Now you see it, now you don't. Reach out to touch and find it gone, back inside her hat. The city room was full of hopefuls, ready to do Marlene, but as far as Martin knew, he himself came closest to trapping the rabbit on a night six years past when both of them worked late and he drove her home, circuitously. Need one explain why he stopped the car, stroked her cheek? She volunteered a small gift of smooch and said into his ear, Oh, Martin, you're the man I'd like to go to Pago Pago with. Whereupon he reached for her portions, only to be pushed away, while she continued nevertheless with bottomless smooch. Twist my tongue but stroke me never. Oh the anomaly. Coquettes of the world, disband; you have nothing to gain but saliva.

"What goodies do you have for us today?" Martin asked her.

"I have a message for you, as a matter of fact. Did you see this morning's paper?"

"I was just about to crack it."

"I have a story in about Melissa Spencer. She sends you greetings and hopes she gets a chance to see you. She also asked about your father."

"Ah. And is she well?"

"She looks absolutely gorgeous. For forty-nine. She is some sexy dame."

"How long will she be here?"

"Just a week."

Martin knew that. He had known for weeks she was starring in the touring production of his father's great work, *The Flaming Corsage*, the play Edward Daugherty had written in order to transform his melodramatic scandal with Melissa and her jealous lesbian lover, and the consequent destruction of his career and his wife, into anguished theatrical harmony. He used both Martin's mother, Katrina, and the young Melissa as models for the two principal women in the play, and, not unnaturally, Melissa, as a young actress, yearned to incarnate the role she had inspired in life.

Now, at forty-nine, no longer disguisable as the pristine Melissa of 1908, she was appearing in the play for the first time, but as the hero's reclusive, middle-aged wife. The casting, the result of assiduous pursuit of the part by Melissa herself, had the quality of aged perfume about it: yesterday's scarlet tragedy revived for an audience which no longer remembered this flaming, bygone sin, but for whom the reversal of roles by the famed Melissa was still quaintly scandalous. Melissa had acted in the play for six months on Broadway before taking it on the road, her comeback after a decade of invisibility: one of the most animatedly lovely stars of the silent screen back once more in the American embrace, this time visible, all but palpable, in the flesh.

"She really is interested in seeing you," Marlene said, opening the morning paper to her interview with Melissa and spreading it on Martin's desk. "She's keeping a ticket in your name at the box office, and she wants you to go backstage after the curtain." Marlene smiled and raised her sexual eyebrow. "You devil," she said, moving away from Martin's desk.

Martin barely managed a smile for the world champion of sexual fatuity. How surprised she would be at what Melissa could do with the same anatomical gifts as her own. He looked at Melissa's photo in the paper and saw Marlene was right. Melissa was still beautiful. When time descends, the ego forfends. But Martin could not read her story now. Too distracted to resurrect old shame, old pleasure. But Martin, you will go backstage one night this week, will you not? He conjured the vision of the naked, spread-eagled Melissa and his phone rang. Chick Phelan on the line.

"I saw you go in across the street, Martin. What'd they say?"

"Not much except to confirm what you said."

"Now they've cut off all the phones on the block. I'm in Tony Looby's store down on Pearl Street."

Chick, the snoop, grateful to Martin for introducing him to Evelyn Hurley, the love of his life, whom he is incapable of marrying. Chick will reciprocate the favor as long as love lasts.

"They probably don't want any busybodies monitoring their moves and spreading the word all over town. Anything else going on?"

"People coming in here know something's up but they don't know what."

"Just keep what you know under your hat, Chickie, for Charlie's sake as well as your own. My guess is they're afraid for his life. And keep me posted."

Martin called Walter Bradley, the Albany police chief.

"Walter, I hear the phones are out on Colonie Street."

"What's that to me? Call the phone company."

"We've been told, Walter, that something happened to Charlie McCall. I figured you'd know about it."

"Charlie? I don't know anything about that at all. I'm sure Patsy'd tell me if something was going on. I talk to Patsy every morning."

"I talked to him myself just a while ago, Walter. And you say there's nothing new? No kidnapping for instance?"

"No, no, no, no kidnapping, for chrissake, Martin. No kidnapping, nothing. Nothing at all. Everything's quiet and let's keep it that way."

"You get any other calls about Charlie?"

"No, goddamn it, no. I said nothing's going on and that's all there is to it. Now I'm busy, Martin."

"I'll talk to you later, Walter."

In minutes Martin's phone rang again, Freddie Dunsbach of the United Press.

"Martin, we've had a tip Patsy McCall's nephew was kidnapped."

"Is that so?"

"It's so and you know it."

"Who said I know it?"

"I called Patsy. He denied it and then said to call you."

"Me? Why me?"

"I thought you could tell me that. Right now we've got an eight-hour jump on you, Martin, or are you putting out an extra? You can't keep a story like this all to yourself."

"There's no story, Freddie."

"You really haven't heard about it?"

"I've heard a wild rumor, but we don't print rumors."

"Since when?"

"Blow it out your ass, Fred." And Martin hung up. The phone rang right back.

"Martin, I'm sorry. That was a joke."

"I accept your groveling apology. What do you want?"

"Why did Patsy tell me to call you?"

"Damned if I know. Maybe to get rid of you."

"I think we're going with the rumor, as an editor's advisory. Our source is a good one."

"That's a bad idea."

"We can't sit on it."

"You can if it means Charlie's life."

"This is too big. Hell, this is national."

Martin snorted. Freddie Dunsbach, boy bureau chief. Arrogant yokel.

"It's all of that. But let me ask you. How long've you been in this town?"

"Almost a year."

"Then you ought to know that if the McCalls are quiet on this thing, and the police are quiet, there's one hell of a reason. Patsy must've sent you to me because I told him I wouldn't print any rumors. I see the significance escapes you, but Patsy's concern is obviously for the safety of Charlie, if Charlie has in fact been kidnapped, which is really not provable if nobody admits it."

"Does he expect us to bury our heads and ignore the story?"

"What Patsy expects is known only to the deity, but I know what I'd expect if I broke this story and Charlie was murdered because of it. Would you know what to expect in a case like that?"

Freddie was silent.

"Freddie, would you?"

"You're talking about reprisals for reporting the news."

"You ever hear about the time Bindy McCall beat a man half to death for insulting his wife? What do you suppose he'd do to somebody who caused the death of his only son? The only child in the whole McCall family."

"You can't run a news organization on that basis."

"Maybe you can't. Maybe a five-minute beat—which is about all you'd get since we'd put it on the I.N.S. wire as soon as the word was out—is worth Charlie's life. Kidnappers are nasty bastards. You know what happened to Lindbergh's kid, don't you? And he was just a baby who couldn't recognize anybody."

"Yeah, there's something in that."

"There's more than you think. We could've had an extra out an hour ago with the rumor. But who the hell wins that kind of game?"

"I see, but—"

"Listen, Fred, I don't run the show here. You talk to Emory when he comes in. He'll be calling the shots for us and I think I know what he's going to do, which is nothing at all until there's a mighty good reason to print something."

"It's going to be all over the world in a couple of hours."

"Not unless you send it."

"I'll talk to Emory."

"You do that."

Martin dialed Patsy, and the great gravelbox answered, again on the first ring.

"Are you sending people to me for a reason, Patsy?"

"You'll keep 'em quiet."

"Hey, this thing is already spreading all over town. Some of these birds don't give a damn about anything but news. They'll blow it wide open unless they're convinced there's a hell of a good reason not to."

Silence.

"Call Max at the office in five minutes."

In five minutes precisely Martin called Max Rosen, law partner to Matt McCall.

"The story is this, Martin," Max said. "I answered a call here forty-five minutes ago. A man's voice told me to tell Patsy and Matt they'd picked up their nephew and wanted a quarter of a million ransom, a ridiculous figure. Half an hour ago we had a letter from them, with Charlie's signature, saying the same thing. They said if we told the police or put out any publicity that they'd kill Charlie. Patsy wants you to inform the rest of the press about this. He won't talk to anyone but you, and neither will I, nor anyone else in the family. We're not telling Chief Bradley much of anything, so don't bother him any more. I don't need to tell you what this means, do I, Martin, this confidence in you?"

"No need."

"When there's something to be said it will be said to you, provided you can convince the rest of the press to preserve silence."

"I'll do what I can, Max. But it's quite a big world out here. Full of nosy, irresponsible newspapermen."

"The family knows that."

"Do they also know I don't work miracles for a living?"

"I think they presume you do now."

*   *   *

Emory Jones's hair was white, with vague, yellowish implications that he might once have been the fair-haired boy of somebody, a mother perhaps, somewhere. He said, whenever the whiteness of his hair arose for discussion, that peabrained reporters who didn't know the doughnut from the hole had given it to him prematurely. For years he had put up with them, he argued, because he had a basically sacrificial nature. He outlasted almost all of them, he argued further, because he had the forbearance of Jesus Christ in the face of the drooling, foaming, dementia praecox activity that passed for reporting on his one and only newspaper. The noted cry: "That son of a bitch doesn't know the goddamn doughnut from the goddamn hole!" emanating from editor Jones's cubicle, meant a short professional life for somebody.

Martin Daugherty placed Emory in this context as he spotted the white hair, saw Emory rumbling across the crooked, paintless, freshly swept wooden floor of the city room. Here he came: pear-shaped, bottom-heavy, sits too much, unhealthy fear of exercise in the man, choler rising, executorially preempted by Martin's pledge, unspeakably happy at the unfortunate turn of events that had already boiled his creative fluids, which fluids, Martin could see, were percolating irrationally in his eyeballs.

Martin remembered a comparable frenzy in Emory's past: the period when Legs Diamond had been an Albany celebrity; the most outlandishly sensational running news event in the modern history of Albany. Emory, who whipped his slaves like a galleymaster to ferret out every inch of copy the story could bear, finally triumphed prophetically the night Diamond was acquitted of a kidnapping charge. He oversaw personally the hand-setting of the great fist-sized wooden type he saved for major natural catastrophes, armistices, and The Chief's sneezes: DIAMOND SLAIN BY ENEMIES; for the rumor had been abroad in Albany for twelve hours, and was indeed current the length of the Eastern seaboard and as far west as Chicago, that Diamond was, on that particular night, truly a terminal target. Emory had the headline made up a full six hours before Diamond was actually shot dead in his bed on Dove Street by a pair of gunmen. It was then used on the extra that sold twenty thousand copies.

Martin had already calculated that the extra that never was on Charlie Boy would have sold even more. When the news on Charlie did break, the coverage would dwarf the Diamond story. There had never been anything like this in Albany's modern history, and Martin knew Emory Jones also knew this, knew it deeply, far down into the viscous, ink-stinking marrow of his editorial bones.

"Did you undo that goddamn pledge?" were Emory's first words.

"No."

"Then get at it."

"It's not possible, Emory."

Emory moved his cigar in and out of his mouth, an unnerved thumbsucker. He sat down in the wobbly chair alongside Martin's decrepit desk, blew smoke at Martin, and inquired: "Why in the sacred name of Jesus is it not possible?"

"Because I don't think you're interested in being the editor who put the bullet in Charlie McCall's brain. Or are you?"

Martin's explanation of the sequence of events forced Emory to recapitulate the future as he had known it all morning. Martin let him stew and then told him: "Emory, you're the man in charge of this silence, whether you like it or not. You're the man with the reputation, the journalistic clout. You're the only one in town who can convince the wire services and whoever's left among the boys up in the Capitol press room to keep their wires closed on this one for a little while. They'll do it if you set the ground rules, make yourself chairman of the big secret. Maybe set a time limit. Two days? Four? A week?"

"A week? Are you serious?"

"All right, two days. They'll do it as a gentleman's agreement if you explain the dread behind it. You'll be a genuine hero to the McCalls if you do, and that's worth money to this newspaper, if I'm not mistaken."

"Keep your venal sarcasm under your dirty vest."

"It's not sarcasm. It's cynical humanism."

"Well, hell, I don't want to murder anybody. At least not Charlie."

"I knew you'd get the picture."

"But what will I tell them?"

"Emory, I have faith that you'll think of something. We both know you've got more bullshit than the cattle states."

"Maybe Dunsbach's already put it out."

"Maybe. Then your problem is solved, even if his isn't. But I doubt it. I was persuasive."

"Then you do it."

"I can't do it, Emory. I'm just a piss-ant columnist, not an omnipotent editor."

"Willard Maney will go along. He's an Albanian."

"And a McCall fancier."

"And Foley at the *News*."

"Another kinsman."

"But those bastards up at the Capitol. I don't know them. You know them. You play cards with them when you're supposed to be out getting under the news."

"Use my name up there if you like."

"The wire services can pass the word up there."

"Exactly. And the boys will very likely follow suit. Despite what you think, they're a decent bunch. And Emory, it's really not your responsibility anyway what out-of-town writers do. Then it's on them, and on their children. And what the hell, even an editor's advisory like Dunsbach's talking about wouldn't be all that bad if they made it clear to their clients that Charlie's life was at stake. Which is now a rotten fact."

"That poor bastard. What he must be going through."

"He may already be gone."

Martin looked at the clippings on his desk, Charlie's face staring up from one as he attends a Knights of Columbus party. On almost any given evening when Charlie walked into the K. of C., somebody would make a fool of himself over this gentle young man who might carry a word of good will back to his father and uncles. Life preservation. Money in the bank for those who make their allegiance known. Shake the hand of the boy who shakes the hand of the men who shake the tree from which falls the fruit of our days. Poor sucker, tied to a bed someplace. Will I live through the night? Will they shoot me in the morning? Where is my powerful father? Where are my powerful uncles? Who will save the son when the father is gone? Pray to Jesus, but where is Jesus? Jesus, Charlie, sits at my desk in the person of an equivocating Welsh rarebit who doesn't understand sons because he never had any. But he understands money and news and power and decency and perhaps such things as these will help save the boy we remember. We are now scheming in our own way, Charlie, to keep you in our life.

"I was putting together a backgrounder on Charlie," Martin said, breaking the silence. "Is there anything else you want me to do? There's also that A.L.P. business today."

"The hell with that stuff now."

"It's pretty big, you know. Quite a show of power."

"They're a handful of reds, that's all."

"They're not reds, Emory. Don't *you* fall for that malarkey. Probably only two or three are really Communists."

"They're pinks, then. What's the difference?"

"We can discuss this fine point of color another time, but it's definitely worth a story, and good play, no matter what else happens along with it."

"Whatever happens I don't want you on it. You stay on Charlie."

"Doing what?"

"Find the kidnappers, what the hell else?"

"Find the kidnappers."

"Check around Broadway. That's where they hang out."

"Check around Broadway."

"And don't get lost. Call me every hour. Every half-hour."

"Every half-hour."

And then Emory Jones, sucking on his stogie, rumbled off and slammed the door of his cubicle, then sat at his desk and picked up the phone to begin spreading the blanket of silence over a story whose magnitude punified even his own recurring glory dreams of news at its colossally tragic best.

IV

Please don't talk about me when I'm gone," Mildred Bailey was singing over WHN, with the Paul Whiteman band behind her. And Billy Phelan, writing horses in his, or, more precisely, his sister's and brother-in-law's living room, wearing pants, socks, and undershirt, no shoes or belt, remembered the time she came to town with Whiteman. Played the Palace. She always sang like a bird to Billy's ear, a hell of a voice. Hell of a voice. Sounded gorgeous. And then she showed up fat. Dumpy tub of lard. Whiteman too, the tub. Billy remembered the night he played games with Whiteman at the crap table in Saratoga. He was dealing at Riley's Lake House, youngest dealer in town that season, 1931, and of course, of course he knew who Whiteman was when the big boy rolled the dice and lost the last of his wad.

"Let's have five hundred in chips, sonny, and an I.O.U.," Whiteman said.

"Who the hell are you? I don't know you," Billy said. Sonny me, you son of a bitch. Hubie Maloy, the crazy, was at the table that night. From Albany. Always carried a gun. But Billy liked him. Hubie smiled when Whiteman called Billy sonny. Big-timer, throwing his weight around, that big gut, and figures everybody on earth knows his mustache.

"I'm Paul Whiteman."

"Wyman?"

"Whiteman. Whiteman."

"Ohhhhh yeah, Whiteman. You're the guy's got that hillbilly band playing over at Piping Rock. You don't mean nothing to me, bud. Go see the manager if you want chips."

They fired Billy twenty minutes later. Orders from above. From those who didn't want to make enemies of Paul the Man. Lemon Lewis came over to the table and said, "I hate to do it, Billy, but we gotta can you. I'll call over to Newman's and the Chicago Club, see what they got going."

And two hours after that Billy was back to work, with cards this time, sleek and sharp, full of unpredictable combinations. Billy, maybe the best dealer around, pound for pound, you name the game, such a snappy kid, Billy.

He was in Saratoga that year because one night a month earlier he was hanging around Broadway in Albany when Bindy McCall came by, Bindy, in the tan fedora with the flowerpot crown, had connections and investments in Saratoga gambling, a natural by-product of his control of all the action in Albany, all of it: gambling houses, horse rooms, policy, clearing house, card games, one-armed bandits, punch boards. Playing games in Albany meant you first got the okay from Bindy or one of his lieutenants, then delivered your dues, which Bindy counted nightly in his office on Lodge Street. The tribute wasn't Bindy's alone. It sweetened the kitty for the whole McCall machine.

Billy touched Bindy's elbow that night.

"Hey, Billy."

"Got a second, Bin? I need some work. Can you fix me up for Saratoga next month?"

"What can you do?"

"Anything."

"Anything at all?"

"Craps, poker, blackjack, roulette. I can deal, handle the stick."

"How good are you?"

"Haven't you heard?"

Bindy chuckled.

"I'll ask around someone who has. See Lemon Lewis."

"All right, Bindy, fine. Obliged. Can I touch you for fifty?"

Bindy chuckled again. Billy's got brass. Bindy reached for the roll and plucked a fifty out of the middle.

"Use it in good health."

"Never felt better," said Billy. "I pay my debts."

"I know you do. I know that about you. Your father paid his debts, too. We played ball together when we were kids. He was one hell of a player. You ever hear from him?"

"We don't hear."

"Yeah. That's an odd one. See Lewis. He'll fill you in."

"Right, Bin."

Billy saw Lewis an hour later at the bar in Becker's and got the word: You deal at Riley's.

"What about transportation?" Billy asked. "How the hell do I get from Albany to Saratoga every night?"

"Jesus, ain't you got a car?"

"Car? I never even had roller skates."

"All right. You know Sid Finkel?"

Billy knew Sid, a pimp and a booster and a pretty fair stickman. Put his kid through dentists' school with that combination.

"Look him up. I'll tell him to give you a lift."

"I'll half the gas with him," Billy said.

"That's you and him. And don't forget your source," and Lemon hit himself on the chest with his thumb.

"Who the hell could forget you, Lemon?" Billy said.

It went fine for Billy for two weeks and then came the Whiteman scene and Billy went from Riley's to the Chicago Club, on earlier hours. The Club got a big play in the afternoon, even though the horses were running at the track. So Billy had to find new transportation because Sid Finkel stayed on nights. Was Billy lucky? He certainly was. Angie Velez saw him dealing at the Chicago Club and when he took a break, she asked him for a light.

"You weren't out of work long," she said.

"Who told *you* I was out of work?"

"I was there when you gave it to Whiteman. Funniest damn thing I've heard in years. Imagine anybody saying that to Paul Whiteman. You're the one with the hillbilly band. I laughed right out loud. He gave me an awfully dirty look."

Billy smiled at this new dish. Then he asked her name and bought her a drink and found she was married but only dabbled in that. Hubby was a gambler, too. Brought her to Saratoga for a week, then left her there to play while he went home to run his chunk of Rochester, what a town. No town like Albany. Rochester is where you might go on the bum, only might, if they kicked you out of Albany. Billy couldn't imagine life outside Albany. He loved the town. And half-loved you too, Angie, now that you're here. "Are you a spic?"

"I'm Irish, baby. Just like you. One of the Gagen girls. My old man's a Cuban."

She was playing kneesies with him by then.

"You keep that up, you're liable to get raped."

"Room two-forty-six in the Grand Union." And she proved it with the key. That was the beginning of Billy's private taxi service between Albany and Saratoga for the rest of the month. Other things began that season in Saratoga: Billy's reputation as the youngest of the hot numbers at any table, never mind the game. Big winner. I could always get a buck, Billy said. What the hell, I know cards and dice.

Of course, at the end of the season Billy was broke. Playing both sides of the table.

Now Mildred Bailey was all through and Clem McCarthy was barking in with the race results on WHN, and can you believe what is happening to Billy? Friar Charles wins, the son of a bitch, five-to-two, the son of a bitch, *the son of a bitch*! Martin Daugherty, what in Christ's name are you doing to Billy Phelan?

Here's how it looked to this point: Martin bet ten across the board on Charley Horse, who wins it, four-to-one; puts a tenner across also on Friar Charles and now wins that one, too; and has a third tenner going across on Hello Chuckie in the sixth at Pimlico, and Hello Chuckie is two-to-one on the morning line. There is more. Martin also *parlayed* the three horses for yet another ten.

Now, Billy knows that Martin is a hell of a sport, always pays, and loses more than he wins, which has always been pleasant for Billy, who takes a good bit of his play. But my Jesus Christ almighty, if he wins the third, plus the three-horse parlay, Billy is in trouble. Billy doesn't hold every bet he takes. You hold some, lay off some. You hold what you think you can cover, maybe a little more, if you're brassy like Billy. Billy lays some off with his pal Frankie Buchanan, who has the big book in Albany. But mother pin a rose on Billy. For bravery. For Billy is holding *all* of Martin's play. Didn't lay off a dime. Why? Because suckers and losers bet three-horse parlays. I'll hold them all day long, was Billy's philosophy until a few minutes ago when Clem McCarthy came on with the Friar Charles news. And now Billy is sitting at his card table in the front room. (Billy came here to Thanksgiving dinner six years ago and never went back downtown to his furnished room.) His money sits on the floor, next to his bridge chair, in a Dyke cigar box, Dykes being the cigar the McCall machine pushed in all the grocery and candy stores in town.

Billy himself sits under the big, shitty print of Mo the Kid in the gold frame. Billy's fingers are working with his number two Mongol pencil on the long yellow pad, and his eyes keep peeking out through the curtains on the front windows in case state cops step on his stoop, in which case Billy would be into the toilet p.g.d.q., those horse bets would be on their way down the city conduits toward the river, and even the most enterprising raider could not then bring them back and pin them on Billy's chest.

Stan whatsisname, the WHN disk jockey, was talking about Bob Crosby and Billy felt good hearing that because he knew Crosby, had heard him in Saratoga, danced to his music with Angie, talked music with him when he played The Edgewood over in Rensselaer. "Between the Devil and the Deep Blue Sea" Crosby was playing now. The phone rang and Billy turned Crosby down. Frankie Buchanan with the results of the fifth at Arlington Park, Friar Charles official now. Billy then told Frankie about Martin Daugherty's very weird parlay.

"You're the weird one," said Frankie, who was as weird as they come. One of the best-liked guys in Albany, Frankie, and yet he couldn't take the public. He'd come out at night for ham and eggs, and you'd have to sit with him in his car behind the Morris diner while he ate off a paper plate. Crazy bastards in this world.

"You want to give me the third horse or part of that parlay?"

"No," said Billy, "I can't believe the son of a bitch can pick three in a row, and parlay them, too. I never seen it done. I believe in luck but not miracles."

"Okay, pal," said Frankie, "it's all yours." And he left Billy wondering if he was really crazy. Billy could cut the mustard if the third horse ran out of the money, because the day's play was good. But if Martin Daugherty wins the parlay, Billy, it's up in the seven, eight hundreds, even if nobody else wins a nickel. And Billy Boy, you don't have that kind of cash. So why, oh why, is darlin' Billy doing it? Well, it's a gamble, after all. And Billy is certainly a gambler. Nobody will argue that. And Billy is already feeling the pressure rise in his throat, his gut, under his armpits, under his teeth and behind his jockey shorts. Christ, it tickles me somewhere, Billy thinks, and the money doesn't matter. Pressure. Sweet pressure. Here we go again, folks.

Crosby was just winding up "Deep Blue Sea." Billy remembered listening to it with Angie, saw her face. And then it was Morey Amsterdam on the radio. Popped into the studio as usual to ad lib with Stan. I gotta go up to the sixth floor, Amsterdam was saying. They're gonna lay a rug up there and I wanna see how they do it.

Telephone. Martin Daugherty.

"Yeah, Friar Charles wins it, Martin, so you got something good going. Shows seven dollars, four dollars, and three-forty. Tote it up, Martin, you're the money machine today."

Stan was telling a caller, if you don't like my show, you crumb, don't listen, but if you want to make more of it than that I'll meet you at five o'clock out in the alley behind the studio and knock your brains out. And he gave the address. Wireheaded bastard, that Stan. Billy liked his style.

Then it was quiet with no phones and only Earl (Fatha) Hines—a kid, really, so why do they call him Fatha?—playing something wild, and somebody in the chorus, when he started to move it, really move it, yelling out, "Play it Fatha . . . play it till nineteen ninety-nine." And

Billy smiles, taps his foot, feels the jazz, feels, too, that good old, good old pressure beginning to cut a pulpy wedge out of his fat-assed day.

*   *   *

Simpson, that bum, rang Billy's bell, looking for his sawbuck. Billy saw him coming up the walk, fished a tenner out of the cigar box, folded it once and put it in his right hip pocket. Ten down the sewer. But Billy had to pay. Tribute to Pop O'Rourke, Democratic leader of the Ninth Ward, who, six months ago, when Billy announced plans to write horses, approved the venture during Billy's formal call. The payoff? Give ten a week to Simpson, Pop said. He's down on his luck. He'll come by every week for it. Fair enough, Billy said. What else could he say? And he was still paying out the tenner.

"Hello, Bill, how you doin'?" Simpson said when Billy opened the door just enough to make it clear that it was not a welcoming gesture. The Simp's sport shirt was at least four days soiled and he needed a shave. Holes in the elbows of his sweater, boozer's look and the breath'd knock over two mules.

"Life's still tough," Billy said to him.

"I thought maybe I'd come in and sit a while," Simpson said as Billy was reaching for the ten in his pocket. And that line stopped Billy's hand.

"What?"

"Keep you company a while. I ain't doin' nothin', just hangin' around Brady's. Might as well chew the fat. You know."

"No, I don't know nothing like that," Billy said. "You ain't coming in now or ever." He opened the door all the way, stepped out, grabbed Simpson's dirty shirt, and lifted him backward down the stairs. "Now get off this stoop and stay off. Next time you put a foot on it I'll knock your ass the other side of Pearl Street."

"Don't get hot, Bill. I just wanna come in and talk."

"I don't let bums in my home. Who the hell do you think you're conning? From now on I don't even want to see you on this side of the street."

"Where's my ten?"

"You blew it, bum."

And Billy slammed the door and called Pop O'Rourke.

"And he says he wants to keep me company for the day, chew the fat. Listen, Pop, I respect you, but that bum is looking to see my action. I have a good half hour, he'll want twenty instead of ten. Don't send him back, Pop, and I mean that. I don't like his slimy looks and I never did. I hit him once, I'll knock him off the stoop altogether. There's five steps and he'd clear the whole five if I hit him. I'll break both his arms, Pop. I don't want the bum ringing my bell."

"Take it easy, Billy. He won't be back. He did wrong. He's a greedy person. I'll tell him."

"Fine, Pop. Do you want me to send you the tenner?"

"No, not at the moment. I'll let you know if there's any other needy case around."

"I'm a needy case, Pop."

"But there are rules, Billy."

"I play by them."

"That's the good boy. Just don't get excited. I underwent a heart attack that way, and I can tell you that getting excited is one of the worst, one of the very worst things a man can do to himself. It takes you over when you don't expect it. Very sudden and we don't anticipate a thing. It's a terrible thing to do to yourself, getting too overly worked up, Billy. I wouldn't do it again for any man."

"I'll catch you later, Pop. Thanks."

"Billy, I'm very glad you called me."

Billy hung up and scraped the horseshit out of his ear.

*   *   *

The first of Billy's family came home at three-forty. Daniel Quinn, age ten, resident little kid returning from fourth grade at Public School Twenty across the street, found his uncle on the couch with *True Detective* open on his chest, the lights out, shades drawn more than usual, the *Telegraph*, the *Armstrong*, the New York *News* and *Daily Mirror* on the floor beside the card table.

"That you, kid?"

"It's me, Unk. Aren't you working?"

"Get lost. I'm half asleep. Catch you later."

And the boy went upstairs. But Billy's eyes were open again, his gaze again on the shitty print of Mo the Kid, more properly titled "The Young Mozart," hanging in an enormous gold frame above the couch. There sat the precocious composer, exceptionally upright, playing, no doubt, a tune of his own making, on a spinet in a drawing room baroquely furnished with gilded mirrors, heavy drapes, fringed oriental rug. The room was busy with footstools, ornamental screens, and music sheets strewn across the floor. The ladies in long, flowered gowns and chokers, clutching single sheets of music, and an older gentleman in a wig, breeches, and buckled shoes like the composer, all sat listening as the young Mo sent out his lifegiving music. The three gave off nonhuman smiles, looking glazed and droopy, as if they'd all been at the laudanum.

The print would not have been on the wall, or in the house, if Billy had had his way. It was a gift to his sister, Peg, from their Aunt Mary, a reclusive old dame who lived in the old family home on Colonie Street, raised canaries, and had a secret hoard of twenty-dollar gold pieces she parceled out on birthdays. The picture always reminded Billy of his ill treatment by the people in that house after his father ran away and left him and his sister and their mother; ran away and stayed away eighteen years, and neither Billy, Peg, nor their mother ever heard from him again. In 1934 he came back, not to his own home but to that goddamn house of his sisters and brothers, his visit culminating in inadequately explained rejection and flight, and further silence. And so Billy hated the house for that reason, and also for the uncountable other reasons he had accumulated during his years as a never-quite-welcome nephew (nasty son of nasty Francis). The house was as worthless as the stupid picture in which Kid Mo offered up his stupid, invisible music to a roomful of dope fiends.

The picture would not leave his mind, even after he'd closed his eyes, and so Billy picked up the magazine and looked again at the about-to-be-raped model, fake-raped, with slip on the rise revealing thigh, garter, seamed stockings. In high heels, with her rouged lips, artful hair, artificial fear on her face, she cowered on the bed away from the hovering shadow of the artificial rapist. The change of vision from Mo to rape worked, and Billy slept the fearful sleep of an anxious loser.

Peg's keys, clinking at the keyhole, woke him.

Plump but fetching, graying but evergreen, Margaret Elizabeth Quinn was returning from her desk in the North End Tool Company, where she was private secretary to the owner.

"It's dark in here," she said. "What happened to the lights?"

"Nothing," Billy said as she switched on the bridge lamp.

"Is Danny home?"

"Upstairs."

"What's new? You have a decent day?"

"Great day."

"That's nice."

"No it's not."

"Did Mama call?"

"No."

"The receiver's off the hook."

"I know it."

"How could she call if the receiver's off the hook."

"She couldn't."

Peg cradled the receiver and took off her black-and-white checked shorty coat and black pillbox hat.

"You want pork chops?" she asked.

"No."

"Liver? That's the choice."

"Nothing, no."

"You're not eating?"

"No, the hell with it."

"Oh, that's a beautiful mood."

"I'm beautiful out of business is what I am."

Peg sat on the edge of the rocker, formidable lady in her yellow, flowered print, full knees up, glasses on, lipstick fresh, fingernails long and crimson, solitaire from husband George small but respectably gleaming under the bridge light, hair marcelled in soft finger wave. Billy's beautiful sister.

"What's this you're saying?"

And he told her the Martin story: that, believe it or not, his three horses all came home. Some joke, eh kid? Sextuple your money, folks. Place your bets with Brazen Billy Boy, who lives the way we all love to live—way, way, way up there beyond our means.

Peg stood up, saying nothing. She pushed open the swinging door to be greeted by a near-frenzied collie, all but perishing from his inability to disgorge affection. From the refrigerator she took out the pork chops and put them into two large frying pans over a low flame on the gas stove. Then she went back to Billy, who was pouring a shot of Wilson's into a soiled coffee cup with a dry, brown ring at the bottom. The phone rang and Peg answered, then handed the instrument to Billy, who closed his eyes to drive out all phone calls.

"Yeah," he said into the mouthpiece. And then, "No, I'm closed down. No. NO, GODDAMN IT, NO! I mean I'm CLOSED. Out of business and you owe me fifty-four bucks and I need it tonight so goddamn get it up. I'll be down." And he slammed the receiver onto the hook.

"Wasn't that Tod?"

"Yeah."

"You don't have to eat *his* head off because you lost some money."

"Lost some money? I'm dumped, broke. I can't work. Do you get that picture?"

"You've been broke before? You're broke most of the time."

"Ah, shut up, this is bad news."

"What possessed you to hold a three-horse parlay? I wouldn't even make that mistake."

"I make a lot of mistakes you wouldn't make."

"It doesn't make sense, with your bankroll."

"I can't explain it."

Billy gulped the Wilson's and the phone rang. Martin Daugherty. Peg handed him the phone.

"Yes, Martin, you're a lucky son of a bitch. Nobody in their right mind bets three-horse parlays. I know it, Martin. Yeah, sure I'll be downtown tonight. I'll have some of it for you. No, I haven't got it right this minute. Collections are slow, nobody paying this month. But you'll get paid, Martin. Billy Phelan pays his debts. Yeah, Martin, I held it all myself. Thanks, I'm glad you feel bad. I wish I could get mad at *you*, you son of a bitch. Knock your teeth out and make you spend your winnings on the dentist. What do I make it? What do you make it? Right. That's exactly right, Martin—seven eighty-eight eighty-five. Yeah, yeah. Yeah. See you tonight around Becker's, or maybe the poker game in Nick's cellar. Yeah, you son of a bitch, you sleep with the angels. What hotel they staying at?"

The kitchen gave off the rich odor of seared pork. Peg came out of it in her apron, carrying a long fork. At the foot of the stairs she called, "Danny," and from a far height in the attic came a "Yeah?" and then she said "Supper," and the door slammed and the steps of Daniel Quinn could be heard, descending from his aerie.

"How much cash do you actually have?" Peg asked.

"About a hundred and seventy," Billy said. "Can you spare anything?"

Peg almost smiled. She sniffed and shook her head. "I'll see."

"George is doing all right, isn't he?" George wrote numbers.

"He's doing swell. He lost three dollars yesterday on the day."

"Yeah. We all got a problem."

"All of us," Peg said. "George wants to talk to you about a new book. Somebody named Muller."

"I'm here if he wants me."

"What about this money you owe? How will you raise it?"

"I can always raise a buck."

"Can you raise six hundred?"

"What does *that* mean, *can* I? I've got to. What do you do when you lose? You pay."

"The Spider never loses," Danny Quinn said as he hit the last step down.

*   *   *

Billy drew the bath water, hot as he could stand for his hemorrhoid, back again. Got to get some exercise, Billy. Three baths a day in the hottest, the doc said, the sweat already forming on Billy's face, as he drew the hottest of hot baths. Has that guy Billy got any money? Has he! He's got piles! And he's in hot water, too, I'll say. Might be all washed up. He really took a bath, all right. But you never can tell about a fellow like Billy, because he runs hot and cold.

Billy eased into the water and spread his cheeks so the heat would rise up the back alley and draw some bloody attention to that oversized worm of a vein which was sticking its nose out, itching the goddamn ass off Billy. Are itchy assholes hereditary? But itchy no more right now. Now soothed. Now hot stuff. Now easy livin'. And Billy settles back against the tub and forgets about his asshole and its internal stresses and considers the evening ahead of him.

He will wear his navy blue gabardine and the new silk shirt he got at Steefel's through Harvey Hess. A fast half-dozen shirts for Billy and six, too, for Harv, who glommed them, wrapped them, and put them down as paid for in Billy's name, and all Billy had to do was go in and pick up his order. How sweet. Billy gave Harvey all his legitimate clothing action, or as much as Steefel's could handle, and why not? For wasn't Harvey Billy's grandest fish?

Harvey.

Why hadn't Billy thought of him before this? Harvey was of the opinion he could actually beat Billy at pool. Even after maybe two hundred games and yet to win even one. Still, Harv could say, I'll beat you yet, Billy, I'm learning and you got to admit that. Billy would admit anything to Harvey as long as he kept coughing up fivers and tenners. Such a mark. Billy remembered the night he and Tod had heavy dates with showgirls from the Kenmore and then Tod says, Billy, we can't keep those dates tonight. Why not? says Billy. Because, says Tod, it's payday at Steefel's.

Billy put Harvey on his list of problem solvers. He already had $170. He would get $54 from Tod. Peg would be good for maybe $10, maybe only $5 if it was as tough with George as she said it was. And it had to be because Peg was no bullshitter. So the arithmetic comes to maybe $234. And if Billy nailed Harvey for, let's be conservative, $25, that's $259, say $260 round figures; which means Billy still has to come up with say $530 round figures to pay off Martin. Quite a challenge, Billy, $530, and the first time in your life you ever went out at night and absolutely had to come up with five big ones. Always a first for everything. But Billy can raise a buck, right, Billy?

Billy saw the top half of his torso in the bathroom cabinet mirror. The vision always reduced him to a corpse, being washed and powdered in an undertaker's basement, like Johnny Conroy. He always turned the image quickly back to life, pulling chest hair to feel pain, pressing a finger against shoulder flesh to see it whiten, then return to rich redness, moving his mouth, showing his teeth, being alive in a way he wasn't sure his father still was. Is death hereditary?

Johnny Conroy: the corpse in Cronin's funeral parlor, 1932, raised with Billy on Colonie Street, wild kid. Used to run with Billy after the action, any action, run to the cliff at the tail end of Ten Broeck Street and leap, leap, faaaaaaaaalllll, and lose the pursuit, faaaaaaaaalllll into the great sandpile in Hogan's brickyard, scramble off, free.

Johnny Conroy, free to die in the gutter over stolen booze, and they waked him at Cronin's.

Billy and Tod were taking Hubie Maloy home that night from Becker's, crazy Hubie who said, Let's stop and see Johnny, my old pal. But they're closed now, it's two in the morning, said Billy. I wanna go in, said Hubert, the wild filbert. And so Tod stopped the car and Hubert got out and went around the back of Cronin's and crawled in a window and in a few minutes had opened the side door for Tod and Billy, and in they went, half drunk or Billy wouldn't have done it. A burglary rap for sure. And there was Johnny in the open coffin with one basket of flowers, only one, ready for planting in the ay-em.

He don't look so bad, Tod said.

He don't look so bad for a corpse, Billy said.

And that's when Hubert undid Johnny's tie. And Billy watched it happen because he didn't understand Hubert's plan. Then Hubert pulled Johnny up from the casket and for the first time Billy really understood the word "stiff." Hubert took off Johnny's coat and shirt, and by then Billy and Tod were out the door and back in Toddy's car, parked safely up the street.

Hubert's nuts, said Tod.

Playful, Billy said and couldn't even now say why that word occurred to him. Maybe because he still, even now, liked Hubert, liked crazies.

Well, I don't play with him no more, said Toddy. He's got no respect.

And Billy said, You could say that. Because he had to admit it was true. Five minutes go by and Hubert puts out the light in Cronin's and comes out with all Johnny's burial clothes under his arm, suit, tie, even the shoes. He owed me, the bastard, Hubert says, and if I waited any longer I'd never even collect this much. And Hubert kept the shirt and tie for his own and sold the suit and shoes for twenty bucks the next afternoon at The Parody Club, to a grifter passing through with a carny. On Broadway they laughed for weeks over poor Johnny and, worse, poor old Cronin, who had an attack and damn near died when he walked in and saw the naked corpse, standing with his back against the coffin, all his bullet holes showing. For Hubert didn't tell folks he also took Johnny's underwear. Always said he wasn't wearing any.

Billy shaved and wet his straight black hair, brushed it back with the little part at the left, and was padding barefoot toward his bedroom, wrapped in a towel, when the phone rang. He waited and listened while Peg got it again. Ma. Billy stayed at the top of the stairs.

"We're fine, Mama, and how are things there? Good. yes, everything is all right. Billy is getting dressed to go out, and George won't be home for an hour. The office is quite busy, yes, which is a nice change. You what, made an apple pie? Oh, I wish I had some. But it burned? Oh that's too bad. But it tastes good anyway. And now Minnie and Josie want to bake pies, too. Well, I hope I get a piece of somebody's pie. I bet yours'll be the best. Yes, Mama, Billy's working. He's going out tonight and pick up some money. Yes, it is nice . . ."

In his room Billy took out the navy blue gabardine and the silk shirt and the newest blue bow tie with the white polka dots. He fished in the drawer for the pair of solid blue socks with the three blue dots on the sides and took his black shoes with the pointed toes out of the closet. Billy never went out without being really dressed. But really. George was the same, and Peg and Ma, too. But George was too flashy. Dress conservative and you'll always be well dressed. George always imitated Jimmy Walker, ever since he worked for him up at the Capitol. He'd see Walker's picture in the paper in a sport coat with patch pockets and he'd be downtown buying one the next day. I never imitated anybody, was Billy's thought. I never even imitated my father. They couldn't even tell me how he looked dressed up, except what Ma said, he was so handsome. George is all right. George is a father. A good one. Billy hoped George would get the new book from Muller, but he didn't know who the hell Muller was.

Billy took his trig gray fedora out of the hatbox and thought: pies. And pictured Pete the Tramp stealing two steaming pies off a kitchen windowsill, then running off and eating them behind a fence.

Billy looked at himself in the full-length mirror on the back of the closet door. He looked good. Maybe handsome to some. Not like a man who owed seven eighty-eight to anybody. Whataya think, because Billy owes a few bucks he can't look good?

"Aren't you eating *anything*?" Peg said when he went downstairs.

"I'll grab something downtown."

She didn't make him ask. She fished in the apron pocket and handed him the bill, folded in a square. A twenty. He kissed her quick and patted her corset.

"That's all I can give you," she said.

"I didn't expect so much. You're a classy dame."

"Class runs in this family," she said.

BILLY GOT OFF THE ALBANY-TROY BUS at Broadway and Clinton Avenue and walked up Clinton, past Nick Levine's haberdashery, where the card game would be. He walked toward the theaters, three of them on Clinton Square, and stopped at The Grand. Laughton in his greatest role. As Ginger Ted. Ragged son of trouble. A human derelict on the ebb tide of South Sea life. Surpassing such portrayals as Captain Bligh, Henry VIII, Ruggles of Red Gap. An experience definitely not to be missed. *The Beachcomber*. Billy made a note to avoid this shit. Fats Laughton in a straw hat on the beach. He walked around the box office to check the coming attractions in the foyer. A Warner Baxter thing. Costume job with that lacy-pants kid, Freddie Bartholomew. Billy had already avoided that one at the Palace, coming back for a second run now. The Grand, then, a wipeout for two weeks. Billy headed for the restaurant.

There were four restaurants within a block of each other on Clinton Square but Billy, as always, went to the Grand Lunch next door to The Grand, for it had the loyalty of the nighttime crowd, Billy's crowd. Dan Shugrue, well liked, ran it, and Toddy Dunn worked the counter starting at six, an asset because he spoke the language of the crowd, which turned up even in daylight for the always-fresh coffee and the poppy-seed rolls, the joint's trademark, and because since Prohibition the place never closed and nobody had to remember its hours. Also there was Slopie Dodds, the one-legged Negro cook, when he worked, for he was not only a cook but a piano player who'd played for Bessie in her early years, and he did both jobs, whatever the market dictated. Nobody believed he'd played for Bessie until it came out in a magazine, but Billy believed it because you don't lie about that kind of thing unless you're a bum, and Slopie was a straight arrow, and a good cook.

The place was brightly lighted, globes washed as usual, when Billy walked in. Toddy, behind the counter, gave him half a grin, and Slopie gave him a smile through the kitchen door. Billy didn't expect the grin from Tod. Billy also saw his Uncle Chick sitting alone at one of the marble-topped booth tables, having coffee and doughnuts before going to work at the *Times-Union* composing room. It was the first time Billy had seen Chick in months, six, eight months, and even that was too soon.

"Hello, Chick," he said, said it aloofly from the side of his mouth, that little hello that hits and runs.

"Howsa boy, Billy, howsa boy? Long time no see."

"All right, Chick."

Billy would have kept walking, but his uncle's gaze stayed on him, looking at those clothes, so spiffy, so foreign because of that; and so Billy spoke compulsively. "How you been?" A man's got to be civil.

"Fine and dandy. Sit down."

"I got some business here a minute," and Billy's hand said, I'll be back, maybe. He walked to the counter, where Tod was already drawing a coffee, dark. Tod also shoved a spoon and an envelope at him.

"Forty there," Tod said, jaunty in his counterman's white military cap of gauze and cardboard. "All I can come up with."

Billy didn't touch the envelope.

"That phone call," Billy said.

"Forget it. Peg called me."

"She tell you what happened?"

"All but the numbers."

"Seven eighty-eight eighty-five. How do you like that, doctor?"

"You got a reason to be edgy."

"I'm through till I pay it off and get another bankroll."

"You got no reserve at all?"

"A wipeout."

"Then what's next?"

"I thought I'd look up Harvey. You want to make the call?"

"For when?"

"When, hell. Now. I'm there if he wants me."

Tod looked at his watch. "Five to six. He's home by now. Shit. I got to work. I'll miss it."

"I'll tell you about it. But I wanna make the game at Nick's."

"How you gonna play with no money?"

"I got almost two bills."

"And you got this forty," and Tod shoved the envelope closer.

"Two-thirty then. I play with half that. I can't afford to lose more than that. I got to save something for Martin, unless I can swing him."

"I'll call Harvey, good old Harv."

"Hey, you hear I rolled two-ninety-nine last night? I beat Scotty Streck and the son of a bitch dropped dead from shock."

"I saw the obituary in the afternoon paper. It didn't mention you. Two-ninety-nine? What stood up?"

"The four pin. Gimme a western." Billy pocketed the envelope and carried the coffee to Chick's table, thinking: I could grunt and Toddy'd get the message. Talk to Chick all week and he'll ask you is this Thursday. Chick wasn't dumb, he was ignorant. Anybody'd be ignorant living in that goddamn house. Like living in a ditch with a herd of goats. Years back, Chick got baseball passes regular from Jack Daley, the *Times-Union*'s sports editor. The Albany Senators were fighting Newark for first place and Red Rolfe was with Newark, and George McQuinn and others who later went up with the Yankees. Chick gave the passes for the whole Newark series to young Mahan, a tub-o'guts kid whose mother was a widow. Billy always figured Chick was after her ass. Chick gave Billy a pass two weeks later to see Albany play the cellar club. Who gave a damn about the cellar club? Billy can't even remember now which club it was. Shove your pass, Nasty Billy told his uncle.

"You're all dressed up," Chick said, chuckling. "Are you going to work?"

"Not to give you a short answer to a snotty question, but what the hell is it to you? What am I supposed to do, dress like a bum? Look like you?"

"All right, Billy, I was only kidding."

"The hell you were."

"Dress any way you want. Who cares?"

"I do what I want, all right."

"Calm down, Billy, and answer me a question. You seen Charlie McCall lately?"

"I saw him last night. He bet against me in a bowling match."

"You hear anything about him?"

"Since last night? Like how he slept?"

"No, no."

"What the hell you asking then?"

"Can you keep a secret?"

"I'd be dead if I couldn't."

"I hear Charlie's in bad trouble. I hear maybe he was kidnapped last night."

Billy stared Chick down, not speaking, not moving except to follow Chick's eyes when they moved. Chick blinked. *Kidnapped.* With Warner Baxter.

"You heard what I said?"

"I heard."

"Don't that mean anything to you?"

"Yeah, it means something. It means I don't know what the hell it means. You got this straight or you making it up?"

"I'm telling you, it's a secret. I shouldn't have said anything, but I know you know Charlie and thought maybe you heard something."

"Like who kidnapped him?"

"Hey, come on, Billy. Not so loud. Listen, forget it, forget I said anything." Chick bit his doughnut. "You heard any news about your father?"

"Wait a minute. Why is it a secret about Charlie?"

"It's just not out yet."

"Then how come you know?"

"That's a secret, too. Now forget it. What about your father?"

"Nothing. You know any secrets about him?"

"No, no secrets. Nothing since he came to see us."

"And you kicked him out."

"No, Billy, we wanted him, I wanted him to stay. Your Uncle Peter and I went all over town looking for him. You know it was your Aunt Sate had the fight with him. They always fought, even as kids. He was gone before we even knew he was out of the house."

"Bullshit, Chick."

"Nobody can talk to you, Billy. Nobody ever could."

"Not about him they can't."

"There's a lot you don't know."

"I know how he was treated, and how I was treated because of him."

"You don't know the half of it."

Somebody said, "Haw! My mother just hit the numbers!" And Billy turned to see a boy with a broken front tooth, about fifteen, brush cut, sockless, in torn sneakers, beltless pants, and a ragged cardigan over a tank-top undershirt with a hole in the front. His jackknife, large blade open, danced in his hand, two tables away.

"Saunders kid," Chick said softly.

"Who?"

Chick whispered. "Eddie Saunders. Lives up on Pearl Street near us. He's crazy. Whole family's crazy. His father's in the nut house at Poughkeepsie."

"She had a dollar on it," Eddie Saunders said. "Four forty-seven.

Gonna get five hundred bucks. Haw!" With his left foot he nudged a chair away from a nearby table, then slashed its leatherette seat twice in parallel cuts.

"Gonna get me some shoes," he said. "Gonna go to the pitchers."

A lone woman in a corner made little ooohing sounds, involuntary wheezes, as she watched the boy. Billy thought the woman looked a little like Peg.

"Who'd she play the numbers with, Eddie?" Billy asked the kid.

The boy turned and studied Billy. Billy stood up. The boy watched him closely as he moved toward the counter and said to Tod, "Where's my western? And gimme a coffee." And then he turned to the kid.

"I asked who she played the numbers with, Eddie."

"The grocery."

"That's big news. Bet your mother feels good."

"She does. She's gonna buy a dress."

Eddie tapped the knife blade on the marble table top and let it bounce like a drum stick. Billy took the ironstone mug of coffee and the western off the glass counter and moved toward the boy. When he was alongside he said, "You oughta close that knife."

"Nah."

"Yeah, you should."

"You won't make me." And Eddie made little jabs at the air about two feet to the right of Billy's stomach.

"If you don't close it," Billy said, "I'll throw this hot coffee in your eyes. You ever have boiling hot coffee hit you in the eyes? You can't see nothing after that."

Eddie looked up at Billy, then at the mug of steaming coffee in his right hand, inches from his face. He looked down at his knife. He studied it. He studied it some more. Then he closed the blade. Billy set his western on the table and reached out his left hand.

"Now give me the knife."

"It's mine."

"You can have it later."

"No."

"You rather have coffee in the face and then I beat the shit out of you and get the knife anyway?"

Eddie handed the knife to Billy, who pocketed it and put the coffee on the table in front of Eddie. He put the western in front of him. "Have a sandwich," Billy said. He pushed the sugar bowl toward the kid and gave him a spoon a customer had left at the next table.

"Now behave yourself," Billy said, and he went back to his table. "Will you for chrissake gimme a western?" he said to Tod.

The dishwasher came in the front door with the Clinton Square beat cop, Joe Riley. Riley had his hand on his pistol. People were leaving quickly. Tod came around the counter and explained the situation to Riley, who took Eddie's knife from Billy and then took Eddie away.

"That was clever, what you did," Chick said.

"Toddy taught me that one. I seen him use it on nasty drunks two or three times."

"All the same it was clever, and dangerous, with that knife and all. You never know what crazy people will do. It was clever."

"I'm a clever son of a bitch," Billy said, and he reached for Chick's check and pocketed it. One up on you, Chick, you sarcastic prick. "Doughnuts are on me, Chick."

"Why thanks, Billy, thanks. Take care of yourself."

Tod came around the counter with two coffees in one mitt and Billy's western in the other. He sat down.

"You play a nice game of coffee."

"I had a good teacher. You call Harvey?"

"Yeah. He'll be down at Louie's." Tod looked at his watch. "Fifteen minutes from now. Damn, I wish I didn't have to work. I love to see old Harvey in action. He makes me feel smart."

"Listen, you know what I heard? Charlie McCall was snatched."

"No. No shit?"

"And I just saw him last night. He backed Scotty against me in this match."

"That'll teach him."

"They must've grabbed him after he left the alleys."

"Wow, that's a ballbuster. Broadway'll be hot tonight."

"Too bad I gotta play cards. Be fun just floatin' tonight." Billy finished his coffee and then gave both his own and Chick's food checks to Tod, who knew how to make them disappear. "Now I gotta go get fresh money."

When Billy walked into Louie's pool room on Broadway across from Union Station, Daddy Big, wearing his change apron and eyeshade, was leaning on a cue watching Doc Fay, the band leader, run a rack. Tomorrow night, Billy would likely face the Doc here in the finals of a six-week-old round robin. There were four players left and Billy and the Doc could beat the other two left-handed. But Billy and the Doc were also near equals in skill. They beat each other as often as they were beaten: Doc, a flashy shooter; Billy, great control through position and safe shots. Doc, as usual, was playing in his vest. Billy watched him mount the table with one leg, flatten out, stretch his left arm as far as it would take him, with the intention of dropping the fourteen ball into the far corner, a double combination shot he'd never try in a match unless he was drunk, or grandstanding. Ridiculous shot, really, but zlonk! He sank it. Sassy shooter, the Doc, no pushover.

Only one of the other ten tables was busy, Harvey Hess at that one, revving up his sucker suction. Billy could feel it pulling him, but he resisted, walked over to Daddy Big, whose straight name was Louis Dugan, known from his early hustling days because of his willingness to overextend the risk factor in any given hustle—once spotting a mark eighty-four points in a game of one hundred—as Daddy Big Ones, which time shortened to Daddy Big. He'd grown old and wide, grown also a cataract on one eye that he wouldn't let anybody cut away. The eye was all but blind, and so focusing on the thin edge of a master shot was no longer possible for him, which meant that Daddy Big no longer hustled. Now he racked for other hustlers and their fish, for the would-bes, the semi-pros, the amateurs who passed through the magically dismal dust of Louie's parlor.

Daddy Big had run Louie's since the week he came out of Comstock after doing two for a post-office holdup flubbed by Georgie Fox, a sad, syphilitic freak with mange on his soul. Because Fox had lifted Daddy Big's registered pistol to pull the job, then dropped it in a scuffle at the scene, Daddy ended up doing the two instead of Georgie, whom the police never connected to the job. But Bindy McCall, Daddy's cousin, made the connection, and sent out the word: Mark Fox lousy; which swiftly denied Georgie the Syph access to all the places the Broadway crowd patronized: the gin mills, the card games, the gambling joints, the pool rooms, the restaurants, the night clubs, even the two-bit whorehouses Georgie had never learned to live without. He lived two years like a mole, and then, the week before Daddy Big was due to return to Albany and perhaps find a way to extract some personal compensation for lost time from him, Georgie walked into Fobie McManus's grill on Sheridan Avenue, bought a double rye for himself and one for Eddie Bradt, the barman, and said to Eddie: "I'm all done now," and he then walked west to the Hawk Street viaduct, climbed its railing, and dropped seventy feet to the middle of the granite-block pavement below, there to be scraped up and away, out of the reach of Daddy Big forever. Bindy's reward to Daddy for time lost was the managership of this pool room, which Bindy had collected during Daddy's absence as payment on a gambling debt. And Daddy had a home ever after.

"Hey, Daddy," Billy said, "the Doc monopolizing the action?"

"He's got an idea he's Mosconi."

"He thinks he can spot Mosconi."

"I know some I can spot. And beat," the Doc said, smiling at Billy. Good guy, the Doc. The ladies love his curls.

"Tomorrow you get your chance," Billy said, "if you got the money to back up the mouth."

"I'll handle all you can put on the table. That's if you don't lose your first match."

"I lose that, I'll get a job," Billy said.

"You want a game here, Billy?" Daddy Big asked. "I'm just keeping a cue warm."

Daddy slurred when he spoke, half in the bag already. By midnight, he'd be knee-walking, with no reason to stay sober any more. Also, his teeth clicked when he talked, prison dentures. Sadistic bastards pulled all his teeth when they had him down. Yet he's still living, and Georgie Fox is gone. Georgie, turned into a cadaver in shoe leather, had hit Billy many a time for coffee money, and Billy'd peel off a deuce or a fin for the bum, even though he was a bum. Georgie was dead long before he hit the pavement, sucked dry by Bindy's order. Why didn't they just beat on him a little, Billy wondered. Lock him up or take away what he owned? But they took away the whole world he lived in. Billy always hated a freak, but he couldn't hate Georgie. I ain't et in two days, Billy. Billy can still remember that line. But Billy also says: You know what you do when you lose, don't you, Georgie? Do you hear me, freak? You pay.

"I already got a game," Billy told Daddy, nodding his head in Harvey's direction.

The Doc heard that and looked up from the cue ball. He glanced at Harv, then smiled at Billy. "So you do have dough, then," he said.

"A hungry chicken picks up a little stray corn once in a while. How much we on for tomorrow night?"

"Fifty all right? And fifty more if my backer shows up?"

"Fifty definite, fifty maybe. You got it."

Billy moved close to Daddy Big and spoke in a whisper. "I heard something maybe you know already. About Charlie McCall."

"Charlie?"

"That somebody put the snatch on him."

"What the hell you say?" said Daddy, near to full volume. "What, what?"

"It's what I hear, a rumor. More than that I don't know."

"Who told you?"

"What am I, a storyteller? I heard it."

"I didn't hear that. I know Bindy good as any man. You hear anything like that, Doc?"

The Doc gave a small shake of his head and listened.

"It's all I know," Billy said.

"I don't believe it. Sounds like goatshit," Daddy said. "If that happens, I'd know about it. I'll call Bindy."

"Let me know," Billy said.

"Hey, Billy," Harvey called across the empty table. "You gonna play pool or you gonna talk?"

Billy looked at the Doc and said under his breath: "Fish get hungry, too." He clapped the Doc on the shoulder and watched Daddy Big waddling toward the pay phone. Then he went over to Harvey's table to reel in the catch.

*   *   *

Harvey Hess, a dude who wore good suits but fucked them up with noisy neckties and loud socks, had bitten the hook one night eight, ten months back when he saw Billy playing in Louie's and asked for a game. Billy recognized him immediately as a sucker. Billy recognized suckers the way he recognized cats. Harvey almost won that first game. The games were for a deuce after the first free one, and on subsequent days went up to five. Hearing rumors of Billy's talent did not put Harvey off. He merely asked for a spot. Ten points, then fifteen, and lately twenty, which made Harvey almost win.

Billy watched Harvey show off for him, finishing off two balls, both easy pickin's. Then Daddy Big came over to rack the balls, mark down the time, and give Billy the word that Bindy's line was busy. Harvey spoke up: "Give me thirty-five points and I'll play you for twenty-five bucks."

"Who the hell you think I am?" Billy said. "You think I'm Daddy Big here, giving the game away?"

"Thirty-five," said hard-hearted Harvey.

"Thirty," Billy said. "I never spotted anybody thirty-five."

"Thirty-five."

"Thirty-two I give you, for thirty-two bucks, buck a point."

"You're on," said Harv, and Billy felt the sweet pressure on the way. Harvey almost won, but it was Billy, finally, one hundred to ninety-two, winging it with a run of thirty-two in mid-game to come from behind twenty points. Daddy Big came back and told Billy: "I knew that was goatshit about Charlie Boy. Bindy said he heard the rumor, too, and to kill it. He talked to Charlie in New York an hour ago."

"What's this about Charlie?" Harvey asked. "I sold him a gray sharkskin last week."

"It's nothin'," said Daddy. "Billy here's spreading the news he was kidnapped, but I just talked to Bindy and he says it's goatshit."

"I took the third degree at the K. of C. with him," Harvey said.

"I'll tell you why I bought it," Billy said, shrugging. "I heard a rumor last summer Bindy was going to be snatched, so the Charlie thing made sense to me."

"Who snatched? I never heard nothing like that," said Daddy.

"It was all over Broadway."

"So was I, but I never heard it."

"I heard it."

"I never heard it either," Harvey said.

"So you bums don't get around. What're we doing here, playing pool or strollin' down memory lane?"

"I'll play you one more, Billy, but I want forty points now. You're hot tonight. I never saw anybody run thirty-two before. You ran my whole spot. That's hot in my book."

"I got to admit I'm feeling good," Billy said. "But if the spot goes to forty, so does the bet."

"Thirty-five," said Harv. "I'm getting low."

"All right," Billy said, and he broke with a deliberately bad safe shot, giving Harvey an opening target. Harv ran four and left an open table. Billy ran ten, re-racked, ran four more, and missed on purpose, fourteen to four, and said: "Harv, I'm on. What can I say? I'll even it up some and give you eight more points, forty-eight spot."

"You give me eight more?"

"For another eight bucks."

Harvey checked his roll, studied the table.

"No, no bet. I got a feelin' I ain't gonna lose this one, even though you got the lead, Billy. I'm feelin' good, too. I'm gettin' limber. Keep the bet where it is. You can't stay lucky forever."

Lucky. The line blew up in Billy's head. He wanted the rest of Harvey's roll, but time was running. Nick's card game at nine-thirty with big money possible, and Billy wanted a cold beer before that. Yet you can't call Billy lucky, just lucky, and get away with it. Billy's impulse was to throw the game, double the bet, clean out Harvey's wallet entirely, take away his savings account, his life insurance, his mortgage money, his piggy bank. But you don't give them that edge even once: I beat Billy Phelan last week. No edge for bums.

Harvey faced the table. The seven ball hung on the lip, but was cushioned, and the cue ball sat on the other side of the bunch, where Billy, you clever dog, left it. No shots, Harv, except safe. Sad about that seven ball, Harv. But wait. Is Harv lining up to break the bunch? Can it be? He'll smash it? Not possible.

"What're you doing?"

"Playing the seven."

Billy laughed. "Are you serious?"

"Depth bomb it. The four will kiss the seven and the bunch'll scatter."

"Harv, are you really calling that, the four to the seven?"

"I call the seven, that's enough."

"But you can't hit it." Billy laughed again. He looked again at the bunch, studying the angle the four would come off the end. No matter where you hit the bunch, the four would not kiss the seven the right way. Not possible. And Harvey hesitated.

"You don't want me to play this shot, do you, Billy? Because you see it's a sure thing and then I'll have the bunch broken, a table full of shots. That's right, isn't it?"

Billy closed his eyes and Harvey disappeared. Who could believe such bedbugs lived in a civilized town? Billy opened his eyes at the sound of Harvey breaking the bunch. The four kissed the seven, but kissed it head on. The seven did not go into the corner pocket. The rest scattered, leaving an abundant kindergarten challenge for Billy.

"You do nice work, Harv."

"It almost worked," said Harv, but the arrogance was draining from his face like a poached egg with a slow leak.

"Why didn't you play a safe shot?"

"When I've got a real shot?"

"A real shot? Willie Hoppe wouldn't try that one."

"I saw you break a bunch and kiss one in."

"You never saw me try a shot like that, Harv."

"If you can do it, I can do it too, sooner or later."

Billy felt it rising. The sucker. Lowlife of Billy's world. Never finish last, never be a sucker. Don't let them humiliate you. Chick's face grinned out of Harvey's skull. Going to work, Billy? Lowlife. Humiliate the bastard.

"Harv, you got to play safe even when you're ahead. Didn't you learn anything playing against me?"

"I learned plenty."

"You didn't learn enough."

And Billy leaned into the action and ran the table and broke a new rack and ran that and part of another. He missed a tough one and Harv sank eight and then Billy got at it and finished it off, a hundred to Harvey's twelve, which, with his forty-point spot was still only fifty-two. Billy put his cue in the rack, feeling he'd done his duty. Suckers demand humiliation and it is the duty of people like Billy to answer their demand. Suckers must be stomped for their love of ignorance, for expecting too much from life. Suckers do not realize that a man like Billy spent six hours a day at pool tables all over Albany for years learning how to shed his ignorance.

Doc Fay watched the finale, shaking his head at what he heard from Harvey's mouth. Harvey paid Billy the thirty-five dollars and put on his hat and suit coat. Billy actually felt something for Harvey then.

"You know, Harv," he said, putting his hand on the sucker's shoulder, "you'll never beat me."

"You're good, Billy. I see how you play safe till the bunch breaks and then you get a streak going. I see how you do it."

"Harv, if you play from now till you're ninety-nine (play it, Fatha), you still won't know how I do it."

"I'll get you, Billy," Harv said, backing toward the door. "One of these nights I'll get you." And then he was gone, only his monkey smirk still hanging there by the door above the image of his orange and purple tie. Doc Fay broke up with laughter.

"I thought for a minute there, Billy, you were wising up the sucker," the Doc said.

"You can't wise up a sucker," said Billy.

"Absolutely. It's what I said to myself when Harv says he knows how you do it. I said, Doc, you know and *Billy* knows."

"What do we know?"

"That a sucker don't get even till he gets to heaven."

"Right," Billy said. "I learned that in church."

III

ED TOM FITZSIMMONS, the four-to-two man at Becker's, a good fellow, stood behind his mustache and amidst his brawn in a fresh apron, arms folded, sleeves rolled, waiting for thirst to arise anew in his four customers. Martin Daugherty sat at the end of the bar underneath the frame of the first dollar Becker's ever made, and at the edge of the huge photo of Becker's thirtieth anniversary outing at Picard's Grove on a sunny day in August of 1932, which adorned the back bar. The photographer had captured two hundred and two men in varying degrees of sobriety, in shirtsleeves, sitting, kneeling, standing in a grassy field, clutching their beer, billowy clouds behind and above them. Emil Becker ordered a wall-sized blowup made from the negative and then spent weeks identifying all present by full name, and writing an index, which he framed and hung beside the blowup, which covered the wall like wallpaper.

Emil Becker died in 1936 and his son, Gus, put a check mark alongside his name, and a gold star on his chest in the photo. Customers then wanted the same done for other faithful departed, and so the stars went up, one by one. There were nineteen gone out of two hundred in six years. Martin Daugherty was in the photo. So was Red Tom. So was Billy Phelan, and Daddy Big, and Harvey Hess. So was Bindy McCall and his son, Charlie. So was Scotty Streck. The star was already shining on Scotty's chest and the check mark alongside his name.

Martin looked at Red Tom, and at his mustache: in the photo and the real thing. It was a mustache of long standing, brooded over, stroked, waxed, combed, pampered.

"That mustache of yours, Fitzsimmons," said Martin, "is outlandish. Venturesome and ostentatious."

"Is that so?"

"Unusually vulgar. Splendid too, of course, and elegant in a sardonic Irish way. But it surely must be unspeakable with tomato juice."

"Give up and have a drink," Red Tom said, pouring a new bourbon for Martin.

"It's pontifical, it's arrogant. It obviously reflects an intemperate attitude toward humankind. I'd say it was even intimidating when found on a bartender, a mustache like that."

"Glad you like it."

"Who said I liked it? Listen," Martin said, now in complete possession of Red Tom's attention, "what do you hear about Charlie McCall?"

Red Tom eyed the other customers, moved in close. "The night squad was here asking your kind of question, Bo Linder and Jimmy Bergan."

"You tell them anything a fellow like myself should know?"

"Only that the word's out that he's gone."

"Gone how?"

"Disappeared, that's all."

"What about Jimmy Hennessey?"

"Hennessey? What's he got to do with it?"

"Maybe something."

"I haven't laid eyes on Hennessey in months."

"Is he all right?"

"Last I heard, he was drying out. Fell down the church steps and landed in front of Father O'Connor, who says to him, Hennessey, you should stop drinking. Hennessey reaches his hand up to the priest and says, I'm waiting for help from the Holy Ghost. He's in the neighborhood somewhere, says O'Connor. Ask him to pick you up. And he steps over Hennessey's chest."

"He must be dried out by now. The McCalls put his name on a go-between list."

"A go-between list?"

"It'll be in the morning paper. Our guess is they're trying to find an intermediary to talk with the kidnappers about the ransom."

Martin put the list on the bar and ran down the names: Joe Decker, a former soft-shoe artist who ran the Double Dot nightclub on Hudson Avenue; Andy Kilmartin, the Democratic leader of the Fifth ward; Bill Shea, a Bindy McCall lieutenant who ran the Monte Carlo, the main gambling house in the city; Barney O'Hare, a champion bootlegger who served four terms as Patsy McCall's man in the State Assembly and no longer had need of work; Arnold Carroll, who ran the Blue Elephant saloon; Marcus Gorman, the town's best-known criminal lawyer, who defended Legs Diamond; Butch McHale, a retired welterweight and maybe the best fighter ever to come out of Albany, who ran the Satin Slipper, a speakeasy, after he quit the ring; Phil Lynch, who ran the candy store that was Bindy's headquarters for numbers collections and payoffs downtown; Honey Curry, a hoodlum from Sheridan Avenue, who did four years for a grocery store stickup; Hennessey, an ex-alderman who was one of Patsy's political bagmen until he developed the wet spot on his brain; Morrie Berman, the ex-pimp and gambler; and Billy Phelan.

"Kilmartin never comes in any more," Red Tom said. "O'Hare comes in for a nightcap after he gets laid. Gorman hasn't been in here since old man Becker told him and Legs Diamond he didn't want their business. Most of the others are in and out."

"Lately?"

"All but Curry. No show for a long while."

"Billy been in tonight yet?"

"He's about due."

"I know. I whipped him today with a parlay. I think I hurt him."

"He knows how to get well. You say this list is in the paper?"

Martin told him how the coded list arrived at the *Times-Union* as a classified ad and was spotted by a lady clerk as oddball enough to send up to Emory Jones for a funny feature story. The message was to CHISWICK, the names in scrambled numbers. Emory solved it instantly: A as 1, B as 2, the moron code. And when Martin next communicated, Emory had him check out everyone on the list. Max Rosen admitted the list was connected to the kidnapping but would say no more and didn't have to. Martin spent an hour in the phone booth discovering that none of those listed was available. Not home. In Miami. Away for the month. Except for Hennessey and Curry, whose phones didn't answer, and Billy and Morrie, whose recent movements Martin knew personally.

"Who's Curry hang around with these days?"

"He's cozy with Maloy, used to be. But he's always with a dame."

"And Maloy?"

"I heard he was hanging out with a bunch down in Jersey. Curry too."

Billy Phelan came in then. Martin saw him touch Red Tom for what looked like a twenty before he even looked the place over. Then he sat down beside Martin.

"Luckiest man in North America," Billy said.

"A connoisseur of horseflesh."

"With a horseshoe up your ass."

"Talent makes its own luck, Billy. Like somebody bowling two-ninety-nine."

"Yeah. I got a partial payment for you." Billy signaled Red Tom for a refill for Martin and a beer for himself, and put an envelope in front of Martin. He kept his hand on it.

"I need a bankroll for Nick's game tonight. If I hold on to this and I win I pay you off entirely."

"And if you lose, I lose this."

"You don't lose. Billy pays his debts."

"I mean this month."

"All right, Martin, you need the cash, take it. I'm not arguing. I just work a little longer."

"Keep the roll and maybe we'll both get our dues paid. But I have a question. What do you hear about Charlie McCall, apart from what we both know about last night?"

"Jesus, this is my big Charlie McCall day. Why the hell does everybody think I know what Charlie's up to?"

"Who's everybody?"

"Nobody."

"Some significant people in town obviously think you might be able to help find him, one way or another."

"Find him? He ain't lost."

"Haven't you heard?"

"I heard he got snatched, but I just found out upstairs that's not straight. Daddy Big got it right from Bindy. Charlie's in New York. All I heard was a rumor."

"Your rumor was right."

"They took him, then? That's it?"

"Correct."

"Daddy Big and his goatshit."

"What goatshit?"

"Just goatshit. What about significant people?"

"Your name's in the paper that comes out tonight, one of twelve names, all in a code in a classified ad, which is obviously a message to the kidnappers about go-betweens. Nobody said anything to you about this?"

"Nobody till now."

"You weren't on the original list. The ad came in about two this afternoon and I just found out your name was added about half an hour ago." Martin told the ad story again, and Billy knew all the names. He signaled for a beer.

"I got a message for you," Red Tom said when he brought Billy's beer. "Your friend Angie was in today. She's at the Kenmore."

"She say anything?"

"She said she needs her back scratched."

"That's not what she wants scratched."

"Well, you're the expert on that," said Red Tom, and he went down the bar.

Billy told Martin, "I don't belong on that list. That's either connected people or hoodlums. I pay off the ward leader, nickel and dime, and I vote the ticket, that's my connection. And I never handled a gun in my life."

"You classify Berman as a hoodlum?"

"Maybe not, but he sure ain't no altar boy."

"You know him pretty well?"

"Years, but we're not that close."

"You know everybody on Broadway and everybody knows you. Maybe that's why you're on the list."

"No, I figured it out. Daddy Big got me on it. If it come in half an hour ago, that's all it could be. Something I said about a plan to snatch Bindy last year. You know that rumor."

"No. What was it?"

"Fuck, a rumor. I'm the only one heard it? What is this? It was all over the goddamn street. Tom, you heard that rumor about Bindy last year?"

"What rumor?"

"Around August. Saratoga season. Somebody was gonna snatch him. You heard it."

"I never heard that. Who was gonna do it?"

"How the fuck do I know who was gonna do it?"

"It's your rumor."

"I heard a goddamn rumor, that's all. I paid no attention, nothing ever happened. Now, because I heard a rumor last August, I'm on the McCalls' shit list?"

"This is no shit list," Martin said.

When Red Tom went to serve another customer, Billy said, "They think I'm in on it."

"I don't think that's true," Martin said, "but it does make you a pretty famous fellow tonight in our little community. A pretty famous fellow."

"Know where I first heard about Charlie? From my Uncle Chick, who don't even know how to butter bread right. How the hell did he hear about it? He asks me what I know about Charlie and all I know is last night at the alleys and then you and all your Charlie horses. You knew it then, didn't you?"

"Maybe."

"Maybe, my fucking noodle."

"Maybe, your fucking noodle then."

"I'm standing with Charlie horses and you know the guy's glommed."

"And that explains why I won?"

"Sure it explains why you won, you prick."

"I didn't win anything yet," and Martin pushed the envelope toward Billy.

"Right. Poker time. Money first, Charlie later."

"Morrie Berman'll be in that game, right?"

"That's what he said last night."

"Look, pay attention to what he says. Anything. It's liable to be very important."

"What do you know that I don't?"

"That's an intriguing question we can take up some other time, but now let me tell you very seriously that everything is important. Everything Morrie says. We'll talk about it later when things aren't quite so public."

"What are you, a cop?"

"No, I'm a friend of Charlie McCall's."

"Yeah."

"And so are you."

"Yeah."

And Billy drank up and stood up. He and Martin moved toward the door, which opened to the pull of Daddy Big as they reached it, Daddy in his change apron and eyeshade, questing sweet blotto at eventide. Billy grabbed his shirtfront.

"You turned me in, you son of a bitch."

"What's got you, you gone nuts?"

"You told Bindy what I said about the snatch rumor."

"I asked about it. Bindy asked me where I heard it."

"And you finked on me, you fat weasel. And I don't know anything worth a goddamn pigeon fart."

"Then you got nothing to worry about."

"I worry about weasels. I never took you for a weasel."

"I don't like you either. Stay out of upstairs."

"I play tomorrow and you don't shut me out and don't try."

"I shut out people who need to be shut."

"Go easy, old man. There's three things you can't do in this world and all three of 'em are fight."

Daddy Big broke Billy's hold on his shirt and simultaneously, with a looping left out of nowhere, knocked him against the front door, which opened streetward. Billy fell on his back on Becker's sidewalk, his fedora rolling into the gutter. Martin picked him up and then went for the hat.

"Not your day for judging talent," Martin said.

Billy put on his hat, blotted his lip. "He hits like he plays pool," he said.

"So, that's new. Something you learned," said Martin, brushing the dust off Billy's suit coat.

*   *   *

Martin walked with Billy up Broadway toward Clinton Avenue, thinking first he would go to Nick's cellar and watch the poker game but not play against his own money. Yet the notion of spectating at a poker game on such an evil day seemed almost evil in itself. His mind turned to thoughts of death: closing Scotty Streck's left eye, Charlie Boy maybe with a bullet in the head, dumped in the woods somewhere.

And passing the United Traction Company building at the corner of Columbia Street he saw Francis Phelan, again cocking his arm, just there, across the street, again ready to throw his smooth stone; and he remembered the bleeding and dying scab, his head laid open, face down on the floor of the trolley, one arm hanging over the top step. The scab had driven the trolley down Broadway from the North Albany barns, and when it reached Columbia Street a mob was waiting. Francis and two other young men heaved a kerosene-soaked sheet, twisted and knotted into a loose rope, over the overhead trolley wire and lit it with matches. The trolley could not pass the flaming obstacle and halted. The militiamen raised their rifles to the ready, fearful that the hostile crowd would assault the car, as it had the day before, and beat the driver unconscious. Militiamen on horseback pushed the mob back from the tracks, and one soldier hit Fiddler Quain with a rifle butt as Fiddler lit the sheet. But even as this was taking the full attention of the military, even before thoughts of reversing the trolley could be translated into action, other men threw a second twisted sheet over the trolley wire to the rear of the car and lit it, trapping the trolley and its strike-breaking passengers between two pillars of flame.

It was then that Francis uncocked his arm and that the smooth stone flew, and the scab fell and died. No way out. Death within the coordinates. And it was the shooting of the innocent onlookers which followed Francis's act that hastened the end of the strike. Violence enough. Martin saw two of the onlookers fall, just as he could still see the stone fly. The first was spun by the bullet and reeled backward and slid down the front of the railroad station wall. The second grabbed his stomach as the scab had grabbed his head, and he crumpled where he stood. Fiddler Quain lay on the granite blocks of Broadway after his clubbing, but the mob swirled around that horseman who hit him, an invasion of ants, and Fiddler was lifted up and swept away to safety and hiding. Like Franny, he was known but never prosecuted. The hands that carried the violence put honest men back to work. Broadway, then and now, full of men capable of violent deeds to achieve their ends.

"Listen, Billy," Martin said as they walked, "that business between you and Daddy Big, that's not really why the McCalls put you on the list. There's something else going on, and it's about Morrie Berman."

Billy stopped walking and faced Martin.

"What Morrie says could be important, since he knows people who could have taken Charlie."

"So do I. Everybody does on Broadway."

"Then what you or the others know is also important."

"What I know is my business. What Berman knows is his business. What the hell is this, Martin?"

"Patsy McCall is making it his business, too."

"How do you know that?"

"I talked to him this morning."

"Did he ask you to snoop around Morrie Berman?"

"No. He asked me to ask *you* to do that."

"Me? He wants me to be some kind of stoolie? What the hell's the matter with you, Martin?"

"I'm not aware that anything's the matter."

"I'm not one of the McCalls' political whores."

"Nobody said you were. I told him you wouldn't like the idea, but I also know you've been friendly with Charlie McCall all your life. Right now, he could be strapped to a bed someplace with a gun at his head. He could even be dead."

Billy made no response. Martin looked at him and saw puzzlement. Martin shaped the picture of Charlie Boy again in his mind but saw not Charlie but Edward Daugherty, tied to a bed by four towels, spread-eagled, his genitals uncovered. Why such a vision now? Martin had never seen his father in such a condition, nor was he in such a state even now at the nursing home. The old man was healthy, docile, no need to tie him to the bed. Naked prisoner. Naked father. It was Ham who saw Noah, his father, naked and drunk on wine, and Noah cursed Ham, while Shem and Japheth covered their father's nakedness and were blessed for it. Cursed for peering into the father's soul through the pores. Blessed for covering the secrets of the father's body with a blanket. Damn all who find me in my naked time.

Billy started to walk again toward Clinton Avenue. He spoke without looking at Martin, who kept pace with him. "Georgie the Syph knocked down an old woman and took four bucks out of her pocketbook. I came around the corner at James Street and saw him and I even knew the old woman, Marty Slyer the electrician's mother. They lived on Pearl Street. Georgie saw me and ran up Maiden Lane and the old lady told the cops I saw him. But I wouldn't rat even on a bum like Georgie. What I did the next time I saw him was kick him in the balls before he could say anything and take twenty off him and mail it to Mrs. Slyer. Georgie had to carry his balls around in a basket."

"That's a noble story, Billy, but it's just another version of the code of silence. What the underworld reveres. It doesn't have anything to do with morality or justice or honor or even friendship. It's a simplistic perversion of all those things."

"Whatever it is it don't make me a stool pigeon."

"All that's wanted is information."

"Maybe. Or maybe they want Morrie for something particular."

"No, I don't think so."

"How the hell do you know what they want, Martin?"

"Suit yourself in this, Billy. I was asked to put the question to you and I did."

"I don't get it, a man like you running errands for the McCalls. I don't figure you for that."

"What else can I tell you after I say I'm fond of Charlie, and I don't like kidnappers. I'm also part of that family."

"Yeah. We're all part of that family."

"I'll be around later to root for our money. Think about it."

"What exactly did Patsy say?"

"He said to hang around Berman and listen. That's all he said."

"That's all. Yeah."

And Billy crossed Clinton toward the alley beside Nick's haberdashery, where Nick, Footers O'Brien, and Morrie Berman were talking. Martin walked up the other side of the street, past the Pruyn Library, and crossed to The Grand Theater when he saw the Laughton film on the marquee. He looked back at the library corner and remembered the death of youth: his cousin's suicide in the wagon. Sudden behavior and pervasive silence. But sometimes living men tell no tales either. Francis Phelan suddenly gone and still no word why. *The Beachcomber*. Martin hadn't told Billy that his father was back in town. Duplicity and the code of silence. Who was honored by this? What higher morality was

Martin preserving by keeping Billy ignorant of a fact so potentially significant to him? We are all in a conspiracy against the next man. Duplicity. And Billy Phelan saw through you, Martin: errand boy for the McCalls. Duplicity at every turn. Melissa back in town to remind you of how deep it goes. Oh yes, Martin Daugherty, you are one duplicitous son of a bitch.

*   *   *

In the drugstore next to The Grand, Martin phoned Patsy McCall.

"Do you have any news, Patsy?"

"No news."

"I made that contact we talked about, and it went just about the way I thought it would. He didn't like the idea. I don't think you can look for much information there."

"What the hell's the matter with him?"

"He's just got a feeling about that kind of thing. Some people do."

"That's all he's got a feeling for?"

"It gets sticky, Patsy. He's a good fellow, and he might well come up with something. He didn't say no entirely. But I thought you ought to know his reaction and maybe put somebody else on it if you think it's important."

"I'll take care of it," Patsy said curtly and hung up.

Martin called the *Times-Union* and got Emory. Yes, the lid was still on the Charlie story. "Everybody went along," Emory said, "including Dunsbach. I seared his ass all right. He wouldn't touch the story now with rubber gloves."

"Heroic, Em. I knew you could do it."

"Have you smoked out any kidnappers yet?"

"You know I don't smoke, Em. What happened with the A.L.P.?"

"I don't give a damn about that piss-ant stuff when I've got a story like this. Here. Talk to Viglucci."

Viglucci, the city editor, explained that some twelve hundred new voters had enrolled in the A.L.P., twice as many as necessary for Patsy McCall to control the young party. No, the desk hadn't reached Jake Berman, the phone constantly busy at the A.L.P. office. Martin volunteered to go there personally, being only two blocks away. Fine.

Jake Berman had been barely a specter all day for Martin, whose sympathy was all with the McCalls because of Charlie. But now Jake could surely use a little consolation. Martin had known Jake for years and liked him, a decent man, a lawyer for the poor, knew him when he was a city judge, appointed by McCall fiat as a sop to the Albany Jews. But that didn't last, for Jake refused to throw out a case against a gouging landlord, an untouchable who was a heavy contributor to the

Democratic Party. Jake quit the bench and the party, and went back to practicing law.

In 1935, when the A.L.P. was founded to gain another line for Roosevelt's second run, Jake spearheaded the party locally and opened headquarters in his father's old tailor shop on Sheridan Avenue, just off North Pearl Street. Old Socialists and laboring men, who wanted nothing to do with the Democrats but liked F.D.R.'s New Deal, made the new party their own, and by 1936 the Albany branch had one hundred and eighty-four members. Patsy McCall tolerated it because it was a stepchild of the Democratic party, even though he had no use for Roosevelt, the snob son of a bitch. The Catholic Church grew restless with the New Party, however, as its ranks fattened with anti-Franco radicals and socialist intellectuals who spat on God. What's more, it promised the kind of growth that one day could be a power balance in local elections, and so Patsy decided it was time to pull the plug.

The word went out to the aldermen and ward leaders of the city's nineteen wards that some sixty voters in each ward should change their enrollment from Democrat to American Labor. As enrolled members, they would then be entitled to vote at A.L.P. meetings, and would vote as Patsy told them to. Jake Berman's few hundred regulars would be dwarfed by the influx, and Jake's chairmanship negated. In time, all in good time, Patsy's majority, of which Chickie Phelan was now one, would elect a new party chairman.

The garmentless tailor's dummy that had been in Berman's tailor shop for as long as Martin could remember was still visible behind the Lehman-for-Governor posters taped to the old store window. The shop had stood empty for several years after the death of old Ben Berman, a socialist since the turn of the century and a leader in the New York City garment industry's labor struggle until strikebreakers fractured his skull. He came to Albany to put his life and his head back together and eventually opened this shop, just off Pearl Street at the edge of an old Irish slum, Sheridan Hollow, where Lackey Quinlan once advertised in the paper to rent a house with running water, and curious applicants found he had built his shack over a narrow spot in the old Canal Street creek. This was the running water, and in it Lackey kept his goose and his gander.

Ben Berman worked as a tailor in the neighborhood, though his clients came from all parts of the city, until he lost most of his eyesight and could no longer sew. He died soon after that, and then his son Jacob rented the shop to another tailor, who ran it for several years. But the new man was inferior to Ben Berman with the needle, and the trade fell away. It remained for the A.L.P. to reopen the shop, and now it looked as if its days were again numbered.

Martin pushed open the door, remembering when Ben Berman made suits and coats for his own father, those days when the Daughertys lived under the money tree. Martin could vividly recall Edward Daugherty standing in this room trying on a tan, speckled suit with knickers and a belt in the back, mottled buttons, and a brown, nonmatching vest. Martin mused again on how he had inherited none of his father's foppery, never owned a tailor-made suit or coat, lived off the rack, satisfied with ready-made. A woman Martin did not know was coming down the inside stairs as he entered. She looked about forty, a matron in style. She was weeping and her hat looked crooked to Martin.

"Jake upstairs?"

She nodded, sniffled, wiped an eye. Martin yearned to console her with gentle fondling.

"Can I help you?" he asked her.

She laughed once and shook her head, then went out. Martin climbed the old stairs and found Jake Berman leaning back in a swivel chair, hands behind head, feet propped up on an open rolltop desk. Jake had a thick gray mustache and wore his hair long, like a serious musician. The elbow was out of his gray sweater, and he was tieless. The desk dominated the room, two rooms really, with the adjoining wall knocked out. Folding chairs cluttered both rooms, and at a long table two men younger than Jake sat tallying numbers on pink pads. The phone on Jake's desk was off the hook.

"Why don't you answer your phone?" Martin asked.

"I'm too busy," Jake said. He moved only his lips and eyes to say that. "What can I do for you?"

"I heard the results."

"You did. And did they surprise you?"

"Quite a heavy enrollment. I was told twelve hundred plus. Is that accurate?"

"Your information is as good as mine. Better. You get yours from McCall headquarters."

"I got mine from the city desk."

"Same thing really, isn't it, Martin?"

"I wouldn't say so. The McCalls do have some support there."

"Some?"

"I for one don't see myself a total McCaller."

"Yes, you write some risky things now and then, Martin. You're quite an independent-minded man in your way. But I didn't see you or anybody else reporting about the plan to take us over. Didn't anybody down on that reactionary rag know about it?"

"Did you?"

"I knew this morning," said Jake. "I knew when I saw it happening. Fat old Irishmen who loathe us, drunken bums from the gutter, little German hausfraus enrolling with us. Up until then, the subversion was a well-kept secret."

Jake's face was battered, his eyes asymmetric, one lower than the other, his mustache trimmed too high on one side. In anger, his lower lip tightened to the left. His face was as off balance as his father's battered and dusty samovar, which sat behind him on a table, a fractured sculpture with spigot, one handle, and one leg broken. Another fractured face for Martin in a matter of hours: Charlie when Scotty died; Patsy and Matt this morning; and now Jake, victim of the McCalls. Interlocking trouble. Binding ironies. Martin felt sympathy for them all, had a fondness for them all, gave allegiance to none. Yet, now he was being accused, for the second time in half an hour, of being in league with the McCall machine. And was he not? Oh, duplicitous man, are you not?

"I came for a statement, Jake. Do you have one?"

"Very brief. May the McCalls be boiled in dead men's piss."

A young man at the tabulating table, bald at twenty-five, threw down his pencil and stood up. "And you can tell the Irish in this town to go fuck a duck."

"That's two unprintable statements," said Martin. "Shall we try for three?"

"Always a joke, Martin. Everything is comic to you."

"Some things are comic, Jake. When a man tells me with high seriousness to go fuck a duck, even though I'm only half Irish, I'm amused somewhere."

The young man, in shirtsleeves, and with Ben Franklin spectacles poised halfway down his nose, came to the desk, hovering over Martin. "It's the religion, isn't it?" he said. "Political Jews stand as an affront to the McCalls and their priests, priests no better than the fascist-dog Catholics who kiss the boots of Franco and Mussolini."

Martin made a squiggle on his notepad.

"Quote it about the fascists," said the young man.

"Do you think the McCalls are fascists, Jake?" Martin asked.

"I know a Jew who's been with them almost since the beginning," said Jake. "He works for a few pennies more than he started for in nineteen twenty-two, sixteen years of penurious loyalty and he never asked for a raise, or threatened to quit over money. 'If I do,' he once said to me, 'you know what they'll tell me? The same they told Levy, the accountant. Quit, then, you Jew fuck.' He is a man in fear, a man without spirit."

"People who don't promote Jews, are they fascists, or are they anti-Semites?"

"The same thing. The fascists exist because of all those good people, like those sheep who enrolled with us today, all full of passive hate, waiting for the catalyst to activate it."

"Your point is clear, Jake, but I still want a statement."

"Print this. That I'm not dead, not even defeated, that I'll take the party's case to court, and that we'll win. If ever the right to free elections was violated, then it was violated today in Albany with this farcical maneuver."

"The McCalls own the courts, too," said the young man. "Even the Federal court."

"There are honest judges. We'll find one," Jake said.

"We won't yield to mob rule," the young man said.

"He's right," Jake said. "We will not. You know an Irish mob threw my grandfather out a third-story window in New York during the Civil War. They were protesting against their great enemy back then, the niggers, but they killed a pious old Jew. He tried to reason with them, with the mob. He thought they would listen to reason, for, after all, he was an intelligent man and had nothing to do with the war, or the niggers. He was merely living upstairs over the draft office. Nevertheless, they threw him down onto the street and let him lie there twitching, dying, for hours. They wouldn't let anyone pick him up or even help him, and so he died, simply because he lived over the draft office. It was a moment of monstrous ethnic truth in American history, my friend, the persecuted Irish throwing a persecuted Jew out the window in protest against drafting Irishmen into the Union Army to help liberate the persecuted Negro.

"But the enormous irony hasn't led to wisdom, only to self-preservation and the awareness of the truth of mobs. My father told me that story after another mob set fire to paper bags on our front porch, and, when my father came out to stomp out the flames, the bags broke and human excrement squirted everywhere. A brilliant stroke by the mob. They were waiting with their portable flaming cross to watch my father dance on the fire and the shit. Fire and shit, my friend, fire and shit. Needless to say, we moved soon thereafter."

"The Klan's an old friend of mine, too, Jake," Martin said. "They burned a cross in front of my house and fired a shot through our front window because of what I wrote in support of Al Smith. You can't blame the Klan on the Irish. Maybe the Irish were crazy, but they were also used as cannon fodder in the Civil War. I could match grandfathers with you. One of mine was killed at Antietam, fighting *for* the niggers."

Jake held a letter opener in his hand like a knife. He poked the point of it lightly at the exposed desk top. Then his arm went rigid. "Goddamn it, Martin, this is a stinking, lousy existence. Goddamn its stink! Goddamn all of it!" And with sudden force he drove the point of the letter opener into the desk top. The point stuck but the blade broke and pierced the muscle of his thumb.

"Perfect," he said, and held his hand in front of his face and watched it bleed. The young man ran to the bathroom for a towel. He wrapped the wound tightly as Jake slumped in his chair.

"Violence solves it all," Jake said. "I no longer feel the need to say anything."

"We'll talk another night," Martin said.

"I won't be less bitter."

"Maybe less bloody."

"And unbowed."

"There's something else, Jake, and you ought to know. It'll be in the paper tonight. Your son, Morrie, is named as a possible intermediary in a kidnapping."

"Repeat that, Martin."

"Bindy McCall's son, Charlie, was kidnapped this morning and the ransom demand is a quarter of a million. The McCalls are publishing a list of names in a simple code, names of men they view as potential go-betweens for the kidnappers to pick from. Morrie is one of twelve."

"God is just," said Jake's young aide. "The McCalls are now getting theirs back."

"Stupid, stupid to say such a thing," Jake snapped. "Know when to be angry."

"I just saw Morrie," Martin said, "getting ready to go into a card game."

"Naturally," said Jake.

"I may see him later. Do you have any message?"

"We no longer talk. I have three daughters, all gold, and I have Morris, a lead slug."

Martin suddenly pictured Jake with a flowing beard, knife in hand on Mount Moriah, cutting out the heart of his son.

"I just had a vision of you holding that letter opener," Martin said to Jake. "You look very much like an engraving of Abraham I've looked at for years in the family Bible. Your hair, your forehead."

"Abraham with the blade."

"And Isaac beneath it," said Martin. He could not bring himself to mention the dissection of Isaac. "The likeness of you to that drawing of Abraham is amazing."

As he said this Martin was withholding; for he now had a clear memory of the biblical engraving and it wasn't like Jake at all. Abraham's was a face of weakness, a face full of faith and anguish, but no bitterness, no defiance. And the knife did not touch Isaac. Abraham's beard then disappeared in the vision. Where he gripped the sacrificial knife, part of a finger was missing. Isaac bore the face of a goat. The vision changed. The goat became a bawling infant, then a bleating lamb. Martin shut his eyes to stop the pictures. He looked at the samovar.

"Isaac," Jake was saying. "God loves the Isaacs of the world. But he wouldn't have bothered to ask Abraham to sacrifice a son as worthless as my Morris."

"Now you even know what God asks," Martin said.

"I withdraw the remark."

With his gaze, Martin restored the samovar, new leg, new handle, new spigot. Steam came from it once again. He looked up to see the 1936 poster: Roosevelt, the Working Man's President. Out of the spigot came the hot blood of centuries.

VIII

BUMP OLIVER WAS A DAPPER LITTLE GUY with a new haircut who played cards with his hat on. Billy met him when he sat down at the table in Nick Levine's cellar, just under the electric meter and kitty-corner from the old asbestos coal furnace which smudged up the cellar air but didn't heat it enough so you could take off your suit coat. New man on Broadway, Nick said of Bump when he introduced him to Billy; no more than that and who needs to know more?

And yet after Bump had dealt twice, Billy did want to know more. Because he sensed a cheater. Why? Don't ask Billy to be precise about such things. He has been listening to cheater stories for ten years, has even seen some in action and found out about it later, to his chagrin. He has watched Ace Reilly, a would-be cheater, practicing his second-card deal for hours in front of a mirror. Billy even tried that one himself to see how it went, but didn't like it, didn't have the patience or the vocation for it. Because cheaters, you see, already know how it's going to end, and what the hell good is that? Also, Billy saw a cheater caught once: a salesman who played in Corky Ronan's clubroom on Van Woert Street, and when Corky saw he was using a shiner, he grabbed the cheater's hand and showed everybody how he wore it, a little bit of a mirror under a long fingernail. Joe Dembski reached over and punched the cheater on the side of the neck, and the others were ready to move in for their licks, but Corky said never mind that, just take his money and he won't come back, and they let the cheater go. Why? Well, Corky's idea was that everybody's got a trade, and that's Billy's idea too, now.

So Billy has seen all this and has thought about it, and because he knows so well how things should be when everything is straight, he also thinks he knows when it's off center, even when it's only a cunt hair off. That's how sensitive Billy's apparatus is. Maybe it was the way Bump beveled the deck and crooked a finger around it, or maybe it was his eyes and the fact that he was new on Broadway. Whatever it was, even though Bump lost twelve straight hands, Billy didn't trust him.

The game was now five-card stud, quarter ante, no limit, and four flush beats a pair. The deal was walking and when it came to Bump, Billy gave him the full eyeball.

"Where you from, Bump?" he asked, just like a fellow who was looking for information.

"Troy," Bump said. "Albia. You know it?"

"Sure, I know it. Who the hell don't know Albia?"

"Well, I was asking. Lot of people know about Troy don't know Albia."

"I know Albia, for chrissake. I know Albia."

"That's terrific, really terrific. Congratulations."

Bump looked at Billy; Billy looked at Bump. The others in the game looked at them both: dizzy-talking bastards. But Billy wanted the cheater thinking about something besides cheating, wanted him edgy. Billy smiled at Bump. Bump didn't smile at Billy. Good.

Billy drew deuce, four, eight and folded. He was ahead $21, which was nice. He'd sat down with about $315 and change, which included his original $170, $20 from Peg, $40 from Tod, another $20 from Red Tom, and $67 from the Harvey Hess Benevolent Association. All he'd spent was carfare and the drinks at Becker's. Roughly speaking he still needed about $455 to get straight with Martin, but he was winging it now, wasn't he, getting where he had to go? And was there ever any doubt? Don'tcha know Billy can always get a buck?

Morrie Berman won the hand with three nines. He was a bigger winner than Billy.

"Your luck's running," Billy said to him.

"Yeah," said Morrie. "Money coming in, name in the paper."

Billy had told him as soon as they met in front of Nick's that both their names were on the list. Morrie already knew. Max Rosen had called around supper to ask him to stay in town, keep himself on tap. Rosen was nice as pie, Morrie said. If you don't mind, Mr. Berman. Naturally I don't mind, Mr. Rosen, and if I can be of any help at all, just call me. What else do you tell a McCall flunky in a situation like this? Neither Billy nor Morrie mentioned the list to anybody else at Nick's. Billy listened carefully to what Morrie said. He didn't say a goddamn thing worth telling anybody.

"What's that about name in the paper?" Nick Levine asked. Nick was his own house player, cutting the game. Nick would cut a deuce out of a $40 pot. Nick also had a nose for gossip when it moved into his cellar.

"Aw nothin', just a thing," Morrie said.

"What thing?"

"Forget it."

"I'll get the paper."

"That's it, get the paper."

But Nick wasn't satisfied. He was a persistent little man with double-thick glasses and he owned more suits of clothes personally than anybody Billy knew, except maybe George Quinn. But then Nick owned a suit store and George didn't, and George looked a hell of a lot better in clothes than Nick. Some people don't know how to wear clothes.

Nick looked across the table at Morrie and gave him a long stare while all play stopped. "They pull you in?"

"No, nothing like that," Morrie said. "Look, play cards. I'll tell you later."

That satisfied Nick and he bet his kings.

Lemon Lewis was a pointy-headed bald man, which was how he got his nickname. Didn't have a hair on his body. Not even a goddamn eyelash. When Lemon, who worked for Bindy McCall, didn't say anything about Morrie's name in the paper, Billy knew he hadn't heard about the list. But Lemon wasn't that close to Bindy any more, not since he overdid it with kickbacks when he handled the gambling patronage. Bindy demoted Lemon for his greed and put him to work on the odds board in the Monte Carlo. Man with the chalk, just another mug.

Lemon was alongside Bump and when the deal reached Lemon, Billy asked for a new deck. If Bump, who would deal next, had been marking cards, beveling them, nicking edges, waiting for his time to handle them again, then the new deck would wipe out his work. Coming at Lemon's deal, the request would also not point to Bump. But it did rattle Lemon, which was always nice.

"New deck, and you're winning?" Lemon said.

"Double my luck," Billy said.

"You think maybe Lemon knows something?" Footers O'Brien asked, and everybody laughed but Lemon. No mechanic, Lemon. Last man in town you'd accuse of cheating. A hound dog around the rackets all his life and he never learned how the game was played.

"Lemon shuffles like my mother when she deals Go Fish to my ten-year-old nephew," Billy said.

Lemon dealt the new cards, delivering aces wired to Billy.

"Ace bets," said Lemon, and when Billy bet five dollars, Bump,

Morrie, and Nick all folded. Footers, a retired vaudevillian who sang Jolson tunes at local minstrel shows, stayed with a king. Lemon stayed with a queen.

On the third card nobody improved. Billy drew an eight and bet again with the ace. Lemon raised and so Billy read him for queens wired, because Lemon rarely bluffed. Footers called with king and jack showing, so probably he had a pair too. Footers wouldn't chase a pair. Too good a player. But whatever either of them had, Billy had them beat.

On the fourth card, Billy paired the eights. Aces and eights now. Neither Lemon nor Footers looked like they improved. Very unlikely. Yet both called, even when Billy bet $20. We can beat your eights, Billy.

Footers's last card was a seven, which didn't help, and Lemon drew a spade, which gave him three spades up. The bet was still to Billy's eights, but before he could bet them, Lemon turned over his hole card and showed the four flush.

"Can you beat it, boys?" he asked, smiling sunbeams.

"Only with a stick," Footers said, and he folded his jacks.

"I bet forty dollars," Billy said.

His hand, showing, was ace, seven and the pair of eights.

"Well that's a hell of a how-do-you-do," Lemon said. "I turn my hand over and show you I got a four flush."

"Yes, you did that. And then I bet you forty dollars. You want to play five cards open, that's okay by me. But, Lemon, my word to you is still four-oh."

"You're bluffing, Phelan."

"You could find out."

"What do you think of a guy like this, Nick?" Lemon said.

"It's the game, Lemon. Who the hell ever told you to show your hole card before the bet?"

"He's bluffing. I know the sevens were all played. He's got a third eight? Aces," Lemon said, now doing his private calculating out loud. "Nick folded an ace, I got an ace. So you got the case ace? That's what you're telling me?"

"Forty dollars, Lemon."

Lemon went to the sandwich table, bit a bologna sandwich, and drew a glass of beer. He came back and studied Billy's hand. Still ace, seven and the eights.

Billy sat with his arms folded. Keeping cool. But folks, he was really feeling the sweet pressure, and had been, all through the hand: rising, rising. And he keeps winning on top of that. It was so great he was almost ready to cream. Goddamn, life is fun, ain't it Billy? Win or lose, you're in the mix. He ran his fingers over the table's green felt, fingered his pile of quarters, flipped through his stack of bills while he waited for the Lemon squash. Goddamn, it's good.

Bump watched him with a squinty eye.

Footers was smiling as he chewed his cigar, his nickel Headline. The Great Footers. Nobody like him. Drinking pal of Billy's for years, always good for a touch. Footers knew how to survive, too. Told Billy once how he came off a four-day drunk and woke up broke and dirty, needing a shave bad. Called in a neighbor's kid and gave him a nickel, the only cash Footers had. Sent him down to the Turk's grocery for a razor blade. The kid came back with it and Footers shaved. Then he washed and dried the blade and folded it back in its wrapper and called the kid again and told him, take this back to the Turk and tell him you didn't get it straight. Tell him Mr. O'Brien didn't want a razor blade, he wanted a cigar. And the kid came back with the cigar.

Billy looked at Footers and laughed at the memory. Footers smiled and shook his head over the mousehole in Lemon's character. Five minutes had passed since Lemon turned up the hole card.

"Thirty seconds, Lemon," Nick said. "I give you thirty seconds and then you call it or the pot's over."

Lemon sat down and bit the bologna. He looked Billy in the eye as his time ticked away.

"You said it too fast when you bet," Lemon said with a mouthful. "You probably got it."

"I'll be glad to show you," Billy said.

"Yeah, well you're good, you lucky bastard."

"Ah," said Billy, pulling in the pot at last. "My mother thanks you, my sister thanks you, my nephew thanks you, and above all, Lemon, I, William Francis Irish Catholic Democrat Phelan, I too thank you."

And Billy shoved his hole card face down into the discards.

Lemon sulked, but life went on. Bump Oliver dealt and Billy came up with kings wired. Very lovely. Also Billy heard for the first time the unmistakable whipsaw snap of a real mechanic at work dealing seconds. Billy watched Bump deal, admiringly. Billy appreciated talent wherever he saw it. Nobody else seemed to notice, but the whipsaw was as loud as a brass band to Billy's ear. It was not Billy's music, however. He did not mind the music cheaters made, so long as they didn't make it all over him. He caught Bump's eye, smiled, and then folded the kings.

"No thanks," was all he said to Bump, but it was plenty. Bump stopped looking at Billy and folded his own hand after the next card. He played two more hands and dropped out of the game. The cheater lost money. Never took a nickel from anybody, thanks to doughty Billy.

Nobody knew Bump was really a wicked fellow at heart. Nobody knew either, how Billy absolutely neutralized him.

Billy, you're a goddamned patent-leather wonder.

x   x   x

Martin arrived at the card game in time to see Lemon Lewis throw the deck across the room and hear Nick tell him, "Pick 'em up or get out. Do it again, I don't want your action." Lemon, the world's only loser, picked up the cards and sat down, bent his shiny bald head over a new hand and continued, sullenly, to lose. Billy looked like a winner to Martin, but Morrie Berman had the heavyweight stack of cash.

"You've been doing all right, then," Martin said, pulling a chair up behind Billy.

"Seem to be doing fine." Half a glass of beer sat beside Billy's winnings, his eyes at least six beers heavier than when Martin had last seen him.

"You coachin' this fella, Martin?" Nick said.

"Doesn't look to me as if he needs much coaching."

"He's got the luck of the fuckin' Irish," Lemon said.

"Be careful what you say about the Irish," Footers said. "There's Jews in this game."

"So what? I'm a Jew."

"You're not a Jew, Lemon. You're an asshole."

"Up yours, too," Lemon said, and he checked his hole card.

"Lemon, with repartee like that you belong on the stage," Footers said, and he looked at his watch. "And there's one leaving in ten minutes."

"Play cards," Nick said.

"The bet," said Morrie, "is eighty dollars."

"Eighty," Nick said.

Morrie smiled and looked nothing like Isaac. he had a theatrical quality Martin found derivative—a touch of Valentino, a bit of George Raft, but very like Ricardo Cortez: dark, slick, sleek-haired Latin stud, as if Morrie had studied the type to energize his own image as a Broadway cocksmith and would-be gigolo, a heavy gambler, an engaging young pimp with one of the smartest whores on Broadway, name of Marsha. Marsha was still in business but had split with Morrie five years back and worked alone now. Pimping is enough to weight down a paternal brow, but Jake's imputation of lead sluggery implied a far broader absence of quality in Morrie, and Martin could not see it.

What he saw was Morrie's suavity, and an ominous reserve in that muscular smile which George Raft, at his most evil, could never have managed; for Raft was too intellectually soft, too ready for simple solutions. Morrie, like Cortez, and unlike the pliant, innocent Isaac, conveyed with that controlled smile that he understood thoroughly that life was shaped by will, wit, brains, a reverence for power, a sense of the comic; that things were never simple; and that the end of behavior was not action but comprehension on which to base action. George Raft, you are a champion, but how would you ever arrive at such a conclusion?

"K-K-K-Katy, he's bettin' me eighty," sang Footers, and he folded. That left Nick, Billy, and Morrie with money to win. The pot fattened, and Nick cut it for the house.

The cellar door opened and a kid, twenty-two maybe, stepped in and was met by Nick's doorman, the hefty Bud Bradt, an All-Albany fullback for Philip Schuyler High in the late twenties. The players looked up, saw the kid getting the okay from Bud, and went back to their cards. Then the kid came down the eight steps, stood with his back to the door that led to Nick's furnace and coal bin, and, taking a small pistol from his sock, told the players: "Okay, it's a holdup."

"Cowboy," Morrie said, and he reached for his cash.

"Don't touch that, mister," the kid said. "That's what I came for," and he threw a cloth bag on top of the pot. "Put your watches and rings in that."

"This isn't a healthy thing to do in Albany, young man," Footers said to him. "They've got rules in this town."

"Do what I say, Pop. Off with the jewelry and out with the wallets. Empty your pockets and then move over against that wall." He pointed with his small pistol toward the bologna sandwiches.

The kid looked barely twenty to Martin, if that. Yet here he was committed to an irrevocably bold act. Psychopathic? Suicidal? Early criminal? Breadwinner desperate for cash? An aberrant gesture in the young, in any case. The kid's shoulders were spotted with rain, a drizzle that had begun as Martin arrived. The kid wore a black fedora with brim down, and rubbers. A holdup man in shiny rubbers with large tongues that protected his shoelaces from the damp night. What's wrong with this picture?

"Come on, move," the kid said, in a louder voice. And Martin felt his body readying to stand and obey, shed wallet, watch, and gold wedding band bought and inscribed in Galway: *Martin and Maire, Together*. Never another like that. Give it up? Well, there are priorities beyond the staunchest sentiment. And yet, and yet. Martin contained his impulse, for the other players still stared at the kid and his .22 target pistol. Gentlemen, do you realize that psychopaths snap under stress? Are you snapping, young crazy? Is blood in the cards tonight? Martin envisioned a bleeding corpus and trembled at the possibilities.

And then Billy reached for the kid's swag bag, picked it off the money pile, and threw it back at the gunny boy. Billy grabbed a fistful of cash from the pot and stuffed it into his coat. The kid stepped behind Bump Oliver's chair and shoved the pistol into the light. "Hey," he said to Billy, yelling. But Billy went back for a second handful of bills.

"That pea-shooter you got there wouldn't even poison me," he said.

Martin's thought was: Billy's snapped; the kid will kill him. But the kid could not move, his response to Billy lost, perhaps, inside his rubbers. The kid's holding position deteriorated entirely with the arrival of a sucker punch to the back of his neck by Bud Bradt, a man of heft, yes, but also of stealth, who had been edging toward the kid from the rear and then made a sudden leap to deliver his massive dose of fist to the sucker spot, sending the kid sprawling over the empty chair, gun hand sliding through the money, gun clattering to the floor on the far side of the table. Lemon pulled the kid off the table, punched his face, and threw him to the floor. Then he and Morrie kicked the kid body in dual celebration of the vanquishing until Nick said, "Shit, that's enough." Bud Bradt took over, kicked the kid once more, and then lifted him by collar and leg up the stairs, a bleeding carcass.

"Don't leave him in my alley," Nick said.

Bud Bradt came right back and Nick said, "Where'd you put him?"

"In the gutter between two cars."

"Good," said Nick. "Maybe they'll run over him."

"I would guess," said Martin, "that that would look very like a murder to somebody. And that's not only illegal, it also requires explanations."

"Yeah," said Nick, crestfallen. "Put him up on the sidewalk."

Martin went outside with Bud in time to see the kid hoisting himself up from the gutter with the help of the bumper of a parked car. The kid drew up to full height, full pain, and a fully bloodied face. He looked toward the alley and saw Martin and Bud, and then, with strength rising up from the secret reservoir fear draws upon, he turned from them and ran with a punishing limp across Clinton Avenue, down Quackenbush Street, down toward the waterworks and the New York Central tracks, and was gone then, fitfully gone into the darkness.

"Didn't kick him enough," Bud said. "The son of a bitch can still run. But he'll think twice before he does that again."

"Or shoot somebody first to make his point."

"Yeah, there's that."

Footers had come up behind them in time to see the kid limp into the blackness. "I was in a crap game once," Footers said, "and a fellow went broke and put a pistol on the table to cover his bet. Five guys faded him."

Martin saw the kid limping into the beginning of his manhood, victim of crazy need, but insufficient control of his craziness. Martin had been delighted to see the kid sucker-punched five minutes earlier, salvation of the Galway wedding band. Now he felt only compassion for a victim, lugubrious emotions having to do with pity at pain, foreboding over concussions, lungs punctured by broken ribs, internal ruptures, and other leaky avenues to death or lesser grievings. Victims, villains were interchangeable. Have it both ways, lads. Weep for Judas at the last gasp. We knew he'd come to the end of his rope. He couldn't beat the fate the Big Boy knew was on him, poor bastard.

"I don't know what the hell to do with this pot," Nick was saying as they reentered the cellar. He was still picking quarters off the floor.

"Give it to Billy," Morrie said. "He deserves it."

"You're a genuine hero," Martin said to Billy. "Like the quarterback who makes the touchdown with a broken leg. There's a heroic edge to such behavior. You think bullets don't kill the single-minded."

"Weird day," Billy said. "I took a knife away from a looney in the Grand Lunch a few hours ago."

The others stopped talking.

"This kid was poking near my belly," and Billy showed them and told them about the coffee game.

"But you had a weapon in the coffee," Martin said. "Tonight you had nothing. You know a twenty-two slug can damage you just as permanently as five rounds from a machine gun. Or is your education lacking in this?"

"I didn't think like that," Billy said. "I just wasn't ready to hand over a night's work to that drippy little bastard. His gun didn't even look real. Looked like a handful of candy. Like one of them popguns my nephew has that shoots corks. Worst I'm gonna get is a cork in the ear, that's how it went. But the money counted, Martin. I owe people, and I was hot for that pot, too. I had kings and nines, ready to fill up."

"Billy should get a chunk of that pot, Nick," Morrie said.

"He got two handfuls," Nick said.

"That was his own dough going back home," Morrie said. "What about the rest? And Bud ought to get something. Without them guys, I'd have personally lost one hell of a bundle."

"Everybody oughta split the pot," Lemon said. "Nobody had a winning hand."

"Especially you," Footers said.

"You folded, Lemon, forget it," Morrie said.

"Fuck you guys," Lemon said.

"Why you gommy, stupid shit," Morrie said. "You might be dead if it wasn't for Billy and Bud. Your head is up your ass."

"While it's up there, Lemon," Footers said, "see if you can see Judge Crater anywhere. He's been gone a long time."

"The only three had the power in that last hand," said Morrie, "was Billy, me, and you, Nick. Everybody else was out of it. So it's a three-way split. I say Billy gets half my share and Bud the other half."

"I got enough," Billy said.

"I'll take it," said Bud.

"It's about forty apiece, what's left, three ways. One-twenty and some silver here." Nick counted out the split, forty to each, and pocketed his own share.

"You really keeping your whole forty, Nick?" Morrie asked, divvying his share between Billy and Bud. "After what those boys did for you and your joint?"

"Whataya got in mind now?"

"The house buys them steaks at Becker's."

"I don't fight that," Billy said.

"I ate," Nick said.

"So eat again, or send money."

Nick snapped a five on the table to Morrie, who looked at it, looked at Nick, didn't pick it up. Nick peeled off another five.

"I give ten to the meal. Eat up. But is the game dead here? What the hell, everybody gonna eat? Nobody gonna play cards?"

"Dead for me," Morrie said, picking up the fivers. And clearly, Billy and Martin were pointed elsewhere when Nick took a good look, and Footers was drawing himself another beer.

"I do believe I'll pass, Nick, me boy," Footers said. "That last one was a tough act to follow."

"I'm still playing," Lemon said, sitting alone at the table.

"You're playing with yourself," Footers said. "As usual."

"Tomorrow night, nine-thirty," Nick said. "Same time, same station."

"Steak time, boys," Morrie said.

Billy found Nick's toilet and pissed before they left. While the old beer sudsed up in the bowl, he consolidated his cash. Out of the coat pocket came the handfuls of bills. He counted it all. Nice. He'd pulled more out of the pot than he put in. He wrapped it all around the rest of the wad. He still needed $275 to pay off Martin, his bankroll now up to $514.

It mounts up. No question about that. Put your mind to it and it mounts up.

UIII

No man who wore socks in Albany felt better in the nighttime than
Billy Phelan, walking with a couple of pals along his own Broadway
from Nick's card game to Union Station to get the papers, including
the paper that was going to make him famous tonight. Maybe he feels
so good that he's getting a little crazy about not being afraid. Martin
was right. A .22 in the eye gives you a hell of a headache.

But now Billy looks around and sees this Broadway of his and
knows he's not crazy, because he knows it all and it all makes sense.
He has known it this way since 1913 when he was six and his father
took him in the rowboat and they rowed down the middle of the street.
The Hudson had backed up over its banks and they were rowing down
to Keeler's Hotel to rescue his Uncle Peter, who had had a fight with
Billy's grandmother and hadn't been home for a month and was caught
now, stranded at the hotel with the big trunk he was taking to New
York, leaving Albany to work in a Manhattan publishing house. But he
could not carry the trunk on his back through two and three feet of
water from Keeler's to the station. And so his brother, Francis, became
the hero who would travel across the waters to the rescue. Francis put
Billy in the boat at the station and right now Billy can see the spot
where he stepped off the curb into that boat, where Steuben Street in-
tersects Broadway. The water was up to the curb there, and toward
State Street it became deeper and deeper.

Billy got into the boat, one of a dozen rowing around on Broadway,
and his father rowed them down the center of the street, down the
canyon of buildings, wearing his cap and the heavy knit sweater with
the collar that Billy remembers. Never a coat; a sweater and gloves

always enough for that man. He rowed Billy half a block and then said: They'll fix this stuff one of these days.

I don't want them to fix it, Billy said.

They've got to, said his father, because they can't let this kind of thing go on.

Billy, sitting in the back of the boat like the captain, said, I hope they never fix it. Then they got the trunk and Uncle Peter, who sat with Billy on his lap, and the trunk standing up in the middle of the boat.

A damn shame, Uncle Peter said, to put up with this, but I suppose you like it, young fellow. And Billy said he liked it better than snow. They rowed to the station, where Uncle Peter got his train and went away.

Now 1913 was gone, too, but Billy was again gliding down Broadway in a craft of his own making, and he relished the sight. There was Albany's river of bright white lights, the lights on in the Famous Lunch, still open, and the dark, smoky reds of Brockley's and Becker's neon tubes, and the tubes also shaping the point over the door of the American Hotel, and the window of Louie's pool room lit up, where somebody was still getting some action, and the light on in the Waldorf restaurant, where the pimps worked out of and where you could get a baked apple right now if you needed one, and the lights of the Cadillac Cafeteria with the pretty great custard pie, and the lights on in the upper rooms of the Cadillac Hotel, where the Greek card game was going on and where Broadway Frances was probably turning a customer upside down and inside out, pretty, tough, busy, knobby lady and Billy's old friend, and the lights in the stairway to the Monte Carlo, where the action would go on until everybody ran out of money or steam, and the lights, too, in Chief Humphrey's private detective office, the Chief working late on somebody's busted marriage, and the light in Joe Mangione's rooms upstairs over his fruit store, and light in the back of Red's barbershop coming through a crack in the door, and Billy knew that Red and others were in there playing blackjack. And look there, too, buddy boy: The lights are on in Bill's Magic Shop, where Bill is staying late, hoping to sell a deck of cards or a pair of dice or a punch board or a magic wand to some nighthawk in search of transport, and the lights are on, too, in Bradt's drug store, where Billy does all his cundrum business.

The lights are on because it's not quite half past eleven on Broadway and some movies are still not out and plenty of people are waiting for the westbound train just now pulling into Union Station, bound for Cleveland and Chicago and carrying the New York papers. Lights are on in Gleason's Grill, which was a soda fountain before beer came back, and lights are shining in the other direction, up toward Orange Street and Little Harlem, like Broadway but only a block long, with the colored crap and card games going strong now, and the Hotel Taft doing its colored business on white sheets, and Prime and Ginsburg's candy store still open, with beer by the bottle and a game in the back and people talking politics there, McCall nigger politics, even at this hour, because that is where the power Democrats gather in Little Harlem.

There is Helen's Lunch, dark now, which feeds the colored hungry and Martha's colored bar all lit up and full of all-night wild music (Play it, Fatha), where Martha wets down the colored thirsty but not *just* the colored. Lights burn in the Carterer Mission, where the colored bums get the same treatment and food the white bums get; and in the colored rooming house run by Mrs. Colored O'Mara, where Slopie Dodds has his rooms and where he keeps his crutches when he's wearing his leg.

There is light still in the triangular sign of the Railroad YMCA, keeping the lamp lit for the conductors and brakemen and engineers who terminate in Albany tonight and want a clean pillow. And next door a light is on in the Public Bath, closed now but where Billy watched his sister, Peg, learn to swim, ducked by Uncle Chick. Peg, older than Billy by eight years, was terrified when she went under. Billy was already a swimmer then, learned in the Basin and in the Hudson when Peg was afraid to go near it. Billy learned everything by himself, everything worth learning. He'd been swimming all that summer when his mother told him to stay away from the river. That August he climbed the Livingston Avenue railroad bridge and dove in—forty feet high, was it?—wearing a straw hat to protect his head. The next summer Billy dove off that trestle without the hat and came up with a fish in his mouth and a mermaid biting his big toe.

Look down Broadway.

Here comes a Pine Hills trolley, and here are the cars coming in to pick up the train people, and there are the Yellow cabs and the gypsies waiting for their long-distance action.

And here comes Mike the Wop ahead of all the passengers, Mike always one of the first off the train because he knows the kids are waiting. Thirty kids anyway. Oughta be in bed, you scurvy little rugrats. But they know Mike is due.

Mike comes out wearing his candy butcher's apron full of change. He has no use for change because he is thick with folding money and bound for the action at the Monte Carlo, and after that he may contract for a bit of the old interrelatedness with Broadway Frances or one of her peers, but for now he is the God Almighty Hero of the Albany rugrats who scream: Here he comes. And of course Mike sees them as soon as he moves across the concourse of the station, the great, glorious, New York Central monument to power, and, feeling perhaps as potent as Vanderbilt, Mike expansively lets his great, pasta-filled stomach precede him toward the door to Broadway.

He then pushes open the station's storm door and enters onto that segment of Broadway Billy and his friends are just now approaching from the north.

Billy pauses and says, Hey, Mike.

Mike turns and is distracted only momentarily from the performance at hand but does say, Eh, Billy, and turns back then to the rug-rats and spins out the change onto the sidewalk under the canopy: dollar, two, five, ten, twenty. Who knows how much change Mike the Wop strews before the rug-rats of Broadway? He gives, they receive. They scramble and pick it up, take it home, and buy the milk and beer.

A man, a grown man, a bum, a wino, a lost derelict from the sewers and gutters of elsewhere, passes and sees Mike's generosity and reaches down for a dime.

Get lost, bum, says Mike, and when the bum does not, Mike raises a foot and pushes the bum over, into the street, where he falls and rolls and is almost run over by a Yellow cab just leaving for Loudonville with a customer and four valises, and is also almost decapitated by the Number Four Pine Hills trolley.

The bum rises, walks on, the dime in his grip.

Mike supervises as the rug-rats clean up every visible nickel and penny, sift in the soft dirt of the gutters for dimes that rolled into the glop. And some will be back, scrounging at dawn for coins that eluded everyone last night. Now they take their cache and disentangle themselves from one another. They run, seethe into the night, and evaporate off Broadway.

Billy watches them go, watches, too, as Mike crosses the street to walk beneath the brightest of the bright lights, one of the many maestros of Broadway power, now heading into the center of the garden in search of other earthly delights.

✳   ✳   ✳

The station was still alive with travelers, with the queers buzzing in and out of the men's room, and the night crowd hot for the papers. When Billy had bought the *Times-Union*, found the ad, decoded what they all knew was there to begin with, then Martin said to Morrie: "I saw your father tonight and told him about this."

"Heh," said Morrie. "What'd he say?"

"Ah, a few things."

"Nothing good, bet your ass on that, the old son of a bitch."

"It wasn't exactly flattering, but he was interested."

"Who's that?" Billy asked, looking up from the newspaper.

"My old man," Morrie said.

"He's a son of a bitch?"

"In spades."

"What'd he do?"

"Nothing. He's just a son of a bitch. He always was."

Well, you got an old man, is what Billy did not say out loud.

They stood in the rotunda, in front of the busy Union News stand with the belt-high stacks of Albany papers, the knee-high stacks of New York *News*es and *Daily Mirrors*, the ankle-high stacks of *Herald Trib*s and *Times*es and *Sun*s. Billy was translating Honey Curry's name from the code. E-d-w-a-r-d C-u-r-r-e-y. They spelled it wrong.

"Honey Curry," Billy said. "Where the hell is *he* these days?"

Martin passed on that, and Morrie said, "Who knows where that son of a bitch is?"

Billy laughed out loud. "Remember when they had the excursion. The Sheridan Avenue Gang. And Curry went wild and hit Healy, the cop, with a crock of butter and knocked him right off the boat and Healy goddamn near drowned. Curry lit out and wound up in Boston and Maloy met him there, downtown, and they're cuttin' it up and Curry's afraid of his shadow. Then a broad walks by, a hooker, and looks at Curry and says to him, Hi ya, honey, how ya doin'? and Curry grabs her with both hands and shoves her up against a tree and shakes the hell out of her. How come you know my name? he says to her."

"That's Curry," said Morrie.

"Where's Maloy? I hear he's in Jersey. Newark, is it?" Billy asked.

"Could be," said Morrie.

"Goddamn," Billy said. "That's where I heard it."

"What?"

"The rumor they were going to kidnap Bindy last summer. We were up in Tabby Bender's saloon. You and me. Remember?"

"No. When was that?" said Morrie.

"Goddamn it, don't anybody remember what I remember? We were sitting at the bar, you and me, and Maloy was with Curry, and Maloy asks if I heard about the Bindy kidnap thing and I didn't. We talked about it, Maloy and Curry shootin' the shit and comin' up to the bar for drinks. And then Maloy tells me, We're gonna take this joint. Now, you remember?"

"I remember *that*," Morrie said. "Screwballs."

"Right," said Billy. "Maloy says, Get out now if you want; we're gonna clean him out. And I told him, I'm comfortable. Clean him out. Take the pictures off the walls. What the hell do I care? And you and me kept drinking."

"Right," Morrie said. "We never moved."

"Right, and they go out and they're gone ten minutes and back they come with handkerchiefs on their faces. Goddamn wouldn't of fooled my nephew, in the same suits and hats. And they cleaned out the whole damper, every nickel. And when they were gone, I said to George Kindlon, the bartender, Let's have a drink, George, and I pushed a fiver at him. I don't think I can change it, he said, and we all busted up because George didn't give a rat's ass, he didn't own the joint. It was Tabby's problem, not George's."

"Right," Morrie said, "and George give us the drink free."

"Yeah," said Billy. "But it was Maloy and Curry really got us the free drink."

"That's it. Maloy and Curry bought that one," and Morrie laughed.

"Son of a bitch," Billy said.

"Right," said Morrie.

Billy pictured Morrie kicking the holdup kid. Vicious mouth on him then, really vicious, yet likable even if he used to be a pimp. He had a good girl in Marsha. Marsha Witherspoon, what the hell kind of a name is that? Billy screwed her before she even went professional. She was a bum screw. Maybe that's why Morrie dumped her, couldn't make a buck with her. But he didn't take up any other whores. Morrie would always let Billy have twenty, even fifty if he needed it. Morrie was with Maloy the night Billy almost lost a match to Doc Fay two years ago. Billy played safe till his ass fell off to win that one, and when he won and had the cash, Morrie and Maloy came over and Maloy said, You didn't have to worry, Billy. If he'd of won the game, we'd of taken the fuckin' money away from him and give it to you anyway. Crazy Maloy. And Morrie was tickled when Maloy said that, and he told Billy, Billy, you couldn't have lost tonight even if you threw the match. Morrie was two years older than Billy and he was a Jew and a smart Jew and Billy liked him. This was funny because Billy didn't like or even know that many Jews. But then Billy thought of Morrie as a gambler, not as a Jew. Morrie was a hustler who knew how to make a buck. He was all right. One of Billy's own kind.

While Billy, Martin, and Morrie ate midnight steaks in Becker's back room, tables for ladies but no ladies, George Quinn came in and found Billy, took him away from the table and whispered: "You hear that Charlie McCall's been kidnapped?"

"I heard that, George."

"Do you know your name's in the paper in some kind of mixed-up spelling?"

"I know that, too."

"The cops were just at the house looking for you."

"Me? What for?"

"They didn't say. Peg talked to them. She asked if you were in trouble and they said no, but that's all they'd tell her."

"Who was it?"

"Bo Linder and somebody else in the car, maybe Jimmy Bergan. That's his partner."

"You see Bo?"

"He came to the door and told Peg for you to call the detective office."

"He didn't say why."

"He said what I told you."

"Right, George. Peg said you wanted to talk to me about a book."

"There's a fellow named Muller works over in Huyck's mill and writes a hell of a good-sized book. I figured you might sit in while I talked to him about taking his layoff. Kind of break the ice a little. I don't know him at all."

"All right, George, I'll do that. When you meeting him?"

"Tonight, one-thirty, quarter to two, when he gets off work. He's coming here."

"I'll probably be here. If I go anyplace, I'll try to be back by then."

"Are you in trouble, Billy? Did you get mixed up with something?"

"No, George. I really don't know what the hell they want."

"You need money? Peg said you took a lickin' today."

"I'm all right on that."

"I can rustle up some if you need it. What do you need?"

"Don't worry about it, George. You need it yourself. I'll be all right. I just got lucky in a card game."

"You're sure you're not in trouble?"

"If I was in trouble, I'd be the first to know."

"All you got to do is ask, whatever it is. And I mean that, even on the money if you're in a jackpot. We'll find it."

"You're a sweetheart, George. Have a drink, relax. I gotta finish my steak."

"Isn't that Jake Berman's kid there?"

"Right, Morrie."

"His name's in the paper, too."

"Right."

"Jake's father made me the first suit of clothes I ever had made."

At the bar a man's voice said, "That's right, I said I hope they don't catch them, whoever they are."

The bar went quiet and Red Tom said, "That's just about enough of that talk," and he took the man's beer away. Billy recognized the talker, name of Rivera, spic like Angie's husband, a pimp. Red Tom poured Rivera's beer in the sink and shoved his change closer to him on the bar. "I don't want your business," Red Tom said. But Rivera wouldn't move. Red Tom came around the bar and grabbed his arm. Rivera resisted. Red Tom reached for the change and shoved it into his pocket. Then he lifted him with one arm, like a sack of garbage, lifted him off the bar stool and walked him out the door.

"The McCalls got everybody scared to do pee-pee," Rivera said over his shoulder. "They think they can treat people like dogs."

"Who's that guy?" George Quinn asked.

"He's a bughouse pimp. Gotta be bugs," Billy said.

Red Tom closed the front door and moved in behind the bar.

"That kind of talk stays out in the street," he said to all in earshot, looking at no one in particular. He pointed twice toward the door with one finger. "Out in the street," he said.

x   x   x

When he'd finished his steak, Morrie Berman stood up and announced he was going off to get laid. Billy thought of tagging along with him but rejected the idea. He envisioned Angie in bed up at the Kenmore, waiting. He would go and see her. He was tired of gambling, tired of these people here. Maybe later he could come back and play some blackjack if the game was still running. Do that when he left Angie. If he left Angie. All right, he would see her, then leave her be and come down and play some blackjack. Billy still owed money. First things first.

"I got a date, Martin," Billy said, pushing away from the table.

"That sounds healthful. Bon voyage."

"I'll keep you posted on the bankroll. We're doing all right."

"I know we are. You've decided not to go along with Patsy's suggestion?"

"I listened all night. He didn't say a goddamn thing."

"What about the Bindy kidnap rumor? He doesn't seem to remember it, but you do. Isn't that odd?"

"That don't mean anything."

"Are you sure?"

"Aaahh," Billy said, and he waved off the possibility and went out onto Broadway and turned up Columbia Street, past the old Satin Slipper, a hot place when Butch McHale ran it during Prohibition and now cut up into furnished rooms. He crossed James Street and was halfway to North Pearl when the car pulled alongside him, Bo Linder at the wheel, Jimmy Bergan with him. Billy. Bo. Been looking for you. Oh yeah?

"Bindy wants to talk to you."

"Bindy? About what?"

"You ask him that."

"Where is he?"

"Up at Patsy's house."

"Patsy who?"

"Patsy who my ass."

"When's he want to see me?"

"Two hours ago."

"If this's got something to do with Charlie, I don't know anything."

"Tell Bindy that. Get in."

"No thanks."

"Get in, Billy."

"You pulling me in? Charging me with something?"

"I can get particular."

"I'm under arrest, I'll get in. Otherwise, I'll take a cab. I know where Patsy lives."

"All right, take a cab. We'll follow so the driver don't get lost."

Billy walked to Pearl Street and at the corner looked up at the Kenmore, maybe at Angie's room. She liked the front so she could look down and see people on Pearl Street after she and Billy had loved all possible juices out of one another. Billy didn't see Angie in any window. She'd be asleep now, wouldn't go on the town alone. Twelve-thirty now, hell of a time to visit the McCalls.

Two cabs stood in front of the Kenmore. Billy whistled and the front one made a U-turn and Billy got in. Bo Linder was idling at the corner, Bo the cop, a good kid when he was a kid. Good second baseman for The Little Potatoes, Hard to Peel. But what can you do with somebody who grows up to be a mean cop? Never was mean on second base. After he went on the force, Bo walked into Phil Slattery's joint and shot Phil's dog when it growled at him. Dog should've bit him on the ass.

"Conalee Street," Billy told the cabbie.

Billy had never learned to pronounce Colonie Street the usual way. But people understood anyway. The driver moved north on Pearl Street, and Bo Linder swung out of Columbia Street and made it a parade.

IX

B ILLY DIDN'T HATE COLONIE STREET ENTIRELY, for it would have meant hating his mother, his greatest friends, Toddy Dunn, for one, even his ancestors. It would have meant hating the city the Irish had claimed as their own from vantage points of streets like Colonie. It was the street where he was born and had lived until adolescence, when he went off to room by himself. It was the street his sister, Peg, left with their mother when Peg married George Quinn and took a bigger and newer house in the North End.

Billy told the taxi driver to leave him off at the corner of North Pearl, and he walked up the hill toward Patsy McCall's house. He passed the old Burns house, where the ancient Joe Burns always sat in the window, ten years in the window at least. Old Joe lived with his son, Kid, the sexton of St. Joseph's Church for years until Father Mooney put him through undertakers' school; and next door to them the Dillons: Floyd, a conductor on the Central, who put Billy and Peg and their mother in a Pullman with only coach tickets when they went to New York to see the ocean for the first time. Across the street was the vacant lot where the Brothers School used to stand, and next to that the Daugherty house, gone, and then the other house: That house Billy did not now look at directly but saw always in his memory and hated, truly did hate that much of the old street.

And it was an old street even when Billy was born on it. It ran westward along the river flats from the Basin, that sheltered harbor that formed the mouth of the Erie Canal, and rose up the northernmost of the three steep ridges on which Albany was built: Arbor Hill. It rose for half a mile, crossed Ten Broeck, the street where the lumber barons had built their brownstones, and, still rising, ran another half mile westward to all but bump the Dudley Observatory, where scientific men of the city catalogued the stars (8241 measured and recorded for the International Catalogue as of 1883) from the top of the same hill on which Mike Mulvaney grazed and daily counted his two dozen goats.

The street took its name from The Colonie itself, that vast medieval demesne colonized in 1630 by an Amsterdam pearl merchant named Kiliaen Van Rensselaer, who was also known as the First Patroon, the absentee landlord who bought from five tribes of Indians some seven hundred thousand acres of land, twenty-four miles long and forty-eight miles wide, out of which a modest seven thousand acres would eventually be expropriated by the subsequent Yankee overlords to create the city of Albany.

Each power-wielding descendant of Van Rensselaer to assume the feudal mantle of the Patroonship during the next two centuries would maintain exploitative supremacy over thousands of farm renters on the enormous manor called, first, Rensselaerswyck, and later, The Colonie. Each Patroon would make his home in the Manor House, which rose handsomely out of a riverside meadow just north of the city on the bank of a stream that is still called Patroon Creek. Mickey McManus from Van Woert Street went rabbit hunting one day near The Patroon's creek and shot a cow. Few can now remember that meadow or even where the Manor House stood precisely. It closed forever in 1875, when the widow of the Last Patroon died there, and it was later moved to make room for the Delaware and Hudson railroad tracks, dismantled brick by brick and reassembled in Williamstown as a fraternity house.

But long before that, North Albany, where Billy Phelan and Martin Daugherty both now lived, and Arbor Hill, where the McCalls and Billy's aunts and uncles still lived, had been seeded in part with the homes of settlers who worked as servants and as farm and field hands for the Patroon. Billy Phelan's great-grandfather, Johnny Phelan, a notably belligerent under-sheriff, was given the safekeeping of the Manor House as his personal charge after four rebellious prisoners barricaded themselves in their cell at the penitentiary and, with a stolen keg of gunpowder, threatened to blow themselves up unless the food improved. Johnny Phelan sneaked a fire hose to the door of their cell, opened the door suddenly, and drenched their powder with a swift blast. Then he leaped over their barricade and clubbed them one by one into civility.

Martin Daugherty's grandmother, Hanorah Sweeney, had been the pastry cook in the Patroon's kitchen and was famed for her soda bread and fruitcakes, which, everyone said, always danced off their platters and onto the finicky palates of the Patroon and his table companions, among them the Prince of Wales, George Washington's grandnephew, and Sam Houston.

Arbor Hill and North Albany continued to grow as the railroads came in, along with the foundries, the stove works, the tobacco factory and the famous Lumber District, which started at the Basin and ran northward two and a half miles between the river and the canal. Processing Adirondack logs into lumber was Albany's biggest business at mid-century, and the city fathers proclaimed that Albany was now the white pine distribution center of the world.

The North End and Arbor Hill grew dense with the homes of lumber handlers, moulders, railroad men, and canalers, and in the winter, when the river and the canal froze, many of them cut ice, fifteen thousand men and boys cutting three million tons from the Hudson in six weeks at century's end.

They all clustered on streets such as Colonie to live among their own kind, and the solidarity became an obvious political asset. Not the first to notice this, but the first to ride it to local eminence, was the fat, bearded, Irish-born owner of the Beverwyck brewery, Michael Nolan, who in 1878 was elected mayor of the city. Coming only three years after the death of the Last Patroon's widow, this clearly signaled a climactic change in city rule: the Dutch and Yankees fading, the American Irish, with the help of Jesus, and by dint of numbering forty per cent of the city's population, waxing strong. And eight years ahead of Boston in putting an Irishman in City Hall.

Nolan had lived on Millionaire's Row, on the east side of Ten Broeck, two and a half blocks from Patsy McCall's home on Colonie Street. Patsy, who could have lived like a millionaire but didn't, was in the Irish descendance of political power from Nolan as surely as the Last Patroon had descended from the first; and was a descendant in style as well as power. When Nolan was elected, he swathed his brewery wagons and dray horses in red, white, and blue bunting and saw to it that Beverwyck beer was sold in every saloon in town. Nolan's example was not wasted on the McCalls. Gubernatorial hopeful Tom Dewey revealed that in October 1938, Stanwix, the McCall beer, was sold in 243 of the city's 249 taverns.

Billy Phelan knew the Patroon only as a dead word, Nolan not at all. But in the filtered regions of his cunning Irish brain, he knew the McCalls stood for power far beyond his capacity to imagine.

They were up from below. And when you're up, you let no man pull you down. You roll your wagons over the faces of the enemy.

And who is the enemy?
It's well you might ask.
Billy pushed the door bell.

Bindy McCall opened the door, smiled, and pulled Billy by the arm, gently, into the house, the first time Billy had entered Patsy's home. The front hall, leading upstairs and also into both front and back parlors, reminded Billy of the hated house across the street, probably built from the same blueprints.

Bindy held Billy's arm and led him into the front parlor with its thick oriental rug, its heavy drapes and drawn shades, where a scowling male ancestor of the McCalls looked down insistently on Billy: a powerful face above a neck stretched by a high collar and string tie, a face not unlike Patsy's, who sat beneath it at a card table, shirtless, reclining in his blue bathrobe in a leather armchair; pads and pencils on the table beside a telephone. An old player piano dominated the room, where Patsy no doubt played and sang the ditties he was famous for, "Paddy McGinty's Goat," for one.

Billy had heard him sing that at the Phoenix Club in the North End on a Sunday years ago when the political notables of North Albany turned out for an election rally. Billy went just to watch the spectacle and barely spoke to anyone, never said, Hello Patsy, as he could have, as thousands did whenever the great leader hove into range. Hello Patsy. Billy just listened and never forgot the song and later learned it himself: *Patrick McGinty, an Irishman of note, fell heir to a fortune and he bought himself a goat.*

A panorama of a Civil War battle, one of Patsy's well-known interests, hung in a gilded frame over the piano. A pair of brass donkeys as bookends, and with Dickens and Jefferson, a biography of Jim Jeffries, and canvasses of Fifth and Eighth Ward voters sandwiched between the but ends of the animals, sat on top of the piano. On an old oak sofa across from Patsy sat a man Billy didn't know. Bindy introduced him as Max Rosen, Matt McCall's law partner.

"You're a tough man to find," Bindy said. "We've been looking for you."

"I wasn't hiding. Just playing cards."

"We heard about the holdup and what you did. You're a tough guy, Billy."

"How'd you hear about it? It just happened."

"Word gets around. We also heard what you did in the Grand Lunch with that crazy kid."

"You heard that, too?"

"That, too," Bindy said.

"Listen, Bin," said Billy, "I'm really sorry about Charlie."

"Are you?"

"Sure I am. You got any word on him yet?"

"We got a little. That's why we wanted to talk to you."

"Me? What've I got to do with anything?"

"Relax. You want a beer?"

"Sure, I'll have a beer with you, Bin."

Bindy, shirtsleeves rolled above the elbow, soup stain on shirtfront, no tie, wearing eyeglasses and house slippers, looked like somebody else to Billy, not Bindy McCall, the dapper boss of the street. He looked tired, too, and Patsy the same. Patsy stared at Billy. Max Rosen, in his suit coat, tie up tight to a fresh collar, also stared. Billy in the middle, a new game. He was glad to see Bindy come back with the beer bottle and glass: Stanwix.

"I heard you took a beating today with the nags," Bindy said, pouring Billy's beer.

"You hear what I had for breakfast?"

"No, but I could find out."

"I ate alone, no witnesses."

"There's other ways."

"Yeah." And Billy took a drink.

"You know where your old man is?" Patsy asked.

"My old man?"

"Yours."

"No. I don't know."

"I heard he was in town," said Patsy.

"My father in Albany? Where?"

"I didn't hear that. Somebody saw him downtown today."

"Goddamn," Billy said.

"You wanna see him?" asked Patsy.

"Sure I wanna see him. I haven't saw him in twenty years. Twenty-two years."

"I'll see if I can track him down."

"That'd be terrific, Mr. McCall."

"Call me Patsy."

"Patsy. That's a terrific thing if you can do that."

"Maybe you can do something for us."

"Maybe I can."

"You heard that kidnap rumor about me," Bindy said, sitting on a folding chair across the card table from Patsy. The card table Billy worked at was in better shape.

"I heard that last summer."

"From who?"

"Jesus, I don't remember, Bin. One of those things you hear at a bar when you're half in the bag, you don't remember. I didn't give it the time of day. Then I remembered it today."

"And got hot at Louie Dugan for telling me about it."

"I didn't expect to have it repeated."

"We heard the same rumor last year and traced it to a couple of local fellows. And maybe, just maybe, that ties in to Charlie. Do you follow me?"

"I follow."

"Neither of these fellows are in town and we don't know just where they are. But they got a friend who's in town, and that's why you're here."

"I'm the friend?"

"No, you're a friend of the friend. The friend is Morrie Berman."

The noise Billy made then was a noncommittal grunt. Maloy and Curry, Berman's pals. On the list, Curry.

"We understand you know Mr. Berman well," Max Rosen said.

"We play cards together."

"We understand you know him better than that," Rosen said.

"I know him a long time."

"Yeah, yeah, we know all about it," said Patsy, "and we also know you didn't give Pop O'Rourke's man his ten dollars today."

"I told Pop why."

"We know what you told him," said Patsy, "and we know your brother-in-law, Georgie Quinn, is writing numbers and don't have the okay for the size books he's taking on."

"Georgie talked to Pop about that, too."

"And Pop told him he could write a little, but now he's backing the play himself. He's ambitious, your brother-in-law."

"What is all this, Bindy? What are we talking about? You know the color of my shorts. What's it for?" Billy felt comfortable only with Bindy, but Bindy said nothing.

"Do you know the Berman family, Mr. Phelan?" Max Rosen asked.

"I know Morrie's old man's in politics, that's all."

"Do you like Morrie Berman?" Rosen asked.

"I like him like I like a lot of guys. I got nothing against him. He's the guy had the idea to buy me a steak tonight. Nice."

"Do you like Charlie?" Patsy asked.

"Do I like him? Sure I like him. I grew up with him. Charlie was always a good friend of mine, and I don't say that just here. I bullshit nobody on this."

Bindy poured more beer into Billy's glass and smiled at him.

"All right, Billy," Bindy said, "we figure we know your feelings. We wouldn't have okayed you for that Saratoga job if we didn't trust you. We know you a long time. And you remember after the Paul Whiteman thing, we gave you that other job, too."

"The Chicago Club?"

"That's right."

"I thought that came from Lemon Lewis. I didn't think you even knew about that."

"We knew. We do Albany people."

"Then it's two I owe you."

"Just one," Bindy said. "We trusted you then, we trust you now. But that don't mean forever."

"Who the hell am I not to trust? What do I know?"

"We don't know what you know," Patsy said.

"It's what you might come to know in the next few days that's important," Max Rosen said. "We're interested in Mr. Berman, in everything he says and does. Everything."

"Morrie doesn't tell me secrets," Billy said.

"We don't expect that," said Max. "If he's involved in the kidnapping, and we're by no means saying that he is, then he's hardly likely to talk about it at all. But you must know, Mr. Phelan, that men sometimes betray themselves indirectly. They reveal what's on their mind merely by random comment. Berman might, for instance, mention the men involved in a context other than criminal. Do you follow me?"

"No."

"You're not stupid," Patsy said, an edge to his voice. He leaned forward in his chair and looked through Billy's head.

"Nobody ever said I was," Billy said, looking back through Patsy's head.

"Billy," said Bindy in a soothing tone, "we're playing in every joint where we can get a bet down. I tell you one thing. Some people wouldn't even put it past Berman's old man to be in on this."

"That's ridiculous," Max Rosen said. "Jake Berman isn't capable of such behavior. I've known him all my life."

"I don't accuse him," Bindy said, "but he don't like us. I just make the point that we suspect everybody."

"People might even suspect you, with your name in the paper," Patsy said.

Billy snorted. "Me?"

"People talk."

"Don't pay attention if you hear that," Bindy said. "We know you're clean. We wanted you and Berman in the same boat. He don't know why you're on the list, but now you and him got that in common."

"You think that'll make him talk to me?"

"It could. What'd he say tonight?"

"We played cards and he kicked the holdup guy a little. He said he talked to Mr. Rosen here, and he said he didn't get along with his old man. We talked about a drink that we had one time."

"Who did he talk about?" Bindy asked. "Who?"

"Tabby Bender. George Kindlon, who tended bar for Tabby."

"Who else?"

"That's all I remember."

"Edward Curry is on the list. Did he mention him?"

"I mentioned Curry, that his name was spelled wrong. And I told a story about him."

"What story?"

"About the whore in Boston called him honey and he asked her, How come you know my name. You think Curry's mixed up in this?"

"What did Berman say when you told the story?" Bindy asked.

"He laughed."

"You didn't talk about nobody else? Nobody? Think."

"I talked about a lot of things but not to Berman."

"Did he say anything about Hubert Maloy?"

"No."

Bindy leaned back in his chair and looked at Patsy. Billy looked at the brothers, from one to the other, and wondered how he would get out of the Maloy lie. He wondered why he'd even bothered to lie. It meant nothing. He saw the faces of strangers he'd known all his life staring him down. In between them, the face of the McCall ancestor was no longer scowling down from the wall but was only stern and knowing, a face flowing with power and knowledge in every line. There was a world of behavior in this room Billy did not grasp with the clarity he had in pool and poker, or at the crap table. Billy knew jazz and betting and booking horses and baseball. He knew how to stay at arm's length from the family and how to make out. He resisted knowing more than these things. If you knew what the McCalls knew, you'd be a politician. If you knew what George Quinn knew, you'd be a family man. They had their rewards but Billy did not covet them. Tie you up in knots, pin you down, put you in the box. He could learn anything, study it. He could have been in politics years ago. Who couldn't on Colonie Street? But he chose other ways of staying alive. There never was a politician Billy could really talk to, and never a hustler he couldn't.

"All right, Billy," Bindy said, standing up. "I think we've made our point. Call us any time." He wrote two phone numbers on the pad and handed the sheet to Billy.

"You come up with anything that means something to Charlie," Patsy said, "you got one hell of a future in this town."

"What if I don't run into Berman again?"

"You don't run into him, then you find him and stay with him," Patsy said. "If you need money for that, call us."

"Berman's a big boy. He goes where he wants."

"You're a big boy, too," Patsy said.

"What Patsy says about your future," Bindy said, "that goes triple for me. For a starter we clear up your debt with Martin Daugherty. And you never worry about anything again. Your family the same."

"What if Berman catches on? He's too smart to pump."

"If you're sure he's on to it, drop it."

"We'll get word to you."

When Billy stood up, Max Rosen put a paternal hand on his shoulder. "Don't worry about anything, Mr. Phelan. Do what you can. It's an unusual situation."

"Yeah, all of that," Billy said.

Bindy shook hands and Patsy gave him a nod, and then Billy was in the hallway looking at the bannister, pretty much like the one he used to slide down in the shithouse across the street until his Aunt Sate caught him and pulled his ear and sent him home. He went out the door and closed it behind him. He stood on the McCall stoop, looking up the street at the Dolan house, remembering the Dolan kid who was kidnapped off this street when Billy was little. An uncle did it. They found the kid in the Pine Bush, safe, and brought him home and put him in the window so everybody could see that he was all right. The kid was only four. Everybody wanted to hang the uncle, but he only went to jail.

Billy walked toward Pearl Street, heading back downtown. He remembered Georgie Fox, marked lousy for what he did to Daddy Big. All anybody on Broadway needed to hear was that Billy was finking on Morrie, and they'd put him in the same box with Georgie. Who'd trust him after that? Who'd tell him a secret? Who'd lend him a quarter? He wouldn't have a friend on the whole fucking street. It'd be the dead end of Billy's world, all he ever lived for, and the McCalls were asking him to risk that. Asking hell, telling him. Call us any time.

When he was halfway to Clinton Avenue, Bo Linder pulled up and asked if everything was all right. Billy said it was, and Bo said, "That's good, Billy, now keep your nose clean." And Billy just looked at the son of a bitch and finally nodded, not at all sure he knew how to do that any more.

x   x   x

When Billy got to Becker's and sat down in the booth beside him (across from Bart Muller), George Quinn was eating a ham sandwich and telling Muller of the old days when he ran dances in Baumann's Dancing Academy and hired King Jazz and his orchestra to play, and McEnelly's Singing Orchestra, and ran dances, too, up in Sacandaga Park and brought in Zita's orchestra, and danced himself at all of them, of course. "They put pins in our heels for the prize waltz," George said. "Anybody bent the pin was out. I won many a prize up on my toes and I got the loving cups to prove it."

"No need to prove it," Muller said.

"We danced on the boat to Kingston sometimes, and the night boat to New York, but mostly we took the ferry from Maiden Lane for a nickel and it went up to Al-Tro Park, Al-Tro Park on the Hudson; they even wrote a song about that place, and what a wonder of a place it was. Were you ever up there?"

"Many times," Muller said.

"We'd take the boat back down to Maiden Lane, or sometimes we'd walk back downtown to save the nickel. One night, three fellows on the other side of the street kept up with me and Giddy O'Laughlin all the way to Clinton Avenue. We didn't know who they were till they crossed Broadway, and one was Legs Diamond. Somebody was gonna throw Legs off the roof of the Hendrick Hudson Hotel that night, but he gave 'em the slip."

"Why are you talking about Legs Diamond?" Billy asked George.

"I'm not talking about Legs Diamond, I'm talking about going to dances. Bart lives in Rensselaer. We both went to dances at the pavilion out at Snyder's Lake."

"George," said Billy, "did you come in here to reminisce or what?"

"We've just been cuttin' it up, me and Bart," George said, "and the business is on, anyway. I'm interested in Bart's book. I'm branching out and Bart knows that. He just took over the night-shift book over at Huyck's mill, and now he's looking for somebody to lay off with. Am I right, Bart?"

"That's right, George."

"Then you made the deal," Billy said.

"I guess we did," said George.

"I'll give you a buzz on it," Muller said. "But I got to get home or the wife worries."

"We'll talk on the phone, Bart," George said. "I was glad to meet you."

"Mutual," said Muller, and he nodded at Billy and left.

George sat back and finished his tea and wiped his lips with his white linen napkin and folded it carefully.

"I don't know what the hell that was all about," Billy said. "Why'd you want me here?"

"Just to break the ice."

"Break the ice? There was no ice. You never shut up."

"I didn't want to push too hard the first time. We'll iron out the details when he calls."

"Calls? He's not gonna call. You made no impression on him. You didn't talk about money."

"He didn't bring it up."

"He came to see you, didn't he? Why the hell does he want to talk about Snyder's Lake, for chrissake? He's writing a book and he wants a layoff and he wants protection. You didn't give him a goddamn thing to make him think you even know what the hell a number is."

"He knows."

"He does like hell. How could he? You didn't talk about having the okay or that you got cash to guarantee his payoffs. You didn't say how late he could call in a play or tell him he wouldn't have to worry getting stuck with a number because you'll give him the last call and get rid of it for him. You didn't tell him doodley bejesus. George, what the hell are you doing in the rackets? You ought to be selling golf clubs."

"Who died and left you so smart?"

"I'm not smart, George, or I'd be rich. But I hustle. You don't know how to hustle."

"I'm not in debt up to my ass."

"You ain't rich either. And let me tell you something else. You don't even have the okay."

"Says who?"

"Says Patsy McCall. I was talking to him, and he says you never got the okay to back numbers. All you got the okay for was to lay off. Twenty per cent, no more."

"Pop O'Rourke knows what I'm doing."

"Patsy said Pop *didn't* know."

"I'll call Pop in the morning. I'll straighten it out. How come you talked to Patsy?"

"It was about another thing."

"Something about your name in the paper?"

"Something about that, yeah."

"Oh, it's a secret. You got secrets with Patsy McCall. Excuse me, let me out. Your company is too rich for my blood."

"Look, George, don't strain your juice. I don't keep secrets I don't have to keep. You know what's going on with Charlie McCall, and you ought to know by this time I'm on your side. For chrissake, don't you know that?"

"Mmmmmm," said George.

"You don't *want* to know what I know, George. Believe me."

"All right, Billy, but you got a nasty tongue."

"Yeah. Have a drink. I buy."

"No, I just had tea."

"Have a drink, for chrissake. Do you good."

"I don't want a drink. I'll take the nickel. What did Patsy say about me? Was he mad?"

"He didn't sound happy. He mentioned you by name."

"I don't want to get in any jackpots with Patsy. I'll call Pop first thing in the morning. I never had a cross word with the McCalls all my life. I give fifteen dollars to John Kelleher for Patsy's first campaign as assessor and Kelleher only asked me for five."

"You'll fix it. Probably you just got to pay more dues."

"I'm not making anything yet. I'm losing money."

"It's goin' around, that problem."

"But I can't afford more."

"You can't afford to stay in business?"

"Pop understands I'm not in the chips yet."

"How does he understand that? You expect him to check your books?"

"No, I don't expect nothing like that."

"Then how the hell does he know your action? All he knows is you're moving into heavier stuff. And you got to pay heavier dues for that. George, you been in this racket fifteen years, and you been in this town all your life. You know how it works."

"I'll pay if Patsy said I got to pay. But Patsy understands a guy being down on his luck."

"Don't cry the blues to them. Don't beg for anything. If they say pay, just pay and shut up about it."

"I don't beg from anybody."

"Tell 'em your story straight and don't weep no tears. I'm telling you be tough, George."

"I know what I'm doing. I know how it works."

"All right. You want that drink?"

"I'll take a rain check."

George went out onto Broadway, and Billy went to the bar for a tall beer, thinking how George couldn't get off the dime. A banty rooster and don't underrate him when he fights. But he don't fight easy enough. Been around tough guys and politicians all his life and he don't know how to blow his nose right. But Billy has to admit George ain't doing bad for a fifty-year-old geezer. Got the house and Peg and a great kid in Danny. Billy's fifty, he'll be what? Alone? Racking balls like Daddy Big? On the chalk like Lemon Lewis? Nineteen years to find out.

"Your lady friend Angie called again, Billy," Red Tom said, as he slid Billy a new, tall, free one. "She says it's urgent."

"I know her urgent."

"And she says it's not what you think. Important, she says."

"Important."

"She sounded like she meant it."

"I'll check her out, Tommy. Have one on me."

"Save your money, Billy. Winter's coming."

"Billy knows where the heat is."

"Up in Angie's room?"

"Some there, yeah. Definitely some up there."

X

'LL SCREW YOU as long as my equipment lasts, Billy once told Angie, but I won't marry you. She repeated the line for Billy after he rolled off her. He sat up, lit a cigarette, and then fixed a scotch with tap water. He put on his white boxer shorts, hiding the ragged scar on the left cheek of his behind. He got that when he was ten, sliding into a second base made from a flattened tin oil can. Almost made him half-assed. But Doc Lennon sewed it up after he poured two bottles of iodine into the slice, which still gives Billy the screaming meemies when he thinks about it. Then Billy's mother bathed the wound and fussed at it for weeks, and the teamwork let Billy grow up with a complete tail.

"Why you bringing that up now?" Billy asked. "You thinking about marriage again?"

"I'm always thinking about marriage, with you."

"Drop it, Ange. I'll never be any good in that husband racket."

"And you couldn't, wouldn't marry a divorcee."

"The hell with that stuff."

"I'm only teasing, Billy. I love to tease you."

Angie stood up and slipped back into her nightgown, sheer white silk with white lace trim where her cleavage would've been if she had any. She was a long, lean, dark-haired Latinesque girl of twenty-five who looked thirty when she talked because she was smart but who grew wispy with a turn of emotion and fled into the look of adolescence. She read sad poetry and went to sad movies in order to cry, for crying at trouble, she told Billy, was almost as good as weeping with love. There was so little love in the world, she said, that people needed substitutes. It's why lonely old people keep pets, she said. Billy was Angie's pet. I can't imagine anyone who didn't sometime want to do away with themselves because of love, she once said to Billy, for chrissake. Billy, she said, stroking him, tickling the back of his neck, if you ever died I'd make sure they put flowers on your grave forever, just like they do for Valentino. This, of course, is just what Billy needs.

But Angie was part of his life now, and had been since her husband slapped her around in the Clubhouse at Saratoga. Billy was watching from the bar when they started their screaming over the car keys. Give 'em to me, you bitch, he said. I haven't got 'em, Angie said. You got 'em, he said. You just wanna hang around here makin' moon eyes at all the studs. Billy was her only stud then, and when her husband was around, she never even gave Billy a nod. So she walked away from the son of a bitch when he said that, and he spun her around by the arm and slapped her twice. Billy wanted to hit him till his teeth fell out, but all he could do was watch. Angie took the whipping and didn't say a word, which beat the bastard. He slammed out of the Clubhouse and left their car in the lot and walked back to the hotel. And found the car keys in his own coat pocket when he was halfway there. Billy bought Angie a drink and smooched her on the cheek where she'd been hit and put her in a taxi and bet twenty on a horse named Smacker in the last race and it showed eight dollars.

Angie came to Albany every other month after that, for a weekend at least and sometimes a week. She'd call Billy and he'd see her and once in a while she'd give him money, which made him feel like a gigolo, but of course that wasn't what Billy was. He only took it when he needed it. Angie called Billy her little wheel of excitement. When I was a kid I used to sit on the stoop and wait for it to roll down the street to me, she said. But it never showed up till I met you.

Why'd ya marry that bum? Billy asked her once, and she said, Because he was like my father and I loved my father, but you're right, he is a bum, he's not like my father at all. He's a bum, he's a bum, and he's got his women, too. He came home one night with the smell of oral sex on his face. Angie never called him on it. She just packed a bag and came to Albany. But he was good in bed, Angie said, he was very good. Angie never told Billy he was very good in bed, but then he didn't hear any complaints out of her either. What got Billy about Angie was the way she was alone so much. Billy was almost never alone. I can stand being alone, Angie told him. Being with him is like being alone. It won't kill you.

Billy looked down on the lights of Pearl Street. No traffic.

"You got aspirin?" he asked Angie. "I got a headache."

"The closet shelf on the left, a small bag," she said. "Why have you got a headache? You never get headaches."

"Whataya mean I never get headaches? Everybody gets headaches. How the hell do you know I never get headaches?"

"All right, you get headaches," Angie said, and she fell back into bed and crossed her feet.

In the closet, Billy looked at her picture hat, black with two white flowers. Billy snatched the hat off the shelf and waved it at her. "When you got a face like you got, you don't need any flowers on your hat." He put the hat back on the shelf and felt for the aspirin and found them. Then he saw her black linen suit with the plaid scarf, and the gray wool suit with the darker gray silk lapels. Goddamn Angie knew how to dress. Like a model. Too goddamn smart. A college dame. Thinks like a man.

"You're too goddamn smart," he said, as he went to the sink.

"What does that mean?"

"The hell with it."

"Billy, come here. Come and sit down."

"Gimme a rest."

"Not that. Just come and sit."

Billy washed his aspirin down and went and sat. She stroked his face and then dropped her hand and eyes and said, "I've got something sad to tell you."

"Your cat got run over."

"Something like that. I had an abortion."

"Yeah?"

"It was ours."

Billy smoked a little and then looked at her. Her eyes were on him now.

"When?"

"About three weeks ago."

"Why didn't you ring me in on it?"

"What would you have done?"

"I don't know. Helped you."

"Helped get it done? A good Catholic boy like you?"

"I mean with your head. It must've been lousy for you."

"You never want to know things like that. Anything that involves you. You really didn't want to know, did you?"

"Half of it's my kid."

"Not a kid, a fetus. And it's gone. Nobody's now."

"Goddamn it, I had a right to know."

"You had a *right*?"

"You bet your ass. What the hell, I don't have a say in my own son?"

"Of course it was a boy. You're really classic, Billy."

"Whatever the hell it was."

Billy looked at his hand and saw the cigarette shaking. Goddamn ton of goddamn bricks. He'd wanted to talk about the Berman business and about his father being back in town. Angie had good sense. He wanted to ask her about money, maybe borrow some, but they got into the sack too fast. You can't ask for money after you've been in the sack with a woman. Now, with this business, he couldn't ask her anything. How do so many things happen all of a sudden? He thought of making nineteen straight passes at Slicky Joyce's in Mechanicville. Almost broke the Greek bankrolling the game. How do nineteen straight passes happen? He stubbed out his cigarette and walked across the room to put on his pants.

"Why are you putting on your pants?"

"I got chilly."

"No. You're ashamed of the part of you that made me pregnant and now you want to cover yourself and hide."

"You know everything about me. My headaches, why I put on my pants. Goddamn it cut it *out*!" Billy screamed. "You don't know the first goddamn thing that's going on with me. You think I'm a goddamn moron like your goddamn dummy husband?"

"All right, Billy. Don't get violent."

"Violent? You kill my kid without even asking me about it. Who made you the butcher?"

"Don't get like this, Billy. I'm sorry I started it this way."

"Started?"

"I'm pregnant."

"Oh, Christ Jesus, what is this game?"

"I wanted to see if you wanted the baby."

"Hell no, I don't want no baby."

"So now it's different."

Billy put on his shirt, unable to speak. He folded his tie and put it in the pocket of his coat, which hung on a black bentwood chair. He sat on the chair and stared at Angie.

"I can take care of it," she said. "I already slept with Joe when I found I had it, just so I could tell him it was his. But I'd never raise it with him. All he wants to raise is money. But I would keep it and give it all the nannies and private schools a kid'd ever need. The only thing it wouldn't have is a real father."

She stood up. "Or I could put it up for adoption."

"No," Billy said.

She came across the room and stroked his face. "Or we could raise it together, somehow. Any way you wanted. I don't mean marriage. I'll go away and have it, and you can come and see us when you want to. The only problem is that if my husband figured it out, he'd probably have all three of us killed. But I don't care, do you?"

"No. Of course not. What the hell do I care?"

Billy walked away from her and sat in the armchair and looked at her standing there barefoot in front of him, the shadow of her crotch winking through the silk nightgown.

"Or you can claim it any time you want, and we could go off then. I've got plenty of my own money. I wouldn't need alimony."

Billy shook his head. "I don't buy it. All this shotgun stuff can go to hell."

"Then you want me to get rid of it?"

"No, I don't want that. I think you oughta have it."

"But you don't want anything to do with it?"

"I'll do something."

"What?"

"I'll go see it."

"Like a cocker spaniel? Why shouldn't I get rid of it?"

"By myself, I don't want to hurt nobody. If you do it, it's you and I can't say don't. I don't even want to know about it."

"That's as far as you go?"

"If you have it, I'll say it's mine."

"You'll do that?"

"I'll do that, yeah."

"Even if Joe says he'll shoot you?"

"He shoots me, he's got big trouble."

"I didn't expect this."

"I'd do it for any kid. You let him into the action, he's got to know who his old man is."

"It's for the kid, not me?"

"Maybe some is for you."

"Birth certificate, baptism, that whole business?"

"Whatever you want."

"I really didn't think you'd do this. You never committed yourself to me on anything. You never even answered my letters."

"Letters? What the hell am I gonna do, write you letters and have you fix up my spelling?"

"I wouldn't do that. Oh God, I love you. You're such a life-bringer, Billy. You're the real man for me, but you're the wrong clay."

"Clay?"

"You can't be molded. Sex won't do it and money won't. Even the idea of a kid wouldn't. But you did say you'd go along with me. That's really something."

"What do you mean the *idea* of a kid?"

"There's no kid."

She was rocking from foot to foot, half-twisting her body, playing with the ends of her hair.

"You did get rid of it."

"I was never pregnant." She smiled at Billy.

"Then what, what the hell, what?"

"I needed to know what you felt, Billy. You really think I'm dumb enough to let you knock me up? It's just that we never talk about things that really matter. This was the first time we ever talked about anything important that wasn't money or my goddamn husband. I know almost nothing about your life. All I know is I love you more now than I did when you walked in the door. I knew I wanted you even before I met you."

Billy was shaking his head. "Imagine that," he said. "You conned me right out of my jock."

"Yes, I know."

"What a sucker."

"Yes, it was lovely. You were wonderful. Now will you take me out for a sandwich? I missed dinner waiting for you."

"Sure. But first get busy with the douche bag. And I'm gonna watch. I'm not going through this noise again."

"Ah, Romeo," Angie said, massaging Billy's crotch.

XI

MARTIN, THINKING OF HIS FATHER, of Charlie Boy, of Noah, all spread-eagled on their beds, of Melissa spread-eagled naked in fatigue on the floor of her suite at the Hampton Hotel, failed to sleep. He faced downward and leftward into the pillow, a trick he played on the fluids of his brain that generally brought sleep, but not now. And so he faced upward, rightward. He closed his eyes, fixating on a point just above his nose, behind the frontal bone, trying to drive out thoughts as they appeared.

But this also failed, and he saw the lonely, driven figure entering the wholly darkened tunnel, so narrow no man could survive the train should it come roaring through before he reached the far exit. He would be crushed by the wheels or squeezed to juice and pulp against the wall. The figure reached the trestle that spanned the bottomless canyon and began to inch across it on hands and knees, fearful of falling, fearful the train would come from beyond the forest curve and bear down on him at mid-trestle. No chance then for backward flight, no chance to sidestep, only to hang from trestle's edge by fingertips. Would vertigo then claim him? Would his fingers hold him?

He sat up and lit the bedside lamp and began to count the ceiling panels again, eleven horizontal, twelve vertical. He multiplied. One hundred and thirty-two panels, including fragments. He counted the sides of the dresser, the number of edges on the six drawers: twenty-four. He counted the edges on the decorative trim on Mary Daugherty's closet. He totaled the edge count: two-seventy-eight. He counted the edges on the ceiling molding. He counted the backs, fronts, and sides of books on his dresser. He lost track of the total.

He could never contain the numbers, nor did he want to. He usually counted sidewalk cracks when he walked, telephone poles when he drove. He remembered no totals except the eighteen steps to the city room, twelve to the upstairs of this house, and remembered these only after years of repetition. If he miscounted either staircase, he would recount carefully on the return trip. He once viewed the counting as a private way of demarcating his place in the world, numbering all boundaries, four counts to the edge of a drawer, four to the perimeter of a tile, an act of personal coherence. On the day he awoke and drawer edges were worth three, tile perimeters five, he would know the rules of his civilization had been superseded.

He switched off the lamp, closed his eyes, and found a staircase. He climbed it and at the turning saw the hag squirming on the wide step, caught in an enormous cobweb which covered all of her except her legs. Beneath her thighs, two dozen white baby shoes were in constant motion, being hatched.

I don't like what everybody is doing to me, she said.

The hag reached a hand out to Martin, who fled up the stairs in terror, a wisp of cobweb caught on his sleeve.

He plucked himself from the scene without moving and felt panic in his heartbeat. He said the Our Father, the Hail Mary, the Confiteor. Deliver us from evil. Blessed is the fruit of thy womb. *Mea maxima culpa.* He had not prayed in twenty-five years except for knee-jerk recitations at funerals, and did not now believe in these or any other prayers. Yet as he prayed, his pulse slowly slackened, his eyes stayed closed. And as he moved into sleep, he knew that despite his infidel ways, the remnants of tattered faith still had power over his mind.

He knew his mind had no interest in the genuineness of faith, that it fed on the imagery of any conflict that touched the deepest layers of his history. Years ago, he'd dreamed repeatedly of hexagons, rhomboids, and threes, and still had no idea why. He understood almost none of the fragmented pictures his mind created, but he knew now for the first time that it was possible to trick the apparatus. He had done it. He was moving into a peaceful sleep, his first since the departure of Peter. And as he did, he understood the message the images had sent him. He would go to Harmanus Bleecker Hall and watch Melissa impersonate his mother on stage. Then, all in good time, he would find a way to make love to Melissa again, in the way a one-legged man carves a crutch from the fallen tree that crushed his leg.

*   *   *

The fountain cherub, small boy in full pee, greeted Martin as he walked through the Hall's foyer. Pssss. *The Golden Bowlful*, by Henry Pease Lotz. Martin remembered seeing Bert Lytell here, the Barrymores and

Mrs. Fiske strutting on this cultural altar. He saw the young Jolson here, and the great Isadora, and when he was only thirteen he saw a play called *The Ten-Ton Door*, in which a man strapped to that huge door was exploded across the stage by a great blast, an epic moment.

"So you made it," said Agnes, the hennaed gum chewer in the Hall's box office. "We expected you last night."

"I was up in Troy last night," Martin said, "walking the duck."

"The duck?"

Martin smiled and looked at his ticket, B-108 center, and then he entered the Hall, a quarter century after the premiere that never was. Edward Sheldon's *Romance* premiered here in 1913 instead of *The Flaming Corsage*, and Sheldon's reputation blossomed. But when the priests and Grundys killed Edward Daugherty's play, calling it the work of a scandalous, vice-ridden man, they made Edward a pariah in the theater for years to come.

In 1928, a bad year for some, Melissa set out to convert the play to a talking picture in which she would star as the mistress, her long-standing dream. She wanted Von Stroheim to direct, appreciative of his sexual candor, but the studios found both the play and the scandal dated, and dated, too, Melissa, the idea of you as a young mistress.

Aging but undauntable, Melissa turned up then with something not so old: Edward Daugherty's journal from the years just before and just after the scandal, full of the drama and eroticism of the famous event, in case, chums, you can't find enough in the play. Still, no studio was interested, for Melissa was a fading emblem of a waning era, her voice adjudged too quirky for talkies, her imperious and litigious ways (when in doubt she sued) too much of a liability for the moguls.

And so *The Flaming Corsage* continued unproduced either as play or film until the Daugherty renaissance, which began with an obscure New York mounting of his 1902 work, *The Car Barns*. George Jean Nathan saw that production and wrote that here was a writer many cuts above Gillette, Belasco, Fitch, and others, more significantly Irish-American than Boucicault or Sheldon, for he is tapping deeper currents, and superior to any of the raffish Marxist didacticists currently cluttering up the boards. Was this neglected writer an American O'Casey or Pirandello? Another O'Neill? No, said Nathan, he's merely original, which serious men should find sufficient.

The Car Barns revival was followed by *The Masks of Pyramis*, Edward Daugherty's one venture into symbolism. It provoked a great public yawn and slowed the renaissance. *The Baron of Ten Broeck Street* followed within a year, a play with the capitalist as villain and tragic figure, the protagonist patterned after Katrina Daugherty's father, an Albany lumber baron. Reaction to the play was positive, but the renaissance might have halted there had not Melissa's need to see herself transfigured on stage been so unyielding.

Six more years would pass before *The Flaming Corsage* entered its new age. By then, three decades after its inspiration, it had become a wholly new play, its old sin now the stuff of myth, its antique realism now an exquisite parody of bitter love and foolish death. The New York production was a spectacular success. Melissa made her comeback, and Edward Daugherty strode into the dimension he had sought for a lifetime as an artist. But he strode with a partial mind. He beamed at the telling when Martin brought the news, but minutes later he had forgotten that he had ever written that play, or any other. What would please him most, he said, squirming in his leather armchair in the old house on Main Street, would be a hot cup of tea, son, with lemon if you'd be so kind, and a sugar cookie.

The theater was already two-thirds full and more were still arriving to see the famed beauty in the infamous play about Albany. Martin positioned himself at the head of an aisle, holding his battered hat in hand, standing out of the way as the playgoers seated themselves. Joe Morrissey nodded to him, ex-assemblyman, tight as a teacup, who lived near Sacred Heart; when the pastor asked him to donate his house to the nuns, old Joe sold the place immediately and moved out of the parish. And there, moving down front, Tip Mooney, the roofer, with the adopted daughter everybody chucklingly says is his mistress. Taboo. Ooo-ooo. The zest for it. And here, as the houselights dim, stands the fellow out for redemption. I'm just as big a sinner as you, Dad. Playboy of the North End, but keeping it in the family. Here to see everybody's favorite honeycomb, who, as Marlene, the reporter, wrote, is out to prove she can plumb the depths of the human heart with her acting, even as she keeps the human spirit all aglow with her dancing, and the human imagination fevered merely by her well-known sensual presence, etc.

The lights went all the way down, the curtain rose and the Daugherty living room on Colonie Street was magically reconstituted from thirty years past, even to the Edison phonograph and its cylinders, the Tiffany butterfly lamp from Van Heusen Charles, the Hudson River landscape on the far wall, and all the other meticulously copied details demanded by the author; for those possessions were inseparable from the woman who sits there among them: the simulated Katrina, remarkably reincarnated by Melissa in a blondish gray wig, unswept into a perfect Katrina crown, her glasses on, her lavender shawl over her legs as she sits in the black rocker, book open in her lap, hands crossed upon it.

"Where will you go?" she asks the young man standing by the bay window.

And the young man, in whom Martin does not recognize anything of his disordered self of 1908, replies, "Someplace where they don't snigger when my name is mentioned."

"Will you go to Paris?"

"Perhaps. I don't know."

"It must be dreary there without Baudelaire and Rimbaud."

"They have that tower now."

"Your father will want to know where you are."

"Perhaps I'll go to Versailles and see where the king kept Marie Antoinette."

"Yes, do that. Send your father a postcard."

And Melissa put her book aside and stood up, sweeping her hand up behind her neck, tapping the wig, smoothing the rattled mind. The gesture was not Katrina's but Melissa's, which generated confusion in Martin. He felt impatient with the play, half fearful of seeing the development a few scenes hence when his father would enter with the awful dialogue of duplicity and defeat, to be met by the witty near-madness of Katrina.

Now the dialogue of mother and son moved the play on toward that moment, but Martin closed out all the talk and watched the silent movement of Melissa, not at all like Katrina, and remembered her in her voluptuary state, drenched in sweat, oozing his semen. The Olmecs built a monument of a sacred jaguar mating with a lustful woman. A male offspring of such a mating would have been half-jaguar, half-boy, a divine creature. The boy-animal of Martin's morning vision, perhaps? Is your mind telling you, Martin, that you're the divine progeny of a sacred mating? But which one? Your father's with your mother? Your father's with Melissa? Your own with Melissa?

The corruption he felt after his time with Melissa came back now with full power: the simoniac being paid off with venereal gifts. He stayed with her three days, she securing her purchase with a lust that soared beyond his own. That body, now walking across the stage, he saw walking the length of the sitting room in The Hampton to stand naked by the window and peer through the curtains at the movement on Broadway and State Street below. He stood beside her and with a compulsion grown weary, slid his hand between her thighs as a gesture. They looked down together, connected to the traffic of other men and women in transit toward and away from their lust. He would stay in the room with her another day, until she said, Now I want a woman. And then Martin went away.

Through the years since then he insisted he would never touch her sexually again. But perceiving now that a second infusion of pain distracts the brain and reduces the pain of the first and more grievous wound, he would, yes, make love to Melissa as soon as possible. He might ask her to wear the blond wig. That would appeal to her twist. He might even call her Katrina. She could call him Edward.

They would pretend it was 1887 and that this was a true wedding of sacred figures. He would tell her of the Olmecs, and of the divine progeny. He would tell her his dream of the divine animal at bedside and suggest that it was perhaps himself in a new stage of being. As they made their fierce and fraudulent love, they would become jaguar and lustful partner entwined. Both would know that a new Martin Daugherty would be the offspring of this divine mating.

The quest to love yourself is a moral quest.

How simple this psychic game is, once you know the rules.

XII

ALL OF A SUDDEN DOC FAY was playing like a champ in Daddy Big's round robin. Billy had been ahead sixteen points and then old Doc ran twenty-six and left Billy nothing on the table. The Doc blew his streak on the last ball of a rack. Didn't leave himself in a position where he could sink it and also make the cue ball break the new rack. And so he called safe and sank the ball, and it was respotted at the peak of the new rack, the full rack now facing Billy.

The Doc also left the cue ball way up the table, snug against the back cushion. Toughest possible shot for Billy. Or anybody. Billy, natch, had to call another safe shot—make contact with a ball, and make sure one ball, any ball, also touched a cushion. If he failed to do this, it would be his third scratch in a row, and he'd lose fifteen points, plus a point for the latest scratch. Billy did have the out of breaking the rack instead of playing safe, as a way of beating the third scratch. But when he looked at the full rack he couldn't bring himself to break it. It would seem cowardly. What's more, it'd set Doc up for another fat run, and they'd all know Billy Phelan would never do a thing like that.

He bent over the table and remembered bringing Danny into this pool room one afternoon. The kid stood up straight to shoot. Get your head down, put your eye at the level of the ball, Billy told him. How the hell can you see what you're hitting when you ain't even looking at it? Get that head down and stroke that cue, firm up your bridge, don't let them fingers wobble. The kid leaned over and sank a few. Great kid. Stay out of pool rooms, kid, or all you'll ever have is fun.

Billy tapped the cue ball gently. He was thrilled at how lightly he hit it. Just right. The ball moved slowly toward the rear right corner of the pack. It touched the pack and separated two balls. No ball touched a cushion.

Scratch.

Scratch number three, in a row.

Billy loses fifteen, plus one for this scratch.

Billy is down twenty-seven points and the Doc is hot. Billy doubts he could catch the Doc now even if he wanted to.

Billy hits the table with his fist, hits the floor with the heel of his cue and curses that last goddamn safe shot, thrilled.

Billy is acting. He has just begun to throw his first match.

The lights in the pool room went out just as the Doc lined up for the next shot. I'll get candles, said Daddy Big. Don't nobody touch them balls. Which balls are they, Daddy? Footers asked in a falsetto. Billy remembered Footers just before the lights went out, licking a green lollipop, and Harvey Hess, his thumbs stuck in his vest, nodding his approval at the Doctor burying Billy. Daddy Big liked that development too, the string of his change apron tight on his gut, like a tick tied in the middle. Behind Billy stood Morrie Berman, who was again backing Billy. Morrie had given Billy fifty to bet on himself with the Doc, and also took all side bets on his boy. Billy heard Morrie softly muttering unhhh, eeeng, every time the Doc sank one.

Maybe a hundred men were standing and sitting around the table when the lights went. Billy saw Martin come in late and stand at the back of the crowd, behind the chairs Daddy Big had set up. Daddy Big lit four candles. They flickered on the cigar counter, on the edge of a pool table covered with a tarpaulin, on a shelf near the toilet. Many of the men were smoking in the half-darkness, their cigars and cigarettes glowing and fading, their faces moving in and out of shadows. Here was the obscure collective power. What'll they do if I fink? Will I see my father? Some of the shadowy men left the room when the lights went out. Most of those with chairs stayed put, but then some of them, too, went down to the street, needing, in the absence of light, at least an open sky.

"Tough shot you had," Morrie said to Billy.

"The toughest."

"You'll pick up. You got what it takes."

"That Doctor's hot as ten-cent pussy."

"You'll take him."

"Sure," said Billy.

But he won't, or else how can he do what he's got to do, if he's got to do it? Wrong-Way Corrigan starts out for California and winds up in Ireland. I guess I got lost, he says, and people say, Yeah, oh yeah, he got lost. Ain't he some sweet son of a bitch?

XIII

THROUGH THE FRONT WINDOW of Louie's, Martin saw that the lights were out on Broadway and in the station. He saluted Billy across the candlelight and went down to the street, which was dark in all directions. He walked to the corner of Columbia Street and looked up. Pearl Street was also dark, candles already dancing in two windows up the block. He walked back and into Becker's and headed for the phone, past customers drinking by the light of the old kerosene lamp that had sat on the back bar for years, unused. Now it illuminated Red Tom's mustache. The test of a real mustache is whether it can be seen from behind. Red Tom's therefore is not real.

The city desk told him that lights were out all over the city and parts of Colonie, Watervliet and Cohoes. All hospitals had been called an hour earlier and told a power failure was possible, and not to schedule any operations unless they had their own generators. Nursing homes were also alerted. But the power company said it hadn't made the calls. Who had? Nobody knew.

Martin went back to the bar and ordered a Grandad on ice and looked at the photo behind the bar. A new star shone on the chest of Scotty Streck, brighter than all others. In the kerosene lamplight the men in the photo moved backward in time. They were all smiling and all younger than their pictures. They were boys and young men under the shirtsleeved, summer sun. None of them was dead or would ever die.

"Lights are out all over town," Martin told Red Tom.

"Is that a fact? I was listening to the radio when they went. Dewey was on, talking about Albany."

"Albany? What was he saying?"

"He mentioned Patsy, and that was all I heard."

"Did he mention Charlie Boy?"

"Not that I heard."

Martin gulped his drink and went outside. People were clustered under the canopy at the station, all cabs were gone, and a West Albany trolley was stalled between Maiden Lane and Steuben Street. Martin could see it in the headlights of cars. The night was a deep, moonless black, with only a few stars visible. It was as if rural darkness had descended upon the city. Faces were unrecognizable three feet away. Albany had never been so dark in Martin's memory. There were gas lamps in his boyhood, then the first few electric lights, now the power poles everywhere. But tonight was the lightless time in which highwaymen had performed, the dark night of the century gone, his father's childhood darkness on new streets cut out of the raw hills and the grassy flats. A woman with a bundle came by, half running toward Clinton Avenue, pursued by the night. Alongside Martin, a match flared and he turned to see Morrie Berman lighting a cigar.

"What news do you hear?"

"Only that they're out all over town."

"I mean about the McCall kid. You fellows at the paper turn up any news?"

"I heard there was another ransom note."

"Is that so?"

"Signed by Charlie Boy. I didn't see it, but from what I gather there'll be another go-between list in the paper tonight."

"They didn't like us on the first list?"

"So it seems."

"You hear anything else?"

Dark shapes moved in behind Morrie, and Martin withheld his answer. The shapes hovered.

"Let's take a walk," Martin said and he took a step toward Steuben Street. Morrie stepped along and they moved south on Broadway, candles in the Waldorf, a bunch of men on the street in front of the Monte Carlo. They stepped around the men in the light of a passing auto. Martin did not want to speak until they had turned the corner onto Steuben. They passed Hagaman's Bakery and Joe's Bookshop on Steuben Street, where Martin knew his father's early novel, *The Mosquito Lovers*, and the volume of his collected plays were sitting in faded dust jackets in the window, and had been for months, ever since the success of *The Flaming Corsage*.

"So what's the secret?" Morrie asked.

"No secret, but I don't want to broadcast it. I know you're a friend of Maloy and the news is they're looking for him. And Curry."

"Why tell me? They got a lot of friends."

"You asked for news. They've both been out of town a week."

"So that ties them in?"

"No, but even their families don't know where they are."

"Hell, I saw Maloy two or three days ago on Broadway. They're apt to be anywhere. Maloy's crazy and Curry's a moron. But they wouldn't mix up in a thing like this, not in their own town."

"Nevertheless, they're looking for them."

"They'll turn up. What else do you hear?"

"The note said they'd starve Charlie Boy till the ransom was paid."

"Tough stuff."

"Very."

Up toward Pearl Street, a window shattered and a burglar alarm rang and rang. Martin saw a silhouette running toward him and Morrie. The runner brushed Martin's elbow, stepping off the curb as they touched, but Martin could not see the face.

"Somebody did all right," said Morrie. "Ain't that a jewelry store there?"

"Right," said Martin. "Just about where Henry James's grandmother used to live."

"Who?"

"An old-timer."

And on the other corner, DeWitt Clinton lived. And across the street, Bret Harte was born. And up Columbia was one of Melville's homes, and on Clinton Square another. An old man had answered when Martin knocked on the door of the Columbia Street house and said, yeauh, he seemed to remember the name Melville but that was next door and they tore that house down and built a new one. Melville, he said. I heard he moved to Troy. Don't know what become of him after that.

Martin and Morrie neared Pearl Street, the glimmerings of light from the cars giving them a fragmented view of the broken window in Wilson's Jewelry Store. When they saw the window, they crossed Pearl. Martin looked down toward State and saw a torchlight parade coming north in support of the nomination of Millard Fillmore. The John G. Myers department store collapsed into itself, killing thirteen and making men bald from flying plaster dust. Henry James, suffused in the brilliance of a sunny summer morning, walked out of his grandmother's house, opened the front gate, and floated like a flowered balloon into ethereal regions. Martin walked in the phosphorescent footsteps of his father and his grandfather.

"Where the hell are we walking?" Morrie asked.

"Just around," said Martin. "You want to go back down?"

"I guess it's all right."

They walked to Clinton Square, where two more trolleys were stalled on the bend. A siren screamed and stopped, back near Steuben and Pearl. Martin and Morrie, their eyes grown accustomed to the darkness, watched the shadowy action in front of the Palace Theater, hundreds waiting to go back inside and see the rest of *Boys' Town* with Spencer Tracy as Father Flanagan, the miracle man. There is no such thing as a bad boy.

"They got some kind of light in the Grand Lunch," Morrie said. "You want some coffee?"

"No, you go ahead. I want to watch the panic."

"What panic?"

"There's got to be panic someplace with this much darkness."

"Whatever you say. See you down below."

In the Sudetenland only last week when Hitler arrived, at nightfall there was an epidemic of suicide.

In France in 1918, Martin had heard a man scream from the darkness beyond a farmhouse where a shell had just hit. Help me, oh God, oh heavenly God, help me, the man yelled, and then he wailed his pain. Martin nudged a corporal and they crawled toward the voice and found an American soldier pinned between two dead cows. The top cow was bloated from inhaling the explosion. Martin and the corporal could not move the bloated cow so they pulled the squeezed man by his arms, and the top half of him came away in their grip. He stopped screaming.

Martin crossed Pearl and went into the K. of C. and called the city desk by candlelight. Viglucci said there was still no explanation for the blackout, but up at Harmanus Bleecker Hall the audience had panicked when the lights went. People shoved one another and Tip Mooney was knocked down and trampled.

Punishment.

x   x   x

"This bum's a Cuban and so's one of the broads," said Morrie as Billy and Martin followed him down two slate steps to the basement doorway beneath the high stoop. Morrie rapped and the pimp peered out in his puce shirt, his hair brilliantined, his shoes pointed and shiny, both ends of him gleaming in the harsh backlight. The lights of the city had come back on an hour earlier.

"Hey, Mo-ree," the pimp said. "Whatchou lookin' for?"

"Pussy," said Morrie.

"You in the right place."

The pimp, the same man Red Tom threw out of Becker's, had a face as pointy as his shoes and resembled Martin's long-snouted animal child. Why should the likes of him concretize a Daugherty abstraction? But why not? Ooze to ooze, slime to slime. Brothers under the sheets.

Two young women sat at the kitchen table drinking sarsaparilla out of jelly glasses. Knives, forks, glasses, and dishes sat in the sink. The stub of a candle stood in a pool of dry wax on a saucer. The pimp introduced the girls as Fela and Margie. Fela, obviously *La Cubana*, was dark, with hair to her kidneys. Margie had carroty red hair, redder by blood weight than Mary Daugherty's crop. Both wore brassieres, Woolworth couture, a size too small, shorts to mid-thigh, with cuffs, and high heels.

"They got shorts on," Morrie said. "Last time I saw a whore in shorts was Mame Fay's."

"I know Mame," said the pimp. "She's got influence up in Troy."

"She used to recruit salesgirls in the grocery marts," Billy said. "She tried to hawk a friend of mine."

"She'd give talks in the high schools if they let her," said Morrie.

"Young stuff is what Mame likes," Margie said.

"Yeah," said Morrie, licking his lips.

"Talk is gettin' hot, *hombres*. Young stuff right in front of you. Who's ready?"

"Don't rush me," said Morrie.

Billy pulled up a chair between Fela and Margie and looked them over. Martin felt a thirst rising.

"You have any beer?"

"Twenty-five cents, *hombre*."

"I'm a sport," said Martin, and the pimp cracked a quart of Stanwix.

"Those broads up at Mame's," Morrie said, "took their tops off when we come in. I'm the best, one of 'em says to us, so take me. If you're the best, says the other, how come your boyfriend screwed me? You? says the other. He'd screw a dead dog with the clap, but he wouldn't screw you. And then they went at it. Best whore fight I ever saw. Bit one another, blood all over the joint, one of their heads split open. Me and Maloy laughed our tits off."

"We don't fight," Margie said. "We like one another."

"That's nice," said Morrie, and he put his hand inside her brassiere. "Soft." He laughed, found a chair, and sat down.

"Maloy," said Billy. "What the hell is he doing in Newark?"

"Who said he was in Newark?" Morrie asked.

"I thought you did."

"He ain't in Newark."

"Where is he?"

"He's someplace else."

"How do you know he ain't in Newark. I heard he was in Newark."

"What the hell'd he be in Newark for?"

"Why not Newark?"

"He don't know nobody in Newark."

"This is a famous guy," the pimp told the girls, putting his hand on Morrie's shoulder. "His name's in the paper this morning. They say that's all about the kidnapping, right Mo-ree?"

"Billy's name's in there, too."

"Very big men in Albany if the McCalls put your name in there," said the pimp.

"You don't like the McCalls," Billy said. "They threw you out of Becker's for bad-mouthing them."

"I never like them," said the pimp. "They make me a janitor at the public bath, then fire me."

"What'd they do that for?"

"For nothing. A little thing. Look at the ladies and pull the old rope. They catch me and tell me I'm all finish. Little thing like that."

"It ain't against the law to pull your rope," Morrie said. "It's against the law to get caught."

"It sure ain't against the law here," Margie said.

"Yeah, you boys come here to talk or screw?" Fela the *Cubana* said.

"Screw," said Morrie, "and you got it, lady. Let's go." He stood up and tongued her ear and she knocked a jelly glass off the table. He took her down the hallway and into a bedroom.

"Hey, Mo-ree," said the pimp, "she's the best blow-job in town." Then he told Martin and Billy: "Margie's good too."

"Is that right?" Billy asked Margie. "Are you good?"

"I ain't had a complaint all week."

Billy washed a glass in the sink with soap and water and poured himself a beer. The pimp came over to Martin.

"What do you like, Mister? Little blow from the best?"

"I'm just along for the ride. I'll stay with the drink."

Martin washed a glass and poured a beer. He stared at the door of the broom closet, then opened the door and saw the notebook for *The Flaming Corsage* hanging from a nail on a short piece of cord. It was inscribed on the cover: *To my beloved son, who played a whore's trick on his father.* Martin closed the closet door and sipped his beer, which tasted like the juice of rotted lemons. He spat into the sink.

Martin dried his mouth and studied Margie, who removed her brassiere for him. Her nipples lay at the bottom of the curves, projecting somewhat obliquely. Martin considered the nipple fetishists of history.

Plutarch, Spinoza, Schubert, Cardinal Wolsey. The doorbells of ecstasy, Curzio Malaparte called them. Billy reached across the table and lifted one of Margie's breasts. People preparing for sexual conflict. The pimp slavered and picked his nose with his thumb.

How had Martin's father prepared for sex? On spindly legs, he stood in his shorts in his bedroom, reading Blake on the dresser top. The shorts seemed unusually long. Perhaps he had short thighs. He looked sexually disinterested, but that was unquestionably deceptive. His teeth carried stains from pipe-smoking. He had a recurring ingrown toenail, clipped with a V, a protruding bone on the right elbow from an old fracture. These things were antisexual.

How would Martin's son ever know anything of his own sexuality? Gone to the priests at thirteen, blanketed with repressive prayer and sacramental censure. How could the tigers of chastity be wiser than the horses of coition?

Ten years ago, a phone call had come for Martin after he'd completed a sexual romp with his wife. The caller, a Boston lawyer, had heard that the notebook of *The Flaming Corsage* was in Martin's possession. Was that true?

Yes.

Was it for sale, or would it be preserved in the trove of Daugherty papers?

The latter, of course.

Well, you may take my name and address, and should you change your mind I want you to know that I will pay a handsome price for that notebook. Like the play made from it, it has a deep significance for my client.

What significance is that?

My client, said the lawyer, was your father's mistress.

"All right," Morrie said, emerging from the bedroom. "Little bit of all right."

"That was quick," Billy said. "You like it?"

"Short but sweet," Morrie said. "How much?"

"Buck and a half," said the pimp.

Morrie snapped a dollar off his roll and fished for the fifty cents. Margie put on her brassiere. Fela picked up the sarsaparilla bottle and looked for a glass.

"Only a buck and a half?" Billy said.

"That's all," said the pimp.

"It must be some great stuff for a buck and a half."

"Go try it."

Fela tipped up the bottle and gargled with sarsaparilla. She spat it into the sink and eyed Billy. The pimp took Morrie's dollar and change.

Martin opened the broom closet and found a dust pan hanging from a nail.

"How the hell can it be any good for a buck and a half?" Billy asked.

"Hey, I ought to know," said the pimp with a rattish smile of cuspids. "She's my sister."

Billy hit him on the chin. The pimp sped backward and knocked over a chair, shook his head and leaped at Billy's throat. Billy shook him off, and the pimp reached for the butcher knife in the sink, but Martin reached it first and threw it out the open window into the alley. Billy hit the pimp again, a graze of the head, but the pimp found Billy's throat again and held on. Martin pulled at the pimp as the whores scrambled away from the table. Morrie pushed past Martin and bashed the pimp with the sarsaparilla bottle. The pimp slid to the floor and lay still. The whores came out of the bedroom carrying their dresses and handbags.

"He looks dead," Billy said.

"Who gives a goddamn?" Morrie said, and he tipped over the kitchen table, opened the dish closet and threw the dishes on the floor. Billy tipped over the garbage pail and threw a chair at the kitchen window. The whores went out the back door.

"Son of a bitch, pimping for his own sister," said Billy.

"She wasn't bad," said Morrie as he swept the contents of the refrigerator onto the floor. "She's got nice teeth."

Martin salvaged a new cold bottle of Stanwix and poured himself a glass. He opened the broom closet so Morrie could empty it. Billy went into the bedroom where Morrie had been with Fela and tore up the bed clothes, then kicked the footboard until the bed fell apart. On the bedside table stood a metal lamp of a nautical F.D.R. at the wheel of the Ship of State, standing above the caption: "Our Leader." Billy threw the lamp through the bedroom window. Martin straightened up two kitchen chairs, sat on one and used the other as a table for his beer, which no longer tasted like rotten lemons. Billy came back and nudged the inert pimp with his foot.

"I think you killed him," he said to Morrie.

"No," said Martin. "He moved his fingers."

"He's all right then," Morrie said. "You ain't dead if you can move your fingers."

"I knew a guy couldn't move his toes," Billy said, winded but calming. "His feet turned to stone. First his feet then the rest of him. Only guy I ever knew whose feet turned to stone and then the rest of him."

Transgressors of good fame are punished for their deeds, was what occurred to Martin. He stood up and opened his fly, then urinated on the pimp's feet. Simoniacs among us.

✳   ✳   ✳

"What'd you make of Morrie's answer about Maloy?" Billy asked.

"I thought he was evasive," Martin said.

"I think he's lying."

"Why would he lie?"

"You tell me," Billy said. "Must be he doesn't want Maloy connected to Newark."

"Maybe he's not connected."

"No. He was lying. I saw it in his face."

They listened to the dismal blues Slopie Dodds was making at the piano. Martin squinted in the dim light of Martha's Place, where they'd come for a nightcap after leaving Morrie. The smoke was dense in the low-ceilinged bar, which was full of Negroes. There were four white men in the place, Martin and Billy, a stranger at the far end of the bar, and Daddy Big, a nightly Negrophile after he reached his drunken beyond. Daddy was oblivious now of everything except hustling Martha, a handsome tan woman in her forties with shoulder-length conked hair, small lips, and a gold-capped canine tooth. Martha was not about to be hustled, but Daddy Big did not accept this, steeped as he was in his professional wisdom that everybody is hustleable once you find the weak spot.

Slopie ended his blues and, as Martha moved to another customer, Daddy Big swung around on his stool and said, "Play me the white man's song, Slopie." Slopie grinned and trilled an intro, a ricky-tick throwback, and Daddy Big sang from his barstool the song he said he had learned from a jailhouse nigger who'd sung it in World War One: *I don't care what it costs, I'll suffer all the loss. It's worth twice the money just to be the boss. 'Cause I got a white man workin' for me now.* The song merged with "The Broadway Rag," into which Slopie passed without comment. Daddy Big opened his arms to the room and said as the ragtime bounced off the walls, "I love all niggers." Looking then to the black faces for reciprocation and getting none, he discovered Billy at the corner table, near the neon-lighted window.

"What're you doing here, Phelan?" he asked. "You ain't a nigger." The words were crooked with whiskey.

"I'm an Irish Catholic," Billy said. "Same thing to some people."

A few who heard this smiled. Daddy Big hurled himself off the barstool and staggered toward Billy, stopping his own forward motion by grabbing the back of a chair with both hands.

"You got your tail whipped tonight."

"Doc was hot," Billy said. "A good player got hot."

"Bet your ass he's a good player. Bet your ass. He'll whip you every time out."

"Then why didn't he whip me the last two matches we played?"

"He'll whip you from now on. He's got your number. All you know how to shoot is safe and you blew that tonight. You ain't got nothin' left, if you ever had anything." Daddy waved his left hand in front of his face like a man shooing flies. He lurched for the door with one word: "Bum," and went out cross-footed, leaving the door ajar. Martin closed it as Daddy Big careened in the direction of Union Station.

"He's got a mean mouth," Martin said.

"Yeah," said Billy. "He's a prick now. Prison got him twisted. But he used to be a nice guy, and at pool he was a champ. Nobody in Albany could beat him. I learned a whole lot watching him sucker chumps who thought they knew something about the game."

The white man from the end of the bar stopped beside Billy. "That guy talks like he wants to wind up dead in the alley. He keeps that up in here, he'll get what he's after."

"He's a cousin of the McCalls," Billy told the man. "Nobody'll touch him."

"Is that so?" The man was chastened. "I didn't know that."

"That pimp," Billy said to Martin when the stranger left, "I don't know why he didn't stay down. I hit him right on the button. They used to stay down when I hit 'em like that."

"Do you suppose he'll try to get even?"

"He'd get worse. You don't come back at Morrie."

"Then you think Morrie's dangerous?"

"Anybody pals around with Maloy and Curry's dangerous." Billy thought about that. "But I like Morrie," he said. "And I like Maloy. Curry's nuts, but Morrie's all right. He saved my ass there."

Slopie finished his ragtime number, a *tour de force* that won applause. Billy signaled to Martha to buy Slopie a drink.

"Can I tell you something, Martin?"

"Anything."

"Positively on the q.t."

"Do you trust me?"

"Yeah, I do. For a straight guy, you know a lot. Why'd you piss on that guy's feet?"

"He seemed worth that kind of attention. I don't meet too many like that. What did you want to tell me?"

"I threw that match tonight."

"Hey," said Martin. "What for?"

"So I wouldn't owe Berman."

"I don't think I follow that."

"He lent me fifty to bet on myself. If I win, then I got money through him, right? But if I lose, I owe him nothing. I already give him back the fifty and we were even. Then the son of a bitch saves my ass."

"So you were going to talk to Patsy about him then?"

"I don't know."

"I could tell them what you want to say. I don't have your qualms."

"They'd know I pumped him and then didn't tell them."

"Then tell them."

"But that puts me full on the tit. Bindy and Patsy paying my debts. Paying you. Me on the tit like Daddy Big. That bastard calls me a bum, but he'd chew catshit if Bindy said it was strawberries."

The stranger who said Daddy Big wanted to die came back into Martha's. "Somebody better call an ambulance," he said. "That drunk guy is outside bleedin' all over the street."

Martha went for the phone, and Billy and Martin ran down the block. Daddy Big lay on his back, his face bloodied badly, staring at the black sky with bugged eyes and puffed cheeks, his skin purple where it wasn't smeared with blood. Two of his front teeth were bent inward and the faint squeal of a terrified mouse came out of his mouth. Billy rolled him face down and with two fingers pulled out his upper plate, then grabbed him around the waist with both arms and lifted him, head down, to release the vomit in his throat. Billy sat down on the sidewalk, knees up, and held Daddy across his lap, face down, tail in the air. Billy slapped his back and pressed both knees into his stomach until his vomiting stopped. Daddy looked up.

"You son of a bitch," Billy said. "Are you all right?"

"Blllgggggggghhh," Daddy said, gasping.

"Then get your ass up."

Billy rolled him off his lap, stood up and pulled the drunken Daddy to his feet. Customers from Martha's stood behind the two men, along with half a dozen passersby. Billy leaned Daddy against the wall of the Railroad Y.M.C.A. and Martha blotted his face with a wet towel, revealing a split forehead and a badly scraped nose, cheek, and chin. A prowl car arrived and two patrolmen helped Daddy into the back seat.

"Where'll you take him?" Martin asked.

"Home. He does this regular," one policeman said.

"You should have him looked at up at the emergency room. He might have aspirated. Inhaled some vomit."

"Nnggggggnnnhhh," said Daddy Big.

The policeman frowned at Martin and got behind the wheel.

"He don't have any teeth," Billy said. Billy found the teeth on the edge of the curb, where a dog was licking the vomit. Billy reached in through the car window and put the teeth in Daddy Big's shirt pocket. As the crowd moved back toward Martha's, Martin saw another car pull up behind the police car, Poop Powell at the wheel.

"Hey, Phelan," Poop called, and both Billy and Martin then saw Bindy McCall in the front seat alongside Poop. Martin patted Billy gently on the shoulder.

"You do lead a full life, Billy," he said.

*   *   *

Martin sat in Martha's window looking at Billy standing in the middle of Broadway, his back to traffic, talking into Bindy's window. The neon sign, which spelled Martha's name backward, gave off a humming, crackling sound, flaming gas contained, controlled. Martin drank his beer and considered the combustibility of men. Billy on fire going through the emotions of whoring for Bindy when he understood nothing about how it was done. It was not done out of need. It rose out of the talent for assuming the position before whoremongers. Billy lacked such talent. He was so innocent of whoring he could worry over lead slugs.

Slopie played "Lullaby of Broadway," a seductive tune. Slopie was now playing in a world never meant to be, a world he couldn't have imagined when he had both his legs and Bessie on his arm. Yet, he'd arrived here in Martha's, where Billy and Martin had also arrived. The music brought back *Gold Diggers* of some year gone. Winnie Shaw singing and dancing the "Lullaby." Come and dance, said the hoofers, cajoling her, and she danced with them through all those early mornings. Broadway Baby couldn't sleep till break of dawn, and so she danced, but fled them finally. Please let me rest, she pleaded from her balcony refuge. Dick Powell kissed her through the balcony door, all the hoofers pleading, beckoning. Dance with us, Baby. And they pushed open the door. She backed away from them, back, back, and ooooh, over the railing she went. There goes Broadway Baby, falling, poor Baby, falling, falling, and gone. Good night, Baby.

Spud, the paper boy, came into Martha's with a stack of *Times-Union*s under his right arm, glasses sliding down his nose, cap on, his car running outside behind Bindy's, with doors open, hundreds more papers on the back seat.

"Paper," Martin said. He gave Spud the nickel and turned to the classifieds, found the second code ad. Footers O'Brien was the top name, then Benny Goldberg, who wrote a big numbers book in Albany and whose brother was shot in his Schenectady roadhouse for having five jacks in a house deck. Martin lost patience translating the names in the dim light and turned to the front page. No story on Charlie Boy, but the Vatican was probing a new sale of indulgences in the U.S. And across the top a promotion headline screamed: "Coming Sunday in the *Times-Union*: How and Why We Piss."

Billy went straight to the men's room when he came back into Martha's and washed off Daddy Big's stink. Then he ordered a double scotch and sat down.

"So I told him about Newark," he said.

"You did? Was he pleased?"

"He wanted more, but I told him straight. I can't do this no more, Bin. I ain't cut out to be a squealer."

"Did he accept that?"

"I don't think so."

"Why don't you think so?"

"Because he says to me, All right, hotshot, you're all by yourself, and he rolls up the window."

XIV

MARTIN, DUCKING HIS HEAD, entered the city room at pristine morning. Across the freshly oiled floor, free now 'from the sea of used paper, shinbone high, that would cover it nine or ten hours hence, he walked softly, playing the intruder, hoping to catch a rat in action. The room was empty except for the clacking, which never deterred the *Times-Union*'s rats. It was their lullaby. They got to be a size, came along a pipe from out back, and ran over the heads of the working stiffs. Benson Hunt, the rewrite man, the star, moved his desk back two feet and never took off his hat again after a three-pounder lost its footing on the pipe and tumbled into his lap. Benson screamed and tipped himself over, breaking a pint of gin in his coat. Martin had no such worries, for no pipes traversed the space over his desk, and he never packed gin. But he too wore his hat to keep his scalp free of the fine rain of lead filings that filtered through the porous ceiling from the composing room overhead.

Martin paused at the sports desk to read a final edition with the story on the blackout. Some sort of sabotage, perhaps, went one theory; though the power company and the police had no culprits. The darkness blacked out, through most of Albany County, the speech by Thomas E. Dewey, aaaahhh, largely an attack on the McCall machine. Sublime. The speech was reported separately. Political monopoly in Albany. Vicious mess of corruption in the shadow of the Capitol. Vice not fit to discuss on the radio. Politics for profit. Packed grand juries. Tax assessments used to punish enemies. Vote fraud rampant. The arrest only today of several men, one for registering twenty-one times.

Martin clicked on the drop light over his own desk and prepared to write a column for the Sunday paper, his first since the kidnapping.

378

In the days since Charlie Boy had been taken, Martin stayed busy chronicling the event as he came to know it, for use when the story finally did break. He had filled his regular space in the paper with extra columns he kept in overset for just such distracted times.

Now he wrote about Billy's two-ninety-nine game and about Scotty dropping dead. Without malice toward Scotty, he discussed the hex, and Billy's response to it. He viewed Billy as a strong man, indifferent to luck, a gamester who accepted the rules and played by them, but who also played above them. He wrote of Billy's disdain of money and viewed Billy as a healthy man without need for artifice or mysticism, a serious fellow who put play in its proper place: an adjunct to breathing and eating.

By comparison, Martin wrote, I find myself an embarrassed ecclesiarch, a foolish believer in luck, fate, magicians, and divine animals. It would serve me right if I died and went to heaven and found out it was a storefront run by Hungarian palm readers. In the meantime, he concluded, I aspire to the condition of Billy Phelan, and will try to be done mollycoddling my personal spooks.

It took him half an hour to write the column. He put it in the overnight folder in a drawer of the city desk, ready for noontime scrutiny by Matt Viglucci, the city editor.

In his mailbox, he found a letter on Ten Eyck Hotel stationery, delivered by hand. Dearest Martin, I missed you at the theater. Do come and call. We have so much to talk about and I have a "gift" for you. Yours always, Melissa.

A gift, oh yes. Another ticket to lotus land? Or was there mystery lurking in those quotation marks? What son eats the body of his father in the womb of his mother? The priest, of course, devouring the host in the Holy Church. But what son is it that eats the body of his father's sin in the womb of his father's mistress? Suggested answer: the plenary self-indulger.

Paper rustled behind him as he stood amid the clackety lullaby. He turned noiselessly to see a large, relaxed rat walking across the scatter of early editions and old wire copy left by the nightside on top of the copy desk. The rat stopped at a paste pot on the desk and nibbled at the hardened outer crust. The pot moved, the rat inched forward, and then, with dexterous forefeet, it lifted the dauber an inch and pushed its own nose into the center of the pot, into the cool, fresh, soft, sweet stickiness of the paste.

Breakfast.

*　　*　　*

Martin counted eighteen steps going out of the building and waved at Rory Walsh, the early man in the sports department, schoolboy football specialist coming out of Steve White's twenty-four-hour bar. Old man Ridley stood in front of his newsroom, burning yesterday's policy slips in the gutter. The window seats of the Capitol Hotel restaurant, reserved for *T-U* folk, were empty. Martin's stomach rolled at the thought of the lobster tail special, three for fifty-five cents. He stopped at Green's stationery store and bought wrapping paper, ribbon, and a card for the present he would give Melissa, tit for tat. The horseroom upstairs over Green's was already open for business. Across the street, Keeler's tempted, as always, and his stomach rolled again. He had slept badly and left the house without waking Mary, without eating. Should he indulge? He did.

Perhaps his decision was colored by his having eaten here in 1928 with Melissa, two breakfasts and one dinner in three days, the only times they left the hotel room, fortifying their bodies with what he considered the equal of the best food on earth, reconstituting themselves for the return to their bed of second-generation concubinage.

He now ordered eggs Benedict, hard rolls and salt sticks, iced butter, marmalade, hashed browns, steaming coffee in the silver pot. A grumpy Jewish waiter in black jacket and long white apron, shuffling on flat feet, served the meal impeccably. Two thirty-five with tip. Gorgeous. He felt stylish, and buoyed by nostalgia. Ready for the lady.

She was registered in a twelfth-floor suite, and he approached it along the carpeted hallway, certain he would rouse her from sleep. He knocked loudly four times before she opened the door, each rap an explosion in the silent corridor.

"I came for my gift," he said.

"You fool. Why didn't you call? Haven't you any thought for a lady's condition at such an hour?"

"Your condition looks fetchingly normal to me. Dressed for bed."

"I must look wretched."

She left the door open and crossed the suite's sitting room, barefoot in a white calf-length negligee, and disappeared into the bedroom. Martin entered and the door swung closed. He put his hat on the coffee table and sat in the love seat. An etching of a step-gabled Dutch house hung on one wall, a Maxfield Parrish print on another wall—*Daybreak*, everybody's favorite picture fifteen years ago. The naked nymph bent over the reclining beauty waking from sleep, the mountain lake and the trees of Arcadia framing the morning confrontation, the brightening sky dappling the mountains and lighting incipient joy. Beneath it on the sideboard Martin saw his father's notebook. It lay flat, a ledger eighteen inches long with canvas and leather cover and binding, and bearing the India ink marking his father had made to identify it by date.

Here was a contrast of low and high art by master achievers: Parrish setting out to entrap popular taste, Edward Daugherty laboring with the death throes of his soul to produce a play that reflected his supreme independence of the crowd. The ledger contained the notation of the history of a masterpiece as well as the revelations of a notorious disgrace. *Daybreak*, with all its dynamic symmetry, made Martin want to throttle Parrish for foisting on the millions the notion that life was tidy, life was golden. Still, the hint of Lesbos had its place on any wall of Melissa's suite, as Edward and Martin Daugherty both knew.

Looking at the ledger, it occurred to him to take it and leave. He had often mused on burglary as a means of retrieving it. He turned his eyes from it only because Melissa re-entered the room in a baby blue satin robe and matching pompommed mules. She had brushed her silvering chestnut hair, colored the cream of her cheeks with a subtle touch of rouge, lifted her eyes from sleep with pale green eye shadow, and powdered away the gleam of her shining morning brow. Her beauty, though controlled by chemistry, was a miracle at forty-nine, given the terror of personal and professional oblivion with which she had lived most of the last decade. Even her wrinkles were now seemly, allowing her to relinquish at last that girlish beauty with which she had lived far too long, keeping her on the cover of *Photoplay*, but sabotaging all her efforts to become a serious actress. For who could believe an anguished spirit lurked behind a face as elegant and proud of itself as Melissa's? No one could, until her role as the cloistered Marina (Katrina) of *The Flaming Corsage* forced a reappraisal of her talent by the critics: Here is a totally new Melissa Spencer . . . acts as if born to the stage . . . confounds critics who said her voice would fail in talkies . . . most fully articulated female presence on the Broadway stage this year, etc.

She went straight to the telephone and ordered breakfast for two: cantaloupe, camembert, croissants, and champagne. Of course. Then she flounced into an armchair across from Martin, framed by *Daybreak* and a cut-glass vase full of white roses opening to the morning with the shining sublimity of their final blooming, only hours left in their life.

"Are you well?" she asked.

"I may be recuperating, but I'm not sure."

"That sounds dreadful, as if you're living in some awful sanitarium."

"That's not far off. I've been on a morose spiritual jag for years, and it's worse these past few days."

"Is it your father? How is he?"

"It's that, but it's not that simple. And he's quite senile but otherwise healthy. It's my son going off to the priesthood, and it's a friend just kidnapped by hoodlums."

"A kidnapping! How fascinating!"

"Oh, Christ, Melissa."

"Well, isn't it fascinating?"

"Everything isn't fascinating. Some things are serious."

"Oh, poo."

"Tell me about you. I suspect you're well. I read your notices."

"It is rather a ducky time."

"You look very fit. For anything."

"Don't be forward now, lovey. It's much too early."

"I've known you, my dear, to throw away the clock."

"Me? Not me, Martin. You must be remembering one of your casual women."

"I could've sworn it was you. That week the taboos came tumbling down. The Hampton, was it?"

"Don't be awful now. Don't. I get shivery about that. Tell me about the play. Did you like it?"

"You were quite splendid. But then you're always quite splendid. And I did find that wig becoming."

"Did I look like her to you? I did try."

"At times. But she was never quite as sensually animated as you played her."

"She must have had her moments."

"I think," said Martin, and he pictured his mother coming down the back stoop naked, walking past the small garbage pail, wearing only her sunbonnet hat and her white shoes and carrying her calico handbag, "that all she ever had was her repressions." Walking into the waiting arms of Francis Phelan? Did they ever make love after that intimacy?

"So sad," said Melissa.

"Very sad. But that's not one of your problems, I've noticed."

"Avoiding things never made any sense to me, none whatever."

"You've done it all."

"I wouldn't go as far as to say that, lovey."

"But it must be difficult to surprise you." Martin resented her use of "lovey." It sounded vaguely cockney, and insufficiently intimate for what they'd had together.

"Surprises are always welcome," said Melissa, "but they're only the interest on the principal, and it's the principal I'm most fond of."

"I have a bit of a surprise for you," Martin said.

"How delicious," said Melissa. "When do I get it?"

"Don't be forward now."

When breakfast came she insisted he sit on the sofa as they had at the Hampton, and she dropped pieces of melon into his mouth, a scene, he presumed, she had copied from a Valentino or Gilbert film. She lifted champagne to his lips, gave him wafer-thin slices of camembert and croissant, and more and more champagne. He thought he had eaten his fill at Keeler's, but satiation too has its limitations, and he accepted all that she offered.

He kissed her when both their mouths were full, shared his champagne with her. He kissed her again when their mouths were empty, stroking the breast of her robe lightly. And then he leaned away.

"What is this gift you have for me?" he said.

"Can't you guess?"

"I've imagined a thing or two."

"I hope you didn't see it," she said, rising from the sofa and crossing the room. She held up the ledger, giving him a full view of the cover with another of his father's date markings: February 1908 to April 1909.

"I didn't mean to leave it here in full view, but you caught me unawares, coming in like that. You didn't see it before, did you?"

"No, no, I didn't. You say you're returning it?"

"It's yours," she said, coming toward him with it. "I took all I needed for my memoirs."

"I thought you wanted it for the film."

"It's not necessary now. They have more than enough in the play, if they really want to do it. They don't deserve any more than that. So it's yours."

"Then I must return your money."

"Of course you must *not*. *Absolutely* you must not."

He had charged her eight hundred dollars for the ledger, an arbitrary price from nowhere, for how could he possibly have set a true dollar value on one of his father's notebooks? He'd said eight hundred for reasons no more explicable than his dream of rhomboids. An odd figure, she said. Oddness, he told her, is my profession.

They had been talking then on the roof garden of the Hampton, where she had taken a suite while she found a way to take possession of the ledger, whose contents she had, at moments, watched being written. The Albany sky was the darkest of blues, swept by millions of stars, the moon silvering the river and the rooftops of buildings on the Rensselaer side. From where Martin and Melissa sat, the Yacht Club, the night boat landing, the Dunn bridge, and much of lower Broadway were blocked from view by a tall, ghostly structure with window openings but no windows, with an unfinished, jagged, and roofless top. This was the "Spite Building," built by a bitter cleric who felt the Hampton had wronged him. And when the hotel opened its roof garden to enormous crowds, the cleric erected this uninhabitable tower of vengeance. It fronted on Beaver Street and nestled back to back with the hotel, and it rose, finally, above the glamorous rooftop cafe, blocking the view and insulting the lofty crowds with its crude bricks and its grotesque eyeless sockets, where squads of verminous pigeons roosted.

Martin and Melissa dined and danced and drank together, abandoning the Hampton roof eventually for the privacy of Melissa's suite. And when the morning came, Martin walked the few blocks to the newspaper, took the ledger from the bottom drawer of his desk, where he'd put it the day before, and brought it back to Melissa. In return he accepted the mysterious eight hundred, and also accepted two and a half more days of lascivious riches from this calculating, venal, and voluptuous incarnation of his psychic downfall.

Melissa now placed the ledger on his lap and sat beside him. He opened it to a page from 1908 and read the words written in his father's upright script, which looked like a wheat field on a windless day.

> The hero will not be a writer. Profession left vague? No. He will be Irish-American foundry owner who came up hard way in commerce, through opportunity and hard work, well educated, from family whose social pretensions were wiped out by influx of '49. Marries daughter of aristocratic Dutch-English family (any near-autobiographical data must be transformed) and secret life of failed marriage is revealed. Wife's aspirations for money and position, not for themselves but out of halcyon yearning, become clear; and these are ineradicable and dementing. Sexually dutiful but her wound in Delavan Hotel fire eradicates even that; early traumas only suggested, yet evident. Eventually she retreats, marriage begins to wither.

Martin turned the pages well forward, stopped, smiled, and read out loud: " 'Clarissa. Valley of veneration. Cave of nuances. Isosceles jungle. Lair of the snake. Grave of the stalker.' " He paused to look at her.

"I know that page by heart," she said.

" 'Grave of the stalker,' " Martin said. "He could be a silly man. I see an erected Hawkshaw. Tell me. Did you ever go round the clock with him for three days as you did with me?"

"That's a very impertinent question. Do you really think I'd tell you?"

"I thought one day you might compare notes on us. I fantasized your reply."

"And naturally you win that contest."

"I didn't think of it as a contest. More a contrast of styles."

"Let me say, and end it here, that exuberance runs in your family."

"Up exuberance," he said, and drank his champagne.

She refilled his glass and raised hers.

"And here," she said, "a toast to my gifts."

"And rare and splendid they are. Up your gifts."

"I was speaking of my gifts to you."

"Gifts, you say. Is there more than one?" And he touched the ledger.

"One more."

"Which one is that?"

"The one and only," she said, and stood up before him and opened her robe to reveal no negligee, only that indelibly remembered torso, with its somewhat graying isosceles jungle trimmed and shaved with supreme care in the contour of a heart.

"It's a bit late in the year," she said, "but will you be my valentine?"

Martin opened his belt, the front buttons of his trousers, the three buttons of the shorts he'd put on clean this morning, and presented to her the second generation stalker, full grown now, oh yes, wrapped in white tissue paper, tied with green ribbon, and tagged with a small card bearing the greeting: Happy Anniversary.

*   *   *

As he made love to Melissa he studied that portion of her neck and breast where his mother had been scarred by the point of a flaming, flying stick in the fire that killed fifteen people, most of them Irish servant girls. Melissa bore no such marks. Her mark was her face, and he kissed it lavishly, loathing both himself and her, loving her with passionate confusion, pitying her the gift of such a face, for it had been her torment. What man could ever think he alone possessed a beauty so famed, so excessive. Who could own Botticelli's Primavera?

His mother's scar had been a white oval with a scalloped circumference where the stitching had drawn her wound together. He closed his eyes as he kissed Melissa, and behind him the white scar grew by itself, a floating ovoid that became witness to his act. The scar swelled, and Martin thought of the flaming ball of tow that had marked the elder Henry James, playing in Albany Academy park, the park on which Katrina's Elk Street home fronted. The young James, then only thirteen, had been flying hot-air balloons, which rose skyward when the flaming tow balls were placed beneath them. One James balloon ascended from the park and when the flaming tow ball fell to earth, someone kicked it and arced it into the hayloft of a livery stable across Washington Avenue. The conscientious James ran to the stable to put out the fire, but his pants leg had been splashed by turpentine from soaking the tow, and it ignited like the tail of a comet. The burns led to amputation, creating a mystic philosopher from an incipient outdoorsman, and changing the future of American culture. Serendipitous movement from Edward to Melissa to Henry to Martin. Bright flaming people in a roundelay of accidental life that alters the world.

The scar grew behind Martin, its center becoming the most brilliant of all possible whites. Martin saw to it that the animal-child was seated on the chair beside the hotel bed in a typical spectator's position.

The animal-child watched the cleansing siege of the taboo, unaware the maternal flame was flirting blindly with his presence. The divine figure saw too late the advent of love's flaming embrace, and he ignited with a rasping, crackling brilliance. He tried to scream but the sound caught in his immaterial throat, and he was suddenly ashes, a spume of sooty flakes flying upward. To heaven? To hell?

Martin ejaculated with an onrush of benediction.

*   *   *

Aware that Melissa had been shorted on the significance of the moment, Martin manipulated her vigorously into a writhing, low-level ecstasy. This, she sadly admitted, was the only estate she could inhabit since her hysterectomy four years before. When her ovaries were taken from her, something else went with them. Oh, she could approach climax, almost peak. But there was a point beyond which nothing would take her. She had tried. Oh, how she had tried. Poor little one. And now she gave what could be given, took what must be taken. Her explanation sounded vaguely biblical to Martin, as if she read Saint Augustine hopefully every time the nuances flooded her cave.

Yet Martin could not escape the notion that his presence here at this altar of hand-me-down flesh was in some way therapistic, that he was expected to remantle the wings of Melissa's passion, that his time with her a decade ago had been as maleficent for her as it had for him, that she was searching in his flaming ashes for a new display of her own lost fireworks. They're not really *all* gone, are they, Daddy?

He rubbed, oh, how he rubbed. She tried, oh, how she tried.

But when she exploded it was only with exhaustion, to save her heart's wearying ventricle.

*   *   *

They dressed and rested and poured new champagne, and Melissa ate a piece of melon standing up. Martin sat on the sofa trying to understand the meaning of what he had just gone through. He was unable to grasp the significance of so many people suddenly webbed in the same small compass of events. He dismissed coincidence as a mindless explanation of anything. Was it his mind discovering patterns that had always existed but that he, in his self-absorption, had never noticed? But how? He was a fairly perceptive man. More than that, he was foresightful. Even now he had the impulse to call the newspaper, for what reason he did not know. Emory would not be in yet, and he had no reason to speak with anyone else.

He went to Melissa's bedroom and sat on the rumpled bed, still damp with drops of love and loathing, and asked the hotel operator to ring the *Times-Union*. When Madge, the crone, answered, all he could think to ask was whether anyone had left him a message. "Yes," said Madge, "some bozo named Franny Phelan called. He's in jail and wants you to bail him out."

Martin went back to the couch.

"Did you ever hear my father speak of having a gift of foresight, or anything comparable?" he asked Melissa.

"I remember he was superstitious," she said. "He used to throw salt over his shoulder when it spilled and he had a lucky pair of pants. They were green with small checks. I can still see them. He almost never wore them except when he needed money, and he swore that when he put them on, money started to trickle in. We were standing in the middle of Fourteenth Street one afternoon and he was wearing a blue suit and he didn't have enough money to buy our lunch at Luchow's. 'Nobody knows I need money,' he said. 'How could they? I don't have my green pants on.' We went to his rooms and he put the pants on, and the next day he got a bank draft in the mail for eleven hundred dollars from a producer."

Martin felt a lazy rapture come over him looking at Melissa, the golden bird of paradise. Yet, he resented the intimacy such a story reflected, and the pain it caused his mother in her grave. It was the first time he'd ever heard of clairvoyance in anyone else in the family. But Martin quickly decided his father, through telepathy with the producer, learned of the money on the way and put on the green pants as a way of turning the vision into something magical but not quite serious. It was not the same gift as his own. No.

"You're going now, aren't you?" Melissa said.

"I had a call at the paper. An old neighbor of mine's in jail and wants my help."

"I could tell by your face you were going to leave me."

"What is it? Do you want to talk? I don't have to go right this minute."

"I don't see you in ten years and you pop in and use me like a Klondike whore."

"Use you? Klondike?" Martin's fingers still ached from the recip- rocal friction.

"You drink my champagne and eat my food and exploit my body and leave me alone with my energy. You use me." She hurled a croissant at him. It missed him and bounced off a lampshade.

"You crazy bitch," he said. "You're as crazy as my mother."

He pulled her robe off her shoulders, pinning her arms to her side. Then he dragged her to the floor and undid his trousers.

x   x   x

How do I use thee? Let me count the ways. As a sacred vessel to be violated. As a thief of Holy Writ. As the transcendent trinity: Melissa- Katrina-Marina, which my father discovered and loved; which I now love. As my father immortalized them all, like the figures on the Grecian urn, so do I now perceive them in all their lambent lunacy. Seeing with my father's eyes and knowing how he was victimized by glory and self- absorption, I now forgive the man his exorbitant expectations, his in- difference, his absence. Once forgiven, it is a short walk to forgive myself for failing to penetrate such passionate complexity as his. For- giving myself, I can again begin to love myself. All this, thanks to the use of the fair Melissa.

As he pronged the dying fire, Martin sensed the presence of his parents in the room, not as flaming balls of tow this time, but as a happy couple, holding hands and watching him do diddle with Melissa for them, just as he had once done proud piddle for them in his personal pot. Clearly, they saw him as the redeemer of all their misalliances, the conqueror of incoherence, the spirit of synthesis in an anarchic family. Martin, in the consanguineous saddle, was their link with love past and future, a figure of generational communion, the father of a son en route to the priesthood, the functioning father of the senile Edward. More than that he had, here, obviously become his own father. He was Ed- ward, son of Emmett Daugherty, father of Martin Daugherty, grand- father of Peter Daugherty, and progenitor of the unchartable Daugherty line to come. Lost son of a lost father, he was now fatherhood incarnate.

Perceiving this, he spent himself in Melissa's ravine of purification.

"You are my yum-yum," she said to him, wholly flattened, the corners of her mouth yanked downward by unseen powers at the center of the earth. She stroked the fluids at the center of herself and sucked the mixture off her middle finger, evoking in Martin a ten-year-old memory of the same act performed at the Hampton. Moved profoundly both by the act and the memory, he loathed himself for his own psychic mendacity, for trying to persuade himself he had other than venereal reasons for jingling everybody's favorite triangle.

Hypocrite!

Lecher!

My boy!

XV

BILLY FOUND MARTIN in the news coop of police headquarters playing knock rummy with Ned Curtin, the *Times-Union*'s police reporter. Martin saw Billy and nodded. Then he drew a card and knocked. Ned Curtin slid a dime to him across the desk.

"How come he called you?" Billy said when Martin came out to meet him. They walked together up the stairs, Billy still smelling the pine disinfectant he always associated with this building. Billy had been here only once, five years ago, for dealing cards on Orange Street. He'd been hired by a punk who said he had Bindy's okay to run the game, but didn't, so they pulled everybody in and held them an hour here and then let the players go. But they kept the punk, who had to pay up and do a night in jail.

"I saw him Thursday down in Spanish George's," Martin said, "and I told him to call me if he needed anything."

"You didn't tell me you saw him."

"He didn't want me to. When you see him, you'll know why."

"Why'd you call me now?"

"It'll be in the paper tonight, or maybe even this afternoon, who he is and used to be. You had to know before that."

They sat down on a long, wooden bench in the empty courtroom. A white-haired man in shirtsleeves came in from the room behind the judge's bench and sniffed at them, then went out again.

"Did you ever know why he left home?" Billy asked.

"I know the gossip. He drank, then the baby died. The one fed the other."

"I was nine."

"Do you remember him well? You could at nine."

"I don't know if I remember his face from seeing it, or from the picture. There's one home in a box of snapshots, about nineteen fifteen, the year before he left. He's standing on our old stoop on Colonie Street."

"He was all done with baseball then. I can remember how he looked. He doesn't look like that any more."

With a magnifying glass, Billy had studied how his father wore his sweater, the same one he wore in the rowboat, and maybe the same cap. He studied the cut of his jaw, the shape of his eyes, and his smile, the lips open and twisted a little to the left. It was a good smile, a strong smile. But Billy's mother said it was a weak thing to leave us and drink so much. A man shouldn't be weak like that, she said. But, oh my, how he cried, she said. How we all cried.

"Here," said Martin, nudging Billy. Through an open door they saw men entering the hallway behind the courtroom. One guard in blue shirt and policeman's cap walked ahead of the prisoner, and one behind him. Billy was not prepared for this sight. It was Pete the Tramp without a hat, without the spiky mustache, without the comedy. When tramps came to the house and asked for a meal, Billy's mother always fed them, and gave them coffee with milk. Now he knew why. Billy and Martin followed the procession. The tramp dragged his feet, slouched, shuffled on fallen arches, or maybe on stumps with toes frozen and gone. Billy kept his father's dirty gray hair in sight. He did not remember hair on his father, he remembered a cap.

The white-haired man who had sniffed at them turned from the large ledger in which he was writing. Billy remembered seeing the man only last month at Foley's pit in Troy, handling fighting cocks for Patsy McCall. His name was Kelly and he was a hell of a handler.

"What's this?" Kelly said, pen in hand.

"Bail. Francis Phelan," said the first policeman.

"Ah, you're the one," Kelly said, putting down his pen and sticking out his right hand to Francis. "Congratulations. Twenty-one, was it?" And everyone laughed.

"So they say," Francis said.

Billy saw his father's smile and recognized the curve of the lips, but the teeth were brown in front, and there were no teeth at all behind them. The mouth was a dark cavity. The smile was dead.

"Somebody got bail money?" Kelly asked.

"Here," said Billy, and he weaved his way through the men. He counted out four hundred dollars and Kelly took it to the next room and put it in a box in the open safe. Billy looked at his father and received a stare of indifference.

"You a bail bondsman? I don't remember you," Kelly said, his pen poised over the receipt book.

"No," Billy said. "Family."

Kelly handed Billy a receipt, and one of the policemen gave Francis a small white envelope with his belongings. Then both guards left the corridor. Billy, Martin, and Francis stood looking at one another until Martin said, "Let's go," and led the way out the door. He stopped at the top of the stairs.

"Martin, thanks for fixing it up," Francis said.

"Not at all. I told you to call me."

"You know a lawyer who'll take me on?"

"I do. Marcus Gorman, the best in town. I already talked to him."

Francis looked at Billy and nodded his head. "You're Billy, ain't you?"

"Yeah," said Billy.

"Thanks for that dough."

"My pleasure."

Francis nodded again. "How you been?"

"Not bad," Billy said. "How about yourself?"

"Well, I ain't in jail." And Francis cackled a throaty laugh, showing his brown teeth and the cavity of his mouth, and fell into a cough that twisted his whole body.

Billy offered him a Camel.

He took it.

*   *   *

They went down the stairs and out the front door onto Eagle Street, confronting a golden October afternoon, the bright sun warming the day with Indian summer's final passion. Men were walking the street in shirtsleeves, and women's dresses still had the look of August about them. The black mood that had fallen on Billy when he first saw his father faded into a new and more hopeful coloration under a sky so full of white, woolly clouds.

The bail almost wiped out Billy's bankroll, but he still had sixty-two dollars and change. It was enough to get the old man a new outfit: shoes, suit, shirt, and tie. Make him look like an American citizen again.

When Martin told Billy about the bail, Billy had immediately said, I got it, I'll go for it. I know it's your money, Martin, but I'll get more. I don't want that money, Martin had said. Forget I ever won that bet. No, I don't forget that, Billy said. What do you do when you lose? You pay.

"I gotta get something in my stomach," Francis said. "I ain't et in two days."

"Didn't they feed you out there in the can?" Billy asked.

"Nothin'd stay down. I still ain't right."

"We can go home. I'll call Peg at the office and have her whip up a meal. She cooks good."

"No," Francis said. "No thanks, no. No."

"Then what do you want?" asked Billy.

"Garlic soup," Francis said. "You know an Italian place? They always got garlic."

"Garlic soup?"

"Lombardo's," Martin said. "First-rate place."

"I don't want no meal," said Francis. "Just garlic soup. Fixes up the stomach. A Mexican bum taught me that in Texas."

"They'll make whatever you want at Lombardo's," said Martin. "But listen, I've got appointments. I'll leave you all to solve the garlic problem."

"No, stick around," Francis said.

"I've got work to do, Fran."

"Nah, nah, nah," said Francis and he grabbed Martin's arm and started to walk with him. "Nah, nah. Stick around a while. It ain't gonna kill you to be seen with an old bum."

"Some of my best friends are bums," said Martin. "The newspaper specializes in them."

"So stick around, stick around."

Billy followed the two men as they all walked down Eagle Street, his father's slouch not so pronounced now, but his shuffle clearly the gimp's gait, left leg dragging. Billy remembered somebody in the family saying Francis was lame, very lame, when he came back to Albany in thirty-five. Whatever it was, he's still got a little of it.

They turned down Hudson Avenue and walked toward the Italian neighborhood, through the farmers' market with its half a hundred trucks, and a scattering of horses and wagons. This had been the city produce market since the days before Francis was born, when everything here was horses and wagons. Billy was maybe six or seven when he gripped his father's hand as they walked among the animals here, smelling the fresh and decaying produce, the fresh and decaying manure, a fluid stench Billy remembered now as clearly as he'd remembered the pine disinfectant. They walked past a spavined animal in its traces, chomping at the feed bag, mashing its leavings with its hind feet, and Billy looked at his father's right hand, the back of it bulging with blue veins and scars Billy did not remember. Then he saw the first two joints were gone from the first finger. Billy pictured them curving around the hand-sewn and soap-rubbed seams of a baseball when his father was instructing him in the ways of an outcurve.

"What happened to your finger?" Billy asked. They were three abreast and he was beside his father.

"What finger?"

"The one that ain't there."

"Oh, that. Some wine bum went nuts and chopped it off. Tried to cut my feet off with a cleaver, but all he got was a piece of the finger."

"Why'd he come after you?"

"He wanted my shoes. I had good-lookin' shoes on and he didn't have none."

"What'd you do to him?"

"I think he went in the river. Somebody told me that."

"When was all this?"

"Hell, I don't know. Ten, twelve years ago. Colorado, I think. Or maybe Idaho."

"You got around some."

"Yowsah. Trains go everywhere."

"Lunch is on me," Billy said.

"Okay by me, Bill."

Bill. That didn't sound right to Billy. People who didn't know him called him Bill. But that's the way it is. He don't know me at all. It then occurred to Billy that he'd known for a day and a half that his father was in town and that he'd made no effort to find him. No effort. None.

*   *   *

"I was never here," Francis said when they walked into the bar of Lombardo's restaurant. "How long's it been here?"

"Must be twenty years," Martin said. "You shouldn't stay away so long."

"Got great Italian roast beef, best in town," Billy said.

"No beef, just soup," Francis said.

They sat in a booth in the bar area, Martin seating himself first, Francis sliding in beside him. At the bar, three young men with black hair and pure white shirts were talking to the bartender. The bar mirror was spotless, and so were the white floor tiles. Only thing old man Lombardo don't have in the joint is dirt. Billy, in his gray gabardine, new last month, and a fresh silk shirt, felt clean to the skin. His father looked dirtier now than he had on the street.

Francis told the chubby waitress the way to make the soup. Boil two garlic cloves in water for five minutes. That's all? No salt, no oregano? No, nothing but the garlic, said Francis.

"You want something to drink?" the waitress asked.

"A double scotch," Billy said.

"I'll have a glass of port," said Martin.

"In that case, muscatel, large," said Francis.

Martin gave Francis the phone number of Marcus Gorman and

explained why the best trial lawyer in town might take his case: because the McCalls, up against the wall from the Dewey attack, would be looking for scapegoats, and who'd care if a drifter and runaway husband took the fall? And Gorman would take any case that needled the McCalls, because they had dumped him as their candidate for Congress after a photo of him vacationing in Europe with Legs Diamond appeared in the local papers.

"The McCall people still owe me money," Francis said. "I could pay the lawyer something. I only collected fifty of the hundred and five I got coming."

"Hundred and five," Billy said. "That ain't a bad day's work at the polls."

"I didn't work the whole day," Francis said.

"I doubt they'll pay you that," Martin said. "They'll be afraid of a setup now."

"If they don't, I'll sing to the troopers and take some of them two-bit sonsabitches to jail with me."

"So we both got our problems with the McCalls," Billy said.

"What's your problem?"

"Did you know Bindy's son, Charlie, was snatched?"

"I heard that out in jail."

"So Bindy and Patsy want me to shadow a guy they think might be mixed up in it. Spy on him, pump him, then tell them what he says."

"What's wrong with that?"

"The guy's a friend of mine."

"Yeah, Bill, but don't forget the McCalls got the power. You do a favor for a guy in power, chances are he'll do you one back. That's why I think they won't do nothin' to me after what I done for them."

"I look at it different," Billy said.

"Did anybody hit on you, or anything like that?"

"Not yet, but I'm waiting."

The waitress brought the drinks and Francis drank half of his wine in one draught. He motioned to her for another and fished in his pocket for the white envelope. He took a crisp five dollar bill from it and put it on the table.

"Not a chance," Billy said. "I told you this was on me."

"You said lunch."

"That's everything."

Francis held the fiver up. "The troopers found I had ten of these and they said, How come a bum like you has fifty bucks in new bills? They was old ones, I said. I just sent 'em out to the Chink's to get 'em washed and ironed." He laughed and showed his cavity.

"You didn't ask about my mother," Billy said.

"No, I didn't. How is she?"

"She's fine."

"Good."

"You didn't ask about my sister, either."

"No. How is *she*?"

"She's fine."

"I'm glad they're all right."

"You really don't give a shit about them, or me either, do you?"

"Keep it cool now, Billy," Martin said.

"I'm not anybody you know any more," Francis said. "It ain't personal. I always liked the family."

"That's why you left us?"

"I been leavin' home ever since I was a kid. Martin knows some of that. And I woulda been long gone even before that if only they'da let me. I wanted to go west and work on the railroad but Ma always said the railroad killed my father. He was a boss gandy dancer, and an engine knocked him fifty feet. But what the hell, he couldn'ta been payin' attention. Maybe he was gettin' deef, I don't know. You can't blame the railroad if a man backs his ass into a steam engine. But Ma did and wouldn't let me go."

"Did you hate my mother?"

"Hate her? No. I liked her fine. She was a great girl. We had good times, good years. But I was one of them guys never shoulda got married. And after I dropped the kid, I knew nobody'd ever forgive me, that it was gonna be hell from then on. So I ran."

"You dropped Gerald? I never knew that."

"No?"

"No. Whataya mean dropped?"

"You didn't know?"

"I told you I didn't."

"Somebody knew."

"Peg never knew it, either. Nobody knows it."

"Somebody knows it. Your mother knows it."

"The hell she does."

"She saw it happen."

"She saw it? She never told none of us if she did."

"Nobody?"

"Not even me and Peg, I'm telling you."

"She musta told somebody. Her brother, or her screwball sisters."

"They all talked about you and still do, but nobody ever mentioned that, and they don't keep secrets."

"That's the goddamn truth."

Francis drank the rest of his wine. When the waitress set a new glass in front of him, he immediately drank half of that and stared at the empty seat beside Billy.

"She never told," he said. "Imagine that." He glugged more wine as tears came to his eyes. "She was a great girl. She was always a great girl." Tears fell off his chin into the muscatel.

"Why don't you come home and see her?" Billy said. "Whatever you did, she forgave you for it a long time ago."

"I can't," Francis said and finished the wine. "You tell her I'll come back some day when I can do something for her. And for your sister. And you, too."

"Do what?"

"I don't know. Something. Maybe I'll come by of a Sunday and bring a turkey."

"Who the fuck wants a turkey?" Billy said.

"Yeah," said Francis. "Who does?"

"Come on home and see them, even if you don't stay. That's something you can do. Never mind the turkey."

"No, Bill, I can't do that. You don't understand that I can't do it. Not now. Not yet."

"You better do it soon. You ain't gonna live forever, the way you look."

"I'll do it one of these days. I promise you that."

"Why should I believe your promises?"

"No reason you should, I guess."

Francis shoved the empty wine glass away and pushed himself sideways out of the booth.

"I gotta get outa here. Tell her I don't want the soup. I gotta get me down to George's and get the rest of my money."

"You're goin'?" Billy said. "You're leavin'?"

"Gotta keep movin'. My bones don't know nothin' about sittin' still."

"You'll get in touch with Gorman yourself, then?" Martin said.

"I'll do that," Francis said. "Righty so."

"That bail money," Billy said. "Don't worry about it. You wanna skip, just skip and forget it. It don't mean anything to me."

"I ain't figurin' to skip," Francis said. "But okay, thanks."

"It doesn't make any sense to skip," Martin said. "You won't do any time with Gorman taking your case. Nobody wants to go to court with him. He turns them all into clowns."

"I'll remember that," Francis said. "Now I gotta move. You understand, Martin."

"I was gonna buy you some new clothes," Billy said.

"Hell, they'd just get dirtied up, the way I bounce around. These clothes ain't so bad."

When he got no response to that, he took a step toward the door and stopped. "You tell the folks I said hello and that I'm glad they're feelin' good."

"I'll pass the word," Billy said.

"Wish you'd let me pay for the drinks. I got the cash." He was halfway into another step and didn't know where to put his hands. He held them in front of his stomach.

Billy just stared at him. Martin spoke up.

"No need for that, Fran. Billy said it was his treat."

"Well, I enjoyed it," Francis said. "Be seein' ya around."

"Around," Billy said.

*   *   *

Billy and Martin sipped their drinks and said nothing.

"He thinks it's all right to fink," Billy said finally, staring at the empty seat.

"I heard what he said."

"He's nothin' like I thought he'd be."

"Who could be, Billy?"

"How could he tell me to rat on a friend?"

"He doesn't understand your situation. He knows better. When he got in trouble in the trolley strike . . . you know about that?"

"He killed a guy."

"Not too many knew, and it never got in the papers who did it. Three of us helped him look for round stones that morning. Patsy McCall, your Uncle Chick, and myself. We were twelve, fourteen, like that, and your father was seven or eight years older and on strike. But we hated the scabs as much as he did and we all had stones of our own. Any one of us might have done what he did, but your father had that ballplayer's arm. He had the fastest throw from third to first I ever saw, and I include Heine Groh. We were down on Broadway in front of the Railroad Y, standing at the back of the crowd. People collected there because they thought the strike talks were going on in the Traction Company building across the street.

"Just then the scabs and the soldiers came along with a trolley and tried to drive it straight through that crowd. It was a bad mistake. There were hundreds ready for them, women too. The women were warriors in the street during that strike. Well, the crowd trapped the trolley between two fires and it couldn't move either way, and that's when the stones flew. Everybody was throwing them, and then Francis threw his. It flew out of his fist like a bullet and caught the scab driver on the head. People turned to see who threw it, but your father was already on the run down Broadway and around the corner of Columbia toward the tracks. The soldiers fired on the crowd, and I saw two men hit. We ran then, too, nobody chasing us, and we saw Francis way off and followed him, and when he saw it was us, he waited. We all thought somebody must've seen him make the throw, so we started running again and went up to the filtration plant in North Albany, about three miles. Your grandfather, Iron Joe Farrell, was caretaker up there then, and he hid Francis in a room full of sinks and test tubes for two hours.

"We all hung around the place while Iron Joe went back up to Broadway and hitched a ride downtown to find out what was up. He learned from a cop he knew that the soldiers were looking for a young man wearing a cap. The cops didn't care about catching your father, of course. They were all with the strikers. But the Traction Company bosses forced them into a manhunt, and so we all knew your father couldn't go back to Colonie Street for a while. Chick went home and packed your father a suitcase and brought it back. Francis said he might head west to play ball somewhere, and if he got a job in a few months, he'd write and tell us.

"He cried then. We all did, over the way he had to go, especially Chick, who worshipped your father. Even Patsy cried a little bit. I remember he wiped his eyes dry with a trainman's blue handkerchief. And then your father walked across the tracks and hopped a slow freight going north to Troy, which was the wrong direction, but that's what he did. And Iron Joe said solemnly that none of us should ever say what we knew, and he told us to go home.

"On the way home, Chick said we should take a blood oath not to talk. Patsy and I said that was okay with us but we didn't know where to get the blood. Patsy wanted to steal a kid from old man Bailey's herd, but Chick said that was against the Seventh Commandment and he suggested Bid Finnerty's one-eyed cat, which everybody on Colonie Street hated as a hoodoo anyway. It took us an hour to find the cat, and then Patsy coaxed it with a fish head and brained it with a billy club so it'd lay still. Chick sliced it open and pulled out its heart and made the sign of the cross in blood on the palms of each of our hands. And I made the oath. We swear by the heart of Bid Finnerty's cat that we won't say what we know about Francis Phelan as long as we live, and that we won't wash this sacrificial blood off our hands until it's time to eat supper.

"The blood was all gone in half an hour, the way we sweated that

XVI

W HEN MARTIN REACHED THE PAPER, he found that Patsy McCall had left three messages since noontime. Martin called immediately and Patsy said he didn't want to go near the newspaper but would pick Martin up by the post office dock on Dean Street in ten minutes. His tone admitted of no other possibility for Martin.

Patsy showed up alone, driving his Packard, and when Martin got in, Patsy gunned the car northward on Quay Street and into Erie Boulevard, a little-traveled dirt road that paralleled the old Erie Canal bed, long since filled in. Patsy said nothing. The road bumped along toward the old filtration plant and led Martin to the vision of Francis running, and to echoes of long-dead voices of old North End canalers and lumber handlers. Immigrants looked out forlornly from the canal boats as they headed west, refused entrance to Albany in the cholera days.

Patsy pulled the car to the side of the road in a desolate spot near the Albany Paper Works. Along the flats in the distance Martin could see the tar-paper shacks hoboes had built. Did Francis have a reservation in one?

"They picked Berman as go-between," Patsy said.

During the morning, Morrie had sent word to Bindy through Lemon Lewis that a letter had been left for him at Nick Levine's haberdashery. "We got Charlie Boy and we want you to negotiate," it said. "If you agree to do this, go to State and Broadway at one o'clock today and buy a bag of peanuts at Coulson's. Cross the street and sit on a bench in the Plaza facing Broadway and feed the pigeons for fifteen minutes." The letter was signed "Nero" and also bore Charlie McCall's signature.

Almost simultaneously Patsy received a letter in his mailbox at the main post office on Broadway, the third letter since the kidnapping. "We want the cash pronto and we are treating your boy nice but we can end that if you don't get the cash pronto. We know all about you people and we don't care about your kind so don't be funny about this." It was also signed "Nero" and countersigned by Charlie.

"You're not surprised they picked Berman?" Martin said.

"Not a bit," said Patsy. "I always thought the son of a bitch was in it."

"But why suspect him out of everybody else?"

"It's an Albany bunch did this, I'll bet my tailbone on that and so will Bindy. They know too much about the whole scene. Berman's always been tied in with the worst of the local hoodlums—Maloy, the Curry brothers, Mickey Fink, Joe the Polack. We know them all, and they'd need Morrie because he's smarter than any of them."

"Me, Patsy. What am I doing here?"

"Morrie's playing cute. He says he really doesn't want to do this thing but he will as a favor. He wants somebody there when they deliver Charlie, a witness who'll take some of the weight off his story. He asked me to pick somebody and when I gave him four or five names, he picked yours. He thinks you're straight."

"What do I do?"

"Go with him. Do what he says and what they tell you to do. If he's their man, you're ours. And take care of Charlie when you get to him."

"When does this happen?"

"Now. Morrie's waiting for me up in the Washington Park lake house. Can you do it?"

"You'll have to tell Mary something to put her mind at ease. And clue Emory in somehow."

"Here's a couple of hundred for lunch money. And put this in your pocket, too." And Patsy handed Martin a snub-nosed thirty-eight with a fold of money.

"I wouldn't want to use a gun."

"It won't hurt to take it."

Patsy then drove north on Erie Boulevard to Erie Street and turned on it toward Broadway, past the car barns Edward Daugherty had written about. Scabs clung to the frame of a trolley as it rocketed through the gauntlet of stone throwers. Across Erie Street from the barns the old wooden Sacred Heart Church once stood, long gone now, Father Maguire on horseback with his whip, his church plagued by pigs and chickens. God be good to Charlie Boy, and all the sick and simple, and all the unhappy dead in Purgatory, and Mama and Papa.

Patsy drove up Broadway through North Albany and up Lawn Avenue to Wolfert's Roost, where the tony Irish played golf. Martin took Peter there one day and the boy fired a hole in one on a par three and thought he'd learned the secret of the game. The car sped along Northern Boulevard, through a rush of memories now for Martin, who considered that on this day, or another very soon, he might be dead. All the history in his head would disappear, the way his father's history was fading into whiteness.

Patsy drove over Northern Boulevard and into Washington Park, past the statues of Robert Burns and Moses, and up to the gingerbread yellow-brick lake house. Patsy parked and Martin got out of the car and stared at a stunning sight: a maple tree shedding its yellow leaves in a steady, floating rain. The leaves fell softly and brilliantly into a perfect yellow circle, hundreds of them constantly in the air, an act of miraculous shedding of the past while it was still golden. The tree was ancient, maybe as old as the park, or older. Martin had walked through the park with his father an age ago. Young people with sleds rolled in the snow and embraced and kissed behind bushes glittering with icy lace. Young people rode together in the summer in open carriages. They held hands and walked around the spectacular Moses fountain. Martin's father stood at the edge of these visions, watching. This is no country for old men, his father said. I prefer, said Edward Daugherty, to be with the poet, a golden bird on a golden bough, singing of what is past.

The land was a cemetery before it was a park. To prepare the park, men dug up the old bones and carted them to new cemeteries north of the city.

"Come on, let's move," Patsy said to Martin.

Martin touched the pistol in his pocket and took a final look at the yellow rain of leaves, a sunburst of golden symmetry. On a day such as this, God rescued Isaac from his father's faith.

*   *   *

Morrie Berman, looking sharp in a gray fedora and blue pinstripe suit, sat alone on a bench inside the desolate lake house, legs spread, elbows on knees, blowing smoke rings at the tile floor. He stood up and stepped on his cigarette when Patsy came through the door. Patsy shook his hand and said, "I brought our friend." Then Martin too shook Morrie's hand, enriching with a quantum leap his comprehension of duplicity.

"They just said a heavy no to the twenty," Morrie told Patsy. "I got the message just before I came up here."

"What else did they say?"

"They think you're trying to chisel them. They called you a muzzler and said they want at least seventy-five."

"I got everything here the family can scrape together," Patsy said, tapping the black leatherette suitcase he carried in his left hand. "Matt just came back from New York with the last five and now there's forty here. And that's all there is, Morrie, that's all there is. I don't even have enough left for a shave. Morrie, you know we wouldn't chisel on Charlie's life. You got to make them know that."

"I'll do my level best, Patsy."

"I know you will, Morrie. You're one in a thousand to do this for us."

Patsy handed Morrie the suitcase. "Count it, make sure."

Morrie opened the suitcase and riffled swiftly, without counting, through the wrapped tens and twenties, then closed it.

"What about their letters?"

Patsy took a white envelope from his inside pocket and handed it to Morrie.

"One more thing. How do I account for all this cash if I get stopped?"

Pat took the envelope back from Morrie and wrote on it: "To whom it may concern. Morris Berman is carrying this money on a business errand for me. To confirm this, call me collect at one of these telephones." And he wrote the numbers of his home and his camp in the Helderberg Mountains, and then signed it. Patrick Joseph McCall.

"Is there anything special I need to know?" Martin asked.

"Morrie will tell you everything," Patsy said. "Just do what needs doing."

"They didn't like it you were a newspaperman," Morrie said, "but I convinced them you were okay."

"Do we need my car?" Martin asked.

"We drive mine," said Morrie.

"You tell them we want that boy back safe," Patsy said.

Morrie smiled and Patsy embraced him.

"They'll know if I'm followed," Morrie said.

"You won't be followed."

And then the three men went out of the lake house, one behind the other. Indian file. The truculent Mohawks once walked this same patch of earth. The Mohawks were so feared that one brave could strike terror into a dozen from another tribe. When the six tribes met to talk of land on Long Island ceded to the white man in exchange for guns and wampum, the lone Mohawk delegate asked whose decision it had been to cede the land. The Long Island chief said it was his. The Mohawk then stood up from his place in the tribal circle, scalped the chief, and left the meeting, a gesture which called the validity of the land transaction into some question.

*　　　*　　　*

In 1921, when Martin walked through the park with his father, they talked of Martin's novel in progress. Martin had just returned from Europe, where he had written about the war. His articles had been published chiefly in the Albany press by Martin H. Glynn, and several of his longer pieces were printed in *The Atlantic* and *Scribner's* and the *North American Review*, which had once printed the writing of his father. Certain editors regarded Martin as a writer of notable talent and encouraged him to challenge it. Accordingly, he wrote two-thirds of a novel about reincarnation.

He traced the story of the soul of the Roman soldier who diced for Christ's cloak, and who was subsequently to live as an Alexandrian fishwife, a cooper in Constantinople, a roving gypsy queen, a French dentist, the inventor of a spring popularized by Swiss watchmakers in the late seventeenth century, a disgraced monk in Brittany, a bailiff in Chiswick, an Irish sailor in the American Fenian movement, and finally a twentieth-century Mexican trollop who marries into the high society of Watervliet.

"You have excellent language at your disposal, and a talent for the bizarre," said the elder Daugherty, "but the book is foolish and will be judged the work of a silly dilettante. My advice is to throw it away and refrain from writing until you have something to say. A novel, Martin, is not a book of jokes."

As a retort, Martin told his father of a former schoolmate, Howie McMahon, who was obsessed with the fate of the oiler in Crane's open boat. Howie taught it to his students at Albany State Teachers College, wrote of it, spoke frequently of it to Martin. My struggle, Howie said, has no more meaning than the life of the oiler with his lifeless head bobbing in the surf after such a monumental struggle to survive. The oiler lived and died to reveal to me the meaning of his life: that life has no meaning. And Howie McMahon, Martin told his father, on a Sunday morning while the family was at high mass, hanged himself from a ceiling hook in the coal bin of his cellar.

"My response to the ravings of a lunatic like your friend," said Edward Daugherty, "is that whether he knows it or not, his life has a meaning that is instructive, if only to illuminate the impenetrability of God's will. Nothing is without purpose in this world."

Martin plucked a crimson leaf from a maple tree and tore it into small pieces.

"That leaf," said the elder writer, "was created to make my point."

XVII

B Y LATE AFTERNOON on Saturday, the Albany newspaper and wire service editors decided they could no longer withhold news of the kidnapping from the world, and they told this to Patsy McCall. He said he understood but had no further comment. At seven o'clock Saturday night, sixty-three hours after Charlie had been taken, his story was told in print for the first time. Headlines seemed not to have been so fat and febrile since the Roosevelt landslide.

The nation's press sent its luminaries of the word to Albany to pursue the story: Jack Lait, Meyer Berger, James Kilgallen, and Damon Runyon among many, forcing comparisons with the 1931 killing of Legs Diamond in an Albany rooming house, the last time America had cast such a fascinated eye on the underside of Albany life.

Shortly after nine-thirty Saturday night, Billy bought one of the last of the *Times-Union* extras, an early edition of the Sunday paper, at the Union Station newsstand. The story of the kidnapping carried Martin's byline. Billy read his own name in the story. No mention was made of any intermediary having been chosen, and no member of the McCall family would speak for publication.

The confirming source for all information was the district attorney, Dick Maloney, who complained that neither he nor the police could convince the McCalls to cooperate with their investigation. Governor Herbert Lehman suggested a reward for the capture of the kidnappers but Patsy told the governor, no, this is between us and them.

Billy folded the newspaper, shoved it into his coat pocket and crossed Broadway to Becker's. The bar was busy, but he found a spot and caught Red Tom's eye. Red Tom nodded but made no move to come near him. "A beer, Tom," Billy finally said, and Red Tom nodded again, drew a beer, and placed it in front of Billy.

"Only one, Billy."

"What do you mean, only one?"

Red Tom put up his hands, palms out, and said nothing. A stranger at the bar looked Billy over, and Red Tom walked away. Billy sipped his beer and waited for enlightenment. When the stranger left the bar, Red Tom came down to Billy and whispered: "Gus don't want your business."

"Why not?"

"I don't know. What'd you do to him?"

"Nothing. I haven't saw Gus in weeks to talk to. And I don't owe him a nickel."

"Tell Billy Phelan we don't want his business is his exact words," said Red Tom. "Why not? I says to him. Because he's no good, he says. Wait a minute, I says to him, Billy is all right, he's a good friend of mine. Okay, you open up your own place and serve him. Here he don't get served, do you get my meaning? I get his meaning. I can't serve you, Billy, and I don't know why. Do you know?"

"Maybe I know," Billy said.

"We're friends, Billy, but I got to work."

"I know that. I don't blame you for anything."

"If I did own the joint, nobody'd keep you out."

Billy managed a small smile and finished his beer. "Have you seen Martin tonight?"

"Not yet. He must be on the story."

"I'll catch you later, Tommy."

And Billy went out of Becker's, feeling a door close on his life when the outside door clicked behind him. He stood looking around Broadway, which was at its Saturday night brightest, bustling with the traffic of cars and people, the usual bunch thickened by the showgoers and nightclubbers.

Not wanted in Becker's? That's like a ball game with no home plate.

Billy walked down Broadway and up the stairs into the Monte Carlo. The horse room was dark but the bird cage, the crap table, and two roulette wheels were all busy, and in the back Billy saw lights on in the card room. He stepped to the crap table, where Marty Mitchell was on the stick and Bill Shea, who ran the Monte Carlo for Bindy, was watching the play. Billy didn't know the shooter, who was trying to make a six. He made it, and then threw an eleven. He doubled his bet to forty dollars and threw a seven. "That's five passes," somebody whispered, and Billy pulled out the exchequer, sixty-two dollars, and put twenty on the come line.

"That twenty is dead," Bill Shea said, and the game stopped.

"What's the problem?" Billy said as the stickman nudged the twenty off the line and back toward Billy.

"No problem," Shea said. "Your money's no good here, Phelan."

"Since when?"

"Since now. And you're not wanted on the premises."

"Is this Bindy's orders?"

"I wouldn't know that. Now, be a good fellow and take your money and get out."

Billy put the twenty around the rest of his cash and backed away from the table under the silent eyes of the players. As he went out the door, the game resumed and the stickman called: "Seven again." Billy walked slowly down to the street.

He found the same response in three more Broadway bars, in Louie's pool room and at Nick Levine's card game. Nick, like Red Tom, apologized. No one gave Billy a reason for turning him away. In Martha's, he sat at the bar and she poured him a double scotch and then told him he'd been marked lousy.

"It was Bindy, I know that much," Billy said. "When did you hear about it?"

"This afternoon," Martha said.

"How?"

"Mulligan, the ward leader, called me. Said you might be mixed up in the kidnapping and to give you the treatment. I said, I got no argument with Billy, and he said, You don't do what I ask, your taxes go through the roof. So bottoms up, honey, and find someplace else to drink."

"That's a lie about the kidnapping. They wanted me to inform on somebody and I wouldn't. That's what it's about."

"Don't make no difference to me what it's about. Them taxes are what this place is about all of a sudden. They go through the roof, Martha goes back on the street, and Martha's too old for that."

"I'm not your problem, Martha. Don't worry."

"You hear about Louie?"

"Louie?"

"Louie Dugan. He died about two this afternoon. Cop who took him to the hospital last night came by and took a statement. I liked that crazy old man. He was mean as a goose but I liked him."

"What'd he die of?"

"Stuff he swallowed in his lungs, the cop says. Drink up, Billy. Don't make me no trouble."

"I'll catch you later, Martha."

"Not till things is straight. Then you catch me all you like."

*   *   *

Billy called Angie at the Kenmore, and while he waited for her room to ring he decided to ask her: How'd you like some fingerprints on your buns? But what he really wanted was to talk to her. Her phone never rang. The operator said she'd checked out and left no message. He went up to the Kenmore anyway and found the bar was out of bounds for him. Wally Stanton, a bartender, said the word came from Poop Powell, not Mulligan. Bindy had a whole team on the street fencing Billy out. Broadway gone, now Pearl Street.

He walked up Pearl toward Clinton Avenue and stopped in front of Moe Cohen's old jewelry store. Now the store was a meat market and Moe was meat, too; hired three punks to get himself killed, gave them five grand in diamonds and two hundred in promised cash. They shot him in the head and all it give him was a headache, and he says, Do something else, I'm dying of cancer and heart trouble, hurry, and they let him have it in the wrist and then in the shoulder and hit him with seven shots before they got one through the eye to do the trick. When they checked his pants for the two hundred, all they found was twenty-eight cents. The bum robbed us. They all went to jail, but nobody could figure out why Moe wanted to die. He didn't have cancer or heart trouble, he had something else.

My father has something else, is what Billy thought.

He thought of Moe among the sausages and turned around and headed toward South Pearl Street. Clinton Avenue would be fenced off by Bindy, too, but he probably wouldn't bother with State Street or South Pearl. That wasn't Billy's territory. Billy might even get a game on Green Street. Dealers didn't know him very well there. But the Cronins ran Green Street for Bindy and they knew Billy and they'd get the word around sooner or later. It'd be a game of recognition. Anybody know Billy Phelan? Throw the bum out. What it came down to was Billy could go anyplace they didn't recognize him, anyplace he'd never been before. Or he could leave town. Or hire some of those fellows like Moe. Or go off the Hawk Street viaduct like Georgie the Syph.

No.

All his life Billy had put himself into trouble just to get himself out of it. Independent Billy. Now, you dumb bastard, you're so independent you can't even get inside to get warm, and it's getting chilly. Night air, like watching the last games of the Albany baseball season. Up high in Hawkins Stadium and the wind starts to whizz a little and you came in early when it was warm and now you're freezing your ass only the game ain't over.

Tommy Dyke's Club Petite? No. Bob Parr's Klub Eagle? No. Packy Delaney's Parody Club? No. Big Charlie's? No. Ames O'Brien's place? No.

Billy didn't want to think about his problem in solitude. He wanted to watch something while he was thinking.

The University Club? Dopey B-girls. Club Frolics? The emcee stinks.

Hey. The Tally Ho on Hudson Avenue. Billy knew the Hawaiian dancer. She was Jewish. And the comic was Moonlight Brady. Billy went to St. Joseph's school with him. He turned off Pearl toward the Tally Ho.

Billy ordered a triple scotch and kept his hat on. The place was jammed, no elbowroom at the bar. The lights were dim while the adagio dancers did their stuff. When the lights went up Billy looked at the half-naked-lady mural among the champagne glasses and bubbles on the wall. Some singer did a medley of Irish songs, for what? It ain't Saint Patrick's Day. The shamrocks are growing on Broadway. Oh yeah. And the Hudson looks like the Shannon. Right. Betty Rubin, the Hawaiian dancer, had fattened up since Billy last saw her and since Billy likes 'em thin, he'll keep his distance and check out the toe dancer.

Billy had been chain smoking for an hour and the tip of his tongue was complaining. He wanted to punish himself for his independence. He could punish himself by going to Bindy and apologizing. Yes, you may kiss my foot. He'd already punished himself by throwing the pool match to the Doc.

Moonlight Brady came on and told a joke about Kelly, who got drunk and fell into an open grave and when he woke up he thought it was Judgment Day and that an Irishman was the first man up. He sang a song: Don't throw a brick at your father, you may live to regret it one day.

Billy's brain was speeding from the scotch, speeding and going sideways. Moonlight came out to the bar when the show ended, a chunky man with a face like a meat pie. All ears and no nose so's you'd notice and built like a fire plug. Billy bought him a drink to have someone to talk to. He would not apologize to Bindy, he decided, but what else he would do was not clear.

"I saw your story in the paper," Moonlight told him.

"What story?"

And Moonlight told him about Martin's column on the two-ninety-nine game and the hex. Billy took the paper out of his pocket and found the column and tried to read it but the light was bad.

"I bowled two-ninety-nine and two-ninety-seven back to back about six years ago," Moonlight said.

"Is that so?"

"Damndest thing. I was in Baltimore and just got red hot."

Billy smiled and bought Moonlight another drink. He was the greatest liar Billy ever knew. You wouldn't trust him if he just came out of Purgatory. He dove into Lake George one day and found two corpses. He put a rope around his chest and swam across Crooked Lake pulling three girls in a rowboat. He was sitting at a table with Texas Guinan and Billy Rose the night Rose wrote the words to "Happy Days and Lonely Nights." He gave Bix Beiderbecke's old trumpet to Clara Bow, and she was such a Bix fan she went to the men's room with Moonlight and he screwed her on the sink. He pimped once for John Barrymore in Miami and got him two broads and a dog. He took care of a stable of polo ponies for Big Bill Dwyer, the rum-runner. Billy's line on Moonlight was that some guys can't even lay in bed straight.

Morrie Berman was probably one of those guys. What if he was in on the kidnap? They took Charlie Boy's world away from him and maybe they'll even kill him. When Billy's father was gone for a year, his Uncle Chick told him he might never come back and that Billy would pretty soon forget his father and develop all sorts of substitutes, because that was how it went in life. Chick was trying to be kind to Billy with that advice. Chick wasn't as bad as the rest of them. And did Billy develop substitutes for his father? Well, he learned how to gamble. He got to know Broadway.

He wanted to see his father and ask him again to come home.

If there was a burlesque show in town he'd go to it.

He watched Betty Rubin, who was beginning to look good.

Billy hated the sons of bitches who closed the town to him, including Red Tom, you prick. Why don't you yell at them that it ain't right to do such a thing?

He would not test out any more places. He would do something else.

Tough as Clancy's nuts.

And to think, Billy, that you were afraid they'd mark you lousy if you finked.

"Oh yeah, I forgot," Moonlight Brady said. "I saw your father's name in the paper. That vote business. Funny as a ham sandwich on raisin bread."

"That's in the paper, too?"

"Same paper. They mentioned how he played ball so I knew it was him."

"Where's *your* father now, Moonlight?"

"He died ten years ago. Left me a quarter of a million he made on the stock market, every nickel he had, and I went through it in eighteen months. But it was a hell of an eighteen months. What a guy he was."

Billy laughed at that. It was one of Moonlight's wilder, more unbelievable lies, but it had what it takes, and Billy's laughter grew and grew. It took on storm proportions. He coughed and tears came to his eyes. He hit the bar with his hand to emphasize the power of the mirth that was on him, and he took out his handkerchief to wipe his eyes.

"What got him?" the barman asked.

"I did," Moonlight said, "but I don't know how." Moonlight was doing his best to keep smiling. "If the line is that funny, I oughta use it in the act," he said to Billy.

"Oh absolutely, Moonlight, absolutely," Billy said. "Use that one in the act. You gotta use that one in the act."

                        *   *   *

Billy walked down Green Street and looked at the whorehouses with their awnings, the sign. They were houses that used to be homes for Irish families like his own. Chinks on the street now, and second-hand clothing stores and the grocery where George used to write numbers upstairs. Bucket-of-blood joints and guinea pool rooms where the garlic smell makes you miscue. Bill Shea lives on Green Street, the son of a bitch. Billy brought him home one night in a cab, sick drunk from Becker's, and he forgets that and says my twenty is dead.

Billy walked into a telephone pole.

Really in the guinea section now. Billy went with a guinea for two years. Teresa. Terrific Teresa. A torch singer. "Along Came Bill," she'd sing when he showed up. She wanted to get married, too.

Angie, you bitch, where are you when I need you?

Would Billy marry Angie? "Frivolous Sal." Peculiar gal.

Angie got Billy thinking about marriage, all right, and now he thinks of Peg and George and the house they've got, and Danny. They can't fence you out of your own house. They can't fence you away from your kid.

His father fenced himself out of the house because he thought they were ready to fence *him* out.

Billy can hear a mandolin being played in a second-floor apartment and he can taste the dago red. He got drunk once on dago red with Red the Barber, dago red and mandolins, and he went out like a light and woke up the next day and lit a cigarette and was drunk all over again. So he don't drink dago red no more.

After he crossed Madison Avenue, the bum traffic picked up. He turned on Bleecker Street toward Spanish George's. It was moving toward eleven o'clock. Hello, Bill.

*　　*　　*

The stench of Spanish George's hit Billy in the face when he walked through the door, the door's glass panel covered with grating on both sides. A dozen bums and a woman were huddled around five round wooden tables, three of the bums asleep, or dead. The stench of their breath, their filth, their shitty drawers, the old puke on their coats and shirtfronts, rose up into Billy's nose like sewer gas.

George was behind the bar in his sombrero, propped against the wall on the back legs of a wooden chair. Billy ordered a scotch, and George delivered it in a shot glass. Billy tossed it off and asked for another.

"You know anybody named Francis Phelan?" he asked George.

George eyed him and touched the handle of his six gun.

"You ain't a copper. I know coppers. Who are you?"

"I'm a relative. The guy's my father."

"Whoosa guy you want?"

"Francis Phelan."

"I don't know nobody that name."

Billy ordered another scotch and took it to the only empty table in the room. The floor beneath his feet had been chewed up long ago by old horses' hooves and wagon wheels. It looked like the faces in the room, old men with splintered skin. The wagons of the old days had rolled over them, too, many times. Most of them seemed beyond middle age, though one with a trimmed mustache looked in his thirties. Yet he was a bum, no matter what he did to his mustache. His eyes were bummy and so were his clothes. He was at the table next to Billy and he stank of old sweat, like Billy's locker at the K. of C. gym. Billy was in the Waldorf one night, and an old drunk was raving on about his life. Not a bum, just an old man on a drunk, and he looked clean. He got Billy's eye and told him, Son, have B.O. and they'll never forget you.

Unforgettable stench of right now. They oughta bottle the air in this joint and sell it for stink bombs.

The man with the mustache saw Billy looking at him.

"You fuck around with me," the man said, "I'll cut your head off." The man could barely lift his glass. Billy laughed out loud and other men took notice of him. He could lick any four of them at once. But if they got him down, they'd all kick him to death. Billy saw that the men had no interest in him beyond the noise he made when he laughed.

The woman at the far table was drinking beer and sitting upright and seemed the soberest one in the room, soberer than Billy. Old bat. Fat gut and spindle legs, but her face wasn't so bad. She wore a beret off to the left and smoked a cigarette and stared out the front window, which was also covered with grating. Bums like to put their hands through windows. And their heads.

The man next to the woman lay with his face on the table. He moved an arm, and Billy noticed the coat and remembered the twill. Billy went across the room and stood beside the woman and stared down at his father. The old man's mouth was open and his lips were pushed to one side so that Billy could see part way into the black cavity that had once been the smile of smiles.

"I don't want any," the woman said.

"What?"

"Whatever it is you're gonna ask."

"Conalee Street."

"I don't want any."

"Neither do I."

"Go way and leave me alone. I don't want any."

"Is he all right?"

"Go way."

"Is he all right? I asked a polite question."

"He's all right if he ain't dead."

Billy grabbed a handful of her blouse and coat just below the neck and lifted her halfway to her feet.

"Holy Mother of God, you're as crazy as two bastards."

"Is he hurt?"

"No, he's passed out, and he'll probably be out for hours."

"How do you know that?"

"Because he drank whiskey. He had money and he drank whiskey till he fell over. He never drinks whiskey. Who the hell are you?"

"I'm a relative. Who are you?"

"I'm his wife."

"His wife?"

"You got very good hearing."

"His wife?"

"For nine years."

Billy let go of her coat and slumped into an empty chair beside her.

*   *   *

When he told his mother he'd met him he made sure Peg was in the room. They sat in the breakfast nook, just the three of them, George still working. Billy was looking out at the dog in the back yard, and he told them all that had happened and how he wouldn't come home. The response of the women bewildered Billy. His mother smiled and nodded her head. Peg's mouth was tight, the way it gets when she fights. They listened to it all. He didn't say anything about Gerald just then. Just the bail and the turkey and the money he had and the way he looked and the change Billy saw from the photograph. I'm goddamn glad you didn't bring him home, Peg said. I don't ever want to see him again. Let him stay where he is and rot for all of me. And Ma said, No, the poor man, the poor, poor man, what an awful life he's had. Think of what a life he could've had here with us and how awful it must've been for him as a tramp. But neither of them said they were sorry he didn't come home. They think of him like he was some bum down the block.

So Billy told them then about Gerald, and Peg couldn't believe it, couldn't believe Ma hadn't told us, and Ma cried because of that and because your father didn't mean it, and how he apologized to her and she accepted his apology, but she was numb then, and he took her numbness for hatred, and he went away. But she wouldn't hold an accident against a man as good as Francis was and who loved the children so and was only weak, for you can hate the weakness but not the man. Oh, we're all so weak in our own ways, and none of us want to be hated for that or killed for that. He suffered more than poor little Gerald, who never suffered at all, any more than the innocents who were slaughtered suffered the way Our Lord suffered. Your father was only a man who didn't know how to help himself and didn't know better. I kept it from you both because I didn't want you to hate him more than you did. You couldn't know how it was, because he loved Gerald the way he loved both of you, and he picked him up the way he'd picked you up a thousand times. Only this time the diaper wasn't pinned right, and that was my fault, and Gerald slipped out of it, and your father stood there with the diaper in his hand, and Gerald was already dead with a broken neck, I'm sure of that, the way his little head was. I'm sure he never suffered more than a pinprick of pain and then he went to heaven because he was baptized, and I thanked God for that in the same minute I knew he was gone. Your father knelt over him and tried to pick him up, but I said, Don't, it might be his back and we shouldn't move him, and we both knelt there looking at him and trying to see if he was breathing, and finally we both knew he wasn't, and your father fell over on the floor and cried, oh, how he cried, how that man cried. And I cried for him as well as for Gerald, because I knew he'd never get over this as long as he lived. Gerald was gone but your father would have to live with it, and so we held one another and in a minute or so I covered him with a blanket and went up the street for Doctor Lynch and told him I put him on the table to change his diaper and then he rolled off and I never knew he could move so much. He believed me and put accidental death on the record, and it surely was that, even though your father was drinking when it happened, which I know is the reason he went away. But he wasn't drunk the way he got to be in the days after that, when he never saw a sober minute. He had just come home after the car barns and a few jars at the saloon, and he wasn't no different from the way he was a thousand other nights, except what he did was different, and that made him a dead man his whole life. He's the one now that's got to forgive himself, not me, not us. I knew you'd never forgive him because you didn't understand such things and how much he loved you and Gerald and loved me in his way, and it was a funny way, I admit that, since he kept going off to play baseball. But he always came back. When he went this time I said to myself, He'll never come into this house again, and he never did, and when we moved here to North Pearl, I used to think, If he does come back he'll go to Colonie Street and never find us, but then I knew he would if he wanted to. He'd find us if he had to.

Sweet Jesus, I never thought he'd come back and haunt you both with it, and that's why I'm telling you this. Because when a good man dies, it's reason to weep, and he died that day and we wept and he went away and buried himself and he's dead now, dead and can't be resurrected. So don't hate him and don't worry him, and try to understand that not everything that happens on this earth has a reason behind it that we can find in the prayer book. Not even the priests have answers for things like this. It's a mystery we can't solve any more than we can solve the meaning of the stars. Let the man be, for the love of the sweet infant Jesus, let the man be.

*   *   *

Billy stared at the woman next to him and smiled.

"What's your name?"

"Helen."

"Do you have any money, Helen?"

"There's a few dollars left of what he had. We'll get a room with that when he wakes up."

Billy took out his money, fifty-seven dollars, and pressed it into Helen's hand.

"Now you can get a room, or get as drunk as he is if you like. Tell him Billy was here to say hello."

Billy tossed the newspaper on the table.

"And tell him he can read all about me and him both in the paper. This paper."

"Who are you?"

"I told you. I'm Billy."

"Billy. You're the boy."

"Boy, my ass. I'm a goddamn man-eating tiger."

He stood up and patted Helen on the beret.

"Good night, Helen," he said. "Have a good time."

"God bless your generosity."

"Generosity can go piss up a rainpipe," Billy said, and he started to laugh. The laugh storm again. The coughing, the tears of mirth. He moved toward Spanish George's door, laughing and telling the old bums who watched him: "Generosity can go piss up two rainpipes for all I give a good goddamn."

He halted in the doorway.

"Anybody here like to disagree with me?"

"You fuck with me," said the bum with the trimmed mustache, "I'll cut your head off."

"Now you're talkin'," Billy said. "Now you're talkin'."

XVIII

BILLY COULD GO ANYWHERE NOW, anywhere in town. He was broke. All the way broke.

He began to run, loping across a vacant lot, where a man was warming himself by a bonfire. It had grown chillier. No place for that fellow to go.

Billy could always get a buck. But where now?

He padded down Madison Avenue to Broadway, where the ramp to the Dunn bridge began. Tommy Kane's garage, where George got his car fixed. He turned up Broadway, still running, putting distance between him and the drunken dead. He wasn't even winded when he reached the Plaza and the D&H building. But he stopped running at Coulson's and went inside for a later edition of the *Times-Union*. The front page was different, but the kidnapping news was the same. He turned to Martin's column and read about himself. A gamester who accepts the rules and plays by them, but who also plays above them. Billy doesn't care about money. A healthy man without need for artifice or mysticism.

What the hell was Martin talking about? Whose rules? And what the hell was that about money? How can anybody not care about money? Who gets along without it? Martin is half crazy, a spooky bird. What is that stuff about mysticism? I still believe in God. I still go to the front.

He folded the paper and went out and crossed State Street and walked north on Broadway past Van Heusen Charles, which always reminded him of the goddamn house on Colonie Street, where they bought their junk. And Cottrell and Leonard and the mannequins in the window. Two bums broke that window one night, drunked up on zodiac juice, everybody's bar dregs, beer, whiskey, wine, that old Lumberg kept in a can and then bottled and sold to the John bums for six bucks a gallon. When the cops caught up with the bums, one of them was dead and the other was screwing the mannequin through a hole cut in its crotch.

Jimmy-Joe's shoeshine stand. Jimmy-Joe told his customers he shined Al Smith's shoes once, and Jack Dempsey's. Everybody's a sucker for big names. Bindy McCall. I kissed Bindy McCall's foot. Suckers.

Broadway was slowing down at one o'clock, all the trains in except the Montreal Limited. Traffic down to nothing, shows all let out. Bill's Magic Shop in darkness. Billy was sweating slightly and breathing heavily. Get the blood pounding and sober up. But he was still drunk as a stewbum, and reeling. Scuse me.

"Where the hell you walkin'?" said Mike the Wop coming out of Brockley's.

"Hey, Mike."

"That you, Billy?"

"Me."

"Whataya know. You got yourself in trouble, I hear."

"What do you hear?"

"That you got yourself in trouble and nobody'll take your action."

"They'll get over it."

"Didn't sound that way."

"Hey, Mike, you got a double sawbuck? I need coffee money and cab fare."

"Double sawbuck?"

"Don'tcha think I'm good for it?"

"You're a bad risk all of a sudden, Billy. You ain't got a connection. You can't even get a drink on this street."

Mike pulled out his roll and crumpled a twenty and tossed it up in the air at Billy. Billy bobbled it and the bill fell to the sidewalk. He picked it up and said nothing. Mike grunted and walked up Broadway and into Becker's. Billy walked toward Clinton Avenue, considering a western at the Grand Lunch. Martha's across the street. Martha's door opened, and Slopie Dodds came out wearing his leg. He saw Billy and crossed the street.

"Hey, man, how you makin' it?"

"I'm coastin', Slope."

"You got a little grief, I hear."

"Little bit."

"How you fixed? You need anything?"

"I need a drink."

"She don't want you over there."

"I know all about that. That ain't the only place in town."

"You ain't mixed up in that snatch, Billy. That ain't true."

"It's bullshit, Slope."

"I knew it was."

"Hey, man. You got a double sawbuck?"

"Sure, I got it. I got fifty if you need it."

"All right, twenty-five. That'll cover me." And Slopie counted it out for Billy.

"Where's your bootlegger?" Billy asked.

"Spencer Street. You want a whole bottle?"

"Yeah. Let me make a visit first and we'll go up."

"Fine with me. I'm done playin'."

They walked back toward the station and Billy went into Becker's. The bar was crowded and Red Tom looked at Billy and shook his head sadly. Oh, Billy. But Billy asked for nothing. He saw Mike the Wop at the bar and went to him. He threw the twenty, still crumpled up, onto the bar in front of Mike and said, "We're even."

"You pay your debts fast," Mike said.

"I pay guys like you fast," Billy said, and he went out. Then with Slopie he walked up to Spencer Street.

The last time Billy needed action from a bootlegger was in Prohibition. And he'd never used a nigger bootlegger before. George had been a bootlegger for about three weeks. Made rye in the kitchen in a wash tub, and Billy peddled it for eight bucks a quart and kept four. Then George got the job writing nigger numbers and gave up the hooch, and a good thing, too, because his rye was moose piss.

The bootlegger was in one of the last houses, a dim light in a first-floor flat. Quarts and pints for five and three, a good price at this hour. The bootlegger was a woolly-headed grandpa, half asleep. Probably made a fortune before it went legal, and now the bottles catch dust. He went to the kitchen to get Billy some Johnnie Walker. Billy opened the bottle and drank and passed it to Slopie.

"Take it outside," the old man said. "This ain't no saloon."

Billy and Slopie went down the stoop and stood on the sidewalk.

"Where you wanna go, Billy?"

"Go someplace and build a fire."

"A fire? You crazy?"

"Gettin' chilly. Need a little heat."

"Go over to my place if you like to warm up. I got some chairs. What the hell you want a fire for?"

"I wanna stay outside. You up for that?"

"Well, I give you a little while. Till my bones freeze over."

"It ain't that cold. Have a drink," and Billy upended the bottle.

"You in a big hurry to fall down tonight, Billy."

"I got a hollow leg, Slope."

"You gonna need it."

Slopie took a swallow and they walked toward the river, crossed the D&H tracks, and headed toward the station on a dirt path under the brightest moon Billy ever looked at. Billy picked up wood as they walked, but a bit of kindling was all he found. They walked past the sidings where Ringling Brothers unloaded every year. Billy had brought Danny down here at four in the morning two years ago and they'd seen an elephant get off the train and walk up to Broadway.

"I'm a little cold, Billy. I ain't sure I'm ready for this."

"Down by the river. There'll be some wood there."

They walked toward the bridge, toward Quay Street, and looked at the Hudson. Just like the Shannon. Billy never swam down this far but he skated on it sometimes when it wasn't all buckled, or snowed over.

"Ever skate on the river, Slope?"

"Never owned no skates."

On the riverbank, Billy found a crate somebody had dumped. He broke it up and made a pile on the flat edge of the bank. He wadded up the *Times-Union*, page by page, and stuck it between the boards. In the moonlight he saw the page with Martin's column and crumpled it. But then he uncrumpled it, folded it and put it in his inside coat pocket. He lit the papers, and then he and Slopie sat down on the flat sides of the crate and watched the fire compensate for the shortcomings of the moon.

"I hear Daddy Big kicked it," Billy said.

"What I hear."

"What a way to go."

"You did what you could, Billy. He'da been dead in the gutter on Broadway, wasn't for you."

"I didn't even like the son of a bitch."

"He was a sorry man. Never knew how to do nothin' he wanted to do. He spit in your eye and think he's doin' you a favor."

"He knew how to shoot pool."

"Shootin' pool ain't how you get where you're goin'."

"Goin'? Where you goin', Slope?"

"Goin' home outa here pretty quick and get some winks, wake up and cook a little, see my woman, play a little piano."

"That where you started out for?"

"I never started out for nowhere. Just grifted and drifted all my life till I hit this town. Good old town."

"How is it, bein' a nigger, Slope?"

"I kinda like it."

"Goddamn good thing."

"What, bein' a nigger?"

"No, that you like it."

Billy passed the bottle and they drank and kept the fire going until a prowl car came by and put its searchlight on them.

"Everything all right here, girls?" one cop asked.

"Who you talkin' to, peckerhead?" Billy said. Slopie grabbed his arm and kept him from standing up. The cops studied the scene and then moved on. The fire and the moon lighted up the night, and Billy took another drink.

✳   ✳   ✳

He woke up sick. Slopie was gone and Billy remembered him trying to talk Billy into going back to Broadway. But Billy just burned the rest of the crate to keep the fire going. He remembered watching the fire grow and then fade, remembered watching the night settle in again without heat, with even the light gone cold. The darkness enveloped him under the frigid moon, and he lay back on the grass and watched the sky and all them goddamn stars. The knowledge of what was valuable in his life eluded him, except that he valued Slopie now as much as he valued his mother, or Toddy. But Slopie was gone and Billy felt wholly alone for the first time in his life, aware that nothing and no one would save him from the coldness of the moon and the October river.

He heard whisperings on the water and thought they might be the spirits of all the poor bastards who had jumped off the bridge, calling to him to make the leap. He became afraid and listened for the voices to say something he could understand, but they remained only whisperings of words no man could understand at such a distance. They could be understood out on the water. He edged himself upward on the bank, away from the voices, and took a drink of whiskey. He was still drunk and he had a headache. He was out of focus in the world and yet he was more coherent than he had been since this whole business began. He knew precisely how it was before the kidnapping and how it was different now, and he didn't give a shit. You think Billy Phelan gives a shit about asskissers and phonies? Maybe they wanted Billy to run. Maybe they thought if he got shut out of a joint like Becker's, he'd pack his bag and hop a freight. But his old man did that, and all he got was drunk.

The fire was out, and so Billy must have slept a while. He felt an ember. Cold. Maybe he'd slept an hour.

What I learned about pool no longer applies.

What Daddy Big learned no longer applies.

He took a swig of the whiskey, looked at the bottle, still half full, and then flung it into the river.

He saw a train coming in over the Maiden Lane trestle and watched the moving lights. He stood up and saw mail trucks moving in the lights of the post office dock on Dean Street. Up on the hill, he could see lights in the Al Smith building, and street lights blazed across the river in Rensselaer. People all over town were alone in bed. So what the hell's the big deal about being alone in the dark? What's the big deal about being alone?

Billy saw the elephant going up toward Broadway; a man walking beside it, holding its ear with a long metal hook on a stick.

Billy brushed off the seat of his pants, which was damp from the earth. He went to touch the brim of his hat but he had no hat. He looked around but his hat was gone. The goddamn river spirits got it. What do they want with my hat? Well, keep it. That's all you're gonna get out of me, you dead bastards.

Billy knew he was going to puke. He kept walking and after a while he puked. Good. He wiped his mouth and his eyes with his handkerchief and straightened his tie. He brushed grass off the sleeves of his coat, then took the coat off and brushed its back and put it on again. He bent over and pulled up his silk socks.

He walked toward Broadway.

No money.

No hat.

No connection.

The street was bright and all but empty, a few lights, a few cars, two trainmen waiting for a bus in front of the station, carrying lunch pails.

The street was closed, not only to Billy.

Billy knew he'd lost something he didn't quite understand, but the onset of mystery thrilled him, just as it had when he threw the match to the Doc. It was the wonderment at how it would all turn out.

Something new going on here.

A different Broadway.

He walked into the station and went to the men's room. He washed his face and hands and combed his hair. The tie was fine. He inspected his suit, his tan glen plaid, for grass and dirt, and he shined the toes of his shoes with toilet paper. He pissed, shat, and spit and went out and bought the New York *News* and *Mirror* with his last half a buck. Forty cents left in the world. He looked at the papers and saw Charlie Boy's picture on page one of each. The news of the day is Charlie McCall. A nice kid, raised like a hothouse flower. He folded the papers and put them in his coat pocket. In the morning, he'd read Winchell and Sullivan and Dan Parker and Nick Kenny and Moon Mullins.

He would have an orange for breakfast to make his mouth feel good.

He went out of the station and climbed into a parked Yellow cab. He rode it to North Albany, to Jack Foy's Blackout on Erie Street and Broadway, and told the cabbie to wait. Jack hadn't heard the news about Billy yet and so Billy hit him for a deuce and paid the cabbie and then hoisted two cold beers to cool his throat. He knew Jack Foy all his life and liked him. When the word came down from Pop O'Rourke, Jack would not let him inside the joint.

Erie Street'd be as dead as Broadway downtown.

The word would spread and every joint in town would be dead.

Billy drank up and walked across Broadway and up through Sacred Heart Park to North Pearl Street, which was deserted, silent at four in the morning. He walked up Pearl, Joe Keefe sleeping, Pop O'Rourke sleeping, Henny Hart sleeping, Babe McClay sleeping.

He was in front of his house when he heard what he heard. First came the quiet snap, then almost simultaneously the streetlight exploded behind him like a cherry bomb, and he ran like a goddamn antelope for the porch.

He crouched behind the solid railing of the porch and listened for new shooting, but the street was already reenveloped by silence. Still crouching, he leaped for the door to the vestibule and, with key at the ready, he opened the inside door and crawled into the living room. He locked the door and peered over the radio, out a front window, then out a dining room and a kitchen window, without moving any curtains, but he saw nothing. He heard movement upstairs and went toward it.

The door to the attic stairway was ajar.

Peg was in bed, but no George. Danny was in bed.

Billy went back to the attic door and climbed the stairs. The upper door to the attic was also ajar. He opened it all the way.

"Hello," he said. Who the hell to?

He smelled dust and old cloth and mothballs. He waited for noise but heard nothing. He went in and pulled the string of the ceiling light and stood in the midst of family clutter that belonged mostly to a child. Boxing gloves and bag, fire engine and steam locomotive, a stack of games, toy animals, skis, two sleds, a collection of matchcovers, a large pile of funny books, a smaller pile of pulps—*Doc Savage*, *The Shadow*, *The Spider*. On a rack in transparent bags hung George's World War uniform, his satin-lapeled tux, a dozen old suits, and, unbagged, a blue woolen bathrobe full of moth holes. Peg's old windup Victrola sat alongside a dusty stack of records, half of which Billy had bought her, or boosted. There was the fake Christmas tree wrapped in a sheet, and the ornament boxes, and a dozen of Peg's hatboxes.

The front window was open. Two inches.

Under it Billy found a flashlight and a copy of *The Spider Strikes*, a pulp Billy remembered buying five years ago, anyway. Richard Wentworth, the polo-playing playboy, is secretly The Spider, avenger of wrong. More than just the law, more dangerous than the underworld. Hated, wanted, feared by both. Alone and desperate, he wages deadly one-man war against the supercriminal whose long-planned crime coup will snuff a thousand lives! Can The Spider prevent this slaughter of innocents?

When he put the magazine back on the floor, Billy found an empty BB package.

He put the light out and went downstairs and met Peg coming out of her bedroom, pushing her arm into her bathrobe.

"What's going on? I heard walking upstairs."

"Is that all you heard?"

"What is it?"

"Somebody shot out the street light out in front."

"Shot it out?"

Billy showed her the BB package.

"The Spider carries the most powerful air pistol there is."

"Oh," she said.

They went into the room of Daniel Quinn, and Billy snapped on the wall switch, lighting two yellow bulbs in the ceiling fixture. The boy pulled the covers off his face and looked at them. Billy held up the BB package.

"Did you shoot out the streetlight?" Peg asked.

The boy nodded.

"Why?"

"I wanted it dark so when Billy came home the police wouldn't see him. I didn't know it was you, Billy. I thought you'd have your hat on."

"The police were here tonight," Peg said. "He was very impressed."

"What'd they want?"

"I don't know. They didn't come in. They just stopped out front and shone their searchlight in the front window. We had all the lights out, because George got a call they were coming to see him."

"Him? What the hell they want with him?"

"Nobody knows."

"Were they looking for me, too?"

"Only George, from what we heard. But they never came in."

"Where is George?"

"He went out for a while." She turned her head away from her son and winked at Billy.

Billy went to Danny's bedside and poked a finger in his ear.

"Thanks for the protection, kid, but you scared the bejesus out of me. I thought I was bushwhacked."

Daniel Quinn reciprocated the remark with a smile.

"You got a hell of an aim with that pistol. That's gotta be twenty-five yards, anyway."

"I had to hit it thirty-two times before it busted."

"An eye like that, you'll make a hell of a dart shooter."

Daniel Quinn reciprocated that remark with another smile.

*   *   *

Billy went to bed after he poured himself a glass of milk. Peg told him George had gone to Troy to stay at the Hendrick Hudson Hotel under the name of Martin Dwyer and would stay there until someone called him and said it was all right to come home. Billy pulled up the covers and thought of taking a trip to Miami or New York, if this was how it was going to be. But where would the money come from? Clean out the kid's bank account? He's been saving since he was in first grade. Probably got fifty by this time. Hock George's golf clubs for train fare?

Billy had a vision of wheat pouring into a grain elevator.

He saw Angie in bed with his twins.

When Billy was a kid he had no attic, no pile of toys, no books. He didn't want books. Billy played on the street. But now Billy has a trunk in this attic with his old spikes and glove in it, and old shirts, and pictures Teresa took of him in his bathing suit out at Crystal Lake. What the hell, it's his attic.

The kid was protecting himself and his mother. George was gone and Billy wasn't home. The kid must've felt he was alone.

Billy thought of the carton of tuna fish Toddy won at a church raffle and how he took a taxi and left the tuna on Billy's stoop because Toddy never ate fish.

Billy thought of all the times he'd been suckered. In high school, it was a blonde who said she would and then didn't after it took him two days to find somebody who'd sell him cundrums. Plenty of bums stiffed him on horse bets, but then Pope McNally, a friend of Billy's all his life, welshed on a fifty-dollar phone bet and said he'd never made it. And that whole Colonie Street bunch. Presents at Christmas and your birthday, and in between you couldn't get a glass of water out of any of them. You think you know how it is with some people, but you don't know. Billy thought he knew Broadway.

He listened to the night and heard a gassy bird waking up. The light of Sunday morning was just entering the sky, turning his window from black to dark blue at the bottom. The house was silent and his brain was entering a moment of superficial peace. He began to dream of tall buildings and thousands of dice and Kayo and Moon Mullins and their Uncle Willie all up in a palm tree, a scene which had great significance for the exhausted man, a significance which, as he reached for it, faded into the region where answers never come easy.

And then Billy slept.

XIX

FREE THE CHILDREN. The phrase commanded the attention of Martin's head the way a war slogan might. Stop the fascists.

Charlie McCall was the child uppermost in his thought, but he kept receiving images of Peter as a priest in a long, black cassock, blessing the world. He'd be good at that. Free Peter. Let him bless anybody he wants to bless.

It was three o'clock Monday morning and Martin was sitting alone in Morrie's DeSoto in an empty lot on Hudson Street in Greenwich Village, Patsy's loaded pistol in his right coat pocket. Hudson Street was deserted, and in the forty minutes he'd been sitting here, only two cars had passed.

This was the finale. Perhaps.

With Morrie, he'd left Albany and driven to Red Hook and then onto the Taconic Parkway. They stopped at the second gas station on the parkway and waited half an hour by the pay phone for a call. The caller told them to go to the Harding Hotel on 54th and Broadway in Manhattan, check in, and wait for another call. They did. They listened to "The Shadow" on the radio, and dance music by Richard Himber and the orchestra, and ordered coffee and sandwiches sent up. They played blackjack for a nickel and Martin won four dollars. Jimmie Fiddler was bringing them news of Hollywood when the phone rang and Morrie was given a circuitous route to deliver the money. Change cabs here and then there, take a bus, take two more cabs, get out at this place and wait to be picked up. Morrie was gone two hours and came back with the money.

"They threw it at me," he said. "They looked at it once and saw right away it was marked."

428

Martin called Patsy, who took two hours to call back. Go to a Wall Street bank on Sunday morning and the manager will give you new, unmarked money. Martin and Morrie slept and in the morning went together to the bank. They were watched, they later learned, by New York detectives, and also by the kidnappers, whose car Morrie recognized. With the new money, Morrie set off again on a new route given in another call. He was back at noon and said they took the money and would call with directions on where to get Charlie.

Martin and Morrie ate in the room and slept some more and exhausted all card games and the radio. Martin ordered a bottle of sherry, which Morrie would not drink. Martin sipped it and grew inquisitive.

"Why did they pick you, Morrie?"

"They know my rep."

"You know them?"

"Never saw any of them before."

"What's your rep?"

"I hung around with guys like them a few years back, tough guys who died with their shoes on. And I did a little time for impersonating a Federal officer during Prohibition. I even fooled Jack Diamond with that one. Our boys had the truck half loaded with his booze when he caught on."

"What'd he do?"

"He congratulated me, with a pistol in his hand. I knew him later and he bought me a drink."

"Were you a street kid?"

"Yeah. My old man wanted me to study politics, but I always knew politics was for chumps."

"The McCalls do all right with it."

"What they do ain't politics."

"What would you call it?"

"They got a goddamn Roman empire. They own all the people, they own the churches, they even own most of the Jews in town."

"They don't own your father."

"No. What'd he tell you when you talked to him?"

"I already gave you that rundown. He said you two didn't get along, but he gets along with your sisters."

"When my mother died, they worked like slaves around the house for him. But he was never there when I was a kid. He worked two jobs and went to college nights. I had to find a way to amuse myself."

"You believe in luck, Morrie?"

"You ever know a gambler who didn't?"

"How's your luck?"

"It's runnin'."

"How's Charlie's luck?"

"He's all right."

"You saw him?"

"They told me."

"And you believe them?"

"Those fellas wouldn't lie."

To free the children it is necessary to rupture the conspiracy against them. We are all in conspiracy against the children. Fathers, mothers, teachers, priests, bankers, politicians, gods, and prophets. For Abraham of the upraised knife, prototypical fascist father, Isaac was only a means to an enhanced status as a believer. Go fuck yourself with your knife, Abe.

When Martin was eight, he watched his mother watching Brother William chastising fourth graders with a ruler. She watched it for two days from the back parlor and then opened her window and yelled into the open window of the Brothers School: If you strike any more of those children, I'm coming in after you. Brother William closed the window of his classroom and resumed his whipping.

She went out the front door and Martin followed her. She went down the stoop empty-handed and up the stoop of the school and down the corridor into the classroom opposite the Daugherty back parlor. She went directly to the Brother, yanked the ruler out of his hand, and hit him on his bald head with it. She slapped him on the ear with her left hand and slapped his right shoulder and arm with the ruler. He backed away from her, but she pursued him, and he ran. She ran after him and caught him at a door and hit him again on his bald head and drew blood. Brother William opened the chapel door and ran across the altar and escaped. Katrina Daugherty went back to the classroom and told the boys: Go home and tell your parents what happened here. The student who was being whipped when she came in stopped to thank her. Thank you, mum, he said, and half genuflected.

The last time Martin went to Hibernian Hall for Saint Patrick's Day a woman danced for an hour with her mongoloid son, who was wearing a green derby on his enormous head. When the music stopped, the boy bayed like a hound.

The call about Charlie came at midnight. Go to Hudson Street near the meat market with your friend and park in the empty lot. Your friend stays in the car. You walk to Fourteenth Street and Sixth Avenue and get a cab and go such and such a route. You should be back in maybe an hour with the property.

Martin felt the need to walk. He got out of Morrie's car and crossed the empty lot. He looked across the street at a car and saw its back window being lowered. Resting on the window as it rolled downward were the double barrels of a shotgun. Martin felt the useless weight of Patsy's pistol in his pocket, and he walked back to the DeSoto.

. At four-fifteen a taxi pulled up to the lot and stopped. When two men got out, the shotgun car screeched off in the direction of the Battery. Martin opened the back door of the DeSoto and helped Charlie Boy to climb in and sit down. Martin snapped on the interior light and saw Charlie's face was covered with insect bites. The perimeter of his mouth was dotted with a rash where adhesive tape had been. He reeked of whiskey, which Morrie said the kidnappers used to revive him from the stupor into which he had sunk.

"Are you hurt anyplace?" Martin asked him. "This is Martin Daugherty, Charlie. Are you hurt?"

"Martin. No. They treated me all right."

"He's hungry," Morrie said. "He wants a corned beef sandwich. He said he's been thinking about a corned beef sandwich for three days."

"Is my father with you, Martin?"

"He's in Albany waiting for you. Your mother, too. And Patsy. Your whole family."

"It's good to see you fellows."

"Charlie," said Martin, "the whole world's waiting for you to go home."

"They hit me on the head and then kept me tied to a bed."

"Is your head all right?"

"One of them put ice cubes on the bump. I want to call up home."

"Were they tough on you?" Morrie asked.

"They fed me and one of them even went out and got me a couple of bottles of ale. But after I'd eat, they'd tie me down again. My legs don't work right."

Martin's vision of his own life was at times hateful. Then a new fact would enter and he would see that it was not his life itself that was hateful but only his temporary vision of it. The problem rests in being freed from the omnipotence of thought, he decided. The avenue of my liberation may well lie in the overthrow of my logic. Not until Charlie Boy was kidnapped did Patsy and Bindy think of electrifying the windows of their homes. Given the benign nature of most evenings on Colonie Street, there is a logic to living with nonelectrified windows. But, of course, it is a dangerously bizarre logic.

"It's time to move," Martin said, and he put out the car light and sat alongside Charlie Boy in the back seat. Morrie took the wheel and moved the DeSoto out of darkness onto the West Side Highway. It now seemed they were all safe and that no one would die. History would continue.

"Stop at the first place that looks like it's got a telephone," said Martin, to whom the expedition now belonged.

We move north on the Henry Hudson Parkway.

When we free the children we also drown Narcissus in his pool.

✳   ✳   ✳

On the day after Charlie Boy returned home, Honey Curry was shot dead in Newark during a gun battle with police, Hubert Maloy was wounded, and ten thousand dollars of ransom money, identifiable by the serial numbers of the bills as recorded by the Wall Street bank, was found in their pockets.

When Charlie Boy was returned to Patsy McCall's cabin in the Helderberg Mountains, Morrie Berman and Martin Daugherty became instant celebrities. The press tracked them everywhere, and even Damon Runyon sought out Martin to interview him on the climactic moments on Hudson Street.

"Martin Daugherty," wrote Runyon, "climbs out of the DeSoto with the aim of stretching his legs. But he does not get very far with his stretching before he is greeted by a double-breasted hello from a sawed-off shotgun peeking out of the window of a parked car. Being respectful of double-breasted hellos of such size and shape, Martin Daugherty goes back where he comes from and ponders the curious ways kidnappers have of taking out insurance on their investments."

Eight hours after Charlie Boy's return, the Albany police arrested Morrie Berman at the ticket office in Union Station, just after he had purchased a ticket to Providence. He was taken to the McCall camp for interrogation, and, Martin later learned, dunked in Patsy's new swimming pool, which was partly filled for the occasion, until he revealed the kidnappers' names. Curry and Maloy were among the names he disclosed, along with the nicknames of four hoodlums from New Jersey and Rhode Island.

The Newark shootout proved not to be the result of Morrie's disclosures, for no amount of dunking could have forced him to reveal a fact he did not know. He thought Maloy and Curry had gone to Providence. Maloy, under interrogation on what he erroneously thought was his death bed, said his flight with Curry from Greenwich Village to Newark was his own decision. He was tired and did not want to drive all the way to Rhode Island at such an hour.

None of the kidnappers had been in Newark before, during, or after the kidnapping. None of them had any way of knowing that the hangouts of criminals in that city had been under the most intensive surveillance for several days.

*   *   *

When Martin heard of Billy's status as a pariah on Broadway, he wrote a column about it, telling the full story, including how Berman saved Billy's life in a brawl, and wondering: "Is betrayal what Billy should have done for Berman by way of saying thank you?" He argued that Billy's information on Newark, and *only* Billy's information, brought Maloy and Curry to justice and saved the McCalls ten thousand dollars. Yet even this was not a betrayal of Berman, for Berman had told Billy the truth about Newark: Maloy was not there, and had no plans to go there.

"Though I doubt he believes it," Martin wrote, "Billy knew Maloy would go to Newark at some point. He knew this intuitively, his insight as much touched with magic, or spiritual penetration of the future, as was any utterance of the biblical prophets which time has proved true. Billy Phelan is not only the true hero of this whole sordid business, he is an ontological hero as well.

"Is it the policy of the McCall brothers to reward their benefactors with punishment and ostracism? Is this how the fabled McCalls gained and kept power in this city of churches for seventeen years? Does their exalted omnipotence in this city now have a life of its own, independent of the values for which so many men have struggled so long in this country? If the McCalls are the forthright men I've always known them to be, they will recognize that what is being done to Billy Phelan is not only the grossest kind of tyranny over the individual, but also a very smelly bag of very small potatoes."

Emory Jones refused to print the column.

"If you think I'm going to get my ass into a buzz saw by taking on the McCalls over a two-bit pool hustler," he explained, "you're a certifiable lunatic."

Martin considered his alternatives.

He could resign indignantly, the way Heywood Broun had quit *The World* over the Sacco-Vanzetti business. But this was not in character for Martin, and he did like his job.

He could send the column in the mail to Patsy or Bindy, or hand-carry it to them and argue the case in person. Possible.

He could put it in the drawer and forget about it and recognize that children must free themselves. True, but no.

The condition of being a powerless Albany Irishman ate holes in his forbearance. Piss-ant martyr to the rapine culture, to the hypocritical handshakers, the priest suckups, the nigger-hating cops, the lace-curtain

Grundys and the cut-glass banker-thieves who marked his city lousy. Are you from Albany? Yes. How can you stand it? I was there once and it's the asshole of the northeast. One of the ten bottom places of the earth.

Was it possible to escape the stereotypes and be proud of being an Albany Irishman?

*   *   *

Martin awoke late one morning, hung over and late for a doctor's appointment. He dressed and rushed and when he stripped for the examination by the doctor, a stranger, he could smell the stink of his own undershirt. He yearned to apologize, to explain that he was not one of the unwashed. Sorry I stink, Doc, but I had no time to change. I got up late because I was drunk last night. Oh yes.

The quest to love yourself is also an absurd quest.

Martin called Patsy and told him he was wrong in what he was doing to Billy.

"I am like hell," said Patsy, and he hung up in Martin's ear.

*   *   *

Mary Daugherty agreed with Patsy McCall.

She sat in the Daugherty living room, reading in the evening paper the latest story on the kidnap gang. When Martin raised the issue of Billy Phelan by way of making polite conversation, she dropped the paper in her lap and looked at him through the top of her bifocals, her gaze defining him as a booster for the anti-Christ.

"The boy is evil," she said. "Only an evil person would refuse to help bring back young Charles from the clutches of demons."

"But Billy gave them the information that caught the demons," Martin said.

"He didn't know what he was doing."

"Of course he knew. He knew he was informing, which was why he refused to inform any further."

"Let him go to hell with his evil friends."

"Your tone lacks charity."

"Charity begins at home," said Mary, "and I feel first for young Charles, my own flesh and blood, and for his father and his uncles. Better men never drew breath."

Martin silently charted the difference between his wife and Melissa. Michelangelo and Hieronymus Bosch, Saint Theresa and Sally Rand. In the sweetness of her latter-day bovinity, Mary Daugherty swathed herself in immaculate conceptions and divine pleasure. And with recourse to such wonders, who has need of soiled visions? Life is clean if you keep it clean. Hire the priests to sweep up and there will be no disease. Joan of Arc and Joan Crawford. Hell hath no fury like a zealous virgin.

"What are we having for dinner?" Martin inquired.

*   *   *

Martin decided to send the column to Damon Runyon, for the recent edict from Hearst on Runyon was still fresh in his mind. Runyon was now the oriflamme of the Hearst newspapers, and yet editors across the country were cutting and shaving his column regularly. "Run Runyon uncut," came the word from The Chief when he heard what was happening.

"If you find a way to get this piece into print," Martin wrote Runyon, "I will try to find it in my heart to forgive you for those four bum tips you gave me at Saratoga in August."

And so, on a morning a week after he wrote it, Martin's defense of Billy Phelan appeared in Runyon's column in full, with a preface reminding his readers who Martin was, and suggesting that if he only gambled as well as he wrote, he would very soon make Nick the Greek look like a second-class sausage salesman.

The day it appeared in the *Times-Union*, the word went out to Broadway: Billy Phelan is all right. Don't give him any more grief.

Red Tom called Billy with the news and Billy called George Quinn at the Hendrick Hudson Hotel in Troy and told him to come home.

And Martin Daugherty bought himself six new sets of underwear.

*   *   *

Martin visited his father in the nursing home the afternoon the Runyon column appeared. His purpose was to read the old man a letter from Peter. Martin found his father sitting in a wheelchair with a retractable side table, having lunch. His hair had been combed but he needed a shave, his white whiskers sticking out of his chin like bleached grass waiting for the pure white lawnmower.

"Papa," he said, "how are you feeling?"

"Glmbvvvvv," said the old man, his mouth full of potatoes.

By his eyes, by the movement of his hands over the bread, by the controlled hoisting of the fork to his mouth, Martin perceived that the old man was clear-headed, as clear-headed as he would ever again be.

"Did I tell you I had lunch with Henry James?" the old man said, when he had swallowed the potatoes.

"No, Papa, when was that?"

"Nineteen-oh-three, I think. He and I had just published some of our work in the *North American Review*, and the editor dropped me a note saying James was coming to America and wanted to talk to me. He was interested in Elk Street. His aunt had lived there when she married Martin Van Buren's son, and he wanted news of the Coopers and the Pruyns and others. I had written about life on Elk Street and he remembered the street fondly, even though he loathed Albany. We had lunch at Delmonico's and he had turtle soup. He talked about nothing but his varicose veins. An eccentric man."

"Mary and I had a letter from Peter," Martin said.

"Peter?"

"Your grandson."

"Oh yes."

"He's gone off to become a priest."

"Has he?"

"He likes the idea of being good."

"Quite a novel pursuit."

"It is. He thinks of Saint Francis as his hero."

"Saint Francis. A noble fellow but rather seedy."

"The boy is out of my hands, at any rate. Somebody else will shape him from now on."

"I hope it's not the Christian Brothers. Your mother was very distrustful of the Christian Brothers."

"It's the Franciscans."

"Well they're grotesque but they have the advantage of not being bellicose."

"How is the food these days, Papa?"

"It's fine but I long for some duck. Your mother was always very fond of duck *à l'orange*. She could never cook it. She could never cook anything very well."

"Melissa was in town this week."

"Melissa was in town?"

"She appeared in your play."

"Which play?"

"*The Flaming Corsage*."

"Melissa appeared in *The Flaming Corsage*?"

"At Harmanus Bleecker Hall. It was quite a success. Well attended, good reviews, and quite a handsome production. I saw it, of course."

"What was Melissa's last name?"

"Spencer."

"Ah yes. Melissa Spencer. Quite a nice girl. Well rounded. She could command the attention of an entire dinner table."

"She asked for you."

"Did she?"

"She's writing her memoirs. I presume you'll figure in them somewhere."

"Will I? How so?"

"I couldn't say. I'll get a copy as soon as they're published."

"I remember her profile. She had a nose like Madame Albani. Exactly like Madame Albani. I remarked on that frequently. I was there the night Albani came to Albany and sang at the Music Hall on South Pearl Street. In 'eighty-three it was. She drew the largest crowd they ever had there. Did you know she lived in Arbor Hill for a time? She played the organ at St. Joseph's Church. She always denied she was named for Albany, but she wouldn't have used the name if she hadn't had a fondness for the city."

"Papa, you're full of stories today."

"Am I? I didn't realize."

"Would you like to hear Peter's letter?"

"Peter who?"

"Your grandson."

"Oh, by all means."

"I won't read it all, it's full of trivial detail about his trip, but at the end he says this: 'Please tell Grandpa that I already miss him and that I am going to pray every day for his good health. I look forward to the day when I will be able to lay my anointed hands on his head in priestly blessing so that he may have the benefit, in the next, of my vocation. I know that you, Papa, and Grandpa, too, have been worldly men. But for me, I am committed to the way of the Cross. "Live in the world but be no part of it," is what I have been instructed and I will try with all my heart and soul to follow that guidance. I love you and Mother and bless you all and long for the time when next we meet. Your loving son, Peter.' "

"Who wrote that?" the old man asked.

"Peter."

"Peter who?"

"Peter Daugherty."

"He's full of medieval bullshit."

"Yes, I'm afraid he is."

"It's a nice letter, however."

"The sentiment is real."

"What was his name?"

"Peter Daugherty."

"Daugherty. That's the same name as mine."

"Yes, it is. Quite a coincidence."

"The Irish always wrote good letters. If they could write."

Martin's view of his meeting with his father was this: that all sons are Isaac, all fathers are Abraham, and that all Isaacs become Abrahams if they work at it long enough.

He decided: We are only as possible as what happened to us yesterday. We all change as we move.

XX

BILLY PHELAN CAME into Becker's at early evening wearing a new hat and a double-breasted gray topcoat. The fall winds howled outside as the door swung closed behind him. He walked to the middle of the bar and stood between Footers O'Brien and Martin Daugherty.

"The magician is among us," Footers said.

"I could've done without that line, Martin," Billy said.

"Magic is magic," said Martin. "Let's call things by their rightful names."

"What're you drinking, Billy?" Red Tom asked.

"You still sellin' scotch?"

"Most days."

"A small one, with water."

"On the house," Red Tom said, setting the drink down in front of Billy.

"Times certainly do change," Billy said.

"Hey, Billy," Footers said, "there's a hustler upstairs looking for fish. Why don't you go give him a game?"

"I'm resting," Billy said. "Too much action all at once gives you the hives. Who's running the pool room now?"

"Nobody yet," Footers said. "Just the helpers Daddy had. Did you hear? They had to take up a collection to pay the undertaker. Bindy bought the coffin, but that still left a hundred and ten due. All they got was seventy-five."

"Who passed the hat?" Billy asked.

"Gus. Lemon. I scraped up a few bucks for the old bastard. Let this be a lesson to us all. He who lives by the tit shall die by the tit."

Gus Becker came out of the kitchen and saw Billy.

"So the renegade hero returns."

"The door was open."

"Give the man a drink on me, Tom," Gus said.

"I already did."

"Then give him another one."

"I don't need free booze, Gus. I got money."

"Don't hold it against us, Bill," Gus said. "When the word comes down, the word comes down. You understand."

"Sure, Gus. You got your business to think of. Your wife and kids. Your insurance policies."

"Don't be difficult, Bill. There was no other way."

"I understand that, Gus. I really understand that now."

"That a new hat, Billy?" Red Tom asked. "It looks like a new hat."

"It's a new hat. The river spirits got my old one."

"The river spirits?" Martin said.

"He's over the edge," said Footers. "You started this, Martin."

"You wouldn't want to explain that, Billy?" said Martin.

"No," Billy said.

"In that case," Martin said, "did you hear that Jake Berman raised two thousand dollars to have Marcus Gorman defend Morrie? It'll be in the paper tonight, without mentioning the fee, of course."

"I thought old Jake didn't like Morrie."

"He doesn't."

"Yeah. What star is that up there?" Billy said. "The one in the back row. That's new."

"That's Curry," Red Tom said.

"Curry? I didn't know he was in that picture. I must've looked at it five thousand times, I never saw him."

"It's him. He hung in here a lot in those days."

Curry was a gen-u-ine crazy," Footers said. "I saw him and another guy steal a billy club away from a sleeping cop one night over in the station. But the billy club wasn't enough so they took the cop's pants and left the poor sucker in the middle of the station in his long underwear."

"And Daddy's got his star, too," Billy said. "That's three in a couple of weeks."

"They go," Red Tom said.

Billy looked at the picture and thought about the three dead. They all died doing what they had to do. Billy could have died, could have jumped into the river to earn his star. But he didn't have to do that. There were other things Billy had to do. Going through the shit was one of them. If Billy had died that night, he'd have died a sucker. But the sucker got wised up and he ain't anywheres near heaven yet. They are buying you drinks now, Billy, because the word is new, but they'll remember you're not to be trusted. You're a renegade, Billy. Gus said so. You got the mark on you now.

Lemon Lewis came in the front door with red cheeks. Never looked healthier.

"Cold as a witch's tit out there," Lemon said.

"Don't talk about witches," Footers said. "The magician is here."

"What magician?"

"Don't you ever read the papers, Lemon?"

"Oh, you mean Phelan. Aaaaah. So they let you back in, eh, hotshot?"

"They just did it to make you feel good, Lemon," Billy said.

"Hey, Phelan," said Lemon, "that card game at Nick's that night of the holdup. Did you really have that ace in the hole?"

All Billy could do was chuckle.

"You'll never know, will you, Lemon?"

"You ready for another?" Red Tom asked Billy. "You got a free one coming from Gus."

"Tell him to give it to the starving Armenians. Footers, what about that guy looking for fish. You ready to back me till I figure him out? Fifty, say?"

"How does twenty-five grab you?" Footers said.

"In a pinch I'll take twenty-five," Billy said.

Billy drank his scotch and said, "Come on, Martin, maybe we'll get even yet."

And with Footers beside him, and Martin trailing with an amused smile, Billy went out into the early freeze that was just settling on Broadway and made a right turn into the warmth of the stairs to Louie's pool room, a place where even serious men sometimes go to seek the meaning of magical webs, mystical coin, golden birds, and other artifacts of the only cosmos in town.

Ironweed

This book is for four good men:
Bill Segarra, Tom Smith,
Harry Staley, and Frank Trippett.

Tall Ironweed is a member of the Sunflower Family (Asteraceae). It has a tall erect stem and bears deep purple-blue flower heads in loose terminal clusters. Its leaves are long and thin and pointed, their lower surfaces downy. Its fruit is seed-like, with a double set of purplish bristles. It flowers from August to October in damp, rich soil from New York south to Georgia, west to Louisiana, north to Missouri, Illinois and Michigan. The name refers to the toughness of the stem.

—Adapted from The Audubon Society's
Field Guide to North American Wildflowers

To course o'er better waters now hoists sail the little bark of my wit, leaving behind her a sea so cruel.

—Dante, *Purgatorio*

I

RIDING UP THE WINDING ROAD of Saint Agnes Cemetery in the back of the rattling old truck, Francis Phelan became aware that the dead, even more than the living, settled down in neighborhoods. The truck was suddenly surrounded by fields of monuments and cenotaphs of kindred design and striking size, all guarding the privileged dead. But the truck moved on and the limits of mere privilege became visible, for here now came the acres of truly prestigious death: illustrious men and women, captains of life without their diamonds, furs, carriages, and limousines, but buried in pomp and glory, vaulted in great tombs built like heavenly safe deposit boxes, or parts of the Acropolis. And ah yes, here too, inevitably, came the flowing masses, row upon row of them under simple headstones and simpler crosses. Here was the neighborhood of the Phelans.

Francis's mother twitched nervously in her grave as the truck carried him nearer to her; and Francis's father lit his pipe, smiled at his wife's discomfort, and looked out from his own bit of sod to catch a glimpse of how much his son had changed since the train accident.

Francis's father smoked roots of grass that died in the periodic droughts afflicting the cemetery. He stored the root essence in his pockets until it was brittle to the touch, then pulverized it between his fingers and packed his pipe. Francis's mother wove crosses from the dead dandelions and other deep-rooted weeds; careful to preserve their fullest length, she wove them while they were still in the green stage of death, then ate them with an insatiable revulsion.

"Look at that tomb," Francis said to his companion. "Ain't that somethin'? That's Arthur T. Grogan. I saw him around Albany when I was a kid. He owned all the electricity in town."

447

"He ain't got much of it now," Rudy said.

"Don't bet on it," Francis said. "Them kind of guys hang on to a good thing."

The advancing dust of Arthur T. Grogan, restless in its simulated Parthenon, grew luminous from Francis's memory of a vital day long gone. The truck rolled on up the hill.

FARRELL, said one roadside gravestone. KENNEDY, said another. DAUGHERTY, MCILHENNY, BRUNELLE, MCDONALD, MALONE, DWYER, and WALSH, said others. PHELAN, said two small ones.

Francis saw the pair of Phelan stones and turned his eyes elsewhere, fearful that his infant son, Gerald, might be under one of them. He had not confronted Gerald directly since the day he let the child slip out of its diaper. He would not confront him now. He avoided the Phelan headstones on the presumptive grounds that they belonged to another family entirely. And he was correct. These graves held two brawny young Phelan brothers, canalers both, and both skewered by the same whiskey bottle in 1884, dumped into the Erie Canal in front of The Black Rag Saloon in Watervliet, and then pushed under and drowned with a long stick. The brothers looked at Francis's clothes, his ragged brown twill suit jacket, black baggy pants, and filthy fireman's blue shirt, and felt a kinship with him that owed nothing to blood ties. His shoes were as worn as the brogans they both had been wearing on the last day of their lives. The brothers read also in Francis's face the familiar scars of alcoholic desolation, which both had developed in their graves. For both had been deeply drunk and vulnerable when the cutthroat Muggins killed them in tandem and took all their money: forty-eight cents. We died for pennies, the brothers said in their silent, dead-drunken way to Francis, who bounced past them in the back of the truck, staring at the emboldening white clouds that clotted the sky so richly at midmorning. From the heat of the sun Francis felt a flow of juices in his body, which he interpreted as a gift of strength from the sky.

"A little chilly," he said, "but it's gonna be a nice day."

"If it don't puke," said Rudy.

"You goddamn cuckoo bird, you don't talk about the weather that way. You got a nice day, take it. Why you wanna talk about the sky pukin' on us?"

"My mother was a full-blooded Cherokee," Rudy said.

"You're a liar. Your old lady was a Mex, that's why you got them high cheekbones. Indian I don't buy."

"She come off the reservation in Skokie, Illinois, went down to Chicago, and got a job sellin' peanuts at Wrigley Field."

"They ain't got any Indians in Illinois. I never seen one damn Indian all the time I was out there."

"They keep to themselves," Rudy said.

The truck passed the last inhabited section of the cemetery and moved toward a hill where raw earth was being loosened by five men with pickaxes and shovels. The driver parked and unhitched the tailgate, and Francis and Rudy leaped down. The two then joined the other five in loading the truck with the fresh dirt. Rudy mumbled aloud as he shoveled: "I'm workin' it out."

"What the hell you workin' out now?" Francis asked.

"The worms," Rudy said. "How many worms you get in a truck-load of dirt."

"You countin' 'em?"

"Hundred and eight so far," said Rudy.

"Dizzy bedbug," said Francis.

When the truck was fully loaded Francis and Rudy climbed atop the dirt and the driver rode them to a slope where a score of graves of the freshly dead sent up the smell of sweet putrescence, the incense of unearned mortality and interrupted dreams. The driver, who seemed inured to such odors, parked as close to the new graves as possible and Rudy and Francis then carried shovelfuls of dirt to the dead while the driver dozed in the truck. Some of the dead had been buried two or three months, and yet their coffins were still burrowing deeper into the rain-softened earth. The gravid weight of the days they had lived was now seeking its equivalent level in firstborn death, creating a rectangular hollow on the surface of each grave. Some of the coffins seemed to be on their way to middle earth. None of the graves were yet marked with headstones, but a few were decorated with an American flag on a small stick, or bunches of faded cloth flowers in clay pots. Rudy and Francis filled in one hollow, then another. Dead gladiolas, still vaguely yellow in their brown stage of death, drooped in a basket at the head of the grave of Louis (Daddy Big) Dugan, the Albany pool hustler who had died only a week or so ago from inhaling his own vomit. Daddy Big, trying futilely to memorize anew the fading memories of how he used to apply topspin and reverse English to the cue ball, recognized Franny Phelan, even though he had not seen him in twenty years.

"I wonder who's under this one," Francis said.

"Probably some Catholic," Rudy said.

"Of course it's some Catholic, you birdbrain, it's a Catholic cemetery."

"They let Protestants in sometimes," Rudy said.

"They do like hell."

"Sometimes they let Jews in too. And Indians."

Daddy Big remembered the shape of Franny's mouth from the first day he saw him playing ball for Albany at Chadwick Park. Daddy Big sat down front in the bleachers behind the third-base line and watched Franny on the hot corner, watched him climb into the bleachers after a foul pop fly that would have hit Daddy Big right in the chest if Franny hadn't stood on his own ear to make the catch. Daddy Big saw Franny smile after making it, and even though his teeth were almost gone now, Franny smiled that same familiar way as he scattered fresh dirt on Daddy Big's grave.

Your son Billy saved my life, Daddy Big told Francis. Turned me upside down and kept me from chokin' to death on the street when I got sick. I died anyway, later. But it was nice of him, and I wish I could take back some of the lousy things I said to him. And let me personally give you a piece of advice. Never inhale your own vomit.

Francis did not need Daddy Big's advice. He did not get sick from alcohol the way Daddy Big had. Francis knew how to drink. He drank all the time and he did not vomit. He drank anything that contained alcohol, anything, and he could always walk, and he could talk as well as any man alive about what was on his mind. Alcohol did put Francis to sleep, finally, but on his own terms. When he'd had enough and everybody else was passed out, he'd just put his head down and curl up like an old dog, then put his hands between his legs to protect what was left of the jewels, and he'd cork off. After a little sleep he'd wake up and go out for more drink. That's how he did it when he was drinking. Now he wasn't drinking. He hadn't had a drink for two days and he felt a little bit of all right. Strong, even. He'd stopped drinking because he'd run out of money, and that coincided with Helen not feeling all that terrific and Francis wanting to take care of her. Also he had wanted to be sober when he went to court for registering twenty-one times to vote. He went to court but not to trial. His attorney, Marcus Gorman, a wizard, found a mistake in the date on the papers that detailed the charges against Francis, and the case was thrown out. Marcus charged people five hundred dollars usually, but he only charged Francis fifty because Martin Daugherty, the newspaper columnist, one of Francis's old neighbors, asked him to go easy. Francis didn't even have the fifty when it came time to pay. He'd drunk it all up. Yet Marcus demanded it.

"But I ain't got it," Francis said.

"Then go to work and get it," said Marcus. "I get paid for what I do."

"Nobody'll put me to work," Francis said. "I'm a bum."

"I'll get you some day work up at the cemetery," Marcus said.

And he did. Marcus played bridge with the bishop and knew all the Catholic hotshots. Some hotshot ran Saint Agnes Cemetery in Menands. Francis slept in the weeds on Dongan Avenue below the bridge and woke up about seven o'clock this morning, then went up to the mission on Madison Avenue to get coffee. Helen wasn't there. She was truly gone. He didn't know where she was and nobody had seen her. They said she'd been hanging around the mission last night, but then went away. Francis had fought with her earlier over money and she just walked off someplace, who the hell knows where?

Francis had coffee and bread with the bums who'd dried out, and other bums passin' through, and the preacher there watchin' everybody and playin' grabass with their souls. Never mind my soul, was Francis's line. Just pass the coffee. Then he stood out front killin' time and pickin' his teeth with a matchbook cover. And here came Rudy.

Rudy was sober too for a change and his gray hair was combed and trimmed. His mustache was clipped and he wore white suede shoes, even though it was October, what the hell, he's just a bum, and a white shirt, and a crease in his pants. Francis, no lace in one of his shoes, hair matted and uncut, smelling his own body stink and ashamed of it for the first time in memory, felt deprived.

"You lookin' good there, bum," Francis said.

"I been in the hospital."

"What for?"

"Cancer."

"No shit. Cancer?"

"He says to me you're gonna die in six months. I says I'm gonna wine myself to death. He says it don't make any difference if you wined or dined, you're goin'. Goin' out of this world with a cancer. The stomach, it's like pits, you know what I mean? I said I'd like to make it to fifty. The doc says you'll never make it. I said all right, what's the difference?"

"Too bad, grandma. You got a jug?"

"I got a dollar."

"Jesus, we're in business," Francis said.

But then he remembered his debt to Marcus Gorman.

"Listen, bum," he said, "you wanna go to work with me and make a few bucks? We can get a couple of jugs and a flop tonight. Gonna be cold. Look at that sky."

"Work where?"

"The cemetery. Shovelin' dirt."

"The cemetery. Why not? I oughta get used to it. What're they payin'?"

"Who the hell knows?"

"I mean they payin' money, or they give you a free grave when you croak?"

"If it ain't money, forget it," Francis said. "I ain't shovelin' out my own grave."

They walked from downtown Albany to the cemetery in Menands, six miles or more. Francis felt healthy and he liked it. It's too bad he didn't feel healthy when he drank. He felt good then but not healthy, especially not in the morning, or when he woke up in the middle of the night, say. Sometimes he felt dead. His head, his throat, his stomach: he needed to get them all straight with a drink, or maybe it'd take two, because if he didn't, his brain would overheat trying to fix things and his eyes would blow out. Jeez it's tough when you need that drink and your throat's like an open sore and it's four in the morning and the wine's gone and no place open and you got no money or nobody to bum from, even if there was a place open. That's tough, pal. Tough.

Rudy and Francis walked up Broadway and when they got to Colonie Street Francis felt a pull to turn up and take a look at the house where he was born, where his goddamned brothers and sisters still lived. He'd done that in 1935 when it looked possible, when his mother finally died. And what did it get him? A kick in the ass is what it got him. Let the joint fall down and bury them all before I look at it again, was his thought. Let it rot. Let the bugs eat it.

In the cemetery, Kathryn Phelan, sensing the militance in her son's mood, grew restless at the idea that death was about to change for her. With a furtive burst of energy she wove another cross from the shallow-rooted weeds above her and quickly swallowed it, but was disappointed by the taste. Weeds appealed to Kathryn Phelan in direct ratio to the length of their roots. The longer the weed, the more revulsive the cross.

Francis and Rudy kept walking north on Broadway, Francis's right shoe flapping, its counter rubbing wickedly against his heel. He favored the foot until he found a length of twine on the sidewalk in front of Frankie Leikheim's plumbing shop. Frankie Leikheim. A little kid when Francis was a big kid and now he's got his own plumbing shop and what have you got, Francis? You got a piece of twine for a shoelace. You don't need shoelaces for walking short distances, but on the bum without them you could ruin your feet for weeks. You figured you had all the calluses anybody'd ever need for the road, but then you come across a different pair of shoes and they start you out with a brand-new set of blisters. Then they make the blisters bleed and you have to stop walking almost till they scab over so's you can get to work on another callus.

The twine didn't fit into the eyelets of the shoe. Francis untwined it from itself and threaded half its thickness through enough of the eyelets to make it lace. He pulled up his sock, barely a sock anymore, holes in the heel, the toe, the sole, gotta get new ones. He cushioned his raw spot as best he could with the sock, then tightened the new lace, gently, so the shoe wouldn't flop. And he walked on toward the cemetery.

"There's seven deadly sins," Rudy said.

"Deadly? What do you mean deadly?" Francis said.

"I mean daily," Rudy said. "Every day."

"There's only one sin as far as I'm concerned," Francis said.

"There's prejudice."

"Oh yeah. Prejudice. Yes."

"There's envy."

"Envy. Yeah, yup. That's one."

"There's lust."

"Lust, right. Always liked that one."

"Cowardice."

"Who's a coward?"

"Cowardice."

"I don't know what you mean. That word I don't know."

"Cowardice," Rudy said.

"I don't like the coward word. What're you sayin' about coward?"

"A coward. He'll cower up. You know what a coward is? He'll run."

"No, that word I don't know. Francis is no coward. He'll fight anybody. Listen, you know what I like?"

"What do you like?"

"Honesty," Francis said.

"That's another one," Rudy said.

At Shaker Road they walked up to North Pearl Street and headed north on Pearl. Where they live now. They'd painted Sacred Heart Church since he last saw it, and across the street School 20 had new tennis courts. Whole lot of houses here he never saw, new since '16. This is the block they live in. What Billy said. When Francis last walked this street it wasn't much more than a cow pasture. Old man Rooney's cows would break the fence and roam loose, dirtyin' the streets and sidewalks. You got to put a stop to this, Judge Ronan told Rooney. What is it you want me to do, Rooney asked the judge, put diapers on 'em?

They walked on to the end of North Pearl Street, where it entered Menands, and turned down to where it linked with Broadway. They walked past the place where the old Bull's Head Tavern used to be. Francis was a kid when he saw Gus Ruhlan come out of the corner in bare knuckles. The bum he was fighting stuck out a hand to shake, Gus give him a shot and that was all she wrote. Katie bar the door. Too wet to plow. Honesty. They walked past Hawkins Stadium, hell of a big place now, about where Chadwick Park was when Francis played ball. He remembered when it was a pasture. Hit a ball right and it'd roll forever, right into the weeds. Bow-Wow Buckley'd be after it and he'd find it right away, a wizard. Bow-Wow kept half a dozen spare balls in the weeds for emergencies like that. Then he'd throw the runner out at third on a sure home run and he'd brag about his fielding. Honesty. Bow-Wow is dead. Worked on an ice wagon and punched his own horse and it stomped him, was that it? Nah. That's nuts. Who'd punch a horse?

"Hey," Rudy said, "wasn't you with a woman the other night I saw you?"

"What woman?"

"I don't know. Helen. Yeah, you called her Helen."

"Helen. You can't keep track of where she is."

"What'd she do, run off with a banker?"

"She didn't run off."

"Then where is she?"

"Who knows? She comes, she goes. I don't keep tabs."

"You got a million of 'em."

"More where she came from."

"They're all crazy to meet you."

"My socks is what gets 'em."

Francis lifted his trousers to reveal his socks, one green, one blue.

"A reg'lar man about town," Rudy said.

Francis dropped his pantlegs and walked on, and Rudy said, "Hey, what the hell was all that about the man from Mars last night? Everybody was talkin' about it at the hospital. You hear about that stuff on the radio?"

"Oh yeah. They landed."

"Who?"

"The Martians."

"Where'd they land?"

"Someplace in Jersey."

"What happened?"

"They didn't like it no more'n I did."

"No joke," Rudy said. "I heard people saw them Martians comin' and ran outa town, jumped outa windows, everything like that."

"Good," Francis said. "What they oughta do. Anybody sees a Martian oughta jump out two windows."

"You don't take things serious," Rudy said. "You have a what-ayacallit, a frivolous way about you."

"A frivolous way? A frivolous way?"

"That's what I said. A frivolous way."

"What the hell's that mean? You been readin' again, you crazy kraut? I told you cuckoos like you shouldn't go around readin', callin' people frivolous."

"That ain't no insult. Frivolous is a good word. A nice word."

"Never mind words, there's the cemetery." And Francis pointed to the entrance-road gates. "I just thought of somethin'."

"What?"

"That cemetery's full of gravestones."

"Right."

"I never knew a bum yet had a gravestone."

They walked up the long entrance road from Broadway to the cemetery proper. Francis sweet-talked the woman at the gatehouse and mentioned Marcus Gorman and introduced Rudy as a good worker like himself, ready to work. She said the truck'd be along and to just wait easy. Then he and Rudy rode up in the back of the truck and got busy with the dirt.

They rested when they'd filled in all the hollows of the graves, and by then the truck driver was nowhere to be found. So they sat there and looked down the hill toward Broadway and over toward the hills of Rensselaer and Troy on the other side of the Hudson, the coke plant spewing palpable smoke from its great chimney at the far end of the Menands bridge. Francis decided this would be a fine place to be buried. The hill had a nice flow to it that carried you down the grass and out onto the river, and then across the water and up through the trees on the far shore to the top of the hills, all in one swoop. Being dead here would situate a man in place and time. It would give a man neighbors, even some of them really old folks, like those antique dead ones at the foot of the lawn: Tobias Banion, Elisha Skinner, Elsie Whipple, all crumbling under their limestone headstones from which the snows, sands, and acids of reduction were slowly removing their names. But what did the perpetuation of names matter? Ah well, there were those for whom death, like life, would always be a burden of eminence. The progeny of those growing nameless at the foot of the hill were ensured a more durable memory. Their new, and heavier, marble stones higher up on the slope had been cut doubly deep so their names would remain visible for an eternity, at least.

And then there was Arthur T. Grogan.

The Grogan Parthenon reminded Francis of something, but he could not say what. He stared at it and wondered, apart from its size, what it signified. He knew nothing of the Acropolis, and little more about Grogan except that he was a rich and powerful Albany Irishman whose name everybody used to know. Francis could not suppose that such massive marbling of old bones was a sweet conflation of ancient culture, modern coin, and self-apotheosizing. To him, the Grogan sepulcher was large enough to hold the bodies of dozens. And as this thought grazed his memory he envisioned the grave of Strawberry Bill Benson in Brooklyn. And that was it. Yes. Strawberry Bill had played left field for Toronto in ought eight when Francis played third, and when Francis hit the road in '16 after Gerald died, they bumped into each other at a crossroads near Newburgh and caught a freight south together.

Bill coughed and died a week after they reached the city, cursing his too-short life and swearing Francis to the task of following his body to the cemetery. "I don't want to go out there all by myself," Strawberry Bill said. He had no money, and so his coffin was a box of slapsided boards and a few dozen tenpenny nails, which Francis rode with to the burial plot. When the city driver and his helper left Bill's pile of wood sitting on top of some large planks and drove off, Francis stood by the box, letting Bill get used to the neighborhood. "Not a bad place, old buddy. Couple of trees over there." The sun then bloomed behind Francis, sending sunshine into an opening between two of the planks and lighting up a cavity below. The vision stunned Francis: a great empty chasm with a dozen other coffins of crude design, similar to Bill's, piled atop one another, some on their sides, one on its end. Enough earth had been dug away to accommodate thirty or forty more such crates of the dead. In a few weeks they'd all be stacked like cordwood, packaged cookies for the great maw. "You ain't got no worries now, Bill," Francis told his pal. "Plenty of company down there. You'll be lucky you get any sleep at all with them goin's on."

Francis did not want to be buried like Strawberry Bill, in a tenement grave. But he didn't want to rattle around in a marble temple the size of the public bath either.

"I wouldn't mind bein' buried right here," Francis told Rudy.

"You from around here?"

"Used to be. Born here."

"Your family here?"

"Some."

"Who's that?"

"You keep askin' questions about me, I'm gonna give you a handful of answers."

Francis recognized the hill where his family was buried, for it was just over from the sword-bearing guardian angel who stood on tiptoe atop three marble steps, guarding the grave of Toby, the dwarf who died heroically in the Delavan Hotel fire of '94. Old Ed Daugherty, the writer, bought that monument for Toby when it came out in the paper that Toby's grave had no marker. Toby's angel pointed down the hill toward Michael Phelan's grave and Francis found it with his gaze. His mother would be alongside the old man, probably with her back to him. Fishwife.

The sun that bloomed for Strawberry Bill had bloomed also on the day Michael Phelan was buried. Francis wept out of control that day, for he had been there when the train knocked Michael fifty feet in a fatal arc; and the memory tortured him. Francis was bringing him his hot lunch in the lunch pail, and when Michael saw Francis coming, he moved toward him. He safely passed the switch engine that was moving slowly on the far track, and then he turned his back, looked the way he'd just come, and walked backward, right into the path of the north-bound train whose approach noise was being blocked out by the switch engine's clatter. He flew and then fell in a broken pile, and Francis ran to him, the first at his side. Francis looked for a way to straighten the angular body but feared any move, and so he pulled off his own sweater and pillowed his father's head with it. So many people go crooked when they die.

A few of the track gang followed Michael home in the back of Johnny Cody's wagon. He lingered two weeks and then won great obituaries as the most popular track foreman, boss gandy dancer, on the New York Central line. The railroad gave all track workers on the Albany division the morning off to go to the funeral, and hundreds came to say so long to old Mike when he rode up here to live. Queen Mama ruled the house alone then, until she joined him in the grave. What I should do, Francis thought, is shovel open the grave, crawl down in there, and strangle her bones. He remembered the tears he cried when he stood alongside the open grave of his father and he realized then that one of these days there would be nobody alive to remember that he cried that morning, just as there is no proof now that anyone ever cried for Tobias or Elisha or Elsie at the foot of the hill. No trace of grief is left, abstractions taken first by the snows of reduction.

"It's okay with me if I don't have no headstone," Francis said to Rudy, "just so's I don't die alone."

"You die before me I'll send out invites," Rudy said.

Kathryn Phelan, suddenly aware her worthless son was accepting his own death, provided it arrived on a gregarious note, humphed and fumed her disapproval to her husband. But Michael Phelan was already following the line of his son's walk toward the plot beneath the box elder tree where Gerald was buried. It always amazed Michael that the living could move instinctually toward dead kin without foreknowledge of their location. Francis had never seen Gerald's grave, had not attended Gerald's funeral. His absence that day was the scandal of the resident population of Saint Agnes's. But here he was now, walking purposefully, and with a slight limp Michael had not seen before, closing the gap between father and son, between sudden death and enduring guilt. Michael signaled to his neighbors that an act of regeneration seemed to be in process, and the eyes of the dead, witnesses all to their own historical omissions, their own unbridgeable chasms in life gone, silently rooted for Francis as he walked up the slope toward the box elder. Rudy followed his pal at a respectful distance, aware that some event of moment was taking place. Hangdog, he observed.

In his grave, a cruciformed circle, Gerald watched the advent of his father and considered what action might be appropriate to their meeting. Should he absolve the man of all guilt, not for the dropping, for that was accidental, but for the abandonment of the family, for craven flight when the steadfast virtues were called for? Gerald's grave trembled with superb possibility. Denied speech in life, having died with only monosyllabic goos and gaahs in his vocabulary, Gerald possessed the gift of tongues in death. His ability to communicate and to understand was at the genius level among the dead. He could speak with any resident adult in any language, but more notable was his ability to understand the chattery squirrels and chipmunks, the silent signals of the ants and beetles, and the slithy semaphores of the slugs and worms that moved above and through his earth. He could read the waning flow of energy in the leaves and berries as they fell from the box elder above him. And because his fate had been innocence and denial, Gerald had grown a protective web which deflected all moisture, all moles, rabbits, and other burrowing creatures. His web was woven of strands of vivid silver, an enveloping hammock of intricate, near-transparent weave. His body had not only been absolved of the need to decay, but in some respects—a full head of hair, for instance—it had grown to a completeness that was both natural and miraculous. Gerald rested in his infantile sublimity, exuding a high gloss induced by early death, his skin a radiant white-gold, his nails a silvery gray, his cluster of curls and large eyes perfectly matched in gleaming ebony. Swaddled in his grave, he was beyond capture by visual or verbal artistry. He was neither beautiful nor perfect to the beholder but rather an ineffably fabulous presence whose like was not to be found anywhere in the cemetery, and it abounded with dead innocents.

Francis found the grave without a search. He stood over it and reconstructed the moment when the child was slipping through his fingers into death. He prayed for a repeal of time so that he might hang himself in the coal bin before picking up the child to change his diaper. Denied that, he prayed for his son's eternal peace in the grave. It was true the boy had not suffered at all in his short life, and he had died too quickly of a cracked neckbone to have felt pain: a sudden twist and it was over. *Gerald Michael Phelan,* his gravestone said, *born April 13, 1916, died April 26, 1916. Born on the 13th, lived 13 days. An unlucky child who was much loved.*

Tears oozed from Francis's eyes, and when one of them fell onto his shoetop, he pitched forward onto the grave, clutching the grass, remembering the diaper in his grip. It had smelled of Gerald's pungent water, and when he squeezed it with his horrified right hand, a drop of the sacred fluid fell onto his shoetop. Twenty-two years gone, and Francis could now, in panoramic memory, see, hear, and feel every detail of that day, from the time he left the carbarns after work, to his talk about baseball with Bunt Dunn in King Brady's saloon, and even to the walk home with Cap Lawlor, who said Brady's beer was getting a heavy taste to it and Brady ought to clean his pipes, and that the Taylor kid next door to the Lawlors was passing green pinworms. His memory had begun returning forgotten images when it equated Arthur T. Grogan and Strawberry Bill, but now memory was as vivid as eyesight.

"I remember everything," Francis told Gerald in the grave. "It's the first time I tried to think of those things since you died. I had four beers after work that day. It wasn't because I was drunk that I dropped you. Four beers, and I didn't finish the fourth. Left it next to the pigs'-feet jar on Brady's bar so's I could walk home with Cap Lawlor. Billy was nine then. He knew you were gone before Peggy knew. She hadn't come home from choir practice yet. Your mother said two words, 'Sweet Jesus,' and then we both crouched down to snatch you up. But we both stopped in that crouch because of the looks of you. Billy come in then and saw you. 'Why is Gerald crooked?' he says. You know, I saw Billy a week or so ago and the kid looks good. He wanted to buy me new clothes. Bailed me outa jail and even give me a wad of cash. We talked about you. He says your mother never blamed me for dropping you. Never told a soul in twenty-two years it was me let you fall. Is that some woman or isn't it? I remember the linoleum you fell on was yellow with red squares. You suppose now that I can remember this stuff out in the open, I can finally start to forget it?"

Gerald, through an act of silent will, imposed on his father the pressing obligation to perform his final acts of expiation for abandoning the family. You will not know, the child silently said, what these acts are until you have performed them all. And after you have performed them you will not understand that they were expiatory any more than you have understood all the other expiation that has kept you in such prolonged humiliation. Then, when these final acts are complete, you will stop trying to die because of me.

Francis stopped crying and tried to suck a small piece of bread out from between the last two molars in his all but toothless mouth. He made a slurping sound with his tongue, and when he did, a squirrel scratching the earth for food to store up for the winter spiraled up the box elder in sudden fright. Francis took this as a signal to conclude his visit and he turned his gaze toward the sky. A vast stand of white fleece, brutally bright, moved south to north in the eastern vault of the heavens, a rush of splendid wool to warm the day. The breeze had grown temperate and the sun was rising to the noonday pitch. Francis was no longer chilly.

"Hey bum," he called to Rudy. "Let's find that truck driver."

"Whatayou been up to?" Rudy asked. "You know somebody buried up there?"

"A little kid I used to know."

"A kid? What'd he do, die young?"

"Pretty young."

"What happened to him?"

"He fell."

"He fell where?"

"He fell on the floor."

"Hell, I fall on the floor about twice a day and I ain't dead."

"That's what you think," Francis said.

"You goddamn right it's all right."

"We gonna eat at the mission? I'm hungry."

"We could eat, why not? We're sober, so he'll let us in, the bastard.
I ate there the other night, had a bowl of soup because I was starvin'.
But god it was sour. Them dried-out bums that live there, they sit down
and eat like fuckin' pigs, and everything that's left they throw in the
pot and give it to you. Slop."

"He puts out a good meal, though."

"He does in a pig's ass."

"Wonderful."

"Pig's ass. And he won't feed you till you listen to him preach. I
watch the old bums sittin' there and I wonder about them. What are
you all doin', sittin' through his bullshit? But they's all tired and old,
they's all drunks. They don't believe in nothin'. They's just hungry."

"I believe in somethin'," Rudy said. "I'm a Catholic."

"Well so am I. What the hell has that got to do with it?"

The bus rolled south on Broadway following the old trolley tracks,
down through Menands and into North Albany, past Simmons Machine, the Albany Felt Mill, the Bond Bakery, the Eastern Tablet Company, the Albany Paper Works. And then the bus stopped at North
Third Street to pick up a passenger and Francis looked out the window
at the old neighborhood he could not avoid seeing. He saw where North
Street began and then sloped down toward the canal bed, the lumber
district, the flats, the river. Brady's saloon was still on the corner. Was
Brady alive? Pretty good pitcher. Played ball for Boston in 1912, same
year Francis was with Washington. And when the King quit the game
he opened the saloon. Two big-leaguers from Albany and they both
wind up on the same street. Nick's delicatessen, new to Francis, was
next to Brady's, and in front of it children in false faces—a clown, a
spook, a monster—were playing hopscotch. One child hopped in and
out of chalked squares, and Francis remembered it was Halloween,
when spooks made house calls and the dead walked abroad.

"I used to live down at the foot of that street," Francis told Rudy,
and then wondered why he'd bothered. He had no desire to tell Rudy
anything intimate about his life. Yet working next to the simpleton all
day, throwing dirt on dead people in erratic rhythm with him, had
generated a bond that Francis found strange. Rudy, a friend for about
two weeks, now seemed to Francis a fellow traveler on a journey to a
nameless destination in another country. He was simple, hopeless and
lost, as lost as Francis himself, though somewhat younger, dying of
cancer, afloat in ignorance, weighted with stupidity, inane, sheeplike,
and given to fits of weeping over his lostness; and yet there was something in him that buoyed Francis's spirit. They were both questing for

the behavior that was proper to their station and their unutterable dreams. They both knew intimately the etiquette, the taboos, the protocol of bums. By their talk to each other they understood that they shared a belief in the brotherhood of the desolate; yet in the scars of their eyes they confirmed that no such fraternity had ever existed, that the only brotherhood they belonged to was the one that asked that enduring question: How do I get through the next twenty minutes? They feared drys, cops, jailers, bosses, moralists, crazies, truth-tellers, and one another. They loved storytellers, liars, whores, fighters, singers, collie dogs that wagged their tails, and generous bandits. Rudy, thought Francis: he's just a bum, but who ain't?

"You live there a long time?" Rudy asked.

"Eighteen years," Francis said. "The old lock was just down from my house."

"What kind of lock?"

"On the Erie Canal, you goddamn dimwit. I could throw a stone from my stoop twenty feet over the other side of the canal."

"I never saw the canal, but I seen the river."

"The river was a little ways further over. Still is. The lumber district's gone and all that's left is the flats where they filled the canal in. Jungle town been built up on 'em right down there. I stayed there one night last week with an old bo, a pal of mine. Tracks run right past it, same tracks I went west on out to Dayton to play ball. I hit .387 that year."

"What year was that?"

"'Oh-one."

"I was five years old," Rudy said.

"How old are you now, about eight?"

They passed the old carbarns at Erie Street, all full of buses. Buildings a different color, and more of 'em, but it looks a lot like it looked in '16. The trolley full of scabs and soldiers left this barn that day in '01 and rocketed arrogantly down Broadway, the street supine and yielding all the way to downtown. But then at Columbia and Broadway the street changed its pose: it became volatile with the rage of strikers and their women, who trapped the car at that corner between two blazing bedsheets which Francis helped to light on the overhead electric wire. Soldiers on horses guarded the trolley; troops with rifles rode on it. But every scabby-souled one of them was trapped between pillars of fire when Francis pulled back, wound up his educated right arm, and let fly that smooth round stone the weight of a baseball, and brained the scab working as the trolley conductor. The troops saw more stones coming and fired back at the mob, hitting two men who fell in fatal slumps; but not Francis, who ran down to the railroad tracks and then north along them till his lungs blew out. He pitched forward into a ditch and waited about nine years to see if they were on his tail, and they weren't, but his brother Chick and his buddies Patsy McCall and Martin Daugherty were; and when the three of them reached his ditch they all ran north, up past the lumberyards in the district, and found refuge with Iron Joe Farrell, Francis's father-in-law, who bossed the filtration plant that made Hudson River water drinkable for Albany folk. And after a while, when he knew for sure he couldn't stay around Albany because the scab was surely dead, Francis hopped a train going north, for he couldn't get a westbound without going back down into that wild city. But it was all right. He went north and then he walked awhile and found his way to some westbound tracks, and went west on them, all the way west to Dayton, O-hi-o.

That scab was the first man Francis Phelan ever killed. His name was Harold Allen and he was a single man from Worcester, Massachusetts, a member of the IOOF, of Scotch-Irish stock, twenty-nine years old, two years of college, veteran of the Spanish-American War who had seen no combat, an itinerant house painter who found work in Albany as a strikebreaker and who was now sitting across the aisle of the bus from Francis, dressed in a long black coat and a motorman's cap.

Why did you kill me? was the question Harold Allen's eyes put to Francis.

"Didn't mean to kill you," Francis said.

Was that why you threw that stone the size of a potato and broke open my skull? My brains flowed out and I died.

"You deserved what you got. Scabs get what they ask for. I was right in what I did."

Then you feel no remorse at all.

"You bastards takin' our jobs, what kind of man is that, keeps a man from feedin' his family?"

Odd logic coming from a man who abandoned his own family not only that summer but every spring and summer thereafter, when baseball season started. And didn't you finally abandon them permanently in 1916? The way I understand it, you haven't even been home for a visit in twenty-two years.

"There are reasons. That stone. The soldiers would've shot me. And I had to play ball—it's what I did. Then I dropped my baby son and he died and I couldn't face that."

A coward, he'll run.

"Francis is no coward. He had his reasons and they were goddamn good ones."

You have no serious arguments to justify what you did.

"I got arguments," Francis yelled, "I got arguments."

"Whatayou got arguments about?" Rudy asked.

"Down there," Francis said, pointing toward the tracks beyond the carbarns, "I was in this boxcar and didn't know where I was goin' except north, but it seemed I was safe. It wasn't movin' very fast or else I couldn't of got into it. I'm lookin' out, and up there ahead I see this young fella runnin' like hell, runnin' like I'd just run, and I see two guys chasin' him, and one of them two doin' the chasin' looks like a cop and he's shootin'. Stoppin' and shootin'. But this fella keeps runnin', and we're gettin' to him when I see another one right behind him. They're both headin' for the train, and I peek around the door, careful so's I don't got me shot, and I see the first one grab hold of a ladder on one of the cars, and he's up, he's up, and they're still shootin', and then damn if we don't cross that road just about the time the second fella gets to the car I'm ridin' in, and he yells up to me: Help me, help me, and they're shootin' like sonsabitches at him and sure as hell I help him, they're gonna shoot at me too."

"What'd you do?" Rudy asked.

"I slid on my belly over to the edge of the car, givin' them shooters a thin target, and I give that fella a hand, and he's grabbin' at it, almost grabbin' it, and I'm almost gettin' a full purchase on him, and then whango bango, they shoot him right in the back and that's all she wrote. Katie bar the door. Too wet to plow. He's all done, that fella, and I roll around back in the car and don't find out till we get to Whitehall, when the other fella drops into my boxcar, that they both was prisoners and they was on their way to the county jail in Albany. But then there was this big trolley strike with shootin' and stuff because some guy threw a stone and killed a scab. And that got this mob of people in the street all mixed up and crazy and they was runnin' every which way and the deputies guardin' these two boys got a little careless and so off went the boys. They run and hid awhile and then lit out and run some more, about three miles or so, same as me, and them deputies picked up on 'em and kept right after them all the way. They never did get that first fella. He went to Dayton with me, 'preciated what I tried to do for his buddy and even stole two chickens when we laid over in some switchyards somewheres and got us a fine meal. We cooked it up right in the boxcar. He was a murderer, that fella. Strangled some lady in Selkirk and couldn't say why he done it. The one that got shot in the back, he was a horse thief."

"I guess you been mixed up in a lot of violence," Rudy said.

"If it draws blood or breaks heads," said Francis, "I know how it tastes."

The horse thief was named Aldo Campione, an immigrant from the town of Teramo in the Abruzzi. He'd come to America to seek his fortune and found work building the Barge Canal. But as a country soul he was distracted by an equine opportunity in the town of Coeymans, was promptly caught, jailed, transported to Albany for trial, and shot in the back escaping. His lesson to Francis was this: that life is full of caprice and missed connections, that thievery is wrong, especially if you get caught, that even Italians cannot outrun bullets, that a proffered hand in a moment of need is a beautiful thing. All this Francis knew well enough, and so the truest lesson of Aldo Campione resided not in intellected fact but in spectacle; for Francis can still remember Aldo's face as it came toward him. It looked like his own, which is perhaps why Francis put himself in jeopardy: to save his own face with his own hand. On came Aldo toward the open boxcar door. Out went the hand of Francis Phelan. It touched the curved fingers of Aldo's right hand. Francis's fingers curved and pulled. And there was tension. Tension! On came Aldo yielding to that tension, on and on and lift! Leap! Pull, Francis, pull! And then up, yes up! The grip was solid. The man was in the air, flying toward safety on the great right hand of Francis Phelan. And then whango bango and he let go. Whango bango and he's down, and he's rolling, and he's dead. Katie bar the door.

When the bus stopped at the corner of Broadway and Columbia Street, the corner where that infamous trolley was caught between flaming bedsheets, Aldo Campione boarded. He was clad in a white flannel suit, white shirt, and white necktie, and his hair was slicked down with brilliantine. Francis knew instantly that this was not the white of innocence but of humility. The man had been of low birth, low estate, and committed a low crime that had earned him the lowliest of deaths in the dust. Over there on the other side they must've give him a new suit. And here he came down the aisle and stopped at the seats where Rudy and Francis sat. He reached out his hand in a gesture to Francis that was ambiguous. It might have been a simple Abruzzian greeting. Or was it a threat, or a warning? It might have been an offer of belated gratitude, or even a show of compassion for a man like Francis who had lived long (for him), suffered much, and was inching toward death. It might have been a gesture of grace, urging, or even welcoming Francis into the next. And at this thought, Francis, who had raised his hand to meet Aldo's, withdrew it.

"I ain't shakin' hands with no dead horse thief," he said.

"I ain't no horse thief," Rudy said.

"Well you look like one," Francis said.

By then the bus was at Madison Avenue and Broadway, and Rudy and Francis stepped out into the frosty darkness of six o'clock on the final night of October 1938, the unruly night when grace is always in short supply, and the old and the new dead walk abroad in this land.

*   *   *

In the dust and sand of a grassless vacant lot beside the Mission of Holy Redemption, a human form lay prostrate under a lighted mission window. The sprawl of the figure arrested Francis's movement when he and Rudy saw it. Bodies in alleys, bodies in gutters, bodies anywhere, were part of his eternal landscape: a physical litany of the dead. This one belonged to a woman who seemed to be doing the dead man's float in the dust: face down, arms forward, legs spread.

"Hey," Rudy said as they stopped. "That's Sandra."

"Sandra who?" said Francis.

"Sandra There-ain't-no-more. She's only got one name, like Helen. She's an Eskimo."

"You dizzy bastard. Everybody's an Eskimo or a Cherokee."

"No, that's the straight poop. She used to work up in Alaska when they were buildin' roads."

"She dead?"

Rudy bent down, picked up Sandra's hand and held it. Sandra pulled it away from him.

"No," Rudy said, "she ain't dead."

"Then you better get up outa there, Sandra," Francis said, "or the dogs'll eat your ass off."

Sandra didn't move. Her hair streamed out of her inertness, long, yellow-white wisps floating in the dust, her faded and filthy cotton housedress twisted above the back of her knees, revealing stockings so full of holes and runs that they had lost their integrity as stockings. Over her dress she wore two sweaters, both stained and tattered. She lacked a left shoe. Rudy bent over and tapped her on the shoulder.

"Hey Sandra, it's me, Rudy. You know me?"

"Hnnn," said Sandra.

"You all right? You sick or anything, or just drunk?"

"Dnnn," said Sandra.

"She's just drunk," Rudy said, standing up. "She can't hold it no more. She falls over."

"She'll freeze there and the dogs'll come along and eat her ass off," Francis said.

"What dogs?" Rudy asked.

"The dogs, the dogs. Ain't you seen them?"

"I don't see too many dogs. I like cats. I see a lotta cats."

"If she's drunk she can't go inside the mission," Francis said.

"That's right," said Rudy. "She comes in drunk, he kicks her right out. He hates drunk women more'n he hates us."

"Why the hell's he preachin' if he don't preach to people that need it?"

"Drunks don't need it," Rudy said. "How'd you like to preach to a room full of bums like her?"

"She a bum or just on a heavy drunk?"

"She's a bum."

"She looks like a bum."

"She's been a bum all her life."

"No," said Francis. "Nobody's a bum all their life. She hada been somethin' once."

"She was a whore before she was a bum."

"And what about before she was a whore?"

"I don't know," Rudy said. "She just talks about whorin' in Alaska. Before that I guess she was just a little kid."

"Then that's somethin'. A little kid's somethin' that ain't a bum or a whore."

Francis saw Sandra's missing shoe in the shadows and retrieved it. He set it beside her left foot, then squatted and spoke into her left ear.

"You gonna freeze here tonight, you know that? Gonna be frost, freezin' weather. Could even snow. You hear? You oughta get yourself inside someplace outa the cold. Look, I slept the last two nights in the weeds and it was awful cold, but tonight's colder already than it was either of them nights. My hands is half froze and I only been walkin' two blocks. Sandra? You hear what I'm sayin'? If I got you a cup of hot soup would you drink it? Could you? You don't look like you could but maybe you could. Get a little hot soup in, you don't freeze so fast. Or maybe you wanna freeze tonight, maybe that's why you're layin' in the goddamn dust. You don't even have any weeds to keep the wind outa your ears. I like them deep weeds when I sleep outside. You want some soup?"

Sandra turned her head and with one eye looked up at Francis.

"Who you?"

"I'm just a bum," Francis said. "But I'm sober and I can get you some soup."

"Get me a drink?"

"No, I ain't got money for that."

"Then soup."

"You wanna stand up?"

"No. I'll wait here."

"You're gettin' all dusty."

"That's good."

"Whatever you say," Francis said, standing up. "But watch out for them dogs."

She whimpered as Rudy and Francis left the lot. The night sky was black as a bat and the wind was bringing ice to the world. Francis admitted the futility of preaching to Sandra. Who could preach to Francis in the weeds? But that don't make it right that she can't go inside to get warm. Just because you're drunk don't mean you ain't cold.

"Just because you're drunk don't mean you ain't cold," he said to Rudy.

"Right," said Rudy. "Who said that?"

"I said that, you ape."

"I ain't no ape."

"Well you look like one."

From the mission came sounds made by an amateur organist of fervent aggression, and of several voices raised in praise of good old Jesus, where'd we all be without him? The voices belonged to the Reverend Chester, and to half a dozen men in shirt sleeves who sat in the front rows of the chapel area's folding chairs. Reverend Chester, a gargantuan man with a clubfoot, wild white hair, and a face flushed permanently years ago by a whiskey condition all his own, stood behind the lectern looking out at maybe forty men and one woman.

Helen.

Francis saw her as he entered, saw her gray beret pulled off to the left, recognized her old black coat. She held no hymnal as the others did, but sat with arms folded in defiant resistance to the possibility of redemption by any Methodist like Chester; for Helen was a Catholic. And any redemption that came her way had better be through her church, the true church, the only church.

"Jesus," the preacher and his shirt-sleeved loyalists sang, "the name that charms our fears, That bids our sorrows cease, 'Tis music in the sinners' ears, 'Tis life and health and peace . . ."

The remaining seven eights of Reverend Chester's congregation, men hiding inside their overcoats, hats in their laps if they had hats, their faces grimed and whiskered and woebegone, remained mute, or gave the lyrics a perfunctory mumble, or nodded already in sleep. The song continued: ". . . He breaks the power of canceled sin, He sets the prisoner free; His blood can make the foulest clean, His blood availed for me."

Well not me, Francis said to his unavailed-for self, and he smelled his own uncanceled stink again, aware that it had intensified since morning. The sweat of a workday, the sourness of dried earth on his hands and clothes, the putrid perfume of the cemetery air with its pretension to windblown purity, all this lay in foul encrustation atop the private pestilence of his being. When he threw himself onto Gerald's grave, the uprush of a polluted life all but asphyxiated him.

"Hear him, ye deaf; his praise, ye dumb, Your loosened tongues employ; Ye blind, behold your Savior come; and leap, ye lame, for joy."

The lame and the halt put their hymnals down joylessly, and Reverend Chester leaned over his lectern to look at tonight's collection. Among them, as always, were good men and straight, men honestly without work, victims of a society ravaged by avarice, sloth, stupidity, and a God made wrathful by Babylonian excesses. Such men were merely the transients in the mission, and to them a preacher could only wish luck, send prayer, and provide a meal for the long road ahead. The true targets of the preacher were the others: the dipsos, the deadbeats, the wetbrains, and the loonies, who needed more than luck. What they needed was a structured way, a mentor and guide through the hells and purgatories of their days. Bringing the word, the light, was a great struggle today, for the decline of belief was rampant and the anti-Christ was on the rise. It was prophesied in Matthew and in Revelation that there would be less and less reverence for the Bible, greater lawlessness, depravity, and self-indulgence. The world, the light, the song, they would all die soon, for without doubt we were witnessing the advent of end times.

"Lost," said the preacher, and he waited for the word to resound in the sanctums of their damaged brains. "Oh lost, lost forever. Men and women lost, hopeless. Who will save you from your sloth? Who will give you a ride on the turnpike to salvation? Jesus will! Jesus delivers!"

The preacher screamed the word *delivers* and woke up half the congregation. Rudy, on the nod, flared into wakefulness with a wild swing of the left arm that knocked the hymnal out of Francis's grip. The book fell to the floor with a splat that brought Reverend Chester eye-to-eye with Francis. Francis nodded and the preacher gave him a firm and flinty smile in return.

The preacher then took the beatitudes for his theme. Blessed are the poor in spirit, for theirs is the kingdom of heaven. Blessed are the meek, for they shall inherit the earth. Blessed are they that mourn, for they shall be comforted.

"Oh yes, you men of skid row, brethren on the poor streets of the one eternal city we all dwell in, do not grieve that your spirit is low. Do not fear the world because you are of a meek and gentle nature. Do not feel that your mournful tears are in vain, for these things are the keys to the kingdom of God."

The men went swiftly back to sleep and Francis resolved he would wash the stink of the dead off his face and hands and hit Chester up for a new pair of socks. Chester was happiest when he was passing out socks to dried-out drunks. Feed the hungry, clothe the sober.

"Are you ready for peace of mind and heart?" the preacher asked. "Is there a man here tonight who wants a different life? God says: Come unto me. Will you take him at his word? Will you stand up now? Come to the front, kneel, and we will talk. Do this now and be saved. Now. Now. Now!"

No one moved.

"Then amen, brothers," said the preacher testily, and he left the lectern.

"Hot goddamn," Francis said to Rudy. "Now we get at that soup."

Then began the rush of men to table, the pouring of coffee, ladling of soup, cutting of bread by the mission's zealous volunteers. Francis sought out Pee Wee, a good old soul who managed the mission for Chester, and he asked him for a cup of soup for Sandra.

"She oughta be let in," Francis said. "She's gonna freeze out there."

"She was in before," Pee Wee said. "He wouldn't let her stay. She was really shot, and you know him on that. He won't mind on the soup, but just for the hell of it, don't say where it's going."

"Secret soup," Francis said.

He took the soup out the back door, pulling Rudy along with him, and crossed the vacant lot to where Sandra lay as before. Rudy rolled her onto her back and sat her up, and Francis put the soup under her nose.

"Soup," he said.

"Gazoop," Sandra said.

"Have it." Francis put the cup to her lips and tipped the soup at her mouth. It dribbled down her chin. She swallowed none.

"She don't want it," Rudy said.

"She wants it," Francis said. "She's just pissed it ain't wine."

He tried again and Sandra swallowed a little.

"When I was sleepin' inside just now," Rudy said, "I remembered Sandra wanted to be a nurse. Or used to be a nurse. That right, Sandra?"

"No," Sandra said.

"No, what? Wanted to be a nurse or was a nurse?"

"Doctor," Sandra said.

"She wanted to be a doctor," Francis said, tipping in more soup.

"No," Sandra said, pushing the soup away. Francis put the cup down and slipped her ratty shoe onto her left foot. He lifted her, a feather, carried her to the wall of the mission, and propped her into a sitting position, her back against the building, somewhat out of the wind. With his bare hand he wiped the masking dust from her face. He raised the soup and gave her another swallow.

"Doctor wanted me to be a nursie," she said.

"But you didn't want it," Francis said.

"Did. But he died."

"Ah," said Francis. "Love?"

"Love," said Sandra.

Inside the mission, Francis handed the cup back to Pee Wee, who emptied it into the sink.

"She all right?" Pee Wee asked.

"Terrific," Francis said.

"The ambulance won't even pick her up anymore," Pee Wee said. "Not unless she's bleedin' to death."

Francis nodded and went to the bathroom, where he washed Sandra's dust and his own stink off his hands. Then he washed his face and his neck and his ears; and when he was finished he washed them all again. He sloshed water around in his mouth and brushed his teeth with his left index finger. He wet his hair and combed it with nine fingers and dried himself with a damp towel that was tied to the wall. Some men were already leaving by the time he picked up his soup and bread and sat down beside Helen.

"Where you been hidin'?" he asked her.

"A fat lot you care where anybody is or isn't. I could be dead in the street three times over and you wouldn't know a thing about it."

"How the hell could I when you walk off like a crazy woman, yellin' and stompin'."

"Who wouldn't be crazy around you, spending every penny we get. You go out of your mind, Francis."

"I got some money."

"How much?"

"Six bucks."

"Where'd you get it?"

"I worked all the damn day in the cemetery, fillin' up graves. Worked hard."

"Francis, you did?"

"I mean all day."

"That's wonderful. And you're sober. And you're eating."

"Ain't drinkin' no wine either. I ain't even smokin'."

"Oh that's so lovely. I'm very proud of my good boy."

Francis scarfed up the soup, and Helen smiled and sipped the last of her coffee. More than half the men were gone from table now, Rudy still eating with a partial mind across from Francis. Pee Wee and his plangently compassionate volunteers picked up dishes and carried them to the kitchen. The preacher finished his coffee and strode over to Francis.

"Glad to see you staying straight," the preacher said.

"Okay," said Francis.

"And how are you, little lady?" he asked Helen.

"I'm perfectly delightful," Helen said.

"I believe I've got a job for you if you want it, Francis," the preacher said.

"I worked today up at the cemetery."

"Splendid."

"Shovelin' dirt ain't my idea of that much of a job."

"Maybe this one is better. Old Rosskam the ragman came here today looking for a helper. I've sent him men from time to time and I thought of you. If you're serious about quitting the hooch you might put a decent penny together."

"Ragman," Francis said. "Doin' what, exactly?"

"Going house to house on the wagon. Rosskam himself buys the rags and bottles, old metal, junk, papers, no garbage. Carts it himself too, but he's getting on and needs another strong back."

"Where's he at?"

"Green Street, below the bridge."

"I'll go see him and I 'preciate it. Tell you what else I'd 'preciate's a pair of socks, if you can spare 'em. Ones I got are all rotted out."

"What size?"

"Tens. But I'll take nines, or twelves."

"I'll get you some tens. And keep up the good work, Franny. Nice to see you're doing well too, little lady."

"I'm doing very well," Helen said. "Very exceptionally well." When he walked away she said: "He says it's nice I'm doing well. I'm doing just fine, and I don't need him to tell me I'm doing well."

"Don't fight him," Francis said. "He's givin' me some socks."

"We gonna get them jugs?" Rudy asked Francis. "Go somewheres and get a flop?"

"Jugs?" said Helen.

"That's what I said this mornin'," Francis said. "No, no jugs."

"With six dollars we could get a room and get our suitcase back," Helen said.

"I can't spend all six," Francis said. "I gotta give some to the lawyer. I figure I'll give him a deuce. After all, he got me the job and I owe him fifty."

"Where do you plan to sleep?" Helen asked.

"Where'd you sleep last night?"

"I found a place."

"Finny's car?"

"No, not Finny's car. I won't stay there anymore, you know that. I will absolutely not stay in that car another night."

"Then where'd you go?"

"Where did *you* sleep?"

"I slept in the weeds," Francis said.

"Well I found a bed."

"Where, goddamn it, where?"

"Up at Jack's."

"I thought you didn't like Jack anymore, or Clara either."

"They're not my favorite people, but they gave me a bed when I needed one."

"Somethin' to be said for that," Francis said.

Pee Wee came over with a second cup of coffee and sat across from Helen. Pee Wee was bald and fat and chewed cigars all day long without lighting them. He had cut hair in his younger days, but when his wife cleaned out their bank account, poisoned Pee Wee's dog, and ran away with the barber whom Pee Wee, by dint of hard work and superior tonsorial talent, had put of of business, Pee Wee started drinking and wound up on the bum. Yet he carried his comb and scissors everywhere to prove his talent was not just a bum's fantasy, and gave haircuts to other bums for fifteen cents, sometimes a nickel. He still gave haircuts, free now, at the mission.

When Francis came back to Albany in 1935, he met Pee Wee for the first time and they stayed drunk together for a month. When Francis turned up in Albany only weeks back to register for the Democrats at five dollars a shot, he met Pee Wee again. Francis registered to vote twenty-one times before the state troopers caught up with him and made him an Albany political celebrity. The pols had paid him fifty by then and still owed him fifty-five more that he'd probably never see. Pee Wee was off the juice when Francis met him the second time, and was full of energy, running the mission for Chester. Pee Wee was peaceful now, no longer the singing gin-drinker he used to be. Francis still felt good things about him, but now thought of him as an emotional cripple, dry, yeah, but at what cost?

"You see who's playin' over at The Gilded Cage?" Pee Wee asked Francis.

"I don't read the papers."

"Oscar Reo."

"You mean our Oscar?"

"The same."

"What's he doin'?"

"Singin' bartender. How's that for a comedown?"

"Oscar Reo who used to be on the radio?" Helen asked.

"That's the fella," said Pee Wee. "He blew the big time on booze, but he dried out and tends bar now. At least he's livin', even if it ain't what it was."

"Pee Wee and me pitched a drunk with him in New York. Two, three days, wasn't it, Pee?"

"Mighta been a week," Pee Wee said. "None of us was up to keepin' track. But he sang a million tunes and played piano everyplace they had one. Most musical drunk I ever see."

"I used to sing his songs," Helen said. " 'Hindustan Lover' and 'Georgie Is My Apple Pie' and another one, a grand ballad, 'Under the Peach Trees with You.' He wrote wonderful, happy songs and I sang them all when I was singing."

"I didn't know you sang," Pee Wee said.

"Well I most certainly sang, and played piano very well too. I was getting a classical education in music until my father died. I was at Vassar."

"Albert Einstein went to Vassar," Rudy said.

"You goofy bastard," said Francis.

"Went there to make a speech. I read it in the papers."

"He could have," Helen said. "Everybody speaks at Vassar. It just happens to be one of the three best schools in the world."

"We oughta go over and see old Oscar," Francis said.

"Not me," said Pee Wee.

"No," said Helen.

"What no?" Francis said. "You afraid we'd all get drunked up if we stopped in to say hello?"

"I'm not afraid of that."

"Then let's go see him. He's all right, Oscar."

"Think he'll remember you?" Pee Wee said.

"Maybe. I remember him."

"So do I."

"Then let's go."

"I wouldn't drink anything," Pee Wee said. "I ain't been in a bar in two years."

"They got ginger ale. You allowed to drink ginger ale?"

"I hope it's not expensive," Helen said.

"Just what you drink," Pee Wee said. "About usual."

"Is it snooty?"

"It's a joint, old-timey, but it pulls in the slummers. That's half the trade."

Reverend Chester stepped lively across the room and thrust at Francis a pair of gray woolen socks, his mouth a crescent of pleasure and his great chest heaving with beneficence.

"Try these for size," he said.

"I thank ya for 'em," said Francis.

"They're good and warm."

"Just what I need. Nothin' left of mine."

"It's fine that you're off the drink. You've got a strong look about you today."

"Just a false face for Halloween."

"Don't run yourself down. Have faith."

The door to the mission opened and a slim young man in bifocals and a blue topcoat two sizes small for him, his carroty hair a field of cowlicks, stood in its frame. He held the doorknob with one hand and stood directly under the inside ceiling light, casting no shadow.

"Shut the door," Pee Wee yelled, and the young man stepped in and shut it. He stood looking at all in the mission, his face a cracked plate, his eyes panicked and rabbity.

"That's it for him," Pee Wee said.

The preacher strode to the door and stood inches from the young man, studying him, sniffing him.

"You're drunk," the preacher said.

"I only had a couple."

"Oh no. You're in the beyond."

"Honest," said the young man. "Two bottles of beer."

"Where did you get the money for beer?"

"A fella paid me what he owed me."

"You panhandled it."

"No."

"You're a bum."

"I just had a drink, Reverend."

"Get your things together. I told you I wouldn't put up with this a third time. Arthur, get his bags."

Pee Wee stood up from the table and climbed the stairs to the rooms where the resident handful lived while they sorted out their lives. The preacher had invited Francis to stay if he could get the hooch out of his system. He would then have a clean bed, clean clothes, three squares, and a warm room with Jesus in it for as long as it took him to answer the question: What next? Pee Wee held the house record: eight months in the joint, and managing it after three, such was his zeal for abstention. No booze, no smoking upstairs (for drunks are fire hazards), carry your share of the work load, and then rise you must, rise you will, into the brilliant embrace of the just God. The kitchen volunteers stopped their work and came forward with solemnized pity to watch the eviction of one of their promising young men. Pee Wee came down with a suitcase and set it by the door.

"Give us a cigarette, Pee," the young man said.

"Don't have any."

"Well roll one."

"I said I don't have any tobacco."

"Oh."

"You'll have to leave now, Little Red," the preacher said.

Helen stood up and came over to Little Red and put a cigarette in his hand. He took it and said nothing. Helen struck a match and lit it for him, then sat back down.

"I don't have anyplace to go," Little Red said, blowing smoke past the preacher.

"You should have thought of that before you started drinking. You are a contumacious young man."

"I got no place to put that bag. And I got a pencil and paper upstairs."

"Leave it here. Come and get your pencil and paper when you get that poison out of your system and you can talk sense about yourself."

"My pants are in there."

"They'll be all right. Nobody here will touch your pants."

"Can I have a cup of coffee?"

"If you found money for beer, you can find money for coffee."

"Where can I go?"

"I couldn't begin to imagine. Come back sober and you may have some food. Now get a move on."

Little Red grabbed the doorknob, opened the door, and took a step. Then he stepped back in and pointed at his suitcase.

"I got cigarettes there," he said.

"Then get your cigarettes."

Little Red undid the belt that held the suitcase together and rummaged for a pack of Camels. He rebuckled the belt and stood up.

"If I come back tomorrow . . ."

"We'll see about tomorrow," said the preacher, who grabbed the doorknob himself and pulled it to as he ushered Little Red out into the night.

"Don't lose my pants," Little Red called through the glass of the closing door.

✻   ✻   ✻   ⚬

Francis, wearing his new socks, was first out of the mission, first to cast an anxious glance around the corner of the building at Sandra, who sat propped where he had left her, her eyes sewn as tightly closed by the darkness as the eyes of a diurnal bird. Francis touched her firmly with a finger and she moved, but without opening her eyes. He looked up at the full moon, a silver cinder illuminating this night for bleeding women and frothing madmen, and which warmed him with the enormous shadow it thrust forward in his own path. When Sandra moved he leaned over and put the back of his hand against her cheek and felt the ice of her flesh.

"You got an old blanket or some old rags, any old bum's coat to throw over her?" he asked Pee Wee, who stood in the shadows considering the encounter.

"I could get something," Pee Wee said, and he loosened his keys and opened the door of the darkened mission: all lights off save the kitchen, which would remain bright until eleven, lockout time. Pee Wee opened the door and entered as Rudy, Helen, and Francis huddled around Sandra, watching her breathe. Francis had watched two dozen people suspire into death, all of them bums except for his father, and Gerald.

"Maybe if we cut her throat the ambulance'd take her," Francis said.

"She doesn't want an ambulance," Helen said. "She wants to sleep it all away. I'll bet she doesn't even feel cold."

"She's a cake of ice."

Sandra moved, turning her head toward the voices but without opening her eyes. "You got no wine?" she asked.

"No wine, honey," Helen said.

Pee Wee came out with a stone-gray rag that might once have been a blanket and wrapped its rough doubleness around Sandra. He tucked it into the neck of her sweater, and with one end formed a cowl behind her head, giving her the look of a monastic beggar in sackcloth.

"I don't want to look at her no more," Francis said, and he walked east on Madison, the deepening chill aggravating his limp. Helen and Pee Wee fell in behind him, and Rudy after that.

"You ever know her, Pee Wee?" Francis asked. "I mean when she was in shape?"

"Sure. Everybody knew her. You took your turn. Then she got to givin' love parties, is what she called 'em, but she'd turn mean, first love you up and then bite you bad. Half-ruined enough guys so only strangers'd go with her. Then she stopped that and hung out with one bum name of Freddy and they specialized in one another about a year till he went somewheres and she didn't."

"Nobody suffers like a lover left behind," Helen said.

"Well that's a crock," Francis said. "Lots suffer ain't ever been in love even once."

"They don't suffer like those who have," said Helen.

"Yeah. Where's this joint, Pee Wee, Green Street?"

"Right. Couple of blocks. Where the old Gayety Theater used to be."

"I used to go there. Watch them ladies' ankles and can-canny crotches."

"Be nice, Francis," Helen said.

"I'm nice. I'm the nicest thing you'll see all week."

Goblins came at them on Green Street, hooded spooks, a Charlie Chaplin in whiteface, with derby, cane, and tash, and a girl wearing an enormous old bonnet with a full-sized bird on top of it.

"They gonna get us!" Francis said. "Look out!" He threw his arms in the air and shook himself in a fearful dance. The children laughed and spooked boo at him.

"Gee it's a nice night," Helen said. "Cold but nice and clear, isn't it, Fran?"

"It's nice," Francis said. "It's all nice."

*   *   *

The Gilded Cage door opened into the old Gayety lobby, now the back end of a saloon that mimicked and mocked the Bowery pubs of forty years gone. Francis stood looking toward a pair of monumental, half-wrapped breasts that heaved beneath a hennaed wig and scarlet lips. The owner of these spectacular possessions was delivering outward from an elevated platform a song of anguish in the city: You would not insult me, sir, if Jack were only here, in a voice so devoid of musical quality that it mocked its own mockery.

"She's terrible," Helen said. "Awful."

"She ain't that good," Francis said.

They stepped across a floor strewn with sawdust, lit by ancient chandeliers and sconces, all electric now, toward a long walnut bar with a shining brass bar rail and three gleaming spittoons. Behind the half-busy bar a man with high collar, string tie, and arm garters drew schooners of beer from a tap, and at tables of no significant location sat men and women Francis recognized: whores, bums, barflies. Among them, at other tables, sat men in business suits, and women with fox scarves and flyaway hats, whose presence was such that their tables this night were landmarks of social significance merely because they were sitting at them. Thus, The Gilded Cage was a museum of unnatural sociality, and the smile of the barman welcomed Francis, Helen, and Rudy, bums all, and Pee Wee, their clean-shirted friend, to the tableau.

"Table, folks?"

"Not while there's a bar rail," Francis said.

"Step up, brother. What's your quaff?"

"Ginger ale," said Pee Wee.

"I believe I'll have the same," said Helen.

"That beer looks tantalizin'," Francis said.

"You said you wouldn't drink," Helen said.

"I said wine."

The barman slid a schooner with a high collar across the bar to Francis and looked to Rudy, who ordered the same. The piano player struck up a medley of "She May Have Seen Better Days" and "My Sweetheart's the Man in the Moon" and urged those in the audience who knew the lyrics to join in song.

"You look like a friend of mine," Francis told the barman, drilling him with a smile and a stare. The barman, with a full head of silver waves and an eloquent white mustache, stared back long enough to ignite a memory. He looked from Francis to Pee Wee, who was also smiling.

"I think I know you two turks," the barman said.

"You thinkin' right," Francis said, "except the last time I seen you, you wasn't sportin' that pussy-tickler."

The barman stroked his silvery lip. "You guys got me drunk in New York."

"You got us drunk in every bar on Third Avenue," Pee Wee said.

The barman stuck out his hand to Francis.

"Francis Phelan," said Francis, "and this here is Rudy the Kraut. He's all right but he's nuts."

"My kind of fella," Oscar said.

"Pee Wee Packer," Pee Wee said with his hand out.

"I remember," said Oscar.

"And this is Helen," said Francis. "She hangs out with me, but damned if I know why."

"Oscar Reo's what I still go by, folks, and I really do remember you boys. But I don't drink anymore."

"Hey, me neither," said Pee Wee.

"I ain't turned it off yet," Francis said. "I'm waitin' till I retire."

"He retired forty years ago," Pee Wee said.

"That ain't true. I worked all day today. Gettin' rich. How you like my new duds?"

"You're a sport," Oscar said. "Can't tell you from those swells over there."

"Swells and bums, there ain't no difference," Francis said.

"Except swells like to look like swells," Oscar said, "and bums like to look like bums. Am I right?"

"You're a smart fella," Francis said.

"You still singin', Oscar?" Pee Wee asked.

"For my supper."

"Well goddamn it," Francis said, "give us a tune."

"Since you're so polite about it," Oscar said. And he turned to the piano man and said: " 'Sixteen' "; and instantly there came from the piano the strains of "Sweet Sixteen."

"Oh that's a wonderful song," Helen said. "I remember you singing that on the radio."

"How durable of you, my dear."

Oscar sang into the bar microphone and, with great resonance and no discernible loss of control from his years with the drink, he turned time back to the age of the village green. The voice was as commonplace to an American ear as Jolson's, or Morton Downey's; and even Francis, who rarely listened to the radio, or ever had a radio to listen to in either the early or the modern age, remembered its pitch and its tremolo from the New York binge, when this voice by itself was a chorale of continuous joy for all in earshot, or so it seemed to Francis at a distance of years. And further, the attention that the bums, the swells, the waiters, were giving the man, proved that this drunk was not dead, not dying, but living an epilogue to a notable life. And yet, and yet . . . here he was, disguised behind a mustache, another cripple, his ancient, weary eyes revealing to Francis the scars of a blood brother, a man for whom life had been a promise unkept in spite of great success, a promise now and forever unkeepable. The man was singing a song that had grown old not from time but from wear. The song is frayed. The song is worn out.

The insight raised in Francis a compulsion to confess his every transgression of natural, moral, or civil law; to relentlessly examine and expose every flaw of his own character, however minor. What was it, Oscar, that did you in? Would you like to tell us all about it? Do you know? It wasn't Gerald who did *me*. It wasn't drink and it wasn't baseball and it wasn't really Mama. What was it that went bust, Oscar, and how come nobody ever found out how to fix it for us?

When Oscar segued perfectly into a second song, his talent seemed awesome to Francis, and the irrelevance of talent to Oscar's broken life even more of a mystery. How does somebody get this good and why doesn't it mean anything? Francis considered his own talent on the ball field of a hazy, sunlit yesterday: how he could follow the line of the ball from every crack of the bat, zap after it like a chicken hawk after a chick, how he would stroke and pocket its speed no matter whether it was lined at him or sizzled erratically toward him through the grass. He would stroke it with the predatory curve of his glove and begin with his right hand even then, whether he was running or falling, to reach into that leather pocket, spear the chick with his educated talons, and whip it across to first or second base, or wherever it needed to go and you're out, man, you're out. No ball player anywhere moved his body any better than Franny Phelan, a damn fieldin' machine, fastest ever was.

Francis remembered the color and shape of his glove, its odor of oil and sweat and leather, and he wondered if Annie had kept it. Apart from his memory and a couple of clippings, it would be all that remained of a spent career that had blossomed and then peaked in the big leagues far too long after the best years were gone, but which brought with the peaking the promise that some belated and overdue glory was possible, that somewhere there was a hosannah to be cried in the name of Francis Phelan, one of the best sonsabitches ever to kick a toe into third base.

Oscar's voice quavered with beastly loss on a climactic line of the song: Blinding tears falling as he thinks of his lost pearl, broken heart calling, oh yes, calling, dear old girl. Francis turned to Helen and saw her crying splendid, cathartic tears: Helen, with the image of inexpungeable sorrow in her cortex, with a lifelong devotion to forlorn love, was weeping richly for all the pearls lost since love's old sweet song first was sung.

"Oh that was so beautiful, so beautiful," Helen said to Oscar when he rejoined them at the beer spigot. "That's absolutely one of my all-time favorites. I used to sing it myself."

"A singer?" said Oscar. "Where was that?"

"Oh everywhere. Concerts, the radio. I used to sing on the air every night, but that was an age ago."

"You should do us a tune."

"Oh never," said Helen.

"Customers sing here all the time," Oscar said.

"No, no," said Helen, "the way I look."

"You look as good as anybody here," Francis said.

"I could never," said Helen. But she was readying herself to do what she could never, pushing her hair behind her ear, straightening her collar, smoothing her much more than ample front.

"What'll it be?" Oscar said. "Joe knows 'em all."

"Let me think awhile."

Francis saw that Aldo Campione was sitting at a table at the far end of the room and had someone with him. That son of a bitch is following me, is what Francis thought. He fixed his glance on the table and saw Aldo move his hand in an ambiguous gesture. What are you telling me, dead man, and who's that with you? Aldo wore a white flower in the lapel of his white flannel suitcoat, a new addition since the bus. Goddamn dead people travelin' in packs, buyin' flowers. Francis studied the other man without recognition and felt the urge to walk over and take a closer look. But what if nobody's sittin' there? What if nobody sees these bozos but me? The flower girl came along with a full tray of white gardenias.

"Buy a flower, sir?" she asked Francis.

"Why not? How much?"

"Just a quarter."

"Give us one."

He fished a quarter out of his pants and pinned the gardenia on Helen's lapel with a pin the girl handed him. "It's been a while since I bought you flowers," he said. "You gonna sing up there for us, you gotta put on the dog a little."

Helen leaned over and kissed Francis on the mouth, which always made him blush when she did it in public. She was always a first-rate heller between the sheets, when there was sheets, when there was somethin' to do between them.

"Francis always bought me flowers," she said. "He'd get money and first thing he'd do was buy me a dozen roses, or a white orchid even. He didn't care what he did with the money as long as I got my flowers first. You did that for me, didn't you, Fran?"

"Sure did," said Francis, but he could not remember buying an orchid, didn't know what orchids looked like.

"We were lovebirds," Helen said to Oscar, who was smiling at the spectacle of bum love at his bar. "We had a beautiful apartment up on Hamilton Street. We had all the dishes anybody'd ever need. We had a sofa and a big bed and sheets and pillowcases. There wasn't anything we didn't have, isn't that right, Fran?"

"That's right," Francis said, trying to remember the place.

"We had flowerpots full of geraniums that we kept alive all winter long. Francis loved geraniums. And we had an icebox crammed full of food. We ate so well, both of us had to go on a diet. That was such a wonderful time."

"When was that?" Pee Wee asked. "I didn't know you ever stayed anyplace that long."

"What long?"

"I don't know. Months musta been if you had an apartment."

"I was here awhile, six weeks maybe, once."

"Oh we had it much longer than that," Helen said.

"Helen knows," Francis said. "She remembers. I can't call one day different from another."

"It was the drink," Helen said. "Francis wouldn't stop drinking and then we couldn't pay the rent and we had to give up our pillowcases and our dishes. It was Haviland china, the very best you could buy. When you buy, buy the best, my father taught me. We had solid mahogany chairs and my beautiful upright piano my brother had been keeping. He didn't want to give it up, it was so nice, but it was mine. Paderewski played on it once when he was in Albany in nineteen-oh-nine. I sang all my songs on it."

"She played pretty fancy piano," Francis said. "That's no joke. Why don't you sing us a song, Helen?"

"Oh I guess I will."

"What's your pleasure?" Oscar asked.

"I don't know. 'In the Good Old Summertime,' maybe."

"Right time to sing it," Francis said, "now that we're freezin' our ass out there."

"On second thought," said Helen, "I want to sing one for Francis for buying me that flower. Does your friend know 'He's Me Pal,' or 'My Man'?"

"You hear that, Joe?"

"I hear," said Joe the piano man, and he played a few bars of the chorus of "He's Me Pal" as Helen smiled and stood and walked to the stage with an aplomb and grace befitting her reentry into the world of music, the world she should never have left, oh why ever did you leave it, Helen? She climbed the three steps to the platform, drawn upward by familiar chords that now seemed to her to have always evoked joy, chords not from this one song but from an era of songs, thirty, forty years of songs that celebrated the splendors of love, and loyalty, and friendship, and family, and country, and the natural world. Frivolous Sal was a wild sort of devil, but wasn't she dead on the level too? Mary was a great pal, heaven-sent on Christmas morning, and love lingers on for her. The new-mown hay, the silvery moon, the home fires burning, these were sanctuaries of Helen's spirit, songs whose like she had sung from her earliest days, songs that endured for her as long as the classics she had committed to memory so indelibly in her youth, for they spoke to her, not abstractly of the aesthetic peaks of the art she had once hoped to master, but directly, simply, about the everyday currency of the heart and soul. The pale moon will shine on the twining of our hearts. My heart is stolen, lover dear, so please don't let us part. Oh love, sweet love, oh burning love—the songs told her—you are mine, I am yours, forever and a day. You spoiled the girl I used to be, my hope has gone away. Send me away with a smile, but remember: you're turning off the sunshine of my life.

Love.

A flood tide of pity rose in Helen's breast. Francis, oh sad man, was her last great love, but he wasn't her only one. Helen has had a lifetime of sadnesses with her lovers. Her first true love kept her in his fierce embrace for years, but then he loosened that embrace and let her slide down and down until the hope within her died. Hopeless Helen, that's who she was when she met Francis. And as she stepped up to the microphone on the stage of The Gilded Cage, hearing the piano behind her, Helen was a living explosion of unbearable memory and indomitable joy.

And she wasn't a bit nervous either, thank you, for she was a professional who had never let the public intimidate her when she sang in a church, or at musicales, or at weddings, or at Woolworth's when she sold song sheets, or even on the radio with that audience all over the city every night. Oscar Reo, you're not the only one who sang for Americans over the airwaves. Helen had her day and she isn't a bit nervous.

But she is . . . all right, yes, she is . . . a girl enveloped by private confusion, for she feels the rising of joy and sorrow simultaneously and she cannot say whether one or the other will take her over during the next few moments.

"What's Helen's last name?" Oscar asked.

"Archer," Francis said. "Helen Archer."

"Hey," said Rudy, "how come you told me she didn't have a last name?"

"Because it don't matter what anybody tells you," Francis said. "Now shut up and listen."

"A real old-time trouper now," said Oscar into the bar mike, "will give us a song or two for your pleasure, lovely Miss Helen Archer."

And then Helen, still wearing that black rag of a coat rather than expose the even more tattered blouse and skirt that she wore beneath it, standing on her spindle legs with her tumorous belly butting the metal stand of the microphone and giving her the look of a woman five months pregnant, casting boldly before the audience this image of womanly disaster and fully aware of the dimensions of this image, Helen then tugged stylishly at her beret, adjusting it forward over one eye. She gripped the microphone with a sureness that postponed her disaster, at least until the end of this tune, and sang then "He's Me Pal," a ditty really, short and snappy, sang it with exuberance and wit, with a tilt of the head, a roll of the eyes, a twist of the wrist that suggested the proud virtues. Sure, he's dead tough, she sang, but his love ain't no bluff. Wouldn't he share his last dollar with her? Hey, no millionaire will ever grab Helen. She'd rather have her pal with his fifteen a week. Oh Francis, if you only made just fifteen a week.

If you only.

The applause was full and long and gave Helen strength to begin "My Man," Fanny Brice's wonderful torch, and Helen Morgan's too.

Two Helens. Oh Helen, you were on the radio, but where did it take you? What fate was it that kept you from the great heights that were yours by right of talent and education? You were born to be a star, so many said it. But it was others who went on to the heights and you were left behind to grow bitter. How you learned to envy those who rose when you did not, those who never deserved it, had no talent, no training. There was Carla, from high school, who could not even carry a tune but who made a movie with Eddie Cantor, and there was Edna, ever so briefly from Woolworth's, who sang in a Broadway show by Cole Porter because she learned how to wiggle her fanny. But ah, sweetness was Helen's, for Carla went off a cliff in an automobile, and Edna sliced her wrists and bled her life away in her lover's bathtub, and Helen laughed last. Helen is singing on a stage this very minute and just listen to the voice she's left with after all her troubles. Look at those well-dressed people out there hanging on her every note.

Helen closed her eyes and felt tears forcing their way out and could not say whether she was blissfully happy or fatally sad. At some point it all came together and didn't make much difference anyway, for sad or happy, happy or sad, life didn't change for Helen. Oh, her man, how much she loves you. You can't imagine. Poor girl, all despair now. If she went away she'd come back on her knees. Some day. She's yours. Forevermore.

Oh thunder! Thunderous applause! And the elegant people are standing for Helen, when last did that happen? More, more, more, they yell, and she is crying so desperately now for happiness, or is it for loss, that it makes Francis and Pee Wee cry too. And even though people are calling for more, more, more, Helen steps delicately back down the three platform steps and walks proudly over to Francis with her head in the air and her face impossibly wet, and she kisses him on the cheek so all will know that this is the man she was talking about, in case you didn't notice when we came in together. This is the man.

By god that was great, Francis says. You're better'n anybody.

Helen, says Oscar, that was first-rate. You want a singing job here, you come round tomorrow and I'll see the boss puts you on the payroll. That's a grand voice you've got there, lady. A grand voice.

Oh thank you all, says Helen, thank you all so very kindly. It is so pleasant to be appreciated for your God-given talent and for your excellent training and for your natural presence. Oh I do thank you, and I shall come again to sing for you, you may be sure.

Helen closed her eyes and felt tears beginning to force their way out and could not say whether she was blissfully happy or devastatingly sad. Some odd-looking people were applauding politely, but others were staring at her with sullen faces. If they're sullen, then obviously they didn't think much of your renditions, Helen. Helen steps delicately back down the three steps, comes over to Francis, and keeps her head erect as he leans over and pecks her cheek.

"Mighty nice, old gal," he says.

"Not bad at all," Oscar says. "You'll have to do it again sometime."

Helen closed her eyes and felt tears forcing their way out and knew life didn't change. If she went away she'd come back on her knees. It is so pleasant to be appreciated.

Helen, you are like a blackbird, when the sun comes out for a little while. Helen, you are like a blackbird made sassy by the sun. But what will happen to you when the sun goes down again?

I do thank you.

And I shall come again to sing for you.

Oh sassy blackbird! Oh!

III

RUDY LEFT THEM TO FLOP SOMEPLACE, half-drunk on six beers, and Francis, Helen, and Pee Wee walked back along Green Street to Madison and then west toward the mission. Walk Pee Wee home and go get a room at Palombo's Hotel, get warm, stretch out, rest them bones. Because Francis and Helen had money: five dollars and seventy-five cents. Two of it Helen had left from what Francis gave her last night; plus three-seventy-five out of his cemetery wages, for he spent little in The Gilded Cage, Oscar buying twice as many drinks as he took money for.

The city had grown quiet at midnight and the moon was as white as early snow. A few cars moved slowly on Pearl Street but otherwise the streets were silent. Francis turned up his suitcoat collar and shoved his hands into his pants pockets. Alongside the mission the moon illuminated Sandra, who sat where they had left her. They stopped to look at her condition. Francis squatted and shook her.

"You sobered up yet, lady?"

Sandra answered him with an enveloping silence. Francis pushed the cowl off her face and in the vivid moonlight saw the toothmarks on her nose and cheek and chin. He shook his head to clear the vision, then saw that one of her fingers and the flesh between forefinger and thumb on her left hand had been chewed.

"The dogs got her."

He looked across the street and saw a red-eyed mongrel waiting in the half-lit corner of an alley and he charged after it, picking up a stone as he went. The cur fled down the alley as Francis turned his ankle on a raised sidewalk brick and sprawled on the pavement. He picked himself up, he now bloodied too by the cur, and sucked the dirt out of the cuts.

As he crossed the street, goblins came up from Broadway, ragged and masked, and danced around Helen. Pee Wee, bending over Sandra, straightened up as the goblin dance gained in ferocity.

"Jam and jelly, big fat belly," the goblins yelled at Helen. And when she drew herself inward they only intensified the chant.

"Hey you kids," Francis yelled. "Let her alone."

But they danced on and a skull goblin poked Helen in the stomach with a stick. As she swung at the skull with her hand, another goblin grabbed her purse and then all scattered.

"Little bastards, devils," Helen cried, running after them. And Francis and Pee Wee too joined the chase, pounding through the night, no longer sure which one wore the skull mask. The goblins ran down alleys, around corners, and fled beyond capture.

Francis turned back to Helen, who was far behind him. She was weeping, gasping, doubled over in a spasm of loss.

"Sonsabitches," Francis said.

"Oh the money," Helen said, "the money."

"They hurt you with that stick?"

"I don't think so."

"That money ain't nothin'. Get more tomorrow."

"It was."

"Was what?"

"There was fifteen dollars in there besides the other."

"Fifteen? Where'd you get fifteen dollars?"

"Your son Billy gave it to me. The night he found us at Spanish George's. You were passed out and he gave us forty-five dollars, all the cash he had. I gave you thirty and kept the fifteen."

"I went through that pocketbook. I didn't see it."

"I pinned it inside the lining so you wouldn't drink it up. I wanted our suitcase back. I wanted our room for a week so I could rest."

"Goddamn it, woman, now we ain't got a penny. You and your sneaky goddamn ways."

Pee Wee came back from the chase empty-handed.

"Some tough kids around here," he said. "You okay, Helen?"

"Fine. just fine."

"You're not hurt?"

"Not anyplace you could see."

"Sandra," Pee Wee said. "She's dead."

"She's more than that," Francis said. "She's partly chewed away."

"We'll take her inside so they don't eat no more of her," Pee Wee said. "I'll call the police."

"You think it's all right to bring her inside?" Francis asked. "She's still got all that poison in her system."

Pee Wee said nothing and opened the mission door. Francis picked Sandra up from the dust and carried her inside. He put her down on an old church bench against the wall and covered her face with the scratchy blanket that had become her final gift from the world.

"If I had my rosary I'd say it for her," Helen said, sitting on a chair beside the bench and looking at Sandra's corpse. "But it was in my purse. I've carried that rosary for twenty years."

"I'll check the vacant lots and the garbage cans in the mornin'," Francis said. "It'll turn up."

"I'll bet Sandra prayed to die," Helen said.

"Hey," said Francis.

"I would if I was her. Her life wasn't human anymore."

Helen looked at the clock: twelve-ten. Pee Wee was calling the police.

"Today's a holy day of obligation," she said. "It's All Saints' Day."

"Yup," said Francis.

"I want to go to church in the morning."

"All right, go to church."

"I will. I want to hear mass."

"Hear it. That's tomorrow. What are we gonna do tonight? Where the hell am I gonna put you?"

"You could stay here," Pee Wee said. "All the beds are full but you can sleep down here on a bench."

"No," Helen said. "I'd rather not do that. We can go up to Jack's. He told me I could come back if I wanted."

"Jack said that?" Francis asked.

"Those were his words."

"Then let's shag ass. Jack's all right. Clara's a crazy bitch but I like Jack. Always did. You sure he said that?"

" 'Come back anytime,' he said as I was going out the door."

"All right. Then we'll move along, old buddy," Francis said to Pee Wee. "You'll figure it out with Sandra?"

"I'll do the rest," Pee Wee said.

"You know her last name?"

"No. Never heard it."

"Don't make much difference now."

"Never did," Pee Wee said.

✲   ✲   ✲

Francis and Helen walked up Pearl Street toward State, the absolute center of the city's life for two centuries. One trolley car climbed State

Street's violent incline and another came toward them, rocking south on Pearl. A man stepped out of the Waldorf Restaurant and covered his throat with his coat collar, shivered once, and walked on. The cold had numbed Francis's fingertips, frost was blooming on the roofs of parked cars, and the night-walkers exhaled dancing plumes of vapor. From a manhole in the middle of State Street steam rose and vanished. Francis imagined the subterranean element at the source of this: a huge human head with pipes screwed into its ears, steam rising from a festering skull wound.

Aldo Campione, walking on the opposite side of North Pearl from Francis and Helen, raised his right hand in the same ambiguous gesture Francis had witnessed at the bar. As Francis speculated on the meaning, the man who had been sitting with Aldo stepped out of the shadows into a streetlight's glow, and Aldo's gesture then became clear: it introduced Francis to Dick Doolan, the bum who tried to cut off Francis's feet with a meat cleaver.

"I went to the kid's grave today," Francis said.

"What kid?"

"Gerald."

"Oh, you did?" she said. "Then that was the first time, wasn't it? It must've been."

"Right."

"You're thinking about him these days. You mentioned him last week."

"I never stop thinkin' about him."

"What's gotten into you?"

Francis saw the street that lay before him: Pearl Street, the central vessel of this city, city once his, city lost. The commerce along with its walls jarred him: so much new, stores gone out of business he never even heard of. Some things remained: Whitney's, Myers', the old First Church, which rose over Clinton Square, the Pruyn Library. As he walked, the cobblestones turned to granite, houses became stores, life aged, died, renewed itself, and a vision of what had been and what might have been intersected in an eye that could not really remember one or interpret the other. What would you give never to have left, Francis?

"I said, what's got into you?"

"Nothin's got into me. I'm just thinkin' about a bunch of stuff. This old street. I used to own this street, once upon a time."

"You should've sold it when you had the chance."

"Money. I ain't talkin' about money."

"I didn't think you were. That was a funny."

"Wasn't much funny. I said I saw Gerald's grave. I talked to him."

"Talked? How did you talk?"

"Stood and talked to the damn grass. Maybe I'm gettin' nutsy as Rudy. He can't hold his pants up, they fall over his shoes."

"You're not nutsy, Francis. It's because you're here. We shouldn't be here. We should go someplace else."

"Right. That's where we oughta go. Else."

"Don't drink any more tonight."

"Listen here. Don't you nag my ass."

"I want you straight, please. I want you straight."

"I'm the straightest thing you'll see all week. I am so straight. I'm the straightest thing you'll sweek. The thing that happened on the other side of the street. The thing that happened was Billy told me stuff about Annie. I never told you that. Billy told me stuff about Annie, how she never told I dropped him."

"Never told who, the police?"

"Never nobody. Never a damn soul. Not Billy, not Peg, not her brother, not her sisters. Ain't that the somethin'est thing you ever heard? I can't see a woman goin' through that stuff and not tellin' nobody about it."

"You've got a lot to say about those people."

"Not much to say."

"Maybe you ought to go see them."

"No, that wouldn't do no good."

"You'd get it out of your system."

"What out of my system?"

"Whatever it is that's in there."

"Never mind about my system. How come you wouldn't stay at the mission when you got an invite?"

"I don't want their charity."

"You ate their soup."

"I did not. All I had was coffee. Anyway, I don't like Chester. He doesn't like Catholics."

"Catholics don't like Methodists. What the hell, that's even. And I don't see any Catholic missions down here. I ain't had any Catholic soup lately."

"I won't do it and that's that."

"So freeze your ass someplace. Your flower's froze already."

"Let it freeze."

"You sang a song at least."

"Yes I did. I sang while Sandra was dying."

"She'da died no matter. Her time was up."

"No, I don't believe that. That's fatalism. I believe we die when we can't stand it anymore. I believe we stand as much as we can and then we die when we can, and Sandra decided she could die."

"I don't fight that. Die when you can. That's as good a sayin' as there is."

"I'm glad we agree on something," Helen said.

"We get along all right. You ain't a bad sort."

"You're all right too."

"We're both all right," Francis said, "and we ain't got a damn penny and noplace to flop. We on the bum. Let's get the hell up to Jack's before he puts the lights out on us."

Helen slipped her arm inside Francis's. Across the street Aldo Campione and Dick Doolan, who in the latter years of his life was known as Rowdy Dick, kept silent pace.

                    *   *   *

Helen pulled her arm away from Francis and tightened her collar around her neck, then hugged herself and buried her hands in her armpits.

"I'm chilled to my bones," she said.

"It's chilly, all right."

"I mean a real chill, a deep chill."

Francis put his arm around her and walked her up the steps of Jack's house. It stood on the east side of Ten Broeck Street, a three-block street in Arbor Hill named for a Revolutionary War hero and noted in the 1870s and 1880s as the place where a dozen of the city's arriviste lumber barons lived, all in a row, in competitive luxury. For their homes the barons built handsome brownstones, most of them now cut into apartments like Jack's, or into furnished rooms.

The downstairs door to Jack's opened without a key. Helen and Francis climbed the broad walnut staircase, still vaguely elegant despite the threadbare carpet, and Francis knocked. Jack opened the door and looked out with the expression of an ominous crustacean. With one hand he held the door ajar, with the other he gripped the jamb.

"Hey Jack," Francis said, "we come to see ya. How's chances for a bum gettin' a drink?"

Jack opened the door wider to look beyond Francis and when he saw Helen he let his arm fall and backed into the apartment. Kate Smith came at them, piped out of a small phonograph through the speaker of the radio. The Carolina moon was shining on somebody waiting for Kate. Beside the phonograph sat Clara, balancing herself on a chamber pot, propped on all sides with purple throw pillows, giving her the look of being astride a great animal. A red bedspread covered her legs, but it had fallen away at one side, revealing the outside of her naked left thigh, visible to the buttocks. A bottle of white fluid sat on the table by the phonograph, and on a smaller table on her other side a swinging rack cradled a gallon of muscatel, tiltable for pouring. Helen walked over to Clara and stood by her.

"Golly it's cold for this time of year, and they're calling for snow. Just feel my hands."

"This happens to be my home," Clara said hoarsely, "and I ain't about to feel your hands, or your head either. I don't see any snow."

"Have a drink," Jack said to Francis.

"Sure," Francis said. "I had a bowl of soup about six o'clock but it went right through me. I'm gonna have to eat somethin' soon."

"I don't care whether you eat or not," Jack said.

Jack went to the kitchen and Francis asked Clara: "You feelin' better?"

"No."

"She's got the runs," Helen said.

"I'll tell people what I got," Clara said.

"She lost her husband this week," Jack said, returning with two empty tumblers. He tilted the jug and half-filled both.

"How'd you find out?" Helen said.

"I saw it in the paper today," Clara said.

"I took her to the funeral this morning," Jack said. "We got a cab and went to the funeral home. They didn't even call her."

"He didn't look any different than when I married him."

"No kiddin'," Francis said.

"Outside of his hair was snow-white, that's all."

"Her kids were there," Jack said.

"The snots," Clara said.

"Sometimes I wonder what if I run off or dropped dead," Francis said. "Helen'd probably go crazy."

"Why if you dropped dead she'd bury you before you started stinkin'," Jack said. "That's all'd happen."

"What a heart you have," Francis said.

"You gotta bury your dead," Jack said.

"That's a rule of the Catholic church," said Helen.

"I'm not talkin' about the Catholic church," Francis said.

"Anyway, now she's a single girl," Jack said, "I'm gonna find out what Clara's gonna do."

"I'm gonna go right on livin' normal," Clara said.

"Normal is somethin'," Francis said. "What the hell is normal any-way, is what I'd like to know. Normal is cold. Goddamn it's cold tonight. My fingers. I rubbed myself to see if I was livin'. You know, I wanna ask you one question."

"No," Clara said.

"You said no. Whataya mean no?"

"What's he gonna ask?" Jack said. "Find out what he's gonna ask."

Clara waited.

"How's everythin' been goin'?" Francis asked.

*   *   *

Clara lifted the bottle of white fluid from the phonograph table, where the Kate Smith record was scratching in its final groove, and drank. She shook her head as it went down, and the greasy, uncombed stringlets of her hair leaped like whips. Her eyes hung low in their sockets, a pair of collapsing moons. She recapped the bottle and then swigged her muscatel to drive out the taste. She dragged on her cigarette, then coughed and spat venomously into a wadded handkerchief she held in her fist.

"Things ain't been goin' too good for Clara," Jack said, turning off the phonograph.

"I'm still trottin'," Clara said.

"Well you look pretty good for a sick lady," Francis said. "Look as good as usual to me."

Clara smiled over the rim of her wineglass at Francis.

"Nobody," said Helen, "asked how things are going for me, but I'll tell you. They're going just wonderful. Just wonderful."

"She's drunker than hell," Francis said.

"Oh I'm loaded to the gills," Helen said, giggling. "I can hardly walk."

"You ain't drunk even a nickel's worth," Jack said. "Franny's the drunk one. You're hopeless, right, Franny?"

"Helen'll never amount to nothin' if she stays with me," Francis said.

"I always thought you were an intelligent man," Jack said, and he swallowed half his wine, "but you can't be, you can't be."

"You could be mistaken," Helen said.

"Keep out of it," Francis told her, and he hooked a thumb at her, facing Jack. "There's enough right there to put you in the loony bin, just worryin' about where she's gonna live, where she's gonna stay."

"I think you could be a charmin' man," Jack said, "if you'd only get straight. You could have twenty dollars in your pocket at all times, make fifty, seventy-five a week, have a beautiful apartment with everything you want in it, all you want to drink, once you get straight."

"I worked today up at the cemetery," Francis said.

"Steady work?" asked Jack.

"Just today. Tomorrow I gotta see a fella needs some liftin' done. The old back's still tough enough."

"You keep workin' you'll have fifty in your pocket."

"I had fifty, I'd spend it on her," Francis said. "Or buy a pair of shoes. Other pair wore out and Harry over at the old clothes joint give 'em to me for a quarter. He seen me half barefoot and says, Francis you can't go around like that, and he give me these. But they don't fit right and I only got one of 'em laced. Twine there in the other one. I got a shoestring in my pocket but ain't put it in yet."

"You mean you got the shoelace and you didn't put it in the shoe?" Clara asked.

"I got it in my pocket," Francis said.

"Then put it in the shoe."

"I think it's in this pocket here. You know where it is, Helen?"

"Don't ask me."

"Look and see," Clara said.

"She wants me to put a shoestring in my shoe," Francis said.

"Right," said Clara.

Francis stopped fumbling in his pocket and let his hands fall away.

"I'm renegin'," he said.

"You're what?" Clara asked.

"I'm renegin' and I don't like to do that."

*   *   *

Francis put down his wine, walked to the bathroom, and sat on the toilet, cover down, trying to understand why he'd lied about a shoestring. He smelled the odor that came up from his fetid crotch and stood up then and dropped his trousers. He stepped out of them, then pulled off his shorts and threw them in the sink. He lifted the toilet cover and sat on the seat, and with Jack's soap and handfuls of water from the bowl, he washed his genitals and buttocks, and all their encrusted orifices, crevices, and secret folds. He rinsed himself, relathered, and rinsed again. He dried himself with one of Jack's towels, picked his shorts out of the sink, and mopped the floor with them where he had splashed water. Then he filled the sink with hot water and soaked the shorts. He soaped them and they separated into two pieces in his hands. He let the water out of the sink, wrung the shorts, and put them in his coat pocket. He opened the door a crack and called out: "Hey, Jack," and when Jack came, Francis hid his nakedness with a towel.

"Jack, old buddy, you got an old pair of shorts? Any old pair. Mine just ripped all to hell."

"I'll go look."

"Could I borry the use of your razor?"

"Help yourself."

Jack came back with the shorts and Francis put them on. Then, as Francis soaped his beard, Aldo Campione and Rowdy Dick Doolan entered the bathroom. Rowdy Dick, dapper in a three-piece blue-serge suit and a pearl-gray cap, sat on the toilet, cover down. Aldo made himself comfortable on the rim of the tub, his gardenia unintimidated by the chill of the evening. Jack's razor wouldn't cut Francis's three-day beard, and so he rinsed off the lather, soaked his face again in hot water, and relathered. While Francis rubbed the soap deeply into his beard, Rowdy Dick studied him but could remember nothing of Francis's face. This was to be expected, for when last seen, it was night in Chicago, under a bridge not far from the railyards, and five men were sharing the wealth in 1930, a lean year. On the wall of the abutment above the five, as one of them had pointed out, a former resident of the space had inscribed a poem:

> Poor little lamb,
> He wakes up in the morning,
> His fleece all cold.
> He knows what's coming.
> Say, little lamb,
> We'll go on the bummer this summer.
> We'll sit in the shade
> And drink lemonade,
> The world'll be on the hummer.

Rowdy Dick remembered this poem as well as he remembered the laughter of his sister, Mary, who was striped dead, sleigh riding, under the rails of a horse-drawn sleigh; as clearly as he remembered the plaintive, dying frown of his brother, Ted, who perished from a congenital hole in the heart. They had been three until then, living with an uncle because their parents had died, one by one, and left them alone. And then there was Dick, truly alone, who grew up tough, worked the docks, and then found an easier home in the Tenderloin, breaking the faces of nasty drunks, oily pickpockets, and fat titty-pinchers. But that didn't last either. Nothing lasted for Rowdy Dick, and he went on the bum and wound up under the bridge with Francis Phelan and three other now-faceless men. What he did remember of Francis was his hand, which now held a razor that stroked the soapy cheek.

What Francis remembered was talking about baseball that famous night. He'd begun by reliving indelible memories of his childhood as a way of explaining, at leisurely pace since none of them had anyplace to go, the generation of his drive to become a third baseman. He had been, he was saying, a boy playing among men, witnessing their talents, their peculiarities, their capacity to dive for a grounder, smash a line drive, catch a fly—all with the very ease of breath itself. They had played in the Van Woert Street polo grounds (Mulvaney's goat pasture) and there were a heroic dozen and a half of them who came two or three evenings a week, some weeks, after work to practice; men in their late twenties and early thirties, reconstituting the game that had enraptured them in their teens. There was Andy Heffern, tall, thin, saturnine, the lunger who would die at Saranac, who could pitch but never run, and who played with a long-fingered glove that had no padding whatever in the pocket, only a wisp of leather that stood between the speed of the ball and Andy's most durable palm. There was Windy Evans, who played outfield in his cap, spikes, and jock, and who caught the ball behind his back, long flies he would outrun by twenty minutes, and then plop would go that dilatory fly ball into the peach basket of his glove; and Windy would leap and beam and tell the world: There's only a few of us left! And Red Cooley, the shortstop who was the pepper of Francis's ancient imagination, and who never stopped the chatter, who leaped at every ground ball as if it were the brass ring to heaven, and who, with his short-fingered glove, wanted for nothing to be judged the world's greatest living ball player, if only it hadn't been for the homegrown deference that kept him a prisoner of Arbor Hill for the rest of his limited life.

These reminiscences by Francis evoked from Rowdy Dick an envy that surpassed reason. Why should any man be so gifted not only with so much pleasurable history but also with a gift of gab that could mesmerize a quintet of bums around a fire under a bridge? Why were there no words that would unlock what lay festering in the heart of Rowdy Dick Doolan, who needed so desperately to express what he could never even know needed expression?

Well, the grand question went unanswered, and the magic words went undiscovered. For Rowdy Dick took vengeful focus on the shoes of the voluble Francis, which were both the most desirable and, except for the burning sticks and boards in the fire, the most visible objects under that Chicago bridge. And Rowdy Dick reached inside his shirt, where he kept the small meat cleaver he had carried ever since Colorado; and slid it out of its carrying case, which he had fashioned from cardboard, oilcloth, and string; and he told Francis then: I'm gonna cut your goddamn feet off; explaining this at first and instant lunge, but explaining, even then, rather too soon for achievement, for the reflexes of Francis were not so rubbery then as they might be now in Jack's bathroom. They were full of fiber and acid and cannonade; and before Rowdy Dick, who had drunk too much of the homemade hooch he had bought, unquestionably too cheaply for sanity, earlier in the day, could make restitution for his impetuosity, Francis deflected the cleaver, which was aimed no longer at his feet but at his head, losing in the process two thirds of a right index finger and an estimated one eighth of an inch of flesh from the approximate center of his nose. He bled then in a wild careen, and with diminished hand knocking the cleaver from Rowdy Dick's grip, he took hold of that same Rowdy Dick by pantleg and armpit and swung him, oh wrathful lambs, against the abutment where the poem was inscribed, swung him as a battering ram might be swung, and cracked Rowdy Dick's skull from left parietal to the squamous area of the occipital, rendering him bloody, insensible, leaking, and instantly dead.

What Francis recalled of this unmanageable situation was the compulsion to flight, the most familiar notion, after the desire not to aspire, that he had ever entertained. And after searching, as swiftly as he knew how, for his lost digital joints, and after concluding that they had flown too deeply into the dust and the weeds ever to be retrieved again by any hand of any man, and after pausing also, ever so briefly, for a reconnoitering, not of what might be recoverable of the nose but of what might be visually memorable because of its separation into parts, Francis began to run, and in so doing, reconstituted a condition that was as pleasurable to his being as it was natural: the running of bases after the crack of the bat, the running from accusation, the running from the calumny of men and women, the running from family, from bondage, from destitution of spirit through ritualistic straightenings, the running, finally, in a quest for pure flight as a fulfilling mannerism of the spirit.

He found his way to a freight yard, found there an empty boxcar with open door, and so entered into yet another departure from completion: the true and total story of his life thus far. It was South Bend before he got to a hospital, where the intern asked him: Where's the finger? And Francis said: In the weeds. And how about the nose? Where's that piece of the nose? If you'd only brought me that piece of the nose, we might be able to put it back together and you wouldn't even know it was gone.

All things had ceased to bleed by then, and so Francis was free once again from those deadly forces that so frequently sought to sever the line of his life.

He had stanched the flow of his wound.

He had stood staunchly irresolute in the face of capricious and adverse fate.

He had, oh wondrous man, stanched death its very self.

*   *   *

Francis dried his face with the towel, buttoned up his shirt, and put on his coat and trousers. He nodded an apology to Rowdy Dick for having taken his life and included in the nod the hope that Dick would understand it hadn't been intentional. Rowdy Dick smiled and doffed his cap, creating an eruption of brilliance around his dome. Francis could see the line of Dick's cranial fracture running through his hair like a gleaming river, and Francis understood that Rowdy Dick was in heaven, or so close to it that he was taking on the properties of an angel of the Lord. Dick put his cap on again and even the cap exuded a glow, like the sun striving to break through a pale, gray cloud. "Yes," said Francis, "I'm sorry I broke your head so bad, but I hope you remember I had my reasons," and he held up to Rowdy Dick his truncated finger. "You know, you can't be a priest when you got a finger missin'. Can't say mass with a hand like this. Can't throw a baseball either." He rubbed the bump in his nose with the stump of a finger. "Kind of a bump there, but what the hell. Doc put a big bandage on it, and it got itchy, so I ripped it off. Went back when it got infected, and the doc says, You shouldn'ta took off that bandage, because now I got to scrape it out and you'll have an even bigger bump there. I'da had a bump anyway. What the hell, little bump like that don't look too bad, does it? I ain't complainin'. I don't hold no grudges more'n five years."

"You all right in there, Francis?" Helen called. "Who are you talking to?"

Francis waved to Rowdy Dick, understanding that some debts of violence had been settled, but he remained full of the awareness of rampant martyrdom surrounding him: martyrs to wrath, to booze, to failure, to loss, to hostile weather. Aldo Campione gestured at Francis, suggesting that while there may be some inconsistency about it, prayers were occasionally answerable, a revelation that did very little to improve Francis's state of mind, for there had never been a time since childhood when he knew what to pray for.

"Hey bum," he said to Jack when he stepped out of the bathroom, "how about a bum gettin' a drink?"

"He ain't no bum," Clara said.

"Goddamn it, I know he ain't," Francis said. "He's a hell of a man. A workin' man."

"How come you shaved?" Helen asked.

"Gettin' itchy. Four days and them whiskers grow back inside again."

"It sure improves how you look," Clara said.

"That's the truth," said Jack.

"I knew Francis was handsome," Clara said, "but this is the first time I ever saw you clean shaved."

"I was thinkin' about how many old bums I know died in the weeds. Wake up covered with snow and some of 'em layin' there dead as hell, froze stiff. Some get up and walk away from it. I did myself. But them others are gone for good. You ever know a guy named Rowdy Dick Doolan in your travels?"

"Never did," Jack said.

"There was another guy, Pocono Pete, he died in Denver, froze like a brick. And Poocher Felton, he bought it in Detroit, pissed his pants and froze tight to the sidewalk. And a crazy bird they called Ward Six, no other name. They found him with a red icicle growin' out of his nose. All them old guys, never had nothin', never knew nothin', stupid, thievin', crazy. Foxy Phil Tooker, a skinny little runt, he froze all scrunched up, knees under his chin. 'Stead of straightenin' him out, they buried him in half a coffin. Lorda mercy, them geezers. I bet they all of 'em, dyin' like that, I bet they all wind up in heaven, if they ever got such a place."

"I believe when you're dead you go in the ground and that's the end of it," Jack said. "Heaven never made no sensicality to me whatsoever."

"You wouldn't get in anyhow," Helen said. "They've got your reservations someplace else."

"Then I'm with him," Clara said. "Who'd want to be in heaven with all them nuns? God what a bore."

Francis knew Clara less than three weeks, but he could see the curve of her life: sexy kid likes the rewards, goes pro, gets restless, marries and makes kids, chucks that, pro again, sickens, but really sick, gettin' old, gettin' ugly, locks onto Jack, turns monster. But she's got most of her teeth, not bad; and that hair: you get her to a beauty shop and give her a marcel, it'd be all right; put her in new duds, high heels and silk stockin's; and hey, look at them titties, and that leg: the skin's clear on it.

Clara saw Francis studying her and gave him a wink. "I knew a fella once, looked a lot like you. I had the hots for him."

"I'll bet you did," Helen said.

"He loved what I gave him."

"Clara never lacked for boyfriends," Jack said. "I'm a lucky man.

But she's pretty sick. That's why you can't stay. She eats a lot of toast."

"Oh I could make some toast," Helen said, standing up from her chair. "Would you like that?"

"If I feel like eatin' I'll make my own toast," Clara said. "And I'm gettin' ready to go to bed. Make sure you lock the door when you go out."

Jack grabbed Francis by the arm and pulled him toward the kitchen, but not before Francis readjusted his vision of Clara sitting in the middle of her shit machine, sending up a silent reek from her ruined guts and their sewerage.

✼ ✼ ✼

When Jack and Francis came back into the living room Francis was smoking one of Jack's cigarettes. He dropped it as he reached for the wine, and Helen groaned.

"Everything fallin' on the floor," Francis said. "I don't blame you for throwin' these bums out if they can't behave respectable."

"It's gettin' late for me," Jack said. "I used to get by on two, three hours' sleep, but no more."

"I ain't stayed here in how long now?" Francis asked. "Two weeks, ain't it?"

"Oh come on, Francis," Clara said. "You were here not four days ago. And Helen last night. And last Sunday you were here."

"Sunday we left," Helen said.

"I flopped here two nights, wasn't it?" Francis said.

"Six," Jack said. "Like a week."

"I beg to differ with you," Helen said.

"It was over a week," Jack said.

"I know different," said Helen.

"From Monday to Sunday."

"Oh no."

"It's a little mixed up," Francis said.

"He's got a lot of things mixed up," Helen said. "I hope you don't get your food mixed up like that down at the diner."

"No," Jack said.

"You know, you're very insultin'," Francis said to Helen.

"It was a week," Jack said.

"You're a liar," Helen said.

"Don't call me a liar because I know so."

"Haven't you got any brains at all?" Francis said. "You supposed to be a college woman, you supposed to be this and that."

"I am a college woman."

"You know what I thought," Jack said, "was for you to stay here,

Franny, till you get work, till you pick up a little bankroll. You don't have to give me nothin'."

"Shake hands on it," Helen said.

"I don't know about the proposition now," Jack said.

"Because I'm a bum," Francis said.

"No, I wouldn't put it that way." Jack poured more wine for Francis.

"I knew he didn't mean it," Helen said.

"I'm gonna tell you," Francis said. "I always thought a lot of Clara."

"You're drunk, Francis," Helen screamed, standing up again. "Stay drunk for the rest of your life. I'm leaving you, Francis. You're crazy. All you want is to guzzle wine. You're insane!"

"What'd I say?" Francis asked. "I said I liked Clara."

"Nothin' wrong about that," Jack said.

"I don't mind about that," Helen said, sitting down.

"I don't know what to do with that woman," Francis said.

"Do you even know if you're staying here tonight?" Helen asked.

"No, he's not," Jack said. "Take him with you when you go."

"We're going," Helen said.

"Clara's too sick, Francis," said Jack.

Francis sipped his wine, put it on the table, and struck a tap dancer's pose.

"How you like these new duds of mine, Clara? You didn't tell me how swell I look, all dressed up."

"You look sharp," Clara said.

"You can't keep up with Francis."

"Don't waste your time, Francis," Helen said.

"You're getting very hostile, you know that? Listen, you want to sleep with me in the weeds tonight?"

"I never slept in the weeds," Helen said.

"Never?" asked Clara.

"No, never," said Helen.

"Oh yes," Francis said. "She slept in the coaches with me, and the fields."

"Never. You made that up, Francis."

"We been through the valley together," Francis said.

"Maybe you have," said Helen. "I've never gone that far down and I don't intend to go that far down."

"It ain't far to go. She slept in Finny's car night before last."

"That's the last time. If it came to that, I'd get in touch with my people."

"You really ought to get in touch with them, dearie," said Clara.

"My people are very high class. My brother is a very well-to-do lawyer but I don't like to ask him for anything."

"Sometimes you have to," Jack said. "You oughta move in with him."

"Then Francis'd be out. No, I've got Francis. We'd get married tomorrow if only he could get a divorce, wouldn't we, Fran."

"That's right, honey."

"We battle sometimes, but only when he drinks. Then he goes haywire."

"You oughta get straight, Franny," Jack said. "You could have twenty bucks in your pocket at all times. They need men like you. You could have everything you want. A new Victrola like that one right there. That's a honey."

"I had all that shit," Francis said.

"It's late," Clara said.

"Yeah, people," said Jack. "Gotta hit the hay."

"Fix me a sandwich, will ya?" Francis asked. "To take out."

"No," Clara said.

Helen rose, screaming, and started for Clara. "You forget when you were hungry."

"Sit down and shut up," Francis said.

"I won't shut up. I remember when she came to my place years ago, begging for food. I know her a long time. I'm honest in what I know."

"I never begged," said Clara.

"He only asked for a sandwich," said Helen.

"I'm gonna give him a sandwich," Jack said.

"Jack don't want you to come back again," Francis said to Helen.

"I don't want to ever come back again," Helen said.

"He asked for a sandwich," Jack said, "I'll give him a sandwich."

"I knew you would," Francis told him.

"Damn right I'll give you a sandwich."

"Damn right," Francis said, "and I knew it."

"I don't want to be bothered," Clara said.

"Sharp cheese. You like sharp cheese?"

"My favorite," Francis said.

Jack went to the kitchen and came back into a silent room with a sandwich wrapped in waxed paper. Francis took it and put it in his coat. Helen stood in the doorway.

"Good night, pal," Francis said to Jack.

"Best of luck," Jack said.

"See you around," Francis said to Clara.

"Toodle-oo," said Clara.

* * *

On the street, Francis felt the urge to run. Ten Broeck Street, in the direction they were walking, inclined downward toward Clinton Avenue, and he felt the gravitational fall driving him into a trot that would leave her behind to solve her own needs. The night seemed colder than before, and clearer too, the moon higher in its sterile solitude. North Pearl Street was deserted, no cars, no people at this hour, one-forty-five by the great clock on the First Church. They had walked three blocks without speaking and now they were heading back toward where they had begun, toward the South End, the mission, the weeds.

"Where the hell you gonna sleep now?" Francis asked.

"I can't be sure, but I wouldn't stay there if they gave me silk sheets and mink pillows. I remember her when she was whoring and always broke. Now she's so high and mighty. I had to speak my piece."

"You didn't accomplish anything."

"Did Jack really say that they don't want me anymore?"

"Right. But they asked me to stay. Clara thinks you're a temptation to Jack. The way I figure, if I give her some attention she won't worry about you, but you're so goddamn boisterous. Here. Have a piece of sandwich."

"It'd choke me."

"It won't choke you. You'll be glad for it."

"I'm not a phony."

"I'm not a phony either."

"You're not, eh?"

"You know what I'll do?" He grabbed her collar and her throat and screamed into her eyes. "I'll knock you right across that goddamn street! You don't bullshit me one time. Be a goddamn woman! That's the reason you can't flop with nobody. I can go up there right now and sleep. Jack said I could stay."

"He did not."

"He certainly did. But they don't want you. I asked for a sandwich. Did I get it?"

"You're really stupendous and colossal."

"Listen"—and he still held her by the collar—"you squint your eyes at me and I'll knock you over that goddamn automobile. You been a pain in the ass to me for nine years. They don't want you because you're a pain in the ass."

Headlights moved north on Pearl Street, coming toward them, and Francis let go of her. She did not move, but stared at him.

"You got some goddamn eyes, you know?" He was screaming. "I'll black 'em for you. You're a horse's ass! You know what I'll do? I'll rip that fuckin' coat off and put you in rags."

She did not move her body or her eyes.

"I'm gonna eat this sandwich. Whole hunk of cheese."

"I don't want it."

"By god I do. I'll be hungry tomorrow. It won't choke me. I'm thankful for everything."

"You're a perfect saint."

"Listen. Straighten up or I'm gonna kill you."

"I won't eat it. It's rat food."

"I'm gonna kill you!" Francis screamed. "Goddamn it, you hear what I said? Don't drive me insane. Be a goddamn woman and go the fuck to bed somewhere."

They walked, not quite together, toward Madison Avenue, south again on South Pearl, retracing their steps. Francis brushed Helen's arm and she moved away from him.

"You gonna stay at the mission with Pee Wee?"

"No."

"Then you gonna stay with me?"

"I'm going to call my brother."

"Good. Call him. Call him a couple of times."

"I'll have him meet me someplace."

"Where you gonna get the nickel to make the call?"

"That's my business. God, Francis, you were all right till you started on the wine. Wine, wine, wine."

"I'll get some cardboard. We'll go to that old building."

"The police keep raiding that place. I don't want to go to jail. I don't know why you didn't stay with Jack and Clara since you were so welcome."

"You're a woman for abuse."

They walked east on Madison, past the mission. Helen did not look in. When they reached Green Street she stopped.

"I'm going down below," she said.

"Who you kiddin'?" Francis said. "You got noplace to go. You'll be knocked on the head."

"That wouldn't be the worst ever happened to me."

"We got to find something. Can't leave a dog out like this."

"Shows you what kind of people they are up there."

"Stay with me."

"No, Francis. You're crazy."

He grabbed the hair at the back of her head, then held her whole head in both hands.

"You're gonna hit me," she said.

"I won't hit ya, babe. I love ya some. Are ya awful cold?"

"I don't think I've been warm once in two days."

Francis let go of her and took off his suitcoat and put it around her shoulders.

"No, it's too cold for you to do that," she said. "I've got this coat. You can't be in just a shirt."

"What the hell's the difference. Coat ain't no protection."

She handed him back the coat. "I'm going," she said.

"Don't walk away from me," Francis said. "You'll be lost in the world."

But she walked away. And Francis leaned against the light pole on the corner, lit the cigarette Jack had given him, fingered the dollar bill Jack had slipped him in the kitchen, ate what was left of the cheese sandwich, and then threw his old undershorts down the sewer.

* * *

Helen walked down Green Street to a vacant lot, where she saw a fire in an oil drum. From across the street she could see five coloreds around the fire, men and women. On an old sofa in the weeds just beyond the drum, she saw a white woman lying underneath a colored man. She walked back to where Francis waited.

"I couldn't stay outside tonight," she said. "I'd die."

Francis nodded and they walked to Finny's car, a 1930 black Oldsmobile, dead and wheelless in an alley off John Street. Two men were asleep in it, Finny in the front passenger seat.

"I don't know that man in back," Helen said.

"Yeah you do," said Francis. "That's Little Red from the mission. He won't bother you. If he does I'll pull out his tongue."

"I don't want to get in there, Francis."

"It's warm, anyhow. Cold in them weeds, honey, awful cold. You walk the streets alone, they'll pinch you quicker'n hell."

"You get in the back."

"No. No room in there for the likes of me. Legs're too long."

"Where will you go?"

"I'll find me some of them tall weeds, get outa the wind."

"Are you coming back?"

"Sure, I'll be back. You get a good sleep and I'll see you here or up at the mission in the ayem."

"I don't want to stay here."

"You got to, babe. It's what there is."

Francis opened the passenger door and shook Finny.

"Hey bum. Move over. You got a visitor."

Finny opened his eyes, heavy with wine. Little Red was snoring.

"Who the hell are you?" Finny said.

"It's Francis. Move over and let Helen in."

"Francis." Finny raised his head.

"I'll get you a jug tomorrow for this, old buddy," Francis said. "She's gotta get in outa this weather."

"Yeah," said Finny.

"Never mind yeah, just move your ass over and let her sit. She can't sleep behind that wheel, condition her stomach's in."

"Unnngghh," said Finny, and he slid behind the wheel.

Helen sat on the front seat, dangling her legs out of the car. Francis stroked her cheek with three fingertips and then let his hand fall. She lifted her legs inside.

"You don't have to be scared," Francis said.

"I'm not scared," Helen said. "Not that."

"Finny won't let nothin' happen to you. I'll kill the son of a bitch if he does."

"She knows," Finny said. "She's been here before."

"Sure," said Francis. "Nothing can happen to you."

"No."

"See you in the mornin'."

"Sure."

"Keep the faith," Francis said.

And he closed the car door.

*   *   *

He walked with an empty soul toward the north star, magnetized by an impulse to redirect his destiny. He had slept in the weeds of a South End vacant lot too many times. He would do it no more. Because he needed to confront the ragman in the morning, he would not chance arrest by crawling into a corner of one of the old houses on lower Broadway where the cops swept through periodically with their mindless net. What difference did it make whether four or six or eight lost men slept under a roof and out of the wind in a house with broken stairs and holes in the floors you could fall through to death, a house that for five or maybe ten years had been inhabited only by pigeons? What difference?

He walked north on Broadway, past Steamboat Square, where as a child he'd boarded the riverboats for outings to Troy, or Kingston, or picnics on Lagoon Island. He passed the D & H building and Billy Barnes's Albany *Evening Journal*, a building his simpleminded brother Tommy had helped build in 1913. He walked up to Maiden Lane and Broadway, where Keeler's Hotel used to be, and where his brother Peter sometimes spent the night when he was on the outs with Mama. But Keeler's burned the year after Francis ran away and now it was a bunch of stores. Francis had rowed down Broadway to the hotel, Billy in the rowboat with him, in 1913 when the river rose away the hell and gone up and flooded half of downtown. The kid loved it. Said he liked it better'n sleigh ridin'. Gone. What the hell ain't gone? Well, me. Yeah, me. Ain't a whole hell of a lot of me left, but I ain't gone entirely. Be god-diddley-damned if I'm gonna roll over and die.

Francis walked half an hour due north from downtown, right into North Albany. At Main Street he turned east toward the river, down Main Street's little incline past the McGraw house, then past the Greenes', the only coloreds in all North Albany in the old days, past the Daugherty house, where Martin still lived, no lights on, and past the old Wheelbarrow, Iron Joe Farrell's old saloon, all boarded up now, where Francis learned how to drink, where he watched cockfights in the back room, and where he first spoke to Annie Farrell.

He walked toward the flats, where the canal used to be, long gone and the ditch filled in. The lock was gone and the lockhouse too, and the towpath all grown over. Yet incredibly, as he neared North Street, he saw a structure he recognized. Son of a bitch. Welt the Tin's barn, still standing. Who'd believe it? Could Welt the Tin be livin'? Not likely. Too dumb to live so long. Was it in use? Still a barn? Looks like a barn. But who keeps horses now?

The barn was a shell, with a vast hole in the far end of the roof where moonlight poured cold fire onto the ancient splintered floor. Bats flew in balletic arcs around the streetlamp outside, the last lamp on North Street; and the ghosts of mules and horses snorted and stomped for Francis. He scuffed at the floorboards himself and found them solid. He touched them and found them dry. One barn door canted on one hinge, and Francis calculated that if he could move the door a few feet to sleep in its lee, he would be protected from the wind on three sides. No moonlight leaked through the roof above this corner, the same corner where Welt the Tin had hung his rakes and pitchforks, all in a row between spaced nails.

Francis would reclaim this corner, restore all rakes and pitchforks, return for the night the face of Welt the Tin as it had been, reinvest himself with serendipitous memories of a lost age. On a far shelf in the moonlight he saw a pile of papers and a cardboard box. He spread the papers in his chosen corner, ripped the box at its seams, and lay down on the flattened pile.

He had lived not seventy-five feet from where he now lay.

Seventy-five feet from this spot, Gerald Phelan died on the 26th of April, 1916.

In Finny's car Helen would probably be pulling off Finny, or taking him in her mouth. Finny would be unequal to intercourse, and Helen would be too fat for a toss in the front seat. Helen would be equal to any such task. He knew, though she had never told him, that she once had to fuck two strangers to be able to sleep in peace. Francis accepted this cuckoldry as readily as he accepted the onus of pulling the blanket off Clara and penetrating whatever dimensions of reek necessary to gain access to a bed. Fornication was standard survival currency everywhere, was it not?

Maybe I won't survive tonight after all, Francis thought as he folded his hands between his thighs. He drew his knees up toward his chest, not quite so high as Foxy Phil Tooker's, and considered the death he had caused in this life, and was perhaps causing still. Helen is dying and Francis is perhaps the principal agent of hastening her death, even as his whole being tonight has been directed to keeping her from freezing in the dust like Sandra. I don't want to die before you do, Helen, is what Francis thought. You'll be like a little kid in the world without me.

He thought of his father flying through the air and knew the old man was in heaven. The good leave us behind to think about the deeds they did. His mother would be in purgatory, probably for goddamn ever. She wasn't evil enough for hell, shrew of shrews that she was, denier of life. But he couldn't see her ever getting a foot into heaven either, if they ever got such a place.

The new and frigid air of November lay on Francis like a blanket of glass. Its weight rendered him motionless and brought peace to his body, and the stillness brought a cessation of anguish to his brain. In a dream he was only just beginning to enter, horns and mountains rose up out of the earth, the horns—ethereal trumpets—sounding with a virtuosity equal to the perilousness of the crags and cornices of the mountainous pathways. Francis recognized the song the trumpets played and he floated with its melody. Then, yielding not without trepidation to its coded urgency, he ascended bodily into the exalted reaches of the world where the song had been composed so long ago. And he slept.

IV

FRANCIS STOOD IN THE JUNKYARD DRIVEWAY, looking for old Rosskam. Gray clouds that looked like two flying piles of dirty socks blew swiftly past the early-morning sun, the world shimmered in a sudden blast of incandescence, and Francis blinked. His eyes roved over a cemetery of dead things: rusted-out gas stoves, broken wood stoves, dead iceboxes, and bicycles with twisted wheels. A mountain of worn-out rubber tires cast its shadow on a vast plain of rusty pipes, children's wagons, toasters, automobile fenders. A three-sided shed half a block long sheltered a mountain range of cardboard, paper, and rags.

Francis stepped into this castoff world and walked toward a wooden shack, small and tilted, with a swayback horse hitched to a four-wheeled wooden wagon in front of it. Beyond the wagon a small mountain of wagon wheels rose alongside a sprawling scatter of pans, cans, irons, pots, and kettles, and a sea of metal fragments that no longer had names.

Francis saw probably Rosskam, framed in the shack's only window, watching him approach. Francis pushed open the door and confronted the man, who was short, filthy, and sixtyish, a figure of visible sinew, moon-faced, bald, and broad-chested, with fingers like the roots of an oak tree.

"Howdy," Francis said.

"Yeah," said Rosskam.

"Preacher said you was lookin' for a strong back."

"It could be. You got one, maybe?"

"Stronger than some."

"You can pick up an anvil?"

"You collectin' anvils, are you?"

"Collect everything."

"Show me the anvil."

"Ain't got one."

"Then I'd play hell pickin' it up."

"How about the barrel. You can pick that up?"

He pointed to an oil drum, half full of wood scraps and junk metal. Francis wrapped his arms around it and lifted it, with difficulty.

"Where'd you like it put?"

"Right where you got it off."

"You pick up stuff like this yourself?" Francis asked.

Rosskam stood and lifted the drum without noticeable strain, then held it aloft.

"You got to be in mighty fair shape, heftin' that," said Francis. "That's one heavy item."

"You call this heavy?" Rosskam said, and he heaved the drum upward and set its bottom edge on his right shoulder. Then he let it slide to chest level, hugged it, and set it down.

"I do a lifetime of lifting," he said.

"I see that clear. You own this whole shebang here?"

"All. You still want to work?"

"What are you payin'?"

"Seven dollar. And work till dark."

"Seven. That ain't much for back work."

"Some might even bite at it."

"It's worth eight or nine."

"You got better, take it. People feed families all week on seven dollar."

"Seven-fifty."

"Seven."

"All right, what the hell's the difference?"

"Get up the wagon."

Two minutes in the moving wagon told Francis his tailbone would be grieving by day's end, if it lasted that long. The wagon bounced over the granite blocks and the trolley tracks, and the men rode side by side in silence through the bright streets of morning. Francis was glad for the sunshine, and felt rich seeing the people of his old city rising for work, opening stores and markets, moving out into a day of substance and profit. Clearheadedness always brought optimism to Francis; a long ride on a freight when there was nothing to drink made way for new visions of survival, and sometimes he even went out and looked for work. But even as he felt rich, he felt dead. He had not found Helen and he had to find her. Helen was lost again. The woman makes a goddamn career out of being lost. Probably went to mass someplace.

But why didn't she come back to the mission for coffee, and for Francis? Why the hell should Helen always make Francis feel dead?

Then he remembered the story about Billy in the paper and he brightened. Pee Wee read it first and gave it to him. It was a story about Francis's son Billy, written by Martin Daugherty, the newspaperman, who long ago lived next door to the Phelans on Colonie Street. It was the story of Billy getting mixed up in the kidnapping of the nephew of Patsy McCall, the boss of Albany's political machine. They got the nephew back safely, but Billy was in the middle because he wouldn't inform on a suspected kidnapper. And there was Martin's column defending Billy, calling Patsy McCall a very smelly bag of very small potatoes for being rotten to Billy.

"So how do you like it?" Rosskam said.

"Like what?" said Francis.

"Sex business," Rosskam said. "Women stuff."

"I don't think much about it anymore."

"You bums, you do a lot of dirty stuff up the heinie, am I right?"

"Some like it that way. Not me."

"How do you like it?"

"I don't even like it anymore, I'll tell you the truth. I'm over the hill."

"A man like you? How old? Fifty-five? Sixty-two?"

"Fifty-eight," said Francis.

"Seventy-one here," said Rosskam. "I go over no hills. Four, five times a night I get it in with the old woman. And in the daylight, you never know."

"What's the daylight?"

"Women. They ask for it. You go house to house, you get offers. This is not a new thing in the world."

"I never went house to house," Francis said.

"Half my life I go house to house," said Rosskam, "and I know how it is. You get offers."

"You probably get a lot of clap, too."

"Twice all my life. You use the medicine, it goes away. Those ladies, they don't do it so often to get disease. Hungry is what they got, not clap."

"They bring you up to bed in your old clothes?"

"In the cellar. They love it down the cellar. On the woodpile. In the coal. On top the newspapers. They follow me down the stairs and bend over the papers to show me their bubbies, or they up their skirts on the stairs ahead of me, showing other things. Best I ever got lately was on top of four ash cans. Very noisy, but some woman. The things she said you wouldn't repeat. Hot, hotsy, oh my. This morning we pay her a visit, up on Arbor Hill. You wait in the wagon. It don't take long, if you don't mind."

"Why should I mind? It's your wagon, you're the boss."

"That's right. I am the boss."

They rode up to Northern Boulevard and started down Third Street, all downhill so as not to kill the horse. House by house they went, carting out old clocks and smashed radios, papers always, two boxes of broken-backed books on gardening, a banjo with a broken neck, cans, old hats, rags.

"Here," old Rosskam said when they reached the hot lady's house. "If you like, watch by the cellar window. She likes lookers and I don't mind it."

Francis shook his head and sat alone on the wagon, staring down Third Street. He could have reconstructed this street from memory. Childhood, young manhood were passed on the streets of Arbor Hill, girls discovering they had urges, boys capitalizing on this discovery. In the alleyways the gang watched women undress, and one night they watched the naked foreplay of Mr. and Mrs. Ryan until they put out the light. Joey Kilmartin whacked off during that show. The old memory aroused Francis sexually. Did he want a woman? No. Helen? No, no. He wanted to watch the Ryans again, getting ready to go at it. He climbed down from the wagon and walked into the alley of the house where Rosskam's hot lady lived. He walked softly, listening, and he heard groaning, inaudible words, and the sound of metal fatigue. He crouched down and peered in the cellar window at the back of the house, and there they were on the ash cans, Rosskam's pants hanging from his shoes, on top of a lady with her dress up to her neck. When Francis brought the scene into focus, he could hear their words.

"Oh boyoboy," Rosskam was saying, "oh boyoboy."

"Hey I love it," said the hot lady. "Do I love it? Do I love it?"

"You love it," said Rosskam. "Oh boyoboy."

"Gimme that stick," said the hot lady. "Gimme it, gimme it, gimme, gimme, gimme that stick."

"Oh take it," said Rosskam. "Oh take it."

"Oh gimme it," said the hot lady. "I'm a hot slut. Gimme it."

"Oh boyoboy," said Rosskam.

The hot lady saw Francis at the window and waved to him. Francis stood up and went back to the wagon, conjuring memories against his will. Bums screwing in boxcars, women gang-banged in the weeds, a girl of eight raped, and then the rapist kicked half to death by other bums and rolled out of the moving train. He saw the army of women he had known: women upside down, women naked, women with their skirts up, their legs open, their mouths open, women in heat, women sweating and grunting under and over him, women professing love, desire, joy, pain, need. Helen.

He met Helen at a New York bar, and when they found out they were both from Albany, love took a turn toward the sun. He kissed her and she tongued him. He stroked her body, which was old even then, but vital and full and without the tumor, and they confessed a fiery yearning for each other. Francis hesitated to carry it through, for he had been off women eight months, having finally and with much discomfort rid himself of the crabs and a relentless, pusy drip. Yet the presence of Helen's flaming body kept driving away his dread of disease, and finally, when he saw they were going to be together for much more than a one-nighter, he told her: I wouldn't touch ya, babe. Not till I got me a checkup. She told him to wear a sheath but he said he hated them goddamn things. Get us a blood test, that's what we'll do, he told her, and they pooled their money and went to the hospital and both got a clean bill and then took a room and made love till they wore out. Love, you are my member rubbed raw. Love, you are an unstoppable fire. You burn me, love. I am singed, blackened. Love, I am ashes.

*   *   *

The wagon rolled on and Francis realized it was heading for Colonie Street, where he was born and raised, where his brothers and sisters still lived. The wagon wheels squeaked as they moved and the junk in the back rattled and bounced, announcing the prodigal's return. Francis saw the house where he grew up, still the same colors, brown and tan, the vacant lot next to it grown tall with weeds where the Daugherty house and the Brothers' School had stood until they burned.

He saw his mother and father alight from their honeymoon carriage in front of the house and, with arms entwined, climb the front stoop. Michael Phelan wore his trainman's overalls and looked as he had the moment before the speeding train struck him. Kathryn Phelan, in her wedding dress, looked as she had when she hit Francis with an open hand and sent him sprawling backward into the china closet.

"Stop here a minute, will you?" Francis said to Rosskam, who had uttered no words since ascending from his cellar of passion.

"Stop?" Rosskam said, and he reined the horse.

The newlyweds stepped across the threshold and into the house. They climbed the front stairs to the bedroom they would share for all the years of their marriage, the room that now was also their shared grave, a spatial duality as reasonable to Francis as the concurrence of this moment both in the immediate present of his fifty-eighth year of life and in the year before he was born: that year of sacramental consummation, 1879. The room had about it the familiarity of his young lifetime. The oak bed and the two oak dressers were as rooted to their positions in the room as the trees that shaded the edge of the Phelan burial plot. The room was redolent of the blend of maternal and paternal odors, which separated themselves when Francis buried his face deeply in either of the personal pillows, or opened a drawer full of private garments, or inhaled the odor of burned tobacco in a cold pipe, say, or the fragrance of a cake of Pears' soap, kept in a drawer as a sachet.

In their room Michael Phelan embraced his new wife of fifty-nine years and ran a finger down the crevice of her breasts; and Francis saw his mother-to-be shudder with what he assumed was the first abhorrent touch of love. Because he was the firstborn, Francis's room was next to theirs, and so he had heard their nocturnal rumblings for years; and he well knew how she perennially resisted her husband. When Michael would finally overcome her, either by force of will or by threatening to take their case to the priest, Francis would hear her gurgles of resentment, her moans of anguish, her eternal arguments about the sinfulness of all but generative couplings. For she hated the fact that people even knew that she had committed intercourse in order to have children, a chagrin that was endlessly satisfying to Francis all his life.

Now, as her husband lifted her chemise over her head, the virginal mother of six recoiled with what Francis recognized for the first time to be spiritually induced terror, as visible in her eyes in 1879 as it was in the grave. Her skin was as fresh and pink as the taffeta lining of her coffin, but she was, in her youthfully rosy bloom, as lifeless as the spun silk of her magenta burial dress. She has been dead all her life, Francis thought, and for the first time in years he felt pity for this woman, who had been spayed by self-neutered nuns and self-gelded priests. As she yielded her fresh body to her new husband out of obligation, Francis felt the iron maiden of induced chastity piercing her everywhere, tightening with the years until all sensuality was strangulated and her body was as bloodless and cold as a granite angel.

She closed her eyes and fell back on the wedding bed like a corpse, ready to receive the thrust, and the old man's impeccable blood shot into her aged vessel with a passionate burst that set her writhing with the life of newly conceived death. Francis watched this primal pool of his own soulish body squirm into burgeoning matter, saw it change and grow with the speed of light until it was the size of an infant, saw it then yanked roughly out of the maternal cavern by his father, who straightened him, slapped him into being, and swiftly molded him into a bestial weed. The body sprouted to wildly matured growth and stood fully clad at last in the very clothes Francis was now wearing. He recognized the toothless mouth, the absent finger joints, the bump on the nose, the mortal slouch of this newborn shade, and he knew then that he would be this decayed self he had been so long in becoming, through all the endless years of his death.

— * * *

"Giddap," said Rosskam to his horse, and the old nag clomped on down the hill of Colonie Street.

"Raaaa-aaaaaags," screamed Rosskam. "Raaaa-aaaa-aags." The scream was a two-noted song, C and B-flat, or maybe F and E-flat. And from a window across the street from the Phelan house, a woman's head appeared.

"Goooo-ooooooo," she called in two-noted answer. "Raaaag-maaan."

Rosskam pulled to a halt in front of the alley alongside her house.

"On the back porch," she said. "Papers and a washtub and some old clothes."

Rosskam braked his wagon and climbed down.

"Well?" he said to Francis.

"I don't want to go in," Francis said. "I know her."

"So what's that?"

"I don't want her to see me. Mrs. Dillon. Her husband's a railroad man. I know them all my life. My family lives in that house over there. I was born up the street. I don't want people on this block to see me looking like a bum."

"But you're a bum."

"Me and you know that, but they don't. I'll cart anything, I'll cart it all the next time you stop. But not on this street. You understand?"

"Sensitive bum. I got a sensitive bum working for me."

While Rosskam went for the junk alone, Francis stared across the street and saw his mother in housedress and apron surreptitiously throwing salt on the roots of the young maple tree that grew in the Daugherty yard but had the temerity to drop twigs, leaves, and pods onto the Phelan tomato plants and flowers. Kathryn Phelan told her near-namesake, Katrina Daugherty, that the tree's droppings and shade were unwelcome at the Phelans'. Katrina trimmed what she could of the tree's low branches and asked Francis, a neighborhood handyman at seventeen, to help her trim the higher ones; and he did: climbed aloft and sawed living arms off the vigorous young tree. But for every branch cut, new life sprouted elsewhere, and the tree thickened to a lushness unlike that of any other tree on Arbor Hill, infuriating Kathryn Phelan, who increased her dosage of salt on the roots, which waxed and grew under and beyond the wooden fence and surfaced ever more brazenly on Phelan property.

Why do you want to kill the tree, Mama? Francis asked.

And his mother said it was because the tree had no right insinuating itself into other people's yards. If we want a tree in the yard we'll plant our own, she said, and threw more salt. Some leaves withered on the tree and one branch died entirely. But the salting failed, for Francis saw the tree now, twice its old size, a giant thing in the world, rising high out of the weeds and toward the sun from what used to be the Daugherty yard.

On this high noon in 1938, under the sun's full brilliance, the tree restored itself to its half size of forty-one years past, a July morning in 1897 when Francis was sitting on a middle branch, sawing the end off a branch above him. He heard the back door of the Daughertys' new house open and close, and he looked down from his perch to see Katrina Daugherty, carrying her small shopping bag, wearing a gray sun hat, gray satin evening slippers, and nothing else. She descended the five steps of the back piazza and strode toward the new barn, where the Daugherty landau and horse were kept.

"Mrs. Daugherty?" Francis called out, and he leaped down from the tree. "Are you all right?"

"I'm going downtown, Francis," she said.

"Shouldn't you put something on? Some clothes?"

"Clothes?" she said. She looked down at her naked self and then cocked her head and widened her eyes into quizzical rigidity.

"Mrs. Daugherty," Francis said, but she gave no response, nor did she move. From the piazza railing that he was building, Francis lifted a piece of forest-green canvas he would eventually install as an awning on a side window, and wrapped the naked woman in it, picking her up in his arms then, and carrying her into her house. He sat her on the sofa in the back parlor and, as the canvas slid slowly away from her shoulders, he searched the house for a garment and found a housecoat hanging behind the pantry door. He stood her up and shoved her arms into the housecoat, tied its belt at her waist, covering her body fully, and undid the chin ribbon that held her hat. Then he sat her down again on the sofa.

He found a bottle of Scotch whiskey in a cabinet and poured her an inch in a goblet from the china closet, held it to her lips, and cajoled her into tasting it. Whiskey is magic and will cure all your troubles. Katrina sipped it and smiled and said, "Thank you, Francis. You are very thoughtful," her eyes no longer wide, the glaze gone from them, her rigidity banished, and the softness of her face and body restored.

"Are you feeling better?" he asked her.

"I'm fine, fine indeed. And how are you, Francis?"

"Do you want me to go and get your husband?"

"My husband? My husband is in New York City, and rather difficult to reach, I'm afraid. What did you want with my husband?"

"Someone in your family you'd like me to get, maybe? You seem to be having some kind of spell."

"Spell? What do you mean, spell?"

"Outside. In the back."

"The back?"

"You came out without any clothes on, and then you went stiff."

"Now really, Francis, do you think you should be so familiar?"

"I put that housecoat on you. I carried you indoors."

"You carried me?"

"Wrapped in canvas. That there." And he pointed to the canvas on the floor in front of the sofa. Katrina stared at the canvas, put her hand inside the fold of her housecoat, and felt her naked breast. In her face, when she again looked up at him, Francis saw lunar majesty, a chilling fusion of beauty and desolation. At the far end of the front parlor, observing all from behind a chair, Francis saw also the forehead and eyes of Katrina Daugherty's nine-year-old son, Martin.

*　　　*　　　*

A month passed, and on a day when Francis was doing finishing work on the doors of the Daugherty carriage barn, Katrina called out to him from the back porch and beckoned him into the house, then to the back parlor, where she sat again on the same sofa, wearing a long yellow afternoon frock with a soft collar. She looked like a sunbeam to Francis as she motioned him into a chair across from the sofa.

"May I make you some tea, Francis?"

"No, ma'am."

"Would you care for one of my husband's cigars?"

"No, ma'am. I don't use 'em."

"Have you none of the minor vices? Do you perhaps drink whiskey?"

"I've had a bit but the most I drink of is ale."

"Do you think I'm mad, Francis?"

"Mad? How do you mean that?"

"Mad. Mad as the Red Queen. Peculiar. Crazy, if you like. Do you think Katrina is crazy?"

"No, ma'am."

"Not even after my spell?"

"I just took it as a spell. A spell don't have to be crazy."

"Of course you're correct, Francis. I am not crazy. With whom have you talked about that day's happenings?"

"No one, ma'am."

"No one? Not even your family?"

"No, ma'am, no one."

"I sensed you hadn't. May I ask why?"

Francis dropped his eyes, spoke to his lap. "Could be, people wouldn't understand. Might figure it the wrong way."

"How wrong?"

"Might figure they was some goin's on. People with no clothes isn't what you'd call reg'lar business."

"You mean people would make something up? Conjure an imaginary relationship between us?"

"Might be they would. Most times they don't need that much to start their yappin'."

"So you've been protecting us from scandal with your silence."

"Yes, ma'am."

"Would you please not call me ma'am. It makes you sound like a servant. Call me Katrina."

"I couldn't do that."

"Why couldn't you?"

"It's more familiar than I oughta get."

"But it's my name. Hundreds of people call me Katrina."

Francis nodded and let the word sit on his tongue. He tried it out silently, then shook his head. "I can't get it out," he said, and he smiled.

"Say it. Say Katrina."

"Katrina."

"So there, you've gotten it out. Say it again."

"Katrina."

"Fine. Now say: May I help you, Katrina?"

"May I help you, Katrina?"

"Splendid. Now I want never to be called anything else again. I insist. And I shall call you Francis. That is how we were designated at birth and our baptisms reaffirmed it. Friends should dispense with formality, and you, who have saved me from scandal, you, Francis, are most certainly my friend."

*   *   *

From the perspective of his perch on the junk wagon Francis could see that Katrina was not only the rarest bird in his life, but very likely the rarest bird ever to nest on Colonie Street. She brought to this street of working-class Irish a posture of elegance that had instantly earned her glares of envy and hostility from the neighbors. But within a year of residence in her new house (a scaled-down copy of the Elk Street mansion in which she had been born and nurtured like a tropical orchid, and where she had lived until she married Edward Daugherty, the writer, whose work and words, whose speech and race, were anathema to Katrina's father, and who, as a compromise for his bride, built the replica that would maintain her in her cocoon, but built it in a neighborhood where he would never be an outlander, and built it lavishly until he ran out of capital and was forced to hire neighborhood help, such as Francis, to finish it), her charm and generosity, her absence of pretension, and her abundance of the human virtues transformed most of her neighbors' hostility into fond attention and admiration.

Her appearance, when she first set foot in the house next door to his, stunned Francis; her blond hair swept upward into a soft wreath, her eyes a dark and shining brown, the stately curves and fullness of her body carried so regally, her large, irregular teeth only making her beauty more singular. This goddess, who had walked naked across his life, and whom he had carried in his arms, now sat on the sofa and with eyes wide upon him she leaned forward and posed the question: "Are you in love with anyone?"

"No, m—no. I'm too young."

Katrina laughed and Francis blushed.

"You are such a handsome boy. You must have many girls in love with you."

"No," said Francis. "I never been good with girls."

"Why ever not?"

"I don't tell 'em what they want to hear. I ain't big with talk."

"Not all girls want you to talk to them."

"Ones I know do. Do you like me? How much? Do you like me better'n Joan? Stuff like that. I got no time for stuff like that."

"Do you dream of women?"

"Sometimes."

"Have you ever dreamt of me?"

"Once."

"Was it pleasant?"

"Not all that much."

"Oh my. What was it?"

"You couldn't close your eyes. You just kept lookin' and never blinked. It got scary."

"I understand the dream perfectly. You know, a great poet once said that love enters through the eyes. One must be careful not to see too much. One must curb one's appetites. The world is much too beautiful for most of us. It can destroy us with its beauty. Have you ever seen anyone faint?"

"Faint? No."

"No, what?"

"No, Katrina."

"Then I shall faint for you, dear Francis."

She stood up, walked to the center of the room, looked directly at Francis, closed eyes, and collapsed on the rug, her right hip hitting the floor first and she then falling backward, right arm outstretched over her head, her face toward the parlor's east wall. Francis stood up and looked down at her.

"You did that pretty good," he said.

She did not move.

"You can get up now," he said.

But still she did not move. He reached down and took her left hand in his and tugged gently. She did not move. He took both her hands and tugged. She did not move voluntarily, nor did she open her eyes. He pulled her to a sitting position but she remained limp, with closed eyes. He lifted her off the floor in his arms and put her on the sofa. When he sat her down she opened her eyes and sat fully erect. Francis still had one arm on her back.

"My mother taught me that," Katrina said. "She said it was useful in strained social situations. I performed it once in a pageant and won great applause."

"You did it good," Francis said.

"I can do a cataleptic fit quite well also."

"I don't know what that is."

"It's when you stop yourself in a certain position and do not move. Like this."

And suddenly she was rigid and wide-eyed, unblinking.

*   *   *

A week after that, Katrina passed by Mulvaney's pasture on Van Woert Street, where Francis was playing baseball, a pickup game. She stood on the turf, just in from the street, across the diamond from where Francis danced and chattered as the third-base pepper pot. When he saw her he stopped chattering. That inning he had no fielding chances. The next inning he did not come to bat. She watched through three innings until she saw him catch a line drive and then tag a runner for a double play; saw him also hit a long fly to the outfield that went for two bases. When he reached second base on the run, she walked home to Colonie Street.

*   *   *

She called him to lunch the day he installed the new awnings. After the first day she always chose a time to talk with him when her husband was elsewhere and her son in school. She served lobster *gratiné*, asparagus with hollandaise, and Blanc de Blancs. Only the asparagus, without sauce, had Francis ever tasted before. She served it at the dining-room table, without a word, then sat across from him and ate in silence, he following her lead.

"I like this," he finally said.

"Do you? Do you like the wine?"

"Not very much."

"You will learn to like it. It is exquisite."

"If you say so."

"Have you had any more dreams of me?"

"One. I can't tell it."

"But you must."

"It's crazy."

"Dreams must be. Katrina is not crazy. Say: May I help you, Katrina?"

"May I help you, Katrina?"

"You may help me by telling me your dream."

"What it is, is you're a little bird, but you're just like you always are too, and a crow comes along and eats you up."

"Who is the crow?"

"Just a crow. Crows always eat little birds."

"You are protective of me, Francis."

"I don't know."

"What does your mother know of me? Does she know you and I have talked as friends?"

"I wouldn't tell her. I wouldn't tell her anything."

"Good. Never tell your mother anything about me. She is your mother and I am Katrina. I will always be Katrina in your life. Do you know that? You will never know another like me. There can be no other like me."

"I sure believe you're right."

"Do you ever want to kiss me?"

"Always."

"What else do you want to do with me?"

"I couldn't say."

"You may say."

"Not me. I'd goddamn die."

When they had eaten, Katrina filled her own and Francis's wineglasses and set them on the octagonal marble-topped table in front of the sofa where she always sat; and he sat in what had now become his chair. He drank all of the wine and she refilled his glass as they talked of asparagus and lobster and she taught him the meaning of *gratiné*, and why a French word was used to describe a dish made in Albany from a lobster caught in Maine.

"Wondrous things come from France," she said to him, and by this time he was at ease in the suffusion of wine and pleasure and possibility, and he gave her his fullest attention. "Do you know Saint Anthony of Egypt, Francis? He is of your faith, a faith I cherish without embracing. I speak of him because of the way he was tempted with the flesh and I speak too of my poet, who frightens me because he sees what men should not see in women. He is dead these thirty years, my poet, but he sees through me still with his image of a caged woman ripping apart the body of a living rabbit with her teeth. Enough, says her keeper, you should not spend all you receive in one day, and he pulls the rabbit from her, letting some of its intestines dangle from her teeth. She remains hungry, with only a taste of what might nourish her. Oh, little Francis, my rabbit, you must not fear me. I shall not rip you to pieces and let your sweet intestines dangle from my teeth. Beautiful Francis of sweet excellence in many things, beautiful young man whom I covet, please do not speak ill of me. Do not say Katrina was made for the fire of *luxuria,* for you must understand that I am Anthony and am tempted by the devil with the sweetness of yourself in my house, in my kitchen, in my yard, in my tree of trees, sweet Francis who carried me naked in his arms."

"I couldn't let you go out in the street with no clothes on," Francis said. "You'd get arrested."

"I know you couldn't," Katrina said. "That's precisely why I did it. But what I do not know is what will be the consequence of it. I do not know what strengths I have to confront the temptations I bring into my life so willfully. I only know that I love in ten thousand directions and that I must not; for that is the lot of the harlot. My poet says that caged woman with the rabbit in her teeth is the true and awful image of this life, and not the woman moaning aloud her dirge of unattainable hopes . . . dead, so dead, how sad. Of course you must know I am not dead. I am merely a woman in self-imposed bondage to a splendid man, to a mannerism of life which he calls a sacrament and I call a magnificent prison. Anthony lived as a hermit, and I too have thought of this as a means of thwarting the enemy. But my husband worships me, and I him, and we equally worship our son of sons. You see, there has never been a magnificence of contact greater than that which exists within this house. We are a family of reverence, of achievement, of wounds sweetly healed. We yearn for the touch, the presence of each other. We cannot live without these things. And yet you are here and I dream of you and long for the pleasures you cannot speak of to me, of joys beyond the imaginings of your young mind. I long for the pleasures of Mademoiselle Lancet, who pursued doctors as I pursue my young man of tender breath, my beautiful Adonis of Arbor Hill. The Mademoiselle cherished all her doctors did and were. The blood on their aprons was a badge of their achievement in the operating room, and she embraced it as I embrace your swan's throat with its necklace of dirt, the haunting pain of young ignorance in your eyes. Do you believe there is a God, Francis? Of course you do and so do I, and I believe he loves me and will cherish me in heaven, as I will cherish him. We shall be lovers. God made me in his image, and so why should I not believe that God too is an innocent monster, loving the likes of me, this seductress of children, this caged animal with blood and intestines in her teeth, embracing her own bloody aprons and then kneeling at the altar of all that is holy in the penitential pose of all hypocrites. Did you ever dream, Francis, when I called you out of our tree, that you would enter such a world as I inhabit? Would you kiss me if I closed my eyes? If I fainted would you undo the buttons of my dress to let me breathe easier?"

✱   ✱   ✱

Katrina died in 1912 in the fire that began in the Brothers' School and then made the leap to the Daugherty house. Francis was absent from the city when she died, but he learned the news from a newspaper account and returned for her funeral. He did not see her in her coffin, which was closed to mourners. Smoke, not fire, killed her, just as the ashes and not the flames of her sensuality had finally smothered her desire; so Francis believed.

In the immediate years after her death, Katrina's grave in the Albany Rural Cemetery, where Protestants entered the underworld, grew wild with dandelions and became a curiosity to the manicurists of the cemetery's floral tapestry. In precisely the way Katrina and Francis had trimmed the maple tree, only to see it grow ever more luxuriant, so was it that the weeding of her burial plot led to an intensity of weed growth: as if the severing of a single root were cause for the birth of a hundred rootlings. Such was its growth that the grave, in the decade after her death, became an attraction for cemetery tourists, who marveled at the midspring yellowing of her final residence on earth. The vogue passed, though the flowers remain even today; and it is now an historical marvel that only the very old remember, or that the solitary wanderer discovers when rambling among the gravestones, and generally attributes to a freakish natural effusion.

✱   ✱   ✱

"So," said Rosskam, "did you have a nice rest?"

"It ain't rest what I'm doin'," said Francis. "You got all the stuff from back there?"

"All," said Rosskam, throwing an armful of old clothes into the wagon. Francis looked them over, and a clean, soft-collared, white-on-white shirt, one sleeve half gone, caught his eye.

"That shirt," he said. "I'd like to buy it." He reached into the wagon and lifted it from the pile. "You take a quarter for it?"

Rosskam studied Francis as he might a striped blue toad.

"Take it out of my pay," Francis said. "Is it a deal?"

"For what is it a bum needs a clean shirt?"

"The one I got on stinks like a dead cat."

"Tidy bum. Sensitive, tidy bum on my wagon."

* * *

Katrina unwrapped the parcel on the dining-room table, took Francis by the hand, and pulled him up from his chair. She unbuttoned the buttons of his blue workshirt.

"Take that old thing off," she said, and held the gift aloft, a white-on-white silk shirt whose like was as rare to Francis as the *fruits de mer* and Château Pontet-Canet he had just consumed.

When his torso was naked, Katrina stunned him with a kiss, and with an exploration of the whole of his back with her fingertips. He held her as he would a crystal vase, fearful not only of her fragility but of his own. When he could again see her lips, her eyes, the sanctified valley of her mouth, when she stood inches from him, her hands gripping his naked back, he cautiously brought his own fingers around to her face and neck. Emulating her, he explored the exposed regions of her shoulders and her throat, letting the natural curve of her collar guide him to the top button of her blouse. And then slowly, as if the dance of their fingers had been choreographed, hers crawled across her own chest, brushing past his, which were carefully at work at their gentlest of chores, and she pushed the encumbering chemise strap down over the fall of her left shoulder. His own fingers then repeated the act on her right shoulder and he trembled with pleasure, and sin, and with, even now, the still unthinkable possibilities that lay below and beneath the boundary line her fallen clothing demarcated.

"Do you like my scar?" she asked, and she lightly touched the oval white scar with a ragged pink periphery, just above the early slope of her left breast.

"I don't know," Francis said. "I don't know about likin' scars."

"You are the only man besides my husband and Dr. Fitzroy who has ever seen it. I can never again wear a low-necked dress. It is such an ugly thing that I do believe my poet would adore it. Does it offend you?"

"It's there. Part of you. That's okay by me. Anything you do, or got, it's okay by me."

"My adorable Francis."

"How'd you ever get a thing like that?"

"A burning stick flew through the air and pierced me cruelly during a fire. The Delavan Hotel fire."

"Yeah. I heard you were in that. You're lucky you didn't get it in the neck."

"Oh I'm a very lucky woman indeed," Katrina said, and she leaned into him and held him again. And again they kissed.

He commanded his hands to move toward her breasts but they would not. They would only hold tight to their grip on her bare arms. Only when she moved her own fingers forward from the blades of his back toward the hollows of his arms did his own fingers dare move toward the hollows of hers. And only when she again inched back from him, letting her fingers tweeze and caress the precocious hair on his chest, did he permit his own fingers to savor the curving flow, the fleshy whiteness, the blooded fullness of her beautiful breasts, culminating his touch at their roseate tips, which were now being so cleverly cataleptic for him.

When Francis put the new shirt on and threw the old one into the back of Rosskam's wagon, he saw Katrina standing on her front steps, across the street, beckoning to him. She led him into a bedroom he had never seen and where a wall of flame engulfed her without destroying even the hem of her dress, the same dress she wore when she came to watch him play baseball on that summer day in 1897. He stood across the marriage bed from her, across a bridge of years of love and epochs of dream.

Never a woman like Katrina: who had forced him to model that shirt for her, then take it home so that someday she would see him walking along the street wearing it and relive this day; forced him first to find a hiding place for it outside his house while he schemed an excuse as to why a seventeen-year-old boy of the working classes should come to own a shirt that only sublime poets, or stage actors, or unthinkably wealthy lumber barons could afford. He invented the ruse of a bet: that he had played poker at a downtown sporting club with a man who ran out of dollars and put up his new shirt as collateral; and Francis had inspected the shirt, liked it, accepted the bet, and then won the hand with a full house.

His mother did not seem to believe the story. But neither did she connect the gift to Katrina. Yet she found ways to slander Katrina in Francis's presence, knowing that he had formed an allegiance, if not an affection, for not only a woman, but the woman who owned the inimical tree.

She is impudent, arrogant. (Wrong, said Francis.)

Slovenly, a poor housekeeper. (Go over and look, said Francis.)

Shows off by sitting in the window with a book. (Francis, knowing no way to defend a book, fumed silently and left the room.)

In the leaping windows of flame that engulfed Katrina and her bed, Francis saw naked bodies coupled in love, writhing in lascivious embrace, kissing in sweet agony. He saw himself and Katrina in a ravenous lunge that never was, and then in a blissful stroking that might have been, and then in a sublime fusion of desire that would always be.

Did they love? No, they never loved. They always loved. They knew a love that Katrina's poet would abuse and befoul. And they befouled their imaginations with a mutation of love that Katrina's poet would celebrate and consecrate. Love is always insufficient, always a lie. Love, you are the clean shirt of my soul. Stupid love, silly love.

Francis embraced Katrina and shot into her the impeccable blood of his first love, and she yielded up not a being but a word: clemency. And the word swelled like the mercy of his swollen member as it rose to offer her the enduring, erubescent gift of retributive sin. And then this woman interposed herself in his life, hiding herself in the deepest center of the flames, smiling at him with all the lewd beauty of her dreams; and she awakened in him the urge for a love of his own, a love that belonged to no other man, a love he would never have to share with any man, or boy, like himself.

"Giddap," Rosskam called out.

And the wagon rolled down the hill as the sun moved toward its apex, and the horse turned north off Colonie Street.

Ⅱ

ᴛELL ME, PRETTY MAIDEN, are there any more at home like you? There
are a few, kind sir, and dum-de-dum and dum-dum too.
So genteel, so quaint.

Helen hummed, staring at the wall in the light of the afternoon sun.
In her kimono (only ten-cent-store silk, alas, but it did have a certain
elegance, so much like the real thing no one would ever know; no one
but Francis had ever seen her in it, or ever would; no one had seen her
take it ever so cleverly off the rack in Woolworth's): in her kimono, and
naked beneath it, she sank deeper into the old chair that was oozing
away its stuffing; and she stared at the dusty swan in the painting with
the cracked glass, swan with the lovely white neck, lovely white back:
swan was, was.

> Dah dah-dah,
> Dah dah-de-dah-dah,
> Dah dah-de-dah-dah,
> Dah dah dah,
> She sang. And the world changed.

Oh the lovely power of music to rejuvenate Helen. The melody
returned her to that porcelain age when she aspired so loftily to a classical career. Her plan, her father's plan before it was hers, was for her
to follow in her grandmother's footsteps, carry the family pride to lofty
pinnacles: Vassar first, then the Paris Conservatory if she was truly as
good as she seemed, then the concert world, then the entire world. If
you love something well enough, Grandmother Archer told Helen when
the weakness was upon her, you will die for it; for when we love with

all our might, our silly little selves are already dead and we have no more fear of dying. Would you die for your music? Helen asked. And her grandmother said: I believe I already have. And in a month she was very unkindly cut down forever.

Swan was, was.

Helen's first death.

Her second came to her in a mathematics class at Vassar when she was a freshman of two months. Mrs. Carmichael, who was pretty and young and wore high shoes and walked with a limp, came for Helen and brought her to the office. A visitor, said Mrs. Carmichael, your uncle Andrew: who told Helen her father was ill,

And on the train up from Poughkeepsie changed that to dead,

And in the carriage going up State Street hill from the Albany depot added that the man had,

Incredibly,

Thrown himself off the Hawk Street viaduct.

Helen, confusing fear with grief, blocked all tears until two days after the funeral, when her mother told her that there will be no more Vassar for you, child; that Brian Archer killed himself because he had squandered his fortune; that what money remained would not be wasted in educating a foolish girl like Helen but would instead finance her brother Patrick's final year in Albany Law School; for a lawyer can save the family. And whatever could a classical pianist do for it?

Helen had been in the chair hours, it seemed, though she had no timepiece for such measurement. But it did seem an hour at least since crippled old Donovan came to the door and said: Helen, are you all right? You been in there all day. Don't you wanna eat something? I'm makin' some coffee, you want some? And Helen said: Oh thank you, old cripple, for remembering I still have a body now that I've all but forgotten it. And no, no thank you, no coffee, kind sir. Are there any more at home like you?

> *Freude, schöner Götterfunken,*
> *Tochter aus Elysium!*

The day had all but begun with music. She left Finny's car humming the "Te Deum"; why, she could not say. But at six o'clock, when it was still dark and Finny and the other man were both snoring, it became the theme of her morning pathway. As she walked she considered the immediate future for herself and her twelve dollars, the final twelve dollars of her life capital, money she never intended to tell Francis about, money tucked safely in her brassiere.

Don't touch my breasts, Finny, they're too sore, she had said again and again, afraid he would feel the money. Finny acceded and explored her only between the thighs, trying mightily to ejaculate, and she, Lord have mercy on her, tried to help him. But Finny could not ejaculate, and he fell back in exhaustion and dry indifference and then slept, as Helen did not, could not; for sleep seemed to be a thing of the past.

What for weeks she had achieved in her time of rest was only an illustrated wakefulness that hovered at the edge of dream: angels rejoicing, multitudes kneeling before the Lamb, worms all, creating a great butterfly of angelic hair, Helen's joyous vision.

Why was Helen joyous in her sleeplessness? Because she was able to recede from evil love and bloodthirsty spiders. Because she had mastered the trick of escaping into music and the pleasures of memory. She pulled on her bloomers, slid sideways out of the car, and walked out into the burgeoning day, the morning star still visible in her night's vanishing sky. Venus, you are my lucky star.

Helen walked to the church with head bowed. She was picking her steps when the angel appeared (and she still in her kimono) and called out to her: *Drunk with fire, o heav'n-born Goddess, we invade thy haildom!*

How nice.

The church was Saint Anthony's, Saint Anthony of Padua, the wonder-working saint, hammer of heretics, ark of the testament, finder of lost articles, patron of the poor and of pregnant and barren women. It was the church where the Italians went to preserve their souls in a city where Italians were the niggers and micks of a new day. Helen usually went to the Cathedral of the Immaculate Conception a few blocks up the hill, but her tumor felt so heavy, a great rock in her belly, that she chose Saint Anthony's, not such a climb, even if she did fear Italians. They looked so dark and dangerous. And she did not care much for their food, especially their garlic. And they seemed never to die. They eat olive oil all day long, Helen's mother had instructed her, and that's what does it; did you ever in all your life see a sick Italian?

The sound of the organ resonated out from the church before the mass began, and on the sidewalk Helen knew the day boded well for her, with such sanctified music greeting her at the dawning. There were three dozen people in the church, not many for a holy day of obligation. Not everybody feels obligations the way Helen feels them, but then again, it is only ten minutes to seven in the morning.

Helen walked all the way to the front and sat in the third pew of center-aisle left, in back of a man who looked like Walter Damrosch. The candle rack caught her eye and she rose and went to it and dropped in the two pennies she carried in her coat pocket, all the change she had. The organist was roaming free through Gregorian hymns as Helen lit a candle for Francis, offering up a Hail Mary so he would be given divine guidance with his problem. The poor man was so guilty.

Helen was giving help of her own to Francis now by staying away from him. She had made this decision while holding Finny's stubby, bloodless, and uncircumcised little penis in her hand. She would not go to the mission, would not meet Francis in the morning as planned. She would stay out of his life, for she understood that by depositing her once again with Finny, and knowing precisely what that would mean for her, Francis was willfully cuckolding himself, willfully debasing her, and, withal, separating them both from what still survived of their mutual love and esteem.

Why did Helen let Francis do this to them?

Well, she is subservient to Francis, and always has been. It was she who, by this very subservience, had perpetuated his relationship to her for most of their nine years together. How many times had she walked away from him? Scores upon scores. How many times, always knowing where he'd be, had she returned? The same scores, but minus one now.

The Walter Damrosch man studied her movements at the candle rack, just as she remembered Damrosch himself studying the score of the Ninth Symphony at Harmanus Bleecker Hall when she was sixteen. Listen to it carefully, her father had told her. It's what Debussy said: the magical blossoming of a tree whose leaves burst forth all at once. It was the first time, her father said, that the human voice ever entered into a symphonic creation. Perhaps, my Helen, you too will create a great musical work of art one day. One never knows the potential within any human breast.

A bell jingled as the priest and two altar boys emerged from the sacristy and the mass began. Helen, without her rosary to say, searched for something to read and found a *Follow the Mass* pamphlet on the pew in front of her. She read the ordinary of the mass until she came to the Lesson, in which John sees God's angel ascending from the rising of the sun, and God's angel sees four more angels, to whom it is given to hurt the earth and the sea; and God's angel tells those four bad ones: Hurt not the earth, nor the sea, nor the trees . . .

Helen closed the pamphlet.

Why would angels be sent to hurt the earth and the sea? She had never read that passage before that she could remember, but it was so dreadful. Angel of the earthquake, who splits the earth. Sargasso angel, who chokes the sea with weeds.

Helen could not bear to think such things, and so cast her eyes to others hearing the mass and saw a boy, perhaps nine, who might have been hers and Francis's if she'd had a child instead of a miscarriage, the only fertilization her womb had ever accepted. In front of the boy a kneeling woman with the palsy and twisted bones held on to the front of the pew with both her crooked hands. Calm her trembling, oh Lord, straighten her bones, Helen prayed. And then the priest read the gospel. Blessed are they who mourn, for they shall be comforted. Blessed are ye when they shall revile you, and persecute you, and speak all that is evil against you, untruly, for my sake: be glad and rejoice, for your reward is very great in heaven.

Rejoice. Yes.

> *Oh embrace now, all you millions,*
> *With one kiss for all the world.*

Helen could not stand through the entire gospel. A weakness came over her and she sat down. When mass ended she would try to put something in her stomach. A cup of coffee, a bite of toast.

Helen turned her head and counted the house, the church now more than a third full, a hundred and fifty maybe. They could not all be Italians, since one woman looked rather like Helen's mother, the imposing Mrs. Mary Josephine Nurney Archer in her elegant black hat. Helen had that in common with Francis: both had mothers who despised them.

It was twenty-one years before Helen discovered, folded in a locked diary, the single sheet of paper that was her father's final will, never known to exist and written when he knew he was going to kill himself, leaving half the modest residue of his fortune to Helen, the other half to be divided equally between her mother and brother.

Helen read the will aloud to her mother, a paralytic then, nursed toward the grave for ten years by Helen alone, and received in return a maternal smile of triumph at having stolen Helen's future, stolen it so that mother and son might live like peahen and peacock, son grown now into a political lawyer noted for his ability to separate widows from their inheritances, and who always hangs up when Helen calls.

Helen never got even with you for what you, without understanding, did to her, Patrick. Not even you, who profited most from it, understood Mother's duplicitous thievery. But Helen did manage to get even with Mother; left her that very day and moved to New York City, leaving brother dear to do the final nursing, which he accomplished by putting the old cripple into what Helen likes to think of now as the poorhouse, actually the public nursing home, and having her last days paid for by Albany County.

Alone and unloved in the poorhouse.

Where did your plumage go, Mother?

But Helen. Dare you be so vindictive? Did you not have tailfeathers of your own once, however briefly, however long ago? Just look at yourself sitting there staring at the bed with its dirty sheets beckoning to you. Your delicacy resists those sheets, does it not? Not only because of their dirt but because you also resist lying on your back with nothing of beauty to respond to, only the cracked plaster and peeling ceiling paint; whereas by sitting in the chair you can at least look at Grandmother Swan, or even at the blue cardboard clock on the back of the door, which might help you to estimate the time of your life: WAKE ME AT: as if any client of this establishment ever had, or ever would, use such a sign, as if crippled Donovan would ever see it if they did use it, or seeing it, heed it. The clock said ten minutes to eleven. Pretentious.

When you sit at the edge of the bed in a room like this, and hold on to the unpolished brass of the bed, and look at those dirty sheets and the soft cocoons of dust in the corner, you have the powerful impulse to go to the bathroom, where you were just sick for more than half an hour, and wash yourself. No. You have the impulse to go to the genuine bath farther down the hall, with the bathtub where you so often swatted and drowned the cockroaches before you scrubbed that tub, scrub, scrub, scrub. You would walk down the hall to the bath in your Japanese kimono with your almond soap inside your pink bathtowel and the carpets would be thick and soft under the soft soles of your slippers, which you kept under the bed when you were a child; the slippers with the brown wool tassel on the top and the soft yellow lining like a kid glove, that came in the Whitney's box under the Christmas tree. Santa Claus shops at Whitney's.

When you really don't care anymore about Whitney's, or Santa Claus, or shoes, or feet, or even Francis, when that which you thought would last as long as breath itself has worn out and you are a woman like Helen, you hold tightly to the brass, as surely as you would walk down the hall in bare feet, or in shoes with one broken strap, walk on filthy, threadbare carpet and wash under your arms and between your old breasts with the washcloth to keep down the body odor, if you had anyone to keep down the odor for.

Of course Helen is putting on airs with this thought, being just like her mother, washing out the washcloth with the cold water, all there is, and only after washing the cloth twice would she dare to use it on her face. And then she would (yes, she would, can you imagine? can you remember?) dab herself all over with the Madame Pompadour body powder, and touch her ears with the Violet de Paris perfume, and give her hair sixty strokes that way, sixty strokes this way, and say to her image in the mirror that pretty is as pretty does. Arthur loved her pretty.

Helen saw a man who looked a little bit like Arthur, going bald the way he always was, when she was leaving Saint Anthony's Church after mass. It wasn't Arthur, because Arthur was dead, and good enough for him. When she was nineteen, in 1906, Helen went to work in Arthur's piano store, selling only sheet music at first, and then later demonstrating how elegant the tone of Arthur's pianos could be when properly played.

Look at her sitting there at the Chickering upright, playing "Won't You Come Over to My House?" for that fashionable couple with no musical taste. Look at her there at the Steinway grand, playing a Bach suite for the handsome woman who knows her music. Look how both parties are buying pianos, thanks to magical Helen.

But then, one day when she is twenty-seven and her life is over, when she knows at last that she will never marry, and probably never go further with her music than the boundaries of the piano store, Helen thinks of Schubert, who never rose to be anything more than a children's music teacher, poor and sick, getting only fifteen or twenty cents for his songs, and dead at thirty-one; and on this awful day Helen sits down at Arthur's grand piano and plays "Who Is Silvia?" and then plays all she can remember of the flight of the raven from *Die Winterreise*.

> The Schubert blossom,
> Born to bloom unseen,
> Like Helen.
> Did Arthur do that?

Well, he kept her a prisoner of his love on Tuesdays and Thursdays, when he closed early, and on Friday nights too, when he told his wife he was rehearsing with the Mendelssohn Club. There is Helen now, in that small room on High Street, behind the drawn curtains, sitting naked in bed while Arthur stands up and puts on his dressing gown, expostulating no longer on sex but now on the *Missa Solemnis*, or was it Schubert's lieder, or maybe the glorious Ninth, which Berlioz said was like the first rays of the rising sun in May?

It was really all three, and much, much more, and Helen listened adoringly to the wondrous Arthur as his semen flowed out of her, and she aspired exquisitely to embrace all the music ever played, or sung, or imagined.

In her nakedness on that continuing Tuesday and Thursday and unchanging Friday, Helen now sees the spoiled seed of a woman's barren dream: a seed that germinates and grows into a shapeless, windblown weed blossom of no value to anything, even its own species, for it produces no seed of its own; a mutation that grows only into the lovely day like all other wild things, and then withers, and perishes, and falls, and vanishes.

The Helen blossom.

One never knows the potential within the human breast.

One would never expect Arthur to abandon Helen for a younger woman, a tone-deaf secretary, a musical illiterate with a big bottom.

Stay on as long as you like, my love, Arthur told Helen; for there has never been a saleswoman as good as you.

Alas, poor Helen, loved for the wrong talent by angelic Arthur, to whom it was given to hurt Helen: who educated her body and soul and then sent them off to hell.

Helen walked from Saint Anthony's Church to South Pearl Street and headed north in search of a restaurant. She envisioned herself sitting at one of the small tables in the Primrose Tea Room on State Street, where they served petite watercress sandwiches, with crusts cut off, tea in Nippon cups and saucers, and tiny sugar cubes in a silver bowl with ever-so-delicate silver tongs.

But she settled for the Waldorf Cafeteria, where coffee was a nickel and buttered toast a dime. Discreetly, she took one of the dollar bills out of her brassiere and held it in her left fist inside her coat pocket. She let go of it only long enough to carry the coffee and toast to a table, and then she clutched it anew, a dollar with a fifteen-cent hole in it now. Eleven-eighty-five all she had left. She sweetened and creamed her coffee and sipped at it. She ate half a piece of toast and a bite of another and left the rest. She drank all the coffee, but food did not want to go down.

She paid her check and walked back out onto North Pearl, clutching her change, wondering about Francis and what she should do now. The air had a bite to it, in spite of the warming sun, driving her mind indoors. And so she walked toward the Pruyn Library, a haven. She sat at a table, shivering and hugging herself, warming slowly but deeply chilled. She dozed willfully, in flight to the sun coast where the white birds fly, and a white-haired librarian shook her awake and said: "Madam, the rules do not allow sleeping in here," and she placed a back issue of *Life* magazine in front of Helen, and from the next table picked up the morning *Times-Union* on a stick and gave it to her, adding: "But you may stay as long as you like, my dear, if you choose to read." The woman smiled at Helen through her pince-nez and Helen returned the smile. There are nice people in the world and sometimes you meet them. Sometimes.

Helen looked at *Life* and found a picture of a two-block-long line of men and women in dark overcoats and hats, their hands in their pockets against the cold of a St. Louis day, waiting to pick up their relief checks. She saw a photo of Millie Smalls, a smiling Negro laundress who earned fifteen dollars a week and had just won $150,000 on her Irish Sweepstakes ticket.

Helen closed the magazine and looked at the newspaper. Fair and warmer, the weatherman said. He's a liar. Maybe up to fifty today, but yesterday it was thirty-two. Freezing. Helen shivered and thought of getting a room. Dewey leads Lehman in Crosley poll. Dr. Benjamin Ross of Albany's Dudley Observatory says Martians can't attack earth, and adds: "It is difficult to imagine a rocketship or space ship reaching earth. Earth is a very small target and in all probability a Martian space ship would miss it altogether." Albany's Mayor Thacher denies false registration of 5,000 voters in 1936. Woman takes poison after son is killed trying to hop freight train.

Helen turned the page and found Martin Daugherty's story about Billy Phelan and the kidnapping. She read it and began to cry, not absorbing any of it, but knowing the family was taking Francis away from her. If Francis and Helen still had a house together, he would never leave her. Never. But they hadn't had a house since early 1930. Francis was working as a fixit man in the South End then, wearing a full beard so nobody'd know it was him, and calling himself Bill Benson. Then the fixit shop went out of business and Francis started drinking again. After a few months of no job, no chance of one, he left Helen alone. "I ain't no good to you or anybody else," he said to her during his crying jag just before he went away. "Never amounted to nothin' and never will."

How insightful, Francis. How absolutely prophetic of you to see that you would come to nothing, even in Helen's eyes. Francis is somewhere now, alone, and even Helen doesn't love him anymore. Doesn't. For everything about love is dead now, wasted by weariness. Helen doesn't love Francis romantically, for that faded years ago, a rose that bloomed just once and then died forever. And she doesn't love Francis as a companion, for he is always screaming at her and leaving her alone to be fingered by other men. And she certainly doesn't love him as a love thing, because he can't love that way anymore. He tried so hard for so long, harder and longer than you could ever imagine, Finny, but all it did was hurt Helen to see it. It didn't hurt Helen physically because that part of her is so big now, and so old, that nothing can ever hurt her there anymore.

Even when Francis was strong he could never reach all the way up, because she was deeper. She used to need something exceptionally big, bigger than Francis. She had that thought the first time, when she began playing with men after Arthur, who was so big, but she never got what she needed. Well, perhaps once. Who was that? Helen can't remember the face that went with the once. She can't remember anything now but how that night, that once, something in her was touched: a deep center no one had touched before, or has touched since. That was when she thought: This is why some girls become professionals, because it is so good, and there would always be somebody else, somebody new, to help you along.

But a girl like Helen could never really do a thing like that, couldn't just open herself to any man who came by with the price of another day. Does anyone think Helen was ever that kind of a girl?

Ode to Joy, please.

> *Freude, schöner Götterfunken,*
> *Tochter aus Elysium!*

Helen's stomach rumbled and she left the library to breathe deeply of the therapeutic morning air. As she walked down Clinton Avenue and then headed south on Broadway, a vague nausea rose in her and she stopped between two parked cars to hold on to a phone pole, ready to vomit. But the nausea passed and she walked on, past the railroad station, until the musical instruments in the window of the Modern Music Shop caught her attention. She let her eyes play over the banjos and ukuleles, the snare drum and the trombone, the trumpet and violin. Phonograph records stood on shelves, above the instruments: Benny Goodman, the Dorsey Brothers, Bing Crosby, John McCormack singing Schubert, Beethoven's "Appassionata."

She went into the store and looked at, and touched, the instruments. She looked at the rack of new song sheets: "The Flat Foot Floogie," "My Heart Belongs to Daddy," "You Must Have Been a Beautiful Baby." She walked to the counter and asked the young man with the slick brown hair: "Do you have Beethoven's Ninth Symphony?" She paused. "And might I see that Schubert album in your window?"

"We do, and you may," said the man, and he found them and handed them to her and pointed her to the booth where she could listen to the music in private.

She played the Schubert first, John McCormack inquiring: Who is Silvia? What is she? That all our swains commend her? . . . Is she as kind as she is fair? And then, though she absolutely loved McCormack, adored Schubert, she put them both aside for the fourth movement of the *Choral* Symphony.

> *Joy, thou spark from flame immortal,*
> *Daughter of Elysium!*

The words tumbled at Helen in the German and she converted them
to her own joyful tongue.

> *He that's won a noble woman,*
> *Let him join our jubilee!*

Oh the rapture she felt. She grew dizzy at the sounds: the oboes,
the bassoons, the voices, the grand march of the fugal theme. Scherzo.
Molto vivace.

Helen swooned.

A young woman customer saw her fall and was at her side almost
instantly. Helen came to with her head in the young woman's lap, the
young clerk fanning her with a green record jacket. Beethoven, once
green, green as a glade. The needle scratched in the record's end groove.
The music had stopped, but not in Helen's brain. It rang out still, the
first rays of the rising sun in May.

"How you feeling, ma'am," the clerk asked.

Helen smiled, hearing flutes and violas.

"I think I'm all right. Will you help me up?"

"Rest a minute," the girl said. "Get your bearings first. Would you
like a doctor?"

"No, no thank you. I know what it is. I'll be all right in a minute
or two."

But she knew now that she would have to get the room and get it
immediately. She did not want to collapse crossing the street. She needed
a place of her own, warm and dry, and with her belongings near her.
The clerk and the young woman customer helped her to her feet and
stood by as she settled herself again on the bench of the listening booth.
When the young people were reassured that Helen was fully alert and
probably not going to collapse again, they left her. And that's when she
slipped the record of the fourth movement inside her coat, under her
blouse, and let it rest on the slope of her tumor her doctor said was
benign. But how could anything so big be benign? She pulled her coat
around her as tightly as she could without cracking the record, said her
thank yous to both her benefactors, and walked slowly out of the store.

Her bag was at Palombo's Hotel and she headed for there: all the
way past Madison Avenue. Would she make it to the hotel without a
collapse? Well, she did. She was exhausted but she found crippled old
Donovan in his rickety rocker, and his spittoon at his feet, on the landing between the first and second floors, all there was of a lobby in this
establishment. She said she wanted to redeem her bag and rent a room,
the same room she and Francis always took whenever it was empty.
And it was empty.

Six dollars to redeem the bag, old Donovan told her, and a dollar and a half for one night, or two-fifty for two nights running. Just one, Helen said, but then she thought: What if I don't die tonight? I will need it tomorrow too. And so she took the bargain rate, which left her with three dollars and thirty-five cents.

Old Donovan gave her the key to the second-floor room and went to the cellar for her suitcase.

"Ain't seen ya much," Donovan said when he brought the bag to her room.

"We've been busy," Helen said. "Francis got a job."

"A job? Ya don't say."

"We're all quite organized now, you might describe it. It's just possible that we'll rent an apartment up on Hamilton Street."

"You're back in the chips. Mighty good. Francis comin' in tonight?"

"He might be, and he might not be," said Helen. "It all depends on his work, and how busy he might or might not be."

"I get it," said Donovan.

She opened the suitcase and found the kimono and put it on. She went then to wash herself, but before she could wash she vomited; sat on the floor in front of the toilet bowl and vomited until there was nothing left to come up; and then she retched dryly for five minutes, finally taking sips of water so there would be something to bring up. And Francis thought she was just being contrary, refusing Jack's cheese sandwich.

Finally it passed, and she rinsed her mouth and her stinging eyes and did, oh yes, did wash herself, and then padded back along the threadbare carpet to her room, where she sat in the chair at the foot of the bed, staring at the swan and remembering nights in this room with Francis.

Clara, that cheap whore, rolled that nice young man in the brown suit and then came in here to hide. If you're gonna sleep with a man, sleep with him, Francis said. Be a goddamn woman. If you're gonna roll a man, roll him. But don't sleep with him and then roll him. Francis had such nice morals. Oh Clara, why in heaven's name do you come in here with your trouble? Haven't we got trouble enough of our own without you? All Clara got was fourteen dollars. But that is a lot.

Helen propped her Beethoven record against the pillow in the center of the bed and studied its perfection. Then she rummaged in the suitcase to see and touch all that was in it: another pair of bloomers, her rhinestone butterfly, her blue skirt with the rip in it, Francis's safety razor and his penknife, his old baseball clippings, his red shirt, and his left brown shoe, the right one lost; but one shoe's better than none, ain't it? was Francis's reasoning. Sandra lost a shoe but Francis found it for her. Francis was very thoughtful. Very everything. Very Catholic, though he pretended not to be. That was why Francis and Helen could never marry.

Wasn't it nice the way Helen and Francis put their religion in the way of marriage?

Wasn't that an excellent idea?

For really, Helen wanted to fly free in the same way Francis did. After Arthur she knew she would always want to be free, even if she had to suffer for it.

Arthur, Arthur, Helen no longer blames you for anything. She knows you were a man of frail allegiance in a way that Francis never was; knows too that she allowed you to hurt her.

Helen remembers Arthur's face and how relieved it was, how it smiled and wished her luck the day she said she was leaving to take a job playing piano for silent films and vaudeville acts. Moving along in the world willfully, that's what Helen was doing then (and now). A will to grace, if you would like to call it that, however elusive that grace has proven to be.

Was this willfulness a little deceit Helen was playing on herself?

Was she moving, instead, in response to impulses out of that deep center?

Why was it, really, that things never seemed to work out?

Why was Helen's life always turning into some back alley, like a wandering old cat?

What is Helen?

Who is Silvia, please?

Please?

Helen stands up and holds the brass. Helen's feet are like fine brass. She is not unpolished like the brass of this bed. Helen is the very polished person who is standing at the end of the end bed in the end room of the end hotel of the end city of the end.

And when a person like Helen comes to an ending of something, she grows nostalgic and sentimental. She has always appreciated the fine things in life: music, kind words, gentility, flowers, sunshine, and good men. People would feel sad if they knew what Helen's life might have been like had it gone in another direction than the one that brought her to this room.

People would perhaps even weep, possibly out of some hope that women like Helen could go on living until they found themselves, righted themselves, discovered ever-unfolding joy instead of coming to lonely ends. People would perhaps feel that some particular thing went wrong somewhere and that if it had only gone right it wouldn't have brought a woman like Helen so low.

But that is the error; for there are no women like Helen.

Helen is no symbol of lost anything, wrong-road-taken kind of person, if-they-only-knew-then kind of person.

Helen is no pure instinct deranged, no monomaniacal yearning out of a deep center that wants everything, even the power to destroy itself.

Helen is no wandering cat in its ninth termination.

For since Helen was born, and so elegantly raised by her father, and so exquisitely self-developed, she has been making her own decisions based on rational thinking, reasonably current knowledge, intuition about limitations, and the usual instruction by friends, lovers, enemies, and others. Her head was never injured, and her brain, contrary to what some people might think, is not pickled. She did not miss reading the newspapers, although she has tapered off somewhat in recent years, for now all the news seems bad. She always listened to the radio and kept up on the latest in music. And in the winter in the library she read novels about women and love: Helen knows all about Lily Bart and Daisy Miller. Helen also cared for her appearance and kept her body clean. She washed her underthings regularly and wore earrings and dressed modestly and carried her rosary until they stole it. She did not sleep when sleep was not called for. She went through her life feeling: I really do believe I am doing the more-or-less right thing. I believe in God. I salute the flag. I wash my armpits and between my legs, and what if I did drink too much? Whose business is that? Who knows how much I didn't drink?

They never think of that sort of thing when they call a woman like Helen a drunken old douchebag. Why would anyone (like that nasty Little Red in the back of Finny's car) ever want to revile Helen that way? When she hears people say such things about her, Helen then plays the pretend game. She dissembles. Helen remembers that word even though Francis thinks she has forgotten her education. But she has not. She is not a drunk and not a whore. Her attitude is: I flew through my years and I never let a man use me for money. I went Dutch lots of times. I would let them buy the drinks but that's because it's the man's place to buy drink.

And when you're a woman like Helen who hasn't turned out to be a whore, who hasn't led anybody into sin . . . (Well, there were some young boys in her life occasionally, lonely in the bars like Helen so often was, but they seemed to know about sin already. Once.)

Once.

Was once a boy?

Yes, with a face like a priest.

Oh Helen, how blasphemous of you to have such a thought. Thank God you never loved up a priest. How would you ever explain that?

Because priests are good.

And so when Helen holds the brass, and looks at the clock that still says ten minutes to eleven, and thinks of slippers and music and the great butterfly and the white pebble with the hidden name, she has this passing thought for priests. For when you were raised like Helen was, you think of priests as holding the keys to the door of redemption. No matter how many sins you have committed (sands of the desert, salt of the sea), you are bound to come to the notion of absolution at the time of brass holding and clock watching, and to the remembering of how you even used to put Violet de Paris on your brassiere so that when he opened your dress to kiss you there, he wouldn't smell any sweat.

But priests, Helen, have nothing whatsoever to do with brassieres and kissing, and you should be ashamed to have put them all in the same thought. Helen does truly regret such a thought, but after all, it has been a most troubled time for her and her religion. And even though she prayed at mass this morning, and has prayed intermittently through-out the day ever since, even though she prayed in Finny's car last night, saying her Now I Lay Me Down to Sleeps when there was no sleep or chance of it, then the point is that, despite all prayer, Helen has no compulsion to confess her sins to gain absolution.

Helen has even come to the question of whether or not she is really a Catholic, and to what a Catholic really is these days. She thinks that, truly, she may not be one anymore. But if she isn't, she certainly isn't anything else either. She certainly isn't a Methodist, Mr. Chester.

What brought her to this uncertainty is the accumulation of her sins, and if you must call them sins, then there is certainly quite an accumulation. But Helen prefers to call them decisions, which is why she has no compulsion to confess them. On the other hand, Helen won-ders whether anyone is aware of how really good a life she lived. She never betrayed anybody, and that, in the end, is what counts most with her. She admits she is leaving Francis, but no one could call that a betrayal. One might, perhaps, call it an abdication, the way the King of England abdicated for the woman he loved. Helen is abdicating for the man she used to love so he can be as free as Helen wants him to be, as free as she always was in her own way, as free as the two of them were even when they were most perfectly locked together. Didn't Francis beg on the street for Helen when she was sick in '33? Why, he never begged even for himself before that. If Francis could become a beggar out of love, why can't Helen abdicate for the same reason?

Of course the relationships Helen had with Arthur and Francis were sinful in the eyes of some. And she admits that certain other liberties she has taken with the commandments of God and the Church might also loom large against her when the time of judgment comes (brass and clock, brass and clock). But even so, there will be no priests coming to see her, and she is surely not going out to see them. She is not going to declare to anyone for any reason that loving Francis was sinful when it was very probably—no, very certainly—the greatest thing in her life, greater, finally, than loving Arthur, for Arthur failed of honor.

And so when crippled Donovan knocks again at eleven o'clock and asks if Helen needs anything, she says no, no thank you, old cripple, I don't need anything or anybody anymore. And old Donovan says: The night man's just comin' on, and so I'm headin' home. I'll be here in the mornin'. And Helen says: Thank you, Donovan, thank you ever so much for your concern, and for saying good night to me. And after he goes away from the door she lets go of the brass and thinks of Beethoven, Ode to Joy,

And hears the joyous multitudes advancing,

Dah dah-dah,

Dah dah-de-dah-dah,

And feels her legs turning to feathers and sees that her head is floating down to meet them as her body bends under the weight of so much joy,

Sees it floating ever so slowly

As the white bird glides over the water until it comes to rest on the Japanese kimono

That has fallen so quietly,

So softly,

Onto the grass where the moonlight grows.

III

FIRST CAME THE FIRE in a lower Broadway warehouse, near the old Fitzgibbon downtown ironworks. It rose in its own sphere, in an uprush into fire's own perfection, and great flames violated the sky. Then, as Francis and Rosskam halted behind trucks and cars, Rosskam's horse snorty and balky with elemental fear, the fire touched some store of thunder and the side of the warehouse blew out in a great rising cannon blossom of black smoke, which the wind carried toward them. Motorists rolled up their windows, but the vulnerable lights of Francis, Rosskam, and the horse smarted with evil fumes.

Ahead of them a policeman routed traffic into a U-turn and sent it back north. Rosskam cursed in a foreign language Francis didn't recognize. But that Rosskam was cursing was unmistakable. As they turned toward Madison Avenue, both men's faces were astream with stinging tears.

They were now pulling an empty wagon, fresh from dumping the day's first load of junk back at Rosskam's yard. Francis had lunched at the yard on an apple Rosskam gave him, and had changed into his new white-on-white shirt, throwing his old blue relic onto Rosskam's rag mountain. They had then set out on the day's second run, heading for the deep South End of the city, until the fire turned them around at three o'clock.

Rosskam turned up Pearl Street and the wagon rolled along into North Albany, the smoke still rising into the heavens below and behind them. Rosskam called out his double-noted ragman's dirge and caught the attention of a few cluttered housewives. From the backyard of an old house near Emmett Street, Francis hauled out a wheelless wheelbarrow with a rust hole through its bottom. As he heaved it upward into the wagon, the odor of fire still in his nostrils, he confronted Fiddler Quain, sitting on an upended metal chamber pot that had been shot full of holes by some backyard marksman.

The Fiddler, erstwhile motorman, now wearing a tan tweed suit, brown polka-dot bow tie, and sailor straw hat, smiled coherently at Francis for the first time since that day on Broadway in 1901 when they both ignited the kerosene-soaked sheets that trapped the strikebreaking trolley car.

When a soldier split the Fiddler's skull with a rifle butt, the sympathetic mob spirited him away to safety before he could be arrested. But the blow left the man mindless for a dozen years, cared for by his spinster sister, Martha. Martyred herself by his wound, Martha paraded the Fiddler through the streets of North Albany, a heroic vegetable, so the neighbors could see the true consequences of the smartypants trolley strike.

Francis offered to be a bearer at the Fiddler's funeral in 1913, but Martha rejected him; for she believed it was Francis's firebrand style that had seduced the Fiddler into violence that fated morning. Your hands have done enough damage, she told Francis. You'll not touch my brother's coffin.

Pay her no mind, the Fiddler told Francis from his perch on the riddled pot. I don't blame you for anything. Wasn't I ten years your elder? Couldn't I make up my own mind?

But then the Fiddler gave Francis a look that loosened a tide of bafflement, as he said solemnly: It's those traitorous hands of yours you'll have to forgive.

Francis brushed rust off his fingers and went behind the house for more dead metal. When he returned with an armload, the scab Harold Allen, wearing a black coat and a motorman's cap, was sitting with the Fiddler, who had his boater in his lap now. When Francis looked at the pair of them, Harold Allen doffed his cap. Both men's heads were laid open and bloody, but not bleeding, their unchanging wounds obviously healed over and as much a part of their aerial bodies as their eyes, which burned with an entropic passion common among murdered men.

Francis threw the old junk into the wagon and turned away. When he turned back to verify the images, two more men were sitting in the wheelless wheelbarrow. Francis could call neither of them by name, but he knew from the astonishment in the hollows of their eyes that they were the shopper and haberdasher, bystanders both, who had been killed by the soldiers' random retaliatory fire after Francis opened Harold Allen's skull with the smooth stone.

"I'm ready," said Francis to Rosskam. "You ready?"

"What's the big hurry-up?" Rosskam asked.

"Nothin' else to haul. Shouldn't we be movin'?"

"He's impatient too, this bum," Rosskam said, and he climbed aboard the wagon.

Francis, feeling the eyes of the four shades on him, gave them all the back of his neck as the wagon rolled north on Pearl Street, Annie's street. Getting closer. He pulled up the collar of his coat against a new bite in the wind, the western sky graying with ominous clouds. It was almost three-thirty by the Nehi clock in the window of Elmer Rivenburgh's grocery. First day of early winter. If it rains tonight and we're outside, we freeze our ass once and for all.

He rubbed his hands together. Were they the enemies? How could a man's hands betray him? They were full of scars, calluses, split fingernails, ill-healed bones broken on other men's jaws, veins so bloated and blue they seemed on the verge of explosion. The hands were long-fingered, except where there was no finger, and now, with accreting age, the fingers had thickened, like the low-growing branches of a tree.

Traitors? How possible?

"You like your hands?" Francis asked Rosskam.

"*Like,* you say? Do I like my hands?"

"Yeah. You like 'em?"

Rosskam looked at his hands, looked at Francis, looked away.

"I mean it," Francis said. "I got the idea that my hands do things on their own, you know what I mean?"

"Not yet," said Rosskam.

"They don't need me. They do what they goddamn please."

"Ah ha," said Rosskam. He looked again at his own gnarled hands and then again at Francis. "Nutsy," he said, and slapped the horse's rump with the reins. "Giddap," he added, changing the subject.

Francis remembered Skippy Maguire's left hand, that first summer away at Dayton. Skippy was Francis's roommate, a pitcher: tall and lefty, a man who strutted when he walked; and on the mound he shaped up like a king of the hill. Why, when he wanted to, Skippy could strut standin' still. But then his left hand split open, the fingers first and then the palm. He pampered the hand: greased it, sunned it, soaked it in Epsom salts and beer, but it wouldn't heal. And when the team manager got impatient, Skippy ignored the splits and pitched ten minutes in a practice session, which turned the ball red and tore the fingers and the palm into a handful of bloody pulp. The manager told Skippy he was stupid and took him and his useless hand off the payroll.

That night Skippy cursed the manager, got drunker than usual, started a fire in the coal stove even though it was August, and when it was roaring, reached in and picked up a handful of flaming coal. And he showed that goddamn Judas of a hand a thing or two. The doc had to cut off three fingers to save it.

Well, Francis may be a little nutsy to people like Rosskam, but he wouldn't do anything like Skippy did. Would he? He looked at his hands, connecting scars to memories. Rowdy Dick got the finger. The jagged scar behind the pinky . . . a violent thirst gave him that one, the night he punched out a liquor store window in Chinatown to get at a bottle of wine. In a fight on Eighth Avenue with a bum who wanted to screw Helen, Francis broke the first joint on his middle finger and it healed crookedly. And a wild man in Philadelphia out to steal Francis's hat bit off the tip of the left thumb.

But Francis got 'em. He avenged all scars, and he lived to remember every last one of them dickie birds too, most of 'em probably dead now, by their own hand maybe. Or the hand of Francis?

Rowdy Dick.

Harold Allen.

The latter name suddenly acted as a magical key to history for Francis. He sensed for the first time in his life the workings of something other than conscious will within himself: insight into a pattern, an overview of all the violence in his history, of how many had died or been maimed by his hand, or had died, like that nameless pair of astonished shades, as an indirect result of his violent ways. He limped now, would always limp with the metal plate in his left leg, because a man stole a bottle of orange soda from him. He found the man, a runt, and retrieved the soda. But the runt hit him with an ax handle and splintered the bone. And what did Francis do? Well the runt was too little to hit, so Francis shoved his face into the dirt and bit a piece out of the back of his neck.

There are things I never wanted to learn how to do, is one thought that came to Francis.

And there are things I did without needin' to learn.

And I never wanted to know about them either.

Francis's hands, as he looked at them now, seemed to be messengers from some outlaw corner of his psyche, artificers of some involuntary doom element in his life. He seemed now to have always been the family killer; for no one else he knew of in the family had ever lived as violently as he. And yet he had never sought that kind of life.

But you set out to kill *me*, Harold Allen said silently from the back of the wagon.

"No," answered Francis without turning. "Not kill anybody. Just do some damage, get even. Maybe bust a trolley window, cause a ruckus, stuff like that."

But you knew, even that early in your career, how accurate your throw could be. You were proud of that talent. It was what you brought to the strike that day, and it was why you spent the morning hunting for stones the same weight as a baseball. You aimed at me to make yourself a hero.

"But not to kill you."

Just to knock out an eye, was it?

Francis now remembered the upright body of Harold Allen on the trolley, indisputably a target. He remembered the coordination of vision with arm movement, of distance with snap of wrist. For a lifetime he had remembered precisely the way Harold Allen crumpled when the stone struck his forehead at the hairline. Francis had not heard, but had forever after imagined, the sound the stone (moving at maybe seventy miles an hour?) made when it hit Harold Allen's skull. It made the skull sound as hollow, as tough, and as explodable, he decided, as a water-melon hit with a baseball bat.

Francis considered the evil autonomy of his hands and wondered what Skippy Maguire, in his later years, had made of his own left hand's suicidal impulse. Why was it that suicide kept rising up in Francis's mind? Wake up in the weeds outside Pittsburgh, half frozen over, too cold to move, flaked out 'n' stiffer than a chunk of old iron, and you say to yourself: Francis, you don't ever want to put in another night, another mornin', like this one was. Time to go take a header off the bridge.

But after a while you stand up, wipe the frost out of your ear, go someplace to get warm, bum a nickel for coffee, and then start walkin' toward somewheres else that ain't near no bridge.

Francis did not understand this flirtation with suicide, this flight from it. He did not know why he hadn't made the big leap the way Helen's old man had when he knew he was done in. Too busy, maybe, figurin' out the next half hour. No way for Francis ever to get a real good look past the sunset, for he's the kind of fella just kept runnin' when things went bust; never had the time to stop anyplace easy just to die.

But he never wanted to run off all that much either. Who'd have figured his mother would announce to the family at Thanksgiving din-ner, just after Francis married Annie, that neither he nor his common little woman would ever be welcome in this house again? The old bat relented after two years and Francis was allowed visiting privileges. But he only went once, and not even inside the door then, for he found out that privileges didn't extend to most uncommon Annie at his side.

And so family contact on Colonie Street ended for Francis in a major way. He vacated the flat he'd rented nine doors up the block, moved to the North End to be near Annie's family, and never set foot again in the goddamned house until the old battle-ax (sad, twisted, wrong-headed, pitiable woman) died.

> Departure.
> Flight of a kind, the first.
> Flight again, when he killed the scab.

Flight again, every summer until it was no longer possible, in order to assert the one talent that gave him full and powerful ease, that let him dance on the earth to the din of brass bands, raucous cheers, and the voluptuous approval of the crowd. Flight kept Francis sane during all those years, and don't ask him why. He loved living with Annie and the kids, loved his sister, Mary, and half-loved his brothers Peter and Chick and his moron brother, Tommy, too, who all came to visit him at his house when he was no longer welcome at theirs.

> He loved and half-loved lots of things about Albany.
> But then one day it's February again,
> And it won't be long now till the snow gets gone again,
> And the grass comes green again,
> And then the dance music rises in Francis's brain,
> And he longs to flee again,
> And he flees.

* * *

A man stepped out of a small apartment house behind Sacred Heart Church and motioned to Rosskam, who reined the horse and climbed down to negotiate for new junk. Francis, on the wagon, watched a group of children coming out of School 20 and crossing the street. A woman whom Francis took to be their teacher stood a few steps into the intersection with raised hand to augment the stopping power of the red light, even though there were no automobiles in sight, only Rosskam's wagon, which was already standing still. The children, their secular school day ended, crossed like a column of ants into the custody of two nuns on the opposite corner, gliding black figures who would imbue the pliant young minds with God's holy truth: Blessed are the meek. Francis remembered Billy and Peg as children, similarly handed over from the old school to this same church for instruction in the ways of God, as if anybody could ever figure that one out.

At the thought of Billy and Peg, Francis trembled. He was only a block away from where they lived. And he knew the address now, from the newspaper. I'll come by of a Sunday and bring a turkey, Francis had told Billy when Billy first asked him to come home. And Billy's line was: Who the fuck wants a turkey? Yeah, who does? Francis answered then. But his answer now was: I sorta do.

Rosskam climbed back on the wagon, having made no deal with the man from the apartment house, who wanted garbage removed.

"Some people," said Rosskam to the rear end of his horse, "they don't know junk. It ain't garbage. And garbage, it ain't junk."

The horse moved forward, every clip clop of its hooves tightening the bands around Francis's chest. How would he do it? What would he say? Nothing to say. Forget it. No, just knock at the door. Well, I'm home. Or maybe just: How's chances for a cupacoffee; see what that brings. Don't ask no favors or make no promises. Don't apologize. Don't cry. Make out it's just a visit. Get the news, pay respects, get gone.

But what about the turkey?

"I think I'm gonna get off the wagon up ahead a bit," Francis told Rosskam, who looked at him with a squinty eye. "Gettin' near the end of the day anyway, 'bout an hour or so left before it starts gettin' dark, ain't that right?" He looked up at the sky, gray but bright, with a vague hint of sun in the west.

"Quit before dark?" Rosskam said. "You don't quit before dark."

"Gotta see some people up ahead. Ain't seen 'em in a while."

"So go."

" 'Course I want my pay for what I done till now."

"You didn't work the whole day. Come by tomorrow, I'll figure how much."

"Worked most of the day. Seven hours, must be, no lunch."

"Half a day you worked. Three hours yet before dark."

"I worked more'n half a day. I worked more'n seven hours. I figure you can knock off a dollar. That'd be fair. I'll take six 'stead of seven, and a quarter out for the shirt. Five-seventy-five."

"Half a day you work, you get half pay. Three-fifty."

"No sir."

"No? I am the boss."

"That's right. You are the boss. And you're one strong fella too. But I ain't no dummy, and I know when I'm bein' skinned. And I want to tell you right now, Mr. Rosskam, I'm mean as hell when I get riled up." He held out his right hand for inspection. "If you think I won't fight for what's mine, take a look. That hand's seen it all. I mean the worst. Dead men took their last ride on that hand. You get me?"

Rosskam reined the horse, braked the wagon, and looped the reins around a hook on the footboard. The wagon stood in the middle of the block, immediately across Pearl Street from the main entrance to the school. More children were exiting and moving in ragged columns toward the church. Blessed are the many meek. Rosskam studied Francis's hand, still outstretched, with digits gone, scars blazing, veins pounding, fingers curled in the vague beginnings of a fist.

"Threats," he said. "You make threats. I don't like threats. Five-twenty-five I pay, no more."

"Five-seventy-five. I say five-seventy-five is what's fair. You gotta be fair in this life."

From inside his shirt Rosskam pulled out a change purse which hung around his neck on a leather thong. He opened it and stripped off five singles, from a wad, counted them twice, and put them in Francis's outstretched hand, which turned its palm skyward to receive them. Then he added the seventy-five cents.

"A bum is a bum," Rosskam said. "I hire no more bums."

"I thank ye," Francis said, pocketing the cash.

"You I don't like," Rosskam said.

"Well I sorta liked you," Francis said. "And I ain't really a bad sort once you get to know me." He leaped off the wagon and saluted Rosskam, who pulled away without a word or a look, the wagon half full of junk, empty of shades.

※   ※   ※

Francis walked toward the house with a more pronounced limp than he'd experienced for weeks. The leg pained him, but not excessively. And yet he was unable to lift it from the sidewalk in a normal gait. He walked exceedingly slowly and to a passerby he would have seemed to be lifting the leg up from a sidewalk paved with glue. He could not see the house half a block away, only a gray porch he judged to be part of it. He paused, seeing a chubby middle-aged woman emerging from another house. When she was about to pass him he spoke.

"Excuse me, lady, but d'ya know where I could get me a nice little turkey?"

The woman looked at him with surprise, then terror, and retreated swiftly up her walkway and back into the house. Francis watched her with awe. Why, when he was sober, and wearing a new shirt, should he frighten a woman with a simple question? The door reopened and a shoeless bald man in an undershirt and trousers stood in the doorway.

"What did you ask my wife?" he said.

"I asked if she knew where I could get a turkey."

"What for?"

"Well," said Francis, and he paused, and scuffed one foot, "my duck died."

"Just keep movin', bud."

"Gotcha," Francis said, and he limped on.

He hailed a group of schoolboys crossing the street toward him and asked: "Hey fellas, you know a meat market around here?"

"Yeah, Jerry's," one said, "up at Broadway and Lawn."

Francis saluted the boy as the others stared. When Francis started to walk they all turned and ran ahead of him. He walked past the house without looking at it, his gait improving a bit. He would have to walk two blocks to the market, then two blocks back. Maybe they'd have a turkey for sale. Settle for a chicken? No.

By the time he reached Lawn Avenue he was walking well, and by Broadway his gait, for him, was normal. The floor of Jerry's meat market was bare wood, sprinkled with sawdust and extraordinarily clean. Shining white display cases with slanted and glimmering glass offered rows of splendid livers, kidneys, and bacon, provocative steaks and chops, and handsomely ground sausage and hamburg to Francis, the lone customer.

"Help you?" a white-aproned butcher asked. His hair was so black that his facial skin seemed bleached.

"Turkey," Francis said. "I'd like me a nice dead turkey."

"It's the only kind we carry," the butcher said. "Nice and dead. How big?"

"How big they come?"

"So big you wouldn't believe it."

"Gimme a try."

"Twenty-five, twenty-eight pounds?"

"How much those big fellas sell for?"

"Depends on how much they weigh."

"Right. How much a pound, then?"

"Forty-four cents."

"Forty-four. Say forty." He paused. "You got maybe a twelve-pounder?"

The butcher entered the white meat locker and came out with a turkey in each hand. He weighed one, then another.

"Ten pounds here, and this is twelve and a half."

"Give us that big guy," Francis said, and he put the five singles and change on the white counter as the butcher wrapped the turkey in waxy white paper. The butcher left him twenty-five cents change on the counter.

"How's business, pal?" Francis asked.

"Slow. No money in the world."

"They's money. You just gotta go get it. Lookit that five bucks I just give ye. I got me that this afternoon."

"If I go out to get money, who'll mind the store?"

"Yeah," said Francis, "I s'pose some guys just gotta sit and wait. But it's a nice clean place you got to wait in."

"Dirty butchers go out of business."

"Keep the meat nice and clean, is what it is."

"Right. Good advice for everybody. Enjoy your dead turkey."

*   *   *

He walked down Broadway to King Brady's saloon and then stared down toward the foot of North Street, toward Welt the Tin's barn and the old lock, long gone, a daylight look at last. A few more houses stood on the street now, but it hadn't changed so awful much. He'd looked briefly at it from the bus, and again last night in the barn, but despite the changes time had made, his eyes now saw only the vision of what had been so long ago; and he gazed down on reconstituted time: two men walking up toward Broadway, one of them looking not unlike himself at twenty-one. He understood the cast of the street's incline as the young man stepped upward, and upward, and upward toward where Francis stood.

The turkey's coldness penetrated his coat, chilling his arm and his side. He switched the package to his other arm and walked up North Third Street toward their house. They'll figure I want 'em to cook the turkey, he thought. Just tell 'em: Here's a turkey, cook it up of a Sunday.

Kids came toward him on bikes. Leaves covered the sidewalks of Walter Street. His leg began to ache, his feet again in the glue. Goddamn legs got a life of their own too. He turned the corner, saw the front stoop, walked past it. He turned at the driveway and stopped at the side door just before the garage. He stared at the dotted white curtain behind the door's four small windowpanes, looked at the knob, at the aluminum milkbox. He'd stole a whole gang of milk outa boxes just like it. Bum. Killer. Thief. He touched the bell, heard the steps, watched the curtain being pulled aside, saw the eye, watched the door open an inch.

"Howdy," he said.

"Yes?"

Her.

"Brought a turkey for ye."

"A turkey?"

"Yep. Twelve-and-a-half-pounder." He held it aloft with one hand.

"I don't understand."

"I told Bill I'd come by of a Sunday and bring a turkey. It ain't Sunday but I come anyway."

"Is that you, Fran?"

"It ain't one of them fellas from Mars."

"Well my God. My God, my God." She opened the door wide.

"How ya been, Annie? You're lookin' good."

"Oh come in, come in." She went up the five stairs ahead of him. Stairs to the left went into the cellar, where he thought he might first enter, carry out some of their throwaways to Rosskam's wagon before he made himself known. Now he was going into the house itself, closing the side door behind him. Up five stairs with Annie watching and into the kitchen, she backing away in front of him. She's staring. But she's smiling. All right.

"Billy told us he'd seen you," she said. She stopped in the center of the kitchen and Francis stopped too. "But he didn't think you'd ever come. My oh my, what a surprise. We saw the story about you in the paper."

"Hope it didn't shame you none."

"We all thought it was funny. Everybody in town thought it was funny, registering twenty times to vote."

"Twenty-one."

"Oh my, Fran. Oh my, what a surprise this is."

"Here. Do somethin' with this critter. It's freezin' me up."

"You didn't have to bring anything. And a turkey. What it must've cost you."

"Iron Joe always used to tell me: Francis, don't come by empty-handed. Hit the bell with your elbow."

She had store teeth in her mouth. Those beauties gone. Her hair was steel-gray, only a trace of the brown left, and her chin was caved in a little from the new teeth. But that smile was the same, that honest-to-god smile. She'd put on weight: bigger breasts, bigger hips; and her shoes turned over at the counters. Varicose veins through the stocking too, hands all red, stains on her apron. That's what housework does to a pretty kid like she was.

Like she was when she came into The Wheelbarrow.

The canalers' and lumbermen's saloon that Iron Joe ran at the foot of Main Street.

Prettiest kid in the North End. Folks always said that about pretty girls.

But she was.

Came in lookin' for Iron Joe.

And Francis, working up to it for two months,

Finally spoke to her.

Howdy, he'd said.

Two hours later they were sitting between two piles of boards in Kibbee's lumberyard with nobody to see them, holding hands and Francis saying goopy things he swore to himself he'd never say to anybody.

And then they kissed.

Not just then, but some hours or maybe even days later, Francis compared that kiss to Katrina's first, and found them as different as cats and dogs. Remembering them both now as he stood looking at Annie's mouth with its store teeth, he perceived that a kiss is as expressive of a way of life as is a smile, or a scarred hand. Kisses come up from below, or down from above. They come from the brain sometimes, sometimes from the heart, and sometimes just from the crotch. Kisses that taper off after a while come only from the heart and leave the taste of sweetness. Kisses that come from the brain tend to try to work things out inside other folks' mouths and don't hardly register. And kisses from the crotch and the brain put together, with maybe a little bit of heart, like Katrina's, well they are the kisses that can send you right around the bend for your whole life.

But then you get one like that first whizzer on Kibbee's lumber pile, one that come out of the brain and the heart and the crotch, and out of the hands on your hair, and out of those breasts that weren't all the way blown up yet, and out of the clutch them arms give you, and out of time itself, which keeps track of how long it can go on without you gettin' even slightly bored the way you got bored years later with kissin' almost anybody but Helen, and out of fingers (Katrina had fingers like that) that run themselves around and over your face and down your neck, and out of the grip you take on her shoulders, especially on them bones that come out of the middle of her back like angel wings, and out of them eyes that keep openin' and closin' to make sure that this is still goin' and still real and not just stuff you dream about and when you know it's real it's okay to close 'em again, and outa that tongue, holy shit, that tongue, you gotta ask where she learned that because nobody ever did that that good except Katrina who was married and with a kid and had a right to know, but Annie, goddamn, Annie, where'd you pick that up, or maybe you been gidzeyin' heavy on this lumber pile regular (No, no, no, I know you never, I always knew you never), and so it is natural with a woman like Annie that the kiss come out of every part of her body and more, outa that mouth with them new teeth Francis is now looking at, with the same lips he remembers and doesn't want to kiss anymore except in memory (though that could be subject to change), and he sees well beyond the mouth into a primal location in this woman's being, a location that evokes in him not only the memory of years but decades and even more, the memory of epochs, aeons, so that he is sure that no matter where he might have sat with a woman and felt this way, whether it was in some ancient cave or some bogside shanty, or on a North Albany lumber pile, he and she would both know that there was something in each of them that had to stop being one and become two, that had to swear that forever after there would never be another (and there never has been, quite), and that there would be allegiance and sovereignty and fidelity and other such tomfool horseshit that people destroy their heads with when what they are saying has nothing to do with time's forevers but everything to do with the simultaneous recognition of an eternal twain, well sir, then both of them, Francis and Annie, or the Francises and Annies of any age, would both know in that same instant that there was something between them that had to stop being two and become one.

Such was the significance of that kiss.

Francis and Annie married a month and a half later.

Katrina, I will love you forever.

However, something has come up.

*　　*　　*

"The turkey," Annie said. "You'll stay while I cook it."

"No, that'd take one long time. You just have it when you want to. Sunday, whenever."

"It wouldn't take too long to cook. A few hours is all. Are you going to run off so soon after being away so long?"

"I ain't runnin' off."

"Good. Then let me get it into the oven right now. When Peg comes home we can peel potatoes and onions and Danny can go get some cranberries. A turkey. Imagine that. Rushing the season."

"Who's Danny?"

"You don't know Danny. Naturally, you don't. He's Peg's boy. She married George Quinn. You know George, of course, and they have the boy. He's ten."

"Ten."

"In fourth grade and smart as a cracker."

"Gerald, he'd be twenty-two now."

"Yes, he would."

"I saw his grave."

"You did? When?"

"Yesterday. Got a day job up there and tracked him down and talked there awhile."

"Talked?"

"Talked to Gerald. Told him how it was. Told him a bunch of stuff."

"I'll bet he was glad to hear from you."

"May be. Where's Bill?"

"Bill? Oh, you mean Billy. We call him Billy. He's taking a nap.

He got himself in trouble with the politicians and he's feeling pretty low. The kidnapping. Patsy McCall's nephew was kidnapped. Bindy McCall's son. You must've read about it."

"Yeah, I did, and Martin Daugherty run it down for me too, awhile back."

"Martin wrote about Billy in the paper this morning."

"I seen that too. Nice write-up. Martin says his father's still alive."

"Edward. He is indeed, living down on Main Street. He lost his memory, poor man, but he's healthy. We see him walking with Martin from time to time. I'll go wake Billy and tell him you're here."

"No, not yet. Talk a bit."

"Talk. Yes, all right. Let's go in the living room."

"Not me, not in these clothes. I just come off workin' on a junk wagon. I'd dirty up the joint somethin' fierce."

"That doesn't matter at all. Not at all."

"Right here's fine. Look out the window at the yard there. Nice yard. And a collie dog you got."

"It is nice. Danny cuts the grass and the dog buries his bones all over it. There's a cat next door he chases up and down the fence."

"The family changed a whole lot. I knew it would. How's your brother and sisters?"

"They're fine, I guess. Johnny never changes. He's a committeeman now for the Democrats. Josie got very fat and lost a lot of her hair. She wears a switch. And Minnie was married two years and her husband died. She's very lonely and lives in a rented room. But we all see one another."

"Billy's doin' good."

"He's a gambler and not a very good one. He's always broke."

"He was good to me when I first seen him. He had money then. Bailed me outa jail, wanted to buy me a new suit of clothes. Then he give me a hefty wad of cash and acourse I blew it all. He's tough too, Billy. I liked him a whole lot. He told me you never said nothin' to him and Peg about me losin' hold of Gerald."

"No, not until the other day."

"You're some original kind of woman, Annie. Some original kind of woman."

"Nothing to be gained talking about it. It was over and done with. Wasn't your fault any more than it was my fault. Wasn't anybody's fault."

"No way I can thank you for that. That's something thanks don't even touch. That's something I don't even know—"

She waved him silent.

"Never mind that," she said. "It's over. Come, sit, tell me what finally made you come see us."

He sat down on the backless bench in the breakfast nook and looked out the window, out past the geranium plant with two blossoms, out at the collie dog and the apple tree that grew in this yard but offered shade and blossoms and fruit to two other yards adjoining, out at the flower beds and the trim grass and the white wire fence that enclosed it all. So nice. He felt a great compulsion to confess all his transgressions in order to be equal to this niceness he had missed out on; and yet he felt a great torpor in his tongue, akin to what he had felt in his legs when he walked on the glue of the sidewalks. His brain, his body seemed to be in a drugged sleep that allowed perception without action. There was no way he could reveal all that had brought him here. It would have meant the recapitulation not only of all his sins but of all his fugitive and fallen dreams, all his random movement across the country and back, all his returns to this city only to leave again without ever coming to see her, them, without ever knowing why he didn't. It would have meant the anatomizing of his compulsive violence and his fear of justice, of his time with Helen, his present defection from Helen, his screwing so many women he really wanted nothing to do with, his drunken ways, his morning-after sicknesses, his sleeping in the weeds, his bumming money from strangers not because there was a depression but first to help Helen and then because it was easy: easier than working. Everything was easier than coming home, even reducing yourself to the level of social maggot, streetside slug.

But then he came home.

He is home now, isn't he?

And if he is, the question on the table is: Why is he?

"You might say it was Billy," Francis said. "But that don't really get it. Might as well ask the summer birds why they go all the way south and then come back north to the same old place."

"Something must've caught you."

"I say it was Billy gettin' me outa jail, goin' my bail, then invitin' me home when I thought I'd never get invited after what I did, and then findin' what you did, or didn't do is more like it, and not ever seein' Peg growin' up, and wantin' some of that. I says to Billy I want to come home when I can do something' for the folks, but he says just come home and see them and never mind the turkey, you can do that for them. And here I am. And the turkey too."

"But something changed in you," Annie said. "It was the woman, wasn't it? Billy meeting her?"

"The woman."

"Billy told me you had another wife. Helen, he said."

"Not a wife. Never a wife. I only had one wife."

Annie, her arms folded on the breakfast table across from him, almost smiled, which he took to be a sardonic response. But then she said: "And I only had one husband. I only had one man."

Which froze Francis's gizzard.

"That's what the religion does," he said, when he could talk.

"It wasn't the religion."

"Men must've come outa the trees after you, you were such a handsome woman."

"They tried. But no man ever came near me. I wouldn't have it. I never even went to the pictures with anybody except neighbors, or the family."

"I couldn'ta married again," Francis said. "There's some things you just can't do. But I did stay with Helen. That's the truth, all right. Nine years on and off. She's a good sort, but helpless as a baby. Can't find her way across the street if you don't take her by the hand. She nursed me when I was all the way down and sick as a pup. We got on all right. Damn good woman, I say that. Came from good folks. But she can't find her way across the damn street."

Annie stared at him with a grim mouth and sorrowful eyes.

"Where is she now?"

"Somewheres, goddamned if I know. Downtown somewheres, I suppose. You can't keep track of her. She'll drop dead in the street one of these days, wanderin' around like she does."

"She needs you."

"Maybe so."

"What do you need, Fran?"

"Me? Huh. Need a shoelace. All I got is a piece of twine in that shoe for two days."

"Is that all you need?"

"I'm still standin'. Still able to do a day's work. Don't do it much, I admit that. Still got my memory, my memories. I remember you, Annie. That's an enrichin' thing. I remember Kibbee's lumber pile the first day I talked to you. You remember that?"

"Like it was this morning."

"Old times."

"Very old."

"Jesus Christ, Annie, I missed everybody and everything, but I ain't worth a goddamn in the world and never was. Wait a minute. Let me finish. I can't finish. I can't even start. But there's somethin'. Somethin' to say about this. I got to get at it, get it out. I'm so goddamned sorry, and I know that don't cut nothin'. I know it's just a bunch of shitass words, excuse the expression. It's nothin' to what I did to you and the kids. I can't make it up. I knew five, six months after I left that it'd get worse and worse and no way ever to fix it, no way ever to go back. I'm just hangin' out now for a visit, that's all. Just visitin' to see you and say I hope things are okay. But I got other things goin' for me, and I don't know the way out of anything. All there is is this visit. I don't want nothin', Annie, and that's the honest-to-god truth, I don't want nothin' but the look of everybody. Just the look'll do me. Just the way things look out in that yard. It's a nice yard. It's a nice doggie. Damn, it's nice. There's plenty to say, plenty of stuff to say, explain, and such bullshit, excuse the expression again, but I ain't ready to say that stuff, I ain't ready to look at you while you listen to it, and I bet you ain't ready to hear it if you knew what I'd tell you. Lousy stuff, Annie, lousy stuff. Just gimme a little time, gimme a sandwich too, I'm hungry as a damn bear. But listen, Annie, I never stopped lovin' you and the kids, and especially you, and that don't entitle me to nothin', and I don't want nothin' for sayin' it, but I went my whole life rememberin' things here that were like nothin' I ever saw anywhere in Georgia or Louisiana or Michigan, and I been all over, Annie, all over, and there ain't nothin' in the world like your elbows sittin' there on the table across from me, and that apron all full of stains. Goddamn, Annie. Goddamn. Kibbee's was just this mornin'. You're right about that. But it's old times too, and I ain't askin' for nothin' but a sandwich and a cupa tea. You still use the Irish breakfast tea?"

*   *   *

The talk that passed after what Francis said, and after the silence that followed it, was not important except as it moved the man and the woman closer together and physically apart, allowed her to make him a Swiss cheese sandwich and a pot of tea and begin dressing the turkey: salting, peppering, stuffing it with not quite stale enough bread but it'll have to do, rubbing it with butter and sprinkling it with summer savory, mixing onions in with the dressing, and turkey seasoning too from a small tin box with a red and yellow turkey on it, fitting the bird into a dish for which it seemed to have been groomed and killed to order, so perfect was the fit.

And too, the vagrant chitchat allowed Francis to stare out at the yard and watch the dog and become aware that the yard was beginning to function as the site of a visitation, although nothing in it except his expectation when he looked out at the grass lent credence to that possibility.

He stared and he knew that he was in the throes of flight, not outward this time but upward. He felt feathers growing from his back, knew soon he would soar to regions unimaginable, knew too that what had brought him home was not explicable without a year of talking, but a scenario nevertheless took shape in his mind: a pair of kings on a pair of trolley cars moving toward a single track, and the trolleys, when they meet at the junction, do not wreck each other but fuse into a single car inside which the kings rise up against each other in imperial intrigue, neither in control, each driving the car, a careening thing, wild, anarchic, dangerous to all else, and then Billy leaps aboard and grabs the power handle and the kings instantly yield control to the wizard.

He give me a Camel cigarette when I was coughin' my lungs up, Francis thought.

He knows what a man needs, Billy does.

❊   ❊   ❊

Annie was setting the dining-room table with a white linen tablecloth, with the silver Iron Joe gave them for their wedding, and with china Francis did not recognize, when Daniel Quinn arrived home. The boy tossed his schoolbag in a corner of the dining room, then stopped in mid-motion when he saw Francis standing in the doorway to the kitchen.

"Hulooo," Francis said to him.

"Danny, this is your grandfather," Annie said. "He just came to see us and he's staying for dinner." Daniel stared at Francis's face and slowly extended his right hand. Francis shook it.

"Pleased to meet you," Daniel said.

"The feeling's mutual, boy. You're a big lad for ten."

"I'll be eleven in January."

"You comin' from school, are ye?"

"From instructions, religion."

"Oh, religion. I guess I just seen you crossin' the street and didn't even know it. Learn anything, did you?"

"Learned about today. All Saints' Day."

"What about it?"

"It's a holy day. You have to go to church. It's the day we remember the martyrs who died for the faith and nobody knows their names."

"Oh yeah," Francis said. "I remember them fellas."

"What happened to your teeth?"

"Daniel."

"My teeth," Francis said. "Me and them parted company, most of 'em. I got a few left."

"Are you Grampa Phelan or Grampa Quinn?"

"Phelan," Annie said. "His name is Francis Aloysius Phelan."

"Francis Aloysius, right," said Francis with a chuckle. "Long time since I heard that."

"You're the ball player," Danny said. "The big-leaguer. You played with the Washington Senators."

"Used to. Don't play anymore."

"Billy says you taught him how to throw an inshoot."

"He remembers that, does he?"

"Will you teach me?"

"You a pitcher, are ye?"

"Sometimes. I can throw a knuckle ball."

"Change of pace. Hard to hit. You get a baseball, I'll show you how to hold it for an inshoot." And Daniel ran into the kitchen, then the pantry, and emerged with a ball and glove, which he handed to Francis. The glove was much too small for Francis's hand but he put a few fingers inside it and held the ball in his right hand, studied its seams. Then he gripped it with his thumb and one and a half fingers.

"What happened to your finger?" Daniel asked.

"Me and it parted company too. Sort of an accident."

"Does that make any difference throwing an inshoot?"

"Sure does, but not to me. I don't throw no more at all. Never was a pitcher, you know, but talked with plenty of 'em. Walter Johnson was my buddy. You know him? The Big Train?"

The boy shook his head.

"Don't matter. But he taught me how it was done and I ain't forgot. Put your first two fingers right on the seams, like this, and then you snap your wrist out, like this, and if you're a righty—are you a righty?"—and the boy nodded—"then the ball's gonna dance a little turnaround jig and head right inside at the batter's belly button, assumin', acourse, that he's a righty too. You followin' me?" And the boy nodded again. "Now the trick is, you got to throw the opposite of the outcurve, which is like this." And he snapped his wrist clockwise. "You got to do it like this." And he snapped his wrist counterclockwise again. Then he had the boy try it both ways and patted him on the back.

"That's how it's done," he said. "You get so's you can do it, the batter's gonna think you got a little animal inside that ball, flyin' it like an airplane."

"Let's go outside and try it," Daniel said. "I'll get another glove."

"Glove," said Francis, and he turned to Annie. "By some fluke you still got my old glove stuck away somewheres in the house? That possible, Annie?"

"There's a whole trunk of your things in the attic," she said. "It might be there."

"It is," Daniel said. "I know it is. I saw it. I'll get it."

"You will not," Annie said. "That trunk is none of your affair."

"But I've already seen it. There's a pair of spikes too, and clothes and newspapers and old pictures."

"All that," Francis said to Annie. "You saved it."

· "You had no business in that trunk," Annie said.

"Billy and I looked at the pictures and the clippings one day," Daniel said. "Billy looked just as much as I did. He's in lots of 'em." And he pointed at his grandfather.

"Maybe you'd want to have a look at what's there," Annie said to Francis.

"Could be. Might find me a new shoelace."

Annie led him up the stairs, Daniel already far ahead of them. They heard the boy saying: "Get up, Billy, Grandpa's here"; and when they reached the second floor Billy was standing in the doorway of his room, in his robe and white socks, disheveled and only half awake.

"Hey, Billy. How you gettin' on?" Francis said.

"Hey," said Billy. "You made it."

"Yep."

"I woulda bet against it happenin'."

"You'da lost. Brought a turkey too, like I said."

"A turkey, yeah?"

"We're having it for dinner," Annie said.

"I'm supposed to be downtown tonight," Billy said. "I just told Martin I'd meet him."

"Call him back," Annie said. "He'll understand."

"Red Tom Fitzsimmons and Martin both called to tell me things are all right again on Broadway. You know, I told you I had trouble with the McCalls," Billy said to his father.

"I 'member."

"I wouldn't do all they wanted and they marked me lousy. Couldn't gamble, couldn't even get a drink on Broadway."

"I read that story Martin wrote," Francis said. "He called you a magician."

"Martin's full of malarkey. I didn't do diddley. I just mentioned Newark to them and it turns out that's where they trapped some of the kidnap gang."

"You did somethin', then," Francis said. "Mentionin' Newark was somethin'. Who'd you mention it to?"

"Bindy. But I didn't know those guys were in Newark or I wouldn't of said anything. I could never rat on anybody."

"Then why'd you mention it?"

"I don't know."

"That's how come you're a magician."

"That's Martin's baloney. But he turned somebody's head around with it, 'cause I'm back in good odor with the pols, is how he put it on the phone. In other words, I don't stink to them no more."

Francis smelled himself and knew he had to wash as soon as possible. The junk wagon's stink and the bummy odor of his old suitcoat was unbearable now that he was among these people. Dirty butchers go out of business.

"You can't go out now, Billy," Annie said. "Not with your father home and staying for dinner. We're going up in the attic to look at his things."

"You like turkey?" Francis asked Billy.

"Who the hell don't like turkey, not to give you a short answer," Billy said. He looked at his father. "Listen, use my razor in the bathroom if you want to shave."

"Don't be telling people what to do," Annie said. "Get dressed and come downstairs."

And then Francis and Annie ascended the stairway to the attic.

*   *   *

When Francis opened the trunk lid the odor of lost time filled the attic air, a cloying reek of imprisoned flowers that unsettled the dust and fluttered the window shades. Francis felt drugged by the scent of the reconstituted past, and then stunned by his first look inside the trunk, for there, staring out from a photo, was his own face at age nineteen. The picture lay among rolled socks and a small American flag, a Washington Senators cap, a pile of newspaper clippings and other photos, all in a scatter on the trunk's tray. Francis stared up at himself from the bleachers in Chadwick Park on a day in 1899, his face unlined, his teeth all there, his collar open, his hair unruly in the afternoon's breeze. He lifted the picture for a closer look and saw himself among a group of men, tossing a baseball from bare right hand to gloved left hand. The flight of the ball had always made this photo mysterious to Francis, for the camera had caught the ball clutched in one hand and also in flight, arcing in a blur toward the glove. What the camera had caught was two instants in one: time separated and unified, the ball in two places at once, an eventuation as inexplicable as the Trinity itself. Francis now took the picture to be a Trinitarian talisman (a hand, a glove, a ball) for achieving the impossible: for he had always believed it impossible for him, ravaged man, failed human, to reenter history under this roof. Yet here he was in this aerie of reconstitutable time, touching untouchable artifacts of a self that did not yet know it was ruined, just as the ball, in its inanimate ignorance, did not know yet that it was going nowhere, was caught.

But the ball is really not yet caught, except by the camera, which has frozen only its situation in space.

And Francis is not yet ruined, except as an apparency in process.

The ball still flies.

Francis still lives to play another day.

Doesn't he?

The boy noticed the teeth. A man can get new teeth, store teeth. Annie got 'em.

x   x   x

Francis lifted the tray out of the trunk, revealing the spikes and the glove, which Daniel immediately grabbed, plus two suits of clothes, a pair of black oxfords and brown high-button shoes, maybe a dozen shirts and two dozen white collars, a stack of undershirts and shorts, a set of keys to long-forgotten locks, a razor strop and a hone, a shaving mug with an inch of soap in it, a shaving brush with bristles intact, seven straight razors in a case, each marked for a day of the week, socks, bow ties, suspenders, and a baseball, which Francis picked up and held out to Daniel.

"See that? See that name?"

The boy looked, shook his head. "I can't read it."

"Get it in the light, you'll read it. That's Ty Cobb. He signed that ball in 1911, the year he hit .420. A fella give it to me once and I always kept it. Mean guy, Cobb was, come in at me spikes up many a time. But you had to hand it to a man who played ball as good as he did. He was the best."

"Better than Babe Ruth?"

"Better and tougher and meaner and faster. Couldn't hit home runs like the Babe, but he did everything else better. You like to have that ball with his name on it?"

"Sure I would, sure! Yeah! Who wouldn't?"

"Then it's yours. But you better look him up, and Walter Johnson too. Find out for yourself how good they were. Still kickin', too, what I hear about Cobb. He ain't dead yet either."

"I remember that suit," Annie said, lifting the sleeve of a gray herringbone coat. "You wore it for dress-up."

"Wonder if it'd still fit me," Francis said, and stood up and held the pants to his waist and found out his legs had not grown any longer in the past twenty-two years.

"Take the suit downstairs," Annie said. "I'll sponge and press it."

"Press it?" Francis said, and he chuckled. "S'pose I could use a new outfit. Get rid of these rags."

He then singled out a full wardrobe, down to the handkerchief, and piled it all on the floor in front of the trunk.

"I'd like to look at these again," Annie said, lifting out the clippings and photos.

"Bring 'em down," Francis said, closing the lid.

"I'll carry the glove," Daniel said.

"And I'd like to borry the use of your bathroom," Francis said. "Take Billy up on that shave offer and try on some of these duds. I got me a shave last night but Billy thinks I oughta do it again."

"Don't pay any attention to Billy," Annie said. "You look fine."

She led him down the stairs and along a hallway where two rooms faced each other. She gestured at a bedroom where a single bed, a dresser, and a child's rolltop desk stood in quiet harmony.

"That's Danny's room," she said. "It's a nice big room and it gets the morning light." She took a towel down from a linen closet shelf and handed it to Francis. "Have a bath if you like."

Francis locked the bathroom door and tried on the trousers, which fit if he didn't button the top button. Wear the suspenders with 'em. The coat was twenty years out of style and offended Francis's residual sense of aptness. But he decided to wear it anyway, for its odor of time was infinitely superior to the stink of bumdom that infested the coat on his back. He stripped and let the bathwater run. He inspected the shirt he took from the trunk, but rejected it in favor of the white-on-white from the junk wagon. He tried the laceless black oxfords, all broken in, and found that even with calluses his feet had not grown in twenty-two years either.

He stepped into the bath and slid slowly beneath its vapors. He trembled with the heat, with astonishment that he was indeed here, as snug in this steaming tub as was the turkey in its roasting pan. He felt blessed. He stared at the bathroom sink, which now had an aura of sanctity about it, its faucets sacred, its drainpipe holy, and he wondered whether everything was blessed at some point in its existence, and he concluded yes. Sweat rolled down his forehead and dripped off his nose into the bath, a confluence of ancient and modern waters. And as it did, a great sunburst entered the darkening skies, a radiance so sudden that it seemed like a bolt of lightning; yet its brilliance remained, as if some angel of beatific lucidity were hovering outside the bathroom window. So enduring was the light, so intense beyond even sundown's final glory-burst, that Francis raised himself up out of the tub and went to the window.

Below, in the yard, Aldo Campione, Fiddler Quain, Harold Allen, and Rowdy Dick Doolan were erecting a wooden structure that Francis was already able to recognize as bleachers.

He stepped back into the tub, soaped the long-handled brush, raised his left foot out of the water, scrubbed it clean, raised the right foot, scrubbed that.

✻   ✻   ✻

Francis, that 1916 dude, came down the stairs in bow tie, white-on-white shirt, black laceless oxfords with a spit shine on them, the gray herringbone with lapels twenty-two years too narrow, with black silk socks and white silk boxer shorts, with his skin free of dirt everywhere, his hair washed twice, his fingernails cleaned, his leftover teeth brushed and the toothbrush washed with soap and dried and rehung, with no whiskers anymore, none, and his hair combed and rubbed with a dab of Vaseline so it'd stay in place, with a spring in his gait and a smile on his face; this Francis dude came down those stairs, yes, and stunned his family with his resurrectible good looks and stylish potential, and took their stares as applause.

And dance music rose in his brain.

"Holy Christ," said Billy.

"My oh my," said Annie.

"You look different," Daniel said.

"I kinda needed a sprucin'," Francis said. "Funny duds but I guess they'll do."

They all pulled back then, even Daniel, aware they should not dwell on the transformation, for it made Francis's previous condition so lowly, so awful.

"Gotta dump these rags," he said, and he lifted his bundle, tied with the arms of his old coat.

"Danny'll take them," Annie said. "Put them in the cellar," she told the boy.

Francis sat down on a bench in the breakfast nook, across the table from Billy. Annie had spread the clips and photos on the table and he and Billy looked them over. Among the clips Francis found a yellowed envelope postmarked June 2, 1910, and addressed to Mr. Francis Phelan, c/o Toronto Baseball Club, The Palmer House, Toronto, Ont. He opened it and read the letter inside, then pocketed it. Dinner advanced as Daniel and Annie peeled the potatoes at the sink. Billy, his hair combed slick, half a dude himself with open-collared starched white shirt, creased trousers, and pointy black shoes, was drinking from a quart bottle of Dobler beer and reading a clipping.

"I read these once," Billy said. "I never really knew how good you were. I heard stories and then one night downtown I heard a guy talking about you and he was ravin' that you were top-notch and I never knew just how good. I knew this stuff was there. I seen it when we first moved here, so I went up and looked. You were really a hell of a ball player."

"Not bad," Francis said. "Coulda been worse."

"These sportswriters liked you."

"I did crazy things. I was good copy for them. And I had energy. Everybody likes energy."

Billy offered Francis a glass of beer but Francis declined and took, instead, from Billy's pack, a Camel cigarette; and then he perused the clips that told of him stealing the show with his fielding, or going four-for-four and driving in the winning run, or getting himself in trouble: such as the day he held the runner on third by the belt, an old John McGraw trick, and when a fly ball was hit, the runner got ready to tag and head home after the catch but found he could not move and turned and screamed at Francis in protest, at which point Francis let go of the belt and the runner ran, but the throw arrived first and he was out at home.

Nifty.

But Francis was thrown out of the game.

"Would you like to go out and look at the yard?" Annie said, suddenly beside Francis.

"Sure. See the dog."

"It's too bad the flowers are gone. We had so many flowers this year. Dahlias and snapdragons and pansies and asters. The asters lasted the longest."

"You still got them geraniums right here."

Annie nodded and put on her sweater and the two of them went out onto the back porch. The air was chilly and the light fading. She closed the door behind them and patted the dog, which barked twice at Francis and then accepted his presence. Annie went down the five steps to the yard, Francis and the dog following.

"Do you have a place to stay tonight, Fran?"

"Sure. Always got a place to stay."

"Do you want to come home permanent?" she asked, not looking at him, walking a few steps ahead toward the fence. "Is that why you've come to see us?"

"Nah, not much chance of that. I'd never fit in."

"I thought you might've had that in mind."

"I thought of it, I admit that. But I see it couldn't work, not after all these years."

"It'd take some doing, I know that."

"Take more than that."

"Stranger things have happened."

"Yeah? Name one."

"You going to the cemetery and talking to Gerald. I think maybe that's the strangest thing I ever heard in all my days."

"Wasn't strange. I just went and stood there and told him a bunch of stuff. It's nice where he is. It's pretty."

"That's the family plot."

"I know."

"There's a grave there for you, right at the stone, and one for me, and two for the children next to that if they need them. Peg'll have her own plot with George and the boy, I imagine."

"When did you do all that?" Francis asked.

"Oh years ago. I don't remember."

"You bought me a grave after I run off."

"I bought it for the family. You're part of the family."

"There was long times I didn't think so."

"Peg is very bitter about you staying away. I was too, for years and years, but that's all done with. I don't know why I'm not bitter anymore. I really don't. I called Peg and told her to get the cranberries and that you were here."

"Me and the cranberries. Easin' the shock some."

"I suppose."

"I'll move along, then. I don't want no fights, rile up the family."

"Nonsense. Stop it. You just talk to her. You've got to talk to her."

"I can't say nothin' that means anything. I couldn't say a straight word to you."

"I know what you said and what you didn't say. I know it's hard what you're doing."

"It's a bunch of nothin'. I don't know why I do anything in this goddamn life."

"You did something good coming home. It's something Danny'll always know about. And Billy. He was so glad to be able to help you, even though he'd never say it."

"He got a bum out of jail."

"You're so mean to yourself, Francis."

"Hell, I'm mean to everybody and everything."

The bleachers were all up, and men were filing silently into them and sitting down, right here in Annie's backyard, in front of God and the dog and all: Bill Corbin, who ran for sheriff in the nineties and got beat and turned Republican, and Perry Marsolais, who inherited a fortune from his mother and drank it up and ended up raking leaves for the city, and Iron Joe himself with his big mustache and big belly and big ruby stickpin, and Spiff Dwyer in his nifty pinched fedora, and young George Quinn and young Martin Daugherty, the batboys, and Martin's grandfather Emmett Daugherty, the wild Fenian who talked so fierce and splendid and put the radical light in Francis's eye with his stories of how moneymen used workers to get rich and treated the Irish like pigdog paddyniggers, and Patsy McCall, who grew up to run the city and was carrying his ball glove in his left hand, and some men Francis did not know even in 1899, for they were only hangers-on at the saloon, men who followed the doings of Iron Joe's Wheelbarrow Boys, and who came to the beer picnic this day to celebrate the Boys' winning the Albany-Troy League pennant.

They kept coming: forty-three men, four boys, and two mutts, ushered in by the Fiddler and his pals.

And there, between crazy Specky McManus in his derby and Jack Corbett in his vest and no collar, sat the runt, is it?

Is it now?

The runt with the piece out of his neck.

There's one in every crowd.

Francis closed his eyes to retch the vision out of his head, but when he opened them the bleachers still stood, the men seated as before. Only the light had changed, brighter now, and with it grew Francis's hatred of all fantasy, all insubstantiality. I am sick of you all, was his thought. I am sick of imagining what you became, what I might have become if I'd lived among you. I am sick of your melancholy histories, your sentimental pieties, your goddamned unchanging faces. I'd rather be dyin' in the weeds than standin' here lookin' at you pinin' away, like the dyin' Jesus pinin' for an end to it when he knew every stinkin' thing that was gonna happen not only to himself but to everybody around him, and to all those that wasn't even born yet. You ain't nothin' more than a photograph, you goddamn spooks. You ain't real and I ain't gonna be at your beck and call no more.

You're all dead, and if you ain't, you oughta be.

I'm the one is livin'. I'm the one puts you on the map.

You never knew no more about how things was than I did.

You'd never even be here in the damn yard if I didn't open that old trunk.

So get your ass gone!

"Hey Ma," Billy yelled out the window. "Peg's home."

"We'll be right in," Annie said. And when Billy closed the window she turned to Francis: "You want to tell me anything, ask me anything, before we get in front of the others?"

"Annie, I got five million things to ask you, and ten million things to tell. I'd like to eat all the dirt in this yard for you, eat the weeds, eat the dog bones too, if you asked me."

"I think you probably ate all that already," she said.

And then they went up the back stoop together.

¤   ¤   ¤

When Francis first saw his daughter bent over the stove, already in her flowered apron and basting the turkey, he thought: She is too dressed up to be doing that. She wore a wristwatch on one arm, a bracelet on the other, and two rings on her wedding ring finger. She wore high heels; silk stockings with the seams inside out, and a lavender dress that was never intended as a kitchen costume. Her dark-brown hair, cut short, was waved in a soft marcel, and she wore lipstick and a bit of rouge, and her nails were long and painted dark red. She was a few, maybe even more than a few, pounds overweight, and she was beautiful, and Francis was immeasurably happy at having sired her.

"How ya doin', Margaret?" Francis asked when she straightened up and looked at him.

"I'm doing fine," she said, "no thanks to you."

"Yep," said Francis, and he turned away from her and sat across from Billy in the nook.

"Give him a break," Billy said. "He just got here, for chrissake."

"What break did he ever give me? Or you? Or any of us?"

"Aaahhh, blow it out your ear," Billy said.

"I'm saying what is," Peg said.

"Are you?" Annie asked. "Are you so sure of what is?"

"I surely am. I'm not going to be a hypocrite and welcome him back with open arms after what he did. You don't just pop up one day with a turkey and all is forgiven."

"I ain't expectin' to be forgiven," Francis said. "I'm way past that."

"Oh? And just where are you now?"

"Nowhere."

"Well that's no doubt very true. And if you're nowhere, why are you here? Why've you come back like a ghost we buried years ago to force a scrawny turkey on us? Is that your idea of restitution for letting us fend for ourselves for twenty-two years?"

"That's a twelve-and-a-half-pound turkey," Annie said.

"Why leave your nowhere and come here, is what I want to know. This is somewhere. This is a home you didn't build."

"I built you. Built Billy. Helped to."

"I wish you never did."

"Shut up, Peg," Billy yelled. "Rotten tongue of yours, shut it the hell UP!"

"He came to visit, that's all he did," Annie said softly. "I already asked him if he wanted to stay over and he said no. If he wanted to he surely could."

"Oh?" said Peg. "Then it's all decided?"

"Nothin' to decide," Francis said. "Like your mother says, I ain't stayin'. I'm movin' along." He touched the salt and pepper shaker on the table in front of him, pushed the sugar bowl against the wall.

"You're moving on," Peg said.

"Positively."

"Fine."

"That's it, that's enough!" Billy yelled, standing up from the bench. "You got the feelin's of a goddamn rattlesnake."

"Pardon me for having any feelings at all," Peg said, and she left the kitchen, slamming the swinging door, which had been standing open, slamming it so hard that it swung, and swung, and swung, until it stopped.

"Tough lady," Francis said.

"She's a creampuff," Billy said. "But she knows how to get her back up."

"She'll calm down," Annie said.

"I'm used to people screamin' at me," Francis said. "I got a hide like a hippo."

"You need it in this joint," Billy said.

"Where's the boy?" Francis asked. "He hear all that?"

"He's out playin' with the ball and glove you gave him," Billy said.

"I didn't give him the glove," Francis said. "I give him the ball with the Ty Cobb signature. That glove is yours. You wanna give it to him, it's okay by me. Ain't much of a glove compared to what they got these days. Danny's glove's twice the quality my glove ever was. But I always thought to myself: I'm givin' that old glove to Billy so's he'll have a touch of the big leagues somewhere in the house. That glove caught some mighty people. Line drive from Tris Speaker, taggin' out Cobb, runnin' Eddie Collins outa the baseline. Lotta that."

Billy nodded and turned away from Francis. "Okay," he said, and then he jumped up from the bench and left the kitchen so the old man could not see (though he saw) that he was choked up.

"Grew up nice, Billy did," Francis said. "Couple of tough bozos you raised, Annie."

"I wish they were tougher," Annie said.

The yard, now ablaze with new light against a black sky, caught Francis's attention. Men and boys, and even dogs, were holding lighted candles, the dogs holding them in their mouths sideways. Specky McManus, as usual bein' different, wore his candle on top of his derby.

It was a garden of acolytes setting fire to the very air, and then, while
Francis watched, the acolytes erupted in song, but a song without sense,
a chant to which Francis listened carefully but could make out not a
word. It was an antisyllabic lyric they sang, like the sibilance of the
wren's softest whistle, or the tree frog's tonsillar wheeze. It was clear to
Francis as he watched this performance (watched it with awe, for it was
transcending what he expected from dream, from reverie, even from
Sneaky Pete hallucinations) that it was happening in an arena of his
existence over which he had less control than he first imagined when
Aldo Campione boarded the bus. The signals from this time lock were
ominous, the spooks utterly without humor. And then, when he saw
the runt (who knew he was being watched, who knew he didn't belong
in this picture) putting the lighted end of the candle into the hole in
the back of his neck, and when Francis recognized the chant of the
acolytes at last as the "Dies Irae," he grew fearful. He closed his eyes
and buried his head in his hands and he tried to remember the name of
his first dog.

   It was a collie.

*   *   *

Billy came back, clear-eyed, sat across from Francis, and offered him
another smoke, which he took. Billy topped his own beer and drank
and then said, "George."

   "Oh my God," Annie said. "We forgot all about George." And she
went to the living room and called upstairs to Peg: "You should call
George and tell him he can come home."

   "Let her alone, I'll do it," Billy called to his mother.

   "What about George?" Francis asked.

   "The cops were here one night lookin' for him," Billy said. "It was
Patsy McCall puttin' pressure on the family because of me. George
writes numbers and they were probably gonna book him for gamblin'
even though he had the okay. So he laid low up in Troy, and the poor
bastard's been alone for days. But if I'm clear, then so is he."

   "Some power the McCalls put together in this town."

   "They got it all. They ever pay you the money they owed you for
registerin' all those times?"

   "Paid me the fifty I told you about, owe me another fifty-five. I'll
never see it."

   "You got it comin'."

   "Once it got in the papers they wouldn't touch it. Mixin' themselves
up with bums. You heard Martin tell me that. They'd also be suspicious
that I'd set them up. I wouldn't set nobody up. Nobody."

   "Then you got no cash."

"I got a little."

"How much?"

"I got some change. Cigarette money."

"You blew what you had on the turkey."

"That took a bit of it."

Billy handed him a ten, folded in half. "Put it in your pocket. You can't walk around broke."

Francis took it and snorted. "I been broke twenty-two years. But I thank ye, Billy. I'll make it up."

"You already made it up." And he went to the phone in the dining room to call George in Troy.

Annie came back to the kitchen and saw Francis looking at the Chadwick Park photo and looked over his shoulder. "That's a handsome picture of you," she said.

"Yeah," said Francis. "I was a good-lookin' devil."

"Some thought so, some didn't," Annie said. "I forgot about this picture."

"Oughta get it framed," Francis said. "Lot of North Enders in there. George and Martin as kids, and Patsy McCall too. And Iron Joe. Real good shot of Joe."

"It surely is," Annie said. "How fat and healthy he looks."

Billy came back and Annie put the photo on the table so that all three of them could look at it. They sat on the same bench with Francis in the middle and studied it, each singling out the men and boys they knew. Annie even knew one of the dogs.

"Oh that's a prize picture," she said, and stood up. "A prize picture."

"Well, it's yours, so get it framed."

"Mine? No, it's yours. It's baseball."

"Nah, nah, George'd like it too."

"Well I will frame it," Annie said. "I'll take it downtown and get it done up right."

"Sure," said Francis. "Here. Here's ten dollars toward the frame."

"Hey," Billy said.

"No," Francis said. "You let me do it, Billy."

Billy chuckled.

"I will not take any money," Annie said. "You put that back in your pocket."

Billy laughed and hit the table with the palm of his hand. "Now I know why you been broke twenty-two years. I know why we're all broke. It runs in the family."

"We're not all broke," Annie said. "We pay our way. Don't be telling people we're broke. You're broke because you made some crazy horse bet. But *we're* not broke. We've had bad times but we can still pay the rent. And we've never gone hungry."

"Peg's workin'," Francis said.

"A private secretary," Annie said. "To the owner of a tool company. She's very well liked."

"She's beautiful," Francis said. "Kinda nasty when she puts her mind to it, but beautiful."

"She shoulda been a model," Billy said.

"She should not," Annie said.

"Well she shoulda, goddamn it, she shoulda," said Billy. "They wanted her to model for Pepsodent toothpaste, but Mama wouldn't hear of it. Somebody over at church told her models were, you know, loose ladies. Get your picture taken, it turns you into a floozy."

"That had nothing to do with it," Annie said.

"Her teeth," Billy said. "She's got the most gorgeous teeth in North America. Better-lookin' teeth than Joan Crawford. What a smile! You ain't seen her smile yet, but that's a fantastic smile. Like Times Square is what it is. She coulda been on billboards coast to coast. We'd be hip-deep in toothpaste, and cash too. But no." And he jerked a thumb at his mother.

"She had a job," Annie said. "She didn't need that. I never liked that fellow that wanted to sign her up."

"He was all right," Billy said. "I checked him out. He was legitimate."

"How could you know what he was?"

"How could I know anything? I'm a goddamn genius."

"Clean up your mouth, genius. She would've had to go to New York for pictures."

"And she'd of never come back, right?"

"Maybe she would, maybe she wouldn't."

"Now you got it," Billy said to his father. "Mama likes to keep all the birds in the nest."

"Can't say as I blame her," Francis said.

"No," Billy said.

"I never liked that fellow," Annie said. "That's what it really was. I didn't trust him."

Nobody spoke.

"And she brought a paycheck home every week," Annie said. "Even when the tool company closed awhile, the owner put her to work as a cashier in a trading port he owned. Trading port and indoor golf. An enormous place. They almost brought Rudy Vallee there once. Peg got wonderful experience."

Nobody spoke.

"Cigarette?" Billy asked Francis.

"Sure," Francis said.

Annie stood up and went to the refrigerator in the pantry. She came back with the butter dish and put it on the dining-room table. Peg came through the swinging door, into the silence. She poked the potatoes with a fork, looked at the turkey, which was turning deep brown, and closed the oven door without basting it. She rummaged in the utensil drawer and found a can opener and punched it through a can of peas and put them in a pan to boil.

"Turkey smells real good," Francis said to her.

"Uh-huh, I bought a plum pudding," she said to all, showing them the can. She looked at her father. "Mama said you used to like it for dessert on holidays."

"I surely did. With that white sugar sauce. Mighty sweet."

"The sauce recipe's on the label," Annie said. "Give it here and I'll make it."

"I'll make it," Peg said.

"It's nice you remembered that," Francis said.

"It's no trouble," Peg said. "The pudding's already cooked. All you do is heat it up in the can."

Francis studied her and saw the venom was gone from her eyes. This lady goes up and down like a thermometer. When she saw him studying her she smiled slightly, not a billboard smile, not a smile to make anybody rich in toothpaste, but there it was. What the hell, she's got a right. Up and down, up and down. She come by it naturally.

"I got a letter maybe you'd all like to hear while that stuff's cookin' up," he said, and he took the yellowed envelope with a canceled two-cent stamp on it out of his inside coat pocket. On the back, written in his own hand, was: *First letter from Margaret.*

"I got this a few years back, quite a few," he said, and from the envelope he took out three small trifolded sheets of yellowed lined paper. "Come to me up in Canada in nineteen-ten, when I was with Toronto." He unfolded the sheets and moved them into the best possible light at longest possible arm's length, and then he read:

" 'Dear Poppy, I suppose you never think that you have a daughter that is waiting for a letter since you went away. I was so mad because you did not think of me that I was going to join the circus that was here last Friday. I am doing my lesson and there is an arithmetic example here that I cannot get. See if you can get it. I hope your leg is better and that you have good luck with the team. Do not run too much with your legs or you will have to be carried home. Mama and Billy are good. Mama has fourteen new little chickens out and she has two more hens sitting. There is a wild west circus coming the eighth. Won't you come home and see it? I am going to it. Billy is just going to bed and Mama is sitting on the bed watching me. Do not forget to answer this. I suppose you are having a lovely time. Do not let me find you with another girl or I will pull her hair. Yours truly, Peggy.' "

"Isn't that funny," Peg said, the fork still in her hand. "I don't remember writing that."

"Probably lots you don't remember about them days," Francis said. "You was only about eleven."

"Where did you ever find it?"

"Up in the trunk. Been saved all these years up there. Only letter I ever saved."

"Is that a fact?"

"It's a provable fact. All the papers I got in the world was in that trunk, except one other place I got a few more clips. But no letters noplace. It's a good old letter, I'd say."

"I'd say so too," Annie said. She and Billy were both staring at Peg.

"I remember Toronto in nineteen-ten," Francis said. "The game was full of crooks them days. Crooked umpire named Bates, one night it was deep dark but he wouldn't call the game. Folks was throwin' tomatoes and mudballs at him but he wouldn't call it 'cause we was winnin' and he was in with the other team. Pudge Howard was catchin' that night and he walks out and has a three-way confab on the mound with me and old Highpockets Wilson, who was pitchin'. Pudge comes back and squats behind the plate and Highpockets lets go a blazer and the ump calls it a ball, though nobody could see nothin' it was so dark. And Pudge turns to him and says: 'You call that pitch a ball?' 'I did,' says the ump. 'If that was a ball I'll eat it,' says Pudge. 'Then you better get eatin',' says the ump. And Pudge, he holds the ball up and takes a big bite out of it, 'cause it ain't no ball at all, it's a yellow apple I give Highpockets to throw. And of course that won us the game and the ump went down in history as Blindy Bates, who couldn't tell a baseball from a damn apple. Bates turned into a bookie after that. He was crooked at that too."

"That's a great story," Billy said. "Funny stuff in them old days."

"Funny stuff happenin' all the time," Francis said.

Peg was suddenly tearful. She put the fork on the sink and went to her father, whose hands were folded on the table. She sat beside him and put her right hand on top of his.

After a while George Quinn came home from Troy, Annie served the turkey, and then the entire Phelan family sat down to dinner.

VIII

"I LOOK LIKE A BUM, don't I?" Rudy said.

"You are a bum," Francis said. "But you're a pretty good bum if you wanna be."

"You know why people call you a bum?"

"I can't understand why."

"They feel better when they say it."

"The truth ain't gonna hurt you," Francis said. "If you're a bum, you're a bum."

"It hurt a lotta bums. Ain't many of the old ones left."

"There's new ones comin' along," Francis said.

"A lot of good men died. Good mechanics, machinists, lumberjacks."

"Some of 'em ain't dead," Francis said. "You and me, we ain't dead."

"They say there's no God," Rudy said. "But there must be a God. He protects bums. They get up out of the snow and they go up and get a drink. Look at you, brand-new clothes. But look at me. I'm only a bum. A no-good bum."

"You ain't that bad," Francis said. "You're a bum, but you ain't that bad."

They were walking down South Pearl Street toward Palombo's Hotel. It was ten-thirty, a clear night, full of stars but very cold: winter's harbinger. Francis had left the family just before ten o'clock and taken a bus downtown. He went straight to the mission before they locked it for the night, and found Pee Wee alone in the kitchen, drinking leftover coffee. Pee Wee said he hadn't seen, or heard from, Helen all day.

"But Rudy was in lookin' for you," Pee Wee told Francis. "He's either up at the railroad station gettin' warm or holed up in some old house down on Broadway. He says you'd know which one. But look, Francis, from what I hear, the cops been raidin' them old pots just about every night. Lotta guys usually eat here ain't been around and I figure they're all in jail. They must be repaintin' the place out there and need extra help."

"I don't know why the hell they gotta do that," Francis said. "Bums don't hurt nobody."

"Maybe it's just cops don't like bums no more."

Francis checked out the old house first, for it was close to the mission. He stepped through its doorless entrance into a damp, deep-black stairwell. He waited until his eyes adjusted to the darkness and then he carefully climbed the stairs, stepping over bunches of crumpled newspaper and fallen plaster and a Negro who was curled up on the first landing. He stepped through broken glass, empty wine and soda bottles, cardboard boxes, human droppings. Streetlights illuminated stalagmites of pigeon leavings on a windowsill. Francis saw a second sleeping man curled up near the hole he heard a fellow named Michigan Mac fell through last week. Francis sidestepped the man and the hole and then found Rudy in a room by himself, lying on a slab of board away from the broken window, with a newspaper on his shoulder for a blanket.

"Hey bum," Francis said, "you lookin' for me?"

Rudy blinked and looked up from his slab.

"Who the hell you talkin' to?" Rudy said. "What are you, some kinda G-man?"

"Get your ass up off the floor, you dizzy kraut."

"Hey, is that you, Francis?"

"No, it's Buffalo Bill. I come up here lookin' for Indians."

Rudy sat up and threw the newspaper off himself.

"Pee Wee says you was lookin' for me," Francis said.

"I didn't have noplace to flop, no money, no jug, nobody around. I had a jug but it ran out." Rudy fell back on the slab and wept instant tears over his condition. "I'll kill myself, I got the tendency," he said. "I'm last."

"Hey," Francis said. "Get up. You ain't bright enough to kill yourself. You gotta fight, you gotta be tough. I can't even find Helen. You seen Helen anyplace? Think about that woman on the bum somewheres on a night like this. Jesus I feel sorry for her."

"Where the wind don't blow," Rudy said.

"Yeah. No wind. Let's go."

"Go where?"

"Outa here. You stay here, you wind up in jail tonight. Pee Wee says they're cleanin' out all these joints."

"Go to jail, at least it's warm. Get six months and be out in time for the flowers."

"No jail for Francis. Francis is free and he's gonna stay free."

They walked down the stairs and back to Madison because Francis decided Helen must have found money somewhere or else she'd have come looking for him. Maybe she called her brother and got a chunk. Or maybe she was holding out even more than she said. Canny old dame. And sooner or later, with dough, she'd hit Palombo's because of the suitcase.

"Where we goin'?"

"What the hell's the difference? Little walk'll keep your blood flowin'."

"Where'd you get them clothes?"

"Found 'em."

"Found 'em? Where'd you find 'em?"

"Up a tree."

"A tree?"

"Yeah. A tree. Grew everything. Suits, shoes, bow ties."

"You never tell me nothin' that's true."

"Hell, it's all true," Francis said. "Every stinkin' damn thing you can think of is true."

*   *   *

At Palombo's they met old man Donovan just getting ready to go off duty, making way for the night clerk. It was a little before eleven and he was putting the desk in order. Yes, he told Francis, Helen was here. Checked in late this morning. Yeah, sure she's all right. Looked right perky. Walked up them stairs lookin' the same as always. Took the room you always take.

"All right," said Francis, and he took out the ten-dollar bill Billy gave him. "You got change of this?" Donovan made change and then Francis handed him two dollars.

"You give her this in the mornin'," he said, "and make sure she gets somethin' to eat. If I hear she didn't get it, I'll come back here and pull out all your teeth."

"She'll get it," Donovan said. "I like Helen."

"Check her out now," Francis said. "Don't tell her I'm here. Just see is she okay and does she need anything. Don't say I sent you or nothin' like that. Just check her out."

So Donovan knocked on Helen's door at eleven o'clock and found out she needed nothing at all, and he came back and told Francis.

"You tell her in the mornin' I'll be around sometime during the day," Francis said. "And if she don't see me and she wants me, you tell her to leave me a message where she'll be. Leave it with Pee Wee down at the mission. You know Pee Wee?"

"I know the mission," Donovan said.

"She claim the suitcase?" Francis asked.

"Claimed it and paid for two nights in the room."

"She got money from home, all right," Francis said. "But you give her that deuce anyway."

Francis and Rudy walked north on Pearl Street then, Francis keeping the pace brisk. In a shopwindow Francis saw three mannequins in formal dresses beckoning to him. He waved at them.

"Now where we goin'?" Rudy asked.

"The all-night bootlegger's," Francis said. "Get us a couple of jugs and then go get a flop and get some shut-eye."

"Hey," Rudy said. "Now you're sayin' somethin' I wanna hear. Where'd you find all this money?"

"Up in a tree."

"Same tree that grows bow ties?"

"Yep," said Francis. "Same tree."

Francis bought two quarts of muscatel at the upstairs bootlegger's on Beaver Street and two pints of Green River whiskey.

"Rotgut," he said when the bootlegger handed him the whiskey, "but it does what it's supposed to do."

Francis paid the bootlegger and pocketed the change: two dollars and thirty cents left. He gave a quart of the musky and a pint of the whiskey to Rudy and when they stepped outside the bootlegger's they both tipped up their wine.

And so Francis began to drink for the first time in a week.

✳   ✳   ✳

The flop was run by a bottom-heavy old woman with piano legs, the widow of somebody named Fennessey, who had died so long ago nobody remembered his first name.

"Hey Ma," Rudy said when she opened the door for them.

"My name's Mrs. Fennessey," she said. "That's what I go by."

"I knew that," Rudy said.

"Then call me that. Only the niggers call me Ma."

"All right, sweetheart," Francis said. "Anybody call you sweetheart? We want a couple of flops."

She let them in and took their money, a dollar for two flops, and then led them upstairs to a large room that used to be two or three rooms but now, with the interior walls gone, was a dormitory with a dozen filthy cots, only one occupied by a sleeping form. The room was lit by what Francis judged to be a three-watt bulb.

"Hey," he said, "too much light in here. It'll blind us all."

"Your friend don't like it here, he can go somewhere else," Mrs. Fennessey told Rudy.

"Who wouldn't like this joint?" Francis said, and he bounced on the cot next to the sleeping man.

"Hey bum," he said, reaching over and shaking the sleeper. "You want a drink?"

A man with enormous week-old scabs on his nose and forehead turned to face Francis.

"Hey," said Francis. "It's the Moose."

"Yeah, it's me," Moose said.

"Moose who?" asked Rudy.

"Moose what's the difference," Francis said.

"Moose Backer," Moose said.

"That there's Rudy," Francis said. "He's crazier than a cross-eyed bedbug, but he's all right."

"You sharped up some since I seen you last," Moose said to Francis. "Even wearin' a tie. You bump into prosperity?"

"He found a tree that grows ten-dollar bills," Rudy said.

Francis walked around the cot and handed Moose his wine. Moose took a swallow and nodded his thanks.

"Why'd you wake me up?" Moose asked.

"Woke you up to give you a drink."

"It was dark when I went to sleep. Dark and cold."

"Jesus Christ, I know. Fingers cold, toes cold. Cold in here right now. Here, have another drink and warm up. You want some whiskey? I got some of that too."

"I'm all right. I got an edge. You got enough for yourself?"

"Have a drink, goddamn it. Don't be afraid to live." And Moose took one glug of the Green River.

"I thought you was gonna trade pants with me," Moose said.

"I was. Pair I had was practically new, but too small."

"Where are they? You said they were thirty-eight, thirty-one, and that's just right."

"You want these?"

"Sure," said Moose.

"If I give 'em to you, then I ain't got no pants," Francis said.

"I'll give you mine," Moose said.

"Why you tradin' your new pants?" Rudy asked.

"That's right," said Francis, standing up and looking at his own legs. "Why am I? No, you ain't gonna get these. Fuck you, I need these pants. Don't tell me what I need. Go get your own pants."

"I'll buy 'em," Moose said. "How much you want? I got another week's work sandin' floors."

"Well shine 'em," Francis said. "They ain't for sale."

"Sandin', not shinin'. I sand 'em. I don't shine 'em."

"Don't holler at me," Francis said. "I'll crack your goddamn head and step on your brains. You're a tough man, is that it?"

"No," said Moose. "I ain't tough."

"Well I'm tough," Francis said. "Screw around with me, you'll die younger'n I will."

"Oh I'll die all right. I'm just as busted as that ceiling. I got TB."

"Oh God bless you," Francis said, sitting down. "I'm sorry."

"It's in the knee."

"I didn't know you had it. I'm sorry. I'm sorry anybody's got TB."

"It's in the knee."

"Well cut your leg off."

"That's what they wanted to do."

"So cut it off."

"No, I wouldn't let them do that."

"I got a stomach cancer," Rudy said.

"Yeah," said Moose. "Everybody's got one of them."

"Anybody gonna come to my funeral?" Rudy asked.

"Probably ain't nothin' wrong with you work won't cure," Moose said.

"That's right," Francis said to Rudy. "Why don't you go get a job?" He pointed out the window at the street. "Look at 'em out there. Everybody out there's workin'."

"You're crazier than he is," Moose said. "Ain't no jobs anyplace. Where you been?"

"There's taxis. There goes a taxi."

"Yeah, there's taxis," Moore said. "So what?"

"Can you drive?" Francis asked Rudy.

"I drove my ex-wife crazy," Rudy said.

"Good. What you're supposed to do. Drive 'em nuts is right."

In the corner of the room Francis saw three long-skirted women who became four who became three and then four again. Their faces were familiar but he could call none of them by name. Their ages changed when their number changed: now twenty, now sixty, now thirty, now fifty, never childish, never aged. At the house Annie would now be trying to sleep, but probably no more prepared for it than Francis was, no more capable of closing the day than Francis was. Helen would be out of it, whipped all to hell by fatigue and worry. Damn worrywart is what she is. But not Annie. Annie, she don't worry. Annie knows how to live. Peg, she'll be awake too, why not? Why should she sleep when nobody else can? They'll all be up, you bet. Francis give 'em a show they ain't gonna forget in a hurry.

He showed 'em what a man can do.

A man ain't afraid of goin' back.

Goddamn spooks, they follow you everywheres but they don't matter. You stand up to 'em is all. And you do what you gotta do.

Sandra joined the women of three, the women of four, in the far corner. Francis gave me soup, she told them. He carried me out of the wind and put my shoe on me. They became the women of five.

"Where the wind don't blow," Rudy sang. "I wanna go where the wind don't blow, where there ain't no snow."

Francis saw Katrina's face among the five that became four that became three.

*   *   *

Finny and Little Red came into the flop, and just behind them a third figure Francis did not recognize immediately. Then he saw it was Old Shoes.

"Hey, we got company, Moose," Francis said.

"Is that Finny?" Moose asked. "Looks like him."

"That's the man," Francis said. Finny stood by the foot of Francis's cot, very drunk and wobbling, trying to see who was talking about him.

"You son of a bitch," Moose said, leaning on one elbow.

"Which son of a bitch you talkin' to?" Francis asked.

"Finny. He used to work for Spanish George. Liked to use the blackjack on drunks when they got noisy."

"Is that true, Finny?" Francis asked. "You liked to sap the boys?"

"Arrrggghhh," said Finny, and he lurched off toward a cot down the row from Francis.

"He was one mean bastard," Moose said. "He hit me once."

"Hurt you?"

"Hurt like hell. I had a headache three weeks."

"Somebody burned up Finny's car," Little Red announced. "He went out for somethin' to eat, and he came back, it was on fire. He thinks the cops did it."

"Why are the cops burnin' up cars?" Rudy asked.

"Cops're goin' crazy," Little Red said. "They're pickin' up everybody. American Legion's behind it, that's what I heard."

"Them lard-ass bastards," Francis said. "They been after my ass all my life."

"Legionnaires and cops," said Little Red. "That's why we come in here."

"You think you're safe here?" Francis asked.

"Safer than on the street."

"Cops'd never come up here if they wanted to get you, right?" Francis said.

"They wouldn't know I was here," Little Red said.

"Whataya think this is, the Waldorf-Astoria? You think that old bitch downstairs don't tell the cops who's here and who ain't when they want to know?"

"Maybe it wasn't the cops burned up the car," Moose said. "Finny's got plenty of enemies. If I knew he owned one, I'da burned it up myself. The son of a bitch beat up on us all, but now he's on the street. Now we got him in the alley."

"You hear that, Finny?" Francis called out. "They gonna get your ass good. They got you in the alley with all the other bums."

"Ngggghhhh," said Finny.

"Finny's all right," Little Red said. "Leave him alone."

"You givin' orders here at the Waldorf-Astoria, is that it?" Francis asked.

"Who the hell are you?" Little Red asked.

"I'm a fella ready to stomp all over your head and squish it like a grape, you try to tell me what to do."

"Yeah," said Little Red, and he moved toward the cot beside Finny.

"I knew it was you soon as I come in," Old Shoes said, coming over to the foot of Francis's cot. "I could tell that foghorn voice of yours anyplace."

"Old Shoes," Francis said. "Old Shoes Gilligan."

"That's right. You got a pretty good memory. The wine ain't got you yet."

"Old Shoes Gilligan, a grand old soul, got a cast-iron belly and a brass asshole."

"Not cast-iron anymore," Old Shoes said. "I got an ulcer. I quit drinkin' two years ago."

"Then what the hell you doin' here?"

"Just came by to see the boys, see what was happenin'."

"You hangin' out with Finny and that redheaded wiseass?"

"Who you callin' a wiseass?" Little Red said.

"I'm callin' you wiseass, wiseass," Francis said.

"You got a big mouth," Little Red said.

"I got a foot's even bigger and I'm gonna shove it right up your nose, you keep bein' nasty to me when I'm tryna be polite."

"Cool off, Francis," Old Shoes said. "What's your story? You're lookin' pretty good."

"I'm gettin' rich," Francis said. "Got me a gang of new clothes, couple of jugs, money in the pocket."

"You're gettin' up in the world," Old Shoes said.

"Yeah, but what the hell you doin' here if you ain't drinkin' is what I don't figure."

"I just told you. I'm passin' through and got curious about the old joints."

"You workin'?"

"Got a steady job down in Jersey. Even got an apartment and a car. A car, Francis. You believe that? Me with a car? Not a new car, but a good car. A Hudson two-door. You want a ride?"

"A ride? Me?"

"Sure, why not?"

"Now?"

"Don't matter to me. I'm just sightseein'. I'm not sleepin' up here. Wouldn't sleep here anyway. Bedbugs'd follow me all the way back to Jersey."

"This bum here," Francis explained to Rudy, "I saved from dyin' in the street. Used to fall down drunk three, four times a night, like he was top-heavy."

"That's right," Old Shoes said. "Broke my face five or six times, just like his." And he gestured at Moose. "But I don't do that no more. I hit three nuthouses and then I quit. I been off the bum three years and dry for two. You wanna go for that ride, Francis? Only thing is, no bottle. The wife'd smell it and I'd catch hell."

"You got a wife too?" Francis said.

"You got a car and a wife and a house and a job?" Rudy asked. He sat up on his cot and studied this interloper.

"That's Rudy," Francis said. "Rudy Tooty. He's thinkin' about killin' himself."

"I know the feelin'," Old Shoes said. "Me and Francis we needed a drink somethin' awful one mornin'. We walked all over town but we couldn't score, snow comin' through our shoes, and it's four below zero. Finally we sold our blood and drank the money. I passed out and woke up still needin' a drink awful bad, and not a penny and no chance for one, couldn't even sell any more blood, and I wanted to die and I mean die. Die."

"Where there ain't no snow," Rudy sang. "Where the handouts grow on bushes and you sleep out every night."

"You wanna go for a ride?" Old Shoes asked Rudy.

"Oh the buzzin' of the bees in the cigarette trees, by the soda water fountains," Rudy sang. Then he smiled at Old Shoes, took a swallow of wine, and fell back on his cot.

"Man wants to go for a ride and can't get no takers," Francis said. "Might as well call it a day, Shoes, stretch out and rest them bones."

"Naaah, I guess I'll be movin' on."

"One evenin' as the sun went down, and the jungle fires were bur-nin'," Rudy sang, "Down the track came a hobo hikin', and said, Boys, I am not turnin'."

"Shut up that singin'," Little Red said. "I'm tryna sleep."

"I'm gonna mess up his face," Francis said and stood up.

"No fights," Moose said. "She'll kick us the hell out or call the cops on us."

"That'll be the day I get kicked out of a joint like this," Francis said. "This is pigswill. I lived in better pigswill than this goddamn pigswill."

"Where I come from—" Old Shoes began.

"I don't give a goddamn where you come from," Francis said.

"Goddamn you, I come from Texas."

"Name a city, then."

"Galveston."

"Behave yourself," Francis said, "or I'll knock you down. I'm a tough son of a bitch. Tougher than that bum Finny. Licked twelve men at once."

"You're drunk," Old Shoes said.

"Yeah," said Francis. "My mind's goin'."

"It went there. Rattlesnake got you."

"Rattlesnake, my ass. Rattlesnake is nothin'."

"Cottonmouth?"

"Oh, cottonmouth rattler. Yeah. That's somethin'. Jesus, this is a nice subject. Who wants to talk about snakes? Talk about bums is more like it. A bum is a bum. Helen's got me on the bum. Son of a bitch, she won't go home, won't straighten up."

"Helen did the hula down in Hon-oh-loo-loo," Rudy sang.

"Shut your stupid mouth," Francis said to Rudy.

"People don't like me," Rudy said.

"Singin' there, wavin' your arms, talkin' about Helen."

"I can't escape myself."

"That's what I'm talkin' about," Francis said.

"I tried it before."

"I know, but you can't do it, so you might as well live with it."

"I like to be condemned," Rudy said.

"No, don't be condemned," Francis told him.

"I like to be condemned."

"Never be condemned."

"I like to be condemned because I know I done wrong in my life."

"You never done wrong," Francis said.

"All you screwballs down there, shut up," yelled Little Red, sitting up on his cot. Francis instantly stood up and ran down the aisle. He was running when he lunged and grazed Little Red's lips with his knuckles.

"I'm gonna mess you up," Francis said.

Little Red rolled with the blow and fell off the cot. Francis ran around the cot and kicked him in the stomach. Little Red groaned and rolled and Francis kicked him in the side. Little Red rolled under Finny's cot, away from Francis's feet. Francis followed him and was ready to drive a black laceless oxford deep into his face, but then he stopped. Rudy, Moose, and Old Shoes were all standing up, watching.

"When I knew Francis he was strong as a bull," Old Shoes said.

"Knocked a house down by myself," Francis said, walking back to his cot. "Didn't need no wreckin' ball." He picked up the quart of wine and gestured with it. Moose lay back down on his cot and Rudy on his. Old Shoes sat on the cot next to Francis. Little Red licked his bleeding lip and lay quietly on the floor under the cot where Finny was supine and snoring. The faces of all the women Francis had ever known changed with kaleidoscopic swiftness from one to the other to the other on the three female figures in the far corner. The trio sat on straight-backed chairs, witnesses all to the whole fabric of Francis's life. His mother was crocheting a Home Sweet Home sampler while Katrina measured off a bolt of new cloth and Helen snipped the ragged threads. Then they all became Annie.

"When they throw dirt in my face, nobody can walk up and sell me short, that's what I worry about," Francis said. "I'll suffer in hell, if they ever got such a place, but I still got muscles and blood and I'm gonna live it out. I never saw a bum yet said anything against Francis. They better not, goddamn 'em. All them sufferin' bastards, all them poor souls waitin' for heaven, walkin' around with the snow flyin', stayin' in empty houses, pants fallin' off 'em. When I leave this earth I wanna leave it with a blessing to everybody. Francis never hurt nobody."

"The mockin'birds'll sing when you die," Old Shoes said.

"Let 'em. Let 'em sing. People tell me: Get off the bum. And I had a chance. I had a good mind but now it's all flaked out, like a heavin' line on a canal boat, back and forth, back and forth. You get whipped around so much, everything comes to a standstill, even a nail. You drive it so far and it comes to a stop. Keep hittin' it and the head'll break off."

"That's a true thing," Moose said.

"On the Big Rock Candy Mountain," Rudy sang, "the cops got wooden legs." He stood up and waved his wine in a gesture imitative of Francis; then he rocked back and forth as he sang, strongly and on key: "The bulldogs all got rubber teeth, and the hens lay soft-boiled eggs. The boxcars all are empty and the sun shines every day. I wanna go where there ain't no snow, where the sleet don't fall and the wind don't blow, on the Big Rock Candy Mountain."

Old Shoes stood up and made ready to leave. "Nobody wants a ride?" he said.

"All right, goddamn it," Francis said. "Whataya say, Rudy? Let's get outa this pigswill. Get outa this stink and go where I can breathe. The weeds is better than this pigswill."

"So long, friend," Moose said. "Thanks for the wine."

"You bet, pal, and God bless your knee. Tough as nails, that's what Francis is."

"I believe that," Moose said.

"Where we goin'?" Rudy asked.

"Go up to the jungle and see a friend of mine. You wanna give us a lift to the jungle?" Francis asked Old Shoes. "Up in the North End. You know where that is?"

"No, but you do."

"Gonna be cold," Rudy said.

"They got a fire," Francis said. "Cold's better than this bughouse."

"By the lemonade springs, where the bluebird sings," Rudy sang.

"That's the place," Francis said.

*   *   *

As Old Shoes' car moved north on Erie Boulevard, where the Erie Canal used to flow, Francis remembered Emmett Daugherty's face: rugged and flushed beneath wavy gray hair, a strong, pointed nose truly giving him the look of the Divine Warrior, which is how Francis would always remember him, an Irishman who never drank more than enough, a serious and witty man of control and high purpose, and with an unkillable faith in God and the laboring man. Francis had sat with him on the slate step in front of Iron Joe's Wheelbarrow and listened to his endless talk of the days when he and the country were young, when the riverboats brought the greenhorns up the Hudson from the Irish ships. When the cholera was in the air, the greenhorns would be taken off the steamboats at Albany and sent west on canal boats, for the city's elders had charged the government with keeping the pestilential foreigners out of the city.

Emmett rode up from New York after he got off the death ship from Cork, and at the Albany basin he saw his brother Owen waving frantically to him. Owen followed the boat to the North Albany lock, ran along the towpath yelling advice to Emmett, giving him family news, telling him to get off the boat as soon as they'd let him, then to write saying where he was so Owen could send him money to come back to Albany by stagecoach. But it was days before Emmett got off that particular packet boat, got off in a place whose name he never learned, and the authorities there too kept the newcomers westering, under duress.

By the time Emmett reached Buffalo he had decided not to return to such an inhospitable city as Albany, and he moved on to Ohio, where he found work building streets, and then with the railroads, and in time went all the way west on the rails and became a labor organizer, and eventually a leader of the Clann na Gael, and lived to see the Irish in control of Albany, and to tell his stories and inspire Francis Phelan to throw the stone that changed the course of life, even for people not yet born.

That vision of the packet moving up the canal and Owen running alongside it telling Emmett about his children was as real to Francis, though it happened four decades before he was born, as was Old Shoes' car, in which he was now bouncing ever northward toward the precise place where the separation took place. He all but cried at the way the Daugherty brothers were being separated by the goddamned government, just as he was now being separated from Billy and the others. And by what? What and who were again separating Francis from those people after he'd found them? It was a force whose name did not matter, if it had a name, but whose effect was devastating. Emmett Daugherty had placed blame on no man, not on the cholera inspectors or even the city's elders. He knew a larger fate had moved him westward and shaped in him all that he was to become; and that moving and shaping was what Francis now understood, for he perceived the fugitive thrust that had come to be so much a part of his own spirit. And so he found it entirely reasonable that he and Emmett should be fused in a single person: the character of the hero of the play written by Emmett's son, Edward Daugherty the playwright: Edward (husband of Katrina, father of Martin), who wrote *The Car Barns*, the tale of how Emmett radicalized Francis by telling his own story of separation and growth, by inspiring Francis to identify the enemy and target him with a stone. And just as Emmett truly did return home from the west as a labor hero, so also did the playright conjure an image of Francis returning home as underground hero for what that stone of his had done.

For a time Francis believed everything Edward Daugherty had written about him: liberator of the strikers from the capitalist beggars who owned the trolleys, just as Emmett had helped Paddy-with-a-shovel straighten his back and climb up out of his ditch in another age. The playwright saw them both as Divine Warriors, sparked by the socialistic gods who understood the historical Irish need for aid from on high, for without it (so spoke Emmett, the golden-tongued organizer of the play), "how else would we rid ourselves of those Tory swine, the true and unconquerable devils of all history?"

The stone had (had it not?) precipitated the firing by the soldiers and the killing of the pair of bystanders. And without that, without the death of Harold Allen, the strike might have continued, for the scabs were being imported in great numbers from Brooklyn, greenhorn Irish the likes of Emmett on the packet boat, some of them defecting instantly from the strike when they saw what it was, others bewildered and lost, lied to by men who hired them for railroad work in Philadelphia, then duped them into scabbery, terror, even death. There were even strikers from other cities working as scabs, soulless men who rode the strike trains here and took these Albany men's jobs, as other scabs were taking theirs. And all of that might have continued had not Francis thrown the first stone. He was the principal hero in a strike that created heroes by the dozen. And because he was, he lived all his life with guilt over the deaths of the three men, unable to see any other force at work in the world that day beyond his own right hand. He could not accept, though he knew it to be true, that other significant stones had flown that day, that the soldiers' fusillade at the bystanders had less to do with Harold Allen's death than it did with the possibility of the soldiers' own, for their firing had followed not upon the release of the stone by Francis but only after the mob's full barrage had flown at the trolley. And then Francis, having seen nothing but his own act and what appeared to be its instant consequences, had fled into heroism and been suffused further, through the written word of Edward Daugherty, with the hero's most splendid guilt.

But now, with those events so deeply dead and buried, with his own guilt having so little really to do with it, he saw the strike as simply the insanity of the Irish, poor against poor, a race, a class divided against itself. He saw Harold Allen trying to survive the day and the night at a moment when the frenzied mob had turned against him, just as Francis himself had often had to survive hostility in his flight through strange cities, just as he had always had to survive his own worst instincts. For Francis knew now that he was at war with himself, his private factions mutually bellicose, and if he was ever to survive, it would be with the help not of any socialistic god but with a clear head and a steady eye for the truth; for the guilt he felt was not worth the dying. It served nothing except nature's insatiable craving for blood. The trick was to live, to beat the bastards, survive the mob and that fateful chaos, and show them all what a man can do to set things right, once he sets his mind to it.

Poor Harold Allen.

"I forgive the son of a bitch," Francis said.

"Who's that?" Old Shoes asked. Rudy lay all but blotto across the backseat, holding the whiskey and wine bottles upright on his chest with both tops open in violation of Old Shoes' dictum that they stay closed, and not spilling a drop of either.

"Guy I killed. Guy named Allen."

"You killed a guy?"

"More'n one."

"Accidental, was it?"

"No. I tried to get that one guy, Allen. He was takin' my job."

"That's a good reason."

"Maybe, maybe not. Maybe he was just doin' what he had to do."

"Baloney," Old Shoes said. "That's what everybody does, good, bad, and lousy. Burglars, murderers."

And Francis fell quiet, sinking into yet another truth requiring handling.

*   *   *

The jungle was maybe seven years old, three years old, a month old, days old. It was an ashpit, a graveyard, and a fugitive city. It stood among wild sumac bushes and river foliage, all fallen dead now from the early frost. It was a haphazard upthrust of tarpaper shacks, lean-tos, and impromptu constructions describable by no known nomenclature. It was a city of essential transiency and would-be permanency, a resort of those for whom motion was either anathema or pointless or impossible. Cripples lived here, and natives of this town who had lost their homes, and people who had come here at journey's end to accept whatever disaster was going to happen next. The jungle, a visual manifestation of the malaise of the age and the nation, covered the equivalent of two or more square city blocks between the tracks and the river, just east of the old carbarns and the empty building that once housed Iron Joe's saloon.

Francis's friend in the jungle was a man in his sixties named Andy, who had admitted to Francis in the boxcar in which they both traveled to Albany that people used to call him Andy Which One, a name that derived from his inability, until he was nearly twenty, to tell his left hand from his right, a challenge he still faced in certain stressful moments. Francis found Andy Which One instantly sympathetic, shared the wealth of cigarettes and food he was carrying, and thought instantly of him again when Annie handed him two turkey sandwiches and Peg slipped him a hefty slice of plum pudding, all three items wrapped in waxed paper and intact now in the pockets of his 1916 suitcoat.

But Francis had not seriously thought of sharing the food with

Andy until Rudy had begun singing of the jungle. On top of that, Francis almost suffocated seeing his own early venom and self-destructive arrogance reembodied in Little Red, and the conjunction of events impelled him to quit the flop and seek out something he could value; for above all now, Francis needed to believe in simple solutions. And Andy Which One, a man confused by the names of his own hands, but who survived to dwell in the city of useless penitence and be grateful for it, seemed to Francis a creature worthy of scrutiny. Francis found him easily when Old Shoes parked the car on the dirt road that bordered the jungle. He roused Andy from shallow sleep in front of a fading fire, and handed him the whiskey bottle.

"Have a drink, pal. Lubricate your soul."

"Hey, old Francis. How you makin' out there, buddy?"

"Puttin' one foot in front of the other and hopin' they go somewheres," Francis said. "The hotel open here? I brought a couple of bums along with me. Old Shoes here, he says he ain't a bum no more, but that's just what he says. And Rudy the Cootie, a good ol' fella."

"Hey," said Andy, "just settle in. Musta known you was comin'. Fire's still goin', and the stars are out. Little chilly in this joint. Lemme turn up the heat."

They all sat down around the fire while Andy stoked it with twigs and scraps of lumber, and soon the flames were trying to climb to those reaches of the sky that are the domain of all fire. The flames gave vivid life to the cold night, and the men warmed their hands by them.

A figure hovered behind Andy and when he felt its presence he turned and welcomed Michigan Mac to the primal scene.

"Glad to meet ya," Francis said to Mac. "I heard you fell through a hole the other night."

"Coulda broke my neck," Mac said.

"Did you break it?" Francis asked.

"If I'da broke my neck I'd be dead."

"Oh, so you're livin', is that it? You ain't dead?"

"Who's this guy?" Mac asked Andy.

"He's an all-right guy I met on the train," Andy said.

"We're all all right," Francis said. "I never met a bum I didn't like."

"Will Rogers said that," Rudy said.

"He did like hell," Francis said. "I said it."

"All I know. That's what he said. All I know is what I read in the newspapers," Rudy said.

"I didn't know you could read," said Francis.

"James Watt invented the steam engine," Rudy said. "And he was only twenty-nine years old."

"He was a wizard," Francis said.

"Right. Charles Darwin was a very great man, master of botany. Died in nineteen-thirty-six."

"What's he talkin' about?" Mac asked.

"He ain't talkin' about nothin'," Francis said. "He's just talkin'."

"Sir Isaac Newton. You know what he did with the apple?"

"I know that one," Old Shoes said. "He discovered gravity."

"Right. You know when that was? Nineteen-thirty-six. He was born of two midwives."

"You got a pretty good background on these wizards," Francis said.

"God loves a thief," Rudy said. "I'm a thief."

"We're all thieves," Francis said. "What'd you steal?"

"I stole my wife's heart," Rudy said.

"What'd you do with it?"

"I gave it back. Wasn't worth keepin'. You know where the Milky Way is?"

"Up there somewheres," Francis said, looking up at the sky, which was as full of stars as he'd ever seen it.

"Damn, I'm hungry," Michigan Mac said.

"Here," said Andy. "Have a bite." And from a coat pocket he took a large raw onion.

"That's an onion," Mac said.

"Another wizard," Francis said.

Mac took the onion and looked at it, then handed it back to Andy, who took a bite out of it and put it back in his pocket.

"Got it at a grocery," Andy said. "Mister, I told the guy, I'm starvin', I gotta have somethin'. And he gave me two onions."

"You had money," Mac said. "I told ya, get a loaf of bread, but you got a pint of wine."

"Can't have wine and bread too," Andy said. "What are you, a Frenchman?"

"You wanna buy food and drink," said Francis, "you oughta get a job."

"I caddied all last week," Mac said, "but that don't pay, that shit. You slide down them hills. Them golf guys got spikes on their shoes. Then they tell ya: Go to work, ya bum. I like to, but I can't. Get five, six bucks and get on the next train. I'm no bum, I'm a hobo."

"You movin' around too much," Francis said. "That's why you fell through that hole."

"Yeah," said Mac, "but I ain't goin' back to that joint. I hear the cops are pickin' the boys outa there every night. That pot is hot. Travel on, Avalon."

"Cops were here tonight earlier, shinin' their lights," Andy said. "But they didn't pick up anybody."

Rudy raised up his head and looked over all the faces in front of the fire. Then he looked skyward and talked to the stars. "On the outskirts," he said, "I'm a restless person, a traveler."

*   *   *

They passed the wine among them and Andy restoked the fire with wood he had stored in his lean-to. Francis thought of Billy getting dressed up in his suit, topcoat, and hat, and standing before Francis for inspection. You like the hat? he asked. I like it, Francis said. It's got style. Lost the other one, Billy said. First time I ever wore this one. It look all right? It looks mighty stylish, Francis said. All right, gotta get downtown, Billy said. Sure, said Francis. We'll see you again, Billy said. No doubt about it, Francis said. You hangin' around Albany or movin' on? Billy asked. Couldn't say for sure, said Francis. Lotta things that need figurin' out. Always is, said Billy, and then they shook hands and said no more words to each other.

When he himself left an hour and a little bit later, Francis shook hands also with George Quinn, a quirky little guy as dapper as always, who told bad jokes (Let's all eat tomatoes and catch up) that made everybody laugh, and Peg threw her arms around her father and kissed him on the cheek, which was a million-dollar kiss, all right, all right, and then Annie said when she took his hand in both of hers: You must come again. Sure, said Francis. No, said Annie, I mean that you must come so that we can talk about the things you ought to know, things about the children and about the family. There's a cot we could set up in Danny's room if you wanted to stay over next time. And then she kissed him ever so lightly on the lips.

"Hey Mac," Francis said, "you really hungry or you just mouthin' off for somethin' to say?"

"I'm hungry," Mac said. "I ain't et since noon. Goin' on thirteen, fourteen hours, whatever it is."

"Here," Francis said, unwrapping one of his turkey sandwiches and handing Mac a half, "take a bite, take a couple of bites, but don't eat it all."

"Hey all right," Mac said.

"I told you he was a good fella," Andy said.

"You want a bite of sandwich?" Francis asked Andy.

"I got enough with the onion," Andy said. "But the guy in the piano box over there, he was askin' around for something awhile back. He's got a baby there."

"A baby?"

"Baby and a wife."

Francis snatched the remnants of the sandwich away from Michigan Mac and groped his way in the firelight night to the piano box. A small fire was burning in front of it and a man was sitting cross-legged, warming himself.

"I hear you got a kid here," Francis said to the man, who looked up at Francis suspiciously, then nodded and gestured at the box. Francis could see the shadow of a woman curled around what looked to be the shadow of a swaddled infant.

"Got some stuff here I can't use," Francis said, and he handed the man the full sandwich and the remnant of the second one. "Sweet stuff too," he said and gave the man the plum pudding. The man accepted the gifts with an upturned face that revealed the incredulity of a man struck by lightning in the rainless desert; and his benefactor was gone before he could even acknowledge the gift. Francis rejoined the circle at Andy's fire, entering into silence. He saw that all but Rudy, whose head was on his chest, were staring at him.

"Give him some food, did ya?" Andy asked.

"Yeah. Nice fella. I ate me a bellyful tonight. How old's the kid?"

"Twelve weeks, the guy said."

Francis nodded. "I had a kid. Name of Gerald. He was only thirteen days old when he fell and broke his neck and died."

"Jeez, that's tough," Andy said.

"You never talked about that," Old Shoes said.

"No, because it was me that dropped him. Picked him up with the diaper and he slid out of it."

"Goddamn," said Old Shoes.

"I couldn't handle it. That's why I run off and left the family. Then I bumped into one of my other kids last week and he tells me the wife never told nobody I did that. Guy drops a kid and it dies and the mother don't tell a damn soul what happened. I can't figure that out. Woman keeps a secret like that for twenty-two years, protectin' a bum like me."

"You can't figure women," Michigan Mac said. "My old lady used to peddle her tail all day long and then come home and tell me I was the only man ever touched her. I come in the house one day and found her bangin' two guys at once, first I knew what was happenin'."

"I ain't talkin' about that," Francis said. "I'm talkin' about a woman who's a real woman. I ain't talkin' about no trashbarrel whore."

"My wife was very good-lookin', though," Mac said. "And she had a terrific personality."

"Yeah," said Francis. "And it was all in her ass."

Rudy raised up his head and looked at the wine bottle in his hand. He held it up to the light.

"What makes a man a drunk?" he asked.

"Wine," Old Shoes said. "What you got in your hand."

"You ever hear about the bears and the mulberry juice?" Rudy asked. "Mulberries fermented inside their stomachs."

"That so?" said Old Shoes. "I thought they fermented before they got inside."

"Nope. Not with bears," Rudy said.

"What happened to the bears and the juice?" Mac asked.

"They all got stiff and wound up with hangovers," Rudy said, and he laughed and laughed. Then he turned the wine bottle upside down and licked the drops that flowed onto his tongue. He tossed the bottle alongside the other two empties, his own whiskey bottle and Francis's wine that had been passed around.

"Jeez," Rudy said. "We got nothin' to drink. We on the bum."

In the distance the men could hear the faint hum of automobile engines, and then the closing of car doors.

*   *   *

Francis's confession seemed wasted. Mentioning Gerald to strangers for the first time was a mistake because nobody took it seriously. And it did not diminish his own guilt but merely cheapened the utterance, made it as commonplace as Rudy's brainless chatter about bears and wizards. Francis concluded he had made yet another wrong decision, another in a long line. He concluded that he was not capable of making a right decision, that he was as wrongheaded a man as ever lived. He felt certain now that he would never attain the balance that allowed so many other men to live peaceful, nonviolent, nonfugitive lives, lives that spawned at least a modicum of happiness in old age.

He had no insights into how he differed in this from other men. He knew he was somehow stronger, more given to violence, more in love with the fugitive dance, but this was all so for reasons that had nothing to do with intent. All right, he had wanted to hurt Harold Allen, but that was so very long ago. Could anyone in possession of Francis's perspective on himself believe that he was responsible for Rowdy Dick, or the hole in the runt's neck, or the bruises on Little Red, or the scars on other men long forgotten or long buried?

Francis was now certain only that he could never arrive at any conclusions about himself that had their origin in reason. But neither did he believe himself incapable of thought. He believed he was a creature of unknown and unknowable qualities, a man in whom there would never be an equanimity of both impulsive and premeditated action. Yet after every admission that he was a lost and distorted soul, Francis asserted his own private wisdom and purpose: he had fled the folks because he was too profane a being to live among them; he had humbled himself willfully through the years to counter a fearful pride in his own ability to manufacture the glory from which grace would flow. What he was was, yes, a warrior, protecting a belief that no man could ever articulate, especially himself; but somehow it involved protecting saints from sinners, protecting the living from the dead. And a warrior, he was certain, was not a victim. Never a victim.

In the deepest part of himself that could draw an unutterable conclusion, he told himself: My guilt is all that I have left. If I lose it, I have stood for nothing, done nothing, been nothing.

And he raised his head to see the phalanx of men in Legionnaires' caps advancing into the firelight with baseball bats in their hands.

✻   ✻   ✻

The men in caps entered the jungle with a fervid purpose, knocking down everything that stood, without a word. They caved in empty shacks and toppled lean-tos that the weight of weather and time had already all but collapsed. One man who saw them coming left his lean-to and ran, calling out one word: "Raiders!" and rousing some jungle people, who picked up their belongings and fled behind the leader of the pack. The first collapsed shacks were already burning when the men around Andy's fire became aware that raiders were approaching.

"What the hell's doin'?" Rudy asked. "Why's everybody gettin' up? Where you goin', Francis?"

"Get on your feet, stupid," Francis said, and Rudy got up.

"What the hell did I get myself into?" Old Shoes said, and he backed away from the fire, keeping the advancing raiders in sight. They were half a football field away but Michigan Mac was already in heavy retreat, bent double like a scythe as he ran for the river.

The raiders moved forward with their devastation clubs and one of them flattened a lean-to with two blows. A man following them poured gasoline on the ruins and then threw a match on top of it all. The raiders were twenty yards from Andy's lean-to by then, with Andy, Rudy, and Francis still immobilized, watching the spectacle with disbelieving eyes.

"We better move it," Andy said.

"You got anything in that lean-to worth savin'?" Francis asked.

"Only thing I own that's worth anything's my skin, and I got that with me."

The three men moved slowly back from the raiders, who were clearly intent on destroying everything that stood. Francis looked at the piano box as he moved past it and saw it was empty.

"Who are they?" Rudy asked Francis. "Why they doin' this?"

But no one answered.

Half a dozen lean-tos and shacks were ablaze, and one had ignited a tall, leafless tree, whose flames were reaching high into the heavens, far above the level of the burning shacks. In the wild firelight Francis saw one raider smashing a shack, from which a groggy man emerged on hands and knees. The raider hit the crawling man across the buttocks with a half swing of the bat until the man stood up. The raider poked him yet again and the man broke into a limping run. The fire that rose from the running man's shack illuminated the raider's smile.

Francis, Rudy, and Andy turned to run then too, convinced at last that demons were abroad in the night. But as they turned they confronted a pair of raiders moving toward them from their left flank.

"Filthy bums," one raider said, and swung his bat at Andy, who stepped deftly out of range, ran off, and was swallowed up by the night. The raider reversed his swing and caught the wobbling Rudy just above neck level, and Rudy yelped and went down. Francis leaped on the man and tore the bat from him, then scrambled away and turned to face both raiders, who were advancing toward him with a hatred on their faces as anonymous and deadly as the exposed fangs of rabid dogs. The raider with the bat raised it above his own head and struck a vertical blow at Francis, which Francis sidestepped as easily as he once went to his left for a fast grounder. Simultaneously he stepped forward, as into a wide pitch, and swung his own bat at the man who had struck Rudy. Francis connected with a stroke that would have sent any pitch over any center-field fence in any ball park anywhere, and he clearly heard and truly felt bones crack in the man's back. He watched with all but orgasmic pleasure as the breathless man twisted grotesquely and fell without a sound.

The second attacker charged Francis and knocked him down, not with his bat but with the weight and force of his moving body. The two rolled over and over, Francis finally separating himself from the man by a glancing blow to the throat. But the man was tough and very agile, fully on his feet when Francis was still on his knees, and he was raising his arms for a horizontal swing when Francis brought his own bat full circle and smashed the man's left leg at knee level. The knee collapsed inward, a hinge reversed, and the raider toppled crookedly with a long howl of pain.

Francis lifted Rudy, who was mumbling incoherent sounds, and threw him over his shoulder. He ran, as best he could, toward the dark woods along the river, and then moved south along the shore toward the city. He stopped in tall weeds, all brown and dead, and lay prone, with Rudy beside him, to catch his breath. No one was following. He looked back at the jungle through the barren trees and saw it aflame in widening measure. The moon and the stars shone on the river, a placid sea of glass beside the sprawling, angry fire.

Francis found he was bleeding from the cheek and he went to the river and soaked his handkerchief and rinsed off the blood. He drank deeply of the river, which was icy and shocking and sweet. He blotted the wound, found it still bleeding, and pressed it with the handkerchief to stanch it.

"Who were they?" Rudy asked when he returned.

"They're the guys on the other team," Francis said. "They don't like us filthy bums."

"You ain't filthy," Rudy said hoarsely. "You got a new suit."

"Never mind my suit, how's your head?"

"I don't know. Like nothin' I ever felt before." Francis touched the back of Rudy's skull. It wasn't bleeding but there was one hell of a lump there.

"Can you walk?"

"I don't know. Where's Old Shoes and his car?"

"Gone, I guess. I think that car is hot. I think he stole it. He used to do that for a livin'. That and peddle his ass."

Francis helped Rudy to his feet, but Rudy could not stand alone, nor could he put one foot in front of the other. Francis lifted him back on his shoulder and headed south. He had Memorial Hospital in mind, the old Homeopathic Hospital on North Pearl Street, downtown. It was a long way, but there wasn't no other place in the middle of the damn night. And walking was the only way. You wait for a damn bus or a trolley at this hour, Rudy'd be dead in the gutter.

Francis carried him first on one shoulder, then on the other, and finally piggyback when he found Rudy had some use of both arms and could hold on. He carried him along the river road to stay away from cruising police cars, and then down along the tracks and up to Broadway and then Pearl. He carried him up the hospital steps and into the emergency room, which was small and bright and clean and empty of patients. A nurse wheeled a stretcher away from one wall when she saw him coming, and helped Rudy to slide off Francis's back and stretch out.

"He got hit in the head," Francis said. "He can't walk."

"What happened?" the nurse asked, inspecting Rudy's eyes.

"Some guy down on Madison Avenue went nuts and hit him with a brick. You got a doctor can help him?"

"We'll get a doctor. He's been drinking."

"That ain't his problem. He's got a stomach cancer too, but what ails him right now is his head. He got rocked all to hell, I'm tellin' you, and it wasn't none of his fault."

The nurse went to the phone and dialed and talked softly.

"How you makin' it, pal?" Francis asked.

Rudy smiled and gave Francis a glazed look and said nothing. Francis patted him on the shoulder and sat down on a chair beside him to rest. He saw his own image in the mirror door of a cabinet against the wall. His bow tie was all cockeyed and his shirt and coat were spattered with blood where he had dripped before he knew he was cut. His face was smudged and his clothes were covered with dirt. He straightened the tie and brushed off a bit of the dirt.

After a second phone call and a conversation that Francis was about to interrupt to tell her to get goddamn busy with Rudy, the nurse came back. She took Rudy's pulse, went for a stethoscope, and listened to his heart. Then she told Francis Rudy was dead. Francis stood up and looked at his friend's face and saw the smile still there. Where the wind don't blow.

"What was his name?" the nurse asked. She picked up a pencil and a hospital form on a clipboard.

Francis could only stare into Rudy's glassy-eyed smile. Isaac Newton of the apple was born of two midwives.

"Sir, what was his name?" the nurse said.

"Name was Rudy."

"Rudy what?"

"Rudy Newton," Francis said. "He knew where the Milky Way was."

*   *   *

It would be three-fifteen by the clock on the First Church when Francis headed south toward Palombo's Hotel to get out of the cold, to stretch out with Helen and try to think about what had happened and what he should do about it. He would walk past Palombo's night man on the landing, salute him, and climb the stairs to the room he and Helen always shared in this dump. Looking at the hallway dirt and the ratty carpet as he walked down the hall, he would remind himself that this was luxury for him and Helen. He would see the light coming out from under the door, but he would knock anyway to make sure he had Helen's room. When he got no answer he would open the door and discover Helen on the floor in her kimono.

He would enter the room and close the door and stand looking at her for a long time. Her hair would be loose, and fanned out, and pretty.

He would, after a while, think of lifting her onto the bed, but decide there was no point in that, for she looked right and comfortable just as she was. She looked as if she were sleeping.

He would sit in the chair looking at her for an amount of time he later would not be able to calculate, and he would decide that he had made a right decision in not moving her.

For she was not crooked.

He would look in the open suitcase and would find his old clippings and put them in his inside coat pocket. He would find his razor and his penknife and Helen's rhinestone butterfly, and he would put these in his coat pockets also. In her coat hanging in the closet he would find her three dollars and thirty-five cents and he would put that in his pants pocket, still wondering where she got it. He would remember the two dollars he left for her and that she would never get now, nor would he, and he would think of it as a tip for old Donovan. Helen says thank you.

He would then sit on the bed and look at Helen from a different angle. He would be able to see her eyes were closed and he would remember how vividly green they were in life, those gorgeous emeralds. He would hear the women talking together behind him as he tried to peer beyond Helen's sheltered eyes.

Too late now, the women would say. Too late now to see any deeper into Helen's soul. But he would continue to stare, mindful of the phonograph record propped against the pillow; and he would know the song she'd bought, or stole. It would be "Bye Bye Blackbird," which she loved so much, and he would hear the women singing it softly as he stared at the fiercely glistening scars on Helen's soul, fresh and livid scars whitening among the old, the soul already purging itself of all wounds of the world, flaming with the green fires of hope, but keeping their integrity too as welts of insight into the deepest secrets of Satan.

Francis, this twofold creature, now an old man in a mortal slouch, now again a fledgling bird of uncertain wing, would sing along softly with the women: Here I go, singin' low, the song revealing to him that he was not looking into Helen's soul at all but only into his own repetitive and fallible memory. He knew that right now both Rudy and Helen had far more insight into his being than he himself ever had, or would have, into either of theirs.

The dead, they got all the eyes.

He would follow the thread of his life backward to a point well in advance of the dying of Helen and would come to a vision of her in this same Japanese kimono, lying beside him after they had made sweet love, and she saying to him: All I want in the world is to have my name put back among the family.

And Francis would then stand up and vow that he would one day hunt up Helen's grave, no matter where they put her, and would place a stone on top of it with her name carved deeply in its face. The stone would say: *Helen Marie Archer, a great soul.*

Francis would remember then that when great souls were being extinguished, the forces of darkness walked abroad in the world, filling it with lightning and strife and fire. And he would realize that he should pray for the safety of Helen's soul, since that was the only way he could now help her. But because his vision of the next world was not of the court of heaven where the legion of souls in grace venerate the Holy Worm, but rather of a foul mist above a hole in the ground where the earth itself purges away the stench of life's rot, Francis saw a question burning brightly in the air: How should this man pray?

He would think about this for another incalculably long moment and decide finally there was no way for him to pray: not for Helen, not even for himself.

He would then reach down and touch Helen on the top of the head and stroke her skull the way a father strokes the soft fontanel of his newborn child, stroke her gently so as not to disturb the flowing fall of her hair.

Because it was so pretty.

Then he would walk out of Helen's room, leaving the light burning. He would walk down the hall to the landing, salute the night clerk, who would be dozing in his chair, and then he would reenter the cold and living darkness of the night.

*   *   *

By dawn he would be on a Delaware & Hudson freight heading south toward the lemonade springs. He would be squatting in the middle of the empty car with the door partway open, sitting a little out of the wind. He would be watching the stars, whose fire seemed so unquenchable only a few hours before, now vanishing from an awakening sky that was between a rose and a violet in its early hue.

It would be impossible for him to close his eyes, and so he would think of all the things he might now do. He would then decide that he could not choose among all the possibilities that were his. By now he was sure only that he lived in a world where events decided themselves, and that all a man could do was to stay one jump into their mystery.

He had a vision of Gerald swaddled in the silvery web of his grave, and then the vision faded like the stars and he could not even remember the color of the child's hair. He saw all the women who became three, and then their impossible coherence also faded and he saw only the glorious mouth of Katrina speaking words that were little more than silent shapes; and he knew then that he was leaving behind more than a city and a lifetime of corpses. He was also leaving behind even his vivid memory of the scars on Helen's soul.

Strawberry Bill climbed into the car when the train slowed to take on water, and he looked pretty good for a bum that died coughin'. He was all duded up in a blue seersucker suit, straw hat, and shoes the color of a new baseball.

"You never looked that good while you was livin'," Francis said to him. "You done well for yourself over there."

Everybody gets an Italian tailor when he checks in, Bill said. But say, pal, what're you runnin' from this time?

"Same old crowd," Francis said. "The cops."

Ain't no such things as cops, said Bill.

"Maybe they ain't none of 'em got to heaven yet, but they been pesterin' hell outa me down here."

No cops chasin' you, pal.

"You got the poop?"

Would I kid a fella like you?

Francis smiled and began to hum Rudy's song about the place where the bluebird sings. He took the final swallow of Green River whiskey, which tasted sweet and cold to him now. And he thought of Annie's attic.

That's the place, Bill told him. They got a cot over in the corner, near your old trunk.

"I saw it," said Francis.

Francis walked to the doorway of the freight car and threw the empty whiskey bottle at the moon, an outshoot fading away into the rising sun. The bottle and the moon made music like a soulful banjo when they moved through the heavens, divine harmonies that impelled Francis to leap off the train and seek sanctuary under the holy Phelan eaves.

"You hear that music?" Francis said.

Music? said Bill. Can't say as I do.

"Banjo music. Mighty sweet banjo. That empty whiskey bottle's what's makin' it. The whiskey bottle and the moon."

If you say so, said Bill.

Francis listened again to the moon and his bottle and heard it clearer than ever. When you heard that music you didn't have to lay there no more. You could get right up off'n that old cot and walk over to the back window of the attic and watch Jake Becker lettin' his pigeons loose. They flew up and around the whole damn neighborhood, round and round, flew in a big circle and got themselves all worked up, and then old Jake, he'd give 'em the whistle and they'd come back to the cages. Damnedest thing.

"What can I make you for lunch?" Annie asked him.

"I ain't fussy. Turkey sandwich'd do me fine."

"You want tea again?"

"I always want that tea," said Francis.

He was careful not to sit by the window, where he could be seen when he watched the pigeons or when, at the other end of the attic, he looked out at the children playing football in the school athletic field.

"You'll be all right if they don't see you," Annie said to him. She changed the sheets on the cot twice a week and made tan curtains for the windows and bought a pair of black drapes so he could close them at night and read the paper.

It was no longer necessary for him to read. His mind was devoid of ideas. If an idea entered, it would rest in the mind like the morning dew on an open field of stone. The morning sun would obliterate the dew and only its effect on the stone would remain. The stone needs no such effect.

The point was, would they ever know it was Francis who had broken that fellow's back with the bat? For the blow, indeed, had killed the murdering bastard. Were they looking for him? Were they pretending not to look for him? In his trunk he found his old warm-up sweater and he wore that with the collar turned up to shield his face. He also found George Quinn's overseas cap, which gave him a military air. He would have earned stripes, medals in the military. Regimentation always held great fascination for him. No one would ever think of looking for him wearing George's overseas cap. It was unlikely.

"Do you like Jell-O, Fran?" Annie asked him. "I can't remember ever making Jell-O for you. I don't remember if they had Jell-O back then."

If they were on to him, well that's all she wrote. Katie bar the door. Too wet to plow. He'd head where it was warm, where he would never again have to run from men or weather.

The empyrean, which is not spatial at all, does not move and has no poles. It girds, with light and love, the primum mobile, the utmost and swiftest of the material heavens. Angels are manifested in the primum mobile.

But if they weren't on to him, then he'd mention it to Annie someday (she already had the thought, he could tell that) about setting up the cot down in Danny's room, when things got to be absolutely right, and straight.

That room of Danny's had some space to it.

And it got the morning light too.

It was a mighty nice little room.